D0960447

RULES
FOR
BEING A
GIRL

RULES

CANDACE BUSHNELL
and KATIE COTUGNO

FOR

BEING A

BALZER + BRAY
An Imprint of HarperCollinsPublishers

GIRL

Balzer + Bray is an imprint of HarperCollins Publishers.

Rules for Being a Girl
Copyright © 2020 by Alloy Entertainment and Candace Bushnell
All rights reserved. Printed in the United States of America.
No part of this book may be used or reproduced in any manner
whatsoever without written permission except in the case of brief
quotations embodied in critical articles and reviews.
For information address HarperCollins Children's Books, a division of
HarperCollins Publishers, 195 Broadway, New York, NY 10007.
www.epicreads.com

Library of Congress Control Number: 2019948010
ISBN 978-0-06-280337-5

Typography by Jenna Stempel-Lobell
20 21 22 23 24   PC/LSCH   10 9 8 7 6 5 4 3 2 1

First Edition

To my sweet, fierce friend Jeanine Pepler
—CB

For Baby Girl Colleran, who lived under my heart
while this book got written
—KC

RULES
FOR
BEING A
GIRL

ONE

"And *that*," Mr. Beckett says, leaning against the edge of his desk in third-period AP English, ankles crossed and dark eyes shining, "is the story of how Hemingway and Fitzgerald became the most famous literary frenemies of the twentieth century. Full disclosure, it probably won't be that useful to you on the AP exam, since for some reason they don't test your knowledge of hundred-year-old publishing gossip. But you can keep it in your back pocket and use it to impress your friends at parties." He grins, standing up and tugging a whiteboard marker out of the back pocket of his dark blue khakis.

"Okay," he says, "let's talk homework."

We let out a collective groan, and Bex—which is what we all call him—waves us off as a bunch of bellyachers, then assigns the first forty pages of *A Farewell to Arms* for us to read that night.

"It'll go fast," he promises, twirling the marker between his fingers like a magician with a deck of cards. "One of the great things about Hemingway—and there are a lot of great things about Hemingway, and we'll talk about them tomorrow—is that he's not much for big words."

"Well, that's good," cracks Gray Kendall, a long-legged lacrosse player who just started here back in September. He's sprawled in his chair a couple of rows behind me, a dimple appearing briefly in the apple of his cheek. "Neither am I."

Eventually the bell rings for the end of the period and we all shuffle toward the door, the scrape of chair legs on linoleum and the smell of chicken sandwich day in the cafeteria wafting down the hallway.

"You ready?" I ask Chloe, stopping by her desk at the front of the room. She's wearing her signature red lipstick and huge hipster glasses, her yellow-blond hair falling in soft waves to her shoulders. A tiny lapel pin in the shape of a pink flamingo is affixed to the collar of her uniform blouse.

"Um," she says, glancing over my shoulder at where Bex is erasing the whiteboard, elegant shoulders moving inside his gray cashmere sweater.

I raise my eyebrows at her blatant gawking, and she makes a face at me in return.

"Yeah."

"Uh-huh. Right." I offer her an exaggerated nod and sling my backpack over one shoulder; we're just about to go when Bex looks up.

"Oh, Marin, hey," he says with a guilty shake of his head. "I managed to space on your book *again* today, if you can believe it. But I'll bring it in tomorrow for sure."

"Oh! No worries." I smile.

Bex has been telling me for the better part of two weeks that he's going to lend me his copy of *The Corrections*, which he says I'll love, but he keeps forgetting to bring it in.

"Whenever is good. Honestly, it's not like I have a ton of time to read for pleasure anyway."

"I know, I know." Bex makes a mischievous face. "You're all too busy posting unboxing videos to your You-Tube channels, or whatever it is you people do for fun."

My mouth drops open. "Not true!" I say, though my whole body is flushing pleasantly. "Getting buried in AP English homework is more like it."

"Yeah, yeah," Bex says, but he's smiling. "Get out of my classroom. I've got lunch duty; I'll see you down there."

"Lucky you," Chloe teases.

"Uh-huh." Bex grins, setting the eraser on the ledge and wiping his hands on the seat of his pants. "You're making fun of me, but joke's on you because you're underestimating how excited I get about chicken sandwich day. Now go."

The cafeteria at Bridgewater Prep is actually a combination auditorium/gym, with a stage at one end and tables that fold down and slide into a storage room during phys ed periods. Ours is already crowded by the time Chloe and I show up, with the same slightly incongruous mix of honors kids from Bex's class and lacrosse bros we've been sitting with since I started dating Jacob.

"Hey, babe," he says now, tweaking me in the side by way of hello. "How's your day?"

"You checking to make sure she's not getting fat?" his buddy Joey cracks, reaching over like he's going to give me a pinch of his own.

I duck out of the way and flip him the finger, rolling my eyes. "Shove it, Joey." Then, nudging Jacob in the shoulder: "Defend my honor, will you?"

"You heard the lady," Jacob says, which is admittedly a little bit weak as far as honor defending goes, but he's pulling me into his lap and pressing a kiss against my cheek, and for a second I forget to be annoyed. Jacob and I have been dating since last spring in AP US History, when we happened to be sitting side by side as Ms. Shah assigned partners for our final research project. I was hoping for somebody who'd let me boss him around and get us both As, which has been my strategy for group projects for basically as long as I've been doing them, but to my surprise, Jacob had actual opinions about which primary sources would be most useful to build a document-based question on the social reforms that led up to the Civil War. We argued for two full weeks before we figured out how to work together. When we got our A he lifted me up and twirled me around right there in the middle of class.

Now I sit down in my own chair and pull a turkey sandwich out of my bag, nodding at Dean Shepherd as he sets his tray down beside Chloe. The two of them went to homecoming together earlier this year and since then he's been not at all subtle about trying to date her.

"You going to this thing at Emily Cerato's on Friday?" he asks, cracking the cap on his bottle of Dr Pepper and offering her the first sip.

Chloe shrugs, peeling her clementine industriously. "I was thinking about it," she allows. "You?"

I miss Dean's answer—and, thankfully, most of Joey's ensuing monologue about how hot Emily and her dance team friends all are—catching sight of Bex perched on the stage at the far end of the room, next to Ms. Klein, a bio teacher who was new back in September. She's youngish, in her late twenties maybe, with curly dark hair and glasses and a wardrobe that seems to consist almost entirely of belted shirtdresses from Banana Republic. She's sitting with her ankles crossed inside a pair of boots with blocky wooden heels, eating a cup of fancy yogurt while Bex laughs at something she said.

Chloe flicks a clementine peel at me. "Now look who's gawking," she says, lifting her chin in Bex's direction.

"I am not!" I whisper-yell.

"Uh-huh. Wipe the drool, why don't you," Chloe says with a laugh.

I sigh dramatically. "I can't help it. You know I'm a sucker for a man in khakis." I glance back at Bex and Ms. Klein. "Do you think there's something going on there?" I'd be lying if I said Chloe and I aren't the tiniest bit obsessed with Bex's romantic life.

"What?" Right away, Chloe shakes her head. "No."

"Why not?" I ask. "Ms. Klein is cute."

"I mean, I guess." Chloe looks unconvinced. "In like, a local newscaster kind of way."

"I'd nail her," Joey puts in helpfully.

"Nobody *asked* you, Joe." I turn back to Chloe. "I'm just saying: long nights grading papers, romantic looks across the teachers' lounge—"

"Oh my god." Chloe pops a wedge of clementine into her mouth. "Are you sure that isn't *your* fantasy?" she asks. "Maybe you should reconsider becoming a journalist. I feel like romance novels are your true calling."

"This is journalism!" I protest, laughing. "Serious, investigative journalism into the never-before-seen love lives of America's most important national treasure—our teachers."

Chloe snorts. "You do that," she says, tucking her clementine peel back into her brown paper lunch bag. "I gotta go though, I've got a dentist appointment this afternoon, so I'm leaving early. Are you good to run the meeting without me?"

Chloe and I are coeditors of the *Beacon* this year and spend basically every available moment in the office with Bex and the rest of the staff, hunched over the sluggish computers and sprawled out on the ragged, sagging couch.

"Yep, totally. I'll text you tonight." I wave goodbye and turn back to Jacob, who's already finishing his second chicken sandwich. "Do *you* want to go to Emily Cerato's party?" I ask.

"Sure," he says with a shrug, opening a cellophane pack of Oreos. "Why not, right?"

"I don't know." I nibble at a piece of kettle corn. "I was also thinking maybe we could do that movie I was talking about the other day, the one about the sisters who inherit the house?"

"The historical thing?" he asks with a frown. "Wouldn't you rather see that with Chloe or your mom?"

I raise my eyebrows pointedly. "By which you mean you'd rather poke out your own eyeballs than sit through it?"

"I didn't say that," Jacob protests, handing me a cookie in an attempt at a peace offering. "If you want to go we totally can."

"Yeah, yeah." I know he means it too—Jacob's a good sport like that—but there's no point in dragging him to something I know he's going to think is totally girly and boring. "You're off the hook, dude. A party sounds fun."

Jacob nods, then gestures over my shoulder at Bex, who's making the rounds through the cafeteria like a groom at a wedding, coaxing easy smiles out of everybody, from debate nerds to the toughest bruisers on the football team. "Your boy's coming over here," he tells me. "Should I ask him if he's giving Ms. Klein the D?"

8

"Oh my *god*," I say, tossing a piece of kettle corn in his direction, "that's disgusting. And also *emphatically* not what I said he was doing." Still, it occurs to me that if Jacob flat out asked Bex if he and Ms. Klein were dating, there's a good chance Bex would tell us the truth. That's one of the nice things about him—he's not obsessed with maintaining some dumb veil of secrecy about his life outside school, like some of the other teachers. He's an actual human being. Like, the other day in class he told us a story about getting a speeding ticket on the way to school after oversleeping because he was out late at a party in Boston for a friend of his who was publishing a collection of short stories. And on picture day he brought in his own senior yearbook so we could all have a laugh at his mid-aughts puka shells and spiky haircut.

Now he stops at our table for a minute, joking around with Dean and asking Jacob about a play from yesterday's lacrosse game. It's not even lacrosse season, technically, but the Bridgewater team is really good, so they have special permission to play in some indoor intramural league and still use the school buses for games. Everyone thinks the lacrosse guys are something special. Maybe I do too, though frankly it always annoys me that they seem to know it.

"You get your chicken sandwich?" I ask Bex.

Bex nods seriously. "Sure did," he says, then reaches over my shoulder and picks up my bag of kettle corn, helping himself to a handful.

"Excuse you!" I protest, though it's not like I actually mind.

Bex just shrugs. "School tax," he says with a grin. "Take it up with your congressman."

I reach for the bag, but he holds it above my head playfully, laughing at my pathetic attempts to grab it, when we hear Principal DioGuardi clear his throat up on the stage at the far end of the cafeteria.

"Attention, ladies and gentlemen," he says, hands fisted on his hips like a cartoon bodybuilder. Mr. DioGuardi was a PE teacher before he got into administration, and he still kind of looks it, with beefy forearms and a torso shaped like an upside-down triangle inside his maroon button-down. He wears a whistle around his neck, which he uses to keep us from getting too rowdy at assemblies and pep rallies and also sometimes randomly pops into his mouth when he's thinking, like a baby with a pacifier. Last year every single member of the lacrosse team went as him for Halloween.

"If I can have a minute of your time, I wanted to talk to you about your favorite topic and mine—the uniform code!"

"Oh, Jesus Christ," Bex murmurs, quiet enough that only I can hear him, then gives my shoulder a quick squeeze through my uniform sweater before straightening up and heading back toward the front of the cafeteria. "Here we go."

I look after him in surprise—it's rare to get that kind of unfiltered reaction from a teacher, even one as chill as Bex. Then again, DioGuardi is notoriously ridiculous about the dress code. I've actually never hated wearing a uniform—there's something to be said for not having to worry about picking a cute outfit every day—but lately DioGuardi has become obsessed, with new rules coming practically every week about everything from skirt length to makeup to how big our earrings can be. Not to mention the fact that the guidelines never seem to apply to the guys.

I glance over at Jacob, but he's scrolling Instagram on his phone under the table, totally unbothered.

"Here we go," I echo, and settle in for the long haul.

That afternoon I'm sitting on the ancient couch in the newspaper room working through a problem set in my calc book when Bex pauses at the open door. It's after five, and our meeting ended a couple hours ago, but I'm stuck waiting for my mom to pick me up. "Hey," he says, glancing at the clock above the whiteboard. "You got a ride?"

"Oh yeah," I tell him. He's wearing a buttery-looking leather jacket, his dark hair curling over his collar. There's a rumor that Bex paid his way through grad school by modeling—supposedly some senior dug up the pictures online last year, though Chloe and I haven't ever been able to find them ourselves—and right now I can believe it. "My mom'll be here in a while. I mean, I have my license, obviously, but—one car. And my sister has a chess thing." I shrug.

Bex raises his eyebrows. "A chess thing?"

"My little sister is a Massachusetts chess champion," I explain, a little embarrassed. "She gets lessons from this crotchety old guy out in Brookline. Normally my dad would just come get me, but he had a meeting, and Chloe had a dentist appointment, so—" I snap my jaws shut, not sure why I feel compelled to bore him with the mundane logistical details of my life. "Anyway. I'm good."

Bex just smiles. "Come on," he says, nodding in the general direction of the parking lot. "I can drive you."

"Oh." I shake my head like an instinct, pulling the scratchy blue sleeves of my uniform sweater down over my hands. "No, that's okay, you don't have to do that."

Bex shrugs. "I wouldn't offer if I didn't mean it," he says easily. "Pretty soon it's going to be just you and Mr. Lyle rattling around this place."

Mr. Lyle is the janitor, who's seven feet tall and almost as wide in the shoulders. Everybody calls him Hodor behind his back.

"Grab your stuff."

I glance out the window, at the dusk falling purple-blue behind the pine trees. Back at Bex. "Okay," I say finally, swallowing down a thrill and reaching for my backpack. "Sure. Thanks."

I text my mom to let her know I've got a ride and follow Bex down the empty hallway and out into the teachers' lot, explaining where I live as we walk. He drives a beat-up Jeep with a peeling Bernie Sanders sticker on the bumper. Inside it smells like coffee; there's a gym bag slouched on the back seat. As he starts the engine the car fills with sad, guitar-heavy indie folk—Bon Iver, I think, although possibly that's just the only artist like that I could name.

"I'm a caricature of myself, I know," Bex says, nodding at the stereo as we pull out of the parking lot. "All I'm missing is the mountain-man beard."

"No, it's fine," I say with a smile. "I mean, I like to stand outside and weep in the pouring rain as much as the next girl."

Bex lets out a loud laugh. "That's what my ex-girlfriend always used to say," he admits. "She used to call it sad-man dead-dog music."

I laugh too, even as the word *ex-girlfriend* sends a tiny electric shock through me. I wonder what she was like, if she was pretty. Most of all I wonder why they broke up.

Bex has always been strangely easy to talk to for a teacher, and he keeps up a pretty steady conversation as we head for my neighborhood—about DioGuardi and the dress code, yeah, but also about a concert he just went to in Boston and a series of author readings at Harvard Book Store that he thinks I should check out.

"So you and Jacob Reimer, huh?" he asks, turning the music down as we cruise along the VFW Parkway, passing the Stop & Shop and the PetSmart. "He seems like a good dude."

"Oh!" I don't know who told him that, and it must show on my face, because Bex mirrors an exaggerated, shocked expression back at me, wide eyes and his mouth a perfect O.

"I know stuff," he says, breaking into a grin. "You guys think teachers are, like, deaf, blind dinosaurs, like we shuffle around with no idea what's going on."

"No, that's not what I think!" I protest.

Bex's lips twist. "Yeah, yeah."

"It's not," I insist, giggling a little. "But yeah. Jacob is awesome."

"Good," Bex says, glancing over his shoulder before

switching into the turn lane, long fingers hooked casually at the bottom of the wheel. "Most high school guys are basically walking mailboxes. You're right to hold out for someone great."

A pleased, unfamiliar blush creeps up my chest, hot and prickly. I'm glad I'm wearing a scarf. "Thanks," I say, fussing with the sticky zipper on the outside pocket of my backpack, yanking ineffectually at the pull.

Bex shrugs. "It's true."

I nod. "Um, this is me up here," I tell him, nodding at my parents' tiny colonial. "Thanks again for the ride."

"Yeah, no problem."

"See you tomorrow," I say, unlatching the door handle.

"Hey, Marin," he says, laying a hand on my arm as I'm getting out of the car; I feel the zing of it clear down my spine, my whole skeleton jangling pleasantly. "Just to be safe, uh. You probably shouldn't mention to anybody at school that I drove you."

"Oh," I say, surprised. "Okay."

"At the last place I worked it was different—it was a boarding school, so I drove students around all the time, you know? I had students over to my apartment for *dinner* like once a week. But here . . ." He trails off. "DioGuardi runs a different kind of ship."

"No, no, I totally get it." I didn't know he worked at a boarding school before he came to Bridgewater. I'm instantly, weirdly jealous of all the students he ever cooked dinner for. "I won't say anything."

"Thanks, pal," Bex says, grinning a little bashfully. "Have a good night."

"You too," I say, shutting the passenger door gently and lifting my hand in a dopey wave. I stand on the darkened lawn until the Jeep disappears out of sight.

TWO

Emily's party is two nights later, so Jacob picks me up in the Subaru his parents got him for his seventeenth birthday and we swing by Chloe's house on the way.

"Hey," I say, turning around in my seat as she settles herself in the back, unwinding her fuzzy scarf from around her neck.

Ancient Whitney Houston croons on the stereo, the air in the car heavy with the scent of the cologne Jacob swears he doesn't spray on the heating vents.

"Where were you this afternoon? I thought we were going to do layout stuff."

Chloe shakes her head. "Covered a shift at work," she explains. "Rosie had a doctor's appointment. Sorry, I meant to text you. It was super last-minute."

Chloe's parents own a Greek restaurant called Niko's; we both started working there in eighth grade, first busing tables and now waiting them.

"Bex wasn't there either," I complain, pulling one leg up underneath me and reaching out to turn the heat down. "It was just me and Michael Cyr in there, which meant I had to listen to him talk for like a full hour about how he just discovered *Breaking Bad* and Walter White is his new hero."

"Just you and Michael Cyr, huh?" Jacob asks, glancing over at me from the driver's seat. "Should I be jealous?"

"Only if you feel threatened by a guy who met all his best friends on Reddit," I say, reaching out to poke him in the rib cage.

Jacob grabs my finger and squeezes. Chloe rolls her eyes.

Emily's house is a sprawling ranch in a midcentury development full of identical sprawling ranches, all of them painted in different pastel colors.

"Once, when I was in second grade, I got off the bus and walked right into the wrong one," Emily says, leading us down the hallway and pulling a couple of beers out of an iceless cooler near the back door. "This old lady Gloria sat me down at her kitchen table and made me soda bread, and then she was my best friend for like three years until she died."

Right away Jacob gets absorbed into a crowd of his lacrosse buddies—Joey and Ahmed, plus Gray Kendall and a few other dudes. The rumor is Gray got kicked out of his fancy prep school last year for throwing the kind of wild parties where people wind up in the hospital for eating Tide PODS. In barely two months at Bridgewater he's fooled around with what seems like basically every girl at school, an unending parade of hopeful-looking underclassmen hanging around outside the locker room on game days. It's deeply embarrassing for everyone, although I can admit he's ridiculously cute.

Chloe and I make ourselves comfortable on the staircase that leads to the second floor, listening to Cardi B rapping tinnily from the Bluetooth speaker on the coffee table. A couple of awkward-looking freshman guys cluster around a video on somebody's cell phone. Slutty Deanna Montalto lounges on the sofa next to Trina Meng.

"Did you hear the thing about Deanna and Tyler Ramos in the auditorium?" Chloe asks quietly, running her thumb around the mouth of her beer bottle. "I feel like she's basically the whole reason behind the new dress-code memo."

"Oh my god, the no-more-knee-socks thing?" Emily asks, plunking down on the stair below us with a can of spiked seltzer in one hand. "So dumb."

"*So* dumb," I agree. "Like, explain to me how these delicate, precious boys are supposedly going to be too distracted by our *knees* of all things to get any work done." I stand up and grab Jacob's arm over the banister, pulling him partway out of the scrum of lacrosse bros. "Can I ask you a question?" I say, lacing our fingers together. "How exactly is us wearing tights instead of knee socks going to help you idiots learn better?"

"It's not," Jacob says immediately, his grin wide and wicked. "What it *is* going to interfere with is Charlie Rinaldi's robust side hustle of taking pictures up your skirts in the cafeteria and selling them online."

Joey and Ahmed bust up laughing. Even Chloe cracks a grin.

"You're disgusting," I inform Jacob, smacking him gently on the elbow, but I can't help but let out a laugh of my own.

The only one who isn't laughing is Gray, who's leaning his lanky body against the post at the bottom of the staircase. "Anybody need a beer?" he asks, holding up his empty bottle. He tips it at us in a salute before he turns and walks away.

"That dude is the fucking weirdest," Jacob says once he's gone, slinging a heavy arm around my shoulders. I watch Gray's broad back disappear into the crowd.

The party breaks up early—turns out Emily Cerato's parents didn't know she was having one to begin with and weren't super thrilled when they came home from dinner and a show down in the Theater District and found two dozen teenagers sprawled all over their furniture.

"How the hell did Emily not realize they were seeing a *one-act* play?" Chloe asks as we dash across the lawn to Jacob's car, her scarf flapping behind her in the sharp autumn wind.

"Maybe we should have tried to convince them they were at the wrong house," I shoot back. That cracks her up, which cracks *me* up; by the time we manage to get our seat belts buckled Jacob looks about ready to leave us both on the side of the road altogether. "Take a little pity on your sober driver, here."

"Sorry, sorry," I assure him, still giggling; I'm pretty sure he finds Chloe and me kind of annoying together, though he's too nice to say so. "Let's go."

Turns out all three of us are starving, so we swing through the twenty-four-hour McDonald's for fries and milk shakes before heading over to Chloe's to drop her off.

"See you at work tomorrow?" I ask, turning around in the passenger seat to look at her. Usually the two of us are on the same Saturday schedule, but tonight she shakes her head.

"I'm off tomorrow," she explains, prying her milk shake out of the cupholder and slinging her bag over one narrow shoulder. "I'm spending the weekend at Kyra's."

I frown. "Really?"

Kyra is her slightly younger cousin, who lives in Watertown and is super into her Greek Orthodox youth group. I know her from years of going to Chloe's birthday parties, and she's cool in a straightedge kind of way, but I definitely wouldn't call them super close.

"Why?"

She shrugs. "My parents want us to be friends, I don't know. They're probably hoping she'll teach me to pray in Greek."

"Oh man," I tease. "Good luck, Kyra."

"Yeah, yeah." Chloe rolls her eyes. "Thanks for the ride, Jacob. I'll see you guys Monday."

Once she's inside, Jacob turns to me, his sharp face

familiar in the light from the dashboard. "You need to get home right away?" he asks.

I glance at the clock, hesitating. I've got a little over an hour before my curfew, truthfully, but I also know what he's actually asking, which is whether I want to go park under the copse of trees at the far end of the Bridgewater parking lot and mess around for a while. "Um."

"We don't have to do anything you don't want to do, obviously," Jacob says quickly.

"Gee, thanks." I make a face.

"Oh, come on." Jacob frowns, wounded. "You know what I mean. I'm not trying to be some, like, pressuring douchebag. I just meant—"

"No, I know." I wave a hand to stop him, a little embarrassed. He's right, actually—Jacob's never given me a hard time about the fact that we haven't had sex yet, even though I can tell he's a tiny bit disappointed every time we're getting up to something and I finally stop him. And it's not even that I don't *want* to, necessarily. I meant what I said to Bex the other day—Jacob is great. He's smart. Everybody is always saying how funny he is. He's the assistant coach of his little brother's peewee basketball team, for God's sake. And if sometimes I feel like I'm still kind of waiting for some crazy *zing* of recognition, some feeling of *Oh, it's you*—well, this is high school, not a Netflix original rom-com. There's no reason to be such a girl about the whole thing.

Finally I sigh, reaching out with one finger and snapping Jacob's seat belt lightly across his chest. "Let's go," I tell him.

Jacob grins.

THREE

Gracie has a chess tournament in Harvard Square the following weekend, so I tag along with my parents to go see her play. The thing about competitive chess is that even at the middle school level—especially at the middle school level—the various matchups are basically more complicated than March Madness seeding, which means that over the years I've spent an awful lot of time sitting around in random auditoriums waiting for it to be my sister's turn to wipe the floor with supposed prodigies from Newton and Andover.

Today the proceedings are even slower than usual; somebody's little brother is kicking the back of my chair periodically, and the dry, forced heat is making me yawn. Gracie sits to my side with her eyes closed and her head tilted back against the red velvet auditorium seat, listening to Christmas music. My phone buzzes with a text from Jacob—a Bitmoji of himself snowboarding, his tongue hanging out like a dog's. I stopped him—again—before things went too far the night of Emily's party, though he didn't actually seem put out about it. He's spending this weekend at his cousin's house in Vermont, so possibly he's too excited about "shredding the mountain"—his words, not mine—to be annoyed about not getting into my pants.

"I'm going to find a coffee shop and do some homework," I finally whisper.

My mom nods. "Don't go too far," she instructs, fishing a ten-dollar bill out of her purse and handing it over. "I'll text you before her match."

In the end I post up at the big Starbucks near the T stop, the windows fogged with the damp chill outside. I pull my laptop out of my backpack and watch the tourists and college kids waiting in line for their coffees, the hipsters with their tattoos and undercuts. Sometimes I think it would be cool to look a little more like them, to try bright pink hair or an eyebrow ring or whatever. Then I imagine the curious looks and snarky comments I know I'd get if

I ever did anything like that at Bridgewater, and it seems safer to just blend in.

"Marin?"

I look up and gasp, almost knocking over my cup at the sight of Bex standing next to my table in jeans and a worn-in hoodie. With his glasses and his coffee cup he looks like a college kid home for the holiday weekend, messenger bag slung over his shoulder and laptop tucked under one arm.

"I thought that was you," he says.

"Oh!" I steady my cup on the table, offering him a smile. "Hi."

"Sorry," he says, "am I traumatizing you right now?" He grins. "I saw my first-grade principal at the pool once, and I don't think I ever really recovered. A nun in a bathing suit, just to burn that image into your mind like it's burned into mine."

I raise my eyebrows. "Nuns are allowed to wear bathing suits?"

"Apparently." Bex shudders, then nods his chin at my computer. "What are you working on?"

I glance down at the screen with gritty eyes, then back at him. "My admission essay for Brown," I admit.

"Really?" He frowns. "Deadline is coming up, right? It's not like you to have put it off this long."

"It's done, honestly," I confess, dumbly pleased that he's been paying close enough attention lately to know what is and isn't like me. "Or, I mean, it's done in that it's a five-paragraph essay with a beginning, a middle, and an end. I just keep noodling on it though. I want it to be absolutely one hundred percent."

"Curse of the perfectionist," Bex says with a knowing smile. "Want me to take a look?"

I shake my head. "You don't have to do that."

"No, seriously," he says. "I want to." He sets his own battered MacBook down on the table. "Come on, hand it over."

"What, right now?"

He shrugs. "Do you have a better time?" He sits down in the empty chair across from me, holding his arms out for my laptop. I click my browser shut—probably there's no reason for him to know that I've been procrastinating by trawling *Riverdale* fan fiction—before passing it across the table, wrapping my hands awkwardly around my empty cup.

"Well, I definitely can't *sit* here while you're reading it," I announce barely five seconds later. I get up and stand in line for another latte—unable to help glancing over my shoulder, searching Bex's face while he reads. His eyes are serious behind his tortoiseshell glasses. The weak afternoon sunlight catches the gold in his hair.

A few minutes later, I walk back to the table, chewing my lip.

"This is fantastic," he says before I even sit down.

I manage to stop my hands before they fly to my mouth, but barely. "Really?"

Bex nods. "Honestly, Marin, I've read a lot of admission essays, and I wouldn't say it if it wasn't true. Your writing is, like, super mature."

"Well, thanks." I glance down at my cup, trying not to smile too widely. He's not the first teacher to tell me that; still, coming from Bex it's like it somehow means more. "I mean, realistically I'm still going to be messing with it until the deadline, but I really appreciate it."

Bex laughs. "I'm the same way. Like I said: curse of the perfectionist," he says, tilting his chair back onto its hind legs as if he's sitting in a classroom himself. "Listen, I don't know if you know this, but I went to Brown. And so did my dad . . . and so did his dad, actually." He smiles a little sheepishly. "When you go for your interview, look out for Beckett Auditorium."

"Oh, wow," I say, eyes widening as I cop on. I had heard his family had money, but I never realized there was *that* much of it. "Yeah, I will."

"Anyway, I just wanted to say that if you ever wanted me to put a call in, try and throw my weight around a little bit, I'd be happy to do it. I don't know if anyone there will give a shit, but it couldn't hurt, right?"

"Thank you," I say, nodding my head and mustering a smile. "That would be amazing."

Bex nods, satisfied. "Honestly, my pleasure. You earned it."

"So, um, what about you?" I ask, motioning with my cup at his laptop. "What are you working on?"

"Oh, Jesus," he says with a rueful shake of his head. "You don't want to know."

I raise my eyebrows. "Well, now you have to tell me."

"My novel." Bex visibly cringes, dropping his face into his hands. "I can't believe I'm even saying that out loud to you right now. Go ahead, have a laugh."

My eyes widen. "You're writing a *novel*? Seriously? What's it about?"

Bex sighs theatrically, lifting his head to look at me again. "I'm trusting you with this, you realize. You could ruin me."

"I wouldn't do that."

"No, I know you wouldn't." He shifts his weight again,

the front legs of the chair hitting the tile floor with a clatter. "It's about a guy who wants to be a theater actor, but he's not a very *good* theater actor, so he's working for a children's theater doing puppet shows about the Revolutionary War and stuff. And then his dad dies." He makes a face. "See, it sounds stupid when I say it out loud."

"It doesn't sound stupid," I promise immediately. "Honestly, it sounds good. Is it, like, autobiographical, or . . ."

Bex makes a face, enigmatic. "My dad is alive," is all he says. "Anyway, I've been writing it since undergrad, and I've got a mostly done draft. But I just keep on . . ."

"Noodling?" I supply with a laugh. "Curse of the perfectionist, right?"

"Exactly," he says, tapping his paper cup against mine.

I'm expecting him to move to one of the other empty tables, but instead he stays where he is while I drink my second latte, caffeine buzzing wildly through my veins. We chat about all kinds of things: our Starbucks orders—Americanos, he tells me—and his parents' aging collie, an exhibit on protest art he saw at the contemporary art museum. I'm struck again by that same feeling I had the day he drove me home after school a couple of weeks ago, that he's weirdly easy to talk to for a teacher.

Not just for a teacher. For a *guy*.

I feel a blush creeping up my chest underneath my sweater, glancing over at the baristas behind the counter and wondering idly if they think Bex and I are on a date. And like, obviously *I* don't think we're on a date—he's my teacher, and he's like thirty years old—but as we sit here I can imagine dating someone like him. Someone who cares about what new plays are workshopping in Boston. Someone who knows the name of the Speaker of the House.

I drink my coffee slowly on purpose, both in an attempt to keep Bex talking and because my hands are starting to shake from all the caffeine. Out the window it's beginning to get dark. I know I should probably get back to the tournament, but part of me feels like I could hang out in this Starbucks all night. That's when Bex's phone dings in his pocket.

"Holy sh . . . ," he says when he looks at it, glancing at me and trailing off before completing the swear. "Is it really after four o'clock? How did that happen?"

I shake my head. "I'm sorry," I say, though I'm not really. "I distracted you. You didn't get any writing done."

Bex shrugs. "Let's be real," he admits, "I probably wasn't going to get any writing done anyway." Then he grins. "Besides, the conversation was worth it."

He stands up and slings his messenger bag over his

shoulder, lifts his empty cup in a salute. "Enjoy the rest of the weekend," he says with an easy smile. "And send that admission essay off before you come into my class on Monday. Noodling time is officially over."

"I will," I promise. I watch his back until Bex disappears into the crowd outside.

FOUR

My dad makes a double batch of chicken noodle soup for dinner on Sunday night, so on Monday after school I head over to Sunrise Senior Living to drop a container of it off for Gram. I know most people think nursing homes are totally creepy, and I guess they're not wrong, but I've been coming here for so long at this point that the bleachy smell and occasional confused, wandering person don't really bother me that much.

"I mean," I pointed out to my mom the last time the two of us came to visit together, "depending on your perspective, it's not actually that different from high school."

I check in at reception before climbing the stairs in the atrium and waving hello to Camille, the nurse supervisor on Gram's floor. She's wearing scrubs printed with wildflowers and a pair of bright green Crocs. Camille has scrubs in a riot of different patterns and Crocs in every color of the rainbow; she's wearing a different combination every time I see her, mixing and matching like she's a walking, talking paper doll.

"Hey, Marin," she says, tilting the plastic tub of cat-shaped Trader Joe's cookies on the counter in my direction. "All those college apps submitted?"

"Yup," I reply, reaching for a cookie. I took Bex's advice and hit send over the weekend, dorkily emboldened by his pep talk. "They're all in."

"And you're going to bring me a T-shirt when you get into Brown, right?"

"A T-shirt, a pennant," I promise her. "One of those big blankets you're supposed to use at football games, maybe."

"See now, you're making fun, but I'm gonna hold you to it." Camille grins. "Go on in, honey."

Gram's door is propped halfway with a doorstop shaped like a Boston terrier, but I knock lightly to give her some warning before easing it all the way open.

"Hey, Gram."

When she first moved into Sunrise back when I was in middle school, Gram still had way more good days than bad days, starting a little rose garden at the back of the building and organizing pinochle tournaments in the rec room. It's about fifty-fifty now; she always remembers me, but according to my mom and Camille it's better not to startle her.

"There she is!" Gram says with a smile, setting her book—a thick, slightly grisly looking mystery—down on the side table. Gram has been a member of the Book of the Month Club since the seventies, and everybody says I get my book-nerd genes from her. "Come here, you."

I bend down to wrap my arms around her narrow shoulders, careful. Gram's always been thin, but in the last couple of years she's gotten downright fragile. She says it's because she doesn't like the food at Sunrise, so a lot of times Mom and Gracie and I will cook her old recipes—chicken parm, baked ziti, her famous meatballs—and bring them over. Still, she's got to weigh less than one hundred pounds. I remember her swinging me up into the waves when I was a little kid at the beach on the Cape, how strong and tan her shoulders were. These days she feels like a bird in my arms.

"Come sit," she says now, motioning to the chair across from her, a roomy upholstered holdover from her house back in Brockton. Her room at Sunrise is suite-style, with a sitting area, a bedroom alcove, and a private bathroom she's outfitted with fancy hand soap from Williams-Sonoma and a curtain printed with arty pineapples. "Tell me about your day."

"It was okay," I say, sticking the soup in the mini fridge and hooking my backpack on the coatrack. "Pretty uneventful."

"Uneventful!" Gram raises her eyebrows, which she fills in every morning with a dark brown Revlon pencil, before getting up and heading over to the tiny kitchenette at the far end of the sitting room, pulling a jug of iced tea from the mini fridge. "How evocative."

"Sorry, sorry." I smile guiltily. "I guess it was just kind of tough to be back in school after the weekend, that's all."

Gram nods. "You know, people always say that high school is the best part of your life," she says, pouring me some without bothering to ask if I want it or not. "But that's just baloney. You're going to go to college, you're going to find out just how much there is for you out in the world. You'll see."

"I just scheduled my interview for Brown, actually," I tell her, taking a sip of my iced tea. "So with any luck, you'll be right."

"See?" Gram beams. "There you go." She went to Brown herself—or to Pembroke, technically, which is what the women's college was called before the university went coed in the seventies. She took me as her date to her fiftieth reunion a few years back, which is when I decided I wanted to go there myself. I still remember the look in her eyes when I told her, the way her whole face seemed to glow.

Now she reaches up with her free hand, tucks my hair behind my ears. "You're such a good girl, my Marin," she says. "You don't always have to be so good though. Lord knows I wasn't."

"Oh no?" I ask, unable to hide a smile.

"Don't laugh," Gram says. "I'm serious."

"I believe you," I say, although actually I don't. For all her style and sophistication, Gram is one of the most buttoned-up people I've ever met: she married my grandpa when she was twenty-two, then raised my mom and her brothers while working part-time as a bookkeeper for a discount mattress company and hosting Tupperware parties on the weekends. I've literally never seen her without lipstick; she's been wearing the same shade of Clinique since at least the eighties. "I want to hear more about this wild and crazy past, Gram."

"Oh," she says, waving her hand, the clear polish on her nails catching the sunlight trickling in through the window.

"Oh," she says again, and just like that I know her mind is wandering. The most surprising thing about Gram's illness is how fast it can make itself obvious, like she's walked out of the room even though she's still sitting right here.

"You want to see if Ina is on?" I ask before she can get flustered, reaching for the remote on the coffee table and clicking over to Food Network. My grandmother is obsessed with the Barefoot Contessa; my mom still buys her all the cookbooks on the day they come out, even though she only has a microwave and an electric kettle in her suite. Still, every once in a while we'll come visit on a special occasion and find she's made candied nuts or a specialty cocktail. I suspect Camille has something to do with it.

"She's not on until four," my gram says now, frowning; her voice has taken on a different quality, thinner and a tiny bit peevish. "And I don't like this other woman with all the cattle." Still, she settles in to watch anyway, her knobby fingers wrapped around her glass of iced tea. I lean my head against the back of the chair.

My mom is prepping chicken cutlets for dinner when I get home from Sunrise late that afternoon, the kitchen warm and cozy even as the early dusk presses against the windows above the sink. The familiar smells of garlic and butter are heavy in the air.

"How was chess?" I ask Gracie, plucking a grape from the bowl on the counter and popping it into my mouth.

"Fine," Gracie says with a shrug. She's sitting at the peninsula, reconnecting my mom's phone to the Bluetooth speaker my dad got her last Mother's Day; no matter how many times Gracie does it for her, my mom always insists it doesn't work. "I won my match."

"She beat the pants off that smug little fish-face Owen Turner," my mom—who has never let anyone's age keep her from declaring them a blood enemy—says gleefully.

I laugh, reaching out and tugging the end of Gracie's ponytail. "Well done."

"Thanks," she says, nodding with satisfaction as the speaker finally connects and the Italian opera music my mom loves fills the kitchen. "He said he was going to have to live the rest of his life in a remote village in Siberia to atone for the shame of losing to a girl."

"Well, fish-face Owen Turner is welcome to do us all a favor and pack his bags," I say brightly.

"That's what I said!" My mom drops a kiss on my temple as she pulls a tub of frozen tomato sauce out of the freezer and sticks it in the microwave. "How was Gram?" she asks, once she's hit the start button. Her voice is carefully casual, but she can't disguise the flicker of worry across her face.

"She was fine," I say, leaving out that one weird moment where she seemed to lose her train of thought. After all, it's not like there's anything anyone can do about it, and there's no point in worrying my mom for no reason. I open the door to the refrigerator, waggle a bag of lettuce in her direction. "You want me to make a salad?"

My mom looks at me for another moment, eyes just slightly narrowed. Sometimes I think she's psychic when it comes to me lying. "Sure," she says finally. "A salad would be great."

FIVE

Chloe wants to get an early start on her Christmas shopping, so we take the T into the city after school on Thursday to poke through the boutiques on Newbury Street. It's feeling like the holidays for real now, the old-fashioned lampposts festooned with evergreen wreaths and all the store windows lined with twinkle lights and sprayed with fake snow. The dusky sky is a purple-blue.

"Did you know Bex is writing a novel?" I ask as we wander through the huge Urban Outfitters, pawing through racks of fuzzy sweaters and scented candles. I pick up a giant pair of white plastic sunglasses with heart-shaped lenses and wear them around the store for a while, making dumb faces into every mirror we pass.

Chloe looks at me over a display of coffee-table books. "How do *you* know that?" she asks.

I raise my eyebrows. "So you did know?"

"No," she says, putting down the question-a-day journal she's been considering and turning toward a rack of organic lipstick. "When did he tell you about it?"

"I saw him at Starbucks in Harvard Square over the weekend," I tell her—aware even as I'm saying it that it sounds a little bit like I'm bragging, and there's a tiny chance that maybe I am. "We wound up sitting there and talking for, like, two hours."

Chloe looks surprised. "Seriously?" she asks. "What the heck did you guys even talk about for two hours?"

From the tone in her voice I can't tell which one of us she thinks would have dragged down the conversation, Bex or me.

"I mean, I don't know," I say, suddenly wishing I hadn't told her. "Random stuff, I guess. His novel, for one thing."

I fill her in on the plot points, which actually do sound a tiny bit ridiculous now that I'm the one doing the explaining. "He does a better job talking about it," I promise finally, putting the sunglasses back on the rack.

I'm expecting her to laugh, or at least be really into it, like she was back in September when we spent the full duration of a Harry Potter marathon on cable trying to figure out if he had a secret Instagram, but Chloe only shrugs, winding her scarf around her neck and nodding toward the exit.

"Come on," she says, "let's go. They don't have anything I want here."

"Okay." I follow her out onto the bustling rush-hour sidewalk; it got all-the-way dark while we were shopping, a raw, icy snap in the air. "Who are you shopping for, anyway?" I ask her, tucking my hands in my pockets to warm them.

"Nobody," she says, and forges ahead of me into the crowd.

Chloe's weird mood lingers all through the hipster bookstore and the fancy coffee shop, though she perks up when we wander into the big mall on Boylston Street, her glasses fogging up in the sudden warmth. She leads me up the escalator and directly into Sephora, her expression faintly beatific as she weaves through the rows of mascara and bronzer, picking up my wrist and spritzing me with perfume samples until I cough.

"Thank you for that," I say, sniffling a bit in a slightly suffocating cloud of vanilla and jasmine.

"You're welcome," she replies sweetly, breathing in deeply and setting the bottle back on the shelf. Sephora is Chloe's own personal happy place. "Come on, I need new lip stuff."

"Speaking of lip stuff," I say, following her through the crowded aisles, "you and Dean seem pretty friendly lately."

"Say what now?" She stops in her tracks beside a stack of metallic eye shadow palettes, her face crinkling up like I've lost my mind. "Me and *Dean*?"

"What?" I ask, kind of put off by her tone—after all, it's not like I'm pulling the idea out of nowhere. He was hanging around her locker literally this morning in an against-dress-code hoodie, munching a family-size bag of trail mix with M&M's. "What's wrong with Dean?"

"I mean, nothing's *wrong* with him," Chloe concedes, shrugging inside her puffy black coat and turning toward the M•A•C display. "And yeah, I guess he's been sniffing around or whatever since homecoming."

"Okay," I tell her. "So?"

"So, nothing." Chloe turns toward the lipsticks.

"Is this about Frank with the Sweatband from the Deli?" I tease. Chloe broke up with Frank with the Sweatband from the Deli back in the summer—which, come to think of it, makes this the longest she's gone without having a boy-friend pretty much since we met. "I mean, sure, he always kind of smelled a *little* like Genoa salami, but I'm not judging. The heart wants what it wants, et cetera."

"Oh my god, he did not!" Chloe smacks me in the shoulder, but she's laughing, which was the whole point. "And no, thank you, this is not about Frank with the Sweat-band from the Deli. I don't know. I just kind of feel like I'm over high school boys, that's all."

"Oh yeah?" I say with a snort. "Gonna start trolling the Saint Xavier's parking lot, maybe pick up a sixth grader or two?"

"Wow, you are just on fire over there." Chloe makes a face. "I'm just saying. We'll be in college soon, and then . . ." She trails off, plucking a pot of lip stain off the rack and holding it up to the light. "I don't know," she says again. "Like, do you think you and Jacob will stay together?"

"I—" Haven't thought about it really, but it feels messed up to say that out loud, even to Chloe. "I guess it depends where we wind up going," I hedge, examining a tube of concealer instead of looking directly at her.

"You mean how close he is to Brown?" she asks with a grin.

"Don't even say it!" I make a face. "We don't know that I'm getting into Brown."

"*I* know you're getting into Brown," Chloe declares, then holds up two red lipsticks. "Which one?"

I squint. "Those . . . are one hundred percent identical."

Chloe huffs. "They are not!" she protests. "Ugh, they have completely different undertones. You're useless, you know that?"

I hold my hands up like, *What can you do?* "You love me."

"I do," she admits, linking her arm through mine and tugging me toward the checkout. "Come on. I'm getting them both."

SIX

I'm heading for my locker after the last bell on Friday when I pass by the newspaper office and spy Bex lounging cross-legged on the sofa.

"Hey," I say, rapping lightly on the open door.

Bex doesn't have an office, per se, but a lot of times he hides out in here if he's got grading to do and doesn't want to deal with the teachers' lounge.

"Hey," he says now, struggling upright. He's wearing khakis and a blue plaid button-down rolled to his elbows, glasses slipping down his face the slightest bit. "Headed out?"

"Almost," I say, pulling my ponytail down over one shoulder. "Although, actually, if you've got a minute, can I run an idea for an article by you really quick?"

Bex nods, gesturing at the other end of the sofa before pulling a desk chair over to use as a footrest. "By all means."

"Thanks," I say, reaching down and pulling my planner out of my backpack. "Okay, so I was thinking—" I break off suddenly as he lets out a giant yawn, dark eyes squinched shut and the pink flash of his tongue. "Sorry," I say with a laugh, a little embarrassed. "Am I keeping you awake?"

"No, no, no, I'm sorry." Bex shakes his head, taking his glasses off and scrubbing a hand over his face before replacing them. "I just haven't been sleeping much."

"Uh-oh," I say, a sharp little thrill running through me. The word *sleeping* feels weirdly intimate coming from him, like even mentioning it opens some invisible door to the thought of . . . whatever else people do in beds. "Too many exciting papers to grade?"

"Obviously," Bex replies with a rueful smile. "No, um, honestly? My ex and I have been trying to work it out, and it's just been . . ." He waves a sheepish hand. "Yeah. It's just been."

I blink. "Oh." I keep my voice neutral, like teachers talk to me about their various romantic relationships all the time and he's the fourth or fifth of the week. I really don't want to think about what getting back together with his ex-girlfriend has to do with him not getting a lot of sleep—or, more truthfully, maybe I do, even if that's totally crossing the line.

"Anyway," Bex continues with a twist of his lips, "we ended it for good last night. Thus"—he gestures down at himself—"the desiccated corpse you see before you today."

I smile. "That sucks."

He shrugs. "It's for the best," he admits. "The thing about Lily is that she's just really—" He breaks off. "I'm sorry. This is literally the last thing I should be talking about right now."

"No, no," I say, totally curious. I can't help it. I pull one leg up underneath me on the sofa. "It's okay."

"I mean, it's not, probably," Bex counters with a shake of his head. "It doesn't exactly win me any points as an authority figure, that's for sure. But I don't know, you just kind of seem, like . . . *older* than other girls in your grade. Has anybody ever told you that?"

Nobody ever has, actually; I think about how I secretly played Littlest Pet Shop until Chloe caught me at it halfway through seventh grade. "I do?"

"Yeah," Bex says, no hesitation at all. "Honestly? I've

taught a lot of teenagers. And I like teenagers, don't get me wrong. But sometimes I listen to what, like, Emily Cerato and her friends are talking about in my classroom, and I think . . . Marin's not like that. It's like you've got an old soul or something."

Pleasure blooms inside my chest, huge and sudden. "Well," I say, ducking my head down and smiling at my planner. "Thanks." When I look up again, Bex is smiling back.

We stay there for the better part of an hour, him grading and me working on a set of calc equations that aren't due until halfway through next week. It's after four when Bex finally stands up and stretches, his shirt coming a little bit untucked, so I can see a flash of smooth bare skin at his hip.

"Okay," he says, stifling another yawn with a guilty smile. "Time to get out of here, Lospato. You need a ride home?"

"Oh!" It's the first time he's offered since that day a few weeks ago, when he told me not to tell anybody. And I didn't tell anyone, not even Chloe, and maybe there's a part of me that's been holding my breath, waiting for him to ask again. "That'd be great, actually. Thanks."

Bex nods, and I grab my stuff before following him out the side door and across the mostly empty parking lot, both of us squinting in the white light. The weather report keeps threatening snow.

"Shoot," Bex says as he's digging his keys out of his messenger bag, smacking the palm of his hand lightly against the hood of the Jeep. "You know what I didn't bring you *again* today?"

"Uh-oh," I say with a laugh. "Let me guess."

"I don't know what's wrong with me," he mutters, buckling his seat belt and turning up the heat. "I mean, sleep deprivation, for one, but that freakin' book has been sitting on my hall table since Halloween, and literally every morning I think, *Don't forget to bring that to Marin.* And every morning I walk out of the house without it."

"Sounds like you should write yourself a Post-it," I tease him.

"If I thought Post-its were enough to get my life in order I'd literally buy stock in 3M," Bex says with a grimace. Then a thought seems to occur to him.

"Actually," he continues as we pull out of the parking lot, "are you in a hurry to get home right now? We could go pick it up on the way."

That surprises me. "You don't have to do that," I say cautiously. On one hand it's not like I'm not curious about where he lives—I'm *super* curious, actually—but on the other I don't want to be a pain in the ass. "You can just bring it to me on Monday, right?"

He stops at a traffic light, fixing me with a dubious look. "Monday, possibly next week. Or next year. Maybe the year after."

"I mean, point taken," I say with a laugh. "Let's go."

Bex lives in a romantically dilapidated Victorian house carved up into three or four apartments. When we pull up to the curb he tilts his head toward the front walk. "Come on in," he says, turning off the engine. "It's freezing out here."

"Oh!" I was fully expecting to wait in the car, peering up at the mismatched windows and trying to figure out which one belonged to him; the thought of seeing the actual inside of his apartment has my heart doing backflips inside my chest. There's a part of me that wants to text Chloe right this second. Another part of me never wants to tell her at all. "Um, okay."

The hallway inside the house is overwarm and violently wallpapered, cabbage roses in aggressive pinks and fuchsias. A dusty chandelier casts dim, dramatic light across his face.

"Watch yourself," he says as I follow him up the staircase, nodding at a place where the maroon carpet is peeling up off the tread. "My mom won't even come visit me here anymore.

She thinks she's going to break her leg or get lead poisoning or something. She sends me real estate listings for these renovated, dorm-looking condos like every single day."

"Aw," I say. An image has started to form in my head of Bex's parents: stern and mostly humorless, the kind of classic New England WASPs we read about in *The Wapshot Chronicle* at the beginning of the year. I feel like he's probably lonely in a family like that. "I think it's great."

As promised, the Franzen book is sitting on the table in Bex's tiny foyer. He hands it over, and I tuck it into my backpack, but instead of herding me back out onto the sidewalk like I'm expecting, he slings his messenger bag over a teetering coatrack and shrugs out of his jacket.

"You hungry?" he asks, putting a hand on my shoulder for the briefest of moments before heading toward the narrow kitchen. "I'm just gonna grab something to drink before we go."

I shake my head. "I'm okay," I say, letting a tiny breath out as I hear him open the refrigerator. I don't want him to catch me gawking, but I can't stop looking around, wanting to commit all of it to memory: the worn leather sofa and the antique desk strewn with papers, the shelves and shelves of books. He's got actual art on his walls—real paintings by actual artists, nothing like the scrolly *Live Laugh Love* canvases my mom is always buying at HomeGoods and hanging on every available surface. A wine crate full of records sits next to a turntable by the window.

I creep farther into the living room, pulling an album out of the pile and turning it over: *Nina Simone Sings the Blues*. The sleeve has gone slightly fuzzy around the corners from being handled. I don't know anything about her, but I make a mental note to google her so I can drop her into conversation later on.

"Whatcha looking at?" Bex asks, coming into the room behind me and peering over my shoulder, a bottle of flavored fizzy water in one hand. His whole house smells like him, coffee and something that might be incense; there are more books stacked in the fireplace, a basket of *New Yorker*s overflowing on the hearth.

I hold up the record, turning to face him. "Do you actually listen to these?" I ask.

Bex smirks. "Yeah, smarty-pants," he says. "Sound quality is way better than Spotify or whatever."

"Is that true?" I ask. "Or is it just, like, what they tell you at Urban Outfitters to make you spend more money?"

Bex's eyes widen. "I don't get my records at Urban fuckin' Outfitters," he says with a laugh, reaching out and taking the album gently from my hand.

"Oh no?" I ask, thrilled and a tiny bit horrified by his language.

Bex grins, a flash of perfectly straight teeth. "No," he says, lacing his fingers through mine and tugging me a step closer to him. "I get them at a record store, like a person with half an ounce of self-respect."

I make a quiet sound then, not quite a laugh, startled by the contact and the movement and the sudden suspicion that something bad is about to happen. He reaches out and pushes a loose strand of hair away from my face.

I don't have time to register any of it though, because that's when Bex puts his free hand on my cheek, ducks his head, and kisses me.

My brain shorts out for a second, lights flickering during a thunderstorm. It's like his mouth is pressed to someone else's, not mine. I stand there frozen and let him do it in the moment, until I feel his hand move down from my face toward my chest. Suddenly every panic response in my body comes screaming to life.

"Um," I yelp, pulling away and taking an instinctive step backward. My neck feels like it's on fire. My skin is two sizes too small. "What are you doing?"

"Easy," Bex says immediately—holding his hands up in surrender, a half smile playing across his face. "I thought you—" He breaks off, clearing his throat. "Easy."

"Um," I say again, taking another step toward the doorway. I remember my mom once describing going out to dive bars in her twenties, how at the end of the night the bartender would suddenly shut off the music and turn the lights all the way up, the fun abruptly over and the whole world in stark relief. "No, I just—I should probably go."

"Oh! Yeah, totally," Bex says. He pats his pockets, flustered. "Lemme just grab my keys and I can—"

"You know what?" I shake my head. "It's not too far from here. I can totally walk."

Bex frowns. "Marin," he says. "Hey. Can we just talk for a—"

"That's okay," I say, my voice canary-bright and maybe a little hysterical. "We're totally good, I swear." I gesture toward the doorway. "I should. Um. Enjoy your weekend!"

I thunder down the narrow stairs and hoof it all the way home, even though it's freezing—my hands jammed in my pockets and a cold wind slicing through my coat. My mom is in the kitchen when I get inside, gathering ingredients for a winter spice cake to bring to my gram while Gracie plays chess on her laptop at the kitchen table.

"Hey," she says, setting the bag of flour on the counter. "I was wondering what happened to you." She looks at me for a moment, eyes narrowing like possibly she can see the blood moving under my skin. "What's wrong?"

I hesitate for a moment, gaze flicking back and forth between my mom and my sister. I have no idea what to say. If I'm being honest with myself, there's always been a tiny part of me that wondered if maybe some of the stuff Bex said wasn't totally aboveboard, if a teacher that chill and funny—and, okay, hot—was too good to be true. If sometimes his attention didn't feel . . . different. But I said yes to the ride anyway, didn't I? I sat with him in the newspaper office.

I agreed to go over to his house.

I mean, what did I *think* was going to happen?

"Nothing," I say now, clenching my fists around the straps of my backpack, then turn on my heels and head upstairs. I shut my bedroom door behind me, digging my phone out of my pocket and scrolling to Chloe's name before realizing I have no idea what to tell her. God, there's probably not even anything *to* tell. I'm blowing this way out of proportion, most likely. Maybe it's not even that big of a deal. After all, it's not like some creepy perv forced himself on me in a dark, deserted alley. It's Bex.

It's *Bex*.

And he *kissed* me.

And maybe I wanted him to, in a way? Except also, I didn't.

I'm still clutching my phone like a weapon when suddenly it buzzes in my hand, startling me so badly I drop it altogether, watching it skitter across the carpet like it's got a mind of its own. I reach down and pick it up, then drop it *again* before finally getting a grip, Jacob's name flashing across the screen. We're supposed to meet a bunch of people at Applebee's tonight, I remember as I hit the button to answer. I'm supposed to go hang out with all our friends.

"Um, hey," I manage, hoping I'm just imagining how fake and squeaky my voice sounds. "How was your practice?"

"It was awesome," Jacob tells me cheerfully, then launches into a long, convoluted story about Joey and Ahmed getting into a fight over whose gym socks were stinking up the locker room that meanders for the better part of five minutes. He's calling from his car, the blare of the radio audible in the background.

"What about you, huh, babe?" he asks finally. "What are you up to?"

"Um," I stall, making a million infinitesimal calculations in the space of a couple of seconds. I can picture him so clearly, his hand slung casually over the steering wheel and everything in his life exactly the same as it was two hours ago. "Not much. Just hanging out."

"You sure?" Jacob asks. "You sound weird."

"I do?" I don't know what it means that I'm surprised that he noticed. "Just tired, I guess."

I can't decide if I'm hoping he'll press it or not, but Jacob just hums along, as usual.

"Take a nap," he suggests cheerfully. "I'm gonna go home and take a shower and then I'll come pick you up for dinner, okay?"

I glance across my bedroom, catching sight of my own reflection in the full-length mirror on the back of the door—my braid and my uniform, the slightly wild expression on my face.

"Sure," I say, looking away again. "Sounds great."

SEVEN

"Okay," I say to Chloe the following night, holding my hand out for the bag of Tostitos she's holding. She came over to my house after our lunch shift at her parents' restaurant, the two of us sprawled out on the floor in my room. "Can I tell you something weird that happened?"

Chloe bites the corner off one triangle-shaped chip, delicate. "Literally always."

"No, I know," I say, rummaging through the bag until I've gathered a salty handful. "This is really weird though, not like, 'Jacob watching those pimple-popping videos' weird."

"Oh, I don't know," Chloe says thoughtfully, "I think those videos are kind of relaxing."

"Oh my god!" I drop my chips back into the bag. "Ugh, you're so gross."

"They are!" Chloe grins. "Okay, okay, go, tell me the weird thing."

I nod, taking a deep breath and telling myself there's no reason to be nervous—after all, it's just Chloe. "Okay," I say again. "So Bex offered to give me a ride home after school yesterday."

Chloe's eyes widen. "He *did*?"

"Yeah," I say, "but that's not the weird part. Or I mean, I guess that's part of what's weird, now that I'm saying it out loud, but—" I tilt my head back against the edge of the bed and tell her the rest of the story, ending with the kiss. "I bailed out super hard right after that, obviously. But now I don't know, like, what to do about it."

Chloe doesn't say anything for a moment. When I look over at her she's breaking a tortilla chip up into a hundred little pieces, arranging them in her lap like a mosaic. "Are you sure?" she finally asks.

I frown. "What do you mean, am I sure? Like, about what happened? Yes, I'm sure. I was there."

"No, I know, I just mean—" She stops. "Like, are you

sure he was actually trying to—like, you didn't just walk into him, or whatever?"

"Yes, I'm sure," I snap, although suddenly there's a tiny part of me that isn't. I sit up a little straighter. "Do you think I'm making it up?"

"Of course not," Chloe says, gathering the chip crumbs up off her lap and tossing them into the wastebasket tucked under my desk.

"Really?" I ask. "Because it sounds like maybe—"

"Marin!" Chloe laughs a little then. "Come on. Hey. It's me. That's not what I think."

"But?" I prompt.

"No buts!" Chloe promises. "That's awful, if he did that. That's totally gross. Was there like—" She breaks off.

"Was there what?"

"I mean, what exactly happened?" she asks, pulling her knees up to her chest and wrapping her arms around them. "Like, was it just a grandma kiss? Was there tongue? What?"

I think of his hand on my face, his palm sliding southward. It feels like somehow I'm not explaining this right. "No," I admit finally. "No tongue."

"Okay," Chloe says, sounding relieved. "Well, that's something, at least."

"I guess." I blow a breath out. "I'm sorry. I'm just—yeah." I spin around on the carpet, lying back on the floor. "Do you think I should tell somebody?" I ask the ceiling.

"You just told me."

"No, like, DioGuardi or someone? I mean, I didn't even tell my parents."

"What," Chloe asks, "to, like, try to get him in trouble?"

"I'm not trying to get anyone in trouble," I say, popping up on my elbows.

"No, of course not," she says quickly. "I didn't mean that how it came out. I guess I just . . . obviously I believe you about what happened, but are you sure he didn't just, like . . . get confused by your vibe, or whatever?"

I startle. "My *vibe*?"

"You know what I mean!" Chloe defends herself. "Or maybe *you* were confused? I'm definitely not saying you were, I'm just trying to figure out—"

"I'm not confused." Ugh, this isn't going how I thought it would at all. I take a deep breath, try to regroup. "It was weird behavior, right? Objectively, for a teacher? It was inappropriate."

"Yes, of course. One hundred percent," Chloe says, even as she's shrugging noncommittally. "But it also sounds a little like maybe you're freaking out a disproportionate amount? I wasn't there, obviously, but, how many times have we talked about how hot he is, or whatever? Maybe he was just picking up what you were putting down, or trying to make it not weird, or—"

"Seriously?" I interrupt. "How does *kissing* me make it less weird?"

"I don't know!" she says. "I'm just trying to make sense of it, that's all. And if you feel like you need to, like, go to the authorities or whatever, then I'm not going to tell you not to."

"But *you* wouldn't," I say, flopping back onto the carpet.

"I mean, no," Chloe says quietly. "I wouldn't try to ruin somebody's whole life over something I wasn't even sure I interpreted correctly."

"I'm not out to ruin anyone's life!"

"Of course not," Chloe says. "But that's what would happen, right?" She shrugs again. "You tell DioGuardi, and they fire him or whatever, and then he can't get another job because he's got this thing on his record that maybe wasn't even . . ." She trails off, reaching out and balancing a tortilla chip on my knee. "I don't know. It's *Bex*, Marin. He's literally your favorite teacher."

And mine, I can hear her adding in her mind. And everyone's.

"It's not like we have a totally normal relationship with him anyway," she says.

"Yeah," I say, closing my eyes for a moment. I don't know why all of a sudden I feel like I might be about to cry. "I guess you're right."

For a long time neither one of us says anything. Finally Chloe rolls up the bag of chips. "I've gotta go," she says, reaching for the plastic clip on my nightstand. "I told my mom I'd have the car back by eleven."

She gets to her feet before offering a hand to help me up, the two of us heading downstairs and past my parents watching an old Tom Hanks movie in the living room. "Have a good night, Mr. and Mrs. Lospato!" she calls brightly, pulling her jacket off the overloaded hook in the foyer before turning to me one more time.

"He really did all that stuff?" she asks now, and her voice is very quiet.

"Yeah," I say, still swallowing down that crying feeling one more time. God, how could I have been so stupid? "He did."

Chloe nods, and for a moment it looks like she's going to say something else, but in the end she just reaches out and unlocks the deadbolt, icy December air slicing into the house. "I'll see you Monday," she promises, and just like that she's gone.

EIGHT

I spend the rest of the weekend helping my parents get the Christmas decorations out of the attic and watching *Home Alone* on cable, trying with extremely limited success not to think about what happened. By the time third period rolls around on Monday morning, I'm a nervous wreck. For a minute I honestly consider skipping English altogether, but that's ridiculous, isn't it? What am I going to do, just cut every day for the rest of the year?

Bex isn't in his classroom as we're filing in, and for a moment I wonder—with a mixture of hope and deep, horrifying dread—if maybe he isn't even here today. Did somebody find out what happened between us? Did Chloe turn around and tell? I'm about to hiss her name across the room when Bex ambles in and shuts the door behind him, raising a hand to say hello.

"Sorry I'm late," he says, dimple popping in his cheek as he slings his messenger bag over the back of his chair. "Vending machine in the cafeteria is eating dollars today, just FYI. Not that I was just in there trying to make breakfast out of some barbecue chips and a KIND bar or anything."

He launches into a detailed biography of Joseph Heller, because we're supposed to start *Catch-22* this week. I feel like someone hit me over the head. I don't know what I was expecting, but it wasn't this bland, aggressive normalcy; for one disorienting moment it occurs to me to wonder if maybe I really did make the entire thing up.

Then I remember the press of his mouth on mine, and shiver inside my uniform blouse.

"First forty pages for tomorrow," he calls as the bell finally rings for the end of the period.

I'm shoving my notes into my backpack when he catches my eye from the front of the room.

"Hey, Marin," he says, the very theology of casual, "stick around for a sec, will you?"

So we *are* acknowledging what happened, then. Right away my skin prickles tightly and my face is on fire. I nod, hanging back as everyone else heads out into the hallway, ignoring the look I can feel Chloe shooting me as she makes for the door.

"So hey," Bex says once we're alone, perching on the edge of his desk and scrubbing a hand over his clean-shaven face. "I feel like we should probably talk, yeah?"

"Um," I say, pulling the sleeves of my uniform sweater down over my hands and crossing my arms like an instinct, shifting my weight in my beat-up Sperrys. "I mean—yeah, I don't know if—"

Bex smiles. "Marin," he says, holding his hands up. "It's just me, okay? You don't have to be afraid of me, or stand here looking like you wish you were dead, or anything like that." He rubs his cheek again, looking sheepish. "Obviously, I . . ." He trails off. "We just . . . I think maybe we had a little bit of confusion there, that's all."

I blink. "Confusion?" I repeat, before I can stop myself.

"Bad communication," Bex continues with a shake of his head. "Mortifying for both of us, obviously. But it happens."

"Um." I swallow. "Sure. Yeah." On one hand, there's something reassuring about the way he's talking about this, like it's just a dumb, awkward thing that happened and not the end of the breathing world. On the other, it occurs to me that he hasn't actually apologized for doing it.

But maybe he doesn't owe me an apology?

69

After all: *I went to his house. I flirted with him. It's not like I hadn't thought about it before.*

"In any event," Bex says now, sliding off the edge of the desk and heading for the doorway, "I just wanted to clear the air and make sure we can both move on without any weirdness. Honestly, you're such a great student, and I'd hate for this to get in the way of whatever amazing thing you're going to do when you get out of this place." He holds his hand out, like we're about to finish a business meeting. "So. We cool?"

"I—yeah, of course," I say as we shake, the touch of his smooth, cool palm sending a fresh wave of ickiness through me. "We're cool."

NINE

Chloe's waiting for me at our usual spot in the cafeteria, her untouched tray sitting on the table in front of her. "What did Bex want?" she asks, as soon as I sit down.

I shrug. "Just to make sure everything was good, I guess. Like, after—" I glance around. "After."

Chloe nods. "And you told him it was?"

"I mean, yeah." I pull a baggie of grapes out of my lunch bag, plucking them all off the stem at once to avoid looking at her. "What else was I going to say, right?"

Chloe frowns, her signature red lipstick slicked neatly across her mouth. "So it's not?" she asks. "Good, I mean?"

"No, it's not that, I just—" I break off. It's . . . confusing. After all, Chloe and I have been obsessed with Bex for the better part of the school year. But people get crushes on their hot teachers, right? That's a thing that happens. It doesn't mean I wanted—that I was *inviting*—anything real to actually happen between us.

Right?

I'm still trying to figure out how to answer when Jacob and a couple of his lacrosse buddies sit down at the table, their trays heaped with mac and cheese so gloppy you could use it to lay bricks.

"Ladies," he says, and I grin. "What's up?"

"Just talking about newspaper stuff," I say, shooting Chloe a look across the table. "We've got a print deadline at the end of the week." I pop a grape into my mouth. "Actually, did you get those article pitches I texted you?"

Chloe nods, noncommittal. "I had a bunch of ideas too," she tells me. Then, nodding at the mac and cheese on Jacob's tray: "Do you want to write something about the new menu, maybe?"

I laugh out loud, I can't help it.

"What?" She shrugs.

"It's not exactly hard-hitting journalism, that's all."

Chloe frowns again. "Is that what you want to be doing now?" she asks. "Hard-hitting journalism?"

"I just—" I break off, not entirely sure why she seems so testy all of a sudden. "Isn't that always what we're trying to do?"

Chloe makes a face at that. "I mean, it's a high school paper, Marin," she reminds me. "Not the *Globe* Spotlight team."

I'm starting to reply when there's a commotion up at the front of the cafeteria—it's Principal DioGuardi yet again, a miserable-looking Deanna Montalto in tow.

"Attention please!" he yells out across the room. "Since apparently some of you ladies have still not gotten the memo about the new uniform guidelines, I thought I'd have my friend Deanna here help me show you all what you should not be doing!"

"Seriously?" I look from Deanna to Chloe and back again. "Is he really about to make an example of her right now in front of everyone?"

"Looks that way," Chloe murmurs, biting her lip.

DioGuardi paces back and forth at the front of the cafeteria like a basketball coach watching a scrimmage. "Now," he begins, "who can tell me how Deanna is violating the uniform code today?" He nods at a freshman girl sitting at a table by the window. "How about you?"

"Um," the freshman says, her small voice barely carrying. "She isn't wearing tights?"

"She isn't wearing tights!" DioGuardi echoes cheerfully. "That's certainly one of the problems here. What else?"

Deanna stands silently as DioGuardi points out all her uniform violations one by one, from her untucked shirt to the too-big hoop earrings she's wearing. He even has Ms. Lynch, the school secretary, bring him a ruler so he can measure the length of her skirt.

"This is awful," I mutter, though when I look over at Jacob for confirmation I realize he's watching the proceedings with a good-natured smirk on his face.

"What are you doing?" I ask, jabbing him in the ribs harder than I necessarily mean to. "This isn't funny."

"Aw," Jacob says with a shrug, "it's a little funny. Besides, Deanna doesn't care. A whole cafeteria full of dudes looking at her at once is probably her dream."

"You're being freaking gross," I tell him, even as his buddies bust up laughing. I look back at Deanna's vacant face. I don't know that I've ever sat back and thought super hard about *why* everyone says she's a slut in the first place beyond the fact that her boobs are big and she had a boyfriend back in seventh grade. Even if she *has* been with a million guys, I think suddenly, even if she *is* dressing to get attention, how is that anybody's business but hers?

"Ms. Montalto," Mr. DioGuardi finishes finally, "I will see you in detention this afternoon. As for the rest of you ladies, please remember to dress yourselves in a way that's befitting of the values we uphold here at Bridgewater."

"Yeah, ladies," Jacob teases. "Have some values, why don't you?"

"I can count three different uniform violations on you right now without even trying," I say. "You're lucky Dio-Guardi didn't drag you up to the front of the cafeteria in front of everyone."

"Eh." Jacob shrugs, unconcerned. I glance over at Chloe for backup, but she's fussing with her phone inside her bag.

"Can I eat these?" Jacob asks, pointing to the rest of my grapes, and I hand them over without protest. Suddenly I'm not hungry at all.

TEN

That night I sit at my desk eating all the pink Starbursts out of a giant bag I picked up at CVS and staring at the blinking cursor on the screen of my laptop, trying with extremely limited success to put together a draft of this article about the new cafeteria menu. Normally I really like writing for the *Beacon*, but now it feels all mixed up with what happened with Bex, all those afternoons we spent in the newspaper office supposedly having such a good time. I mean, we *were* having a good time. At least I was. But now . . .

Also, damn if it isn't a tall order to make grilled chicken on top of limp romaine lettuce sound exciting and novel.

Finally I push my chair back from my desk, catching sight of myself in the mirror on the back of my closet door. My hair has gotten long, the ends still bearing traces of last summer's sun-and-lemon-juice highlights. When I was little I wanted to look like a mermaid—I remember how Chloe and I used to sleep in braids the night before a beach trip, then hole up in her bathroom or mine slathering on self-tanner, spending way longer getting ready than we ever did messing around in the waves. All at once it occurs to me how much time I've wasted in my life trying to make it look like I haven't spent any at all.

I stand up and face myself full-on in the mirror, taking in my cropped shirt and the sliver of belly that peeks up over my high-waisted jeans and wondering briefly what I'd think if I was a stranger and saw a picture of myself on Instagram. What would I say to Chloe about that girl's flat butt and smudgy mascara? Probably not "She looks smart and like a good friend," that's for sure.

I glance over at the empty place on the carpet where Chloe sat the other night, our conversation replaying like some bad radio earworm inside my head: *You're freaking out a disproportionate amount.* I got so amped up at the thought of it, but what if she's right? I went to his house, I remind myself again. I reapplied my ChapStick right there in his front seat. But was that an invitation? I didn't mean it that way—at least, I don't think I did—but maybe we did just have *bad communication*.

And then I remember: *it happened*. I was there. God, it's like even *I* want to make myself doubt myself. How messed up is that? But there are so many unspoken rules for navigating high school—for navigating life, maybe—that I can't help but try to figure out which one I broke to get myself into this situation. There are so many rules for girls.

I stretch my arms over my head and think again about what happened to Deanna at lunch today, the caught-animal look in her eyes as DioGuardi called her out in front of everyone. The longer I think about it the angrier I get—at DioGuardi, sure, but also at myself. I want to tell Deanna I'm sorry for all the casually nasty, sexist stuff I've ever heard about her, for all the times I could have said *That's not funny* and didn't. I want to tell her how unfair the whole thing is. Like, every guy wants to hook up, but if you actually do hook up, you have to worry about *this*? I want to ask her if she also feels like there are all these guidelines we're supposed to be following in exchange for the alleged privilege of walking around this world as a teenage girl: Be flirty but not *too* flirty. Be confident but not aggressive. Be funny but in a low-key, quiet way. Eat cheeseburgers, but don't get fat. Be chill, but don't lose control. I feel like I could keep on going, like a full list would cover one of those old-fashioned scrolls from cartoons about Santa Claus.

I dig through the bag and unwrap another Starburst, chewing thoughtfully for a moment before laying my hands back down on the keyboard.

RULES FOR BEING A GIRL

I type frantically for the better part of an hour, my fingers flying over the keys and my tongue caught between my teeth. I'm just finishing up when Gracie knocks on the door. "Are you going to come watch TV?" she asks, leaning against the jamb in her buffalo-check pajama pants and fuzzy slippers. "Dad's making popcorn."

"I— What?" I feel wrung out like a washcloth; I glance at the clock in the corner of the screen, sure that hours have passed and it's the middle of the night, but to my dazed surprise it's barely nine o'clock. "Um. Sure."

"Okay." Gracie looks at me for another minute. "Are you all right?"

I glance at my editorial, back at my sister. "I'm good," I tell her, smiling a little. And for the first time since that day in Bex's apartment, it actually feels like the truth.

RULES FOR BEING A GIRL

BY MARIN LOSPATO

It starts before you can remember: you learn, as surely as you learn to walk and talk, the rules for being a girl. You are Princess. You are Daddy's Little Girl. Are you ticklish? Give him a hug. You're sweet, aren't you? You're a good little girl.

You don't remember those early days, but here's what you do remember: You remember ballet class, the way your tummy stretched your pink leotard and your parents fretted over some future eating disorder, and then you were trying tap, or soccer, or what about a musical instrument? You remember "We just want you to be happy!" and you remember you said you were happy because you knew that's what they wanted to hear. How long have you been saying what everyone else wants to hear?

Time went on, and GIRLS CAN DO ANYTHING! So speak up, I can't hear you! But also: Manners, young lady. A boy is bothering you at school? Stand up for yourself! A boy is bothering you at school? He's just trying to get your attention. Do you like sparkles and unicorns and everything pink? Oh that's stupid now. Can you play in this game? Sorry, no girls allowed.

Put a little color on your face. Shave your legs. Don't wear too much makeup. Don't wear short skirts. Don't distract the boys by wearing bodysuits or spaghetti straps or knee socks. Don't distract the boys by having a body. Don't distract the boys.

Don't be one of those girls who can't eat pizza. You're getting the milk shake too? Whoa. Have you gained weight? Don't get so skinny your curves disappear. Don't get so curvy you aren't skinny. Don't take up too much space. It's just about your health.

Be funny, but don't hog the spotlight. Be smart, but you have a lot to learn. Don't be a doormat, but God, don't be bossy. Be chill. Be easygoing. Act like one of the guys. Don't *actually* act like one of the guys. Be a feminist. Support the sisterhood. Wait, are you, like, gay? Maybe kiss a girl if he's watching though—that's hot. Put on a show. Don't even think about putting on a show, that's nasty.

Don't be easy. Don't give it up. Don't be a prude. Don't be cold. Don't put him in the friend zone. Don't act desperate. Don't let things go too far. Don't give him the wrong idea. Don't blame him for trying. Don't walk alone at night. But calm down! Don't worry so much. Smile!

Remember, girl: It's the best time in the history of the world to be you. You can do anything! You can do everything! You can be whatever you want to be!

Just as long as you follow the rules.

ELEVEN

I'm headed for my locker the following morning when someone calls my name from down the hallway; I turn, and there's Bex poking his head out of the newspaper room, the collar of his plaid flannel button-down just slightly askew.

"Hey," he says cheerfully, gesturing me over. "You got a minute?"

"Um," I say, glancing at the ancient clock in the hallway. A week ago I wouldn't have thought twice about being alone in the newspaper room with Bex—would have welcomed it, even, the chance to have his whole and undivided attention—but it isn't a week ago. "Sure."

Bex nods and heads back inside the office, perching on the edge of the desk, but I hover awkwardly in the open doorway, crossing and uncrossing my arms.

"So," he says, in that same cheery voice—and am I imagining it, or does it sound just the tiniest bit hollow? "I just wanted to chat really quick about the editorial you uploaded last night."

"Sure," I repeat cautiously. The essay was the last thing I thought about before I fell asleep and the first thing I thought about when I woke up—I think it's one of the strongest things I've ever written—but something about that tone in his voice has me second-guessing myself all of a sudden. "Why, are you not into it?"

"No, no, I think it's great," Bex says quickly, holding his hands up. "It's really smart, and thoughtful, and edgy— and obviously the writing is top-notch. I guess I just wanted to make sure you'd thought through all the angles before we published it, that's all."

I frown. "What's there to think about?"

"Well, I don't know," Bex says, tilting his head to the side. "You're taking some pretty bold positions, don't you think?"

"I guess," I say slowly. "I mean, I didn't think they were *that* bold."

"Look, Marin, don't get me wrong." Bex smiles. "It's a stellar piece. This school is just full of a bunch of dopes, that's all. As your adviser, I want to make sure you're prepared for whatever blowback might come your way."

"You think I'm going to get blowback?" I ask, surprised. The idea hadn't actually occurred to me, and all at once I wonder if that makes me completely naive. "From who?"

"I have no idea," Bex says immediately. "Not from me, obviously. I just don't want you to be taken off guard if people aren't crazy about what you have to say, that's all."

I nod, crossing my arms a little bit tighter until it almost feels like I'm hugging myself. I'm getting the distinct impression he thinks I should pull the piece altogether, and part of me wants to agree with him—after all, the last thing I want is for people around school to think I'm some kind of militant feminist.

The other part of me can't help but wonder if somehow this is related to what happened in his apartment.

"Isn't that the point of being the editor of the paper?" I ask finally, forcing myself to relax my posture, to stand up straight and push my shoulders back like someone who knows her own mind and isn't afraid to speak it. "Saying stuff that makes other people uncomfortable sometimes?"

Bex looks at me for a long moment, an inscrutable expression on his face. "Fair enough," he says, as the warning bell rings for homeroom. "We'll put it in the next issue."

The seed of doubt Bex planted in my head spends all morning growing roots and leaves and flowers; by the time third period rolls around, it's practically a national park. I'm hoping for a pep talk from Chloe before the bell rings, but when she scurries into Bex's classroom her painted eyebrows are knitted tightly together.

"Okay," she says, making a beeline down the aisle and perching on the edge of my desk, blowing a tendril of yellow hair out of her eyes and dropping her electric blue leather tote bag on the linoleum with a quiet thump. "Can we talk about your editorial for a sec?"

My heart sinks. "You don't like it either?" I ask.

"No, it's not that, I just—" Chloe frowns. "Wait, who else doesn't like it?"

I shrug, glancing over my shoulder up at the front of the room and lowering my voice. "Bex was weird about it this morning. I don't know."

"He was probably just looking out for you."

"Why do I need looking out for though? Like, what about this piece is so bad that—"

"It's not bad!" Chloe interrupts. "It's just . . . a little . . . shrill."

My mouth drops open, stung. "What's shrill?"

"I mean, your *voice* is shrill right now, for one thing," Chloe teases gently, laughing a little. "Easy, tiger. I don't know. It just kind of sounds like you hate all boys, first of all. Or like you think you're experiencing some great oppression because you have to shave your legs. Or like you're about to turn into one of those girls who *doesn't* shave her legs in the first place."

"Of course I'm still going to shave my legs!" I protest. "That's not what I'm—"

"Look," she tells me, "I'm not saying we should pull it. And I'm not even giving you a hard time for going rogue on me, even though I thought we were supposed to be coeditors of this whole thing. I just think you should be ready for blowback, that's all."

"Blowback?" My eyes narrow, suddenly suspicious. That's the same word Bex used. "Did you talk to Bex about this?"

"What?" Chloe shakes her head. "No!"

For some reason I don't entirely believe her, though it's possible I'm just being paranoid. I don't totally trust my own judgment today. Make that lately.

"Okay," I say slowly. "So we'll run it?"

"We'll run it," she promises with a smile. She bumps my shoulder with hers before she sits down.

My editorial runs on the front page of the *Beacon* the following Monday, right next to the results of last week's swim meet and this week's lunch menu.

I find Jacob in the cafeteria before first period, where he's eating an egg sandwich and scrolling through Snapchat on his phone. "Hey," I call, relieved by the sight of him. I was up half the night wondering if I was making a huge mistake—opening myself up to all kinds of unnecessary drama, upsetting the status quo—but that's ridiculous, isn't it? After all, it's just an editorial. And really, is any of it even that controversial? I mean, the rules for being a girl are ridiculous. Anyone can see that.

Jacob doesn't smile back. "Hey," he says, and that's when I notice the paper spread out in front of him like a placemat.

"Don't tell me," I say, sitting cautiously down in the chair beside him. "You're not a fan."

Jacob shrugs. "It's not that I'm not a fan," he says. "It just . . . didn't make me feel very good, that's all."

"It didn't?" I ask, momentarily confused. "Why not? I mean, it's not about you."

"Maybe not," Jacob counters, "but everybody's going

to think it is. Like, is this really what you think all guys are like?"

"The piece isn't even *about* guys though," I protest. "It's about the expectations on girls, that's all."

"I guess," Jacob says, sounding wholly unconvinced.

"You know, you could try to say something nice about it," I snap, suddenly irritated. "Since I'm ostensibly your girlfriend and all."

"Ostensibly my girlfriend?" Jacob's eyes narrow. "What does *that* mean?"

I glance around the cafeteria, uneasy; it's pretty empty at this hour, but we're hardly alone. I can see a pair of freshmen a few tables over pretending not to listen. "It means I would love if you could try to be a little bit more supportive, that's all," I say, lowering my voice to a murmur. "I'm sorry. I'm just not a hundred percent sure about how people are going to react to it, so—"

"So then why did you publish it in the first place?" he interrupts. "And also, like, you obviously don't care what I think either way, since you didn't even give me a heads-up— I had to hear about it from freakin' Joey, which—"

"I don't need your permission to write an editorial."

"That's not what I'm saying!" Jacob shakes his head. "Do you hear me saying that right now?" He sighs.

"Come on," he says, reaching for my hand and squeezing. "I'm sorry you're stressed out about it. If it makes you feel better, it's not like people are exactly clamoring to read the *Beacon* the second it comes out."

"Seriously?" I ask, pulling away. "Probably nobody even read it? *That's* the best you can do?"

Jacob's shoulders stiffen. "What's your *problem* this morning, huh?" he asks, sounding honestly baffled. "Are you on the rag or what?"

I blink at him for a moment. "Okay," I blurt, shoving my chair back with a loud, grating screech. Suddenly I don't care who's paying attention. "You know what? I don't think this is working."

"Wait a second." Jacob's eyes widen. "What's not working?"

"This." I gesture between us. "You and me, all of it. I think . . . maybe I just need some space. From you. Like, permanently."

I'm actually shocked to hear the words come out of my mouth, and from the look on Jacob's face, I can see he is too. Ten minutes ago, breaking up with him wasn't even on my radar. But suddenly it seems like the only logical choice.

"What the hell, Marin?" Jacob stands up too, so we're

eye to eye, his chair clattering. "Where the hell is this coming from? Like, okay, I'm sorry I said that thing about you having your period. That was fucked. But it's nothing to break up over."

"Isn't it?" I ask, although now that I'm actually thinking about it, it feels like so much more than that one stupid comment. It's the list his lacrosse buddies made last year ranking freshman girls in order of hotness. It's how he laughed at Deanna in the cafeteria. It's his smirk when we talk about the dress code, and the way he always assumes I want Froyo and not ice cream. It's a million little things that I told myself didn't matter, except for all of a sudden they completely do.

"I don't know, dude."

"Fine," Jacob says, throwing his hands up. He's pissed now, his mouth gone thin and his cheeks an angry pink. "We're done, then. You know, it's probably better we break up anyway, if this is what you're going to be like now."

"Oh?" I raise my eyebrows. "And what exactly am I like?"

"Like this," he says, waving at me vaguely. "You write some weird article and start acting like a total psycho and . . . what? Turn into some crazy feminist?"

I laugh out loud at that, a mean hollow bark. "Some

crazy— You know what, Jacob? Maybe that's exactly what I'm turning into. And maybe you can go screw yourself."

For a moment Jacob just stares at me, his mouth opening and closing. I've never said anything like that before—to him, or to anyone. I'm waiting for the surge of horror, but instead I just feel kind of powerful. Maybe I should tell people to screw themselves more often.

"Okay then," he finally says, crumpling his sandwich wrapper up into a ball and chucking it into the bin at the front of the cafeteria. "See you never."

"See you never," I echo, slinging my backpack over my shoulder and heading to my first-period class.

Jacob's reaction to my editorial is a pretty good litmus test for the rest of the morning, all told. Dean Shepherd makes a big show of cowering like he thinks I'm going to hit him. Hallie Weisbuck makes a Hillary Clinton joke.

"Maybe it's a good thing," Chloe says consolingly at the beginning of Bex's class. "Honestly, this is the most people have talked about the *Beacon* since we started editing it."

"Headlines don't sell papes, Marin's crazy editorials sell papes?" I ask, riffing on *Newsies*, which we used to watch all the time back in middle school. Then I frown. "Oh, also, I just broke up with Jacob."

"Wait, what?" Chloe's hands drop. *"Why?"*

"Because—" I break off. All of a sudden *His casual sexism randomly started to bother me when he said he didn't like my piece* doesn't feel like the banner cause it did this morning. "Because—"

Chloe shakes her head. "Marin, what is going *on* with you?"

"Okay," Bex calls before I can answer, leaning against his desk up at the front of the room. "You guys ready to get started?"

I slink low in my chair as he goes over this week's vocab unit, then assigns a response paper due the following week. "I've got a new reading list for you all to take a look at," he says, passing out a stack of papers. "I want you guys to pick one of the short stories on this list, then write two to three pages on one of the literary techniques the author uses."

It's an easy assignment, the kind of thing I'll be able to knock out in an hour or two, but as I scan the list of authors I find myself frowning: John Updike, Michael Chabon, John Cheever. Before I can quell the impulse, my hand is up in the air.

"Yep," Bex says, nodding in my direction. "Uh, Marin."

"I'm sorry, I just—" I look around a little nervously. Dean Shepherd already has a smirk on his face. "Shouldn't there be some female authors on this list? Or authors who aren't white?"

Bex looks surprised for a moment; he glances down at the list, like possibly he hadn't noticed the omission. He tsks quietly, then looks back up at me. "Ooookay then, Marin," he says brightly. "Not into the list, huh? What do you think I should add?"

"Oh—um." I hesitate, my mind going completely, terrifyingly blank. In this moment I honestly couldn't name a single short story if my life depended on it, let alone one written by somebody other than a dead white guy. "I guess I hadn't really thought it through that far," I admit finally.

"Well," Bex says in that same cheerful voice—slightly plastic, I think now, more sarcasm than actual friendliness. It's the first time all year he's seemed anything less than 100 percent chill about an assignment—although I guess it's also the first time I've complained. "Make sure you let us know if you come up with anything, yeah?"

The class kind of chuckles, and I nod miserably, feeling my whole body prickle with embarrassment. Chloe shoots me an incredulous look. God, why couldn't I just have kept my mouth shut? It's not like I wasn't drawing enough attention to myself already.

Bex is turning back to the whiteboard when there's

a knock on the open door. I glance over, and there's Ms. Klein in the doorway in her navy-blue shirtdress and her big round glasses, her dark hair in a tidy bun on top of her head.

"Mr. Beckett," she says, gaze flicking from him to me and back again in a way that makes me wonder if she heard the whole exchange. "I've got your attendance forms from Ms. Lynch. I told her I'd drop them off."

"Oh!" Bex nods, shooting her a megawatt smile. "Thank you."

By the time he gets back to his desk he seems to have forgotten about me, thank God. Still, I spend the rest of the period slouched in my seat, aching to disappear. Chloe makes a beeline for me once the bell rings for the end of the period, grabbing my arm and steering me out into the hallway.

"Okay, did you seriously need to add picking a fight with Bex in front of the whole class to the list of dramatic things you did today?" she asks, joking, but also not really. "Do you have raging PMS or what?"

"Oh, come on." I don't tell her I dumped Jacob for basically saying that exact thing to me not three hours ago. "I wasn't picking a fight," I defend myself instead. "It just felt like—"

"Marin!"

I flinch. I cannot take one more person giving me shit

today. But when I turn around it's Ms. Klein, holding her water bottle in one hand and a slim white paperback in the other. "Can I talk to you for a minute?"

"Um." I look from her to Chloe and back again. "Sure," I say, and follow Ms. Klein down the hall.

"I overheard your conversation with Mr. Beckett," she tells me, and I grimace.

"I don't know that I'd call that a conversation," I admit. "I totally froze."

Ms. Klein smiles. "It happens," she says. "But it was a good impulse on your part—an all-white, all-male reading list is ridiculous. Next time you'll have to be better prepared, that's all. Here"—she holds out the book for my inspection—"this might be a good place to start."

I look down at the title: *Bad Feminist*, by Roxane Gay.

"You know," she says, looking at me thoughtfully, "if you're not happy with the way things are around here, you ought to do something about it."

She heads down the hallway before I can ask her what she means exactly, then turns back to face me. "By the way," she calls, "I really liked your piece."

I read *Bad Feminist* in the library at lunchtime and in between classes and tucked into my bed late at night, and two mornings later I go to see Ms. Klein before the first-period bell rings. She's sitting in the bio lab going over lesson plans, classical music playing softly on her phone beside her. Her shirtdress is a deep hunter green.

"Hi, Marin," she says, smiling. "How'd it go with the book?"

"I think I have an idea," I tell her, instead of answering. "But I need your help."

TWELVE

"I'm just warning you now, I don't think anyone's going to come," I tell Ms. Klein two weeks later, perching nervously on the edge of a lab bench after the eighth-period bell. When I first had the idea for a feminist book club, the night after she gave me the Roxane Gay book, it seemed almost brilliant—what a great *fuck you* to Mr. DioGuardi's ridiculous dress code and Bex's sexist reading list, right? What a great *fuck you* to everything that's been going on. I made fliers and agonized over our first book before finally deciding on *The Handmaid's Tale* because that was what the library had the most copies of; I filed new-student-organization paperwork with Ms. Lynch in the admin suite.

Now that it's the day of our first meeting though, I just feel like the host of a party nobody wants to come to: even Chloe begged off in favor of an extra shift at the restaurant, which probably shouldn't have surprised me at this point but still sort of sucked. The fact that I couldn't convince my own best friend that a feminist book club was a good idea doesn't bode super well for its success.

Ms. Klein shrugs. "So then no one comes," she says. "You and I can talk about the book ourselves." She nods at the Dunkin' Donuts box on the desk beside her. "And eat twenty-five Munchkins apiece."

I laugh, which calms me down a little; I'm about to ask her if she's read anything else by Margaret Atwood when a couple of nervous-looking freshmen I vaguely recognize as members of the jazz band sidle into the classroom. My heart leaps when I realize they're both holding copies of the book.

"Hey," the taller one says, a white girl with her blond hair in two Princess Leia buns, looking around with no small amount of trepidation. "Um, is this the book club?"

"Sure is," Ms. Klein says. "Have a seat."

It's a little bit awkward, but to my surprise, a handful of other people trickle in one by one: this kid Dave, an AV dude with carroty hair and a pale face full of freckles, and Lydia Jones, who's black and works on the lit mag. Elisa Hernandez, the five-foot-tall captain of the girls' volleyball team, shows up with a couple of her teammates.

"You guys have a big game coming up, right?" Ms. Klein asks, and Elisa beams.

"We were state champs last year," she explains with a nod. "We're defending our title."

"Seriously?" I ask. I don't exactly have my ear to the ground around school lately, but I've heard exactly nothing about this. I think of how everybody—me included—always shows up to cheer for our sucky football team, even though they won like twice all of last season. "How come they're not doing a pep rally for you guys?"

"Are you kidding?" Elisa asks as her teammates giggle. "We can barely even get a bus for away games most of the time."

I frown. "That's so obnoxious." It's like now that I'm looking for inequality, I'm seeing it everywhere, categorizing a thousand great and small unfairnesses everywhere I go. Why didn't I really see this before?

"Sounds like a great topic for your next op-ed, Marin," Ms. Klein says pointedly, popping a Munchkin into her mouth.

Which—huh. I look over at Elisa, raising my eyebrows.

"You want to do an interview?" I ask, and Elisa grins.

Eventually Ms. Klein steers us back around to *The Handmaid's Tale*. I've never been in a book club before, and I printed a list of discussion questions off the internet in case there were any horrifying lulls in the conversation, but it turns out we don't even need them: Lydia and Elisa are big talkers, and Dave is quietly hilarious, with a sense of humor so darkly dry it takes me a full beat to realize when he's joking. We're talking about the similarities between the Republic of Gilead and modern-day America when somebody knocks on the open door. I look up, and there's Gray Kendall in his Bridgewater Lax hoodie, backpack slung over one bulky shoulder.

"Uh," he says, his dark eyes flicking around the room. "Sorry I'm late. Is this the book club meeting?"

Right away I sit up a little straighter. "Why?"

"Marin," Ms. Klein chides mildly. "You're looking at it, Gray."

"Cool," Gray says. He looks at me a little strangely, then holds up a book—a battered paperback copy of *The Handmaid's Tale*, a bright orange USED SAVES sticker peeling off the spine. "Can I, uh—?"

"You did not read that book," I blurt before I can stop

myself. I know I'm being hugely rude, but he's obviously got some kind of ulterior motive. For one insane second I wonder if Jacob sent him to mess with me.

"Um." Gray huffs a laugh, good-natured but slightly disbelieving. "Yeah, I did."

My eyes narrow. "The whole thing?"

"Yeah."

I look at him skeptically, trying to figure out what on earth his game is. A random lax bro showing up here like some kind of Trojan horse who's acting all interested to try and . . . what? Infiltrate my book club? That makes no sense.

Everyone else is watching silently. Dave clears his throat.

"Fine," I say eventually. "You can stay."

Gray smiles then, saluting me with his tattered paperback and making his way to an empty seat across the circle. Ms. Klein asks a question about Offred and the Commander, and the discussion is pretty animated from there. I'm expecting Gray to try to dominate the conversation, but to my surprise, he mostly keeps his mouth shut; when I glance over in his direction he's leaning slightly forward in his seat, listening to Elisa with a furrowed brow. He's *so* quiet, in fact, that as we're about to wrap up, Ms. Klein nods in his direction.

"You've been keeping to yourself over there, Gray," she says pleasantly. "Anything you took from the book that we haven't covered?"

"Um." Gray clears his throat. "I mean, I'll be honest, I thought it was terrifying. My heart was pounding the whole entire time. I almost peed my pants when that girl's plane to Canada got stopped on the runway."

I frown. That definitely didn't happen in the book, unless I somehow missed it. "Which girl?" I ask; Lydia and Elisa look at him curiously.

"The main one," he explains, for once in his life looking vaguely uncomfortable at the prospect of this much female attention at once. "You know, the one who was on *Mad Men*."

And there it is. "Uh-huh," I say, satisfied. "That's what I thought."

"All right," Ms. Klein says, barely hiding a smile. "We should break up for today anyway, but I'll meet you all back here next week." We're going to read mostly short stories and essays, we decided, for the sake of being able to meet more frequently. "Any of you who want to take leftover Munchkins home, feel free."

I pocket a couple of glazed and head out to the parking lot, where I'm surprised to catch Gray pacing back and forth in front of the building, stopping every few feet to frown down at what looks like his watch.

"You okay over there?" I call out.

Gray nods sheepishly. "Step counter," he calls by way of explanation, waggling his wrist in my direction. "But it's not working."

I laugh, I can't help it. "Seriously?" I don't know what it is about this guy that makes me want to heckle him.

"What's wrong with a step counter?"

I shake my head, walking closer. "I mean, nothing, if you're my mom."

"Is your mom extremely physically fit?" Gray fires back.

"If Zumba counts, absolutely she is." I nod at his wrist. "What's your goal?"

"Twenty thousand."

I raise my eyebrows and shrug my peacoat around my shoulders. "Every day?"

He shrugs. "It's not that much, really."

"You don't have to have false modesty about your step count," I say with a smile. "I'm not that impressed."

"Clearly," Gray says, grinning back. I can't tell if he's flirting with me or not. Even if he is, I know it doesn't mean anything. Gray is notorious for flirting with everyone.

"So what were you really doing in there, huh?" I can't resist asking, nodding my head back toward the building. "With the book club, I mean."

Gray makes a face. "College apps," he admits. "I need to bulk up extracurriculars." He tilts his head to the side. "I thought it was ballsy how you fought with Mr. Beckett though. So I came to support. Or like—" He frowns. "I guess *ballsy* isn't the right word, huh?"

"*Ballsy* is fine."

"*Brave* is what I meant."

I smile again, more slowly, and this time nothing about it is a tease. "I'm sorry I gave you a hard time in there," I tell him.

"It's cool," Gray says. "I get it." The strangest part is how it seems like maybe he does. I think of his serious expression when Jacob made that stupid joke at Emily's party, the way he always sort of seems to keep his distance from the rest of the lacrosse guys. Just for a moment, I wonder if possibly there's more to Gray Kendall than I thought.

My phone rings inside my backpack—the kicky little trill that means it's my mom—but when I go for it the busted zipper on the bottom pouch catches again. I swear quietly, yanking with absolutely no success whatsoever.

"It's just stuck," I explain, a little awkwardly. "I probably just need a new one."

Gray shakes his head. "You got ChapStick? Actually, you know what, never mind. I do." He digs a tube of it out of his pack pocket and uncaps it with his teeth, rubbing the stick along the zipper until it slides open without a problem. "There," he says, dimple flashing as he hands it back over. "Good as new, right?"

"Yeah," I say, smiling back in spite of myself. "Good as new."

THIRTEEN

"Hey there, Marin," Chloe's dad says, grinning at me from behind the bar when I come into Niko's that night. "I read your editorial. Very good."

I grin back, rolling my eyes a little. "Thanks."

"I'm serious," he says cheerfully.

I've always liked Steve, with his thick eyebrows and beer belly and incessantly corny dad jokes.

"You go, girl."

"Oh my god," Chloe says, brushing by behind me and heading for the kitchen. "Dad, can you stay out of feminist politics for today?"

Steve frowns, rubbing a hand over his bushy beard as he watches her go. I just shrug.

I catch up with her back by the wait station, where she's tying on her apron.

"Hey." I offer a sheepish smile. "I hardly saw you today. Everything okay?"

"I'm fine," Chloe says immediately, offering me a quick smile back. "It's just been super busy."

I feel my lips twist; I've never *not* spent so much time with Chloe as I have this past week. "You sure?"

"Totally," she says. "How was your book club?"

"Good!" I say, surprised to find that I mean it, and launch into a detailed description of our meeting. I'm telling her about our plan to make *Nolite te bastardes carborundorum* T-shirts for next week's dress-down day before I realize she isn't listening at all.

"You should think about joining," I finish weakly. Then, "Chlo, what's *wrong*?"

Chloe sighs. "Look," she says, "this is probably going to sound bitchy, and I honestly don't mean for it to, but like. You're just so *different* lately. Like, where's Marin? My fun, cool best friend Marin?"

She holds her hands up, glancing over her shoulder toward the dining room. "I know you've had some . . .

stuff . . . ," she says meaningfully. "But I thought you were going to put all that behind you. And instead you're just like . . . rolling around in it, I don't know."

I blink. "Rolling around in what, exactly?"

"Don't get mad," Chloe says. "I just—"

"Ladies!" Steve calls, deep voice booming from behind the bar. "Tables, please."

We don't talk for the rest of the night, orbiting around each other like two competing moons. Yes, I've had some *stuff*, I think to myself, a little bitterly. And I have put it behind me, obviously. I didn't tell anyone. I'm still doing everything I was doing before. But I'm also thinking about things a little differently. Is there something wrong with that?

By nine thirty, I've had enough. This is ridiculous, I decide finally. *Where's Marin? I'm right* here. I drop the check for the last of my tables, two middle-aged guys I'm pretty sure were celebrating their anniversary. It's *me*. It's *Chloe*. I'll see if she wants to get a late-night Starbucks on the ride home. We'll listen to the new Sia album on Spotify and talk it out.

When I stow my apron and head out into the parking lot though, I look around for a long moment before I frown. Chloe has driven me home from every shift since she got her license last summer, but I don't see her SUV—a tan Jeep with a cartoon sloth bumper sticker affixed to the back window—anywhere.

I yank my phone out of my backpack. *Did you leave?* I text.

Her reply comes thirty seconds later. *ACK I'M SO SORRY! Asked my dad to tell you, but he must have spaced. Kyra's having a boy crisis so I said I'd go see her. Can you find a ride???*

If I think too much about the likelihood that Chloe has really ditched me for her dorky cousin Kyra, I might lose it, so instead I sit down on a bench outside the restaurant and consider my options for getting home: it's too far to walk. My parents are at a scholarship fund-raiser Grace's chess teacher throws every year all the way in Burlington. And I sure as shit can't call Jacob. I scroll through my phone, trying to figure out which of my friends I haven't alienated recently who might also have access to a car. Nothing like standing alone in the parking lot of a strip mall outside a Greek restaurant at ten on a Friday night to put your life choices in glaring perspective.

I'm about to go back inside and throw myself on Steve's mercy when a thought occurs to me. I bite my lip, swiping through my contacts until I find Gray's name. He put his number in there himself after the book club meeting today, then texted himself so he'd have mine: "In case I need help with the big words," he explained, handing my phone back to me with a flourish.

Hey, I text now, hitting send before I can talk myself out of it. *Are you busy?*

He shows up fifteen minutes later, pulling up to the curb outside the restaurant in a ten-year-old Toyota with a bobblehead dog affixed to the dashboard. "Somebody call an Uber?" he asks as I climb in.

"Hey," I say with a grateful grin. "Thank you. You're totally saving me right now."

"No problem." His car smells like cinnamon Altoids and a little bit like a gym bag; his phone is upside down in the cupholder, Kendrick Lamar echoing quietly from the tinny speaker. "No Bluetooth," he explains, a little sheepish.

"I'm going to have to dock you a star," I tease, nudging aside a half-dozen empty Pepsi bottles and setting my backpack on the floor between my feet. "Seriously, though, I mean it. Thanks. I didn't think you'd be around."

"Because I'm so popular?"

I make a face. "I mean, you're more popular than me right now, that's for sure."

Gray doesn't comment. "I was out with some friends,"

he admits, glancing over his shoulder before pulling out onto the main road, "but I was tired of them anyway."

"You were, huh?"

"Yeah," he says easily. "I'll be honest with you, Marin. I've been thinking I need a change."

He's full of shit, clearly, but I smile anyway. I lean my head against the back of the seat rest. "You and me both."

"So, um," he says. "Where to?"

"Oh, crap!" I laugh and give him my address. "You can just drop me at the corner of Oak if you don't want to deal with the roundabout. I can walk the rest of the way."

"Now what kind of Uber driver would I be if I did that?" Gray asks with a grin. Then: "Hey, are you hungry?"

I literally just ate half a tray of spanakopita, but . . . "Are *you*?"

"I mean, I'm seventeen," he says, grinning crookedly. "I'm literally always hungry."

We stop at the Executive Diner on Route 4, following a stern-looking waitress to a booth by the window. I order a peanut butter milk shake while Gray gets a cheeseburger with onion rings and a side of chocolate chip pancakes. "I've never actually been in here at night before," he says, looking around at the chipped Formica tables, the few schleppy middle-aged dudes posted up at the bar.

"Oh no?" I ask, wrinkling my nose at him over my milk shake. "Too busy wining and dining the ladies of Bridgewater Prep?"

"Or writing feminist op-eds," he counters with a smile.

"Or getting kicked out of fancy schools for being a degenerate?"

I'm teasing, but Gray flinches a little. "Is that what I did?" he asks, raising his dark eyebrows across the table.

"Isn't it?" I ask. "I mean, I heard . . ." I trail off. "Shit. I'm sorry. I'm an asshole."

"Nah, you're fine." Gray smiles, dunking one of his onion rings in a ketchup/mayo/hot sauce concoction of his own making. "I don't know how that rumor got started. I mean, I do, I like to throw parties, but that's not what I got expelled for."

"So what happened, then?" I ask, stirring my milk shake with a long metal spoon instead of looking at him. "I mean, you don't have to tell me, obviously."

"No, it's cool." He shrugs. "I was too dumb."

My head snaps up. "You're not dumb," I say immediately.

Gray waves a hand. "I mean, sure, not *dumb*, but . . . I've got, like, ADHD and stuff, and was not meeting Hartley's, uh, rigorous academic standards."

I frown. "Don't they have to accommodate you for that?" I ask. "It's a learning disability, no?"

"I mean, sure," Gray says. "But you also have to like . . . do your work every once in a while."

"Ah," I say, feeling my face relax into a smile. "Right. I can see how that would be part of the bargain."

"Yeah. Anyway," Gray continues, "people are going to think what they want to think about you, right? So I just kind of . . . let them think it. It's a better story, in any case."

"But don't you ever want to set the record straight?" I dip my fork in his ketchupy sauce, tasting cautiously. Not bad.

Gray shrugs. "Sure, sometimes," he says, "if it's somebody whose opinion I give a shit about. But mostly I feel like: it's only a few more months, right? What do I care?"

"I guess," I say slowly. "Where are you headed next year, do you know?"

Gray groans, pretending to upend his plate of pancakes and slither onto the floor underneath the booth—only then he almost *does* knock over his Pepsi, grabbing the big plastic cup at the last second. His reflexes are impressive, I've got to give him that much.

"Uh-oh," I say with a laugh. "Sorry. Touchy subject?"

Gray sighs, scrubbing a hand over his face. "Both my moms are lawyers, right? Or actually, it's worse—one of them is a lawyer, and the other one is a law *professor*. And both of them went to St. Lawrence, and both of them want me to go there and play lacrosse, because they donate a ton of money there every year, so it's like the one place I'm guaranteed to get in even though I'm an idiot."

"Stop saying that," I tell him, kicking him under the table before I quite know I'm going to do it. "You're not an idiot. What do *you* want to do?"

"Paint," Gray deadpans, his face heartbreakingly serious for a moment before it busts wide open into a goofy grin. "No, I'm kidding. I kind of don't want to go at all, honestly. I had to volunteer at this after-school program in Fall River for community service last year—which, yeah, I'm not saying that everything you heard about my partying was a lie."

"Laundry detergent?" I ask, raising my eyebrows.

"I didn't tell anyone to eat laundry detergent!" Gray says, sounding outraged. "Like, Jesus, I'm the one with fucking ADHD, and even I know enough not to eat soap."

I snort. "Fair enough."

"Anyway, I had to go there three times a week and play games with these little kids, and at first it was a total drag, but I actually really liked it, so I still go, even though I did all my hours. And they like me too, I guess, because they offered me a full-time gig after graduation if I want it."

"That's awesome," I say—picturing it before I can stop myself, trying not to find it charming and failing completely. "But your parents—your moms, I mean—aren't on board?"

Gray grimaces. "Oh, no way. Not go to college? As far as they're concerned I might as well sell my body for drug money. Or like, go work for the US government."

Gray finishes his burger-and-pancake feast, plus a slice of questionable cheesecake from the spinning case near the cashier; his shoulder bumps mine as we head outside into the raw, chilly night.

"Can I ask you a rude question?" I say as we cross the parking lot. "If your grades are really that bad, what are you doing in AP English?"

Gray snorts. "It was the only language arts requirement that would fit in my schedule," he explains, clicking the button to unlock the doors to the Toyota. "They made an exception so I could play lacrosse. Which," he says, obviously reading the expression on my face in the neon light coming off the diner sign, "I recognize is probably the same special treatment that makes it so the girls' volleyball team doesn't get a bus."

"Wait—" I start, remembering Gray wasn't even there when we started talking about that.

"I was standing outside the door before I came in," he explains. "I was nervous."

I smile at that, sliding back into the passenger seat. "It's a fucked-up system, that's all. And for what it's worth, I'm really glad you're in that class with me. And I'm glad you came to book club."

"Yeah," he says. "I'm glad I am too."

We ride to my house mostly in silence, just the sound of Gray's tinny iPhone speaker and the slightly labored hum of the Toyota's engine.

"Thanks again," I tell him when we pull up in front of my house. "You really bailed me out."

"Yeah, no problem," he says. "I'll see you Monday."

"See you Monday," I echo, reaching down for my backpack. I've got my hand on the car door when he touches my arm.

"Hey, Marin, by the way?" Gray clears his throat, like maybe he's a tiny bit nervous again. "I, um. Really liked your article."

I laugh out loud, surprised and weirdly delighted, but then it's like the laugh jangles something loose in me, and for a moment I think I might be about to burst into tears.

Instead, I take a deep breath and smile at him in the green glow of the dashboard.

"Thanks."

FOURTEEN

Saturday night finds me sitting at my desk in my pajamas, trying to keep my eyes from glazing over as I scroll boringly through an ancient SparkNotes guide to the symbolism in "The Swimmer." Chloe ended up spending the weekend with Kyra, so instead of hitting Starbucks or driving around singing along to her latest Spotify masterpiece like we usually would, I'm listening to Sam Smith, picking at my short-story paper for Bex's class, and—okay, I can admit it—thinking about Gray. I'm not looking for a new boyfriend, obviously. But still. I liked talking to him. I liked the feeling that he actually cared about what I had to say.

I'm making zero progress on this paper, meanwhile.

Part of me just wants to say screw Bex and go rogue and write it on the Hunger Games essay from *Bad Feminist*, but what good would that do? I'd just be hurting myself in the end.

Grace knocks on my open door. "Will you do that thing with the flat iron?" she asks, holding it up and rotating it in a circle to demonstrate.

"Sure," I say, feeling my eyebrows flick before I can quell the impulse. She's dressed in skinny jeans and a crop top I'm not entirely sure my mom is going to let her wear out of the house, plus a pair of wedge booties that are definitely mine. "Where are your glasses?" I ask, ignoring the petty theft for now in favor of getting up and rolling the desk chair in front of the full-length mirror on the back of my closet door.

Grace shrugs, a quick jerk of her shoulders. "I don't need them."

That is . . . some magical thinking if ever I've heard it. "Gracie," I say, struggling not to laugh, "you're basically straight-up blind without your glasses. You're going to be walking into walls like Mr. Magoo."

Grace flops down into the chair, sighing loudly in the direction of the hallway. "Well if Mom would just let me get contacts, that wouldn't matter."

"Why *does* it matter, huh?" I ask, frowning a little as I reach down to plug the flat iron into the wall. "Where are you even going?"

"Just to the movies with some people in my class."

"Some people . . . ," I echo, scooping my own hair out of my face and sensing there's more to the story here. "Any person in particular?"

Gracie tilts her head back, her long brown hair reaching almost to the carpet. "I mean, there's a boy," she admits grudgingly. "But it's not a big deal."

"Oh yeah?" I gather up her hair in both hands, raking through the tangles and betting on the fact that she'll say more if and only if I act like I'm not curious. "Grab me that claw clip, will you?"

Sure enough: "His name is Louis," she continues, handing it over; I divide her hair into sections as I wait for the iron to heat up. "And he's so cute. And when we talk in Spanish I think he likes me—like, he's always laughing at my jokes and stuff—but he's popular." She screws her face up in the mirror, or maybe she's just squinting to try to see herself. "And just, with the glasses, and the chess—"

"You *love* chess!" I blurt, unable to help it. "And you're fucking amazing at it, so—"

"That's not the point!" Grace interrupts. "The other

girls in my class . . ." She trails off. "They have boobs, and one of them has eyelash extensions. And I basically still look like a little kid."

You are *a little kid*, I think immediately, but at least I know better than to say it out loud. I gaze at Gracie in the mirror, her clear skin and straight eyebrows, the scar on the edge of her mouth from the time she took a header off her skateboard when she was seven. I want to tell her that Opal Cosare was the first person to get boobs in my class and the boys made her life a living hell over it. I want to tell her that getting older isn't everything it's cracked up to be. But I don't want to scare her off.

I'm quiet for a moment, clamping her hair in the flat iron and pulling gently. Chloe taught me this trick, I think with a tiny pang behind my rib cage, patiently doing it for me until I figured it out for myself.

"Anybody who doesn't think you're adorable in your glasses isn't worth it anyway," I say finally, flicking my wrist to make a perfect fashion-blogger wave.

"You have to say that," Gracie retorts, rolling her eyes. "It's like, in the big-sister constitution. Next thing you'll be telling me is I'm perfect just the way I am."

"I mean, you *are* perfect the way you are," I tell her. "But it's not like I didn't go through this exact thing in eighth grade. Remember when I begged Mom to let me get a belly button ring before that pool party at Tamar Harris's house?"

"Oh my god, I forgot about that," Grace says, grinning goofily. "You kept threatening to do it yourself with a sewing needle."

"I don't even think there *are* any sewing needles in our house," I say with a laugh. "Like, when was the last time you saw Mom sew something? But I just thought that belly button ring was the key to my glamorous teenage life or something, I don't even know." I remember the run-up to that party with a kind of visceral embarrassment—the girl who searched high and low for the perfect two-piece and attempted to contour a six-pack onto her stomach with makeup, wanting to prove how chill and fun and sexy she was on the eve of her middle school graduation—and at the same time I wish I could go back and protect her.

"Anyway," I say now, tilting Grace's head to the side to get to the section of hair behind her ear, "if you honestly don't want to be wearing glasses anymore because you personally like how you look better without them, I'll help you pitch it to Mom for this summer. But if you're just doing it to try to impress Louis—or anybody else—I can promise you that tripping down a flight of stairs at the Alewife multiplex is not going to get you the kind of attention you're after."

"I *guess*," Grace grumbles, visibly unconvinced.

Then she turns her face to look at me. "I thought your article was really good, PS," she says suddenly. "I don't know if I told you that or not."

"Really?" I peer at her in the mirror, surprised. "How did you even read it?"

"My friend McKenna had a copy," she explains. "Her sister goes to your school."

"Oh." I nod. "Cool. Thanks, Gracie." I think about that for a moment, busying myself with the flat iron to hide my smile. Realistically, I know that my feminist book club and my editorials in the paper probably aren't going to make a whole lot of difference to the world at large. But if they made some kind of difference to my sister, that would be something.

"Promise me you'll wear your glasses tonight, okay?" I ask her, pulling the barrette out of her hair and clamping it onto the pocket of my hoodie for safekeeping. "If only so that I don't have to visit you in the ER instead of finishing this paper."

Gracie hums noncommittally, her fuzzy gaze flicking to the open laptop sitting on my desk. She doesn't say anything, but for a moment I can see her thinking it, weighing the cost of everything I've been up to lately: no boyfriend. No plans on a Saturday night. Big-sister constitution or not, I'm half expecting her to tell me to mind my own business.

"Fine," she finally declares. "I'll wear them."

This time I don't bother to hide my smile. "Good," I tell her, satisfied. "Now stop moving around so I can finish your hair."

FIFTEEN

I drop my paper on "The Swimmer" on Bex's desk on Monday, then spend the rest of class slouching silently in my seat while everyone else discusses the different point-of-view characters in *As I Lay Dying*, which we were supposed to finish over the weekend. I used to look forward to AP English all morning, but the last few weeks it's like I spend the entire period holding my breath and hoping to disappear.

Today I feel like maybe I actually have turned invisible, until nearly the very end of the period, when Bex catches my eye across the room.

"Marin," he says, "you've been quiet today. Any thoughts you'd like to share on our old friend Billy Faulkner?"

"Um." I swallow hard, my heart skittering like a mouse along a baseboard. I don't like this version of myself. I don't recognize her. "Nope," I say, clearing my throat a bit. "I don't think so."

"Really?" Bex raises his eyebrows in surprise that might or might not be genuine. "Nothing to add?"

I shake my head. A month ago, I would have fallen all over myself to come up with something witty and intelligent and impressive. This morning, I can't bring myself to try. "I think everybody else has pretty much covered it," I manage to say.

I'm expecting him to leave me alone after that—Bex has never been the kind of teacher who's interested in embarrassing anybody for the sake of proving a point—but instead he keeps his gaze on mine, steady. "Did you not do the reading or something?" he asks.

"What?" I ask, hearing an edge in my voice. "Of course I did."

"Okay." Bex shrugs. "Then what?"

"Then nothing," I snap, suddenly out of patience for whatever game he's trying to play. "I'm just saying, it's hard to get worked up about the literary themes in a book where one woman character dies in the first twenty pages and the other one spends the whole time getting taken advantage of by creepy men while she tries to get an abortion, that's all."

For a second the classroom is so quiet I can hear my own heartbeat. Then a chorus of laughs and *ooh*s break out. Chloe whirls around to stare at me, her eyes shocked and wide-looking; Gray lifts his chin in a wry, delighted nod.

Only Bex's face is completely impassive, and that's how I can tell I've gone too far. Sure, we've always joked around in his class, made fun of the books we're reading and the authors who wrote them, but this . . .

This wasn't that.

I'm opening my mouth to apologize, but he holds up a hand to stop me.

"See?" is all he says, and his voice is so, so even. "I knew you'd have an opinion." He nods at the door as the bell rings for the end of the period. "Class dismissed."

My interview at Brown is first thing Saturday morning. I wake up as dawn is dragging itself blue and gray over the horizon, then spend close to an hour obsessing over my outfit: if I wear a dress, does that make me seem unserious? If I *don't* wear a dress, am I saying something else? I finally decide on a pair of skinny black pants and a lacy blue button-down, plus an off-white cardigan that belongs to my mom. I add a lucky bracelet that used to be my gram's, then steal my wedge booties back out of Gracie's room and head downstairs, where my parents are drinking coffee at the kitchen table.

"You look fierce," my mom says with an approving nod.

"'Though she be but little,'" my dad says, raising his mug in a salute. "That's Shakespeare, in case you want to work it into your interview. You know, show 'em how smart you are, tell 'em you got it from your old dad."

"She's not so little anymore," my mom reminds him, rolling her eyes affectionately before turning to me. "You ready to go?"

I hesitate for a moment, all the uncertainty that has been building up the last couple of weeks cresting inside me like a wave. "I mean," I say, and I'm only half kidding, "I don't actually *need* the Ivy League, right?"

"Get out of here," my dad says, pulling me close with his free hand and dropping a kiss on top of my head. "No time for cold feet."

My mom pours the rest of her coffee into a travel mug before ushering me out into the garage and turning on both seat warmers. Theoretically I could drive myself—Providence is only about forty-five minutes away—but I'm happy for the company. I lean my head back against the seat and watch the barren trees out the window, listening to the hum of the college station out of Boston she likes to listen to.

Eventually we pull off the highway and into downtown Providence, past the big mall and the river and the cute shops and restaurants nestled along Thayer Street.

"I'm going to go find a Starbucks to read in," my mom says once she finds a place to pull over near campus, leaning across the gearshift and wrapping me in a lavender-scented hug. "Text me when you're done."

She leans back and looks at me for a moment—tucking a piece of my hair back behind my ear, then smiling. "You nervous?" she asks.

"Nah," I lie.

"Mm-hmm. Just be yourself," she says—unfooled, clearly, and reaching over to hug me one more time. "If they're smart, they'll love you for it."

I can't help but smile as I shut the passenger door behind me: after all, it's exactly what I told Grace the other night, isn't it? *Just be yourself.* Never mind the fact that lately I'm not 100 percent sure who that is.

I've got a little time to kill before I meet my interviewer, so I take a lap around the bustling campus—I do find Beckett Auditorium, and my stomach turns a bit—before taking a seat on the student center steps to wait. I spy a girl in a head scarf with a guitar case strapped to her back and a dopey-looking white guy with an absurd hipster handlebar mustache and two pretty brunettes sharing a green-tea doughnut, their gloved hands intertwined. The best part is the way none of them are gazing back at me with any particular interest, like in this place I could be whoever I want.

My interviewer is a Brown alum named Kalina who graduated a few years ago but stayed on campus to work in the admissions office; she's tall and willowy-looking, her dark hair in long dreads down her back. We sit in the café on campus while she asks me about my classes and my extracurriculars, what projects I'd worked on that meant the most to me.

"I read the piece you sent," she says, taking a sip of her latte. She's wearing a bright orange silk blouse and a slouchy pair of wool pants, and I immediately want to be exactly like her when I grow up.

"'Rules for Being a Girl.' I have to tell you, I was really impressed."

I smile and duck my head, pleased but not wanting to seem too cocky—which, I think suddenly, is probably something I wouldn't worry about if I were a guy. I force myself to lift my face again, looking her square in the eye.

"Thanks," I say, and my voice hardly shakes at all. "I worked hard on it."

"I could tell." Kalina nods. "What prompted you to write something like that?"

I hesitate. *Well, my AP English teacher kissed me at his apartment* doesn't seem like a great story to lead with in a college interview—but that's not even the whole reason I wrote it, really.

"It feels like there are all these double standards for guys and girls," I explain finally, wrapping my hands around my coffee cup. "In life, I mean, but especially in high school. Once I started noticing them, it was like I couldn't stop. And it seems to me like before we can do anything—before we can, like, start to undo them—at the very least we need to point them out."

Kalina nods at that, jotting something down in her Moleskin notebook. She asks me what I see myself doing after college—journalism, I explain, though I know it's hard to make a living that way—and eventually the conversation meanders around to living in Providence and whether it's actually going to snow here later like the forecast says.

"I hope not," she says with a grimace. "I'm from Texas, and I'd never even owned a pair of snow boots before I moved here. I'm still getting used to New England winters."

"Was it a difficult adjustment?" I ask.

"I was definitely homesick at first," Kalina says, sitting

back in her chair and seeming to consider it. "And honestly, this campus is pretty white. It's better now than it was when I was a student, but there's still a long way to go."

I think of the students I saw milling outside—to be honest, it seems a lot more diverse than my high school, and it occurs to me with a jolt how little I've thought about that. The same way most guys don't realize what it's really like just *being* a girl, I realize now, I definitely haven't given enough thought to what it's like just *being* black or brown, or speaking another language, or being from another place.

"I can appreciate that."

Kalina nods. "So I think that's all I've got for you," she says, shutting her notebook and offering me a wide smile. "Here, let me give you my card, so you can be in touch if anything comes up. I'd wish you luck, but honestly, Marin—with your grades and extracurriculars, you shouldn't really need it."

"Really?" I can't keep the dorky excitement out of my voice. "You think so?"

"Really," she says, reaching across the table to shake my hand like a promise.

SIXTEEN

The next day I head over to Sunrise to see Gram. She's working on the *Globe* crossword puzzle when I knock on the door of her suite, tapping a ballpoint pen idly against her lipsticked mouth.

"Granola bars," I report, setting the Tupperware on the coffee table in the sitting area. "Gracie made them."

Gram raises her eyebrows. "Sounds healthy," she says ominously.

"They've got chocolate chips," I tell her, settling down beside her on the narrow love seat and breathing in her familiar grapefruit and tropical-flower smell. "You can hardly taste the chia."

Gram smirks. "Here," she says, handing me the paper and sitting back against the throw pillows. "Help me with this. I'm useless at the pop culture clues."

I glance down at the puzzle, surprised to see it's almost all the way filled in already. "Looks like you've been doing fine without me."

Gram waves her hand. "The *Globe* puzzle is easy," she demurs, though I can tell she's a little bit pleased with herself. "They say it keeps your brain sharp, for all the good that'll do me."

"No, it will!" I say, smiling a little awkwardly. I never know exactly how to react when Gram mentions being sick. The reality is that Alzheimer's is progressive; she isn't ever going to get better, or move out of Sunrise and back into her own place. The trick, my mom always says, is to enjoy her while we have her—which, I remind myself, is exactly what I came here to do.

I open the tub of granola bars—Gram's right, they do taste a little on the healthy side—and grab the pitcher of iced tea from the fridge. We fill in the rest of the crossword while I tell her about my Brown interview.

"She basically said I was a shoo-in," I finish with a grin.

"Damn right you are," Gram says, raising her glass in an iced tea cheers. "I'd expect nothing less from you, Marin-girl."

"What were *you* like back in college?" I ask, remembering suddenly what she told me about not having been such a good girl when she was my age. "Were you really a hell-raiser?"

"I had my moments." She glances at me over the tops of her glasses. "I got arrested in Boston once, protesting the Vietnam War."

"What?" My jaw drops. "You did *not*."

"Why is that so difficult to believe?" Gram looks openly delighted with herself now, her blue eyes bright and canny. "Oh, I swore to your grandpa I'd never tell anyone. I don't even think your mother knows."

"No, I don't think she does either." I try to imagine it— Gram with her pearl stud earrings and sensible slacks from Eileen Fisher. "You were a badass."

"Well." Gram breaks a granola bar in half. "I suppose I was. But it didn't feel like that at the time. It just felt necessary, that's all. Doing what I could to right what was wrong."

"Did you burn your bra too?" I laugh.

Gram raises her eyebrows.

I clap a hand over my mouth. "Gram!"

"Oh, it was the sixties," she says, waving her hand with a shrug. "No one was wearing a bra to begin with."

I laugh at that. "Anything else you want to tell me about

this secret life you've been hiding for the last, oh, seventeen years?"

Gram considers that for a moment. "Well, my first protests were during the civil rights movement," she tells me. "I went down to Washington for Dr. King's speech, with my church group, but you knew that."

"Grandma, I most certainly did *not* know that." I gawk at her, dumbfounded.

"Well," she says, brushing crumbs off her lap. "I suppose I always felt I could have done more—I *know* I could have done more, actually—so it didn't seem right to go around flying my own flag about it."

I nod slowly, thinking of one of the essays in *Bad Feminist*—the one about the movie *The Help* and how it was a work of science fiction, not historical fiction. I remember watching it with my mom when I was home sick once; I'm embarrassed to admit I thought it was really inspiring, not realizing there was this whole racist narrative about a white lady swooping in to heroically combat inequality, when in reality of course the black women had been fighting their own battles for years and years. The more I read and learn lately, the more work I know I have to do.

"So what happened?" I ask now, tucking one leg under me. "How come I never knew about any of this?"

She shrugs, like she's never really considered it. "Well, Grandpa and I got married. It's a pretty common story, I think. Your mom and her brothers needed me, and the rest of it . . ." She trails off. "Or that could just be excuses, of course. I guess there's no way to say for sure."

"Did you miss it?" I ask, picking the chocolate chips and cherries out of my granola bar before setting the rest of it down on a napkin. "Like, protesting?"

"Well, I suppose I was just protesting in different ways," she says thoughtfully. "Calling my senators, writing letters, donating money to causes I believed in. I was on a first-name basis with the staffers at Senator Kennedy's office back in the nineties." She looks at me meaningfully. "I like to think there are different ways of being a rebel. Doing what you can with what you have, and all of that."

"Wow," I say, shaking my head. "I had no idea."

"Well," she teases, "maybe you're not asking your old gram enough questions." She smiles. "Better do it now, while I can still remember the answers."

I frown. The idea that Gram won't always be here burns behind my ribs. "Gram," I start, but I think she can see that she rattled me, because she holds up one elegant hand.

"I'm just teasing, Marin-girl." She reaches out and squeezes my arm, then glances out the window; it's not quite so cold today, a surprising reprieve. "Now," she says, clapping her hands together. "You want to go for a walk to the bakery, see if we can get a halfway decent cookie?"

Do what you can with what you have, I remind myself firmly. "I'd love that," I say, snapping the lid back on the granola bars and standing up. Gram slips her hand into mine.

SEVENTEEN

The girls' volleyball championship is the following Wednesday, and weirdly people are actually talking about it. A couple of underclassmen have even told me they liked the piece I wrote about the school's glaring lack of support for the team.

"I feel like we should make a banner or something," Dave says, unwrapping his turkey sandwich at our table near the back of the cafeteria. The book club has been sitting together more lately—not every day, but a couple of times a week, which is nice considering Chloe seemingly wants nothing to do with me and otherwise I've been spending my lunch period in the library, working on my Title IX editorial.

"There are a bunch of supplies left over from the pep rally," Lydia puts in. She's a class rep for student council and always has the line on extra balloons or poster board or chocolate chip cookies floating around. "We could meet up after school."

I nod. "I've got my mom's car today," I say, smiling, as Lydia offers me one of her carrot sticks, "so I can drive some people over."

"No need," Gray says. "I got us a ride."

I turn to look at him. I hadn't even noticed him coming up behind me, and my skin prickles like it always does when I haven't had time to properly prepare for the sight of him. "What?"

He grins, all mischief. "You'll see. Just meet me out front after eighth period."

It's freezing outside when classes let out, the barren trees waving their branches at the far end of the parking lot and our breath visible in the chilly air. I find Gray with the rest of the book club over by the picnic tables at the side of the building; he is hard at work on a sign that reads, GO BRIDGEWATER, his bottom lip caught between his teeth as he concentrates.

"What?" he asks when he looks up and catches me smiling.

"Nothing," I say with a shake of my head. "Nice sign."

"Shut up," he says, blushing—blushing!—just the faintest bit. "Not all of us can be fancy, clever writer types."

"I'm not fancy," I assure him, though it's not like I'm mad about it.

"I think you're kind of fancy," Gray says.

I'm about to reply when a school bus pulls into the parking lot, the driver tooting the horn in cheery greeting.

"Oh, good," Gray says, putting the finishing touches on his sign and straightening up. "Our ride's here."

"Wait, what?" I blink at him. "You got us a . . . school bus?"

"I got us the lacrosse team's school bus," he admits, looking the slightest bit pleased with himself, "but there's a catch."

"And what's that?"

"We're not the only ones riding it over there." Gray nods at the gym entrance, and my eyes widen. The entire lacrosse team is trickling out of the locker room and toward the bus. Well, almost the entire lacrosse team—Jacob makes a point of scowling at me and walking off in the opposite direction.

"Seriously?" I gape at Gray. "You convinced them to come support?"

"They wanted to," Gray says, and I shoot him a dubious

look. "Well, okay, maybe *wanted* to is the wrong way to put it, but still."

I laugh out loud as the rest of the club looks on in wonder. Even Ms. Klein looks surprised. "That's really decent of you, Gray."

"Well," he says. "I think you'll find that if you get to know me, I'm a pretty decent guy."

I open my mouth, not sure how to answer. He's not who I thought he was, that's for sure.

"You guys ready to load up?" Ms. Klein asks, saving me from my own awkward silence. I toss the leftover art supplies into the trunk of my mom's car and climb onto the bus, sliding into the empty seat beside Gray before I can talk myself out of it.

The game is at St. Brigid's, a fancy all-girls' school a couple of towns over, with floor-to-ceiling windows and state-of-the-art science labs. Gray heads over to the snack bar—an actual snack bar, not the crappy vending machines that are lined up outside our school—and comes back with a giant soda for himself and a bunch of bags of peanuts for everybody. "Are you, like, book club dad right now?" I ask, grinning as he passes them out.

"Maybe," he says. "Everybody needs to behave or I'll turn this volleyball game around, et cetera."

I snort, helping myself to a peanut. "You're kind of a nerd, huh? Is that, like, your big secret?"

Gray shrugs. "One of them," he admits, his eyes steady on mine. The back of his hand brushes mine. I can convince myself it's an accident until it happens again a few minutes later—the skate of his knuckles over my fingers, his pinky nearly hooking with mine. I bite my lip.

"Gray . . ."

He raises his eyebrows. "Marin," he says, exactly mimicking my tone.

I blow a breath out, debating. It's not that I'm not interested, obviously. If I'm being honest, I've been interested since the day of our first book club meeting, when he fixed the zipper on my backpack in the parking lot outside of school. Or before that, even. It's not like I never noticed him, always surrounded by admiring onlookers—it's just, I promised myself I'd never be one of them.

"You know what everybody says about girls when they hook up with you, right?" I ask him finally.

I'm expecting him to play dumb, but right away Gray nods. "I do know, actually," he says. "And it's fucked-up. I don't know why it's anybody's business. We're all just having a good time."

That surprises me, although probably it shouldn't. I'm

guilty of it myself, aren't I? How many times did Chloe and I sit around on my front porch complaining about girls with the audacity to kiss boys we had crushes on, or how skanky some sophomore looked at the Valentine's Day dance? I have to admit, for all of Gray's alleged conquests, I've never heard a peep about him being anything less than gentlemanly to anyone. And I've certainly never heard him running his mouth.

"Anyway," he says now, cracking a peanut shell and offering me a cheeky smile. "Who says I'm trying to hook up with you to begin with?"

"I—" Suddenly I'm back at Bex's apartment: sure I misread the situation, confused his intentions. "I'm not saying—"

The panic must register on my face, because Gray nudges me gently in the shoulder. "I mean, no, I'm definitely trying to hook up with you," he admits. Then he shrugs. "But—and listen, I know this is going to sound like a line, and it's not—I'm not *only* trying to hook up with you, okay?"

I raise my eyebrows. "Oh no?"

"No," Gray says. "I meant what I said to you. I think it's cool, what you're doing here. You kind of blow me away a little bit."

I consider that for a moment. I've spent the last few weeks feeling like such an outsider, it's hard to imagine Gray could think that what I'm doing is something cool. "Well," I say finally, "I will keep that in mind."

"You do that," Gray says, eyes warm and steady on me. "Now, if you'll excuse me, I'm trying to watch this volleyball game."

I snort. "Oh, sorry, am I distracting you?"

"Yes, actually," he says, but he's grinning.

I can't help but grin back.

It's weird, watching the girls' volleyball team defend their title—after all, I know it's just a game. But something about it makes me feel hopeful, and when Elisa makes the winning point at the very end of the final set, the rest of us leap to our feet like lunatics, hooting as the ref blows his whistle and the team floods onto the court. Lydia and Dave are slapping each other five in all different configurations. Ms. Klein is screaming like a drunk football fan.

"Oh my god!" I fling my arms around Gray's neck before I totally know I'm going to do it, nearly knocking him clear off his feet, and when he ducks his head to kiss me, it feels like the most surprising win of all.

EIGHTEEN

Bex hands our response papers back the following morning. I'm so prepared for an A that for a second I think that's what I'm seeing before I realize there's actually a bright red *D* at the top.

Wait, *what?*

I flip the paper over as fast as humanly possible, glancing around to make sure nobody saw it as my whole body burns with shame and disbelief. I've never gotten a D in my life, let alone on something that involved writing. Let alone on something for *Bex*. It just . . . doesn't happen.

Except that apparently now it does.

We've got a vocab lesson this morning, but I barely hear anything anyone says the entire period over the horrified roar echoing inside my head. By the time class ends I've crafted an argument in my own defense worthy of Ruth Bader Ginsburg herself, but when I finally make it up to the front of the empty classroom all that comes out is a sputter.

"What happened?" I manage, holding the wrinkled paper out of in front of me, carefully typed pages drooping like so many white flags.

"I'm sorry, Marin," Bex says, looking disappointed. "But this essay just wasn't up to your usual standards."

"Wha—" I shake my head. "Why not?"

"It was rushed, and it was sloppy," he says. "It just felt like you didn't try at all. I know you've been spending a lot of time on your editorials. Maybe you've been distracted."

"That's not true," I say. "I mean, maybe it wasn't my best work. But seriously, a D?"

Bex just shrugs. "If you need to make it up, we can talk about extra credit."

Something about his attitude has the skin on the back of my neck prickling unpleasantly. This isn't about the essay. This feels personal.

"What is this really about?" I say.

"Excuse me?" Bex's eyebrows almost crawl off his face entirely.

"I don't deserve this grade. I just . . . I don't."

We both just stare at each other for a minute until Bex blows a breath out.

"What's up with you, huh?" he asks me, leaning back against his desk and scrubbing a hand through the hair at the back of his neck; for a moment he's the same Bex I recognize, whose class was my favorite part of the day.

That stops me. "What?"

"You've been a really tough crowd lately. With the reading list and your attitude in class . . . And you know, I didn't want to say this about your essays in the *Beacon*, but honestly . . ." He trails off.

I frown. "Honestly what?"

His eyes narrow. "I thought you said everything was cool."

I take a step back. "If everything was cool, would I not be getting a D on this paper?"

The words are out before I can think better of them. For a moment they hang there between us like a dare. Finally Bex presses his lips together, a muscle twitching once in his jaw.

"Easy, Marin," he says, and his voice is all warning. "I'm your teacher."

"Yeah," I say, shoving my useless paper into my backpack, turning around, and heading for the door. "I know."

I don't mention the paper to my parents. I don't know what stops me, exactly; I can't figure out who I'm protecting— me or Bex. It's my turn to clear the table after dinner that night, and I hold the plates distractedly under the faucet to rinse them, wondering if I made the smart move confronting him. Just once I'd like to be sure I was doing the right thing.

I stick the leftover cheese and sour cream back in the refrigerator—my dad made tacos tonight, Gracie loading hers up with enough jalapeños to have my eyes watering clear across the table—and wipe the counters with a slightly-grungy yellow sponge. My mom comes up behind me as I'm finishing up, resting her chin on my shoulder and wrapping her arms around my waist.

"Oh, hi there, daughter of mine," she says, squeezing gently. "I'm proud as hell of you, you know that?"

I glance at her out of the corner of my eye. I don't know how she senses when I need the extra encouragement. "Thanks."

"I mean it," she says, planting a kiss against my cheek before straightening up again. She gives the counter a perfunctory wipe with a dish towel, then glances at the clock on the stove. "*Grey's Anatomy* doesn't start for twenty minutes," she says thoughtfully. "You think that's enough time to run to Seven-Eleven for ice cream and get back?"

I consider it. "If we speed," I conclude after a moment.

My mom nods, scooping her keys off the hook near the doorway. "Let's go."

NINETEEN

Gray takes me skating at the Frog Pond on Boston Common on Friday night, his big hand warm against my chilly one as we weave our way through the crowded rink. Little kids in hockey skates whiz past clusters of college students in fur-collared parkas while Ariana Grande blasts over the speakers; a giant Christmas tree winks with colored lights.

Once the session ends we get hot chocolates in a tiny coffee shop overlooking the park, all Edison bulbs and basket-weave tile, a heavy velvet curtain hung across the doorway to keep out the chill. Gray folds his bulky body basically in half to sit in a wobbly chair by the window, his knees bumping the mosaic tabletop, which isn't much bigger than a dinner plate.

"You okay over there?" I ask with a laugh, grabbing my mug before its contents go sloshing over the sides.

"Oh, I'm great," he says, and I think he's joking around until I glance up and catch how he's looking at me, his gaze calm and steady. My whole body gets warm.

"Well," I say, taking a sip of my cocoa to hide my blush. I never felt like this with Jacob, like my actual bones were glowing deep inside my body just from being near him. "Good."

Gray breaks a massive snickerdoodle into two pieces, handing me half. "My moms make these every Christmas," he tells me. "They have this whole baking day they do—they both have a bunch of sisters, so my aunts and all my girl cousins come over and make like a million different kinds."

"And you taste test?" I joke.

Gray snorts. "You think my moms would let me get away with sitting on my ass while a bunch of womenfolk make me food?" he asks with a laugh. "I do my fair share. I'll have you know I'm an excellent measurer."

"I don't doubt that," I say with a smile. "So you have a big family?"

"Huge," Gray says, finishing his cookie in two bites. "Like, twenty-two first cousins. And some of them have kids now too. It's a zoo."

"That sounds nice," I tell him, using a teaspoon to scoop a mound of whipped cream out of my hot chocolate before it can sink to the bottom of the mug. "It's always just been Gracie and me and our parents. It's part of why we're so close to our gram."

"Oh yeah?" Gray looks interested. "Is she cool?"

"She's the best," I say immediately, leaving out the part where she's not always reliably herself these days. "And I actually just found out she's got this whole secret Riot Grrrl past I never knew about."

"That's awesome," Gray says with a grin.

We sit in the coffee shop for a long time, until the crowd thins out and it's just us and a glamorous-looking middle-aged woman nursing an espresso, and still I'm in no hurry to get home. Gray's a good question asker, full of self-deprecating stories about being the only guy in a family full of ladies; he's got a sister named Alice who's studying political science in Chicago.

"You guys will like each other," he says, totally confident, and I can't help but smile at his use of the future tense.

Finally the baristas start wiping down the tables in a

way that feels like a hint. We head out and make our way down Charles Street, our footsteps echoing on the cobblestones. Laughter spills out the doors of the bars. It should feel festive—Christmas break is only a few days away, and there are fairy lights and garlands strung up over the empty street—but out here in the cold and the dark I can feel the cloud of dread that's been following me around lately come sulking back. I'd forgotten about yesterday's conversation with Bex while Gray and I were hanging out—I'd forgotten about all of it, actually—but forgetting only works for so long. This whole thing is still a baffling, humiliating mess. God, what am I going to *do*?

Gray can tell something's up: he's been rambling cheerfully on, holding up the conversation for both of us, but as we tap our cards at the entrance to the brightly lit T station he pauses.

"Everything okay?" he asks, his cheeks gone pink from the cold. "It feels kind of like you just . . . went somewhere."

I shake my head. "It's nothing," I promise as we take the escalator to the elevated train platform, the dark expanse of the Charles River visible in the distance. The giant neon Citgo sign glows white and orange and blue. "It's dumb."

"It's nothing, or it's dumb?"

I hesitate. "Both?" I try, glancing down the track for

any sign of the train, even though the arrival board on the platform says we've got ten minutes to wait. "Neither?" I sigh, my breath just visible. "I don't know."

Gray nods, tucking his hands into his coat pockets. "You don't have to tell me jack shit, obviously," he says, rocking back on the heels of his boots. "But like, just FYI, you can if you want to. I get that this might come as a shock to you, but I'm actually a pretty good listener."

I snort, I can't help it. "You do realize that people who self-identify as good listeners are never actually good listeners, don't you?"

"Oh, really?" Gray shoots back, all mischief. "Did you come up with that theory while I was telling you my life story just now and you were like, reorganizing your sock drawer in your mind?"

"Rude!" I protest, elbowing him in the bicep. I tip my head back, look at the sky.

"Yeah, yeah," Gray says, dimples flashing. Then he shakes his head.

"Marin," he says, quiet enough that nobody else on the platform can hear him. "Try me."

I sigh, and then I just . . . tell him. I tell him everything—about Bex and about how Chloe has been so busy it feels sometimes like she's avoiding me and about lying to my parents and about the paper and the creeping feeling that somehow all of this is my fault.

"I don't want to get anybody in trouble," I finish finally, shivering a little inside my peacoat. "But I also feel like ignoring it hasn't made it go away so far."

Gray's quiet for a long time when I'm finished. Then he shakes his head. "Holy shit, Marin," he says, and I'm surprised by how angry he sounds. "That dude is a total dick."

I bark a laugh, so loud and surprising that a woman looks at us curiously from the other side of the platform. All at once I realize it's what I was expecting Chloe to say when I told her. What I kind of *needed* for Chloe to say.

"Yeah," I reply, swallowing down that now-familiar tightness in my throat, that feeling of trying to keep it together. "I guess he kind of is."

"Not kind of," Gray says decisively. "A hundred percent."

I glance down at my boots on the concrete. "Do you think I should tell somebody?"

Gray thinks about that one for a moment. "I have no idea," he finally says, and he sounds very honest. "I think this is probably one of those times where my mom would say you have to decide what you can live with, which is seriously one of my least favorite mom-isms because it means there's no right answer." He shrugs. "But I can tell you I'll have your back no matter what you decide."

The train comes rumbling into the station then, fast and noisy. Gray reaches out and takes my hand.

TWENTY

I make an appointment to see Mr. DioGuardi during my free period on the Monday before Christmas break, perching on the very edge of his fake-leather visitor's chair and tucking my hands under my thighs to keep them from shaking. It's a small office, cluttered: the desk is heaped with file folders. A potted plant droops on the windowsill. There's a photo of Mr. DioGuardi's kids on the bookshelf, two college-aged guys with red hair and freckles clowning around at a camp-site. A part of me can't help but wish he had a daughter too.

"Just, ah, give me one more second here," he says vaguely, holding up a finger and squinting at his computer screen; judging by the beeps and honks the thing has let out in the six minutes I've been sitting here, he's either attempting to hack into a government database or trying unsuccessfully to send an email attachment.

"Take your time," I say, though the truth is the longer he keeps me waiting the more I feel like I'm about to jump clear out of my skin and take off down the hallway, shedding muscle and viscera in my wake. I breathe in and force myself not to fidget. *Calm and quick*, I remind myself.

Finally Mr. DioGuardi folds his hands on top of his keyboard, frowning and jerking back as he hits the space bar by mistake. The computer dings in protest, and I bite the inside of my cheek to hold back a nervous giggle.

"So," he says. "Marin. What can I do for you?"

I take a deep breath. "Well—"

"I've been reading your editorials in the paper, by the way," he tells me, raising his eyebrows in a way that I'm not sure how to interpret, exactly. "I hadn't realized you had quite so much to say about the gender politics here at Bridgewater."

"Yeah." I muster a smile, cheerful and nonthreatening. "It's something I've been thinking about lately, I guess."

Mr. DioGuardi nods. "So it would seem." He clears his throat. "Now. What's on your mind?"

I swallow hard, digging my nails into my nylon-covered knees. "It's about Mr. Beckett," I admit.

"Oh?" Mr. DioGuardi's eyebrows twitch, cautious. "What about him?"

I take a deep breath and keep things as factual as possible, starting with the first day he drove me home and ending with the afternoon in his apartment.

"He kissed me," I say, cringing; God, I can't believe I'm using that word in front of Mr. DioGuardi. I can't believe I'm using that word about *Bex*. Everything about this is humiliating.

When I'm finished Mr. DioGuardi doesn't say anything for a long time, whistle clicking rhythmically against his two front teeth.

"These are serious allegations, Marin," he tells me finally. "You realize I'm required to report them to the school board. They'll want to do a full investigation."

"Okay," I say slowly, not sure if he's trying to warn me off or not. It kind of feels like maybe he is. "I just—what else is there to investigate?" I shake my head, confused. "I mean, I just told you what happened."

Mr. DioGuardi's impassive expression flickers, just barely. "Well, this is a process, Marin. We'll need to gather more information before we decide on a course of action.

They'll want to interview you themselves, first of all. And I imagine they'll want to speak to Mr. Beckett as well."

"And what if he says I'm making the whole thing up?"

Mr. DioGuardi frowns. "*Are* you?"

"What? No!" I say, more sharply than I mean to. "Of course not!"

"Watch the tone, please," Mr. DioGuardi reminds me, reaching for the whistle around his neck like he's checking to make sure it's still there in case he needs to foul me out. "I know this is an . . . emotional situation, which is exactly why there's a procedure in place." He smiles again—reassuring, dadlike. "These things take time, Marin. But the board will be thorough. You can trust us all to do our jobs."

I wrap my hands around the arms of the chair, knowing somehow—the way he said *emotional situation*, maybe— that there's no room to argue without proving his point.

"Okay," I say instead, reaching down for my backpack before standing up so quickly I get lightheaded. It's claustrophobic in here all of a sudden, the air too hot and thick to breathe properly. "Well. Um. Thank you. I should get back to class."

Mr. DioGuardi frowns. He was expecting me to be more grateful to him, I realize. And I'm not following the playbook.

"Marin—" he begins, but I paste another bland smile on my face before he can say anything else.

"I appreciate your help with this, Mr. DioGuardi." I promise. "Really."

"Of course," he says, mollified. I'm somebody he recognizes again: good student, reliable coeditor of the *Beacon*, not one to make a fuss. A nice girl.

"Feel free to come to my office with any questions. We're here to support you."

I thank him one more time, keeping the smile plastered on my face as I head out of his office. I wave to Ms. Lynch, who's scrolling industriously through Facebook on her office computer. I wait until I'm out in the empty hallway to let the mask slip off my face, leaning against a bank of sophomore lockers and taking deep breaths, trying to swallow down the whirlpool of dread rising in my chest. I wanted telling Mr. DioGuardi to put an end to this whole miserable episode.

But now it looks like it's barely begun.

Gray's waiting by my locker at the end of last period, tie already loosened and a charmingly ridiculous reindeer beanie—complete with pompom—shoved down over his wavy hair.

"Hey," he says, with a smile that makes me shiver in spite of the sense of impending doom I've been carting around since my meeting with DioGuardi. "How did it go?"

I shrug. "Okay, I guess?" I fill him in as quickly and factually as possible, trying not to sound like a person at the mercy of her own *emotional situation*. "It sounds like I'll know more after the break."

"Well, that's good, right?" Gray asks. "That he's bringing it to the school board?"

"No, it is," I agree, though in fact the very idea makes me want to dig a hole in the nearest snowbank and live inside it till spring. Already I feel like an idiot for having ever imagined I could tell my story to DioGuardi and that would be the end of it. It feels like a theme in my life lately: what did I *think* was going to happen? "It is."

"Good," Gray says again, like it's just that simple; still, I know he's just trying to be encouraging. "You coming to pizza?"

I shake my head. Everybody at Bridgewater always goes for slices at Antonio's on the last day of school before Christmas break; normally it's one of my favorite afternoons of the year, the line spilling out onto the chilly sidewalk and the smell of cheese and pepperoni warm in the air. Today, though, I can't face the thought of being around that many people. "There's something I gotta do," is all I say.

My mom is working on her laptop at the dining room table when I get home, paperwork spread out in messy piles all around her; my dad is already prepping the Feast of the Seven Fishes for Christmas Eve tomorrow night.

"Hey, guys?" I say, setting my backpack down in the mudroom, tucking my hair behind my ears. I steel myself against the panicky feeling of having set a series of events into motion, when I'm not even sure it was the right thing to do. "I think we probably need to have a talk."

TWENTY-ONE

I'm expecting fireworks from my mom in particular—after all, this is the same woman who marched down the street in her pajamas and put the fear of god in Avery Demetrios when she was mean to me at day camp the summer after fourth grade—but instead she just sits stock-still at the table and listens, one hand in my father's and one hand in mine.

"He did *what*?" she asks when I get to the part about the kiss, but my dad's grip tightens around her fingers, and she immediately presses her lips together.

"I'm sorry," she says, shaking her head like she's trying to clear it, and I see her eyes getting watery. "Keep going."

So I do, staring down at the table and telling them about my editorial and the response paper and ending with today and my conversation with Mr. DioGuardi. When I'm finished all three of us are quiet for a long moment.

"God*damnit*, Marin," my mom says, and when I look up at her I'm surprised to see she's wiping tears away with her whole palm. "I am so, so sorry he did that to you."

We sit at the table for a long time, all three of us talking. My dad makes us a snack of cheese and crackers and grapes. They don't ask any of the questions I'm expecting: *Are you sure you weren't confused? Did you give him the wrong impression? What the hell were you doing in his apartment to begin with?* I don't know why I feel a tiny bit guilty about that, like maybe they're letting me off too easy.

All of us startle when the back door opens and Gracie ambles through, back from her carpool with her cheeks gone pink from the cold.

"I'm starving," she announces, then registers all three of us sitting around the table like we're conducting a séance. "What's wrong?"

I hesitate for a moment, then take a breath and smile. "Nothing," I promise, offering her a cracker; sitting here between my parents it feels like maybe it could be the truth. "Everything's okay."

◆ ◆ ◆

I go to Chloe's the day after Christmas, pulling my mom's car into the driveway and skirting past the enormous blow-up snow globe on her parents' front lawn. Every year the two of them get more and more into the holidays, three-foot-tall candy canes lining the flower beds and a motorized, light-up Santa waving from beside the chimney. To Chloe it's literally the most embarrassing thing on the planet—none of our other friends are allowed to come over between Thanksgiving and New Year's—but I've always thought it was kind of great.

Once her mom lets me in I wave to Chloe's brothers, who are sprawled on the carpet in front of the Christmas tree playing Battleship, and find Chloe still in her pajamas in her bedroom, watching an eyeliner tutorial on her laptop.

"Hey," she says, looking surprised when I knock on the mostly closed door.

I frown. "We're doing the mall, aren't we?" Chloe and I have done the mall the day after Christmas for the last four years, returning ugly sweaters from our various family members and taking advantage of the clearance sales. We always end with a peppermint mocha at the scruffy hipster coffee shop in Inman Square.

"Oh." Chloe shakes her head, like this is totally new

information and not something we've been doing since before we got our periods. "Yeah, I guess. I don't know. I just figured you'd be with Gray."

"What?" I didn't even realize she knew about me and Gray, and it stings to think how little we've been hanging out. "Gray's in New Hampshire with his cousins until New Year's. But also, why would I be with Gray? This is our day, right?"

"Right." Chloe shrugs. "I don't know."

I frown. "Do you not want to go?" I mean, obviously I know things have been weird with us, and I don't 100 percent believe all the time she's been spending with Kyra, but it would just be so much weirder to *not* do this.

"No, we can," she says, shutting her laptop with a look on her face like I just invited her for a rousing afternoon of digging a hole in the frozen earth. "I just have to shower."

"I mean, we don't have to." Suddenly it does feel like a bad idea, actually: Chloe's lousy mood, yeah, but also the crowds, the chance of running into people we know from school. Running into *Bex*. I sit down on the edge of her unmade bed.

"Can I tell you something?" I ask, picking at a loose thread in the quilt her mom made out of all her old day camp T-shirts. "Without you, like, freaking out?"

Chloe raises her eyebrows. "Is it that you got Bex in trouble with DioGuardi?" she asks immediately.

"I—" My eyes widen. "How do you know that?"

"Everybody knows that," Chloe says, sliding the laptop onto the mattress and climbing out of bed. "Like, the entire school."

"What? Seriously?" My heart drops. I purposely talked to Mr. DioGuardi on the last day before vacation to buy myself time before the gossip mill started grinding. "How?"

"I have no idea," she says, though she's not quite looking at me.

"Well, I mean, who told *you*?"

"Does it matter?"

"I mean, yeah, Chloe. If people are going around saying—"

"Can you stop messing with that?" she interrupts, nodding at the quilt. "The whole thing is going to fall apart any second."

"Sorry." I set it down, wiping my suddenly sweaty palms on the knees of my jeans. "Are you mad at me?" I ask, although the answer is pretty obvious. What I can't figure out is the why.

Chloe scoops her bathrobe off the back of the closet door, draping it over her arm. "I just don't understand why you even bothered asking what I thought you should do," she says, shrugging inside her Bridgewater hoodie. "When, like, you obviously had your own agenda this whole entire time."

"Wait, wait, wait," I protest. "I don't have an agenda. What does that even mean?"

Chloe huffs like I'm being dense on purpose. "It means you, like, decided you had this vendetta against him, and now—"

"Against *Bex*?" I shake my head. "That's not even—"

"You know he's probably going to get fired, right?" Chloe cuts in. "And we'll be stuck with some hundred-year-old sub for the rest of the year who's going to make us read a bunch of boring crap and write, like, detailed sequence-of-events responses, just because you couldn't drop the rock about some dumb misunderstanding."

"Holy shit, Chloe." I feel my throat get tight, my eyes stinging; in the whole entire history of our friendship, she's never talked to me like this before. "What the hell is your problem?"

"I don't have a problem," Chloe snaps; then, looking over her shoulder at the hallway, she lowers her voice. "I just don't understand why you're being like this, that's all. Like, why can't you just admit you made a mistake—"

"I didn't make a mistake!"

"So what, you think he's in love with you?" Chloe laughs meanly. "Like he brought you to his apartment as part of some super-secret plan to make you his girlfriend?"

"No, of course not." My eyes are filling for real now, my vision blurring. I glance up at the overhead light, take a deep breath. "You realize you're supposed to be my best friend."

"I *am* your best friend," Chloe says immediately. "And part of my job is to tell you when you're making a total fool of yourself."

"Is that what you think I'm doing?"

"I think you've lost all connection with reality, yeah."

"Well . . ." And I shrug, because what else can you say to that? I stand up and sling my bag over my shoulder, wiping my face with the heel of my hand. "I guess today's not such a good mall day after all."

"No," Chloe says, still clutching her bathrobe in front of her like a shield. "I guess not."

I head downstairs and let myself out, dodging her mom in the kitchen. The boys are still playing in the living room, their trash talk just audible over the clatter of the Cartoon Network.

"Sunk!" one of them says, gleeful. The sound of them laughing is the last thing I hear before I shut the door.

TWENTY-TWO

My parents and I meet with Principal DioGuardi and the school board over break, all of us sitting around a folding table on the stage in the auditorium. I wonder if they made Mr. Lyle come in specifically to set it up. I give the board my full statement, feeling weirdly like I'm performing in a play I never auditioned for; they assure us that they're taking the matter very seriously, that they'll be talking to Mr. Beckett as well.

The rest of Christmas vacation is achingly quiet. Gray gets back from New Hampshire and takes me to breakfast at Deluxe Town Diner. Gracie and I go see *The Nutcracker* with my mom. My dad sits through about a million

Hallmark Christmas movies without complaining, getting up periodically to get us more homemade marshmallow hot chocolate cookies, which I know is code for *I love you and I'm here.*

My mom lets me take her car in my first morning back after break, the security blanket of knowing I could make a quick exit if I needed to. I slam the driver's door shut before dashing across the parking lot, the pavement sleet-slippery under my boots. Icy rain slides underneath the collar of my winter coat, and I almost wipe out hard on the concrete staircase, catching myself on the railing just in time.

I shake my hair out once I make it through the senior entrance and scan the bright, crowded hallway. Harper Russo raises her eyebrows, then whispers something to Kaylin Benedetto. Michael Cyr shoots me a giant, shit-eating grin.

I duck my face and head for my locker, telling myself I'm being dramatic—this is my actual high school, not the establishing shot of a nineties teen movie. Still, I grab my books as quickly as humanly possible, edging past Cara St. John and Aminah Thomas in the bottleneck in the hallway.

"—always hanging out with him in the newspaper office," Cara is saying, scooping her shoulder-length hair into a stubby blond ponytail. "I don't know what she thought was going on."

"I *wish* Bex would try something with me," Aminah chimes in with a snort, then happens to glance over her shoulder and spot me right behind her. The embarrassment on her face is nothing compared to the hot, prickly wave of nausea that rolls through my entire body.

So. Everybody really does know, then.

I shuffle dazedly through my first two classes, feeling like my head has been wrapped in gauze and I can't see or hear or even breathe properly. All morning I try to imagine what I'll do if Bex is in his classroom at the start of AP English, and all morning I try to imagine what I'll do if he's not.

"You ready?" Gray asks, slipping his hand into mine as we head down the hallway, and I nod.

I've been telling myself I'll be fine no matter what happens, but I can't deny the way my knees go wobbly with relief when I see the sub standing up in front of Bex's classroom, a nerdy-looking middle-aged guy with a comb-over and a paunch.

"Nice," Gray murmurs, a smile spreading over his face as we take our seats. "See? Dude's gone. Nothing to worry about."

"Yeah." I muster a small smile of my own. It falls as Chloe comes in, stopping short at the sight of the sub.

"Hey," I say quietly, as she passes by my desk. "Can we talk?"

Chloe ignores me.

The sub introduces himself as Mr. Haddock—"like the fish," he clarifies, looking visibly pained when nobody laughs—and launches into this week's vocab lesson. He's dry as toast and just as achingly boring as Chloe predicted. But I don't care at all.

Apparently, I'm the only one.

"This guy suuucks," Dean Shepherd mutters from the back of the room.

"At least Marin won't try to screw him," Michael Cyr cracks in response. "I mean . . . probably."

I stare fire down at my notes, my face flaming. Gray fixes them both with a look.

"Excuse me?" Chloe pipes up at the front of the room, raising her hand primly. "When will Mr. Beckett be back?"

Mr. Haddock frowns. "He should be here tomorrow, I believe—but I have no intention of wasting the time I've got with you folks, so if you'll open your books—"

I lose the rest of what he says underneath the sudden roar in my head. For a moment I honestly think I've heard him wrong.

Tomorrow. He'll be back . . . tomorrow?

God, I'm such an idiot.

This isn't finished at all.

Once the bell finally rings I'm out of my seat like a sprinter at the starting gun, ignoring Gray as he heads toward me and stumbling down the hall toward the admin suite, where Ms. Lynch is eating a bag of Famous Amos cookies and hungrily scrolling a gossip site on her computer. "Is Mr. DioGuardi here?" I blurt.

Her eyes narrow. "Excuse you," she says, quickly minimizing the window; I wouldn't have pegged her for a Rihanna fan, but I guess we all contain multitudes. I can't wait to tell Chloe, until I remember Chloe and I aren't speaking.

"Do you have an appointment?"

You keep his calendar, I think but don't say. *You know I don't.*

"Um, nope," I manage, aiming for bright and winding up somewhere in the neighborhood of totally deranged. "Just a quick social call."

Ms. Lynch frowns. "I'll tell him you're here."

I take a seat in the outer office to wait, watching the seconds tick by on the ancient clock out in the hallway. It's the better part of ten minutes before the door opens and Mr. DioGuardi comes out.

"Marin!" he says, looking not at all pleased to see me. "Come on in. You were on my list of students to touch base with this morning."

175

I bet I was, I think bitterly.

"Mr. Beckett is coming back tomorrow?"

Mr. DioGuardi frowns. "Have a seat," he says, gesturing to the chair across from him. "That's what I wanted to talk to you about. The school board investigated your . . . allegations over the break. Ultimately, the disciplinary committee found no conclusive evidence of wrongdoing, so he'll be returning to his classes for the remainder of the year."

"I *told* you about the wrongdoing," I say, and it comes out a lot more like a wail than I mean for it to. I swallow hard, digging my nails into the armrests. *Don't be hysterical. Don't be a crazy girl.* "I just mean—"

"I understand that, Marin," Mr. DioGuardi says. "But without any corroborating statements, without evidence—"

"No evidence—" I break off as the larger implications here start to make themselves clear. "So you think I'm *lying*?"

"Now hold on just a moment," he says. "No one is saying that."

"Well then what *are* you saying?"

"Marin—" Mr. DioGuardi pops his whistle into his mouth for a moment, then pulls it out again. When he speaks his voice is suddenly gentle.

"Look," he says, "is it at all possible you misinterpreted

what was happening? With Mr. Beckett, I mean? No one would blame you, obviously. He's one of our younger faculty members, and I see so many girls hanging around his classroom, or in the newspaper office. It would be perfectly understandable if you somehow misunderstood—"

"Oh my god." It's out before I can stop it. I shove my chair back and jump upright. "I'm not listening to this."

Mr. DioGuardi's eyes narrow across the desk. "Marin," he says sharply. "I understand you're upset, but may I remind you who you're talking—"

Stop using my name, I want to scream loud enough to shatter the windows. Instead, I press my lips together, remembering my manners. Swallowing down my own rage and fear.

"You're right," I manage, the words like gravel in my mouth. I hold my hands up, forcing a cowed smile. "I'm sorry. I shouldn't have—you're right."

Mr. DioGuardi nods with a thin smile—pleased, I think, to be in the position of being able to give me a pass in this trying time. "All I mean is that these things happen," he continues. "And sometimes, once we've had time to cool off and reconsider a situation from all angles, we find we see things differently than we might have at first."

"Sure," I say. I focus on the bookcase, on that photo

of DioGuardi's sons at the campsite. I want to rip it off the shelf and hurl it directly at his head, then encourage him to take some time to cool off and reconsider the situation from all angles. "I get it."

"Now," he says, standing himself, "if you don't have any further questions—?"

"Um, nope," I say, backing up toward the doorway. What else could there possibly be to ask? "I guess that's it. Thanks for letting me know."

"Of course," Mr. DioGuardi says, and his smile is genuine relief as he shuffles me out into the admin suite. "I'm glad we had this talk."

TWENTY-THREE

"This is un-frickin'-acceptable," my mom announces that night, slamming pots and pans around the kitchen like she's thinking of starting a percussion ensemble.

"I mean it. I've had it. I'm going to march in there and stick my boot so far up that man's ass that he'll be able to open up his mouth and read the L.L.Bean logo in the mirror. Then I'm calling a lawyer."

"Dyana," my dad says from his perch at the kitchen table, sounding faintly weary. I cringe at the sight of the bags under his eyes. "Go easy, will you?"

"You go easy!" my mother snaps, yanking open the

fridge and brandishing a Styrofoam package of ground turkey like a weapon. "This is ridiculous. And frankly I don't think there's anything wrong with showing our daughter it's okay to get worked up over injustices." She drops the turkey in the pan with a wet thud. "Which this is."

"Nobody's saying it isn't an injustice," my dad puts in, getting up to check the potatoes in the oven. "I'm just saying that I don't see how violence is going to help—"

"It's metaphorical violence, Dan." My mom makes a face as she jabs at the turkey with a wooden spoon. "Mostly."

"Guys," I protest weakly. "Please. I can handle this."

My dad scrubs a hand over his face. "Can you transfer out of the class?" he asks me. "I feel like that should be the first step, right?"

I bite the end off a baby carrot and think about that for a minute, surprised by how simple he makes it sound. And it *would* be simple, really: there's a non-AP senior English class that meets at the same time, two rooms over. They're reading *The Art of Fielding*. It would probably be fine.

I take a deep breath. "No," I tell them, calm as I can manage.

My mom raises one thick brow. "Why not?"

I shrug, popping the rest of the carrot into my mouth and crunching hard. "Because then he wins."

My parents are both quiet then, the two of them exchanging a look across the kitchen. I think it might be worry. I think it might be pride. My mom sets the wooden spoon down on the counter, then comes over and slides an arm around my waist.

"Go get your sister," she says, squeezing once before letting me go. "It's almost time to eat."

I'm finishing up some homework later that night when Gracie gallops down the hallway, grabbing hold of the doorjamb and swinging her gangly body into my room. Her nails are painted a bright, sparkly blue. "There's a boy here for you," she reports.

"What?" I had my earbuds jammed into my ears in an attempt to block out the rest of the world entirely. I didn't even hear the doorbell ring. "Seriously?"

"Yep," Gracie says, popping the *P* delightedly. "And he's hot."

"Oh god." I check my hair in the mirror—end-of-the-day greasy, but there's nothing to be done about it now—then slick on some ChapStick and head downstairs.

Gray is standing near the front door, his hands shoved into the pockets of his oversize sweatpants as he chats gamely to my parents about *We Should All Be Feminists*, which we're going to be discussing at book club on Thursday. My mom looks completely enamored. My dad looks completely confused.

"So," I say brightly. "You've met Gray."

My mom raises her eyebrows. "We have," she tells me, in a voice that unmistakably communicates the fact that up until this moment I've entirely failed to mention him. *I didn't think he was for real*, I want to explain to her, although seeing him standing here like a friendly giant in my parents' tiny foyer, it occurs to me again how wrong I was.

My mom looks like she'd be more than happy to settle in and spend the rest of the evening with Gray watching Chimamanda Ngozi Adichie's TED Talk, but thankfully, my dad lays a hand on her arm.

"We were just about to head upstairs," he says. "There's ice cream in the freezer, if you kids are interested."

"Sorry," Gray says, making a face once it's just the two of us in the foyer. "Is this okay? I didn't mean to get you in trouble or anything like that."

"Oh no, you're fine." I shake my head. "They're not those kind of parents." They are, however, the kind of parents who are probably lurking around the corner hoping to accidentally-on-purpose overhear us, so I grab my coat off the overflowing rack, zipping it over my leggings and Bridgewater hoodie and leading Gray out onto the porch.

"So what's up?" I say, tucking my hands into my pockets and shivering a little; January in Massachusetts is brutal, single-digit temperatures and the kind of shrieking wind that chaps your face and stings the insides of your ears. "Everything okay?"

"Yeah, totally." Gray shrugs. "I just wanted to check on you, I guess. I mean, not that you can't take care of yourself or anything, but I wanted to make sure you were hanging in there after . . ." He trails off, a little awkwardly. "You know. After."

I raise my eyebrows and smile. "You could have done that over text," I point out.

Gray nods. "I could have," he agrees. "I didn't want to."

"Oh no?" I'm grinning for real now, I can't help it. I've never met anyone like him before. "Why not?"

Gray's fingertips brush the hem of my coat, just lightly. "You know why not."

"Well. I'm glad you did." I look down at my fuzzy slippers, suddenly shy. "I'm okay, I guess. I feel a little bit like I just made the biggest mistake of my life, possibly? But other than that, super."

"It wasn't a mistake," Gray says immediately. "I mean, easy for me to say, right? But I don't think it's ever a mistake to tell the truth."

It *is* easy for him to say, probably. Still, I appreciate the sentiment.

"Maybe not," I allow. But then I think of the look on Chloe's face this morning, the whispers that followed me down the hallway. "It just feels like the truth didn't mean anything, you know? Like I put myself out there, I opened myself up to all this shit, everybody staring at me and making their judgments, and it didn't even change anything."

Gray considers that. "Maybe not," he says. "But it kind of changed you, right?"

That stops me; I'm quiet for a moment, turning it over in my mind. On one hand, there's no silver lining here—it's not like I'm *glad* this all happened, but I guess it's true that I'm tougher than I was a couple of months ago. It's true that I see things differently now.

"Maybe," I say again, shivering a little in the bitter cold.

"Come here," Gray says; for a moment I think he's going to kiss me, but in the end he just wraps me in his arms. We stand there for a long time in the glow of the porch light, the winter wind calling down the empty street.

TWENTY-FOUR

I barely sleep that night, picking half-heartedly at an Eggo on my ride to school the following morning and letting my coffee go cold in the cup holder. I may have been ready to raise hell in the kitchen of my parents' house last night, but this morning all I want is to run right out the door and disappear into the woods behind the football field. Forget switching classes, I think miserably. At this point I'm ready to try homeschooling for the rest of the year.

Gray finds me in the hallway before third period. "Hey," he says, reaching for my hand and squeezing. "How you doing?"

"Me?" I paste the world's fakest smile on my face, then realize it's just Gray and let it melt into an exaggerated grimace, crossing my eyes and baring my teeth. "I'm super. Why, do I not look super?"

"Oh no, totally super," Gray says grandly, bumping his shoulder against mine before we head inside and take our seats. I tell myself I'm imagining the low murmurs as I make my way down the aisle. Chloe, meanwhile, will barely look at me.

"Hey," I try, kicking lightly at her chair from across the aisle; she offers me a smile even faker than the one I tried on Gray a minute ago, then turns back to her bullet journal. I sigh and pull my notebook out of my bag.

Bex isn't in class by the time the bell rings for the start of the class period. For a second I let myself hope for dorky Mr. Haddock, but a moment later Bex strolls through the door with his reusable coffee cup in hand, like possibly he was lurking outside in the hallway just waiting for the exact right time to make his entrance.

"There he is," Dean calls, slouched in his chair near the window. "Thought you abandoned us, man."

Bex flashes the dimple in his cheek, easy. "Me?" he asks, all innocence. "Never."

He's wearing dark khakis and one of his signature

chambray shirts, a fresh new haircut that makes him look even younger than usual.

"Now, tell me: did you guys manage to actually learn anything yesterday, or not so much?"

He takes attendance and asks if anybody's read anything good lately, just like always, then opens up a detailed discussion of some Joyce story with absolutely no fanfare whatsoever. The weirdest part is how into it everyone gets—Dean Shepherd offers surprising insight into the story's symbolism. Chloe raises her hand about a thousand times. I don't know what I was expecting, but it wasn't this: it's like he's going to make things normal again through sheer force of will, and everybody has decided to go along with it. It makes me feel more than a little crazy. More than that though, I'm *furious*—the kind of anger that could light fires and power cities, the kind that laughs at the limits of my nice-girl self-control. *Why doesn't anybody care about what happened?* I want to shriek, loud enough to rattle the windows. *Why doesn't anybody care about* me?

I scribble in the margins of my notebook and pray he doesn't call on me to make some kind of point about how fine everything is between us. It feels like years before the end of the period.

"All right, that's it for today," he says as the bell rings. "Marin, can you stay after for a sec? Yeah, yeah," he says, shaking his head at the assorted snorts and snickers from the back of the room. "Get out of here, the rest of you animals."

I startle at that, gaping at Bex as everyone files out of the classroom—everyone, that is, except Gray, who leans against the doorjamb, backpack slung over one broad shoulder like he's waiting for the public bus.

"What are you doing?" I ask, my gaze darting from him to Bex and back again.

"I'm gonna stay," he announces.

"I'm fine," I lie. "Go."

Gray shakes his head. He's taller than Bex, and broader; he fills almost the whole doorway. "Nah, I'm good here."

I know he means well, but it feels like he's peeing a circle around me.

"Go," I tell him through gritted teeth. "Gray, seriously."

Gray goes, but not before shooting Bex a look that could take the bark right off a tree. "See you at lunch, Marin," he says.

Bex watches him go for a moment before turning back to me. "Well!" he says, faux-brightly, and there's that sheepish smile again. "I guess we know where I stand with your friend Gray."

I take a step backward; the backs of my legs bump awkwardly against a desk. "He's just—"

"I'm kidding," Bex says, holding both hands up. "It was a joke." Then he makes a face.

"Okay," he says, perching on the edge of his desk, "Marin. Can we just . . . reset?"

"Reset?" I repeat dumbly. That . . . is not what I was expecting him to say. "Like . . . between us?"

"Yeah," Bex says. He picks a rubber band up off his desk, stretching it between his thumbs. "Listen, I'm sorry I came down so hard on you about that paper."

Wait, *what*?

"It wasn't about the paper," I blurt, faintly horrified. Holy shit, is that what he thinks? "I mean, I didn't go to Mr. DioGuardi just because—"

"No, no, no, of course not," Bex says. He's still fidgeting with the rubber band. "That's not what I'm saying."

Then what are *you saying?* I want to ask, but even as I have the thought it feels extremely unwise to argue. I think of the way everyone's been staring at me since yesterday morning. I think of Mr. DioGuardi and *maybe you were confused*.

"Okay," I say finally, edging toward the doorway. My heart is thudding. "Yeah. Um. A reset would be great."

"Good," Bex says, finally dropping the rubber band

back into a jar on the desk and getting to his feet. "Glad to hear it."

"Okay," I say again. "Um. Thanks."

"No problem," he says, with a brisk, businesslike nod. "Have a good day."

I pull my backpack up on my shoulder and book it out of Bex's classroom. Gray's leaning cross-ankled against a bank of lockers across the hall.

"How'd it go?" he asks, standing upright and reaching for my hand.

I shrug, weirdly reluctant to talk about it. "Fine?"

"Fine like he's going to move to Saskatchewan and never talk to you again?"

"No, fine like . . ." I shake my head, fighting a flash of annoyance. I know he's just trying to be supportive, but I need a second to myself to try to figure out what just happened. "Forget it."

"No, hey, talk to me." Gray puts a hand on my arm, but I shrug him off, harder than I mean to. He takes a step back, hands up.

"Sorry." I feel like a shaken-up soda bottle, like if anyone even looks at me wrong I might explode in every direction. "I think I just need some air."

"Marin—" Gray frowns. "You're not coming to lunch?"

"Not hungry," I say. "I'll see you later, okay?" I don't wait for him to answer as I head down the hallway.

I'm so focused on getting away from him—on getting away from everyone—that I've made it almost all the way to the far end of the building before I realize I have no idea where I'm actually headed. It feels like there's nowhere to hide. Two months ago I would have hightailed it directly to the newspaper room, flung myself down on the couch—and complained at great length to Bex himself, probably. It's grossly surprising to realize I miss him—or at least, I miss the person I thought he was. All at once I'm furious he's taken that from me too.

Finally I make my way to the bio lab, where Ms. Klein is sitting at her desk grading papers and eating peanut butter out of the jar with a spoon.

"Hey, Marin," she says, surprise flickering briefly over her features. "You okay?"

"Yep!" I say. "I just, um—" I break off, trying to come up with some kind of plausible book-club-related excuse for being in here and coming up empty.

Ms. Klein doesn't seem to need one: "Do you want to talk?" she asks quietly, putting down her pen. "About . . . what everyone is talking about?"

"Um," I say, struggling to keep my voice even. God, I

can't believe even Ms. Klein knows. "Not really. Can I just, like, hang out in here for a bit?"

Ms. Klein lifts her chin in the direction of the lab benches. "Sure thing," she says, and her voice is very even. "Have a seat."

TWENTY-FIVE

Weekend afternoons are notoriously slow at Niko's if there isn't a bridal shower or a christening booked in the sunroom, which is bad news for tips but good news in that it'll give me four long, boring hours' worth of chances to try to smooth things over with Chloe. We've been avoiding each other since we got back from break—or, more to the point, Chloe's been avoiding me. On the rare occasions I've made it into the cafeteria, she's been eating with some girls from the drama club. We've been putting the next issue of the *Beacon* together entirely via a string of extremely tense, polite emails.

When I get to the restaurant though, I find Chloe's monosyllabic cousin Rosie rolling silverware at the wait station instead, chunky rings on every one of her fingers and a diamond stud glittering in her nose.

"She changed up her schedule," Steve explains when I ask about it, looking vaguely uncomfortable. "Some new club she's in."

I sincerely doubt that—after all, it's Saturday—but it's not like I'm about to argue with her dad of all people. I shuffle my way through my shift, then swing by Sunrise with two plastic clamshells of baklava tucked under my arm. I drop one with Camille at the nursing station and bring the other into Gram's room, where we sit on the love seat with the window cracked to let a tiny bit of cold, fresh air in, brushing flakes of puff pastry off our laps.

"Oh, you know what, Marin?" she says suddenly, getting up off the sofa and heading for the closet, surprisingly spry in her cardigan and khakis. "I've got something for you."

I raise my eyebrows. "You do?"

"I do!" She stands on her tiptoes and rummages along the top shelves for a moment; when she turns around she's holding a fabric-covered storage box, the kind you buy at craft supply stores. We must have moved a hundred of them from her house in Brockton, full of old papers and mementos and slightly creepy locks of hair from when my mom and uncles were little kids. When she brings this one back to the love seat and pulls the top off though, I see it's full of old photos—and not the ones from the seventies that I'm used to seeing, my mom with pigtails riding her bike and my uncles' hair curling down over their collars. These are older: my grandpa at his high school graduation, looking grave and serious even as a teenager. The narrow brick apartment building in the North End where my grandma grew up. And—

"Is that *you*?" I ask, grabbing a faded photo out of the pile and holding it up to get a better look.

"Damn right it's me," Gram says with a laugh. Her shiny brown hair is longer than I've ever seen it. She's standing in a crowd in a leafy green park, dressed in bell-bottoms and huge sunglasses and a sleeveless white T-shirt, a clunky beaded necklace nestled in the deep V of the collar. She looks ferocious, her arms flung in the air and her mouth opened in a howl.

"What is— I mean, what are you—" I break off, not even sure which question to start with. "Is this in the city?" I finally ask.

She nods. "Right on Boston Common," she says. "I

took the bus in with a bunch of girlfriends for a civil rights demonstration. Your grandfather almost lost his mind."

"He didn't want you to protest?" I ask, eyebrows raised.

"Well, I wouldn't say *that*, exactly." Gram takes the picture from my hand, gazes at it appraisingly. "But he was worried about me, I think."

"Well, if this was when you got arrested, I guess he was right to be."

Gram waves a hand. "Oh, please," she says with a smirk. "First of all, this wasn't the protest where I got arrested. Second of all, maybe worried isn't the right way to put it. We were coming from different places, that's all. He didn't always understand why certain things were important to me, or why I reacted to things the way I did." She smiles at the picture, almost to herself. "He tried though. And that was the most important thing."

I think of Gray then. He and I haven't talked much either, the last couple of days, and I feel crummy about the way we left things outside Bex's classroom. I know he just wanted to take care of me, back in Bex's classroom. I didn't know how to explain how important it felt for me to take care of myself.

I'm about to ask Gram what she thinks I should do about him when Camille knocks on the door, poking her head in.

"That baklava is delicious," she reports with a smile. "How are you ladies doing in here?"

"We're great," Gram says, beaming, the box of photos still balanced in her narrow lap. "My daughter is visiting."

"Granddaughter," I remind her gently.

"Of course," Gram says. "My granddaughter. Ah . . ." She trails off then, a flash of panic skittering across her face; I can see she's lost her train of thought.

"Marin," I say, trying to keep my voice casual. She's never forgotten my name before. It's a fluke, that's all. "But Camille and I know each other already, remember?"

"We're old friends," Camille says. She's smiling, but her tone is slightly wary, her gaze flicking from me to Gram and back again. "You girls just yell if you need me, okay?"

"We will," I promise, and smile back.

I'm waiting in the bio lab Monday morning before first period when Gray appears in the doorway, looking around the empty room and back at me with confusion written all over his face. "Hey," he says. "Am I early?"

I shake my head. "Nope," I say. "Right on time."

Gray nods slowly. "There was a note taped to my locker this morning," he says, the faintest of smirks appearing at the very edges of his mouth. "Said there was an emergency book club meeting before first period. You wouldn't happen to know anything about that, would you?"

I tilt my head to the side for a moment, pretending to consider. "It's possible," I admit, holding up the Dunkin' Donuts box I picked up on the way in this morning, "that you're pretty much looking at it."

"Ah." Gray smiles a real smile now, all straight white teeth and sheepish expression. "You know, as I was coming over here I was wondering what the hell an emergency book club meeting could possibly be about. But I figured, what do I know, right? I'm new."

"There could conceivably have been some time-sensitive literary issue," I protest with a laugh. Then I shake my head. "I'm sorry I lost it like that the other day," I tell him. "Outside Bex's classroom."

Gray snorts. "That was you losing it?" he asks, sitting down on the sagging sofa beside me.

I shrug. "You know what I mean."

Gray nods. "You can tell me, you know," he says, leaning his head back against the threadbare cushions. "If you need space. I know I can be, like, a lot sometimes. Just say, 'Gray, with respect, go fuck off.' Easy as that."

I laugh. "With respect, obviously."

"The key to any successful relationship," he shoots back.

"Is that what this is?" I ask, before I can think better of it. The fluorescent lights overhead feel unforgivingly bright all of a sudden. "A relationship?"

Gray raises his eyebrows. "You tell me."

I bite my lip. On one hand, I'd be lying if I said I didn't feel something for him, that being with him doesn't light a spark inside me, doesn't fill my heart like a balloon inside my chest. On the other hand . . .

"I don't think you're a lot," I tell him finally, which isn't really an answer to his question. "Or I mean, okay, you can be. A lot, I mean. But in a good way." I reach for his hand, the calluses on his palm scraping gently against my skin. "I would never tell you to fuck off. I mean, I'd never tell anyone to fuck off, let's be real. But especially not you."

Gray smiles. "Too polite, huh?"

"Something like that," I tell him.

"Well," he says, "you never know. You might surprise yourself. Maybe one of these days you'll snap and start telling people to fuck themselves left and right."

"Maybe." I hold up the doughnut bag. "Peace offering?"

"There better be bear claws in there," he says, and kisses me before I can reply.

TWENTY-SIX

I'm in the bathroom near the gym on Friday morning when the door to the stall beside me opens and Chloe comes out.

"Oh! Sorry," I say, motioning at the sinks; there are only two in this bathroom, and only one of them has any water pressure. "Go ahead."

Chloe shakes her head, blond hair bouncing; today the lapel pin on her uniform collar is shaped like a tiny palm tree. "No," she says, "you can go."

"No, really."

"Marin," Chloe says, an impatient edge creeping into her voice. "Just go, okay?"

"Okay. Sorry." I wash my hands as fast as humanly possible, wrinkling my nose at the smell of the cheap green soap and grabbing a paper towel from the dispenser.

"So, um," I try, sensing an opening. "How's your day going?"

As an opening gambit it's pretty pathetic; Chloe's expression makes that much abundantly clear.

"It's fine. No complaints."

"That's good." I pull the sleeves of my uniform sweater down over my hands, wanting to howl at the thought of things being this awkward and impossible between us forever. *It's just me*, I want to tell her. *I'm still the same person I was before.*

"Look," I tell her, "I know this is a long shot, but there's a book club potluck tonight, if you're interested."

Chloe blinks at me. "A potluck?" she repeats.

"I know," I say, suddenly embarrassed by the earnestness of it—it's the kind of thing we probably would have made fun of, three months ago. "It's kind of like, very Midwestern mom of us? But it could be fun, right? And you don't have to be in the book club to come, so . . ."

Chloe nods slowly. "Um, thanks," she says. "I've got other plans, but . . . sounds fun."

I wince. *Other plans*, like she's some vague acquaintance

on the T who doesn't want to come to my weird church group and not the person who knows me best and longest, who always comes into a one-person bathroom with me when we're out together and whose house I've thrown up in on two separate occasions.

"Sure thing," I tell her. "Maybe another time, then."

"Maybe," Chloe says, leaning over the sink to reapply her lipstick. Neither one of us says goodbye before I go.

After Gray's practice, we head over to the potluck together, his heavy hand on mine. I've always kind of liked being in school when it's dark out, how it feels weirdly festive; Lydia and Elisa made decorations for the bio lab, brightly colored paper bunting hung up above the whiteboard, and a bunch of desks are pushed together and draped with a purple plastic cloth. Gray brought brownies one of his moms made, studded with walnuts and caramel chips and topped with flaky sea salt. Dave stopped at McDonald's and got like five dozen Chicken McNuggets, and Chloe's dad sent me with a huge to-go container of lamb meatballs with a yogurt dipping sauce from the restaurant. Even Ms. Klein brought something, though she's always talking about how she doesn't ever turn her oven on—tiny crostini spread with herby cheese and dolloped with fancy blackberry jam.

This is the first time we've all hung out where we didn't have a specific book to talk about, and I was worried it might be as awkward as it was back at the very beginning, but to my surprise the room is echoing with conversations: Bri and Maddie, the jazz band freshmen who've been showing up since the very beginning, are debating whether cheerleading is inherently sexist, while Dave and Gray scroll through Gray's phone, putting together a playlist of pump-up jams.

"My boyfriend is obsessed with this one," Dave says, hitting play on what I think is the new Halsey. He dates a super cute guy on the track team who's dropped in on a couple of our meetings and knew a shocking amount about feminist film theory.

"It's also important to think about the ways that women of color are left out of the conversation," Ms. Klein is saying when I drift over toward the dessert table. "Like when people say that women make seventy-seven cents on the dollar, what they mean is white women. For black women it's sixty-three cents on the dollar. And for Latina women it's even less."

"It's fifty-four cents," Elisa pipes up from across the room, then goes back to talking with Fiona Tyler, a sophomore who joined the club a couple of weeks ago, about some musical show on the CW they both like.

"No offense," Lydia says, crossing her ankles and leaning back on the desk she's perched on, "but when it comes to feminism, or whatever, it feels like white ladies always kind of want to make the conversation about them. Like they're the only ones whose ideas or priorities anyone should listen to."

My first reaction is to feel defensive—that's not what I'm doing, is it?—but then I take a breath, thinking about everything I thought I knew about feminism before I started the book club. I know that I've still got a ton left to learn.

"I can see that," I admit. "Like I remember reading an article about the original name of the Women's March being a rip-off of the Million Man March, and when black activists pointed that out a bunch of white women got all offended."

"Yeah, that's one example," Lydia says, though from her expression I can tell it's nowhere near the most important one. "But basically it's just that a lot of white women have this idea that feminism can be separated out from race or sexual identity or ability or any of that—and it can't. If you're going to go in, you have to go all in, you know?"

"The Audre Lorde essay we're going to be talking about next week is a great example of how different identities and marginalizations intersect and inform each other," Ms. Klein says, nibbling the corner of a brownie. "And you guys put *Her Body and Other Parties* on the list of books you might want to tackle, right?"

"That book is awesome," Gray says immediately. "And, like, super gory."

I look at him in surprise. "You've read it?"

He shrugs. "My mom got it for me, 'cause I said I liked Stephen King."

The conversation wanders from there—from *Pet Sematary* to who bought winter formal tickets and who they're taking, to the new werewolf show that just went up on Netflix, to a short biography of Ida B. Wells that Fiona pulls up on her phone when Dave admits to not knowing who she is. She's just finishing up when I notice Gray sneaking a look at his messages.

"You got another date?" I ask, nudging him gently in the side.

He shakes his head. "There's a party at Hurley Dubcek's," he admits. "I was going to ask you if you wanted to go after this, but I didn't want you to think I didn't want to be here." Gray looks around. "Because I do," he says resolutely, like he thinks he's running for political office. "Want to be here."

"Okay, big feminist," I say, patting him reassuringly on the shoulder. "We believe you."

"I was going to swing by that party too, actually," Lydia pipes up. "If anybody wants a ride."

There's a moment of awkward quiet then, all of us looking around at each other, none of us wanting to be the first to bail.

Finally Ms. Klein lets out a snort. "Get out of here," she says, popping one last meatball into her mouth before snapping the lid back onto the take-out container. "Make good choices, et cetera. I'll see you guys next week."

TWENTY-SEVEN

Hurley Dubcek lives in one of those quintessential Massachusetts houses that's been around since the colonies, with a steeply pitched roof and no real front porch, like maybe they didn't have time for things like that back then because there was too much butter to be churned. As we walk past an antique china cabinet in the narrow hallway all the delicate-looking dishes rattle ominously.

"I always feel like a frickin' monster in places like this," Gray murmurs over my shoulder.

I nod. "I was just thinking that exact same thing about you."

He looks at me, mock horror on his handsome face. "Rude!"

I grin at him. "I'm kidding." I reach back and take his hand, lacing our fingers together and squeezing once before releasing him. "Come on."

We pull a couple of warm cans from a thirty-pack in the kitchen, watching as Elisa grabs Lydia a Diet Coke from the fridge before pulling Dave in the direction of the backyard. Gray lets out a low whistle.

"Check out book club," he says with a smile. In the end almost everyone who was at the potluck wound up coming, all of us rolling down the windows in Lydia's mom's van and singing along to the radio at the tops of our lungs. "Ready to rage."

"I was surprised they all showed up tonight," I admit as we edge through the crowd into the living room, where someone has pushed aside what looks like a hundred-year-old leather sofa to make room to dance on the knotty wood floors. "To the potluck, I mean. Honestly, I'm surprised they show up at the actual meetings too, but you know what I'm saying."

"Kind of." Gray shrugs, tilting his head back against the wall in between two ancient-looking botanical prints. "They're showing up because of you though."

I laugh. "Maybe *you* are."

"I'm serious," Gray counters with a frown. "It's not just me. It's cool, what you started."

"Well," I say, suddenly self-conscious. I look out in the living room, where Dean Shepherd is attempting an extremely rudimentary pop-and-lock situation near the enormous stone fireplace. "Thanks."

"Don't mention it." Gray lifts his chin. "You want to dance?"

I raise my eyebrows. "Do *you*?"

"Always." He takes my hand, pulling me into the living room. "Come on."

Gray is the most enthusiastic dancer I've ever met, which in no way means he's good at it—arms and legs everywhere, a goofy, uncoordinated shuffle. I wonder what it's like not to care about what people think—although, yes, it's certainly easier not to care what people think when you're a six-foot-tall lacrosse star with a reputation for getting a million girls.

Just for tonight though, I don't want to worry about that. I close my eyes and shake my hair and let Gray twirl me around—liking the winter-woods smell of him, the feeling of his chest pressed against my back.

Eventually Dave comes and rounds us up for a game of book club beer pong; I promise to meet them outside before detouring toward the powder room tucked underneath the staircase in the front hall. I twist the creaky glass knob, pulling the door open—and almost trip right over Chloe, who's sitting with her knees pulled up on the tile. "Whoops," I say, holding up my hands to show I come in peace. "Sorry."

"It's fine," Chloe mumbles, tipping her head back against the peeling toile-patterned wallpaper. Her eyeliner is migrating down her face. "I was just leaving."

She curls her fingers around the sink, pulling herself unsteadily to her feet. "I—whoops." She stumbles a little, bracing her free hand against the wall.

I frown. So this was what she meant by "other plans." I haven't seen her this drunk since fall of freshman year, when we experimented with the peach schnapps at the back of my parents' liquor cabinet and wound up throwing up all over my basement by 9:00 p.m.

"Are you okay?" I can't help asking.

"I'm fine," she snaps, then immediately turns and barfs up a stomach full of bright blue party punch. She makes the toilet, thank God, but just barely; I reach over and gather her hair back like an instinct, just like she did for me last year when I puked in the bushes behind her house after spring formal. Both of us can just barely fit in here at once.

When she's finally finished I pass her a wad of TP to wipe her mouth with, tucking my hands in my pockets and looking discreetly away as she pulls herself together.

"Um," she says, clearing her throat and swiping her thumbs under her eyes to wipe the makeup away. "Thanks."

"No problem," I say, with the kind of polite *Don't worry about it* smile you offer someone when they've only got one item at the grocery store and you're letting them cut ahead of you in line. "You got a ride home?"

I'm prepared for some variation of *You're not my fucking mother*, but instead Chloe just nods.

"Emily is going to take me," she says, and I nod back.

"That's good." We stand there for a moment, looking at each other. This is *Chloe*, I remind myself, who taught me how to do an understated cat eye and is allergic to apples unless you microwave them for ten seconds first and can recite the entire second season of *Parks and Rec* from memory. I know her like I know Gracie; I know her like I know myself. But it feels like I'm looking at a stranger.

"Okay," I say finally. "Well. Have a good night, then."

"You too," Chloe says. She looks at me for a long moment, her eyes suddenly clear and focused. "Listen, Marin—" she starts, then abruptly breaks off. "Never mind," she says, and it's like I can see the moment she changes her mind about saying whatever it is she's got to say to me. "I'll see you."

"No, hey, wait." I've been edging out of the tiny bathroom, but suddenly I stop. "What's up?"

Chloe shakes her head. "It's nothing," she says, curling her fingers around the doorjamb for balance and brushing past me. "I'll see you around."

So . . . That's that, I guess.

I pee and wash my hands and make my way out into the backyard, which boasts a statue of a gnome holding a gazing ball, a tiny wishing well complete with crank and wooden bucket, and one of those little decorative ponds you can fill with Japanese koi. In this case it seems to be mostly filled with muck, which isn't stopping a bunch of people from playing catch across the diameter of it, one of those old Nerf footballs with the fin on the back of it sailing through the air. Gray and the rest of the book club are still negotiating the rules of this alleged beer pong tournament, though suddenly the last thing I want to do is play some dumb drinking game.

"I'm not having fun anymore," I announce, and Gray frowns.

"Can't have that," he says. Then, more seriously: "Everything okay?"

"Yeah." I offer him a smile; I want to explain about Chloe, but I don't want to do it here. "You want to maybe bail though?"

There's a part of me that's expecting him to be kind of a dick about it, but instead Gray just nods right away, taking my hand as we turn to go. That's when I hear a scoff off to my left, and when I turn I see Jacob. A bottle of Coors dangles from his fingers.

"Can I help you?" I ask.

"Just enjoying this little lovefest," he calls from the edge of the mucky pond. He's even drunker than Chloe, if that's possible. There's a mean, hard glint in his eye. He turns to Gray, his nasty smirk morphing into a faux-magnanimous smile.

"It's cool if you want my sloppy seconds, dude," he says, slurring just a little. "And Bex's too, I guess."

I take an instinctive step back, shocked as if he'd slapped me. There's a moment when I feel, horribly, like I'm about to cry.

"What did you just say?" Gray asks. His voice is perfectly pleasant—friendly, even—but he lets go of my hand as he takes a step closer to Jacob, who squares his shoulders and holds his ground.

"You heard me," he says, lifting his arrogant chin.

213

Gray nods easily. "I did," he agrees, taking a step closer, then another; now Jacob *does* back up, only he's misjudged how close he is to the side of the algae-covered pond. A slippery rock gives way under his foot and he goes pinwheeling backward, landing in the chilly, smelly water with a splash so noisy and dramatic half the party breaks into applause.

Gray looks at Jacob for a moment, then back at me, trying not to laugh and doing an overall admirable job of it.

"Sorry," he says, sounding a little sheepish. "I know you don't need me to protect you."

I reach to cup his face with both hands, stamping a kiss on his mouth like a seal of approval. "You know," I say, "I think I can make an exception just this once."

I don't have to be home for an hour yet, so we swing by Gray's house, a tidy Cape Cod with carefully tarped rose-bushes planted underneath the windows and a porch light shaped like a star hanging over the red front door. Inside it's warm, the air fragrant with the scent of sandalwood incense; I spy the orange flash of a cat as she darts up the stairs.

"Home!" Gray calls, hanging our coats on a hook by the doorway.

"In here!" a woman's voice calls back.

Gray leads me through the living room, which is lined

with bookshelves on two walls and art prints on the others, a blue velvet couch facing a pair of architectural-looking chairs. It's not how I pictured his house, and it must show on my face, because Gray nudges me in the side. "Were you imagining like, the whole place decorated in the colors of the New England Patriots?" he asks.

"Shut up," I say, though he's definitely on to me at this point. "No."

"You totally were," he says with a laugh, then nods at the bookshelves. "How exactly did you think I came up with a copy of *The Handmaid's Tale* so fast?"

He leads me through the formal living room and into a den, where two women are sitting watching *Brooklyn Nine-Nine* and drinking wine, a second orange cat purring on the sofa between them.

"Hey, baby," one of them says, lifting her face so that Gray can drop a kiss onto her cheek.

"This is Marin," he says. "These are my moms, Heather and Jenn."

"*This* is Marin!" the brunette—Jenn, I think—crows, like she's heard about me before.

I smile.

"Mom," Gray says, looking faintly embarrassed. "Jesus."

We chat for a little while, about the book club and about my editorials for the *Beacon*, which I guess he also mentioned.

"How was the party?" Heather asks.

"Kind of boring," Gray says, though I'm not entirely sure if he means the potluck or Hurley's; either way, he leaves out the part about Jacob and the algae pond. "We're gonna get some food and go upstairs."

"Door open!" Heather calls after us, and Gray makes a face for my benefit.

"Noted!" he calls back. Then, more quietly, "Jesus *Christ*, Mom."

"We heard that!" Heather yells.

We head into the kitchen, which looks like it was recently redone, with stainless appliances and a big window above the sink overlooking the yard.

"Can I ask you something?" I say, hopping up onto a stool. "Do you call both your moms 'Mom'?"

That makes him smile. "I mean, yeah," he says, opening a box of Cheez-Its and digging out a bright-orange handful. "What else would I call them?"

"No, I just mean, how do you keep them straight?"

Gray gives me a weird look, like possibly he's never stopped to think about it before. "Well, I mean, there's only two of them," he says. "And my sister always just kind of . . . knows which one I'm talking about? I don't know. I didn't think it was weird until right this minute, so thanks for that, I guess."

"You're welcome," I say with a smile, taking the box of crackers from his outstretched hand. "Also, I gotta say— obviously I don't know them, but those guys don't seem like the type to get super worked up over whether you play lacrosse in college."

Gray's eyes narrow. "In the five minutes you talked to them?" he asks pointedly, and I can tell I've hit a nerve.

"Okay, fine," I say, "Fair enough."

"They just . . . want me to be a college guy, that's all." Gray shrugs. "And if I can't get in on my grades, then . . ." He trails off. "I don't know," he says, picking the box of Cheez-Its up off the counter and using it to usher me out of the kitchen. "I'll figure it out."

"You will," I promise, and follow him up the stairs.

Gray's room is less of a surprise than the rest of the house, with white walls and bluish carpet and a signed Tom Brady jersey hanging in a poster frame above the desk. The bed is unmade, with rumpled flannel sheets melting off the edge of it. Gray scoops a pair of boxers off the floor and chucks them into the closet, looking goofily embarrassed.

"Sorry," he says. "If I knew you were coming—" He breaks off, seeming to think about it for a moment. "Well, no, honestly. I probably still would have been a total slob."

"Monster," I tease, glancing around the room at the half-empty water glasses clustered on every available surface, paperbacks for book club stacked haphazardly on the desk. On the dresser is a photo of his moms standing on either side of a little boy with a slightly uneven bowl cut, his front teeth bucked like a cartoon character's.

"Oh my gosh," I say, reaching for it before I can stop myself. "Is this you?"

"Nah," Gray says immediately, "it's just some other little kid I keep pictures of in my bedroom."

"Shut up," I tell him, completely unable to keep the grin off my face. "You were cute."

"I was . . . desperately in need of a haircut and twelve thousand dollars' worth of orthodontia," Gray counters, sitting down on the edge of the bed and leaning back on his palms. "That picture keeps me humble."

"Oh, right," I say seriously, crossing the carpet to stand between his knees, his shoulders warm and broad and solid underneath my hands. "Because otherwise your ego would just explode all over the place, huh?"

"Oh, totally out of control," Gray confirms with a smile.

"I mean, what with my athletic achievements, my outstanding academic record—"

"Your legendary prowess with the ladies," I put in.

"I'm also tall," he says, curling his fingers around my waist and pulling me closer. "Don't forget about that."

"I would never," I murmur, wrapping my arms around his neck and angling my face down until he gets the message and kisses me. I breathe a tiny sigh against his mouth. We've done this enough over the last few weeks that it's starting to feel normal, which isn't to say the thrill of it has worn off—the opposite, actually. Kissing Gray isn't like anything else I've ever done. It's not that I never enjoyed myself, fooling around with Jacob, but the truth is I never totally got what the big deal was. Half the time in my head I'd be somewhere else entirely—worrying over a missed problem on that morning's calc test, replaying an argument with my mom—and I don't think he ever actually noticed.

With Gray I feel achingly, deliciously alert.

Eventually he eases us back onto the mattress, the smell of detergent and sleep and boy all around me. The door is still open, but his room is far enough from the top of the stairs that the effect is the same as if we were the only ones in the house. Gray's fingertips creep up under the hem of my T-shirt, touching the sensitive skin of my waist and tracing the very bottom of my rib cage. I shiver, and Gray's eyes fly open.

"This okay?" he asks, gaze searching.

I pull back and look at him for a moment, hit by that sudden zing of recognition I never felt before.

I see you, I want to tell him. *I think you see me too*. "Yeah," I tell him. "This is good."

TWENTY-EIGHT

Gray's got a lacrosse game the following Thursday, so I head off to book club without him—we read "Age, Race, Class and Sex," this week, and I was thinking about suggesting we watch the PBS documentary about Audre Lorde, but when I walk into Ms. Klein's classroom after eighth period Dave looks surprised to see me at all.

"You're here?" he asks, pulling a bag of pretzels and a tub of onion dip out of his backpack. It was his turn to bring snacks today. "Doesn't Gray have that big game against Hartley?"

"I mean, yeah," I say, ignoring the twinge of guilt I feel

at missing it—the same twinge I've been feeling all day, truth be told. "But he gets it."

"Really?" Elisa puts in, dropping her shoulder bag on the floor and plunking down in an empty seat next to Ms. Klein. "That's the school he got kicked out of, isn't it? Feels like kind of a big deal."

"Thanks a lot," I say, snagging a couple of pretzels out of the bag and crunching thoughtfully. "I don't know. I guess I didn't want to be that girl, you know? The one who drops her commitments to go cheer on some dude."

"I don't think there's anything wrong with supporting somebody you care about," Elisa says, holding her hand out for the pretzel bag and waggling her long fingers until I pass it over. "I mean, you guys all came to my game, didn't you?"

"I mean, sure," I say, "but that's different."

"Why, because she's a girl?" Dave asks. "Isn't that reverse sexism?"

"Reverse sexism is one hundred percent not a thing," Lydia says immediately.

"Well, let's dig into that," Ms. Klein says, setting her book of essays down on the desk like she suddenly suspects we won't be getting to it anytime soon. "Can anyone explain to me *why* it's not a thing?"

"Because men unequivocally have more power than

women in our society," Maddie says easily, and I look at her in surprise—she's been pretty quiet at meetings up until now, but her voice is confident and clear. "It's like how racism against white people isn't a thing."

Ms. Klein nods. "Racism—and sexism, and ableism—are all power structures," she explains. "They're systems of oppression that are larger than any one interaction. So when we're thinking about them, it's important for us to ask ourselves what groups of people have historically been in charge in our society, and how the ways that our institutions are set up make it possible for those same groups to hold on to that power."

"So, just to throw out a random, totally hypothetical example," Elisa says, "a system where the entire school dress code is way more restrictive for girls than it is for guys—that would be sexism. Whereas Marin not going to Gray's game because she's trying to prove some point about something—"

"That's just dumb," Lydia finishes triumphantly.

"Hey!" I protest, but I'm laughing. After all, it's not like they're wrong. As much as I love this book club, I can't act like I don't wish I was somewhere other than here today. I care about Gray, as much as I've tried to keep myself from admitting it. I want to be there to cheer him on.

Elisa glances at the clock about the doorway. "Game doesn't start till four, right?" she asks, raising her eyebrows. "I propose a field trip."

"All in favor?" Dave asks, and a half-dozen hands go up around the classroom.

I feel myself grin.

Hartley is only about twenty minutes away, the bleachers packed with onlookers and the whole place smelling faintly of locker room. Ms. Klein tagged along too in the end, following us in her tidy little Volkswagen, and the group of us find spots on the Bridgewater side, the fluorescent lights casting everyone's face slightly green.

"There's Gray!" says Maddie, throwing a hand up to wave as we get ourselves settled near the top of the bleachers. I duck my face to hide my own instinctive eye roll at how swoony she sounds, but when I look up again Gray's gazing right at me, and just like that the expression on his face erases any weirdness I felt about coming here. He looks—there is no other way to describe this, or the way it sets something burning warmly in my chest—*delighted*.

Even after dating Jacob for the better part of a year, I have no idea what the rules of lacrosse are, honestly, but I like watching Gray running around down there—the easy way his body moves inside his red-and-gold uniform, the concentration on his handsome face. I know he's got mixed feelings about playing for St. Lawrence next year, but it's obvious he could if he wanted to: he's a natural leader, shouting casual encouragement at his teammates even as he bolts down the length of the gym.

Our team's leading 3–2 and Gray's heading for another goal when one of the guys from Hartley juts his lacrosse stick out in what looks to me like a purposeful jab. Gray spots it and tries to sidestep, but he's not quite fast enough, and all at once he trips and hits the floor with a thud I feel in my spine. Beside me, Ms. Klein gasps, the kind of sound you never really want to hear from an authority figure. Lydia lets out a low, quiet swear.

For a moment Gray lies still, unmoving; the ref blows his whistle, and a murmur goes up in the stands. Before I even know I'm going to do it I'm out of my seat and scrambling down the bleachers, darting through the crowd and out onto the field.

"You can't be out here!" one of the refs calls to me, but I'm not listening. Normally this is never something I would do—purposely drawing attention to myself, making a scene—but lately I've been realizing exactly what I *will* do, with a good enough reason.

And Gray is a good enough reason.

He's struggling to sit up as I reach him, another ref and Coach Arwen and a bunch of guys from the team circled around him in concern. His ankle is already starting to swell.

"I'm calling an ambulance," Coach is saying, digging his cell phone out of his pocket.

"No, no, no, I definitely don't need that," Gray protests, but when he tries to get to his feet his whole face goes sweaty and ghost pale.

"Okay," he says, sitting back down hard on the floor with a grimace. "Maybe I do."

He seems to register me for the first time then. "Hi," he says.

"Hi," I say. "You want me to call your moms?"

Gray shakes his head. "You can, but it's going to be hard to get them," he tells me. "My mom's got a late-afternoon class. And my mom's in court." He looks at me, offering a weak smile; he's hurting badly, that much is clear, though he's trying not to show it.

"See, this would be one of those times where it would be useful for me to call them two different things."

The ambulance arrives a few minutes later, a pair of tersely efficient paramedics peppering Gray with questions, moving his ankle gently this way and that. The one who's a woman doesn't look much older than us.

Do you know what you're doing? I want to ask her, flinching as Gray grimaces in obvious discomfort. *Do you know how important he is?*

Finally they seem to agree it's likely broken and he needs to get an X-ray, boosting him to his good foot and loading him up onto a stretcher. He's taller than both of them, and broader; they remind me of a couple in a fairy tale trying to transport a fallen giant.

"I'll get over there as soon as I can," Coach Arwen tells Gray, taking off his hat and scrubbing a nervous hand through his salt-and-pepper hair so it sticks up in all directions like the scientist from *Back to the Future*. "Do you want to have one of the guys ride along with you, keep you company?"

"I'll go," I hear myself say.

The crowd of faces turn to look at me at once. "Who are you?" the male EMT asks.

"I'm his girlfriend," I blurt.

Gray raises his eyebrows with a smile. This is the first time I've used the g-word in front of him. Actually, it's the first time I've used it at all.

I leave messages for both his moms on our way to the

hospital, then settle myself in a waiting room chair while the nurse takes him for X-rays, texting my own parents and the rest of the book club to let them know what's going on.

Tell Gray we love him! Elisa texts back, along with a string of on-theme emojis. *We won the game.*

Finally the nurses let me go and hang out with him while we wait for the X-rays to come back.

"Hi," I say, sitting down in the visitor's chair beside his hospital bed. He's still in his lacrosse uniform, a stretch of painful-looking turf burn on his forearm from where he fell.

"I'm on a lot of drugs," Gray announces grandly. "So, you know. No funny business."

"I would never," I assure him, looking down at my hands for a moment. Lately I've been biting my fingernails again, a habit I kicked back in second grade when my mom took to painting them with white vinegar, and my cuticles are ragged and raw.

Gray smiles a lazy, loopy smile. "It was nice hearing you call yourself my girlfriend back there."

I grin and roll my eyes. "It seemed faster than identifying myself as, like, founder of your feminist book club and new pal who sometimes hangs out in your bedroom."

He leans his head back against the pillow, his gaze surprisingly keen. "It does have kind of a ring to it, I guess.

Then again, so does girlfriend." He reaches for my hand. "I like you so, so much, Marin," he tells me. "And not just because I'm a little stoned at this particular moment, and not just because I can't get enough feminist theory in my life. I think you're smart. I think you're funny. And I think you're fierce as all hell."

I try to stave off the sudden rush of emotion—fear of getting hurt again, relief that he's okay, and something altogether bigger and warmer than that, something that fills my chest until it feels like I might burst from the sheer expansive size of it. "I bet you say that to all the girls," I finally say.

I'm kidding, but Gray doesn't smile.

"I don't, actually," he says as he sits up in his hospital bed. "I really don't." He tugs on my hand then, pulling me forward until our faces are nearly touching.

"You my girlfriend?" he asks, and his voice is so quiet.

I'm too busy kissing him to reply.

TWENTY-NINE

Second-semester seniors are allowed to leave campus during their free periods, so on Tuesday I run out to Panera for bagels and lattes, then come back and meet Gray in the common area outside the library, where he's reading *A Room of One's Own* for book club with his busted ankle propped up on a bench. It's just a bad sprain, but he's on crutches for a couple of weeks at least.

"Eh," he said when the doctor told him, "only a couple of games left anyway."

I couldn't help but notice he didn't sound all that broken up about it. He still hasn't talked to his moms about college.

"My hero," he says now, taking his bagel and lifting his face to kiss me before holding the book up for my inspection. "This one's super fucking boring," he reports.

"Oh, shush," I chide, though the truth is I read the first fifty pages last night and it's not like he's wrong, exactly. I sit down on the bench beside him, taking a sip of my latte before reaching into my backpack and clicking the mail icon on my phone. If Mr. DioGuardi catches you even looking at your phone during school hours he'll take it for the rest of the day, where it sits in a big basket in the admin suite labeled with a picture of an anthropomorphic iPhone crying enormous cartoon tears that he must have printed off the internet, but Brown notifications are going out this week, and I've been refreshing my email every fifteen minutes. I checked while I waited at Panera, and then again before I came back into school, but this time when I click over I can't hold back a quiet gasp: there's BROWN UNIVERSITY OFFICE OF ADMISSIONS in the sender line.

Gray looks up from his book. "Hm?"

I shake my head instead of answering. When I pictured this moment—and let's be real, I've been picturing this moment more or less since freshman year—I was always sitting calmly at home on my laptop, a mug of tea beside me and a cat curled in my lap, the hugeness and inevitability of the occasion somehow managing to overcome the inconvenience of the facts that I don't drink tea or have a cat. Now I force myself to take a breath, to take in the scene around me—the crispy January grass out the window, the faintly medicinal smell of Gray's face wash, the crinkly brown Panera bag in my lap. I want to remember exactly how this feels.

> *Dear Marin,*
> *Thank you for your interest in Brown University.*
> *Unfortunately, I'm very sorry to inform you that we*
> *are unable to offer you admission for the upcoming*
> *academic year.*

I feel the blood drain out of my face, pins and needles prickling in the tips of my fingers. For a long, disorienting moment, I can't get the words to compute.

I didn't get in.

I didn't even make the *wait* list.

The letter goes on from there, explaining how many applications they receive and how rigorous the admission process is, reassuring me that just because I didn't get into Brown doesn't mean I don't have a bright academic future ahead of me, but it's like the whole thing is written in a language I don't understand. My heart slams against my rib cage. My hands and feet are cold and numb. This is just one more situation I totally misjudged, I realize grimly: I was overconfident, too sure I was in control of what was happening. I played it all wrong.

Gray glances over at me again, a tiny divot appearing between his thick, straight eyebrows. "Everything okay?" he asks.

"Um," I say, swallowing down a lump the size of a pair of gym socks stuck at the back of my throat. "Yup." I can't bring myself to tell him, and as soon as I have that thought I remember that somehow I'm going to have to tell my parents—God, that I'm going to have to tell *Gram* when it's all she's ever wanted for me—and that's when I start to feel like I might throw up.

I thought I was a shoo-in. How could I have been so dumb?

Wait a minute, I think, my head clearing briefly. I thought I was a shoo-in because my interviewer essentially told me I was.

"Um," I say, getting to my feet so quickly the paper bag slides to the tile; I bend down and scoop it up before thrusting it in Gray's direction, swinging my still-open backpack onto one shoulder. "I just remembered I left my notes for next period in the car. I'll see you at lunch, okay?"

"Uh, yeah." Gray's eyes narrow a little. "Sure."

Then, laying one big hand on my arm: "Marin," he says, "Are you sure you're okay? You just got, like, super weird all of a sudden."

"Yup," I call over my shoulder, pulling gently away and darting down the hallway toward the exit. "Everything's fine!"

Out in the parking lot I dig wildly through my backpack until I find the business card Kalina gave me on the day of the interview; it's crumpled at the bottom, crumb-stained and soft around the edges. I dial her office number with shaking hands, squinting up at the midmorning sunlight.

"Marin," Kalina says, once the front desk assistant puts me through to her office. Right away she sounds uncomfortable, and I wonder if any authority figure is ever going to be happy to hear from me again. "How are you?"

"Um, not great, actually." I dig the nails of my free hand into my palm, trying not to sound hysterical. I've only got six more minutes until I have to be in class. "I just got a rejection letter from your office."

Kalina makes a sympathetic sound. "Oof, I'm sorry to hear that," she says. "You know, the university gets over thirty thousand applicants each year, and there's such a limited number of spots that often even when a candidate is qualified—"

"No, I know," I interrupt. "It says so in the letter. And I'm sorry if it's inappropriate to be calling you like this. I know it's probably bad form. But I just wanted to know what happened. For, like, the future."

"Unfortunately I can't really speak to the specifics," Kalina says. "We've got a policy of not commenting on individual applicants—again, the pool is just so large—"

"Kalina," I say, and my voice is dangerously close to be breaking. "Please? You had all the information when we met, right? And you said—"

"I shouldn't have," she interrupts me. "I know you and I had a rapport, but I was speaking out of turn, and I'm sorry if I—"

"Was it my grades?" I ask. "My extracurriculars? What?"

Kalina doesn't say anything for a moment. It's like I can feel her debating something with herself on the other end of the line. "Look, Marin," she says, and her voice is very quiet. "Ultimately the admissions board received some information that made us feel like you might be a better fit elsewhere, that's all."

All at once I stand up a little straighter, a sensation like a spider scuttling up along my spine. "What information?"

"Marin, I really can't—"

"What information? Kalina, if somebody said something about me that made it so I can't get into *college*—" I shake my head, catching a glimpse of the window of the newspaper office out of the very corner of my eye; then, all at once, the penny drops. "Oh my god. Was it Bex?"

"I'm sorry?"

"Mr. Beckett," I say. "Jon Beckett, my English teacher. He—he and I—his family are these huge donors, and—" I break off. "Is that who it was?"

For a long time Kalina doesn't answer, and that's how I know that it's true.

"For what it's worth, I went to bat for you," she tells me finally. "I'm really sorry it didn't work out."

"Yeah," I say, dimly aware of the bell for the end of the period ringing in the distance. I tilt my head back and look up at the tree line, my eyes blurring with tears. "Me too."

THIRTY

I stumble back into the building, my chest tight and my breath coming in frantic, ragged gulps. I feel like I could rip tree trunks in half with my bare hands or burst into flames in the middle of the hallway. In the back of my mind I know that not getting into my first-choice Ivy League university is the very definition of a champagne problem: after all, there are plenty of other colleges. There are plenty of other paths.

But this is the one I wanted. This is the one I *earned*.

And he just . . . took it.

There's only one concrete thought in my head as I careen down the hallway:

I have to find him.

I know from back when we used to be friends, or whatever it is I thought we were, that Bex doesn't have a class this period. I head for the newspaper office, but the room is dark and empty when I arrive, the Bridgewater screensavers glowing vacantly on the computer screens.

I try the cafeteria next, then the admin suite where the copier is, coming up empty. I'm fully prepared to march right into the teachers' lounge, to interrupt whatever secret, sacred stuff they all do in there with their microwave and their electric kettle, but instead, when I turn the corner near Ms. Klein's lab there he is strolling down the hallway in my direction, his stupid messenger bag slung across his chest.

I gasp, freezing for one icy moment before I manage to make any words. "Um," I announce, the sound coming out phlegmy and garbled. "I need to talk to you."

Bex frowns. "Marin," he says, with this tiny pause like I'm some random student he's never taught before and he needs to search his mental contacts list for my name. "Shouldn't you be in class?"

"I don't think it really matters at this point, does it?" I shoot back. "You made sure of that."

Bex's eyes narrow for the briefest of moments. "Well, it's pretty obvious you're upset," he observes mildly, like the emotion has nothing whatsoever to do with him, like I'm a character on a TV show he doesn't much like. "Do you want to go somewhere and talk?"

"Somewhere like your apartment, you mean?"

It's out before I can stop myself, and I think I shock us both in equal part: Bex's lips thin, a muscle twitching erratically in his jaw.

"This is really inappropriate," he murmurs with a shake of his head, turning away and making to brush past me down the hallway. "If you want to have a conversation related to your schoolwork, you know where to—"

I laugh out loud, hysterical and cackling like the witches from *Macbeth*. I know I sound exactly as crazy and ungovernable as everyone in this school already thinks I am, but for the first time since this all started I 100 percent do not care.

"Seriously?" I can't help asking. "*I'm* inappropriate?"

"*Enough*." All at once Bex turns around again, grabbing me by the arm and steering me down the hallway into the south stairwell, the door slamming shut behind us with a startling *chunk*. "Jesus *Christ*, Marin," he says, bewildered. "What is your problem right now?"

In the back of my head it occurs to me to be afraid of him. Instead, I stand my ground, planting my feet on the linoleum and willing my voice not to shake. "Did you talk to the Brown admissions board about me?"

Bex's expression doesn't change, smooth and innocent as a Boy Scout's, but his hands twitch at his sides.

"I— What makes you think that?" he asks, and then he clears his throat, and that's when I know I've got him.

"You did." Even after everything that's happened there's a part of me that didn't believe it until right this moment, like surely no adult—no *teacher*—could be that awful and petty and mean. "Oh my god."

"First of all—"

"How could you do this to me?" I interrupt, trying like all hell to swallow the sob I feel rising in my throat. Sounding a little emotional is one thing. Letting him see me cry is quite another. "Brown has been my dream my entire freaking life."

Bex lets out a low, mean scoff. "I ruined your *dream*?" he echoes contemptuously, like I'm a little kid who still believes in Santa Claus. "You tried to ruin my *life*, Marin."

For a moment I'm totally stunned. "I—what?"

Bex rolls his eyes, scrubbing a hand through his hair like he honestly cannot believe me. "My god," he says, "you are so spoiled. Everyone in this school is spoiled, but especially you."

I blink at him for a moment, caught up short. No adult has ever talked to me that way before. "How am I spoiled?" I ask, more baffled than offended. "You're the one who—"

"You can play victim all you want, kiddo," Bex interrupts. "You can act like you had nothing to do with any of this. But you and I both know the truth."

I feel myself get very still. "What does that mean?"

"Oh, don't look at me like that. You're not a baby deer." Bex rolls his eyes. "You were always around, Marin. Hanging out in the office. Making up excuses to ask for rides."

"Wait a second," I protest. "I never—"

"Sitting on my fucking desk, for Christ's sake," Bex continues. "What vibe did you think you were giving off, exactly? You wanted it, Marin. And maybe you freaked out and regretted it afterward, but I'm not going to sit around and let you make me out to be some kind of fucking sex predator when we both know you were every bit as responsible for what happened as I was. More, probably."

I am crying now, I can't even help it, tears slipping fast and silent down my face. For the first time in my life it's like I'm all out of words.

"Fuck you," is all I can manage. I don't wait for him to reply before I turn and walk away.

THIRTY-ONE

I tear down the hallway toward the south exit, slamming the push bar and exploding out into the parking lot even though it's the middle of the day. After all, it's not like it matters— what are they possibly going to do to me at this point if they catch me skipping my afternoon classes? Tell me I can't go to Brown?

The parking lot is strangely quiet, just a couple of birds chattering away in the trees and the occasional car cruising by out on the street. I unlock the car with shaking hands, jamming the key into the ignition and nearly clipping a red Passat as I peel out of the parking lot, everything

I should have said to Bex echoing meanly in my head. *I'm* spoiled? He's the one with his name on the auditorium at an Ivy League university. *I'm* responsible for what happened between us? He's the asshole who drove me to his fucking apartment.

Hot tears blur my view of the road in front of me. I head down Juniper Hill Avenue, midday traffic thinning out as I pass the municipal baseball fields and the golf course development, the function hall where we had my eighth-grade graduation party. I don't have any real destination in mind. I can't go home and face my parents. I can't turn around and go back to school. There's a part of me that wants to just keep on driving—to speed right out of this stupid town, to keep my foot pressed to the pedal until I get all the way to the Atlantic Ocean.

Finally I head for Sunrise without ever quite making the conscious decision to do it, instinct and muscle memory taking over. My gram is the only person I can imagine being around right now.

Camille is coming out of a suite down the hall as I step off the elevator, a blood-pressure cuff dangling from one hand. Her scrubs have rubber ducks parading across them today, her Crocs the same bright, cheery yellow.

"Marin," she says, looking surprised—and there's that

uncomfortable look again, that flicker of trepidation at the sight of me. "What are you doing here, hm? Shouldn't you be in school?"

"Reading day," I tell her, surprised at how smoothly the lie comes out of my mouth. "I just need to talk to my gram real quick."

"It's not really a good time, sweetheart. You should come back later."

That surprises me—in all the years I've been coming here, Camille has never said anything like that to me before. "Why?" I ask, frowning. "What's going on?"

"She's having a tough day, that's all. She was a little agitated this morning. It's probably better if you just let her rest."

Camille's tone is light—friendly, even—but there's an underlying warning I've never heard from her before. "What do you mean, agitated?" I ask, trying to keep my own voice even. "Is she okay?"

Camille nods. "She's fine, sweetheart. She just—you know. Needs to take it easy until she's feeling more like herself."

"What, like she's not remembering stuff?" I shake my head. "That's okay though. I don't mind."

"Marin—"

"She knows who I am," I promise. "It's fine, Camille, honestly. I'll be quick."

Camille takes a step closer then—to try to block my path down the hallway, maybe, or to catch me by the arm—but I'm too fast and too determined and possibly a little too wound up, skirting past her and slipping down the brightly lit corridor to the door of Gram's suite. It's all the way closed today, which is unusual, but I knock lightly before pushing it open, same as always.

"Hi, Gram," I call, all slightly manic sunshine—then stop where I'm standing in the doorway, caught short. The woman sitting vacantly on the love seat doesn't look anything like my grandmother. She's not wearing any lipstick, her mouth so pale it's nearly vanished into the rest of her face. Her white hair is a matted mess. She's still in her pajamas, the undone top button revealing her sharp, jutting collarbones. Most of all she just looks *frail*.

"Who are you?" she asks, her blue eyes watery and suspicious.

I bite my lip. "Hey Gram," I say again, careful to keep my voice breezy. "It's me. Marin."

Gram shakes her head, stubborn. "I don't know you."

"I'm your granddaughter," I remind her, working hard to swallow down the sudden lump in my throat, knowing instinctively that getting emotional is only going to make this worse—which, I think bitterly, is something of a theme in my life lately. "I'm Dyana's daughter, remember?"

I take a step closer, but Gram holds her hands up, like the victim in an old murder mystery on the classics channel.

"Who? I don't *know* you," she repeats. "Where's the nurse?" Then, raising her voice toward the open door: "Hello! There's a strange woman in here! I need help!"

"Gram," I plead, "come on," but Camille is already here, laying a firm, gentle palm on my back.

"Well, hey there, Ms. Fran," she says calmly. "You're okay, I'm right here. I'm just going to take a stroll with our friend here, and then I'll be right back to get you some iced tea, how about?"

"I don't *know* her," Gram insists again—sounding more irritated than scared now, like I'm more inconvenience than threat. I don't actually know which one is worse.

I shouldn't have come here, I think dully. All I do is wreak disaster everywhere I go.

"I know," Camille says, wrapping an arm around my shoulders and squeezing once before steering me toward the door. "Come on, sweetheart."

"I'm sorry," I say once we're out in the hallway. "I'm sorry, I know you tried to tell me, I just—" *Thought I knew better*, I realize, feeling abruptly like an idiot on top of everything else. "I'm sorry."

"Marin, honey." Camille lets a breath out—not *mad* at

me, exactly, but not as warm as she usually is either. "Why don't we call your mom, okay?"

Right away I shake my head. "It's fine, I'll just—I'll go. I'm sorry. You can go back in there and check on her. I didn't mean to make things worse."

"Marin—" Camille starts, and I know she's going to try to comfort me, even though it's not her job to do that. I hold my hands up to stop her, then turn and make a beeline for the stairs, tears aching at the back of my throat.

Down in the parking lot I sit in the car for a long time, wiping tears and snot and so much sadness from my face. I remember when I was a kid, before Gracie was born, even, when I used to stay with Gram overnight at her house in Brockton. It wasn't long after Grandpa Tony had died and she used to let me sleep in the big bed with her, the two of us watching reruns of nineties sitcoms while the AC unit hummed in the window. She used to pet my hair until I fell asleep.

Finally, exhausted, I pull out of the parking lot and head for home. The fastest route takes me back by school, and I glance over at the parking lot as I'm idling at the red light: eighth period got out a while ago, and the grounds are mostly empty. In fact, I realize with a quick, nasty jolt, Mr. Beckett's Jeep is one of the only cars still parked in the lot. It's sitting there smugly under a blooming dogwood tree not far from the senior entrance, his stupid Bernie Sanders sticker fading on the bumper.

I think, very clearly: *Don't be such a good girl.*

That's when I turn into the lot.

I pull up beside the Jeep and yank the emergency brake, leaving the engine running while I pop the trunk and jump out onto the concrete. I haven't even really articulated a plan to myself when I grab the poster paint left over from the day of Elisa's volleyball game—still sitting in the trunk next to my mom's first aid kit and a couple of overdue library books, like deep in the back of my own secret brain I knew I might need it again. It feels like a relic from a totally different past.

I clamp a dry, crusted-over paintbrush in my teeth and twist the lid off the tub of paint with shaking hands, glancing over my shoulder to make sure no one is coming; the parking lot is deserted, even the birds have gone home for the day. It's like I'm totally outside myself as I scrawl the first word I can think of, the letters huge and red and dripping across Bex's back windshield. When I'm done I throw the rest of the paint at the car for good measure before standing back for a moment, admiring my handiwork.

Then I get back in my car and drive away.

THIRTY-TWO

I've barely made it through the door of my first-period French class the following morning when Madame Kemp nods in my direction.

"Marin," she says distractedly as she lopsidedly scrawls this morning's irregular verbs on the whiteboard, "there's a pass for you on my desk over there. Ms. Lynch says they want you down in the office."

I freeze where I'm standing, fingers curled tightly around the strap of my backpack. All at once I think of *Thelma & Louise*, this old movie my mom and I watched last year on cable about two friends who kill a guy in self-defense and then go on the run. The movie ends with the two of them driving into the Grand Canyon rather than giving themselves up to the police—this incredible, shocking freeze-frame of the car flying over the cliff that I couldn't get out of my head for weeks after I saw it. It was weirdly exhilarating, the idea of these two women refusing to engage with an unfair system. Looking at a menu of shitty choices and deciding to go out on their own terms.

Of course: we never saw the actual crash.

I shuffle down the senior stairs to the admin suite, where Ms. Lynch is diligently adding balloon emojis to the birthday wishes she's composing on someone's Facebook.

"Marin," says Mr. DioGuardi when I knock on the open door of his office, not bothering to say hello this time. I guess we're officially past formalities at this point. "Sit."

I plunk down obediently as Mr. DioGuardi pops his whistle into his mouth, the faintest, shrillest shriek filling the air every time he breathes. Finally he pulls it out again and eyes me across the desk. "So," he says, meaty hands folded. "Do you want to start, or should I?"

"Um," I say, not sure of the protocol here. In my entire life, I've never really gotten in trouble—and I'm pretty sure that's what's about to happen here, though I'm not sure who possibly could have seen me. "You can start."

I don't mean to sound sullen, exactly, but I can tell that's how Mr. DioGuardi takes it.

"All right," he says crisply. "Have it your way." He turns his computer monitor around so that it's facing me, hitting the space bar on the keyboard so the grainy security camera footage on the screen starts to move.

Yup, I think with surprising numbness, watching in silence as my car pulls up beside Bex's, as I hop out of the driver's seat and open my trunk. *Definitely about to get in trouble.*

I stare at the screen, transfixed by my yesterday-self as one by one the letters appear on the back of Bex's car: *S*, then *C*, then *U*, then the dark red curves of the *M*. It occurs to me, if I was going to get caught anyway, that I could have gone ahead and picked a longer word.

"What were you thinking?" Mr. DioGuardi asks, and I look at him, startled. For a second I almost forgot he was there. "Quite seriously, Marin, what on earth was going through your head?"

"Well," I say, truly considering it. "I wasn't thinking about the security cameras, I can tell you that much."

That's the wrong thing to say: Mr. DioGuardi glowers at me across the desk, his dark eyebrows nearly connecting. "Is this funny to you?" he demands.

"No," I promise immediately, and it's the truth. "I don't think it's funny at all."

"Then I would be very careful how you handle this situation," he instructs me.

Clearly, I've exhausted his store of patience.

"Your future is in your hands right now. We're suspending you for two weeks, effective immediately. Unless you want to turn that into an expulsion—"

"I'm sorry, *what*?" I shove my chair back, jumping to my feet like I'm trying to escape a burning building. "You're—?"

"What did I *just* say, Marin?" Mr. DioGuardi's cheeks redden. "Lucky for you, Mr. Beckett has agreed not to press criminal charges."

I sit back down, not so much because he's telling me to as because I think my legs might actually give out underneath me.

"Um," I say again, wrapping my hands around the armrests in a pathetic attempt to ground myself. I can taste this morning's orange juice rising dangerously at the back of my throat. "Okay."

"He and I are both willing to acknowledge the emotional stress you've been under," Mr. DioGuardi continues, "and we understand the possibility that you weren't entirely yourself."

Not myself, I think dully, staring down at my hands like they're somehow completely separate from my body.

"The suspension is effective immediately," Mr. Dio-Guardi says again. "I'll be calling your parents to inform them of the situation, and Ms. Lynch can escort you to your locker to get your things."

"I don't need an escort," I tell him, forcing myself to my feet again. Nothing about this conversation seems real. *Suspended.* Me. He might as well be telling me he's sending me off to the moon.

"Marin—"

"I said I don't need one!" I snap, and it comes out a lot more like a wail than I mean for it to. Right away I hold my hands up in surrender, like a bank teller being held hostage. "I'm going, okay? I'm going."

Just for a moment Mr. DioGuardi looks at me with something like sympathy. "All right," he says quietly. "Go get your things, then."

The bell rings just as I stumble dazedly out of the admin suite, classroom doors slamming open like they're spring-loaded and the entire student body spilling out into the hallway. I almost crash right into Jacob, his immaculate Top-Siders gleaming white under the fluorescents and an against-dress-code Sox hat cocked on his head, not that anybody's going to say anything to him about it.

"Hey, Marin," he says, smiling a twisty, unpleasant smile. Then he nods at the admin office. "You making some alone time with DioGuardi now too?"

It's like something in me just breaks then, like everything I've been holding in with varying degrees of success in the last few months comes exploding out all at once. Before I even know I'm going to do it I'm lunging at him, shoving him as hard as I can in the chest and shoulders, the heels of my hands connecting with a satisfying thud. It's ridiculous—I'm emphatically not a fighter, Gracie and I never even pulled each other's hair as little kids—but Jacob's not expecting it; I shove him again, even harder this time, knocking him loudly into the bank of lockers behind him.

"What the fuck, Marin?" he yells, arms coming up to try and defend himself. "You're fucking insane!"

"And you're an asshole!" I can hear assorted gasps and shouts all around us, my vision blurred at the corners of my eyes. "And I've had it with letting you all just get away with saying shit like that!"

It's a spectacle, the exact kind of thing I've tried to avoid since I got back to school after break—hell, like I've tried to avoid my whole entire *life*. Maybe he's right. Maybe I am insane, hysterical, attention-hungry, desperate. Maybe I'm everything everyone thinks I am, but I can't bring myself to care. This whole little rebellion was a stupid idea to begin with.

And all at once I've got nothing left to lose.

I'm about to go after him again when Gray swoops in out of nowhere, dropping his crutches to the ground and wrapping his arms around my waist. "Let me go!" I order, trying to pry his arms off me. I don't want another guy touching me right now. I don't want anyone holding me back.

"Hey, hey, hey," Gray says, hauling me away from the crowd with a few choice words for the scrum of onlookers. He's twice my size, but I'm thrashing; I reach back and catch him on the side of his jaw before he finally deposits me in the hallway that leads to the library and nurse's office, quiet and dark in comparison to the rest of school.

"Let me *go*," I insist, though he's already done it, hobbling sideways on his walking cast, pain visible in the twist of his handsome features. The bell rings for the start of class, though it sounds strangely far away.

Gray shakes his head. "What *was* that?" he asks, bewildered. "Are you okay?"

"I'm fine," I snap, making to brush past him; he reaches for my arm, and I hiss. "Stop. Can you stop? I am so *sick* of this."

God, I have to get out of here. As soon as DioGuardi

hears about this, I know I'm going to be facing an expulsion; I want to run as far as I can and never come back.

"Marin," Gray says, reaching for my hand again; I yank myself away, and he holds his palms out. "I'm sorry. I'm sorry, I just—"

"I said *stop*!" I tell him, my voice echoing down the hallway. "Stop trying to fix everything, or protect me, or whatever it is you think you're doing. Just leave me alone for once, okay?"

"Okay," Gray says, hands still up like I'm a wild animal—like maybe I'm dangerous, and need to be contained. "I won't touch you again, I promise. I'm sorry. But can you please just talk to me for a sec?"

I shake my head. I can't take his affable good-guy act right now—because let's be real, that's probably what it is, right?

"You're not helping," I inform him. "Nothing you've done this whole time has helped, actually, so—" I break off. I don't know why I'm saying this. Part of me doesn't know what I'm saying, but I can't stop.

"Look," I try again. "This has been fun. But I just don't think it's a good idea to keep—"

"To keep what?" Gray frowns. "What's not a good idea?"

"You and me."

"Seriously?" He looks baffled. "I don't—why? Because Jacob is a dick?"

I gape at him. "*That's* what you think this is about?"

"No, no," he amends quickly. "Of course not, but—"

"No." I cut him off. I'm just so done. We're so done. "It's over."

"I—"

"*No*," I say again—and there's something that feels satisfying about it, finally, even if there's a voice in my head that's already wondering if this is really the bridge I want to burn. His instructions from weeks ago come tumbling back to me then, and before I can stop myself I tell him: "With respect, Gray? Fuck off."

For a second Gray just stares at me, eyes flickering with recognition, and my heart breaks a little bit. Then his face falls.

"Yeah," he says, and his voice is so quiet. "I can do that."

THIRTY-THREE

I manage to make it home and get into bed without talking to anybody, pulling the covers up over my head and closing my eyes. I know Mr. DioGuardi is going to call here. It's only a matter of time.

Sure enough, when the knock on my door comes it's both of my parents, hands linked, their faces twin pictures of worry.

"So," my mom says. She sounds remarkably calm—calmer than I've heard her since this whole thing started, actually, her dark hair pulled neatly off her face. "Do you want to talk about it now, or do you want to talk about it later?"

"Later," I mumble into the pillows.

To my surprise, she nods.

"Okay," my dad says. "We love you."

That's when I start to cry.

Both of them are across the room in a second, like I'm a toddler who fell down learning to walk.

"Sweetheart," my dad says, while my mom sits down beside me on the mattress, "what the hell happened?"

I take a deep breath, the whole sad story spilling out of me all at once: the email from Brown and the call with Kalina, the visit with Gram, what I did to Bex's car.

"Everything you guys did. The SAT tutors. Those stupid piano lessons. Everything Gram wanted for me. I blew it all," I tell them.

My mom shakes her head. "You didn't blow anything."

"Really?" I ask tearfully. "Honestly, name one thing I haven't totally ruined in the last couple of months. Brown. My friendship with Chloe. Gray. And it's all my fault." I swipe at my face with the back of my hand, angry and embarrassed. "All of this is my fault."

"What?" My mom shakes her head, baffled. "No, sweetheart. That's not true. How could any of this possibly be your fault?"

"Because I had a crush on him!" It comes out like a keen, high-pitched and humiliating. "I did! And I *did* hang around all the time, and it did give him the wrong idea, and—"

"Hold on a second," my mom says, wide-eyed. "No way. That's not how this works, okay? That's not how any of this works."

She shakes her head one more time. "Sweetheart, do you know how many people get crushes on their teachers? Do you know how many teachers *I* had crushes on, growing up?"

"It's not the same," I insist. "If I hadn't—"

"It's the teacher's job to set the boundary," my dad says firmly. "Because the teacher is the adult."

Logically, of course, I know they're right. Bex and I weren't equal partners in some doomed flirtation; he was the authority figure, and I was a kid in his class. But looking around at the total wreckage of my life right now, it's hard to make myself believe it.

"Still," I say—shrugging half-heartedly, unconvinced. "I should have known better."

"*He* should have known better." My mom puts her arms around me then, gathering me close and stroking a hand through my hair. "And he *did* know better. And all of this is so unfair."

On that last point, at least, it's difficult to argue, so

instead I let her hold me, closing my eyes against a sudden wave of exhaustion.

"I hate him," I mutter into her neck.

"I know," my mom says, her grip tightening reassuringly. "I fucking hate him too."

THIRTY-FOUR

The first couple of days of my suspension aren't actually so terrible. I watch a bunch of low-budget rom-coms on Netflix. I take myself on a long, winding walk. I heft Gram's old *The Silver Palate Cookbook* off the shelf in the kitchen and fumble my way through the recipe for orange-pecan loaf, leave it on the counter for my mom to bring to her and the nurses in the morning.

That's when the boredom sets in.

I lie on my bed and stare at the ceiling for a while. I will myself not to check my phone. I'm contemplating cleaning out my closet—which is how you know I'm truly desperate—when I hear the doorbell chime downstairs.

"Marin, honey!" my mom calls a moment later, the faintest hitch of surprise just barely audible in her voice. "You've got company!"

I'm startled too: seriously, is there anybody in my entire life I haven't somehow alienated lately? I shuffle out into the hallway and down the steps, making it as far as the landing before I stop on the matted carpet. Chloe is standing in the foyer in a silky top and a pair of open-toed booties, hands shoved into the back pockets of her dark skinny jeans. Her eyeliner is as perfectly applied as always, but for the first time in a long, long time her lips are pale.

"What are you doing here?" I ask, but then I notice the hunch of her narrow shoulders like she's shielding herself from a blow, and some dormant best-friend instinct sputters creakily to life. "Are you okay?"

Chloe shrugs, squinting at the 3D sea-glass sculpture on the wall in the hallway instead of looking at me. "Can we talk?" she asks.

I glance from her to my mom, who's slipping discreetly into her office, then back to Chloe again. "Sure."

I pull a hoodie off the row of hooks next to the front door and we head outside to sit on the porch swing, the chain link groaning quietly as we rock back and forth. We've had almost every important conversation of our friendship out here: sixth grade, the two of us trying valiantly to decipher the primitive dick-and-balls cartoon Brandon Farrow had scribbled on the back cover of her notebook; freshman spring when she told me her sister was leaving college to do inpatient eating-disorder treatment; last year when I was deciding if I wanted to lose my virginity to Jacob. I used to think I could tell Chloe anything. But now I don't know what to say.

In the end it turns out I don't have to.

"Can I ask you a question?" she begins, picking at the polish on her freshly painted thumbnail. She still isn't looking at me. "Why did you trash Bex's car?"

I whirl around, shocked all over again. "*That's* what you came here to yell at me about?" I demand. "His douchey car? Because if it is you can just—"

"Can you calm down?" Chloe interrupts, finally turning to look at me. Her eyes are hot as flame. "I'm not yelling at you. Do you hear me yelling at you? I'm just asking you why you did it."

I shrug. "Why do you even care?"

Chloe huffs a breath out. "Marin," she says, tilting her head back against the swing. "Come on."

"You come on." I'm being a baby—I know I'm being a baby—but I can't help it. I don't know how to not be hurt by what she did.

"Look." Chloe peels a flake of polish off her pinky nail, flicking it onto the floor of the porch. "I know I haven't been a very good friend to you lately—and I know that's even an understatement, probably," she says, holding a hand up when I let out a sound of protest. "And you don't owe me any kind of explanation. But I'm listening, if you want to tell me."

So: I tell her. I tell Chloe everything, from Bex's first day back to my call with Kalina, to his grip on my arm that day in the stairwell. "He wanted to get back at me for telling, and he did," I finish finally. "So I guess I just wanted to . . . get back at him too." I reach one foot out and push off the porch railing harder than I mean to, and we go swinging forward quickly. "But the only person I actually ruined anything for was myself."

The swing creaks back and forth, back and forth, and Chloe doesn't say anything. When I glance in her direction her face is almost as white as the clapboard on the front of the house.

"I'm sorry," she says, her eyes filling so suddenly with tears that I can't keep from gasping. "Marin. I'm so, so sorry."

Right away I shake my head. "Hey," I say, holding my hands up, palms out in shocked surrender. Our friendship has felt like one bizarre, inexplicable missed connection after another lately. But I wasn't prepared for this. "It's . . . okay."

"It's not!" she says, and she's up off the swing now, pacing across the porch. "It's a lot of things, Marin, but it is definitely not okay."

"Chloe," I say, curling my fingers around the edge of the porch swing. My voice is quiet. "What's going on?"

Chloe shakes her head, her eyes flicking to her car in the driveway like she can't decide if she wants to dive behind the wheel and peel away into the sunset or just take off on foot and never, ever stop. I know that look—I've seen it in the mirror a lot lately—but in the end she just sits back down beside me, clearing her throat like she's preparing to give testimony in a courtroom. She takes a deep breath.

"I thought he loved me," she confesses, then immediately digs the heels of her hands into her eye sockets, rubbing until her mascara smudges. "Oh my god, I can't believe I'm saying that out loud right now. I sound like a fucking idiot. I thought he *loved* me."

"Who?" I ask—even though I already know, in some secret part of my brain. Maybe I always did.

Chloe rubs her thumbs underneath her eyes, wiping the mascara away. "Who do you think?"

It started in October, she tells me. He took her to his apartment, in the Victorian house with the built-in book-shelves on either side of the fireplace. He wanted to lend her a book. They listened to records; he cooked her pasta. She told her parents she was at the library.

He told her she had an old soul.

"When you told me what happened between you guys I just kind of lost it," Chloe admits. "The way you described it, him being a creep—it didn't feel like that to me. Or not at the time, at least. I thought we were . . . a couple." She rolls her eyes and another tear slips down her cheek. "We did couple stuff. Like—I went with him to the Cape back in the fall."

My eyes widen. "You did what?"

"Can you not?" Chloe shakes her head. "I know now it was stupid."

"I don't think it's stupid," I promise. "I just—what, to a *hotel*?"

She shrugs. "His family has a house."

"Of course they do." I run my fingers through my hair. "I'm sorry. I'm being an asshole. I just—when?"

"The weekend I told you I was with Kyra."

"Oh my god, I *knew* there was no way you were vol-untarily spending a weekend with her!" For a moment I'm weirdly, horribly vindicated—that I knew her that well, at least, that I wasn't totally fooled—and then I realize how messed up that is. "What did you tell your parents?" I ask.

"School trip," she says miserably. "I made a fake permission slip and everything."

"Weren't you worried I'd say something to them about it when I was at work?"

"Are you kidding me?" Chloe exhales sharply. "I was *terrified*. It was all I could think about all weekend, only I didn't want to tell him that, because I didn't want to remind him—"

"That you're *seventeen*?"

"All right!" Chloe explodes, shocking us both into silence for a moment. When she speaks again her voice is barely more than a whisper. "After you went to his apartment . . . he told me he'd just tried to be nice to you." Her nail polish is mostly gone by now, pale pink dust scattered across her lap. "Like, that it was this totally harmless thing, and you'd gotten the wrong idea, or whatever. But then he broke up with me."

"And that's why you were so pissed?"

Chloe nods. "He said it was too dangerous now, and I blamed you," she admits. "I'm sorry, I know it's like I've never seen a movie or watched a TV show or read a book in my entire life, but I just . . . I did. I thought this was different, and I blamed you. I felt like you took him away from me."

"I get it," I say. "I mean, it sucks, but I do."

"And I hate telling you this, but then after a while, we started back up again, but it wasn't the same. *He* wasn't the same, and there was, like, this part of me that knew he was going to do something to you. I just . . . I should have been there for you," she says, voice breaking. "You're my best friend, and I was—you had to do all this stuff by yourself."

I shake my head, trying to push away the picture of everything she's telling me now. "I wasn't by myself," I promise her, thinking of my parents and the book club and Ms. Klein. Thinking, with a pang behind my rib cage, of Gray. "But I really did miss you."

"Yeah," Chloe says, wiping her face with a heel of her hand. "Me too."

We swing for a while, neither one of us saying anything. I look out at the late-winter street. Jayden next door is pushing a plastic shopping cart up and down the front path, determined; Mrs. Lancaster is salting her sidewalk three houses down.

"Do you think I should report him?" Chloe asks finally. "To Mr. DioGuardi, I mean?"

I shrug. "I don't know," I tell her. "You have to do what feels good to you, I guess. Or, like, not even good, necessarily—just, least bad. I mean, I thought reporting was the right thing in the moment, and maybe I still do. But honestly, I don't know if it was worth it, you know? Half the school still thinks I made it up."

I tell her about the process with DioGuardi and the school board and how that didn't work. How, no offense, but they'd probably make it into Chloe's fault. "I'm not saying you shouldn't do it. It's not my place at all. I just . . . I don't know. I wish I could say it would work."

Chloe thinks about that for a moment, brushing the nail polish crumbs carefully off her jeans. Then all at once her head pops up.

"You know what?" she asks, turning to me with something like a smile passing across her expression. "I think I've got a better idea."

LETTER FROM THE EDITORS:
THE WHOLE TRUTH
BY MARIN LOSPATO AND CHLOE NIARCHOS

Dear Fellow Students, Faculty, and Administration of Bridgewater Preparatory,

Over the past several weeks, many of you may have heard rumors regarding allegations against a much-beloved teacher here at Bridgewater. As a community, it's safe to say we have struggled to separate information from innuendo and reconcile our own personal experiences with others' lived realities. It is never easy to come to terms with the idea that someone we admire—even adore, even perhaps love— may not be worthy of our continued esteem.

However: as the coeditors of the Beacon and young journalists ourselves, we are committed to the integrity of this newspaper and to using its power to speak truth. We believe in the power of the press to bring about positive change in the communities it serves, and it is in this spirit of truth telling that we write to you today.

The allegations against this teacher—that he has had inappropriate emotional and physical relationships with his students; that he has invited students into his home under academic pretexts and made advances of a sexual nature; that he has retaliated against students who have spoken up about his behavior—are true. We report this information with confidence in our sources, because our sources are each other. Both of us have experienced this teacher's behavior firsthand.

We trusted him. We looked up to him. We found him charming and charismatic. And he took advantage of us. We were not special. We were not, as he told us, "old souls." We were simply his students.

When one of us came forward with these allegations, Bridgewater Preparatory's official position was that the administration did not have enough credible information to pursue further disciplinary action against this teacher. When the other of us admitted her strikingly similar situation, we could not help but question if she would be met with the same response. Would she, too, be asked if she was simply "confused" by the situation? Would she suffer the same rumors? Would she, too, be accused of looking for attention?

We write this letter today to shine a light on a dark place at Bridgewater, and also in the hope that any other student who has had a similar encounter—be it with this particular teacher, another authority figure, or someone else at this school—will feel safe and supported should they choose to come forward.

We believe you.

Sincerely,
Marin + Chloe

THIRTY-FIVE

Our piece goes to print on the front page of the paper the following Monday, my first day back at school after suspension. I take care of the editing and Chloe somehow manages to keep the whole thing a secret from the rest of the staff, including, of course, Bex.

Newly unsuspended or not, there's no way I can sit through Bex's class this morning, so I head outside as the bell is ringing for the start of third period. It's almost spring now, the cold air laced with the smell of something damp and briny. I cross the muddy field and make my way up the bleachers, climbing halfway to the top before sitting down and tilting my head back toward the weak midday sunshine, like a new plant desperate to grow.

I don't know how long I'm sitting there, the light making patterns on the insides of my eyelids, before somebody calls my name from the other side of the field. I open my eyes and there's Gray crossing the fifty-yard line below me, backpack slung over one broad shoulder. He's off his crutches now, but he's still walking with just the tiniest limp, the kind you wouldn't even notice if you hadn't spent the whole semester noticing things like the way he normally walks.

"Hey," I call back, holding up one hand in greeting as he makes his way carefully up the wide metal steps. He's wearing a Bridgewater hoodie over his uniform, his ridiculous step counter fastened securely around one wrist. "You back up to twenty thousand per day yet?"

"Getting there," he reports with half a smile. He hesitates a moment like he's asking for permission before I nod, and he settles himself down beside me, stretching his long legs out in front of him.

"I read your piece," he says, nodding at the *Beacon* sticking out of his bookbag. "I think it's awesome. I mean, it's shit what happened to your friend Chloe, obviously, but . . . That was really brave of you guys."

I muster a smile. "Thanks." The truth is, it doesn't feel brave at all: I'm glad Chloe had the chance to talk about what Bex did to her. I'm a little nervous I'm going to get expelled. But mostly I'm just sort of numb. It's like I keep waiting for some cinematic moment to signal I'm totally over everything that happened, that means it's all done and dusted. But the hard, frustrating reality is that all I can do is move on one day at a time.

Both of us are quiet for a minute, watching as a couple of Canada geese totter across the field, honking irritably at each other. A chilly wind rustles the budding branches on the trees.

Finally Gray takes a breath. "I told my moms I don't want to go to St. Lawrence," he confesses.

"You *did?*" I whip around to look at him, everything that's happened between us momentarily forgotten. "How'd they take it?"

Gray shrugs. "I mean, they weren't thrilled," he admits. "They lawyered me pretty hard. But eventually we made a compromise—I can take the job at Harbor Beach as long as I'm also taking college classes someplace local, Bunker Hill or UMass or someplace. So I think I'm gonna do that."

"Good for you," I say, reaching out to squeeze his arm like a reflex before remembering myself and dropping my hand awkwardly. "I'm, um. Really proud of you."

"Thanks," he says, smiling a little sheepishly. "You're kind of the person who inspired me to do it, actually. I guess I figured if you could put yourself on the line, then at the very least I could nut up and tell my moms I didn't want to play sports at college."

I laugh, I can't help it, and then my face abruptly falls. "Gray, I'm really sorry." This time I do touch him, just the tips of my fingers against the sleeve of his shirt. "About like . . . everything. I was a total asshole to you, and you didn't deserve it at all."

Right away, Gray shakes his head. "Hey," he says, "don't even sweat it. You were going through a thing, you know?"

"I mean, I guess so," I say, unwilling to let myself off the hook quite so easily. "But that's not an excuse. You were a really, really good boyfriend, and I took a bunch of stuff out on you that wasn't actually your fault. And I'm sorry."

"Really, Marin, don't worry about it." Gray waves me off. "We had fun, right?"

"I—yeah." That stings a little—both the words themselves and his casual shrug as he says them; just like that, he's the guy I thought he was back in October, a vaguely douchey lacrosse bro only looking for a good time. I think it could have been more than just fun, whatever there was between us. I guess I thought it was. But I'm pretty sure I missed my chance now. "Yeah," I say again, brushing some imaginary lint off my jeans. "We had fun."

Gray nods, like he's glad that's all settled. "So, um, what about you?" he asks, clearing his throat. "You figure out where you're headed in the fall?"

"Amherst," I report, aiming for excited and mostly getting there—it's still an awesome school, even if it's not the one my gram went to, and I know I'm incredibly lucky to have the option at all. "Sent in my deposit yesterday, actually."

"You're going to be amazing wherever you go," Gray predicts easily, like it's just a given. "Amherst's not too far either."

I look over at him in surprise, not sure what he means— not too far from here? Or from him? The miracle of Gray was always how easy he was to talk to. But now it's like I don't know how.

"No," I agree finally, careful. "Not too far."

Gray smiles. For a second it feels like he's going to say something else, or maybe like I am—like there's unfinished business here and both of us can feel it. But the bell rings for the end of the period before either one of us can find the words.

"Shit, I've got a trig exam," Gray says, getting to his

feet and reaching down for his backpack. "Take care of yourself, okay? With the article and everything, I mean. I'll see you around."

"Yeah," I say. "I will." Then, suddenly: "Gray—"

"Hm?" He turns around. "What's up?"

I open my mouth, then close it again. Of everything I've lost in the last few months, somehow this feels like the worst.

"Nothing," I tell him finally. "You take care of yourself too."

THIRTY-SIX

School is strangely quiet the rest of the day. Chloe and I were fully prepared for a fallout of epic proportions—we even drafted emergency letters to our respective colleges in the event we were both expelled—but other than my conversation with Gray on the bleachers, no one says anything to me about it. I take a calc quiz. I sit with the book club at lunch. Even Michael Cyr leaves me alone.

On one hand it feels like a massive relief—that editorial was the riskiest thing I've ever written, and even though I might have been prepared to sacrifice what's left of my future, I wasn't exactly looking forward to the consequences.

On the other hand, it's hard not to feel a tiny bit disappointed too. Like, does seriously no one even care?

Chloe picks me up the following morning, the two of us listening to the latest episode of our favorite creepy podcast and taking the long way so we can swing by the Starbucks drive-through for iced coffees and slightly dry croissants. By the time we pull into the Bridgewater parking lot it almost feels like it did last fall before everything happened.

That is, until we actually get inside.

I've become something of an expert in gauging the energy in the south hallway the last few weeks, and this morning it definitely feels like something unusual is happening, that sharp electric bite in the air. Sean Campolo's gaze cuts in between us. Allie Chao whispers something behind her hand.

"Oh, what the hell is this?" I can't keep myself from muttering. It feels like my first day back after break all over again, right down to the icy feeling creeping down my backbone. I thought I was immune to this, to the shame of being singled out and stared at. I guess, even after all this time, I was wrong.

I'm about to bolt—directly to first period, or possibly right out the door again—but Chloe reaches down and hooks her elbow in mine.

"Relax," she says, with all the easy intuition of seven years of best friendship. Her voice is perfectly level. "Whatever happens, we're together, right?"

I force a nod. "Right," I manage, and to my surprise, I do feel a tiny zing of confidence, my spine straightening the slightest bit. "We're together."

We head toward our lockers, gather our books; down the hall I can see a gaggle of book clubbers sprawled in the lounge outside the cafeteria, and as we weave through the crowded hallway in their direction, I can see that Elisa is grinning. Lydia lifts her chin in a nod.

"Okay, no, seriously," I murmur, quiet enough that only Chloe can hear me. "What the hell is this?"

Before she can reply I spy Principal DioGuardi coming down the hallway from the direction of the admin suite in a blue button-down so shiny it's nearly iridescent. He catches my eye and motions us over, popping his whistle into his mouth.

"Girls," he says, pulling it out again as we approach him. "Can I speak with you for a moment?"

I take a breath. "Mr. DioGuardi," I begin, just like we practiced in Chloe's bedroom, "Chloe and I are happy to discuss whatever concerns you had about this week's issue. But I should let you know that we looked at the organizational paperwork for the *Beacon* before we published, and it says very clearly that the administration shall not interfere with the editorial page unless there's an egregious violation of—"

Mr. DioGuardi shakes his head. "It's not about that," he tells me. "Or it is about that, but—" He jams the whistle back into his mouth, looking visibly pained. "I just wanted to let you both know that Mr. Beckett has been removed from the faculty."

For a second I just blink at him dumbly. That is . . . not what I was expecting him to say.

"Really?" I blurt.

Mr. DioGuardi nods. "Other students have already come forward," he explains miserably. He looks exhausted, greenish bags under his eyes and a day's worth of beard on his chin; if things had gone a little bit differently between us, I'd almost feel sorry for him. "It seems there was . . . well. More of a problem with Mr. Beckett than we realized, certainly. Both here and at the last school he worked at."

The last school he worked at. I remember the first day Bex drove me home, that line about cooking dinner for students in his apartment, and can't keep from shaking my head.

"He's really gone?" I ask, still looking for the catch somewhere, but Mr. DioGuardi nods again.

"Effective immediately," he reassures me. "He won't be back."

"Wow." It's more than I ever dreamed would happen, honestly. "That's . . . wow."

Chloe seems to consider that for a moment; to my surprise, she doesn't actually look satisfied. "So, Mr. Dio-Guardi," she says politely, cocking her head to the side, her eyes sharp and keen behind her glasses. "It sounds like what you're saying is that you were wrong not to believe Marin when she came to you in the first place, hm?"

Mr. DioGuardi frowns. "Well, it wasn't a question of belief or not," he explains, his gaze cutting from her to me and back again. "The board was working with the information they had at the time—"

"Including the information she gave you, right?"

"I . . . yes," Mr. DioGuardi admits. "But without corroborating—"

"So it almost kind of feels like you owe her an apology."

For a moment Mr. DioGuardi looks like he's going to argue, but in the end he just sort of sags.

"I'm sorry, Marin," he says, the words as stiff and awkward in his mouth as if he's trying to speak Klingon. "I know you've been through a lot these last couple of months."

It's not exactly stellar, as far as apologies go, and it turns out that I don't actually give a shit if he's sorry or he's not. I told the truth. Bex is gone. And Chloe and I are friends again. All told, I could have done worse. "Thanks," I say, cool as a glass of my gram's iced tea on the hottest day of summer. "I appreciate that."

Once he's gone I look around the hallway, then back at Chloe. Her expression is a shocked, delighted mirror of my own. "You wanna skip first period and go to the diner for breakfast?" I ask her. "Just you and me?"

"You know," Chloe says thoughtfully, "I think that is the best idea I've heard all year."

We link arms again and head back out into the parking lot. The sun is warm on the back of my neck.

THIRTY-SEVEN

I go by Sunrise after school on Friday and find Camille standing at the nurses' station, humming quietly to herself while she fills out some paperwork. Her Crocs are hot pink today, her scrubs printed with toucans and flamingos. An enormous Dunkin' iced coffee sweats at her side.

"I've got something for you," I tell her, digging around in my backpack for a moment before pulling out an Amherst T-shirt.

Camille's mouth drops open. "Oh, Marin, you didn't have to do that!"

"A promise is a promise," I say with a shrug. "I'm just sorry it's not from Brown."

"Are you kidding?" she says. Her grin is wide and white. "I'm so proud of you, honey." She raises her eyebrows. "Are you proud of yourself?"

I consider that for a moment. "You know," I say finally, "I actually really am."

"Good," Camille says, reaching out and squeezing my shoulder before nodding down the hallway toward Gram's suite. "Let me know if you need anything, okay? She had a pretty good morning, but just in case."

I nod. It's the first time I've been back here on my own since the day Gram didn't recognize me—Mom and I went together one morning, and Gracie tagged along with me the time after that—and I can feel my heart thumping unpleasantly as I make my way down the hallway.

It's just Gram, I remind myself firmly. *Whether she remembers you or not, it doesn't change who she is to you.*

"Hey there," I say, knocking lightly on the door.

"Hi, Marin-girl."

I let a breath out, relief coursing through me at the sound of my own name. Gram is sitting on the love seat with a biography of Katharine Graham in her lap. She's wearing a linen shift dress and a pale pink cardigan, her hair pulled into a wispy knot at the base of her neck. The line of her lipstick is a tiny bit wobbly, but otherwise she looks like herself.

"Dad made a ciambellone," I tell her once I've kissed

her hello, hefting the Tupperware carrier up as evidence. It's an Italian tea cake that she used to make when I was a kid, lemony and dense. I remember wandering around her yard with a hunk of it in my fist, Grandpa Tony's toy poodle Lola trying to nibble bits of it out from in between my fingers. "He used your recipe, so he said he wants your honest opinion about how it turned out."

"Oh, that's lovely!" she says, sounding genuinely pleased. "I got that recipe from my mother-in-law, did I ever tell you that? She was not a nice lady, your great-grandmother, but the woman knew her way around a kitchen."

I laugh, cutting us both slices and bringing them over to the coffee table, running my thumb over the edge of the delicate scalloped plate. "You got a crossword around here anywhere?" I ask. "I've been practicing."

We pass the better part of our visit that way, filling in the puzzle and catching up on my last few weeks of school. I'm telling her about the dress I got for spring formal when something about her expression, a wary uneasiness, stops me. "Everything okay?" I ask.

Gram nods. "You know," she says, and it sounds almost like an accusation, "I used to make a cake just like this."

I bite my lip, trying to keep my face neutral. "I know,

Gram," I say gently. "It's your recipe, remember?"

She narrows her eyes then, and I know all at once that I've lost her.

"It's delicious, isn't it?" I ask, instead of trying to get her to remember. It's better not to push her when she gets like this, Mom explained after that last disastrous solo visit; she'll come back on her own when she's ready. It might be this afternoon, or it might not be. At some point she might not come back at all. "It tastes like spring."

I spend the rest of my visit chattering on, cheerful, keeping my voice light and full of air: about summer finally coming and the tulip beds in front of Sunrise; about Katharine Graham, who I know from Ms. Klein was the first female publisher of a major American newspaper. Gram, for her part, seems content to listen to me, nibbling at her cake and nodding politely at appropriate breaks in my monologue like I'm a particularly gregarious stranger in a train station. As I'm getting up to leave, she touches my hand.

"I like you," she says, her smile warm but somehow completely unfamiliar. "You remind me of myself."

I tilt my head to the side, swallowing hard. "I do?"

Gram nods. "You're a good girl," she continues, "but you don't always have to be *so* good." Then she raises her eyebrows, mischievous. "Lord knows I wasn't."

For a second she looks like herself again, Gram who bought me my first journal and grew prize-winning roses and taught me to separate eggs over her immaculately polished stainless steel sink; then she blinks and it's gone. I turn my hand over and squeeze hers for a moment, just gently, before letting go.

"I know," I promise. "I'll remember."

EPILOGUE

The year's final meeting of the feminist book club is on a warm Thursday afternoon at the beginning of June, a breeze blowing in through the open windows of Ms. Klein's classroom and the trees exploding into verdant green outside. Elisa's mom sends homemade tamales. Grace and I baked seven-layer bars. We read Warsan Shire's *Teaching My Mother How to Give Birth*, which was Lydia's pick—and which comes with the benefit of letting us watch Beyoncé's *Lemonade*, which is playing on a loop on a laptop at one corner of the room. Maddie and Bridget have an impromptu dance party going in one corner of the classroom, and I catch Dave singing along to "Formation" under his breath when he thinks no one is paying attention.

"You did something really good here, Marin," Ms. Klein says quietly, coming to stand beside me with a paper cup of seltzer in one hand. The club is going to keep meeting next year, the underclassmen decided; Lydia nominated Elisa to be president, and she ran unopposed. I like the idea of the club continuing on without me—it's dumb, maybe, but it kind of makes me feel like I'll have a real legacy at Bridgewater beyond just being the girl who got Bex fired.

Of course, I'm not mad if that's part of my legacy too.

Chloe and her parents pressed charges, which was hard for Chloe, but she felt like it was the right thing to do. The town paper ran a huge article on Bex, and Bridgewater caught a lot of heat for how they handled the whole situation. People were shocked by the administration's actions—or lack thereof.

"How could something like this still happen today?" everyone said—but I guess that's the reality, right? It does still happen.

Now I look around the classroom, my chest warm. Even Chloe came today, though she hadn't read the book.

"Are you sure it's okay?" she asked on the way over here, hesitating in the hallway. "To be crashing?"

"It's not really about the book," I promised, reaching for her hand and pulling her into the classroom. "I mean, it is and it isn't." Now I see her chatting with Elisa about the makeup artist who works on all Beyoncé's videos, and I can tell she's glad she came.

The only person who's missing is Gray.

I sigh, smiling half-heartedly at Ms. Klein before drifting over to the food table. I thought he might show up for nostalgia's sake—it's our last meeting, after all—but I guess I chased him away for good. And sure, I apologized that day on the bleachers. But I know better than most people that sometimes an apology isn't enough.

I'm just about to drown my sorrows in another tamale when I sense a movement behind me in the doorway; I turn around and there he is in his uniform and a Sox cap, smile as sheepish and crooked as the first day he joined the club. He catches my eye and grins.

I smile back, wide and honest.

It occurs to me that our story, whatever it might turn out to be, is far from over.

"Sorry I'm late," he says, shrugging a little shyly. "I needed to finish the book."

3

THE SKY FISHERMAN

BOOKS BY CRAIG LESLEY

Winterkill

River Song

The Sky Fisherman

THE SKY FISHERMAN

CRAIG LESLEY

A MARC JAFFE BOOK

Houghton Mifflin Company

BOSTON   NEW YORK

For information about permission to reproduce selections from this
book, write to Permissions, Houghton Mifflin Company,
215 Park Avenue South, New York, New York 10003.

For information about this and other Houghton Mifflin trade and
reference books and multimedia products, visit The Bookstore at
Houghton Mifflin on the World Wide Web at
(http://www.hmco.com/trade/).

Library of Congress Cataloging-in-Publication Data

Lesley, Craig.
The sky fisherman / Craig Lesley.
p.   cm.
"A Marc Jaffe book."
ISBN 0-395-67724-6
I. Title.
PS3562.E815S58 1995
813'.54 — dc20   94-47493
CIP

Book design by Anne Chalmers
Text type: Trump Medieval (Adobe),
Trio-Light (Castle Systems)

Printed in the United States of America

MP 10 9 8 7 6 5 4 3

For

KATHERYN ANN STAVRAKIS

and our daughters,

ELENA and

KIRA

PROLOGUE

THE NEON TROUT blinks off and on, advertising my uncle Jake's guide service and store. Near the railroad tracks, wheat elevators and a flour mill mark the biscuit company where my mother worked. Early sunlight flashes off a silver passenger train crossing the trestle. From the high bluffs, Gateway looks about the same.

After the steep descent into town, I see change. The Oasis offers espresso for the river rafters. Homer's bakery has moved into a modern grocery store, and I want a jelly roll, but they stopped making them when Homer retired. The shabby house where my mother and I hoped to start a new life has been razed for a fast-food chain. The Phoenix stands dark.

At least my mother's new place contains the old icons: Ivory soap, Lipton tea, yellow curtains, a separate hand towel for each guest. Later I will visit my uncle's store. Even now, I know baseball gloves' rich leather smell, the ice machine's whir and clink, the worm beds' earthy odors, fishing tackle's bright allure. An old moosehead trophy has replaced Juniper Teewah's haunting painting of Kalim at the All-Indian basketball tournament.

Seated at the weekly *Gazette*, I pore over yellowed newspapers to see if memory matches facts, or whether my imagination has transformed those past events into myths. Pleased, the young editor offers her help and a cup of herbal tea. "Which year was it?" she asks.

I can't believe she doesn't know. If not for Billyum Bruised-Head and Jake, the entire town might have been lost.

Reading old accounts, I nod as detail after detail rings true. I recognize familiar faces among volunteers who braced shoulders against the disasters. One photo astonishes me. A tiny biplane emerges from billowing thunderheads of smoke. How could it survive that inferno? The photographer is longdead, but he left one hell of a shot. I hear the Stearman's radial engine whine, the warning shouts of ruddy-faced men. I smell char.

Buzzy has given up flying, I learn. Impossible. For me, he remains forever bursting from the smoke, caught in time.

Billyum could be right. "You white guys have a screwball notion," he says. "For you, time's a damn straight line. For us, it's more like a wheel turning 'round. Everything you call the past is still happening right now. No use running."

THE SKY FISHERMAN

1

MY STEPFATHER, Riley Walker, worked for the Union Pacific Railroad, and it was a steady job, but uncertain, because trucking had hurt the railroad by then and they were cutting back. Riley had only a little seniority, and he was always getting "bumped," a railroad term that meant moving to another job when you were forced out by someone with more seniority who wanted yours. In turn, my stepfather bumped someone with less seniority than he had. As a result, my childhood was spent moving from one railroad town to another, each one smaller and more remote than the one before. This constant moving gave me a sense of restlessness, of always being near the edge of something, but of freedom, too, and loss. I learned that I didn't have to feel attached to anyone, except my mother, stepfather, and my uncle Jake, and even that changed eventually.

My mother faced these frequent moves with patience and relentless good cheer for the most part. Her first item of business was to measure the new windows. Then she sewed bright, colorful curtains and seemed even cheerier once they were hung. "That civilizes the place a bit," she'd say, and Riley would nod and agree. "Just like home."

I'd glance up from the railroad housing linoleum — it was my task to scrub the floors with disinfectant, trying to remove any trace of germs left by the former tenants — and I'd try to say something encouraging. But the packing and loading were always difficult, and we worked like coolies, if you want to know the truth.

The moving pattern was recognizable. After we'd been in a place about a year, one night Riley would delay coming home while he stopped off for a couple hours at a tavern near the railroad depot commiserating with the buddies he'd be leaving, and working his nerve enough to tell my mother. Supper finished, she'd stand anxiously by the door, sipping a cup of hot tea and watching the twilight settle. Riley always carried a small gift when he arrived late — candy or scented candles, perhaps, and she'd thank him and reheat dinner while I went into the front room to watch TV and sulk.

They'd talk with lowered voices at the kitchen table, and I'd hear the clink of Riley's fork and knife, my mother fixing more tea. Her voice always caught a few times, and one phrase I'd hear was "Riley, when's all this going to stop?" Then he'd attempt to say soothing, comforting words, such as he was building up seniority all the time, or he'd heard the schools were good in Harney or Grass Valley, small towns near the railroad sidings where we lived. When the towns became too small to offer comfort, he'd say it was good for a boy to have room to roam, and rural people still had good values.

After they went to bed, I usually didn't hear anything except a few sighs, until the night my stepfather announced we were moving clear across the state to Griggs. Then my mother cried.

In the morning hours I went to the bathroom sink for a cold glass of water and found her lying naked on the tile floor. A wet washcloth covered her face, and her skin seemed flush, as if she had a fever. My turning on the light had startled her, and she bolted upright for a moment, whipping the washcloth from her eyes and calling out, "Griggs! Griggs!" Then she settled back like a child in a restless sleep.

We'd usually have about two weeks before the actual move, enough time to make arrangements for the mail, utilities, and phone. I'd mope around school a little, wringing sympathy from my teachers and a few classmates. Most of the kids had lived on family farms, generation after generation, and I was just a newcomer to them anyway. The teacher might suggest a going-away gift, and the class would bring dollars to buy a book or a basketball. They'd dutifully sign their names and I'd promise to remember them and write, but of course I never did.

My mother always conferred with my teachers and took careful notes about my subjects, so I wouldn't fall behind in the shuffle. She dressed well for those conferences, and when I saw her standing alongside my teachers, I was surprised how pretty she was and how her ash blond hair shone in the sunlight. "Pretty enough for Hollywood," Riley always teased, but my mother claimed it wasn't true, on account of her nose, which was a little sharp.

Riley tried to ease the strain of displacement by buying some things my mother treasured. A love seat with matching needlepoint chair and a drum table with a leather top come to mind. These nice pieces of furniture were always purchased on time, and I remember how odd they looked in the small plain houses where we lived.

My uncle Jake usually helped with the moves. He was my father's brother and had been fishing with my father when he drowned in a boating accident on the Lost River. After that, Jake tried to keep an eye on us, but he was a bachelor by nature, and I always thought he was relieved when my mother remarried. I knew my mother blamed Jake and his recklessness for my father's death — but she never said much. The Griggs move was our seventh, and my mother didn't call Jake to tell him about it because she knew he was so involved with his sporting goods store and guide business that he couldn't spare the time.

My mother always tried to appear happy while packing, and occasionally she whistled. Before each move, she made a triple batch of her three-bean salad, because you could eat it hot or cold, and her oriental sesame chicken for the same reason. Sometimes the power wasn't turned on at the new place, and it took a while to settle.

For the Griggs move Riley hired two casual laborers from the hall in town, and that pair hardly moved at all. One had high-water pants that barely grazed the top of his runover boots, and the second owned a stomach as big as a flour sack, so he had to sit down frequently to wait out his "woozy" spells. Each man heaped several helpings of chicken and salad on his plate, and the first said the chicken reminded him of being in the Philippines during his tramp schooner days. The other kept pushing the food around his plate with a piece of white bread. "Mighty good fixings," he said. When they were out of earshot and gouging the drum table while loading the truck, my mother glared at Riley and muttered, "I guess we've still got a ways to slip."

☆ ☆ ☆ ☆ ☆

Moving to Griggs was a slide. We lived in railroad housing at the siding itself. The reality was I'd have to take the school bus thirty-five miles to Pratt for my junior year. My mother would have to do without the comforts of a nearby town. "I'll just catch up on my reading," she said when she realized the situation.

3

As always, we started out hopeful, but as we traveled across miles and miles of desolate country, a pall fell over our little band. Riley gripped the U-Haul truck steering wheel as if trying to seize control of his life. I sat staring out the window at sagebrush and sparse juniper trees, a few jackrabbits, and an occasional loping coyote. "Good hunting around here, I'll bet," Riley said when we saw a covey of chukars eating gravel at the roadside.

Griggs was one of those remote railroad sidings with three buildings and a lot of dust. All painted leprous yellow, the buildings varied in size with the largest for the stationmaster and the smallest for the track-walker. Ours was the middle house and sported a strip of cheatgrass-infested lawn. In the early June heat, the buildings appeared to undulate, and my mother said, "Riley, we're going to need some fans."

Beyond the railroad tracks was a sluggish, dirty brown river with a fringe of willows. Close to the river, the air seemed rank and stagnant, offering little relief from the heat. The one outstanding item I noticed at Griggs was a decent basketball hoop and backboard fastened to one of the telegraph posts just beyond the trackwalker's shack. The hoop had a new nylon net. I had been the sixth man for the Grass Valley team the past year and figured I could have started my junior year, especially with two senior guards going off to college. But Pratt was smaller, and I knew I could play B-league ball with no trouble at all, maybe even move to forward, so I planned to keep my shooting touch sharp over the summer.

That basket was the only thing I felt good about. Still, we started fixing our house with a vengeance — hanging curtain rods and curtains, lining the shelves with contact paper, covering the pitted Formica table with a bright blue tablecloth.

My mother's face had dropped when she saw the bathroom, though, which had only a shower unit. She was accustomed to long baths, soaking away her worries and doubts. When she pointed out this lack of a tub to Riley, he just spread his hands wide. "It's only temporary, Flora," he said. "I'm building seniority all the time."

Dwight Riggins, the Griggs station agent, was a burly man with black hair the color of creosote. He kept four or five cigars tucked into the bib pocket of his striped coveralls. The day we arrived in Griggs he was away, but he showed up later that evening just in time to help us unload some heavy items like the refrigerator from the front of the truck bed. My mother had put lamp shades in the refrigerator to keep them from getting crushed, and Dwight thought that was a pretty nifty trick. "After you move a few times, you learn some little shortcuts," she told him.

"I'm sure you do at that," he said. He seemed friendly enough, and I was glad for his help, because by that time we were all getting pretty tired. Still, I didn't care for the way he kept sneaking sidelong glances at my mother, and I thought maybe his laugh came just a little too easy. It turned out that he was batching a couple weeks because he had dropped off his wife and daughter at a fancy art camp.

"They're taking painting classes at the coast," he explained. "Both of them together. It's a mother-daughter deal."

"It must be cool at the coast," my mother said, and I could hear the touch of envy in her voice. "I'll bet it's quite lovely."

"It better be, for what I'm paying for that program," he said. "My wife doesn't have a lick of talent, but Dwy-anne, my daughter, there's another story. Of course, the teacher tells them both they're gifted. That's how he affords living on the coast in summer."

After Dwight left to have dinner in town with some friends, my mother strolled through the house, checking the layout. Even though the boxes hadn't been unpacked, the beds were made and the furniture set out, so you had a sense of the place. She ran her fingers over the dusty doorsill and looked out over the dry countryside. "We're going to need some fans, Riley, if this is going to be tolerable."

"I'll put them on my list, Flora," he said.

"There's more to Dwight than meets the eye," Riley told me later. At first I thought he was talking about Dwight's sidelong glances at my mother, but then Riley said, "He's a nudist. Word has it the whole family is — even the daughter. And she's just a couple years older than you are."

I stopped unpacking one of my suitcases. He had piqued my interest. "How do you know that?" I asked.

"Railroad telegraph," he said. "Word gets around."

"He had clothes on today."

Riley shook his head. "He's not a nudist on railroad time. They'd dock him. But you'd better keep an eye on his daughter."

In his job as section foreman, Riley drove the speeder car twenty miles either side of Griggs, checking for loose or rotten ties. After he found them, he ordered a section crew out from Pratt to replace the ties while he supervised their work. At times they had to delay the trains a few hours to complete repairs. Riley always carried his shotgun with him in the speeder. The shotgun was a Remington Model 870 pump with a barrel cut down to exactly the legal eighteen inches. Over the years he'd brought home a lot of game with it, and I've got memories of Riley hunching over the outside faucets cleaning birds because my mother didn't want blood and feathers in her kitchen sink, although she enjoyed eating the birds out of the pan, if they were fried crisp.

During the first two weeks we were in Griggs, Riley had me ride with him in the speeder as far as Barlow, a siding almost identical to Griggs but twenty miles east. On the return trip, we saw a covey of chukars eating gravel on the railroad bed, and Riley handed me the shotgun. "Sluice them, Culver," he said.

Usually I wait for birds to fly, but chukars prefer to run, and these started racing down the track. With the first shot I stopped two, and as the rest flew I got one bird but missed completely with my third shot. At home Riley bragged a little about my deadeye aim. He held up birds for my mother to inspect. "By God, they look like bandits don't they?" he said, referring to the markings around their eyes.

"You know it's not the season, Riley," she said.

As we were cleaning them out back, he spoke slowly. "Your mom's acting pretty quiet."

I had noticed but I said, "Maybe she's just tired."

"She's always adjusted before, but this place takes a little more getting used to."

I wanted to say something comforting but I couldn't think of anything.

"Well," he said, "it's only temporary. I'm building up seniority all the time." A BB fell out from underneath the skin of one of the chukars, plinking against the metal pan. "Watch your teeth, Culver. We can't afford any trips to the dentist."

Late that evening, when the fierce heat of the day slacked, a cool breeze came up from the river. In the twilight before dark, it seemed momentarily pleasant in Griggs. After returning from town, Dwight sat on his screened porch reading the paper. A match spurted, and after a while we could smell his cigar in the evening air. My mother, Riley, and I walked out to a little knoll overlooking the river. Ducks rose from the shallows and winged overhead with that soft whistling ducks make as the wind catches their feathers.

"That water looks good enough for a swim," Riley said. "Anybody want to join me?"

"I don't feel that adventuresome," my mother said. "Anyway, my swimsuit is still packed somewhere."

"No one's going to see much way out here," Riley said, stripping down to his undershorts and wading in. "Hey, this feels great."

He was trying to have a good time so I joined him, even though my

6

heart wasn't in it. The water did feel good and I liked the way the mud squished under my toes.

Just after ten, the Coastal Flyer came by, its cars shining silver under the summer moon. We saw the people inside — first the coach cars and then the lounge car and diner. White-jacketed waiters hovered over the people eating dinner, and by looking close I could glimpse the single red rose on each table. I envied the people on the train because they seemed to be going somewhere, and I could imagine how Griggs must have appeared to them in the moonlight — just a little no-'count railroad siding with the three of us looking like stick figures. And then Riley surprised me, surprised us all, by dropping his undershorts and grabbing his ankles, flashing those passing diners a full moon.

I heard my mother suck in her breath, then say, "Don't be so uncouth, Riley. Remember, you actually *work* for the railroad."

"I don't work for *them*," he said, meaning the diners.

"Well, of course, you're setting a poor example for the boy," she said. "In any case, Culver and I have ridden on the train and we have enjoyed a wonderful dinner. And I'm certainly glad my appetite wasn't spoiled by seeing some man's hind end."

Riley didn't answer but managed to wink at me as he pulled up his shorts.

My mother sighed, and I knew she was thinking about the time we rode the train to see my uncle Jake in the beautiful, mountainous part of the state. I was nine. She intended to talk with him about my father's death — "To clear the air," as she put it.

My mother had saved some money so we could eat in the dining car. Before dinner I went into the men's lounge and slicked my hair back. She had brought along my Sunday school white shirt and an old tie that had belonged to my father. The tie was blue with a hand-painted leaping red fish. She had cut the tie and resewn it to fit, although it remained a little long.

The waiter provided us with menus and stubby pencils to mark our choices. The pencils had no erasers, so I was careful not to make a mistake. She ordered lamb chops with spearmint jelly, and when the chops came, each one had a little parsley ruffle around the blackened bone, and I didn't think I'd ever seen anything so elegant before. My mother had me taste the jelly, which came in a small white paper cup. "They make it from crushed mint leaves," she said. "It's nice when they go out of their way to make things special."

It was good, sweet and pungent at the same time, although I preferred my cheeseburger.

We sat at the window a long time, watching the countryside roll by. Once I saw a farmer changing hand line in his alfalfa field. Glancing up from his work, he took off his red cap and waved it at the train. I waved back, even though I doubted he saw anything but the train sliding by sleek as wind.

"I could get used to this," my mother said, pouring herself another cup of tea. Out the window, scenery rushed by and the setting sun lengthened the shadows of tall pines. Farmhouse lights were beginning to wink on.

Now, standing by that remote siding, my mother stared at the Coastal Flyer's brake lights dimming in the distance.

"Better times are coming," I said because I couldn't think of anything else.

After a moment, she said, "I expect they're just around the corner."

☆ ☆ ☆ ☆ ☆

The third Friday after we'd moved in, my stepfather was away on the speeder, checking on the tie repairs the section crew was making near Barlow. Dwight watched me shooting baskets for a while from his front porch, then came off and challenged me to a game of one-on-one. I figured he'd be easy because he looked slow and clumsy in his usual coveralls and clodhoppers. But today he was wearing tennis shoes, and when he stripped down to a T-shirt and shorts, I saw he was no pushover. He was remarkably quick for a man his size, and I could seldom drive on him, so I had to rely on my outside shot, which was always streaky. If Dwight had the ball, he backed in, using his bulk to keep me away, then put up soft hooks or twisting jump shots. Luckily, he was rusty and soon became winded, or I might have lost.

My mother brought a chair from inside the house and placed it in the yard, first turning on the lawn sprinkler to get a little cool moisture. She'd made sun tea by leaving a pitcher of teabags and water in the sun, and she poured some of this over a tumbler of ice. She sat, sipping her tea and reading Hollywood gossip magazines.

After finishing the game, Dwight approached my mother's chair and tried to make conversation, but he was awkward at it. "This kid is a regular whiz," he said. "All he needs is to pack a few more pounds." He dribbled the ball a couple times and tried to palm it, but it slipped away. "I used to play college ball myself at a Mormon school in Utah. But I'm not Mormon."

8

"That explains the cigars then, doesn't it," my mother said. "We're not Mormon either."

"No, I didn't think you were," he said. "Not for a minute."

She offered him a glass of tea, but he declined and then unwrapped the cellophane from one of his cigars. "Cuban. I've got a friend who flies down there on business. He tells me these cigars are rolled on the damp thighs of young Cuban girls. Fidel sees to it they're all under sixteen. That's the rule."

I had never heard anyone make such a remark in front of my mother before, and I didn't know how she would react. She placed the glass of iced tea against her cheek and laughed softly. "I imagine that's why you enjoy them so much," she said. "You and your friend must have *extremely* active imaginations."

He seemed pleased that he had impressed her and turned to me. "What do you think, sport? You want to try one of these dusky beauties? Let's see, those girls would be just about your age."

"I don't believe he'd care for one," my mother said. She held the glass of tea against her forehead. "Culver's interests lie in an entirely different direction, don't they, Culver?" Before I could answer she added, "So perhaps you should hang on to the cigars you have."

"You got a point there all right," he said.

It seemed for a minute he was going back to his house, but then he spoke again. "When I see you sitting out in this heat just reading those magazines, it makes me wonder if there isn't something else you might do. Develop some interests."

She ran her finger around the sweaty beaded outside of the glass and touched it lightly to her lips. "I have interests," she said. "There's the boy." She tipped the glass slightly in my direction. "And I'm very interested in travel. Now you must excuse me. I've got to think about supper." With that she folded her magazine and headed into the house.

From Griggs, it was three miles to Griggs Junction, a combination restaurant and truck stop crested with a blue neon eagle whose flashing wings imitated flying. On paydays, Riley enjoyed taking us there for what he called a fling, and as we drove in he'd wave at all the truck drivers and call out, "How's it going, George?" He had greeted strangers the same way ever since I had known him, and when I was younger, I had marveled that he knew so many men named George.

This night my mother had put on a cool green dress that emphasized the green in her hazel eyes. As she looked out the window at the parking lot filled with trucks, she seemed restless. When she put on a pair of new sunglasses she must have bought in town, I swear she could have been a movie star, sharp nose or not.

Grinning, Riley looked at me as if to say, "How'd you think I ever got so lucky?"

"Do you have any fresh fruit?" my mother asked the waitress when she came to take the orders. "It's so hot today, I'm feeling like a fruit salad would be just the thing."

The waitress scowled at the question. "We had some bananas but the flies got them." She tapped her pen against the pad to get the ink going. "Sure has been hot. Earlier, they couldn't get the kitchen fans working, and it's like a boiler room back there. Honey, let's see now, we've got some canned peaches and cottage cheese. Or some pears."

"Pears and cottage cheese would be just fine," my mother said and handed her the folded menu.

"I sure do like that dress," the waitress said. "It probably doesn't come in my size."

Riley and I had cheeseburgers as always, and I had a large chocolate shake. This was only late June, and I figured July and August were going to be unbearable. I'd written a letter to my uncle Jake about trying to fix me up with a job in the sporting goods store, and I was wondering if it was air conditioned. I hadn't told Riley or my mother, but if the job came through, I knew she'd approve.

A golden curtain above the counter opened and a little puppet band played music along with the juke box. My mother tapped her fingers to the tunes.

"We should go dancing sometime," Riley said. "We haven't been dancing since that night in Black Diamond. Geez, that seems years ago."

"It was," my mother said. "Black Diamond was Culver's first year in junior high school — five moves back."

Riley winced a little. "I'm getting old fast."

My mother glanced in his direction, but she didn't say anything.

When the food came, Riley and I started eating ours, but my mother asked for a salad plate and then separated the pears from the cottage cheese. The cottage cheese did appear affected by the heat, and when she held a forkful to her nose, she wrinkled it. She cut the pears into very small bites and ate slowly. When she had finished and laid down her fork, Riley asked, "How was your salad, Flora?"

"It's a sorry business, Riley," she said. "A very sorry business altogether. Excuse me, I'm going to need the ladies' room."

After she was gone, Riley put another quarter in the jukebox, so the puppet band played again. "She's in a mood," he said.

"It's been hot," I said, and sucked on my milk shake.

He tried singing along with the music but he gave it up shortly. After what seemed a long time, he took the railroad watch from his pocket. "She must be having a session in there." A few more minutes passed. "She had one of those after we ate Chinese food that time in Grass Valley. You remember? She was gone over half an hour that time."

"I remember all right," I said. I was only eleven then and didn't remember too clearly.

He put a couple quarters on the table. "You pick them. Play something that snaps along a little. I'm going back there to see if I can speed things up. I've got to head out to Barlow early tomorrow."

I asked for a glass of water at the counter because my throat was dry. Out on the river a small sailboat caught the last rays of the sun, and I couldn't imagine who might be out there sailing in this desolate place.

Riley returned, his mouth set in a thin line. "I can't figure where she's got herself off to."

"Maybe she walked home," I said. "Maybe she wanted to be on her own a while."

"Darned crazy thing to do, if she did."

Riley asked the waitress to check the women's bathroom and make certain Mom hadn't fainted from the heat, but she came back out shaking her head. We hung around another half hour and Riley tried not to look at the waitress. "She didn't say anything?" he asked me.

I spread my hands. "Not to me."

Finally, Riley went outside to talk with one of the kids pumping gas. I could tell how much Riley hated doing it, because they were the kind of wiseasses you always see at gas stations — ripped jeans, dirty caps tipped back on their heads — kids just waiting to drink a couple six packs after work.

"Saw a gal climb into a big old Bekins moving truck and head north," one kid said. He stuffed part of a candy bar into his mouth and tossed the wrapper at the trash bucket. "I suppose that could have been her."

"Was she wearing a green dress?" Riley asked. "Sunglasses?"

"Can't say for sure," the kid said. "Wasn't looking much at the dress." Smirking now, he winked at his buddy.

"Good legs for an old gal," the buddy said.

Anger flushed my face, and even though they were a couple years older than me, I wanted for Riley and me to take them, but he let it drop.

"I'm sure that wasn't Flora," Riley said as we headed for the car. "That's not one bit like her."

The speedometer stayed under ten miles per hour all the way to Griggs. "Look sharp," he told me. "She might have took sick and be lying in the ditch somewhere. Those pears looked touched. She saw that right off. I wished she'd ordered the peaches instead."

"I'm keeping my eyes peeled, Riley," I said. And I was, but when I got to thinking about the new green dress and the sunglasses, I didn't think she was in any ditch. As we pulled off the main road and into Griggs, the Coastal Flyer came by, and I thought of the time I had ridden across the state with my mother. Now I half wished she might be on that train, heading somewhere exciting.

As the train passed, Riley opened the car door to spit, so I spotted them first. The crossing gate was still going up, its red lights blinking, and I had to strain my eyes a little to make out the two white figures against the shadowy background of willows at the river edge. The moon had just risen above the basalt cliffs and covered everything with an eerie pale light.

Dwight had taken off all his clothes, including the railroad cap, but his size and shape were unmistakable, even at that distance. She was naked too, and they were in the shallows but wading toward deep water.

Riley hadn't closed the car door; his arm remained straight out from his side and seemed frozen stiff. Then he muttered, "Flora, by God."

When he looked at me, Riley's eyes were widened in amazement and confusion. I realized then that he understood nothing about his life or circumstances; chances were slim he ever would. And I believed he was capable of some desperate act, the kind you read about in newspapers.

He got out of the car, and the gravel crunched beneath his feet as he began striding toward the two waders. "Hey," he shouted, but they didn't hear him. "Hey, God damn it!"

I climbed out too, thinking I could stop him. I slammed the car door and broke into a run, hoping I could catch up.

2

 As RILEY APPROACHED, Dwight's head snapped up. "What in thunder are you doing intruding on us like this?" Dwight said. "We want a little privacy!"

The woman was glaring at us, too, and up close you could tell right off she wasn't my mother, although at a distance they bore some resemblance. When I looked back and saw a second car in Dwight's yard, I knew how wrong we'd been.

Riley's mouth opened, but he didn't say anything, so I mumbled an apology and tried to look anywhere but directly at Dwight and his wife, even though I'd already seen pretty much what there was to see.

"Maybe you'd better head back to your place and let us be," Dwight said. "She's been away two weeks."

Taking Riley's elbow gently, I turned him back toward Griggs and our little place. After undressing without saying a word, he carried a pillow and blanket out to the couch so he could be near the phone.

I had trouble falling asleep and kept thinking about Dwight and his wife down at the river. In the middle of the night, Riley shook me from the fretful sleep, and my heart raced when I figured there'd been bad news.

"What is it, Riley?" I asked, gripping his shoulders.

"Do you think she took any money with her? Do you?"

"I don't know, Riley," I said, then relaxed my hold. "I really don't have any idea."

.   .   .

Riley headed to Barlow early the next morning after first making me promise to stay close by the phone. "Women will find a way to frost your balls every time, Culver," he said. "Remember that. She's having herself some kind of genuine fit, but I can't hang around and take a chance on losing this job."

"I hear you, Riley."

I fixed some corn flakes and then went outside to shoot baskets. All the windows were open, so I could hear the phone if it rang. The morning was still cool and the red-winged blackbirds fluttered in the willows at the river edge. When I looked at the place where Dwight had been swimming with his wife, I blinked a couple of times to make certain I hadn't imagined the whole thing.

About nine, my mother called.

"We were worried plenty," I said. "Are you all right?"

"Where's Riley?" she asked.

"Gone off to Barlow," I said.

"That's good. Your uncle Jake and I are coming with a truck, and I don't care to see Riley just now. You understand, don't you, honey?" She paused and when I didn't answer, she continued. "So you better start getting your things together. We're going to have a brand-new life, Culver. An absolutely fresh start."

Her enthusiasm seemed genuine and I didn't want to spoil her mood, but to be honest, I wasn't looking forward much to the fresh start. We hadn't finished unpacking from the last one.

"Say hi to your uncle Jake. He can't wait to see you."

Jake got on the phone. "Hey, Culver, I've got some good news. The store's air conditioned and the job's yours."

He sounded hearty and confident, the way I remembered him. I tried to seem upbeat. "That's terrific."

"These rich dudes keep hiring me to go fishing, and I need a good man to hold down the store. We're busier than a one-armed fry cook. Gateway's going through quite a boom. You'll love it."

"Sounds great." I held the phone away from my ear a little. "Say, where are you, anyway?"

"Having breakfast in Pratt. See you in an hour. This call is burning money."

"In an hour," I said, but he had already hung up.

Almost by habit, I packed my clothes in two battered blue suitcases that had belonged to my father. Then I carried in some of the empty moving boxes. They were still marked according to what they had held for the Griggs move, and I started stuffing sheets and pillowcases into the "linen" box. After a few minutes I stopped because I couldn't understand how to divide things.

Five long honks announced the truck's arrival, and I went outside to see the U-Haul bouncing over the tracks. It was a small truck with a twelve-foot bed and I knew at least they had the size right. We didn't have all that much stuff.

Jake backed the truck to the front door, and even though I gave him some hand signals, he didn't need them. Jumping out, he revealed a quickness that made him seem younger than forty. His arms and face were tanned from spending so many hours on the river, and his gray eyes were slightly bloodshot from the sun's glare. When he shook my hand, he grinned and exclaimed, "Look at this scrapper. He's grown into a good-looking devil."

"Isn't he handsome?" my mother said. "I'm not just saying that because he's my son. *Everybody* thinks he's handsome." Smiling, she hugged me. "I'm sorry you were so worried. When's Riley due back?"

I shrugged. "He didn't say, but it sounded like they had a big day."

"Perhaps we should get started," she said, looking at Jake.

"All right," he said. "I'm anxious to have this boy see Gateway."

As we packed, he talked with great enthusiasm about the town. "Lots of construction. Gateway's building two new subdivisions and the plywood mill's going a hundred ten percent. Three shifts — 'round the clock. And they're building a big dam on the Upper Lost for power and flood control. The workers are hunting and fishing fools — spend half their paychecks in my store."

"It sounds great," my mother said.

"Even the Indians are doing okay," my uncle said. "They're finishing a big lodge and resort on the reservation. Got piles of federal money. Eighteen-hole golf course smack by the river. The Frybread Tournament's scheduled this summer. Pretty soon they're going to tear down a bunch of reservation houses and put up new ones. I tell you, this whole country's booming."

"And we're going to be part of it," my mother said. "It sounds wonderful, doesn't it, Culver?"

Jake punched my shoulder. "You'll love the high school's new gymnasium. University-style hardwood floors and glass backboards. I got the contracts for the uniforms and shoes, too." He grinned. "Of course, I had to show the superintendent and athletic director a couple of secret fishing holes on the Lost. The fix was in, but don't worry; I saved the very best for family."

"I'm sure it will all be lovely," my mother said.

She directed our packing and didn't seem to hesitate about what to leave and what to take. "We'll buy some new furniture," she said. "This has gotten so shabby." Of course, she took the love seat and drum table.

Dwight's wife never left the house, but he wandered over to check things out. From his casual manner, you couldn't tell anything had happened the night before. "I see you're leaving us," he said to my mother. "What about Riley?"

"They're splitting the sheets," Jake said.

"An opportunity came up for a job in another town," my mother said. "A wonderful opportunity."

"Is that right," Dwight said. "I'm sorry to see you go."

He didn't offer to help with the loading, but maybe it was just as well. We were doing fine by ourselves. As we were finishing, I thought about my mother's word "opportunity." Maybe she was referring to my job or one she planned to get, but the word sounded good and my mood improved a little. With Riley, it seemed we had been slipping downgrade for a long time. Now Jake's enthusiasm and my mother's good cheer convinced me better times really were coming.

Still, I felt low spirited about running out on Riley, leaving him to bach at that miserable little siding. After the truck was loaded, I went back into the house a moment, and it struck me how bare it looked. I sat at the kitchen table and tried to write a note, but nothing much came to mind. Finally, I printed, "Riley, we went to Jake's. You take good care now," signing it with just my name. I didn't feel like adding "love" or "your son," because that would have been close to outright lying and perhaps make both of us feel worse.

Before climbing into the truck, I stood on the tracks and stared long and hard toward Barlow. Maybe I expected to see the speeder car, just a speck in the distance at first, then growing larger and larger as it approached with Riley at the wheel. However, I didn't see anything except the long empty track and scattered blackbirds along the telegraph wires.

On the long trip to Gateway, Jake spent the first couple of hours talking about the town's boom, what with the tourists, plywood mill, lodge, and construction projects. "Some days, I take in fifteen hundred dollars, and that's not hay. You'll find a job there easy, Flora, and the boy can be my right-hand man."

My mother hugged her knees, and even then I could see her arms were trembling. "It's exciting, isn't it. A fresh start. I just had a tremendous feeling."

After a while she leaned back and closed her eyes, but a slight smile lingered on her face and she seemed to relax. She looked younger, I thought, and I was struck again at how pretty she was. Maybe it was possible for us to improve things, get ahead a little, especially with Jake leading the way.

Frowning suddenly, she opened her eyes and turned to my uncle. "Can you blame me?" Something about the way she said it made me shrink back in my seat a little, because I sensed a sorrow and anger older and deeper than anything Riley had caused.

Jake might have sensed it, too. After a few moments he said, "Hey, nobody blames you for anything."

"He just didn't have any gumption," she said, and I realized she was now focusing on Riley. "What kind of an example is he for a boy like Culver, one with so much potential."

"You're doing the right thing," Jake said. "No question."

"Absolutely right," she said, setting her mouth straight across.

"Think of this kid." Jake grinned at me. "You've done a great job with him. A smart kid, good looking; he'll be running Gateway in a couple years — the whole enchilada."

"Of course," she said, reaching over to tousle my hair. "Everything's going to be better."

Pleased with the praise, I closed my eyes and leaned back to rest. The truck vibrations were soothing, and I felt good that we were getting somewhere at last. Mother's perfume mingled with Jake's aftershave and the smells of crops outside — alfalfa, wheat, onions — and the good moist smell of water in ditches.

We all sounded so optimistic, and I realized how long it had been since I had believed anyone who talked in such a hopeful way about things. Sometimes, when Riley had tried to sound hopeful, his words were hollowed with doubt, like a kid calling out on a dark night, pretending not to be afraid.

"What is it?" I asked, waking up. The truck was still running, but Jake had stopped it on the shoulder.

"Smell that," he said.

I took a deep breath, but couldn't place the pungent odor.

"Mint," he said. "Right in this county we grow half the peppermint in the whole damn United States."

"No kidding," I said. "What do they use it for?"

"Candy, toothpaste. Some old fart opens his Pepsodent, he's got Jackson County to thank for the flavor."

"Hang on a second," I said. "I want to get some." Climbing out of the truck, I remembered how much my mother had enjoyed the lamb with mint sauce. Reaching through the fence, I grabbed some of the dark green stems and leaves, bruising them between my fingers to release a stronger scent. In the distance a yellow biplane swooped low, crop dusting an emerald green field. When I climbed back into the truck, I handed several sprigs to my mother. "Doesn't this smell great?"

"Delicious. I wish we lived in the South so we could all sit out on the veranda and drink mint juleps."

"You can put it in iced tea," I said. "Or spoon it over lamb chops."

"That's a lovely idea," she said, holding the peppermint beneath her nose. "But I believe that mint sauce actually requires spearmint."

We settled into a small rental house across from the high school where my mother planned to enroll me in the fall. Although smaller than the place in Griggs, it had a combination bathtub and shower. She seemed excited about being on her own — except for me — and working again. She made curtains for the windows and bought some secondhand furniture in Central, about fifty miles away. So many people were moving to Gateway because of the boom, all the decent local furniture had been picked over, she said.

Jobs were easy to come by, and she got hired as a receptionist at Sunrise Biscuits. She had to go to work early, but the hours were regular and she wasn't on her feet. Anything was better than being a waitress was how she looked at jobs. "This pay's steady and you don't have to take anyone's lip."

As he had promised, my uncle put me to work, starting with simple things around the sporting goods store like packaging worms and fixing flats on kids' bicycles. The hours were long but the pay was low, as he liked to say, and I enjoyed working there, meeting the people coming through on vacation or planning their yearly fishing trips.

Except for Riley's occasional calls and the awkwardness they caused, things got back to normal. He had started calling as soon as we had a phone installed. A couple of times he had long conversations with my mother and talked about getting back together, but she shook her head firmly and told him that wasn't an option. Once he said, "Put the boy on," and she handed me the phone.

He talked about old times awhile, then asked, "Seems like her mind's set, huh, Culver?"

"It does seem that way, Riley."

"The best years of my life, gone to hell in a handbasket." He paused. "Well, anyway, I'd like to see you, buddy. Maybe do some fishing. Remember those salmon we caught on the coast? One was pretty near as big as you."

"Those were fish to remember all right," I said.

"By golly, we'll go again sometime then," he said, brightening. "Well, that's it for now. Don't take any wooden nickels."

I hung up, feeling a little low but wondering exactly why I didn't feel more torn up.

One morning, after we'd been in Gateway about two weeks, my mother was just ready for work when my uncle Jake showed up, pounding on the door. He pushed in past her and slapped the newspaper down on the kitchen table. I was finishing my shower but I could hear them talking with excited voices.

When I came out of the bathroom, my mother sat at the table reading the newspaper spread out before her. A strange look was on her face, one I can only describe as vindicated, but she seemed fierce, too.

"Would you believe it?" Jake said.

She stood and swept her hand across the table. "I knew it. I could see it coming." She paced around the kitchen, clearly agitated but somehow pleased, too, the way a person is when proven right. Stopping at the sink, she got a glass of water and took a long drink. "We got out of there just in time," she said.

"Do you want me to do something, Flora?" Jake asked.

"Just take me to work," she said, picking up her purse. "This is only my second week and I don't want to be late."

Jake started to gather up the newspaper, but she stopped him. "Let him read about it," she said, meaning me. "I got him out of there just in time." She thumped her small fist on the table. "Just in time."

When they had gone, I poured a glass of orange juice and sat, braced for the worst. I feared that Riley had blown off his head, or someone else's, but that wasn't the story.

He had burned Griggs to the ground, every building standing, including the trackwalker's outhouse. And he had planned it carefully, waiting until the trackwalker left on a binge and the stationmaster and his wife headed to the movies in Pratt. After dousing the buildings with railroad kerosene, Riley had burned them. The arson investigator said Riley had left three cans around as evidence.

By the time the county's outlaw fire engine raced to the scene from Pratt, all the buildings were fully involved and the fire burned out of control toward the river. Only the water stopped it.

Remarkably, Riley had driven to Griggs Junction, drunk coffee, and eaten doughnuts while watching the spectacle below. "He was calm as a cucumber," the waitress was quoted as saying. "I never suspected him at all. He left a generous tip and said 'Good evening' as polite as pie." In the newspaper quote, Dwight called Riley "a very disturbed and sneaky bastard," but I guess that wasn't too bad, considering his house and all its belongings were gone. The paper went on to say the alleged arsonist had not been apprehended but the authorities were following leads.

In addition to the story, the paper carried "before" and "after" photos of Griggs. Nothing remained in the after photos except the buildings' charred foundations and the basketball hoop hanging from a blackened telegraph pole.

After studying the pictures awhile, I smiled because I realized that the first photo wasn't of Griggs, but of Barlow, the siding thirty miles east, and somehow it made me happy to think that probably no one had a picture of Griggs, except for how it looked after my stepfather burned it.

I fixed a bowl of corn flakes and sat at the table, reading and rereading the story just to see if I could fill in any of the gaps, but the story remained pretty much the same as when I had first read it. Neither my mother nor I was mentioned, and that made me feel relieved somehow, as if I had a special secret. Of course, I figured the authorities would contact us eventually to see if Riley had been in touch, but I didn't plan on telling them anything, even if I knew. Having a stepfather on the run made me feel exhilarated and I decided not to go to work.

When I went outside, the morning was bright and fresh. Two girls were hitting a tennis ball on the high school court, and their tennis outfits gleamed white in the sun. Even at this distance, I could see both were better looking than any girl in Grass Valley.

Beside the tennis court was a basket with five guys playing a pickup game. Two of them were Indians from the reservation nearby, and after we shot for sides, I was on their team. I realized the three big farm boys on the other team had missed on purpose, so they could play together, but I didn't mind. Still, I said to myself, Culver, you remember this is how things work in Gateway.

Knowing a man I had lived with for eight years was now a felon on the run gave me a streak of recklessness, and that day I shot red-hot hoops. Every shot seemed to fall. Each time I released the ball it flew like a wild bird to its nest, and when the farm kids tried to double-team me, I made quick passes to my open teammate for easy layups.

After a while the girls stopped playing tennis and watched us, the way girls do when they're interested but trying not to show it. The dark-haired one smiled a couple times like she knew something special, and after I made a long fadeaway jumper, I gave her a little wave. She half waved back, and not long after, they left.

"Don't even think about it," one of the Indian boys told me. "That's heartbreak city."

"Is that right," I said. "I'm new in town."

"What's your name, anyway? Maybe you're gonna make the team."

"Culver," I said. "I live right across the street." I nodded toward the house. My mother had left her bedroom window open, and in the breeze, the bright curtains seemed to wave a greeting, but I couldn't say if it was hello or farewell.

$$3$$

THE GATEWAY SPORTING GOODS sign featured a leaping blue trout with a red neon rainbow along its side. The sign was illuminated twenty-four hours a day, and we stayed open most of those hours during fishing season. Gateway was the closest town to the Lost River Wilderness Area, and all the Chamber of Commerce brochures proclaimed "Gateway to Recreational Paradise."

Uncle Jake was the kind of stand-up guy a small town relies on. Before going into the sporting goods business, he had worked at the weekly newspaper, so he was acquainted with nearly everyone in town and on the nearby reservation. He had driven ambulance and fought fires as a volunteer when he wasn't guiding on the river. In short, he was everything my stepfather Riley was not.

As soon as the store opened at seven, we had to take the bicycles from the aisles and line them along the sidewalk just outside the plate glass windows that ran the length of the store. By clearing the aisles, we made a path to the worms, which were kept in a big refrigerator at the back of the store. It took fifteen minutes or so to clear the path, especially if one of us had to stop to write a couple of fishing licenses or boat permits for the Lost. During that time, the worm customers would browse and pick up hooks, weights, nets, and lures. Even the most dedicated bait fisherman sometimes became frustrated when the fish refused to bite on natural bait and would try trailing the worm behind an Indiana or Colorado spinner. I came to realize there was no particular hurry in getting the worms for the customers, because the longer they were forced to browse in the store, the more likely they would buy other equipment. We actually lost money on the worms but made it up on all the tackle.

Three quarters of the worms came from Lucky's worm farm in the valley, where it was cooler and they had more rainfall. Lucky stopped by every two weeks with a small refrigerator truck loaded with worms. The truck had green shamrocks on the side but Lucky wasn't Irish. We'd buy six thousand on the spot because we kept another refrigerator in back that could hold twelve large boxes. They came five hundred to a box.

I guess we must have been his best customers, at least in that part of the state, because after each delivery he'd sit an hour or two in back, shooting the breeze and helping me package worms. We put them in Buss Bedding, adding a little moss to hold the moisture. The bedding was a dry grayish compound that resembled the dumpings from a vacuum cleaner bag. Moistened, it felt like bits of clay. In the refrigerator worms could last a month, but if someone left the worms unprotected in a sweltering car, they'd die in a couple hours. Backpackers who put them in their packs, then hiked five or six miles to some remote mountain lake, found the worms dead when they arrived. "You sold me lousy worms," they'd complain a couple weeks later. To prevent this sort of thing, each time I sold a package, I'd lift the lid and show them the worms, perfectly alive and wiggling.

Jake also bought worms from kids who caught them at night on the high school lawns after the big rotating sprinklers soaked the ground. The kids filled coffee cans or milk cartons, and we paid them a penny a worm, as long as they hadn't used electrodes. Shocked worms turned mushy and died after a couple days, so Jake never had me package kids' worms until they'd been in the refrigerator a few days and we could see how they were holding up. If a kid lied about them, we didn't buy any more from him. Only a couple tried to cheat.

As soon as we had wheeled the bikes onto the sidewalk, clearing a path to the bait refrigerators, and served the initial surge of customers, Homer Baxter delivered a tray of doughnuts, bear claws, and jelly rolls. Like most bakers, he got up around two A.M. so he could be to work at three, and as he was fond of pointing out, by the time we opened the store he was halfway to quitting time. Homer took great pride in his simplest goods such as cake doughnuts, but his passion was to create a perfect raspberry jelly roll. He rolled up long sponge cake strips into tight circles oozing jam and sprinkled the outside with confectioners sugar; then he sliced the cake in sections two fingers thick. No matter what I was doing, when I saw Homer bearing a tray of jelly rolls, I stopped my task and headed to the back of the store. Once in a while, Homer would try a slice of his roll and grin. "I've almost got it right," he'd say.

My uncle nailed an old wicker creel to the wall by the coffeepot, and people tossed in dimes for coffee, quarters for bakery goods. Once a week he took out enough cash to buy another five-pound can of Folgers. The rest he gave to Homer.

Gigantic Gabriel Webster had sparkling blue eyes and a smile wide as a Cadillac grill. The station manager for KRCW, he chose the handle "Gab" for his radio work — everything from selling advertisements and promotions to covering high school events. Gab could talk, as Jake pointed out, and he constantly kept a string of patter going. A tireless promoter of local businesses and events, he firmly believed radio spots could push merchandise.

But for all his boosterism, Gab had a melancholy streak, the residue of years' selling door to door until he'd finally hustled his way into the heart of the station owner's daughter. By that time, he felt he'd missed his big opportunity, television. Handsome enough for the small screen, he had grown a little long in the tooth, and when he quit grinning, Gab appeared tired.

Even so, his voice was rich and confident, making him seem bigger than he actually was, just a shade over six one. "This is Gigantic Gab on the radio giant KRCW-Gateway," he'd announce as he did his radio promotions, and listeners could imagine him as big as they wanted. "When I talk, I fill up their entire front rooms and kitchens," he liked to say. "Radio offers the power of imagination."

Gab usually arrived a few minutes after Homer, and he put a pretty big dent in the pastry selections. When several locals had gathered to lounge in the back room, Gab would run four or five of his promo ideas by them. Big network stations did professional surveys, according to Gab; the smaller ones had to fly by the seat of their pants.

Buzzy Marek, usually the next to arrive, was the best crop duster in six counties, according to Jake. "Most dusters brag about treetop level," my uncle said. "Buzzy swoops so low he's got to burp to clear the barbed-wire fences! His propwash flips over the plant leaves, so he dusts both sides with one pass."

On first approaching Gateway, I'd seen Buzzy's yellow biplane, a Stearman World War II trainer he'd converted to crop dusting by replacing the forward seat with a hopper for chemicals.

The optimum time for crop dusting was at first light, when dew still clung to the plant leaves. Buzzy started dusting around five or so, and by eight-thirty he'd stop for a bear claw and a cup of coffee. Goggles perched high on his aviator's helmet, Buzzy entered the back room, a faint odor of chemicals clinging to his gray-striped jumpsuit.

"Damn, but I wish you'd change clothes before you walk in here," Jake would say. "You just go walking past the refrigerator and the worms drop dead."

"It's good for your health, Jake," Buzzy might retort. "Sit next to me and you kill all the cooties you pick up from your girlfriends. Besides, you don't have any trouble with scorpions."

The scorpion reference usually drew a hoot. One of Jake's selling gimmicks was to shake out any boots or hip waders before the customers tried them on, just in case some none-too-cozy creature had curled up inside. He expected spiders or maybe a beetle, but one day a good-size scorpion dropped out of a left hip boot, surprising everyone. Hitting the floor, the varmint curled his stinger and rushed the shocked customer. Shoeless, the dude jumped onto a chair and began yelling, thereby getting Jake flustered. Instead of stomping the insect as he should have, Jake tried whacking it with the hip boot, but swung awkwardly and missed. After missing twice more, he remembered to stomp, but by that time the scorpion had scooted among the piles of tennis shoe boxes and Jake had no luck finding it, even though he cautiously moved every box.

Sniffy St. John, night watchman and glue mixer at the plywood mill, had witnessed the entire show, and by the time he retold the story to the mill boys, the scorpion had grown to lobster size and Jake was packing a short-handled shovel to deal it a lethal whack. For the next couple weeks, the mill boys came in to rib Jake about hunting scorpions, asking what sort of rifles worked best for large insects and trying on pair after pair of hip boots, looking for the critter.

In self-defense Jake claimed there had never been a scorpion and reminded Sniffy's coworkers that St. John had sworn he'd spotted a flying saucer on Shaniko Flats early that spring.

"I got out to pee and there it was, hovering and making this strange high-pitched whine." Sniffy had still shivered when he retold the story to me. "Looked like a baseball cap covered with aluminum foil. And when it accelerated, the foil glowed orange-blue."

Jake had asked him if he'd shut off his truck engine and doused the lights. "Your own headlights can play funny tricks out there. Clouds and shadows make light warp."

"I know what I saw," Sniffy insisted. "Followed me five miles until I hit the outskirts of Sherman. Each time it got close, I smelled ozone."

The ozone detail didn't make sense according to my uncle. "All the benzene and formaldehyde Sniffy smells making glue have bent his nose clear out of whack. He can't smell liver and onions from a foot away."

Back-room speculation concluded that Sniffy had seen too many double features at the Eltrym Theater. Weekends featured Japanese movies about space invaders — all with the same rocket-ship footage — as well as stories of gigantic mutant grasshoppers, ants, and crabs, the frightening results of radioactive experiments gone haywire.

Although my mother turned up her nose at these movies, I was at least pleased Gateway had a downtown theater in addition to a drive-in. For us, that was a step up.

Seaweed Swanson, retired chief petty officer, USN, smelled like warm wool and his marble-eyed sheep dog, Skipper. Without the bosun's whistle to wake Seaweed each dawn, his hours were irregular; he usually arrived late but never complained about cool pastry or coffee dregs. Anything beat Navy chow, he figured.

According to Jake, Seaweed always had trouble with the clock and actually spent two extra years in the Navy before realizing he could retire with full pension after twenty. Seaweed blamed his personal time warp on too many trips across the international date line. "Those crossings added years to my service, but I've always been dedicated to God and country." Saying the last, he'd suck in his belly and salute with a tattooed hand.

Although capable of speaking without swearing, Seaweed seldom did, and his speech was peppered with what Gab called potty-mouth.

"Do you know the twelve basic kinds of farts?" Seaweed demanded the first time we met. After I confessed my ignorance, he rattled them off. "Recruit, remember these: the fizz, the fuzz, the fizzy fuzz; the blower, the bender, the binder, the blinder; the ripsnorter, the tear ass, the sneaker, the rattler; and the one that goes pooooooh." The last he drew out like a long sigh.

Such was his sense of humor. However, like many men who hadn't spent much time around women, Seaweed had an exaggerated sense of chivalry. Whenever a woman entered the store, he'd head outside so as not to chance offending her. Usually he'd take Skipper behind the ice-house and throw sticks until the customer had finished her business.

His command to fetch was "Dead soldier!" since he'd been in innumerable Army-Navy bar brawls.

His booming voice made Seaweed's gallant attempts ill fated. Although Seawood imagined he was beyond earshot, we could hear him swearing at the dog. "Fetch the stick, Skipper. Dead soldier! You sonofabitching seadog. Dead soldier! Miserable mutt."

Even on hottest days, my instructions were to close the front door whenever Seaweed headed outside to avoid offending a woman customer.

A little addlepated after years of booze and brawls, Seaweed never could grasp the idea I wasn't Jake's son. No matter how many times I explained, he always called me Little Jake.

Gab's most recent promotional scheme involved a group called the Bitterwater Boys, who were scheduled at the Grange. Ticket sales had been slow and he was offering some free to the merchants who increased their radio advertising budgets. In turn, Gab claimed the merchants could lure customers with the tickets.

"What do you say we go a hundred this month, Jake?" Gab had his receipt book in hand. "Twenty free tickets if you double your advertising dollars."

"Whatever happened to George Jones?" my uncle asked. "I remember you promised George and Tammy Wynette this year for sure."

"That's blood under the bridge, Jake. You know when Jones didn't show, I almost lost my shirt. His agent said he had sinus problems."

"Sure," Jake said. "Got his nose stuck in a whiskey bottle."

Everybody laughed at that one.

"Trust me. The Bitterwater Boys are skyrocketing. Now they're off the launch pad gaining speed. Pretty soon . . . *whoosh!*" He gestured toward the ceiling.

"That group was on a USO tour," Seaweed said. "Called themselves the Bilgewater Boys back then." He ignored Gab's glare. "I should have stayed in the Navy. Bob Hope was actually on my ship. And Anita Bryant. But I tell you who might come to Gateway. Don Ho! He's related to Ace — shirttail cousin or something. On R and R in Honolulu, I climbed right up on the stage and sang with him." Seaweed closed his eyes. "Tiny bubbles . . . in the wine."

"You should have stayed in the Navy all right," Gab said. "We wouldn't have to worry so much about drowning in your bullshit around here."

"Sounds like the pot calling the kettle black," Seaweed said. "At least

I keep my bullshit confined to the room I'm in. But you're on every damn radio in town."

"That's music to my ears, Seaweed." Gab grinned. "Sound promotion."

"My wife says the Bitterwater Boys are pretty good," Buzzy said. "If Jake buys more ads, I'll take some free promotional tickets."

Gab took a bite of Homer's bear claw. "What about it, Jake?"

"You can sign me up for sixty if you promise to stop looking like your best friend stole your truck and dog but left the wife. Put some of those ad spots right before Paul Harvey."

Gab brushed pastry flakes from his lap and nodded. "Sixty is small potatoes, but you got it."

"Put me down for fifty, too," Homer said. "Better run them first thing in the morning. People don't buy doughnuts for dinner. And crank up the volume."

Gab glanced at Buzzy, but he shook his head. "Not me. Crop dusting is all word of mouth. And if you're not good, you're dead."

Gab nodded at Homer. "I'll stop by around two when you knock off and we'll work out the lingo." He seemed pretty cheerful. "I'm going to tell you boys something straight arrow. As soon as this concert's over, I'm chartering a bus to Reno. Take all my preferred customers for a spree."

"Why go all the way to Reno?" Jake asked. "I can walk to Ace's."

"Reno, the biggest little city of them all," Gab said, warming to the subject. "Bigger jackpots, better food, more scrumptious babes. They import women from California. Everyone knows California grows the world's best-looking women. And Reno has first-class entertainers. You think I could get Johnny Mathis to come to Ace's?"

"Only if you told them Seaweed was singing along," Buzzy said, and everybody laughed.

"No offense," Jake said. "But I wouldn't want to head to Reno with this bunch. I'd plan to cut a wide swath, and who needs wagging tongues later on."

"At your age, a dragging tongue is more like it," Gab said. "But I'm lining a bus up anyway. Whether you want to tag along or not is your business." He stood. "Well, I got to go and look up some real customers. Gibb Morris at the Feed and Seed has deep pockets. Maybe he wants to move some fertilizer and garden hoses. I've never seen it this damn hot and dry."

"I'm heading out that way, too," Buzzy said. "Can't jawbone all day. Got to get a couple hundred pounds of parathion."

Seaweed cocked an eyebrow. "You got the crabs again?"

"I've got to go out and talk to some of the ag boys about thrips," Buzzy said. "Those little varmints have been invading their carrots, but parathion should knock them for a loop.

"Thrips?" Seaweed said. "I think I caught those one time in the Philippines. Tell the farmers to wash it good and piss quick."

★ ★
★ ★ ★

Mule Mullins, foreman at the Gateway Plywood Mill, also coached the Loggers, a league championship American Legion baseball team. When younger, Mule had played Double-A ball for the Tacoma Braves, and he entertained the back-room boys with dirty jokes and stories of his misadventures in Spokane, Portland, and Calgary. A fringe of orange hair peeked from beneath his green baseball cap, but when he removed the cap, he was almost bald. Mule stirred his coffee with a wide carpenter's pencil that seemed fragile in his large hands. His thick shoulders and lumpy wrists showed he'd spent early years pulling lumber on the green chain before he became night foreman.

The Loggers kept an open charge account because Jake knew they were good for the bill at the beginning of each month. Mule purchased baseballs by the gross, bats by the dozen, and extra gloves, resin bags, and baseball shoes. He had convinced Hall Tangent, who owned the mill, that a winning team was top advertising, and Tangent spared no expense.

With the building boom in Gateway and across the state, the mill ran twenty-four hours a day, seven days a week. In front of the mill was what Mule called the biggest cold deck in the West, stacks of logs twenty feet high and deep enough to cover two football fields. At night, showers of sparks rose from the mill's wigwam scrap burners, turning the south end of town into a glowing Fourth of July display.

"What with coaching and overtime, I'm going eighteen or twenty hours a day," Mule said. "I don't know how much more of this fun I can take."

"Stop complaining," Jake said. "Cry all the way to the bank. I heard you beat Central pretty good. Sorry I was on the river."

"It wasn't a close game," Mule said, "because I kept in my best pitcher. It's always fun to beat those snooty Central people. Especially a double-header."

Mule owned a powder blue Ford pickup with stepside bumpers, and after the victory he drove through town, honking the horn. Ten or eleven cheering ballplayers rode in the bed or stood on the bumpers, waving brooms to show they'd swept Central.

"We'll beat them in the tournament, too," Mule said, then yawned. "Unless I'm so tired from all the work I can't stand up to coach. Did you hear we got the plywood contract for Hollywood?"

"No, but I figured you would," Jake said.

"Gonna rebuild most of the reservation from what I hear. Hollywood is just the start. Tangent knows all the mucky-mucks on the tribal council. All the big-shot chiefs." Mule picked up a new baseball glove and slipped it on his hand. He squinted at the tag. "Pricey."

"Kangaroo leather," Jake said. "Top quality."

"Some of those featherheads complained about the plywood prices, but somebody's always grumbling on the reservation. The loggers think they get cheated at the scaling station." Mule pounded his fist into the glove pocket. "Anyway, we got the Hollywood contract but we can't get to it for six months. We're way behind on orders."

"I'm glad they're rebuilding that eyesore," Jake said. "Floods got parts of it a couple times, but it really needs a bulldozer and torch." He chuckled. "You new ambulance guys will have to learn street numbers or something. When I was driving, they just said the purple house or the chartreuse place. Screwball colors."

"We could sure use you to drive ambulance again," Mule said. "Some of the young volunteers don't know shit from Shinola."

Jake shook his head. "I earned my twenty-year certificate. Those last runs got longer each time. We'd load some groaning guy in back while his poor kids watched, their scared faces pressed against the window. One of us stayed with him, while the other drove like hell, trying to beat death's door. And the miles stretched out. Gateway needs a hospital. Central's too damn far."

Mule picked up one of the Spaulding baseballs and worked it into the glove. "I hate those Hollywood runs. Been inside a couple places you wouldn't believe. One had about five hundred empty Dinty Moore beef stew cans, and a scrawny cat for each can."

"A lot of those people have pride," Jake said. "Just not much means."

"Well, the tribe and BIA are building them all new houses," Mule said. "Indian fringe benefit. Of course, your taxes and mine are paying for those places. But at least I'll get a little back in overtime."

"Don't forget to spend some here," Jake said. "Cash makes no enemies."

"Put this on the team's account." Mule tucked the glove and ball under his arm. "Hollywood," he muttered. "To most people it's the end of the rainbow. Around here, it's more like the end of the line."

The Phoenix stood just beyond Gateway's northside city limits and featured a blinking neon bird that resembled a pheasant more than a phoenix. The restaurant served the best steaks in town, including a seventy-two-ounce porterhouse special, and what passed for Chinese food. Opaque Chinese lanterns with dangling red tassels hung from the light fixtures, and golden dragons adorned the walls. The Lucky Dragon Lounge featured twenty-five-cent beers and half-dollar well drinks during happy hour, double shots from six to eight. Dance bands played four nights a week, country and western and rock and roll getting equal billing.

Ace Ho's Stardust Resort stood adjacent to the Phoenix and offered deluxe modern rooms and a giant outdoor pool. Everyone stayed at the Stardust, from construction engineers and dam inspectors to traveling salesmen. Those with a hankering for poker and blackjack found games of chance in the motel's back suites. I heard girls were available in some of the units.

Ace Ho owned both places and was the biggest operator in town, except for Hall Tangent. Although his places were fancy, Ace himself kept a low profile. He had spent his teen years working on Hawaiian pineapple plantations, and he didn't have any fingerprints because the pineapple acid had eaten away the whorls of his skin. Rumors circulated about Ace's connections with Honolulu's racketeering and gambling, but no one actually knew where he got his start-up money.

Occasionally, Ace came into the store to buy ammunition for the .32 automatic he carried. When he helped himself to coffee in the back room, the conversation lulled. Although almost fifty, he moved with the litheness of a jaguar and had the coldest blue-green eyes I'd ever seen. Jake called them iceberg eyes, claiming they were the exact color of the new icebergs calved from the glacial fields near Sitka.

The town felt ambivalent about Ace, and once or twice some blue-noses talked about picketing his establishment, but it didn't come to anything because no one wanted to confront him directly. The city police wouldn't deal with the club since it lay beyond their jurisdiction, and the county sheriff, Grady Simmons, gave Ace a wide berth.

"You can't argue with success," Jake told Grady one morning at the Oasis, and Grady replied, "People might as well spend their wad in Gateway. Why have them cart their business off to Central?"

Jake usually recommended that the wealthy dudes he guided stay at Ace's, especially if they had a yen for the fast lane. And some nights we went there, too. Anytime we sold seven hundred dollars' worth of sporting goods, Jake treated me to a boys' night out. We celebrated by eating steaks at the Phoenix. He always ordered the Top Hand for himself and the Wrangler for me. Both were T-bones, but the Top Hand was bigger.

A couple of times Jake asked my mother along, but she declined, saying that eating heavy food so late at night disturbed her rest and made her feel logy the next day at work.

We almost always saw Gab at a small table in the bar, seated with a different attractive woman. He'd send over a Seven and Seven for Jake and a Coke Virgin for me. When the woman excused herself for the powder room, Gab would slip over and say, "She's a client from Central. Owns a furniture store and takes out lots of advertising. Don't want you guys getting the wrong notion." He'd glance around. "This is a business meeting."

By the time we'd be ready to leave, Gab might be holding hands with the woman or dancing close.

"Wonder what kind of business?" I'd ask.

Jake scowled. "None of yours."

Some nights Jake decided to stay and check out the action, so I walked home alone. I didn't mind, because it gave me a chance to study the town at night and consider how I fit in it.

Once I wandered to the back of the motel, seeing what I could glimpse through the open doors. The gambling suites had big-game trophies displayed on the walls, and I guessed Ace had shot the animals on safari. Dozens of gamblers clustered around the tables. Some wore mill hats or farm clothes; others had white shirts and ties. Most of the dealers were women wearing short fringe dresses and white caps with an ace of clubs design. Cigarette smoke and chatter drifted out of the rooms.

The girls' quarters were quiet, the doors closed and the windows covered with dark green drapes. I stood staring at the rooms a few minutes when two tall men approached carrying flashlights. They were Indians and wore the black and crimson satin jackets of the RedWings, the reservation's semipro basketball team.

One shone the flashlight in my face. "What's up, kid?"

I shrugged. "Not much. I had dinner, now I'm just walking around."

"You a guest? Your folks checked in?"

I shook my head. "I'm here with my uncle Jake. He owns the sporting goods store."

"Sure, we know Jake," he said, lowering the light from my face. "See him all the time. Jake wouldn't want you hanging around here." He shifted the flashlight beam to the front of my pants. "Take your stiffie home. Come back when you're twenty-one."

The other one laughed and held up his hand. "Say hello to Rosie Palm."

I could feel the heat rise in my neck, and I wanted to say something but couldn't think what, so I just walked away. Seeing my uncle's empty pickup with the blinking neon phoenix reflecting off the windshield made me feel alone and sad. My mother and I were newcomers to Gateway, I realized, connected to the town only by our ties to my uncle.

That night I walked a long way until I had wrung out the anger and emptiness. I found myself inside the train depot, hanging around listening to the clack-clack of the telegrapher's key, smelling the cigar butts and chewing tobacco in the brass spittoons. At 11:40 the night freight rolled by, and I went outside to watch the boxcars for open doors, imagining the hoboes inside. The moon was nearly full, and I saw a flatcar carrying three John Deere tractors chained to its deck. A hobo perched on one tractor seat, pretending he was driving, and in the indistinct light his face resembled Riley's. The hobo's long matted hair blew back in the wind and he was grinning as if he owned the world. As the freight passed, he waved at me, fingers waggling from the torn holes in his gloves.

☆ ☆ ☆ ☆

Four days a week, Jake guided on the Lost. Parts of the other three, he worked in the store. He was building a reputation, and his guide calendar was almost full the entire summer. When he found out how fast I grew savvy about the business, he started relying on me more and more. After a couple of weeks, I could even close out the till and make the night bank deposit.

On those occasions, I got home just before midnight, and sometimes found my mother still up reading. "Jake shouldn't take advantage of you," she'd say. "Just because you're related doesn't mean he should work you like a slave."

The fact was, I liked working at the store. The back-room boys put me at the heart of the town. I also enjoyed visiting with the tourists who stopped and listening to the dam workers retell their adventures. Most of all, I liked the excitement of meeting the dudes.

The dudes, as my uncle called them, fell into two types. Doctors, architects, or businesspeople from the city comprised the first. These had lots of money, and their fishing clothes were so new they still had package creases in the shirtsleeves. Usually, one of the dudes knew my uncle from a trip the year before and had returned with his clients or friends. Most likely it was a tax write-off, according to my uncle. The second group were working people who had saved their money for the three-day trip. Sometimes a couple wives gave their husbands trips for Christmas gifts. My uncle understood these men might have preferred salmon fishing in Alaska or a couple weeks in Canada, but they couldn't afford it, so they settled for three deluxe days on the Lost.

"Treat 'em right, treat 'em the same" was his motto, and I never saw him deviate from it.

The groups came in around ten and spent an hour or so getting outfitted. The first group wore sunglasses and bright caps from places like Sun Valley and Aspen. They smelled of aftershave and breath mints. The others wore battered caps from the mills and plants where they worked: Cenex, John Deere, Freightliner. Their eyes creased with worry lines but they were out to have a good time. Jake called everyone fella because he was bad at names. Among the wealthy dudes, usually one was poorly equipped, having tried to match a borrowed fly rod with a spinning reel, so Jake would get him taken care of while the others ribbed him. Nearly everybody needed new monofilament, and we also checked the guides and tips on their rods. A worn tip could cut the monofilament so they'd lose a nice fish.

Sooner or later most dudes would head for the baseball equipment, pull a thirty-four-inch Louisville Slugger from the bat boxes, and take a few practice cuts, placing the hundred-dollar fly rods in jeopardy. Although they never actually hit one, the danger made me wince.

Moving from behind the counter and stepping in their direction, Jake would say, "Fellas, I hope your insurance covers those pricey rods. I hate to tell you, mine doesn't." Taking a quick look at the small price tags hanging from the metal eyes, he'd shake his head. "A hundred dollars. That's pure graphite but it sure seems expensive."

Grinning and looking a little foolish, the dudes would lower their bats. Knowing he had their full attention, Jake would say, "You're welcome to carry that bat outside, try a few swings." Sometimes they'd take up his offer; others, they'd replace the bats into the box and look around a little more, hands jammed in pockets.

I worried that someone might actually break a rod when Jake was on the river, but he winked and said, "The insurance covers it, but I don't want my premiums jacked."

.   .   .

Jake actually outfitted the dudes, and I helped in small ways, but they always wanted to hear advice straight from him. I could explain to the fly fishermen that the trout were taking spent-wing stones, Adams, and Rhoda specials, tell the lure plunkers to use silver Mepps spinners and frog flatfish, but they wouldn't buy a thing until Jake confirmed my picks. Then they'd take a dozen.

I loaded the big Igloo ice chests with blocks from the ice house outside, six-packs of pop, Hamm's beer, and lots of sandwiches. Jake also took the best food from Gateway lockers — steaks, chops, and a baron of sirloin roast beef to cook in the cast-iron Dutch oven. They could have caught enough fish to fill everyone, but they usually ate fish only once on a trip. We iced another big cooler for the catch, because the dudes wanted to return home with impressive trout.

By eleven-thirty, they left the parking lot in Jake's Dodge crew-cab pickup towing one of the drift boats. I had half an hour until the noon rush started, and I'd thumb through one of the old *Outdoor Life* or *Sports Afield* magazines Jake piled on shelves in the bathroom.

Some days I'd stare at the large black and white photograph of Jake, my father, and mother that hung on the wall behind the cash register. A two-day limit of trout — sixty fish — were spread across a fallen barn door in front of them. Thick-sided rainbows native to that region, the fish had fattened all summer with Salmon flies and crayfish.

The brothers wore battered straw cowboy hats, lures dangling from the brims, and my mother wore a woman's felt hat — too stylish for the river. She stood squarely before the camera and seemed genuinely happy. Jake's hat tipped forward at a jaunty angle.

My father held his right hand beside his cheek, shielding the sun. His face was shadowed, but his eyes were distinct and seemed fixed on something far away the others could not see.

The first time I took the picture down for a better look, I shuddered. My father had penciled the word "Lunkers" and then in my mother's neater hand: "We had such a marvelous time. A perfect day!" The small date marked in the corner showed it was taken the autumn before my father drowned.

At times when the store was quiet, I studied the picture, trying to determine the meaning of my father's expression. Much later, I came to realize it resembled the faces of high school students featured on the annual's In Memory page, those who die before they graduate. Victims of car accidents or mysterious diseases the small-town doctors cannot fathom, they seem to be gazing into the future they will not share with those around them.

4

 WHEN JAKE was guiding on the Lost, I answered the phone at the store several dozen times a day, but one call made me jump. It was Riley, calling just before lunch.

"Culver? Is that you? How's my boy?" He paused. "Listen. Make sure no one's eavesdropping."

I quickly surveyed the parking lot and store. "No one's here right now."

"Good. I tried calling a couple days ago, but Jake answered. I don't think I should call the house anymore because the phone might be tapped." He didn't sound frightened or upset, just careful, like a parent explaining something to a child.

"Are you all right, Riley? Taking care of yourself?"

He started chuckling. "She never thought I had it in me. Damn railroad ground me down, but not out. I got their attention, didn't I. What did your mother say?"

"She was surprised," I said after a moment's hesitation. "I think it's fair to say she didn't see it coming." She had said a lot of things, critical and harsh, but I didn't want to go into that right now.

"I sent you a postcard. But I'm not at that location anymore. Got to keep moving for a while yet."

"You be careful, Riley."

"A couple minutes," I heard him say to someone on the other end. "Some bastard needs to use the phone," he said. "Probably calling his girlfriend so his wife can't hear. Listen, tell your mom I love her. And tell her . . . I'm just a little short of cash. Otherwise, I'd send some along to help you out."

"It's all right," I said. "We're both working."

"I knew Jake would take care of you. He's a stand-up guy. One more quick question. Does she talk about me?"

"Yes," I said. "Quite a bit, really."

"I knew it," he said. "Darkness over Arizona."

"You take care," I said again, but he had already hung up. After a couple of moments, I replaced the receiver, too. My right ear, the one I had listened with, seemed hot, so I rubbed it a little. I was trying to figure out what he meant about Arizona, but a customer came in about then and I had to make out a fishing license.

No postcard came to the store that day, and when I went home at night, I debated about telling Mom that Riley had called. When I hit the door, she was all smiles, so I couldn't bring myself to say anything.

"Sit down," she said. "Sit down. I've got some wonderful news."

"Did they make you president of Sunrise Biscuits already?" I asked. I sat in one of the wooden chairs because I'd gotten my jeans dirty fixing some bicycle flats that afternoon. I was eager to hear her news, but I was trying to figure out dinner. Something smelled like fish.

She sat in the love seat, hands folded. Her cheeks were flushed, and for a moment I thought maybe Riley had called her, too, but that wasn't it. "A wonderful opportunity has come up. A truly wonderful opportunity. My supervisor wants me to go to Minneapolis for a training seminar so I can become an office manager."

"That sounds great, Mom."

"It's for ten days. Are you sure you won't mind? Jake can watch out for you."

"You got to get ahead, and it's just us now. You said so yourself."

"That's exactly right," she said. "I leave in two days, then. I've never been to Minneapolis. Maybe I'll have a chance to look around."

Dinner was halibut au gratin and cheese muffins. She claimed it was one of my favorites, but that was news to me, and I didn't think Riley had liked it either. Maybe she was thinking of my father. She was so excited about the Minneapolis seminar, I took a second helping and pretended to like the fish.

"You haven't said much about work today. Anything exciting happen?" She tore open one of her muffins and the steam escaped from the pockets of cheese.

"Packed dozens and dozens of worms," I said. "A few dangerous ones escaped, but I managed to round them up."

She laughed and touched the back of my hand lightly with her fingertips. "You've always had a great sense of humor. That goes a long way in life. That, and an eager attitude." She picked up the cheese muffin but set it down again. "I'm too excited to eat. Maybe later."

When I finished my second helping of halibut, I asked my mother about the photograph of the fishing trip.

"Oh, good heavens," she said. "I hadn't thought about that picture in years."

"That was your handwriting," I pointed out. "You said you had a marvelous time, a perfect day."

"Did I?" Her face grew troubled. "Well, perhaps I did say something like that in the excitement of the moment, but I never really cared for fishing. That was your father's interest. And Jake's."

"Sure looks like you were having a great time. I never saw so many big fish."

She folded her hands, holding them at the edge of the table. "It probably was fun all right . . . in those days. But I don't believe I ever went fishing again."

After supper I helped clear the table, then watched television awhile. When the news came on, I shut it off and went to the bathroom to brush my teeth. Mom had set up the ironing board and was ironing her blouses. The house was filled with the scent of warm cotton.

About ten, someone knocked on the door and I answered. Both of us figured it would be my uncle Jake stopping to see how the business had been. But there stood Grady Simmons, the county sheriff. I was stunned.

He held his hat and looked past me, toward my mother, who seemed startled. Her iron paused in midair. "Excuse me for coming in so late, Mrs. Walker, but there was an accident just this side of the reservation."

She touched her free hand to her heart. "Not Jake."

"No, no, nothing like that. I apologize for worrying you." He ran his hand through his hair. "A couple Indian kids rolled their car, but don't you worry. A broken leg, maybe a couple cracked ribs. Nothing too serious. By now the Gateway volunteers have taken them to the hospital in Central."

"Oh dear," she said. "This town could use a hospital. There are so many wrecks."

"The way we're going, that's going to come through in a couple years. Especially the way the Jaycees are pushing for it." Grady had stepped inside and I remembered to shut the door. My hand trembled a little, but I don't think he noticed because he was looking at my mother.

I think she realized he was watching her because she set down her iron, and after turning it off, just stood a moment with her hands in front of her stomach. "Sit down; just sit, please," she said then. "I've forgotten my manners. Would you like some tea, officer? It'll only take a minute. The water's still hot."

"I'd appreciate that, Mrs. Walker. I'm just a little cold. To tell the truth, accidents give me the shivers. You get the call, but you never know what might have happened, who might be in the wreck. The phone rings, and you just never know."

When my mother went into the kitchen, Grady smiled at me a moment, then finished surveying the room. He studied the painting above the love seat a long time before leaning toward me. "How are things working out at the store?"

"Real busy," I said, trying to calm my voice. "Jake's on the river a lot so that leaves me with a big responsibility." I told him about selling a hundred-dollar fly rod to a tourist and taking a down payment on a bicycle. I realized I was talking a lot to cover my nervousness, but Grady just kept smiling.

Returning to the room, my mother handed him a cup of tea. "See, that was only a jiffy."

He didn't take the cream and sugar she offered. "Monet, isn't it?" Grady nodded at the painting. "You don't see much of that in Gateway."

"Renoir. You were pretty close." She stirred her tea. "Of course, that's a reproduction. *From the Terrace*. I've had it forever."

"I doubt you're that old, Mrs. Walker," he said. "It looks good there. The colors pick up the print of that love seat."

"Are you interested in art?" she asked.

"Well, it's not quite up my alley, you see. But when I was at the police academy, I did take an art appreciation course at the women's college nearby. We had to take something in the humanities, and frankly — art class — that's where a lot of the most attractive women were, so it was a popular elective among the cadets."

Mom smiled, but I could tell by the way her brow furrowed she was worried.

In Grady's hands the teacup seemed fragile. "Most of the art game went over my head. But I did like Monet. All those haystacks. You see, I grew up on a ranch, and they really do look different in different light, the way the shadows are . . ."

My mother twisted abruptly and set her teacup down. "He's dead, isn't he? That's what you've come to say. Did your people shoot him?"

Grady stiffened. He seemed genuinely puzzled. "Jake? No, he's fine."

After a moment he said, "Oh, you mean Riley Walker, your husband." He set his cup down and leaned forward, his big hands resting on the thighs of his blue polyester uniform. "The reason I came by was just to check. The railroad authorities keep pestering me . . . so I wanted to ask if you've heard anything from him. It's just routine . . . my asking."

"Not for me," she said, her voice brittle. "It's nothing like my usual routine." She squeezed her eyes tight and rubbed her forehead with her thumbs. Her eyes remained closed as she said, "He hasn't called for weeks. Not since that unfortunate business in Griggs. No, I don't have any new leads for you."

I didn't say anything when Grady glanced at me. I tried to swallow but I couldn't work up enough spit.

"I'm sure you haven't," Grady said. "No doubt he's lying pretty low right now, maybe staying with friends or relatives. The railroad officials have checked his possible contacts, at least the ones they know."

My mother opened her eyes. "I imagine they're very thorough."

"Yes," he said. "I was just wondering about southern California. Do you know anybody there he might look up? He was in the service, wasn't he? Maybe an old Navy buddy."

"I can't think of a soul," she said. "Don't you people have anything better to do than hound that poor man?"

Grady took a pair of reading glasses out of his shirt pocket, slowly unfolded them, and put them on. When he removed a postcard from his jacket pocket, my blood turned to ice.

"This card was addressed to the boy at the store. The postmaster turned it over to us." He studied the card a moment. "Sure, I recognize that place. Disneyland. Took the grandchildren there one summer and waited in line over an hour for the Matterhorn. They're growing up fast. The time just slips by."

"Perhaps you can take them again," my mother said. "May I see that card?"

"That's a good thought," he said, handing it to her. "You can see the card's not signed. But I expect it's Riley's handwriting."

"Not a doubt," she said after a minute. "He doesn't say much, but then he never did."

She handed the card to me. I could tell it was Riley's handwriting all right, but my eyes wouldn't focus.

"I'm sure you don't know anything about this, do you, Culver?" she asked.

"I've always wanted to go to Disneyland," I said, half smiling. "No, it's news to me."

"You haven't received any other cards, then? Or had any phone calls?" Grady glanced at the canary yellow phone Mom had installed to match the love seat tapestry.

"Not a single word," she said. Her eyes flashed indignation. "That postmaster should be ashamed for reading people's mail. We might as well live in Russia. Who ever thought we'd have the police barging into our lives at all hours. I've got half a mind to get a lawyer and stop this harassment."

Grady scooped up his hat and stood. "I didn't mean to get you upset. It's just routine, like I said, nothing personal. I thought you might know something more that could help us."

"And if I did, who's to say I'd tell you? A wife needn't testify against her husband or have you forgotten that?" She shook her head. "When you think about it, what's so terrible about burning down a crummy railroad siding? I wish I had a big enough torch to burn them all down — squalid little eyesores. Sometimes I wish I had done it myself, I truly do, the way those railroad people shoved us from place to place like a bunch of damned gypsies. Anyway, no one was actually hurt."

After my mother's outburst Grady tried to say a few words about the potential danger of the arsonist, but he was no match for her and soon left, still carrying his hat. Closing the door behind him, she leaned against it, as if bracing for wind.

"Culver," Mom said later, after drinking two cups of tea with generous measures of rum and sugar, "I want you to promise me something."

"What is it?"

"Even if you get truly desperate at times, promise me you won't burn down a railroad siding and get yourself into this kind of jam."

"All right," I said. "I won't, then." It seemed an easy kind of promise to make because at that age, desperation seems unlikely.

"I'm glad that's settled," she said, draining the last of her tea. "Now I'm going to bed."

I stayed up a little, trying to watch something on television, but all the situations seemed too contrived and my mind wandered. This entire business with Riley kept hitting me off guard. Of course, I should have realized he'd be back in touch, like a bad penny showing up. It wasn't too likely a man would live with my mother for eight years and then just vanish.

But what puzzled me was her reaction. She seemed to be sticking up for him now. I didn't know much about love, but I suspected she might have fallen in love with him after these strange events. I didn't believe that she had loved him earlier, but something about that desperate act of burning down the siding had demonstrated the strength of his desire for her, and perhaps she had succumbed to it, somehow. Maybe his act had even burned away some of the residual love I thought she carried for my father. I believed he had always stood like a shadow between them.

Thinking of that shadow, I realized finally what Riley's remark "darkness over Arizona" had meant. It involved one of the weird news articles from my mother's gossip magazines. In the account, a man's wife had left him because he was spending too much time at a tavern, not paying her enough attention. This was in the Southwest, and they were both Catholics, as I recall. Distraught over the abandonment, he had himself crucified on a wooden cross in the desert to show his desperate love for her. A couple of women from the tavern, casual acquaintances according to the article, helped by pounding the nails through his hands.

It wasn't a complete crucifixion though, because he stood on a ladder so as not to suffocate. The women kept climbing the ladder, bringing him beer, pretzels, pickled eggs, hot sausages, and other bar foods to help ease the pain and keep up his strength.

I remembered Riley finishing the article and slapping the magazine against his knee. "Craziest story I ever heard. Bunch of damn nuts, the lot of them," he had said.

But it had worked. A newspaperman wrote up the guy's plight and the story got syndicated. The wife read about her husband and went back to him when she realized the depth of his love.

She took an ambulance rescue unit out in the desert to save him, but the attendants were afraid to remove the nails without a doctor, and the cross wouldn't fit into the ambulance. So she returned to town, hired a flatbed truck and got him to the hospital that way. A few days later he was released, and they renewed their marriage vows. So the guy's plan worked, crazy or not.

"Can't you go to bed? The TV's bothering me and I've got a headache." My mother stood in the doorway.

"Sorry," I said. "Still unwinding from this goofy day." I turned off the set.

"You said it. Disneyland. That about takes the grand prize." We both moved to the kitchen table and she began picking at the leftover cheese muffin. "What's next? Knott's Berry Farm? If I wrote this to 'Dear Abby' she wouldn't believe it. And she's heard just about everything."

I watched her across the table. "I think he did it for you, Mom. Burning that place down was Riley's way of showing love."

42

She stared at me as if I were an alien. "Do you know what you're saying? What kind of crazy talk is that?"

I took a breath. "Riley wanted to show he loves you. Maybe you love him."

She fixed her burning eyes on me and there was a long pause. Then slowly, as if thinking of the right words, she said, "I understand what it means to be pushed to your limit. To be shoved from pillar to post. That's all." She stood abruptly. "But I am not one to squander my opportunities. Now let's get some sleep."

I watched my mother retreat down the hall, a small figure silhouetted in the doorway, holding herself straight.

5

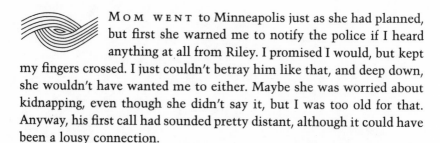 M O M   W E N T to Minneapolis just as she had planned, but first she warned me to notify the police if I heard anything at all from Riley. I promised I would, but kept my fingers crossed. I just couldn't betray him like that, and deep down, she wouldn't have wanted me to either. Maybe she was worried about kidnapping, even though she didn't say it, but I was too old for that. Anyway, his first call had sounded pretty distant, although it could have been a lousy connection.

I started taking my meals at the Oasis Cafe with Jake, and I got a kick out of it because he knew everyone in town, and they swapped extravagant yarns or told off-color jokes in low voices, raising the punch lines just loud enough for the waitresses to catch. One named Doreen had her eye out for Jake and usually traded the others for our table. She wore several pieces of turquoise jewelry and kept the top two buttons of her uniform undone. She called us Big Sweetie and Little Sweetie, and always smelled like Doublemint.

Nearly everybody in the Oasis had a nickname labeling their coffee cups, which hung on wooden racks behind the counter. I enjoyed trying to match the customers with their colorful monikers: Big Joe, Babe, Grasshopper, Heavy Duty, Short Stack, Skook. A few cups were turned upside down, honoring the patrons who had died. Although I didn't have a cup, Jake introduced me to the others as Shotgun, because I was always riding with him now. If we were talking to some of the local cowboys, he called me Number One Rowdy, the guy who hangs out behind the rodeo bucking chutes and cheers on the riders.

The cops ate in the Oasis too, usually sitting at the counter for sandwiches and coffee, then swiveling half a turn on the stools as if to survey the diners for suspects. Grady was in a few times and Jake nodded toward him, but you could tell things were cool. Mom had told Jake about Grady coming over, and the next morning when he stopped by the store for coffee, Jake told him off, concluding with the warning "Election's coming soon." After that, Grady stayed out of the store, although some of the other policemen came in to buy fishing gear and tennis shoes. To tell the truth, it made me a little jumpy to see them. They might have traced Riley's call, although I don't think I broke any laws by keeping quiet.

Mom called a couple times, telling me the seminar was going well. Once she was particularly excited. "After our training session for the day, we got to ride a riverboat down the Mississippi, a big old sternwheeler, just like Mark Twain wrote about."

"That's great, Mom. Are you sure it was the Mississippi? I thought it was farther east."

She clucked her tongue. "What are those schools teaching you? Don't you learn any geography? When I get back we're going to put a big map of the U.S. in your bedroom."

"I was just kidding, Mom," I said. A map would look horrible alongside the pictures of basketball players I kept up there.

"I haven't told you the best part," she said. "There was a dance band right on the boat, and I had several dances with one of the men from the seminars." Her voice got a little lower, taking on a confidential tone. "Not one of the participants — most of us are women. He's one of the actual directors, a big muck-a-muck who works right here in Minneapolis."

"Don't let him sweep you off your feet, Mom. Winters are pretty cold back there." I tried to picture him, a blond, no doubt.

"Don't you go worrying. He's not really my type. But it was fun, and it's nice to know a little bloom's still left on the rose."

"You haven't lost a thing, Mom," I said, and she seemed pleased with the compliment.

"Everything all right there? You eating okay? Be sure to get enough vegetables."

"I've got it covered, Mom. Don't *you* work too hard."

"I won't, but I'm ringing off for now. Got to run for class. Just one more thing. Any word of Riley?"

I shook my head. "Not a bit, unless the post office is keeping his cards tacked up with the Most Wanted posters. I haven't looked."

Her voice got lower. "Don't even kid about that. This is a dorm phone and I don't want anyone to know we've got the law mixed up in this. It's a sorry business." She paused. "Well, love you." She hung up, as usual, without pausing to say good-bye, as though her thoughts had already outpaced the conversation.

☆ ☆ ☆ ☆

Three days after my mother had left, a tribal policeman driving a white pickup with the reservation insignia stopped by the store. Getting out, he seemed huge, solid and tall, like an upright freezer.

Jake introduced us. "You haven't met my nephew, Culver. He's riding shotgun around here now. Number two man. This is Billyum Bruised-Head. His people were from Alberta, but moved out here. We go back a long way — high school football."

"Jake was the slowest halfback Gateway ever had," Billyum said. His hand was calloused and rough, but he shook lightly, the Indian way.

"I thought I was half fast," Jake said, pronouncing it like "half-assed."

"Not anymore," Billyum said. "You should see how you look from behind. Two hogs fighting under a sheet. Aaay." Turning to me, he said, "This boy's a lot better looking."

"Takes after his father." Jake pointed to the picture above the cash register. "Culver and his mother moved to town three weeks ago."

Billyum squinted at the picture a moment, then motioned us to the back of the store.

Jake poured three coffees and turned over an ammunition box to sit on. He pointed Billyum to the good chair. "Take a load off."

When Billyum sat, I saw he was wearing black cowboy boots with silver toeplates.

The two men talked about high school football, fishing, the progress of building the dam on the Upper Lost. I sipped my coffee and waited. Their talk seemed casual, but something about the way Billyum acted made me realize he was here on business. Jake knew it, too, but just waited politely until Billyum got around to it.

Eventually, he put his coffee cup down on the workbench and examined the Snap-On Tool calendar hanging above the bench. Miss June was holding a crescent wrench and wearing an orange bikini. Billyum pointed to the calendar's words. "Make your tool a Snap-On," he said.

"I'm always afraid mine's going to snap off," Jake said. "I'm way past the warranty" — and we all grinned.

Then Billyum got down to business. "Twenty-eight days is what I'm thinking. Kalim Kania's been in the river twenty-six days now."

Billyum sat down again and took out a small pocketknife. He began trimming his nails, picking each small sliver off his whipcord trousers and placing it in his olive shirt pocket. "His people want that boy back. Old Sylvester Silvertooth went down to the water and chanted. His grandmother threw in a medicine bundle."

"You think he's about ready to pop up, then?" Jake asked.

Billyum nodded. "Sure. After twenty-eight, twenty-nine days. He'll come up all right."

"Medicine works every time, doesn't it?" Jake sipped his coffee. "Pretty darned slow though."

Billyum shrugged. "Everybody's not in a hurry. But we need to start looking for that boy again, and I was hoping you could help."

"I'm full up with guide trips," Jake said. "This is my peak season." He spread his hands and shrugged. "Sorry, I'd like to help . . ."

"Suit yourself," Billyum said. He snapped the knife closed and put it in his pocket. "Did you know Kalim's aunt was Juniper Teewah? She might come back for his funeral, if we find him." He sipped his coffee and studied Jake.

My uncle put down his cup. "I didn't know that. She still in New Mexico, or what?"

"Albuquerque. Going on two years now. Hanging out with fancy artists. I hear she's part owner of a gallery." Billyum carried his cup to the sink and washed it out. "Well, I better go see about rounding up some more help."

"Never mind." Jake pushed aside some broken reels and a couple of snapped fly rod tips. He spread a map of the Lost River Wilderness Area on the workbench. "Lots of water to search, but most of them get found eventually, once they float."

Billyum traced a stretch of the river with his large finger. "I'll take some of the reservation boys and cover Whiskey Dick's down to Bakeoven. We got good access there from the reservation back roads."

"All right," Jake said. "I'll cover the stretch between Bakeoven and the Bronco."

"Think you can watch the rapids and the shore both?" Billyum asked.

"I'll row. Shotgun here can keep his eyes peeled. We won't let him slip by."

"No we won't," I said, excited about the prospect of a river trip with Jake.

Billyum studied me. "Your father had great eyes. He could see a doe's ear flick in a juniper flat. You got good eyes?"

"Pretty good." I was curious about this talk of my father and wondered how Billyum had known him. And I was also curious about the woman Juniper.

"You're both hired, then," Billyum said. "Double trouble."

"It's a deal," Jake said. "How much you paying?"

"Same as the last time. Next Ceremonial Days, you can eat all the salmon and elk you want."

"I'm afraid I'll jump an income tax bracket," Jake said.

"That's only a problem for you white guys." Billyum stood and put on his cap. "Well, better get back to the rez. Stop the damn crime wave." He touched my shoulder. "Good meeting you. I won't hold Jake against you. A man can choose his friends, but gets stuck with his relations."

"We'll be on the river in two days," Jake said. "I've got to call old Jed to cover the store. He's a retired salesman, but he'll help us out."

"I'm stopping by to tell the sheriff," Billyum said. "He should put a boat on the water."

"Tell him if you want, but there's not much point," Jake said. "Grady couldn't find his butt in the bathtub."

After Billyum left, Jake and I stayed at the back of the store and talked. No customers came in for over half an hour. I was so excited about going on the Lost with my uncle, I could barely keep quiet, but I did because I didn't want to seem like a dude. I knew my mother wouldn't approve, that she'd worry herself sick every minute if she knew, so I thought I'd have to think up some excuse.

According to my uncle, the Lost claimed a lot of lives year round, but summers were the worst. Fishermen stepped in deep holes with the ankle straps of their waders tied too tightly to wriggle free; boaters failed to fasten the lower cinches of their life vests, so when they went into whitewater, the force ripped the vests over their heads like wet T-shirts; drunks waded into fast water and lost their footing, then banged their heads against the rocks.

But Kalim's circumstances appeared to be different. The young man was only a few months past twenty-one when a troop of Boy Scouts had seen him standing on the railroad bridge at White River Junction. He had waved as the boats passed beneath the bridge, and they noticed he was wearing a crimson and black RedWing jacket. Some heard a shout, and when they looked back to the bridge it was empty. One boy reported he thought that he had seen someone else standing in the Russian olives along the riverbank, but he couldn't be certain. The scouts had stopped for lunch at Whiskey Dick's, two miles below the bridge, and while eating they were startled to see someone floating down the river face first. They had tried to get out to the body, but they were too slow. Later they had stopped downstream and searched the banks, but found no sign. Everyone agreed the body was wearing a RedWing jacket.

"Once they go down in the Lost, they stay under about four weeks," Jake said. "Sometimes longer. Bloat depends on the water temperature, whether they drank beer and ate a pizza." His voice trailed. "Maybe they don't come up at all. There's sections that have old lava tubes. Some are blind — no outlets. It's always better if you get a floater before he goes down."

"Yes," I said. I figured we were both thinking about my father.

"Well, we better get some gear together. Those scouts planted a lot of Bureau of Land Management saplings hoping they'll get big enough to stop soil erosion. We'll take buckets and water them along the way. It gets mighty hot and it's good to have some shade."

"And we can fish a little?" I asked.

"You bet. We'll cook them up in the pan. I got to call Jed. He'll probably want time and a half."

"You pay time and a half? What about me?"

He grinned. "You're still learning. Hell, I ought to charge for showing you the ropes. Anyway, you're family and that makes it special."

"You can't spend special."

"You're keeping me broke in Pepsi and jelly rolls. Listen, be sure to pack a sweatshirt and windbreaker. It gets cold at night."

"What about that guy on the bridge? Think he jumped?"

"It's hard to say." Jake dumped the grounds from his coffee cup. "I imagine Billyum asked around, talked to his family, guys he works with, and girlfriend. Kalim was a damn good high school basketball player. Second team all-state. But he flunked out of college and started working in the woods."

"Seems like a waste," I said.

Jake wiped his cup with a paper towel. "Billyum probably checked the riverbank to see if he left anything behind. A good cop makes sense of that stuff . . ."

"What kind of stuff?"

Jake picked up a broken fly rod from the repair rack. We were waiting for the new tip section from Fenwick. He flicked it back and forth a couple of times, but the action was too stiff without the tip. "Say a fellow has some trouble with the wife or business — just decides to end it." Jake scowled at the rod. "He leaves a bottle and his fly rod on the riverbank. Now a lot of guys drink too much, go out in deep water, and lose their footing — but they're planning to fish. A rod on the bank is a dead giveaway, see?"

"I get it," I said. "You're like a regular detective."

Jake shook his head. "It's pretty simple. Take a real drowning. Some guy steps into a deep hole. His waders fill with water, but the air pocket at the bottom flips him upside down, just like that." He tapped the rod butt against the floor. "Let's say the dummy tied his ankle straps too tight and he can't kick free. Then his head hits a rock." Jake held out the broken rod. "Four weeks later you find that guy still gripping the rod butt like a vice. Can't pry open his fingers."

"And the creel might still be on him, but the body's so bloated there's no way to get it off until the coroner cuts the straps. Old Doc Paisley, Gateway's retired coroner, used to brag he never bought a fly — just took the ones he found in drowned guys' creels."

I shook my head. "Unbelievable."

"Well, he was a windy old fart, so who knows. He never bought any here." Jake put the rod back in the holder. "Sometimes there's crawdads inside the creel, eating the guy's catch. In the valley, they have crawdad festivals and people line up to eat those scavengers. Not me."

Thinking about it, I shivered a little. Not me either, I thought.

"But if you find that creel on the bank, along with all the fancy flies and special tackle he's bought over the years, then you think it over. Maybe this guy's been to Idaho and fished the Silver, Oregon for the Deschutes, the Gallatin in Montana. Each place he's picked up some local flies, special lures. He isn't planning to take all that stuff down with him. That's a waste, so he leaves it on the bank — maybe for a relative, maybe for the next fisherman that happens along. Who knows exactly what someone's thinking before he takes the plunge."

I nodded. I was giving the creel above the coffeepot a long, hard look, and Jake saw me.

He picked it up, rattling that morning's coffee change. "Don't worry. This didn't come off a floater. It belonged to your granddad. I just keep it here to remind me . . . of the good times we all used to have."

A customer came in and Jake started for the front of the store, then stopped. "When you find them," he said, "it never matters how tall they are or how much money's in the bank account, or how much the kids love them. They all look pretty small floating facedown in two feet of water."

I had thought it over while Jake was talking. "That guy wouldn't have been fishing from a railroad bridge. That's not how you fish the Lost."

"No, he wasn't fishing," Jake said. "We know that for damn sure."

6

 AFTER TWO DAYS on the river, I stopped imagining that every odd-shaped log was the drowned boy. I had conjured him so many times, straining my eyes to search the deadfall at the water's edge, that I believed I might be a little disappointed when we found him. Jake had grown quieter, that good humor and confidence he had always shown in the store wearing down to a dark moodiness. During the long stretches when conversation lulled, I just kept quiet and studied the river banks. Twice I had sounded false alarms, and each time my uncle had shipped the oars while his gaze followed my quivering finger. "Log," he muttered, then rowed to shore anyway, emphasizing my mistake. "I can't describe it, how a floater looks," he said, "but you'll know when your gut clenches. That's how you tell." Even so, I saw him pull close to shore a couple times, searching some debris along the eddies. He imagined he'd seen the boy, too.

"Maybe he didn't drown after all," I said. "Maybe he was just stunned and crawled out along the bank somewhere."

"Where would he be now, then?" my uncle asked. "Don't you think he'd show up?"

"Maybe he's got amnesia. Maybe a snake bit him."

"You're so damn raw." He chuckled, the glum mood broken. "You've been watching too much TV. Hardly anybody gets amnesia. And no one dies of snakebite. They just get puke sick."

Twice we saw buzzards, and he pulled to shore for a closer look. Once it was a bloated cow poisoned in a patch of ragwort, and the second was a small deer that had gotten a back leg tangled in fence wire. The coyotes had been there first, and the buzzards were eating only the scattered remains.

We had four large buckets in the boat and two short-handled shovels. Stopping every couple hours, we carried water to the BLM saplings. The bureau had selected ponderosa pines, black alders, Russian olives, and Jake had argued with the regional director because not all the species were indigenous to that area. Less than half survived the withering heat away from the riverbank, and these had to be watered regularly by passers-by. We used the shovels to dig little trenches around the saplings so the water we carried wouldn't run downhill.

Before nightfall we came to a sagebrush and juniper flat containing one old abandoned prospector's cabin. Someone had spray-painted a sign on one weather-beaten wall: RATTLESNAKE TEST AREA. PLEASE ENTER AND BE PART OF OUR SURVEY.

After dinner the wind blew, and clouds scuttled across a sky lighted by a gibbous moon. Coyotes howled from the flatland above the steep basalt canyons, and birds whistled in the willows a quarter mile upstream.

"You hear that?" my uncle asked.

"The coyotes?" They sounded so mournful, but I shivered when I thought of the deer they had torn apart.

He shook his head. "The other sound. Like birds."

"What are they? Chukars?"

"The Indians say they're *Steah-hah.* Stick Indians. According to the legend, *Steah-hah* come when you're in some kind of trouble, spiritual trouble maybe. Or when you're lost in the darkness, they whistle like night birds. If you're a good person, they lead you to safety. And if you're bad . . ." He drew a finger across his throat and made a gurgling sound. "Well, it's better to be a good person." He laughed. "Of course, it's all a bunch of hokum, but the dudes like it. A story to take home from the trip."

"You got any trouble?" I asked.

"Nothing two drinks won't fix." He laughed. "How about you? I figure you made up a big story to tell your mom."

I shrugged. "I just said I'd been working too hard and was going off camping for a couple days."

"I hope you kept your fingers crossed," he said. "Well, I guess we know *Steah-hah* are calling for you. I can sleep tight."

Jake took a handful of wooden matches and walked a few yards away from the fire, then tossed the matches out toward the darkness. "Here." He handed me some. "Give them a toss."

"Are you serious?" I held on to the matches because I didn't want to seem foolish. "Is this a snipe hunt?"

"I have the fellas do this." He walked to the other side of the fire and threw some other matches downstream. "Stick Indians like matches because they live in darkness. When Billyum takes his nieces and nephews up huckleberrying, he always gives them matches to throw. That way if the kids get lost, the Stick Indians will bring them home safely."

"All right, then," I said and tossed a few into the underbrush.

After we had settled down, he poured a couple cups of coffee and added a shot of Seagram's Seven to each. "You do get some desperate characters down here. A few years back, a trapper shot a game warden not far from here. The warden came into his camp to check his license and gear, see if he had any illegal camp meat."

"Riley told me about it," I said. "He was interested in the trial. It took them a long time to catch that guy." I hadn't paid much attention to Riley because I was only twelve then.

"That's right. Old Wilbur — that was his name — covered most of the West before they caught him. The state police and game wardens were combing everyplace, but he could survive in the wilderness. That's what he did best. A couple times before I took a trip downriver, the cops tried to show me wanted posters. But I refused to look. If I was way off in the wilds and a guy came into my camp, I'd just pour him a drink, hand him a hunk of steak left over from supper, and act natural as pie. I'd rather think he was just another fisherman or boater instead of some desperado that dropped a game warden, if you see what I mean."

"Yes," I said. "I see what you're getting at."

"I don't want to be a dead hero." He poured himself another half cup of coffee, then filled the cup with Seagram's. Nodding my way, he asked, "Just a splash?"

"Sure," I said, "but I'm getting a little tired."

"You're relaxing," he said, stirring the fire. "The dudes I bring down here finally relax after a day or two. It's calming to get away from the day-to-day routine. Some of those guys work their butts off fifty-one weeks a year so they can feed their families, buy the kids new shoes, get their teeth filled. They're the real heroes, just meeting the bills each month and praying the kids don't grow too fast or need braces. They get one week off a year and I show them a good time.

"I set up a little booth at the sportsman's shows, take a few brochures and some pictures of the river and big fish. The other booths have guides from Canada and Alaska showing fancier brochures. Some of the hard-working stiffs want to go north. Hell, who blames them? But they can't afford to, so they come with me."

He held the coffee cup in his hands as if feeling its warmth. "Once they're down here awhile, maybe they get to talking. Usually the old dreams are sliding away. Everybody's losing ground. One of their kids goes bad on booze; Daddy's sweetheart gets knocked up by some no-'count. These men start talking a little, real quiet at first, because they're not used to spilling their guts at the plant or shop. Here on the river they can say what they feel. No danger of it getting back."

"What about Riley?" I asked when he paused. "Do you think they're going to catch him?"

Jake's eyes gleamed in the firelight. "Riley was long suffering. I'm not saying what he did was exactly square, but he made a break. I'm sure it wasn't easy for him — always living in your father's shadow like that. Your mother's a gem — don't get me wrong — but she's not a saint." He lifted his cup and drank.

"Maybe you've got something there," I said after thinking about it a moment. I realized there had been times when Riley seemed to want to get closer. But I treated him indifferently, always figuring he wasn't really my father, but just a nice guy my mother had married. "You ever think of making a change yourself?"

"This river and I go pretty far back," Jake said. "Your grandfather taught us boys how to fish. In the old days we all rode the train up after the old man finished putting out the paper. After dark, when our creels were bulging with fish, we'd wait on the tracks and ride the night freight back. During those waits, Dave and I hatched big plans to start up a guide business."

He finished his whiskeyed coffee and set down the cup. "Right now, I'm just here to have a good time and treat the dudes square. And if you want to learn a few tricks, get to know this river, you might think of spelling me." He winked. "Partners in a way. The Top Hand and the Little Wrangler."

We turned in shortly after that. The wind died and the coyotes quit howling. The night birds were quiet, too, and after a while, when the fire quit hissing, all I heard were Jake's snores and the lap of the small waves against the boat. I thought of what he had said about the *Steah-hah* and the working guys being heroes. Maybe Riley was a kind of hero, too, and I never gave him enough credit. He did go out of his way to help. One time after a Grass Valley bully bloodied my nose, Riley bought boxing gloves and took me into the basement. We boxed each night until my wrists ached, even though my mother called it barbaric. Riley insisted it was survival, and after I thumped that kid, Riley handed me ten dollars and instructed me not to tell Mom.

Thinking of the times Riley had been good to me, I slipped out of my sleeping bag and crawled from the tent, so as not to disturb Jake. I grabbed a handful of kitchen matches and carried them a few yards out into the sagebrush. I didn't really believe in such *Steah-hah* stuff, but what could it hurt? If a guy like Billyum did it, maybe there was something to it.

I tossed the handful of matches out toward the tall sagebrush thicket, which gleamed silvery white in the moonlight. "Take care of Riley, you guys," I whispered. "Take good care."

☆ ☆ ☆ ☆ ☆

We were just finishing breakfast the next morning when my uncle put a plate of pancakes and sausages on a flat rock, along with a cup of coffee. "Come and get it!" he yelled, and except for the coffee, I thought he was talking to a couple of scolding magpies in a broken juniper.

An old Indian emerged from the tall sagebrush patch near the cabin. He was carrying a fishing pole and a light sleeping bag. Two creels hung from his shoulders, each one so heavy with fish the tails hung out and he couldn't fasten the leather straps. Although he smiled at Jake, his eyes were hidden behind dark round sunglasses.

"Thought it might be you," Jake said. "This was always one of your favorite stretches. Culver, this is Sylvester Silvertooth, one of the top men on the reservation. And a pretty decent fisherman."

"Good to meet you," I said.

Sylvester shook hands, then started eating. "Your uncle's a pretty decent cook, too," he said. "Make somebody a good wife, if he wasn't stump ugly." He concentrated on his food, remaining quiet until he had nearly cleaned his plate. "All I brought was pemmican and some Hershey bars. Damn chocolate melted."

"You could eat your fish." Jake nodded at the catch.

The old man shook his head. "Gonna sell these to the restaurant at the lodge. Tourists want them fresh caught by real Indians." He grinned. "That's me. One hundred percent full blood."

"You drowning worms?" Jake asked.

Sylvester drank some of his coffee. "The big ones are lying deep. I weight Salmon flies, bump them along the bottom." He finished his sausage, then pointed the fork at the last pancake. "Anybody want that?"

"Go ahead," Jake said. "But I thought you were supposed to live off the land."

"I do. Soon as I got up this morning, I knew some white guy was fixing my breakfast."

Sylvester finished his pancake. As he held the coffee cup, his hand trembled a little. "I know you're down here looking for my nephew. Thanks for helping out."

"Sure," Jake said. "We're sorry about the boy."

The old man set down his cup. "He was a good kid, but after high school, he sort of slipped away . . . Tried a little gypo logging, odd jobs at the mill. After a while, he should have straightened out."

"You're looking for him, too," Jake said.

Sylvester nodded. "I built a little sweat house right where Deer Creek comes in. It's hid pretty good but you can stop by anytime, Jake. The boy, too."

"Thanks. I appreciate that," my uncle said.

"Last night, I had a good sweat, used sage and juniper to get out the impurities. When I was cooling off in the river, I heard them talking. Kalim's down around South Junction."

Jake nodded. "That's pretty far down. If you're right, we've got to run through Bronco Rapids." He squinted at Sylvester.

"My hearing's still good, but I can't walk that far."

Sylvester picked up the creels. "Going to the lodge while these are still fresh. Thanks, Jake." He disappeared into the tall sagebrush.

"How did you know he was out there?" I asked.

"Shh. Listen."

We were quiet for a good two minutes. I didn't hear anything but the river and some magpies scolding downstream. "I don't hear him," I said.

"I didn't know Sylvester was coming," Jake said. "But somebody was. First, it's what you *don't* hear. Things get quiet in a direction. Frogs quit croaking. The blackbirds hush. Something's coming. Then the magpies start scolding and you know company's arrived."

"I'll try to remember that," I said. "You think Sylvester is right about Kalim?"

Jake shrugged. "He's got to be someplace."

"Sylvester was talking about the *Steah-hah*, wasn't he? He was listening to the Stick Indians."

Jake snorted. "You catch on pretty fast. He *thinks* he was. Sylvester didn't want to say their name — speak it aloud. Indians are superstitious like that." Shaking his head, my uncle added, "I really didn't want to go through Bronco Rapids this trip. Chancy."

7

 AFTER BREAKING CAMP we drifted downriver toward the Bronco and South Junction, leaving the tree-lined shore and occasional green meadows of the upper run. Now the landscape turned somber, with spindly junipers dotting the gray-brown talus slopes. The Lost entered sullen canyons where steep basalt walls squeezed the water into a series of deep channels. "The Narrows," Jake said, using the oar to push away from a boulder. "No fishing here. If Kalim's caught in a deep channel, the current will keep him down."

I nodded but didn't say anything. We both felt glum at the idea of not finding him.

With few places to search for a floater, we made good time. Just before noon, we left the Narrows and entered some of the best country on the Lost, according to Jake.

Blue-green firs timbered the high canyons and tall ponderosas bordered the riverbanks. Occasionally the sweet smell of mock orange drifted in the air. Chutes and rooster tails alternated with deep holes and slick eddies. The rich landscape lifted our spirits, and I was aching to break out the fishing poles.

Jake beached the boat at a small meadow dense with pines and shaggy trees I didn't recognize. Where sunlight penetrated the canopy, thick elk grass grew. Someone had fashioned a picnic table with weathered wood, and it rested on a thick pine-needle carpet. "How'd that table get here?" I asked.

"Hard work. This place used to be knee-deep in garbage from an old homesteader's dump, but Dave and I hauled it out two gunnysacks at a time. That's all we could fit in our boat. Just one if the fish grew too big." He winked at me. "After cleaning up, we built that table so we could sit down to a half-civilized meal."

"What do you call this place?"

"Barn Hole. I thought you'd recognize it from that picture in the store. Some damn good fishing water."

I wouldn't have recognized the setting because the barn had fallen the way they do after one too many winters or windstorms. In Black Diamond we had rented a place with a dilapidated dairy barn, and even though Riley warned me to stay out, I played there whenever I had the chance. One morning I was amazed to discover the barn down; I hadn't heard it tumble in the night.

"Take a look," Jake said, and I poked among the weathered boards until I found the barn door they had almost covered with thick-sided fish. The door still held a rusty horseshoe, and I was surprised I had missed it in the photo.

When I returned to the boat, Jake had brought out two crayfish viewers from the storage compartments under the seat. The viewers were made from a pane of glass fifteen inches square and had wooden sides six inches high. He demonstrated how to hold the wooden sides and set the glass flat in the shallow water near the barn. It was like looking at the river bottom through a window.

"Roll over the rocks real careful," he said. "Don't muddy the water. Underneath are crayfish, some with soft shells. Right after they molt, they need protection and hide. Don't let Sylvester fool you. He wasn't using Salmon flies to catch those lunkers. I saw the way his pole was rigged. Crayfish."

If the crayfish had soft, flexible shells, we put them in a coffee can. Hard-shelled crayfish we left in the river. After forty-five minutes, we had a dozen. "Let's give these a try," Jake said, straightening and grabbing his back. "Got a damn cramp."

We carried the crayfish and spinning gear to the deep pools at the lower end of the sagebrush flat, a couple hundred yards below the barn. Jake rigged the crayfish by cutting a small piece of surgical tubing and running the spinning line through it. With his pliers he cut a two-inch strip of lead and shoved it into the surgical tubing, wedging the line between the lead and the tubing. "If the lead hangs on the bottom," he said, "you can pull it out of the tubing without losing the crayfish. This early in the season, good soft ones are hard to come by."

Jake tied a loop in the end of the monofilament line. Then he took an ice pick with a flattened, notched end. Placing the loop in the notch, he stuck the pick into the crayfish behind the first section of tail, then shoved the pick through the middle of the crayfish, bringing the loop out just under the head. After withdrawing the pick, he tied a #6 treble hook to the line and pulled it back into the soft flesh of the crayfish.

Handing me the pole, he said, "Cast upstream and let it bounce along the bottom. When a fish takes the crayfish, he'll sort of mouth it to see if it's soft, and if it is, he swallows it. But if he feels the line drag, that odd pull, he lets go. So when it stops, you've got to give slack. Back off three turns, count to five, and set the hook."

The first try, I made an awkward cast that sent the crayfish and lead splashing into the water about twenty feet offshore. "That's a damn awkward rigging."

"Try again. Take a wide swing and let it sail. You got to cast farther and more upstream."

I flung off two of the precious crayfish before I got a cast right where Jake wanted, and I could feel the lead tick the gravel bottom during the drift. Jake watched the pole tip; the little bob showed the lead was bouncing along the rocky bottom. I felt the bobbing stop before the end of a drift and feared a snag, but Jake said, "Back it off now. Three turns."

I turned the handle backwards, feeding three coils off the spool and through the guides.

"Now!"

Snapping my wrist back, I set the hook. The pole bent nearly double.

"Loosen the drag, damn it!"

The pole jerked again and again, while I fumbled to release the drag screw. The line screamed out and the reel smoked as the fish coursed downstream with the current.

"Turn that bastard while you still got line."

I snubbed the fish, then began reeling slack as it turned back.

When it was in the deep pool, Jake warned, "Don't let him get snagged on the bottom. Keep the pole tip up."

I knew by the way the fish had run it was a lunker, and Jake didn't want it to die snagged on the river bottom, the crayfish and treble hook deep in its gut.

I played it for another five minutes, trying to force it to the surface, but it stayed deep. "Why won't he jump?"

"Hooked too deep. He's got a bellyache."

When the fish played out, I eased it to shore, and Jake moved quietly below him, wading in the shallow water. His hand and forearm submerged, he held the net close to the river bottom. I backed away from the river, forcing the trout into the shallows. A silver flame spurting out of the dark green pool, the fish paused in the current.

Taking care not to foul the line, Jake brought the net up, and as the fish lunged, he swept it into the net. Holding high the threshing fish, he grinned. "You caught a log!"

"What a fish!" It was as large as a steelhead, but thicker.

"A dandy." Jake clubbed the fish while it still struggled in the net. "Four and a half pounds. Maybe five."

"That's the biggest fish I ever caught," I said. And it was a beauty. The deep red rainbow covered half of its silver side.

"Get a couple more," he said. "I'll clean this one and toss it in the ice chest. Back home, we'll have a barbecue."

Before we ran out of crayfish I caught two smaller trout; each one was close to three pounds. Bringing them out in the net, Jake whooped and shouted like a boy at a circus.

"Good grits," Jake said, finishing the last bite of fish on his plate. He had baked them in the Dutch oven, adding brown sugar and onions for flavor. "Hats off to the fisherman." He removed his cap, then put it back on his head. "You caught some lunkers, damn nice fish."

"The chef didn't do a bad job of cooking them either," I said. Fish had never tasted so good. "I wish we could stay three days. Maybe we could cover the barn door with trout, like in the picture. Think so?"

He grinned. "These are damn nice fish, no flies on them. But to be honest, the fish were bigger in the old days. Now there's so many people. A lot more pressure on the river."

"We've only seen a couple other boats," I said. "And Sylvester."

He nodded. "It's still good water, don't get me wrong. But in the old days, maybe you wouldn't see anyone else for three or four days. Listen, you'll like this story. One time Dave and I were heading out to fish and we ran into a guy who spent opening day elbow to asshole with other fishermen on some pissy stream near the city, jockeying for eight-inch hatchery trout the fish commission planted. Now this guy was trying to do some serious fishing. Planned to go to Deep Creek. That's way up above here. Dave told him, 'Don't go there. It's all fished out.' This dude looked crestfallen. 'What do you mean?' he asked. Dave scowled and said, 'A guy was up there just *last* week.'"

We both laughed. "That would be something," I said.

"You know, I've got this idea about your dad — had it for a long time.

We'd bring down some cement, mix it up, and then think of fancy words to put on a plaque. See, we'd build a memorial for your father. Maybe say something about your grandfather and the old-time guides."

"That's a great idea," I said. "Mom could help us, too. She's got a way with words."

He held up his hands, palms facing out. "Whoa. Let's not bring her in quite yet, until we get the blueprint. Then we can surprise her. You know, she's pretty touchy about this river."

I broke a stick and tossed it into the fire. "She sure looked happy in that picture. But she told me she never went fishing again."

He squinted. "That was a great trip. A classic." Looking around, he took a deep breath. "Smell those pines. Dave loved this place. He claimed he could hear those big ponderosas breathing. And if you move a few yards away from the fire, you can see a couple trillion stars."

He stepped away, tilting back his head to stare into the night sky. I did the same, and my eyes swam at the sheer beauty of it. "What are those other trees? The shaggy ones?"

"Good eyes," he said. "Those are Lebanon cedars. This is the single place they grow on the river. Originally, they came from the holy land, but no one knows how those got here."

"One of the early guides could have planted them."

"It's a puzzler." He was still staring into the sky. "Flying saucers, maybe. One of Sniffy's buddies."

"On the bottom of that picture, Mom wrote she had a marvelous time."

"Did she?" He glanced at me. "I haven't taken it down in years."

"The date's on the picture. Dad drowned later that year."

Jake nodded and raised his hands to the stars. "Old Dave is looking down on us, I imagine."

I paused. "She almost never talks about his death anymore."

"She's carrying it deep, like a piece of flint way inside her belly."

☆
☆ ☆ ☆
☆

"Right there," I said, pointing at a deadfall alder. "In the shadows." My gut had tightened exactly the way Jake had said it would as soon as I had seen the floating body.

Jake squinted a moment, then nodded. "Looks like we found him. Good eyes." He had to bring the boat around against the current, and as he rowed closer, I could see the body nudging back and forth against the deadfall. The jeans and jacket were muddy and camouflaged with leaves, but a bit of one crimson sleeve showed each time the current gently rolled the body.

The floater was turned facedown in the murky water, and I was glad for that. The shadows and light made the river bottom difficult to see, so Jake measured the depth with an oar, just to be sure there were no deep holes. After snubbing the boat on a branch close to the shore, he took out the heavy rubber body bag from the storage compartment beneath the seat, stepped out of the boat, and carried the bag up the steep cutbank. Then he unfolded the bag and unzipped the wide, waterproof zipper. The dull gray rubber had blocked letters: JACKSON COUNTY SHERIFF'S DEPARTMENT.

"Too bad there's no beach here," he said. "We'll have to pull him to shore and heave him up the cutbank."

"Can't we just put him in the boat?" I asked.

"We could, but it's better to let him drip dry a little." He slid back down the cutbank.

When I got out of the boat, I almost fell on the slippery rocks.

"Watch your goddamn footing," Jake said. "I don't need another casualty." He waded over to the body and grabbed the jacket between the left shoulder and the arm.

"Take a hold," he said. "You got to free that one foot, the way it's caught in the brush."

I broke a brittle limb off the tree and tried prying the wedged foot clear. Somehow he had lost one shoe, although the sock was still on. The tennis shoe on the other foot had a crimson lace, matching the jacket sleeve.

"Grab hold, for Christ's sakes. You've had a tetanus shot."

I grabbed the calf. The flesh beneath the wet denim felt soft and slippery from being in the water so long. I'll bet you never get used to this, I thought. When I jerked, the leg came free and the current swung both legs against my waders.

"Let's reel him in." Jake began wading toward the shore, towing the sodden body along. I just followed, keeping a light grip on the calf, halfway steering.

As he neared the cutbank, he slowed. "In the shallows, he'll get real heavy. No buoyancy. We'll need to rest a minute before we heave him up the bank."

"All right, then." I wiped my forehead, a little surprised at how hard I was sweating. Glancing across the river, I saw two red-headed canvasbacks flash low over the water.

Jake took a couple deep breaths. "Lift the legs high. Grab just below the knees and lift. No pussying around."

When I lifted the legs, the jacket hiked up a little so I could see the beaded belt that spelled out K A L I M — red letters against dark blue.

Jake grunted as he lifted the heavy chest and shoulders; I realized he had given me the lighter end. "We'll swing twice, then heave him up," he said. "Here goes. One!"

The body was heavy as hell, and for the first time, I smelled the stench.

"Two!"

I tried swinging harder but couldn't get the rhythm.

"Heave."

We got the body part way up the cutbank, but not to the flat grassy part. As it started slipping back down, Jake ducked, catching the weight with his shoulder. "Give a hand here, Culver. God damn it!"

With my left hand, I grabbed Kalim's belt and lifted his butt with my right, and we rolled him up on the flat spot somehow, but the head flopped around, revealing where the face should have been.

Even though I tried averting my eyes, I had seen too much, something straight out of nightmares. "Jesus." I choked. "What happened to his face?"

Jake took a large blue bandanna from his pocket and covered the head. "Crayfish chewed on him. It's better if you don't look."

I stumbled over to a flat rock and sat for a few minutes, fighting off the urge to puke. With the bloat and no face, the body could be anyone. It's not my father, I thought. This is a young Indian man. Running my fingers through the thick warm grass, I kept repeating, His people want him back, his people want him back.

"Come take a squint at this, Culver."

After a couple of minutes, I stood and stepped closer to my uncle. The grass around Kalim was all wet, and I didn't notice the smell so much anymore, but the flies were starting to gather and Jake kept brushing them away with his hand. "Take a close look." He squatted beside the body, pointing at the letterman's jacket.

I saw the small hole high up on the back, just to the right of the spine. "What's it about?"

"You tell me."

"Caught a snag maybe. Barbed wire."

"Barbed wire makes a tear, not a hole. Help me turn him. Don't look at the face now."

As I got my hands under the small of his back and rolled him, I felt something hard and heavy, bulging his jacket pockets.

Kalim was on his back, and Jake pulled the bandanna over the face.

"He's still wearing his medicine pouch." Jake touched the leather bag that hung from a thong around his neck. "But it didn't help him much."

I saw the pouch all right, but I was staring to the side of it, at the jagged hole in his shirt.

Jake lifted the shirt and let out his breath. "Somebody shot him all right. He was stone dead when he hit the water."

"What the hell happened, I wonder!"

Jake shook his head. "Just be glad we found him. Otherwise, somebody gets by with murder."

He stood, slapping me on the back. "You're going to be a hero — name in the paper, all that sort of thing."

I felt a rush of elation. It was a good thing we had done, I decided. Even though I hadn't known him, I felt as if maybe I could have, because he was only a few years older than I was, and if things were a little different we might have played ball together, something like that. Kalim's relatives were going to be pleased that he wasn't still lost, and whoever was responsible for shooting him would have to pay.

We put Kalim in the body bag and Jake zipped it closed. Then we slid the bag down to the boat and lifted him in. "I guess we'd better get this down to South Junction," Jake said. "We're losing the light, and I don't want to find any new rocks in the Bronco."

☆ ☆ ☆ ☆

Just before we went into the rapids, Jake shifted the oars and cinched his life vest tight. "Make sure," he said, nodding at me, and I gave my cinches another pull, too. "All set," I said.

The Bronco was treacherous. I could see jagged rocks teething out of the whitewater. Jake kept to the middle to avoid the rocks at the head of the run and the smooth boulders lining the main chute. Each rapid slammed the boat with a loud *chunk*, throwing the nose high and tugging at the bow, trying to spin us onto the rocks. The seat jarred my spine, but I kept grinning at Jake, like I was having fun.

He fought the rapids' pull with long, deep oar strokes, keeping the boat away from the rocks until it was sucked into the long curling chute of slick water.

The chute hurled the boat downstream like a toboggan, skimming past the large boulders. In spite of Jake's efforts to keep the nose downstream, we were gripped by a momentary eddy and flung sideways against one of the large rocks.

64

Water poured over the side of the boat, soaking my right forearm. When Jake tried to push off the boulder with an oar, the blade snapped. "God damn it," he shouted, his eyes widening with fury as he flung the broken oar with such force it sailed onto the riverbank. "Bail!" he yelled, and I quit clutching the gunwale long enough to grab one of the floating coffee cans.

Plunging his hand through the ankle-deep water, he grabbed the spare oar from the boat bottom and stood, using his full strength to push the water-laden boat off the boulder and into the chute once again.

I bailed furiously, pushing the body bag aside and flinging half cans of water over the side.

As I glanced at Jake, his face was red. "Goddamn but she's heavy," he said.

I bailed harder, until the body bag quit floating and rested on the bottom planks.

When we made it through the rooster tail at the lower end of the rapids, Jake pulled the boat into shore. Both of us got out for a minute and stood in the sand.

"Sonofabitching oar," he said. "Damn near cost me my boat."

"I thought we'd bought the farm," I said.

"You never go through that fucking rapids the same way twice, no matter where you start. Those currents shift with the water levels. Sometimes you can slide through slick as a whistle. Others you hang on every rock." He looked me over a minute. "You look like hell," he said. "You really do. A kid is supposed to look good." He sat on a rock and laughed, and we both felt better. After a couple of minutes he got up and pulled out a pint of Yukon Jack from under the seat. Taking off the lid, he handed me the bottle. "Your first time through the Bronco. And you're here to tell the tale."

When the bottle was almost gone and the shadows on the water were angling toward the far shore, I asked, "How was it when my father drowned?"

Jake stood, brushing off his pants. For a moment, I thought he was going to get back in the boat without speaking. But he cleared his throat and started telling the story, measuring each word to get it right.

"We could have walked up from South Junction. That's how the other fishermen were doing it, because the water was too high that spring. But we were in our twenties and had a new boat and thought nothing could stop us. So we decided to fish the Barn Hole, then run the Bronco — save ourselves lots of walking.

"The water was so high you could barely see the rocks, but we slipped by them fine and slid into the chute. Just before the rooster tail, the boat hit something, part of a big tree trunk washed down in the spring floods. We both tried pushing off, but a wall of water flipped the boat. I was swept around, but Dave went underneath. The current banged me against rocks and kept sucking me under. Each time I came up looking for Dave. He finally surfaced but without a jacket. Maybe it wasn't on tight and the water tore it off, but probably it caught on a branch, holding him under, so he had to shed it to get clear."

I shuddered a little, thinking of the tough choice to wriggle out of a life jacket in the Bronco.

"Fighting for every inch, I closed the distance, until I grabbed his shirt and we spun a moment, locked together. His arm seemed broken, I remember that, and when the current tumbled us against a big rock in the rooster tail, things went black. I came to, choking on water, and I had a hunk of flannel clutched in my fist."

Jake stared at his hands, thick with calluses and rough from years on the river. "I tried, but I just couldn't hold him. Below the rapids, I crawled ashore and searched the riverbank until way past dark. I kept shouting and cursing but there was no Dave.

"I hiked to South Junction and called the sheriff. The worst part was calling your mother later that night. When I heard her voice go dead on the other end of the line, I felt cold all over, like it was me lying on the river bottom, drowned."

He started untying the boat line. "It hurt me most we never found him. When I do find them, like Kalim here, it eases the hurt just a bit."

I understood a little of what he meant. Although the discovery of Kalim's murder was terrible, at least his relatives would know the outcome. With my father, things never seemed to settle. "Thanks, Uncle Jake. Thanks for telling me. I never believed it was your fault."

He nodded. "Your mother does, though, even if she stays quiet. I remember that time she came on the train. We had it out." He threw the tie line into the boat. "I lived, so I get the blame. That's how she is."

8

AT SOUTH JUNCTION, we unloaded the body bag and made camp. Jake hiked up the dirt-track fisherman's road to the nearest farmhouse while I "stood watch," as he called it — not that Kalim was going anywhere. Before leaving, Jake suggested that I catch some trout for dinner, and he pointed out some good water with grassy hummocks extending into the river.

Fishing with an Adams fly as he had recommended, I caught six nice fish in an hour. By that time it was getting so dark I could hardly see the small fly against the gray water. Bats darted out from the basalt cliffs, and a couple made quick passes at my fly on the back cast, flicking aside at the last second.

Returning to camp, I quickly cleaned the fish near the boat. I was getting hungry but didn't want to cook until Jake returned, so I ate a couple handfuls of Fig Newtons, washing them down with sodas from the ice chest. Still hungry, I ate half a box of crackers, then built a fire to take off the chill.

After sitting that close to Kalim awhile, I got to thinking about the contents of his jacket pockets, how when we rolled him over I felt something heavy and hard. Curiosity got the better of me, and I took a flashlight over by the body bag. No one was within miles of camp, but I looked around good, just to be sure, then unzipped the bag. Holding my breath, I checked the pockets. They were filled with quarters, silver dollars, and soggy paper. Putting the contents on the ground, I examined them with a flashlight. Among the papers were wadded bills, mostly twenties and fifties. Counting quickly, I guessed he had over three hundred dollars on him.

I know I didn't plan to take the money — I was just curious — but right then I saw headlights flicker as a vehicle wound down the steep canyon road. It was still a long way off, too far for anyone to see me, even in the campfire's glow, but I could see it fine. I stuffed the paper money from Kalim's pockets into my creel and covered it with fishing tackle, then checked to make certain the pockets of his jacket weren't turned out. I closed the body bag and returned to the campfire.

As the pickup got closer, I was surprised to see it was a white tribal vehicle rather than one of the dark blue rigs the sheriff drove. Then I remembered how much Jake hated Grady. After Billyum shut off the engine, both men got out of the truck. "How you two been keeping?" Jake asked me. "Kalim didn't give you any trouble, did he? Sonofabitching farmer had the gate locked up there so no fishermen could drive down. I couldn't catch a ride and had to hike a long way for a phone."

"I caught some fish," I said. "You hungry?"

"In a minute," Jake said. "Better fry up a couple for Billyum, too."

Billyum shook his head. "I had me a big steak at the Phoenix."

"Sweet deal," Jake said. "Some of us were working hard while others were hardly working."

"That's why I picked you," Billyum said. "Delegate authority. Anyway, I knew you were a firecracker."

As Billyum went over to the body bag, he raised his right arm in the air. Holding his palm up, open to the sky, he turned slowly in a circle.

Jake winked at me and shook his head slowly. "Mumbo-jumbo," he mouthed.

Squatting by the body bag, Billyum took a flashlight from his belt. He unzipped the bag and studied Kalim for a while. "Not pretty anymore. The girls wouldn't smile to see him now." I thought I saw his hands slide into Kalim's pockets but my view was partially blocked by Billyum's size. "Still wearing his basketball jacket. You remember that outside shot he had. Sweet."

"I remember the state tournament," Jake said. "It was sour, that championship game."

"Anybody can have an off night," Billyum said.

"I lost five hundred dollars on that game," Jake said. "Some people claimed Kalim threw it."

"People are always buzzing about something," Billyum said. "Especially when it concerns the reservation." Taking a pouch of tobacco out of his pants pocket, he pinched some and began sprinkling it over the body. "You always want to be careful about Wet Shoes," he said.

"Don't tell me you believe in that hokum," Jake snorted. "Wet Shoes and leprechauns."

"It doesn't hurt anything." Billyum zipped the bag closed and stood, then sprinkled tobacco in a circle around the body. "Kalim's grandma and old Sylvester might feel better, knowing I did this right. Anyway, Juniper would have my hide if I didn't."

"They're going to be pretty shook," Jake said. "You think Juniper will come back for Kalim's funeral?"

"Most relatives do," Billyum said.

When he tried sprinkling some of the tobacco on Jake, my uncle shrugged, but didn't jerk away. "I guess it won't hurt none."

"You still got a few things to learn, Jake." Billyum's tone was testy. He put shreds of the tobacco on my shoulders and a little in my hair. "Some of the old people believe that when a person drowns, if his spirit isn't treated right, the ghost comes back out of the water to claim another. If that happens, you hear the spirit walking around the campfire in wet shoes. When I was growing up, lots of fishermen drowned, and all us kids were told to stay close to the fire or the Wet Shoes would get us."

"I doubt Kalim drowned," Jake said, "unless it was in his own blood. That bullet never gave him a chance."

"You're right," Billyum said. "Pretty big caliber, too."

"Either that or a crayfish got him that's big enough to swallow a boat," Jake said.

Billyum grinned at my uncle's joke. "Might be." Taking a pack of Juicy Fruit out of his pocket, he offered me a stick.

"No thanks," I said, shaking my head. Shreds of tobacco clung to his fingers, and I imagined I could smell Kalim on his hands.

Jake took the offered stick and both men started chewing on the gum. "I never have liked this stretch of river," Billyum said. "Nothing but a shitpot full of trouble."

"Don't I know it," Jake said, and I thought he might have been thinking about my father.

"I appreciate you and the boy helping out." Billyum slapped my knee, a little too hard. "Grady's never much interested in missing Indians."

Jake spit at the fire. "Well, hell. I'm going to start cooking that fish." Turning to me, he asked, "What did you use, anyway?"

"Adams," I said.

Jake winked at Billyum and started banging around the cooking gear. "You're not as dumb as you look, Culver."

Billyum chose a rock close to mine and sat in silence a few minutes while we watched as Jake put some corn meal and Krusteaz in a flat pan, then rolled the fish in the mixture. Billyum took the gum from his mouth and threw it in the fire. "Tastes funny."

Jake fried up the trout, squeezing fresh lemon juice over them, and they were delicious. When I salted the tail and ate it, the thin brittle crackled in my mouth. Inside the papery skin, the pink flesh was moist and hot. More lemon made the fish taste even better.

"You better try one," Jake said to Billyum. "They're never so good as when you eat them on the river."

"That's what you said last night," I said. It was true then, too.

"Watching you guys makes me hungry," Billyum said, helping himself to the fish. "Must have been something puny about that steak. I'm starved already."

After we finished eating, Jake poured steaming cups of coffee from the pot on the coals at the fire's edge. He took a flask of whiskey out of the cooking supplies and poured a shot and a half into each cup. Billyum took the one Jake handed him, sipping it slowly and smiling. I took one, too. It tasted good, and I began to relax.

"Times like these, I know I can never leave this river," Jake said.

"It's pretty peaceful," I said.

Billyum helped himself to more coffee and whiskey. "Did your uncle ever tell you about the time he played in the All-Indian band? Back then, he thought he was going to be one hotshot musician."

"Hell, you don't have to tell the kid everything," Jake said. He was smiling at the memory.

"Remember that little goatee you had?" Billyum asked. "All of about three hairs. He wanted to be Boots Randolph or somebody like that. How he got started was the music teacher asked if anyone wanted to play sax and he thought he said *sex*. After playing awhile, though, he got to be second chair.

"When we were out of school, my cousin Harney had this All-Indian band and they were supposed to play at Jordan Mountain, a pretty rough place. Harney thought about the crowd of loggers and cowboys and railroaders and asked if I knew anybody who wanted to be onstage. Of course, I thought of old Jake. He always wanted to be up there."

"Can you blame me?" Jake asked. "The good-looking women always go for the band guys."

"He figured as soon as he stepped on the stage, women would faint, but there weren't any good-looking women at Jordan Mountain. Just a lot of double uglies, the kind you might invite to tractor pulls, if you didn't have a tractor. And you should have seen the look on your uncle's face when he saw Harney's half-brother Bruno was already there playing saxophone."

"They didn't want me to play anything," Jake complained. "They just wanted a white guy to keep the drunks off the stage."

Billyum cut Jake off. "It's my story. He was supposed to play the folding chair. His job was to stand up on the stage with this heavy metal chair and bash any loggers or cowboys that tried to scramble onto the stage and grab the mike away from Harney. Meantime, those local boys were getting liquored up and shouting, 'Do you Redskins know "Ira Hays?"' or 'I can play better than any goddamn Indian.' One drunk cowboy had buddies that tried pushing him onto the stage five or six times."

"I've seen some tough hombres," Jake said. "He was the worst. After I clobbered him a couple good ones, they carried him out for stitches, but he promised to come back the next week and kill me."

"If you were Indian," Billyum said, "his buddies would have killed you right there."

Jake shook his head. "The next weekend, that rowdy bastard showed up stone sober. He came after me with an ax handle out behind the dance hall. I rolled under a pickup and yelled bloody murder to keep him from beating me to death."

Billyum nodded. "We heard this screaming inside the dance hall and rushed out to save your uncle. That cowboy had the hardest head I ever slugged." He held up his fist and flexed it. "We packed the band and cleared out before things got really ugly."

"He got in a few solid pokes with that ax handle," Jake said. "My ribs hurt for months." He laughed. "I figured a musician's life was too dangerous, so I took up guiding."

"Taking a bunch of slick dudes fishing," Billyum said. "Old Easy Money." He sighed, leaning back against the rock.

"Harney played a pretty fair guitar and his singing wasn't half bad," Jake said. "I thought maybe he'd make it to Reno or something."

"Me, too." Billyum turned the cup in his hands. "Come back with a big old Caddy and a couple of blond showgirls."

"Couldn't he make the music business?" I asked.

Billyum shook his head. "He got shot up near the Yakima Reservation. This guy who worked swing shift at the fruit-packing plant lipped off once too often and got fired. Came home early, double bent, and found Harney with his wife. Harney ran like hell, but there's no cover around there, and the guy shot him with his deer rifle. Maybe he was a good guitar player, but Harney couldn't keep his pants zipped."

Jake shook his head. "Too damn bad about Harney. Tough luck. Drunks don't usually shoot straight, except around Yakima."

Just then the moon peeked over the basalt rim, bathing the river and canyon in a cold light. Nobody said anything for a few minutes while we watched the moonrise. Then I asked, "You suppose that's why Kalim got shot? Maybe he was involved with some woman."

"The kid might have something there." Jake half winked at Billyum and a look passed between them that I couldn't fathom. "You suppose Kalim couldn't keep his zipper up?"

Billyum stood and stretched. "You know the rez. Anything's possible. But all this yammering has made me sleepy. I'm gonna throw out my bedroll."

"What about the dishes?" Jake asked. "The kid caught the fish and I cooked them. That means you wash up."

Billyum groaned. "I'm too damn tired. Make you a deal, Culver. You wash up and I'll take you to a couple secret lakes on the rez. We got fish to drool over, but you gotta have a special invitation to get in."

"It might be worth it," Jake told me. "They do have some blue-ribbon trout."

I began gathering the dirty dishes, figuring I could wash up in twenty minutes. "Sounds good." After carrying the dishes and flashlight down to the riverbank, I began scouring the frying pan with sand to cut the grease. The wind was coming upriver, and away from the fire I grew chilled.

Jake and Billyum teased one another as they rolled out the sleeping bags. Billyum looped a horsehair rope around his bag to keep snakes away, and when Jake wisecracked about the Wet Shoes, I turned to watch.

Billyum half swung at Jake, but he ducked away and both men laughed. Everything appeared okay, just a couple of old friends making camp and kidding around. But when I noticed they had put my sleeping bag closest to Kalim, I shivered.

Turning back to the dishes, I saw one of the tin cups floating away. It bobbed toward the boat, just out of reach. "Shit," I said as it filled with water and sank. Picking up the flashlight, I waded out to the spot, but it was deeper than I thought and the cold water swirled around my thighs. Playing the beam onto the river bottom, I didn't see the cup, but I was startled to see a large crayfish scuttle between rocks, dragging a piece of fish gut. Stepping back, I bumped my arm against the boat. The flashlight fell into the water, winking out.

I reached for it, but stopped when my fingers touched the water. I was afraid to grope among the dark rocks at the river bottom. The Wet Shoes business was just a crazy superstition, I knew, but I felt as if some icy hand could reach up from the river bottom and claim mine. Standing in the cold water, my legs grew numb and I grabbed the boat, clutching its side for balance.

I wanted to call out, but waited until my fear passed, leaving me with emptiness and disappointment. Deep in the marrow of my bones, I felt that nothing was going to turn out as we had hoped, and I felt sick for all of us, especially my mother.

9

THAT SUMMER lightning ignited so many fires it seemed half the West was burning. Everyone remembers the big Montana fires, because of the destroyed wildlife, and the Hell's Canyon burn that charred a lot of eastern Oregon and Idaho, but there were hundreds of others, too, so many the smoke-jumping Hot-Shots couldn't get to half of them. Smoke from the fires close by drifted over Gateway skies, dimming the sun and hanging like a pall.

A rash of mysterious barn fires erupted across the West, isolated wooden barns blowing like tinderboxes. The work of arsonists, according to the authorities. Some farmers lost their structures and hay but others lost the stock. One described the horrible smell of burning horse-flesh.

Timber and grass fires swept across the reservation, and some Gateway residents said the Indians set them on purpose, trying to make firefighting jobs for themselves, but Jake said that was just mean talk, although he acknowledged the Alaskan natives were known for that. Everybody worried about the cold deck at the plywood mill, and the company kept giant sprinklers circulating on top of the stacked logs soaking the top layer's bark, even though the lower layers were so dry a carelessly tossed cigarette would ignite the entire deck. Mule Mullins claimed once those logs started, nothing could stop them until the entire deck was destroyed.

The ground was parched as baked clay, and puffs of dust rose from my feet wherever I walked. The fires kept me jittery thinking about Riley. Our house was so hot we slept with the doors open, although we kept the screens locked for security.

Some nights I'd dream I was choking on smoke. Riley hunched over a square metal can pouring kerosene and the thick fumes filled the room. He shuffled along, dousing the floors and furniture. Turning in my direction, his eyes danced with reflected flames, while outside, beyond the smoke-darkened windows, fires consumed so many houses, I could tell this place was larger and more dangerous than Griggs.

When Riley held out the can, I seized it, inhaling the fumes. He led me to the bedroom he'd shared with my mother and showed me where to pour. After he stripped back the covers, I soaked their mattress, then the clothes hanging in their closet, finally the gaping bureau drawers that held her nightgowns and underwear.

Suddenly the entire room was burning, although I never struck a match, and when I turned to run from the fire, they were all watching: Riley, my mother, Jake, even Dwight and his wife. Someone else, too, an obscure figure backlit by the flames. The shadowy face could have been my father's.

I'd awaken with my heart boxing my chest, my hand jammed in my mouth to stifle a yell. After a few minutes I'd go into the kitchen and let the water run a long time, splashing some of it onto my face to make certain I was good and awake. Then I'd just listen awhile and hear a train off in the distance, and I'd think, yes, that's the three-eighteen night freight coming to the trestle. And even though I knew by then it was just a dream, I sometimes smelled kerosene on my hands after I awoke, and I washed them until they smelled like the lemony dish soap we kept in the kitchen.

I was glad none of these episodes woke my mother, for she was a heavy sleeper most of the time. Some nights I'd stand at the doorway to her bedroom, listening for her steady breathing and gentle snore, watching the easy rise and fall of bedcovers. Then I'd return to my bedroom hoping everything was all right for now but knowing Riley could show up at any time. And wondering, too, who was setting fire to those barns all across the West with no regard to property or life, imagining someone out there as wild and unhinged as Riley, maybe not a bad man, really, but one who was pushed by circumstances beyond his limits.

Later, the fires got worse — not bigger, but more horrible. When part of the hobo jungle under the railroad trestle east of town burned, the wind carried a foul smell like charred tennis shoes, and greasy ashes clung to my skin and clothes, leaving a dark smear as I tried to brush them away.

A couple of fellows from the Gateway volunteer ambulance squad told my uncle the story in lowered tones that gave me shudders. A recent shantytown resident had finally drunk himself to death, and his buddies stuffed the body into a fifty-gallon barrel and attempted a do-it-yourself cremation with gasoline siphoned from tourists' cars. The fire got away from them and several were burned badly enough to be taken to the hospital in Central. No one wanted to deal with what remained in the barrel, especially the coroner, who just put "posthumous immolation" on the death certificate.

Every evening after supper I'd check and recheck the stove knobs, making certain the burners were off. And when my mother finished ironing her blouses for work, I'd see that the iron was unplugged.

Some evenings my mother stood in the doorway to catch a faint breeze. Touching her fingers to her throat, just above where the robe gapped, she'd say, "So many fires. That's all they could talk about at work. When I think of all those poor animals in Montana burning up . . ."

"Maybe we'll get some early rains," I offered, although I doubted we might.

Her nose wrinkled as the smoke smell grew stronger. "In the office they mentioned an Indian woman who makes masks of all the animals. Raku masks, I think they said. Deer and elk, foxes and wolves. This woman carries them out to the scorched land and leaves them to put the animal spirits back." She took a breath. "That's a beautiful and remarkable thing to do, don't you think, Culver? Imagine how wonderful things could be if everyone made such a contribution."

"It would sure help all right," I said.

"A truly lovely gesture." She took a deep breath and turned from the door. "It seems as if the entire West might be on fire."

"The West is pretty big, Mom," I said. I was still thinking about the artist carrying her masks to the woods.

☆ ☆ ☆ ☆

The reservation grade school had a broad expanse of green lawn, but it was so hot that afternoon, no children were playing. The sky was hazy from the reservation fires, and the haze seemed to contain the heat and quiet the breeze. Jake pulled the pickup in front of a yellow pumice-block building that said RUBY'S TRADING POST.

"I'm parched," he said, handing me a dollar. "Get us a couple Cokes, would you?" His suit coat lay folded on the seat between us. Sweat showed under the arms of his dress shirt, and he had loosened the knot in his tie. The tie was bright and too wide. "And ask the guy how to get to the old tribal church and graveyard. I only half remember."

Inside, a few young kids clustered around a pinball machine. After passing some turquoise jewelry, moccasins made in Maine, and a dusty display of arrowheads, I took two Cokes from the cooler and returned to the front counter.

"Live around here?" the man asked as he took the money. He had two thin braids tied with a rubber band and wore a T-shirt that said CUSTER GOT SIOUXED.

"Gateway," I said. "I'm going to Kalim Kania's funeral."

"You a friend or something?" Curiosity tinged his voice.

"I found him," I said trying to keep it casual. "I work for my uncle Jake, help him out on the river."

He nodded. "I heard something about it."

"How do you get to the old tribal graveyard, anyway?"

"That your rig?" He indicated the pickup with his chin, and I nodded. "Turn it around and drive straight past the fairgrounds and Hollywood. Go right at the pink house. It's about four miles."

"Thanks," I said. "I've heard of Hollywood."

When I handed Jake his Coke and change, I wanted to tell him about taking the money in Kalim's pockets, but I thought he'd get sore. At home, I had wrapped the money in plastic and hidden it among old school papers in a small suitcase. Kalim must have been gambling, playing the slots at the Stardust. Maybe someone had shot him for his winnings, but he had jumped into the river before they could grab him. It was hard to figure.

Near the fairgrounds, big circulating sprinklers were watering the lawn and it seemed a little cooler. A teenaged boy kept shoving his girlfriend into the pulsing stream. She laughed, trying to break away, but he held her in the water while they both got soaked.

"It's a wet T-shirt contest," Jake said. "Too bad I can't see that good."

A fringe of tepees circled the fairground arena. One had two yellow suns painted above the door flap and a sign in front: WE BUY PORCUPINES. As we passed, an old man came out.

Jake stopped the pickup and thumped on the door with his fist. "Hey, Yazzie, how do I get to Hollywood?"

He squinted at Jake and waved. "Get a face-lift."

Jake laughed. "Go to hell. At first I mistook you for a star."

Yazzie shuffled toward the pickup, then staggered to the right, widening his eyes. "That tie about blinded me. When will the rest of the band show up?"

"Yazzie, this is my nephew, Culver. We're just headed out to Kalim's funeral. That's why I'm so decked out. Culver, Yazzie Tapoah here used to be one mean guitar player. Had his own band and toured the West. Even opened for Buck Owens a couple of times."

"That's going way back," Yazzie said. "Before arthritis bit me." He held up his hands so I could see the swollen joints. "Rheumatoid. I should have been a singer."

"What's going on here?" Jake asked, pointing toward the tepees.

"Just hanging around." Yazzie shrugged. "Pretty soon they'll come by with some commodity foods."

"Take care, Yazzie," Jake said. "I don't want to miss the doings."

"It's been a regular parade around here," Yazzie said. "Even saw Juniper Teewah looking all citified."

"So she made it," Jake said as he pulled away. Yazzie half waved.

"He's going downhill," Jake said, "and it's too bad. Ten years ago he was headlining in Reno. Came back to town once in a cowboy Cadillac, big old bull horns on the hood and six-shooters for door handles. The dashboard was inlaid with silver dollars. He swaggered around town, a showgirl dangling from each arm. That must have cost him a mint. They were all legs and smiles, I remember that."

"What happened?" I asked.

"Crooked agent, bad luck." Jake shrugged. "Things change."

"What's he do with the porcupines?"

"His wife uses them to make Indian jewelry, decorate dancing outfits. If you want a part-time job, they'll buy porkies dead or alive."

"Forget it, I'm not touching porcupines."

Crossing the wooden bridge over Kooskia Creek, we entered Hollywood. Ramshackle two-story dwellings and quick-built government houses covered several acres of lowland between the creek and the river. As if defying the leaning porches and sagging roofs, each house was painted bright colors different from the rest. My favorite, a chartreuse house with lavender trim, perched near the riverbank. Broken-down pickups and rusting cars littered the brown lawns and cracked roads. Someone had nailed up a green and white California freeway sign that said ENTERING HOLLYWOOD.

"If you lived here, you'd be home," Jake said. "Floods carried off chunks of this place a time or two. But now prosperity will sweep it clean. Go figure." He slowed down, shaking his head. "Some people think these Indians have it made in the shade. Ask Yazzie. He needs more than a new place to get back on his feet. Hollywood. What happens to the old stars?"

☆ ☆ ☆ ☆ ☆

Shaded by a grove of tall cottonwoods, we were sitting at the boundary of the reservation cemetery while inside the weathered church Kalim's service was being held. The church windows were open because of the intense heat, and I heard the words but couldn't understand because they were in the tribal language. The hymns were unfamiliar, too.

Jake picked a bachelor button and put it in his lapel. Then he hung the suit coat on a branch. "The old man liked these and always brought your grandmother bunches of them. She had milk-bottle bouquets all over the house."

"Tell me something about him," I said. "I don't know many stories."

He gave me a quizzical look, then nodded as he realized I had never heard anything about him from my father.

"The old man was a hell of a fly fisherman," Jake said, "and for a long time he knew the Lost better than anyone else, every hole and riffle. He'd smoke an old crook-stemmed pipe, and each time he tied on a new fly, he'd blow Prince Albert smoke on it, 'For good luck,' he said. In April he fished with Royal Coachmen and Adams flies but that was just practice, although he landed some nice ones. Late May, when the Salmon flies hatched, he started fishing for real, using tied-down Caddis flies. He favored the yellow bodies but he'd use orange, too. He caught lunkers then. And he stayed on the river until it got completely dark and cave bats going after the night hatch chased his flies on the back cast. Those bats made him mad, especially when the hook caught 'em and he had to bring them in. He carried leather gloves so they couldn't bite him when he pulled out the hook with his fishing pliers. But they screeched and hissed and flapped their wings."

"Did it kill the bats?" I asked.

He shook his head. "They always veered at the last second, so the hook caught the fur just below their mouths or maybe snagged a wing. When the old man started catching more bats than fish, he headed home."

"I don't like bats," I said. "There's something creepy about them."

"I can't stand them myself," Jake said, then went on.

"The old man was kind of a show-off, but in a good sort of way. After a couple of dudes gave up fishing a nice riffle, he loved to wade out and land a couple nice fish under their noses. He'd clench that pipe between his teeth, trying not to grin, while the dudes shook their heads. Then he'd reach in his fishing vest for a package of Fig Newtons. He'd say, 'Darn tootin', I like Fig Newton.'

"Midafternoon, when the evening paper was finished, he'd grab his fishing gear and head out to the river, flag down a train, and ride upstream eight or ten miles. In the old days, railroaders gave fishermen lifts. Everyone liked the old man, especially when he took them the paper and a bottle now and then. Around eight, when he had enough fish, he'd catch the night freight back to town. Sometimes he'd eat the cold supper your grandmother left, but if she was mad at him and had cleared the table, he'd fry up some fish. Dave and I would sneak downstairs and he'd give us the crackling tails and a couple Fig Newtons, then shoo us back to bed."

"Sounds good." I was getting hungry and could almost taste it.

"Delicious." Jake winked. "Some weekends he'd take us with him. If we were staying over on the river, he'd fry those fish in Krusteaz, adding a little lemon. They never tasted so good as when we ate them on the river with the old man.

"He was devoted to your grandmother. They'd come out from Minnesota together — Stillwater, where the state pen is. After things went bad in the woods, he worked at the state pen about a year but said he couldn't stand to see those boys walled in, so they set out together, and it was damn hard, until he landed a steady job with the newspaper. But she stuck by him and she hardly ever complained. I never heard her gripe, except a few times about the fishing. Once she got really mad and complained he should keep a fancy woman instead of that river.

"Then he stayed home two weeks straight. But he told us boys fishing was a little slack anyway. Each night after supper was finished, he'd light his pipe and start reading the paper to see how it looked. Since he'd set the type, he was pleased when he couldn't find any mistakes. 'I do damn good work,' he'd say. Pretty soon he'd start to nod off, and his head would sink lower and lower on his chest. Finally, Dave and I would wink to each other, taking bets as to how long it would be before some of the hot ashes spilled out of the pipe bowl onto his shirt. When that happened, he'd yell and jump, slapping his chest to knock away the smoldering ashes. Your grandmother would come rushing in from the kitchen and scold us for not waking him up sooner. We'd lie through our teeth and say we were so involved in our homework, we didn't notice."

I laughed.

"Every shirt he owned was burned through with holes. When we buried him, the funeral director wanted to put a new shirt on him, one without burns, but we said hell no. We buried him with an old shirt, his fishing vest, and that pipe.

"They were fine people," he said. "And both went too soon. Her heart gave out, and when the old man got throat cancer from that pipe, it spread and riddled his bones. They got so fragile he couldn't walk, so Dave and I carried him from room to room in a blanket."

The singing had stopped inside the church, and when Jake grew quiet, all I could hear was the rustle of wind high in the cottonwoods and the occasional whir of a large grasshopper sailing across the fields. "I'll bet you miss him," I said.

"Hell, I miss all of them. Sometimes when I drive up to the house, for a moment, it's like they're all there just as they used to be, but then I look again and they're gone." Jake stood, taking his suit coat from the tree limb. "We've got to do that memorial. Listen, I'm glad you live closer now — your mother, too."

The church door opened. "Party time," Jake said.

The first person to come out was Sylvester, ringing a large brass bell. His long white hair was pulled back in a ponytail, and he wore buckskin trousers and a black ribbon shirt. Carrying a wooden coffin draped with a Pendleton blanket, the pallbearers followed. Two wore RedWing jackets; one had sunglasses and a medicine bundle hanging around his neck. I felt a little jolt when I recognized the second as one of the bouncers at the Stardust. Elderly men and women followed the pallbearers, younger ones next, and children last. In spite of the heat, several old people draped colorful blankets across their shoulders.

Juniper wore a shawl over her head when she emerged from the church, but as the only mourner wearing city clothes, she was easy to spot. Her plaid skirt and matching jacket resembled the outfits my mother wore when she wanted to look "sharp" at the office. Outside, Juniper lowered the shawl and shook her head, freeing her shoulder-length dark hair. A few steps from the church, she paused and turned toward us as surely as if she'd been a compass point swinging north. She didn't smile, but raised one hand slightly, spreading her fingers. When a stooped old woman walking beside her stumbled, Juniper took her by the arm.

We followed the procession toward the freshly dug grave at the far edge of the cemetery. Standing behind the others, we waited for the ceremony to finish. Sylvester held an eagle feather to the sky and spoke the old language. Whatever he said was short, and I was glad because I felt like an intruder, especially when the old people raised their right hands to the sky and cried, "Ahhhhh." After the pallbearers folded the Pendleton blanket and gave it to the stooped old woman, I figured she was Kalim's grandmother. One of the RedWings removed his satin jacket and placed it on the coffin before they lowered it into the grave.

Jake hadn't taken his eyes off Juniper, but she glanced our way only once. Soon people started drifting toward their cars for more food or heading into the church to eat. Jake and I stood alone, and he scuffed his foot against the dirt, toeing a pebble into the hole. I stared at the large plastic flowers arranged by the headstone. A miniature basketball was among the artificial blossoms.

Juniper took the blanket from the old woman and guided her toward the church. She seemed too frail to make it on her own.

Jake nodded at the two women. "I'm going to pay my respects," he said. "You go check out the parking lot. Someone's fooling around. Don't want some kid jacking my car."

"I didn't see anybody," I said.

Jake seemed annoyed. "Go have a look. Then come back and we'll eat. If we leave now, these people will be insulted."

When I reached Jake's pickup, I saw it was only Billyum moving from vehicle to vehicle, writing down the license plate numbers. Now and then he'd kick some dirt off so he could read them correctly. Flecks of ash dotted his uniform, and I guessed he'd been out to the reservation fires. After he'd written down Jake's number, he glanced at me and put two fingers against the brim of his cowboy hat as a kind of salute.

"What's up?" I asked, following him as he moved along the line of cars.

"Routine stuff. Going by the book. A lot of times the killer shows up at the funeral. So I'm taking down everyone's plate numbers. I had some special training at the state police academy. Top-level stuff."

"But you know Jake," I said. "We found the body."

Billyum tilted his head to one side. "I know everybody here. Known 'em for years. That's what makes this job so tough." He tapped the pencil against the notebook. "You're about the only stranger. As for Jake, he knew right where to look, didn't he?"

Billyum studied me for an uncomfortably long moment before breaking into a grin. "Ayyy," he said to show he was kidding. "I'm just practicing in case I ever go big time."

He looked past me and I followed his gaze to Jake and Juniper. They were still standing by the church, talking, but the old woman had gone inside. Billyum shook his head. "Too bad it took a funeral to get her back home." Flipping the notebook closed, he put it in his shirt pocket. "Wish I had a big break, something to cheer her up."

"What kind of break?" I asked.

"Who knows?" He spread his hands. "Three months after Bryce Chamas got killed, his shooter showed up at a rodeo wearing his boots and belt buckle. Even hung Bryce's fuzzy dice from the rearview mirror. Lime green. Only pair like it on the rez." He shook his head. "That was one for Ripley's *Believe It or Not*."

"Maybe you'll get lucky," I said.

"Better lucky than good." He nodded. "Two weeks from now or two months, someone will talk. Ninety percent of reservation police work is just waiting for mouths to open. Like fishing." He hooked his finger, sticking it inside his mouth until his cheek bulged. Taking the finger out again he wiped it on his pants. "They talk, and I reel them in."

"Time will tell then, I guess."

Billyum nodded. "You know, I thought old Kalim should be cashy, considering how he threw money around, but he was almost tapped. Nothing but silver dollars and pocket change."

My tongue felt thick; I kept my mouth closed.

When Billyum gripped my shoulder with his big hand, I flinched, but he didn't seem to notice. Steering me toward the church, he said, "Can't round up crooks on an empty stomach, Culver. We might as well go eat."

BILLYUM GOT SIDETRACKED by the RedWings and Juniper had gone inside already, so Jake and I entered the church basement through the back door. The room was a combination kitchen-cafeteria, and two tables were loaded with food. All the older Indians had taken off their blankets; now the women wore bright cotton dresses and moccasins or tennis shoes. Gray braids hung below the colorful bandannas they wound around their heads. As we moved through the line, the old women serving the food laughed and joked. One had a blue cap with bright pink pom-poms that said, "The cook is always right." "How you been keeping, Cora?" Jake asked, winking at her.

"I'm still grinning," she said, "but they're all false."

We sat next to an old man wearing mismatched slacks and vest. "Planning to get your elk this year, Delvis?" Jake asked, but the old man shook his head. "Too damn much walking." He pointed to the cane beside the bench. "Let the young guys chase 'em." Finishing his plate of food, Delvis lit a pipe and wandered off.

Billyum came in from outside and grabbed two plates. I heard him say, "Doing the best I can, ladies. There's only one of me," as he moved down the line. "That sure looks good, Lettie. How about another piece of salmon? I worked up quite an appetite at those fires."

He joined us and started shoveling the food down. Glancing toward the cooks, he said, "Those old magpies make me nervous." He sopped up some remaining stew with a piece of fry bread. "They may not look tough, but those old women run the show. Every guy on the tribal council has a grandmother or aunt pecking at him."

Finishing his food, Billyum shoved the plates away. "Good snack. Now when do we eat?" He went to the dessert table, returning with three large pieces of huckleberry pie. Shoving two in front of Jake and me, he said, "Lettie Black-Eye makes these. You'll never taste better. She uses leaf lard from elk intestines."

"You're kidding," I said, but the pie was delicious. Juice had bubbled out and baked crisp on top of the crusts. "You got to come to the Huckleberry Feast," Billyum said. "The men work up an appetite sitting on tule mats, and when the women dance in wearing beaded buckskin dresses and balancing woven baskets filled with huckleberries on their heads, that's something to see."

Jake twisted in his seat. "Where'd Juniper go, anyway?"

"Back room, I imagine." Billyum nodded toward a salmon-colored door. "She's probably still talking with Kalim's grandmother. Old woman's pretty shook up." He ate another mouthful of pie. "I saw Juniper when she got in last night. You take a close look? She's packing some weight."

"Looks good on her though," Jake said.

Billyum winked at me. "You know what they say, kid. The thicker the cushion . . . Ayyy."

"Don't go talking about your old girlfriend like that," Jake said.

Billyum glanced up from his plate, and I thought a look passed between him and my uncle, but I couldn't be sure. "Naw," Billyum said. "Too high style for me. Her old man was a Simnasho chief, big fish in a little pond. She'd go to a dance with me if she needed an escort. That's as far as it got."

Jake spread his hands. "Things change. Now she probably owns an art gallery. Maybe she can support you."

Ignoring him, Billyum stood. "These cooks can't expect me to solve a case hungry." He snuck past them for two more pieces of pie and slid one across the table. "Culver's a growing boy."

"Here she comes." Jake nodded toward the salmon-colored door as Juniper stepped out. She had taken off her jacket and wore a sky blue blouse with her plaid skirt.

As she approached, Billyum scooted over and motioned to the seat beside him. "Take a load off."

Jake stood and smiled.

Up close, I could tell she was a handsome woman, but now she seemed bone tired. Deep shadows haunted her eyes. Hazel colored, almost green, they showed red rims from fatigue and sorrow.

Setting her coffee down, she reached across the table to shake my hand. "You've got to be Culver. I'm sorry to say you resemble your uncle

Jake." Smiling, she seemed a little younger. "I already thanked these two for helping find Kalim. Now I want to thank you."

Her long fingers had blunt nails; a couple were chipped. Working hands, I thought. "Glad to help out," I told her.

She took the seat Billyum offered and sipped her coffee. "I've got to rest a few minutes, then get back to Stella. She was devoted to that boy."

"Sorry about missing the funeral," Billyum said. "I hated to do it, but I had to check those fires." He brushed some ash off his shirt front. "Can't get rid of this stuff."

"Anything promising with Kalim's investigation?" she asked Billyum.

Uncomfortable, he poked the pie crust sliver with his fork. "I've talked to lots of people. Something will break pretty soon."

She laughed but without humor, then added some sugar to her coffee and stirred it with Billyum's fork. "Things never change around here, do they?"

Billyum shrugged and didn't answer, so Jake said, "The new resort's finished and they're planning to rebuild Hollywood. I'd say things are improving."

"Just cosmetics," she said. "Underneath, nothing really changes." She rolled her shoulders and stretched. "But maybe I'm just tired. And I had a tough time getting someone to watch my place on such short notice."

"How is the art game, anyway?" Jake asked. "I hear you own a big gallery in Albuquerque."

"The art game." She laughed, and for the first time her face relaxed. "I don't *own* an art gallery. Things always get blown out of proportion around here. I *rent* a space. It's tiny, Jake — itty-bitty. If you stretch out your arms, you can touch both walls — like this." She held out her arms, moving them up and down slightly.

"But after all the years of selling at powwows and Indian rodeos, at least my work doesn't get dusty or knocked over by horses." She paused. "So you could say the art game's improving, I guess. But I'm not setting my expectations too high. Ask me again in a couple of years."

"Maybe you could sell some of your paintings at the lodge," Billyum said. "They have a gift shop."

After hesitating a moment, she said, "I might just do that."

"How long can you stick around?" Jake asked.

"We'll see," she said. "I don't come back much, so I want to see people while I'm here, especially the old ones. I can't believe how many are already gone." She put her hand on Billyum's shoulder. "I'm sure the case will be wrapped up by then." Shaking her head, she seemed about to cry. "Kalim was always a little wild, but who expected this? Maybe a logging accident . . ."

"Some wild streak." Billyum leaned back in his chair, remembering. "When he set fire to that chicken coop, Hollywood stunk for days like Colonel Sanders gone bad." He grinned. "You took after him with that shoe. Pounded him good."

Juniper frowned. "Damn it, Billyum. Don't go hanging out dirty laundry. He was just smoking in there. It was an accident."

"Now don't get all sore on me," Billyum said. "I was just remembering how strange it smelled."

She stood and grabbed her cup. "I've got to take some food to Stella. Get her to eat." Looking at me, she added, "I only hit him twice. I never could make him mind. That's how he was." Juniper turned toward Billyum. "Please watch your mouth, Billyum. And keep me posted about Kalim."

None of us spoke until Juniper had loaded a plate and carried it into the back room, closing the salmon-colored door behind her. Then Jake said to Billyum, "Check your boot heel, buddy. You stepped in something."

Billyum grabbed both sides of his hat brim, tipping it down until his eyes were covered. "Jesus. That woman always made me sweat." He lifted the brim and squinted at us. "Even so, how could I say anything so stupid? I completely forgot her grandparents burned up."

"It wasn't in that fire Kalim started, was it?" I asked.

Billyum shook his head. "A lot earlier. Hollywood wiring, or maybe they smoked in bed. Who knows? Hoot Toopah was the cop then, and he couldn't investigate a traffic ticket."

"Funerals make everybody edgy," Jake said. "It'll blow over."

"I'm going outside before these old ladies get after me." Billyum stood. "Maybe I can find a suspect, make it look like I'm questioning somebody."

"We'll keep you covered," Jake said. "Got to head back to town, anyway. This boy needs his shut-eye."

Outside, as we neared the pickup, Billyum said, "Damn woman, always catches me off guard. Remember that homecoming stunt she pulled our senior year? Just threw down her carnation bouquet and stalked off the stage. Pretty soon, the rest of the Indian princesses followed."

Jake laughed. "I was stunned all right." He turned to me. "All the homecoming princesses got boxes of flowers at the dance. Nobody knew who was queen until they saw her open the box containing the roses. The runners-up got carnations. It was supposed to be a big secret."

Billyum said, "The deal was, some blonde from town or one of the farm girls always won. Hell, we Indians knew it was rigged, but Juniper was the first to walk away."

Jake punched Billyum's shoulder. "This guy was supposed to be her escort, but she stormed out the door and he was stuck on stage with his thumb jammed up his ass."

"Yeah, stuck with some bawling blonde holding roses. No one cared about the queen. Everyone was staring after Juniper. Finally I scooped up the carnations and headed out to catch her."

"He's always been a little slow on the uptake," Jake said. "That's why he's a cop."

Billyum touched his hand to his chest. "Look at me. Twenty years later she's still got me ducking for the exit."

☆ ☆ ☆ ☆

My mother was standing at the screen door when Jake dropped me off. "You're later than I expected," she said. "I was just starting to worry." She opened the door. "Now come on in. You too, Jake. I've made some tea."

I got out but my uncle only raised his arm and waved. "Another time, Flora. I'm beat and need some shut-eye."

As he drove off, my mother glared at the pickup. "He needs to work on his manners."

Inside, she insisted that I tell her all about it, and I tried to think of everything, even though I was tired. We drank tea and I described the church and the graveside ceremony, the people's dress, the salmon, venison, and roots. Throughout, her eyes shone with excitement, and she stopped me now and again to clarify a detail. "What an experience for you. Learning about different cultures always helps you get along," she said. "The world's changing."

When I told her about Juniper, she listened with complete attention, and as I finished the homecoming story, my mother smiled and nodded. "She must be a remarkable woman." Putting down her teacup, she added, "I'm certain your father told me something about her. Parts of that story sound familiar."

"Did he really?" I asked.

"I'm positive," she said. "There might be something else. Jake used to be sweet on an Indian girl. Your father said so. I wonder if she's the one."

"I don't think so, Mom."

She spilled a little of her tea on the robe. "Look at me slop. I don't know why I'm so messy." After dabbing the tea with a napkin, she said, "We'll just have to wait and see about Juniper. But renting gallery space makes her pretty unusual. I wonder how she got started."

"Billyum used to be interested in her," I said. "Jake went on about it."

She laughed, but her face seemed troubled and she rose, carrying the cup and saucer to the kitchen. "You're too young to know about these things, Culver."

In my bedroom, I lay awake going over the events of the day and thinking of Juniper. After meeting her, I felt worse about taking Kalim's money and wondered if Billyum suspected me. Turning on a flashlight, I quietly checked the suitcase. The money was there all right, but somehow the whole search for Kalim seemed unreal, like a movie.

When I awakened in the night, I was surprised to see the table lamp still on in the front room. As I looked in, my mother was holding the phone to her ear but she wasn't saying anything. This went on for what seemed like a long time, until I finally entered and asked, "Mom, is everything all right?"

Startled, she rose a little from the love seat and put the phone receiver down hard. "My God, Culver, you scared me half to death." Her face showed how upset she was. "Don't go sneaking up on me like that again or you'll be a complete orphan."

"I wasn't sneaking," I said. "Who were you talking to so late? Did Riley call or something? I never heard the phone ring."

She looked agitated but pretended to laugh. "Honey, I was just calling the operator to see what time it was. I believe the kitchen clock's slowing, and I was afraid I'd be late to work. Would you check it, please?"

I stepped back into the kitchen. "It's not slow, Mom."

When I returned to the front room, she was going into her bedroom. "Well, it seemed that way to me. I had intended to call earlier, but it slipped my mind. Now I need some sleep. You, too. We both work in the morning." She closed her door almost completely.

She hadn't turned off the table lamp, so I did, checking near the phone for a number or message about Riley, but there wasn't one. However, a damp Kleenex lay on the floor beside the love seat. "Damn him," I muttered.

I didn't believe her story about the clock and went to bed angry at Riley because I figured he had called up to pester her, but she didn't want to upset me by saying anything. I turned this over for a long time, when suddenly the angry feeling changed to surprise as another idea struck. She might have been trying to call my uncle Jake, checking to see if he ever went home and letting the phone ring and ring inside the empty house.

11

 OVER THE NEXT TWO WEEKS, while Jake stayed busy with Juniper, my mother started dating a man named Franklin Worthington II who drove a brand new Chevrolet Bel Air and smelled of English Leather. Franklin worked at Sunrise Biscuits with my mother, but not in the same office, as she was quick to point out. That was against company policy.

The first time Franklin came to dinner, she made shrimp salad and cheese muffins, her standard fare. The second time, she served Rancho pork chops broiled in the oven — ketchup, slice of lemon, and onion on the top. Adding a little brown sugar to the ketchup sweetened the dish. Working on my second pork chop and studying Franklin across the table, I wondered if this was going to become steady. If my mother made Hawaiian ham, Riley's favorite, that meant serious.

Franklin seemed okay, not mean or anything, but too prissy. His clothes were color matched, his cologne too strong, and his hands accountant smooth. He vigorously sucked breath mints, and when he'd crunch them, I'd see my mother's face tighten. Franklin's car was terrific, though — two-tone beige and navy blue with a hula girl air freshener jiggling from the rearview mirror.

Two Saturdays in a row, Franklin took us for a spin and we tried a little fishing on the Lost, the accessible part you could drive along, where broad paths were beaten to the river and the banks were littered with fishing debris and beer cans. He wasn't much of a fisherman although he had new equipment, a discounted spinning rod and reel set that came shrink-wrapped in plastic.

A lure plunker, Franklin splashed out from shore, scaring the feeding fish as he bumped rocks or stirred up the mud with a wading stick he had purchased in Scotland. He claimed to have caught salmon there, but never offered to show pictures.

Jake's rule of thumb was ten percent of the fishermen catch ninety percent of the fish. Nice rainbows populated this overfished stretch of the Lost, but few people caught them. Using Jake's tips like casting a fly into the foam line where the fish wait for food, I caught some fairly nice ones. Showing up Franklin was fun. I let him try my fly rod a few times but he couldn't get the hang of it.

For these "outings," as she called them, my mother packed a picnic lunch in a wicker basket she and my father had received as a wedding gift. She prepared deviled ham sandwiches, fruit cup in icebox dishes, neatly sliced carrot and celery sticks. She spread pimento and cream cheese on the celery, but I couldn't eat mine that way. Beer for Franklin, sodas for me, a thermos of tea for herself.

She spread the picnic on an old blue Pendleton blanket and we'd eat after Franklin and I had fished a couple hours. We didn't talk much, although I remember Franklin going on about a trip he planned to see the castles on the Rhone River.

Lunch finished, I'd head back to the river while she and Franklin sat on the blanket. They'd study the sky and remark on cloud shapes — one of my mother's picnic pastimes. As I fished, I glanced back every so often, but nothing was going on. Even so, I kept them in sight.

I pretended to think that if Franklin didn't know more about fishing than he did, he was equally inept at other activities and thus of little interest to my mother. Still, I knew she wanted to come up in the world, have things a bit easier. She remained beautiful. "A bit of bloom lingered on the rose," she might comment when she felt good about herself. As soon as we had moved to Gateway, she had taken off her wedding band, and now her tan lean fingers didn't show a trace of white line.

Whether or not she told Franklin about Riley I considered her business. I realized that if she did marry again, Mother would most likely select someone professional. She as much as said so herself. Once, when I told her the story of how Riley thought she had been swimming nude with Dwight Riggins, she threw back her head and laughed. "Why don't you give me some credit? Dwight lived in Griggs and smelled like cigars and creosote." She shook her head. "Can you imagine his poor wife? No, Culver, the whole point was to get away from Griggs and get around some professional people."

She meant white-collar. I could imagine Franklin at the office, taking off his suit coat to show how hard he was working, rolling up his shirtsleeves two turns to display the fine brown hairs on his forearms.

"A person could do worse than Franklin," she had remarked the evening after he dropped us off from the first picnic. "I'm certain any house he lived in would have screen doors." She raised her chin for emphasis. "When they came and told me your father had drowned, we were stuck in a little place that swirled with flies each time you opened the door. Jake and the policemen stood right there holding it open, and I couldn't keep the flies out."

On the river, she had felt comfortable enough with Franklin to fall asleep. I knew how much she liked the soothing sound of rushing water. When I splashed ashore late afternoon with a couple decent trout, she was asleep on the blanket, one tan arm across her eyes, hair fanned out against the blue wool.

I don't know how long she had been asleep, but long enough to appear deeply relaxed. Her lips were parted, revealing her fine white teeth. I had the idea Franklin had been admiring her for a long time.

Raising his head toward me, he said, "Your mother's a remarkably pretty woman."

I gazed at her a few seconds and replied, "Pretty enough for Hollywood."

☆ ☆ ☆ ☆

While Mom stayed busy with Franklin, and Jake with Juniper, I worked my tail off at the store, writing licenses, packaging worms, sacking ice, assembling and repairing bicycles. A Gateway kid never brought in a bike unless it had two flat tires and several busted spokes. Schwinn made over seventy spokes in those days, so it was never easy finding the right match. Replacing inner tubes was faster than repairing them with glue and patches, and while it was a waste, I tossed the old ones, unless the kids insisted on a repair. If they had bought a repair kit from us, often the tubes had been fixed at home half a dozen times already. With all the commotion, I seldom took time to eat lunch or go to the bathroom. Even so, I couldn't keep up.

By the time Jake drove in from the reservation, he was often an hour late for the guide trips, and both of us would scurry around the store in a half panic. Checking over the disarray, he'd shake his head and comment, "Going to hell in a handbasket."

"There's only one of me," I'd mutter.

One time we ran out of coffee and the back-room boys carried on like the end of the world. That had happened only once before, when Jake was away at elk camp for ten days. To ease the strain a little, Jake hired Jed to help out again, but he hardly ever left the stool behind the cash register. Every blue moon, he'd package a dozen worms or make coffee, and even that was weak. Jed claimed that growing up in the Depression had taught him to tolerate coffee like his relatives — thin and bitter.

Of course, the less Jake was around, the more people insisted on talking with him. Sports reporters called up to ask where the fish were biting and what lures or flies worked best. I'd tell them exactly the same information Jake would, but they brushed me off. Once a man phoned to talk about the dam and how it might affect the fishing when it was completed.

"Terrific fishing in the lake behind the dam," I said. "Boating, too, and water skiing. Mention Jake's as recreational headquarters."

"Can I quote Jake on this?" he asked.

"From the horse's mouth. This is his nephew."

But they never ran the article.

Eventually Jake became so frazzled that he asked me to call and cancel half a dozen guide trips. "Tell them I'm under the weather. Make up some bullshit. Ask them to reschedule." His eyes were bloodshot and the lines in his face seemed deeper. "Too much burning the candle at both ends, some in the middle."

"You want me to lie straight out?"

"No, lie crooked." He grinned. "That's why you're getting paid big bucks."

Most of the dudes sounded mad when I called to tell them Jake was canceling their trip. After their initial anger cooled, I'd say, "He's suffering from gallstones." Then I'd lower my voice. "We're praying and keeping fingers crossed it's no more than that. Exploratory surgery in two weeks. Meanwhile, he's just fighting the pain."

The voice would soften at the other end. "Gee, I'm sorry to hear that."

"It's rough, all right. Still, he doesn't want to be rowing you fellas through some class-five rapids and suffer an attack." And here I'd pause a moment as Jake had suggested, to allow them time to imagine the situation. "He feels terrible about letting you fellas down. But he wants to reschedule in October when the big steelhead come in. If that squares with your party." Another pause. "No extra charge to you fellas. He insists. And your deposit locks in the trip." They always took the bait and we'd fix the schedule. "Understand, I got to write this in pencil for now. Just in case . . ."

No one asked for his deposit back, and we got a sprinkling of get-well cards, some chocolates, several bottles of liquor, one bouquet of flowers. I took the flowers home to Mom, considering them a bonus for covering Jake's ass.

☆ ☆ ☆ ☆ ☆

One afternoon Jake and Juniper showed up at the store with five of her paintings carefully wrapped so they hadn't been damaged in the pickup bed. "We need to take down some of the trophies," Jake told me. "We're hanging these."

I got out the stepladder and tried to share Jake's enthusiasm, but I wasn't sure our customers gave a hoot about art.

After climbing the ladder, Jake handed me the trophies, making a show of blowing dust off each one. "Here I go and pay my nephew union scale, and look how filthy he keeps this place." The last to come down was a mangy moosehead. For each holiday, Jake decorated the critter, now sporting Fourth of July stuff — Uncle Sam's tricolored hat, sunglasses, three skyrockets clenched between its teeth.

Juniper laughed at the getup. "I never knew you were so patriotic, Jake." Turning to me, she said, "Why did I let him talk me into this?"

"Don't worry," he said. "A little culture won't hurt these dudes. Isn't that right, Shotgun?" Without waiting for me to answer, he said, "Anyway, I own enough of this outfit to say what goes."

She handed him the first painting, wild horses on the reservation prairie. Two stallions were Appaloosas. I was amazed at how lifelike the animals appeared — almost like a photograph. Standing back, she measured the distance. "The right side needs to be lower." She crossed her arms as Jake made the adjustment. "That's fine, but I still don't know about hanging them in your store."

"All the rich dudes stopping by, we'll sell these faster than you can paint," he said.

Next they hung a painting of Fancy Dancers at a celebration. The lead dancer carried a swan feather fan and seemed to be moving.

Each painting was terrific. I could appreciate that and was eager to have my mother come see them. For the most part, she didn't like the rough-and-tumble atmosphere of the store, but this gave it another dimension beyond "slaughtering poor dumb animals," as she put it.

In the third painting, three old men fished from treacherous scaffolds on the lower Lost. This was traditional Indian fishing with long-handled hoop nets they lowered into the white water. One man was lifting a salmon out; another clubbed a fish on the bank.

"What do you think of that, nephew? It's so real you can smell the fish."
I nodded. "Wish I could catch some that big."

The next painting hit me. A man sat in a pickup, perhaps headed for town. In the doorway of a log cabin, a woman wearing a blue print dress waved good-bye. A boy cradling a rifle stood beside an empty rail corral. Nobody had to tell me the boy was Kalim.

"I painted that one from an old family picture," she said. "And memory." She unwrapped the last painting. "This one really gets me."

Kalim and the RedWings were at a tournament, and by their dark uniforms you could tell they were the visitors. While the coach diagrammed a play on chalkboard, the team huddled. But Kalim wasn't studying the play with the others. His head was raised, and his eyes held a faraway gaze that saw beyond the scoreboard and crowd. With a shudder, I realized this was the same look my father wore in the fishing photo. On Kalim, the expression made me uncomfortable, and I hoped the painting would sell soon.

Jake seemed a little surprised by it, too. "That's different from the others," he pointed out. "No landscape and it's off the rez."

She nodded. "I like Kalim's eyes. Startling, aren't they? I worked hard to get those just right."

"It's something all right," I said. "Where were they playing?"

"Browning. The All-Indian Tournament. They came in second, but he scored more points than anyone else." Her eyes glistened. "Unstoppable."

"It's a hell of a likeness," Jake said. "Reminds me of when he played for Gateway."

"That's right. I thought if we hung it here, someone might remember. Come forward about his death."

"Maybe you should hang it at the lodge," Jake said.

She handed him the painting. "I've got some others at the lodge, but this seems right here. Anyway, they don't sell guns at the lodge."

Jake half turned and started to say something but stopped, then climbed the ladder and hung the painting.

I don't think Juniper intended to insult Jake with her remark and I was glad he let it slide. She had a point though. Whoever had shot Kalim probably had come into the store to buy a rifle or ammunition. Just thinking about it made my stomach churn.

When I returned from carrying the trophies to the storeroom, the two of them were still admiring her work.

96

I could tell how proud Juniper was. Even though she wore paint-spattered coveralls and a white painter's hat, she glowed. "Beautiful," Jake said under his breath, and I realized he was looking at her.

"Do we need to put price tags on them?" I asked.

Jake scowled. "This is art, not a garage sale."

Juniper handed me some brochures from her purse that explained her life and work, listed her shows. "Keep these at the front counter," she explained. "If anyone's interested, give him one to read."

"Each painting's two hundred dollars," Jake said. "That's a bargain. In a big city, you couldn't touch her work for that."

"At Jake's art gallery of the West, overhead is low." She lowered her voice. "I'll take less. A girl's got to eat. In a couple days, I'm going up to Central. One of the art galleries there plans a show of new artists."

At the mention of Central, Jake made a face. "Central doesn't deserve these," he said. "A bunch of retired blue-haired schoolteachers fussing around with watercolors."

"Think of all the tourists who come for the Water Pageant. They like visiting the galleries."

"Waste of time," Jake said.

While Juniper excused herself to use the restroom, I asked Jake, "You're taking her to art galleries and the Water Pageant?"

He held a finger to his lips, shushing me. "Some of her friends over there play the art game. I'm just helping out. You wouldn't catch me at Central's Water Pageant, for Christ's sake."

When Homer finished working his bakery shift, he came over, coffee cup in hand. He still had on his baker's clothes and smelled of baked bread and yeast. Flour powdered his dark eyebrows. "Jake said he did some decorating."

Homer took his time, studying each painting carefully. "Wow! Those horses look like they're running across the prairie!" He touched two fingers to his baker's cap as a kind of salute. "Never thought Jake was such a classy guy."

"One of these would look real good hanging in your bakery, Homer. Maybe that one of the old Indian man and the sheep. When Indians come into your shop, I bet they'd like seeing that painting."

"It's a beaut all right," he said, squinting at the painting. "No price tag on it. That means too rich for my blood."

☆ ☆ ☆ ☆

Some days, before work, I'd hike the half mile to the hobo jungle under the railroad tracks. This featured cardboard and tin lean-tos and a cooking fire. Riley had warned me that sometimes hoboes grabbed young boys to bugger them, so I never got too close. When I grew older and knew what Riley meant, I carried a stockman's knife with two strong blades, just in case. But the hoboes were buried deep in bedrolls and never stirred. I heard their snoring as I hiked back toward the store.

Still, one time a young hobo, just a few years older than I was, got close without my knowing. His tennis shoes and jeans were soaked with early dew and his lips were blue from the cold. Frizzy blond hair sprouted from beneath his Minnesota hat. He carried a broken-down fishing rod and a bait can. "Any fishing round here, 'bo?"

The simplicity of his question disarmed me. "Willow Creek is okay further down," I said, "but you've got to use grasshoppers. Cast them in the swirls close to the bank and stay out of sight."

He shook the bait can a little. "Worms is all I got. The grasshoppers are too fast. Tried that yesterday afternoon."

"Not this early. Slap them with your hat. Fish don't mind if the 'hoppers get banged around a little."

"I hate it when they spit," he said. "Right when you stick the hook in them. But I'm wanting breakfast." He paused. "Listen, 'bo. You carrying smokes?"

"No," I said, "but I got a candy bar." I handed him a PayDay.

"Thanks," he said. "These got smaller, didn't they? They used to be big as your fist."

"My stepdad might be riding the rails. Name's Riley Walker. You ever hear of him?"

He shook his head. "Hardly anybody uses his real name. There was a Riley up around Spokane. Short and heavy."

"That's not him," I said, "but thanks."

"If I see him, who should I say is looking?"

"That's okay," I said. "I'm not looking very hard."

☆ ☆ ☆ ☆

Central's Water Pageant was the biggest annual event in our part of the state. For weeks their newspaper featured items highlighting the colorful water floats, the queen and her court, the grand marshal — one of the first seven astronauts. Franklin had invited my mother and she was excited, already planning what to wear. This year's theme was Venice West, so she was thinking Italian.

Jake hated the ballyhoo. "Chamber of Commerce gangsters up there," he muttered. "Buy them for what they're worth; sell them for what they *think* they're worth. I'd make my first million."

On those rare occasions when the back-room boys caught Jake at the store, they razzed him about the pageant because it never failed to get his goat.

Gab perched on an ammunition box, munching one of Homer's fresh bear claws. "Sold five thousand dollars' worth of pageant advertising yesterday, Jake. Scout's honor." He flashed the Boy Scout salute. "How many radio spots do you want?"

"Bullshit. You never sold that in a week, much less a day. And you never were a scout."

"Sounds like Jake needs an outlook overhaul." Sniffy St. John, the glue man at the plywood mill, shifted forward in his chair, eager to watch a verbal sparring match.

"Nobody buys fishing equipment when they're headed to a damn water pageant," my uncle said.

"Jake, Jake, Jake." Gab rolled his eyes and spread his hands. "I'm disappointed in your small-town thinking. This isn't *just* a sporting goods store. It's *recreation* headquarters. See, we emphasize your ice chests, sun visors, thermos bottles. And what about that stack of picnic tables outside? Each time I drive by they look more forlorn. You better discount those or you'll be using them for firewood after Labor Day."

Jake had bought two dozen knocked-down cedar tables, but we couldn't sell them. Gab had laughed when he first saw the stack because the legs and seats for the tables had to be attached. "People hate the phrase 'Some assembly required,'" he said.

Sniffy hooted. "You took a lickin' on those tables all right, Jake." He was enjoying himself.

"Not necessarily," Gab said. "Have the boy pound together a couple of those tables and benches, set up a nice display of merchandise. People will line up for blocks." Gab stood pointing out the window at the icehouse. "Right about there. And don't forget ice. Gets mighty warm at the festival until nightfall." He took his pad and pen out. "Couple hundred?"

Jake shook his head. "Things are all screwed up this week. I'll go back to my regular schedule when this pageant nonsense settles down."

Sniffy selected a chocolate-covered cake doughnut. "Nice and warm still. Talk about screwed up, the damn Water Pageant fucks the mill over like you can't believe. Everybody wants to switch shifts and schedules. Some dumb bastards tried swapping three or four days' vacation for Festival of Floats night off. Me, I always take the wife. She wouldn't miss it for the world. By planning ahead, cooking up enough glue, I won't even get docked. I'm indispensable around there."

Jake sipped his coffee. "Must be nice to be so tight with the boss."

Sniffy winked at Gab. "Not as good as the fishing racket."

Gab rinsed out his cup and hung it on the peg rack. He used his forefinger as a toothbrush, running it back and forth across his teeth. Finishing, he smiled at himself in the mirror. "Boys, I hate to leave but there's cats to kill and fish to fry. Some of us, a very few, actually *work* for a living. Jake, last chance and we'll say it right: 'Gateway's Water Pageant Headquarters — ice chests, thermos bottles, suntan oils . . .'"

"No suntan oil," Jake said. "This isn't a damn drugstore."

"I knew that." Gab stopped under Juniper's paintings. "Not a drugstore but an art gallery. I'm glad you've chosen to diversify. A real entrepreneur." Gab sauntered toward the door.

"Hey," Jake called after him. "You never put a quarter in the creel for coffee or paid for that bear claw."

Gab just waved and kept walking. "Did I charge you for consultant's fees? I tossed out a thousand dollars' worth of merchandising tips. Pearls before swine."

Jake gave Sniffy and me a stern look. "I'm hiding his cup."

Laughing, Sniffy stood and tossed a dollar in the creel. "I'll cover him. Good show today — worth the price of admission. I'd say Gab won this round."

"Go sniff some glue," Jake said. "Close the doors tight and take deep breaths."

Sniffy stopped under the paintings. "Art." He shook his head. "Next thing, it'll be goddamn wine tasting. Little hunks of cheese with colored toothpicks. Lah-de-dah."

After Sniffy and Gab had gone, Jake muttered in their direction, "Suckers." He put his arm on my shoulder, looking me square in the face. "Nephew, it's hard to swim with the salmon when you're bogged down with bottom feeders."

☆ ☆ ☆ ☆

Shortly after I opened the store one morning, Ace strolled in. It seemed odd to find him out so early. "Jake around?" he asked.

"Not yet." I didn't know whether to expect him at all.

"He been feeling poorly?"

I shrugged. "Kind of punk." I couldn't imagine where Ace could have heard anything. "Can I help you?"

He didn't answer but drummed his fingers on the counter. Each knuckle was big as a walnut. His iceberg eyes gave me the chills.

"If you need something, maybe I can help?"

His eyes shifted to the paintings. "Jake getting into the art business or what?"

"Those are Juniper's paintings. He thought the dudes might go for them."

"Which dudes?" His eyes swept the store like he could conjure up some fishermen. "A bunch of the boys have canceled their reservations out to my place. If they don't show, they can't eat, drink, play cards. It's running into serious money. Tell your uncle I hope he gets to feeling better fast."

Ace started out but stopped at the sunglasses and tried on a pair. Even then, I could feel those eyes.

He replaced the glasses. "Maybe it's too much Indian cooking. That fry bread can really twist your gut."

I didn't say anything.

"Tell Jake he better stick to rainbows. I hear he's chasing those *brown* trout now. Browns are tricky. They stick to deep water. Sometimes you can't see the bottom. Might fall into something."

My throat was dry, but I knew he expected me to answer. "I'll tell him you stopped by."

When Ace returned two days later, Jake came out of the back. I didn't know what was on his mind after I had told him about Ace's first call. Two mornings in a row Jake had arrived at work before I opened and assembled bicycles. Grease streaked his face, and he held a ten-inch crescent wrench.

"Did my nephew show you these paintings, Ace? She's pretty good. You might want to buy a couple for your place."

Both men smiled at each other, but you could cut the tension.

Jake went along, pointing out the features of each painting, suggesting which ones Ace might like.

Some kids came in to buy worms and hooks, so that distracted me a little, and as they left Jake was showing Ace the painting of the Indians fishing from scaffolds. "They're catching salmon, don't you think, Ace. I don't see any browns, do you?" Jake pointed with the wrench.

Ace half turned, raising his arms, but Jake struck fast, and Ace sprawled across a display of stacked cool cans and picnic baskets. They all tumbled, Ace with them. He was out cold, but the coolers broke his fall.

Jake winced in pain and jammed the bleeding knuckles of his right fist into his mouth. Only then did I realize he hadn't used the wrench, but held it as backup.

"Jesus, Jake!"

"That hurts," he said, looking at his scraped knuckles and flicking his hand a few times. "Hope it doesn't screw up my fly fishing." He put the wrench down and motioned for me to help drag Ace.

"Do you think he's got brain damage or anything?"

Jake grinned. "He's a tough old bird. Anyway, that was just a love tap."

We dragged Ace outside by the arms and somehow lifted him into the pickup. He moaned a little and Jake turned Ace's head sideways. "You ride in the back," he told me. "If he throws up, make sure he doesn't strangle on his vomit."

I climbed in and hunkered beside Ace, wishing hard to keep him from throwing up. Jake slipped back into the store and returned wearing a windbreaker. For a moment I thought maybe he planned to ride in back himself, but then I saw the gun butt under the breaker.

At the Phoenix, Jake got a couple of the RedWings to help unload Ace and carry him into a unit. They stayed pretty calm, although one of the women came out and started getting excited.

"Don't you think a doctor should look at him?" she asked.

"Ace doesn't believe in hospital bills," Jake said. "Anyway, he's coming around. When he can swallow, give him four aspirin."

"His mouth is bleeding," she said. "What happened?"

"He slipped on some ice, fell into some cool cans," Jake said. "Pretty clumsy."

On the way back, Jake pointed out he felt some better and mentioned it was neighborly for Ace to check on him. At the store, he put the .38 back in the holster below the cash register. "You remember about this," he said and I nodded. "If anyone acts funny, stay behind the counter."

Then Jake took off, and I was on my own for two days. I half expected Ace to come back at any time packing a pistol and bringing trouble. Over and over, I imagined what I would do, but the fact was I didn't have the slightest idea.

Jake's warning made me spooky and I even had one false alarm. After I'd wheeled in the bikes one night and was preparing to close, a tall, flat-faced man who reeked of beer came in and wandered about the store. He had parked his car across the lot and was acting jittery, so I stayed behind the counter.

"Hey, kid. You want to come over and unlock this case? I like that pearl-handled pistol."

"Just a minute," I said. "I'm finishing up some license reports. That handle's pure abalone. Costs a lot."

While I was trying to decide what to do, someone in the car honked a couple times, then again. The man grinned as he headed out. "Another time, kid. Right now, I've got to eat some chicken."

☆ ☆ ☆ ☆

When trouble did show, Franklin brought it. He slunk in, looking like hell. The left side of his face resembled a swollen plum about to burst. Both eyes were blackened and his nose scraped raw. I was certain he'd been in a wreck, until I realized the Bel Air was scratchless. Still, I asked about a wreck, but Franklin shook his head.

"Fall down some steps?"

He pointed to the display case full of pistols. "Let me see that three fifty-seven Magnum."

After I handed him the Blackhawk, he tried spinning the cylinder and dry firing. I winced because the spinning scored the pistol, making it appear used, and dry firing might break the pin.

"How much?"

I told him, explaining we throw in a box of ammunition with each new gun purchase. I was eager to make the sale — usually people purchased pistols only from Jake — but I was even more eager to hear about Franklin's condition.

"Got in a fight with a tramp," he said finally. "Big sucker."

"Hope he looks worse than you do."

Franklin gripped the gun. "He looked worse to start with. But I got in my licks. He won't try me again."

"Good for you, Franklin." His unmarked knuckles showed he hadn't landed a blow, at least none that counted. "What was the beef?"

"Strange." Franklin shook his head. "He accosted me just as I was leaving for work. I tossed my briefcase in the car, glanced up, and there he was. Came out of nowhere."

"Did he say anything?" Suddenly I had a feeling about this tramp.

"Crazy son of a bitch! I thought he planned to rob me. But he yelled out, 'Marriage is sacrosanct.'"

I held my breath, wondering if he'd make the connection to my mother, but he just said, "Maybe he was a religious nut." Franklin pushed the gun at me. "I want hollow points in case he shows up again or brings friends."

"You've got to wait three days before you can actually take that pistol," I said. "The police have to check your background."

"Shit. The police in this town can't read."

"You have to fill out a form anyway," I said. "Have you ever been convicted of a felony? Are you crazy? That sort of thing."

"Can't we just bypass all that?" Franklin was becoming agitated. "Do I seem crazy to you?"

"Maybe," I said, trying to lighten the mood. "You are going out with my mother."

He didn't seem ready for kidding around.

After Franklin filled out the papers and left, I called Mom at work. "Don't get excited, but Riley might be in town."

I heard her catch her breath.

"If it is Riley, he beat up Franklin."

"He called in sick today," she said. "I thought it was just a bug."

"A tramp knocked the shit out of him. The description could match Riley's." I paused but she didn't answer. "Franklin just came in and bought a pistol."

"Don't sell them all," she said after a moment. "I might want to buy one myself."

☆ ☆ ☆ ☆

"Sell any picnic tables?"

Jake had started using that greeting whenever he called to check on things at the store. The stacked tables looked more weather beaten every day.

"Maybe I'll give them away," I said. "Everybody thinks I bought the store. You ever coming back?"

"Don't be a smart-ass like your uncle. Listen, make out the night deposit, would you? I don't want a bunch of cash hanging around." He paused. "Take the pistol with you."

"It's only four blocks to the bank."

"Most robberies occur near home."

When things slowed down a little before nine, I started wheeling in the bikes. I enjoyed the store — the hum of the air conditioner, the bright merchandise, the rich-leather smell of baseball gloves and spiked shoes, the pungent linseed oil and gun cleaner. I liked Juniper's paintings, too, except for Kalim's haunting eyes.

I locked the front door, bought a Pepsi with till change, calculated the night's deposit in the back office. The cash register drawer containing twenty-five dollars stayed open. If someone broke in wanting money for a toot, Jake hoped they wouldn't smash the expensive register or break into the gun cases.

Carrying the night bag in one hand and a padlock in the other, I stopped outside to lock the icehouse door. While leaning over to fasten the lock, I thought I felt a gun in my ribs.

"Freeze."

Panic grabbed me. I was sure Ace was back or had sent a RedWing.

"Stack of picnic tables makes a pretty good hiding place, Bucko. I don't think you're ever going to sell them."

"Jesus, Riley. You scared me to death." I felt out of breath. "You cost me a year's growth."

"Good thing you're wearing dark pants. Something leaked a little in front. Check it out."

Instinctively, I checked, but he was only kidding. Riley was thinner, with darker hair than I remembered. He wore sunglasses, a Detroit Tigers baseball cap, and a shit-eating grin. To tell the truth, I was glad to see him, not that I felt like giving him a big hug or anything. "You seem pretty fit, Riley."

"Feel this." He flexed his bicep.

I touched it. "Hard as stone."

He punched my shoulder then, a pretty good blow, but I didn't move. "You're packing more muscle, too, but I can probably still take you. For another year or two, anyway."

He meant it as a compliment.

"How you been keeping, Riley?" I asked.

"Lots of fresh air and wide open country. I've missed seeing you, Bucko. And your mom. But that's blood under the bridge now. Anyhoo, I'm getting by."

"We've been getting by, too," I said.

He nodded. "Saw the place. Yellow curtains. Does it have a tub or shower?"

"Combination," I said, a little relieved he hadn't been peeking in the windows. "You come around very often?"

"Sometimes. It gives me crampy feelings. Lots of guys walk through towns at night, look in windows, imagine the people inside. Maybe you want to stay, settle down, but then the feeling passes and you're glad to move on." He sighed. "I suppose the people inside the windows are stuck, too."

"Sure," I said, knowing I'd felt the same way at times, but I thought you outgrew it.

Riley's eyes shifted and I thought he might be embarrassed at saying too much, but he was watching a passing police car. Grady was driving, and I half waved, trying to appear natural. He didn't seem to notice us.

"On his way to coffee," Riley said. "Fat-ass."

"You stirred things up when you pounded Franklin. What was that about?"

"I didn't know I was going to hit him at first. Then I smelled his sickening cologne."

The last came out mean, and I sensed a streak in Riley I hadn't noticed before, so I waited to see if it passed. After a moment, he sauntered over to the picture window and studied Juniper's work. "That's new."

"One of Jake's old girlfriends is a painter," I said.

"She's pretty good," Riley said. "Is Jake going to sell those?"

"He thinks the rich dudes will buy them. Doctors, lawyers."

Riley tipped back his baseball cap. "You know, when I torched Dwight's place, they had rooms full of paintings. You never saw such horrible stuff. Burned like hell, though. Lots of oil."

Until Riley mentioned the paintings, I hadn't thought of Dwight's wife and daughter all that much. From a distance, I had just remembered the crummy railroad siding, not the people who lived there. Now Riley's act seemed like a personal violation.

"You actually went inside their house?"

"Sniffing around. Seeing how the other half lived. I can tell you right off, this stuff Jake has hanging is the real ticket."

"Riley, what did it feel like to burn that place down? I'm just curious."

His eyes widened and he tilted his head slightly so the blinking neon fish illuminated the left side of his face.

"It was something," he said. "You should try it."

☆ ☆ ☆ ☆

Approaching the hobo camp, I had my stockman's knife handy, and Mom was armed with a bulldog's determination and a Gideon's New Testament Bible. A gray-haired man in an electric blue suit had given a copy to every student in Grass Valley, except the Mormons and the Seventh-Day Adventists, who preferred their own. I didn't know what Mom planned with the Bible and I didn't believe I'd have to use the knife. Her determination would suffice.

Three hoboes huddled around the campfire: Minnesota, a bearded old man in a tan cap, a red-haired man with a lazy eye. The lot seemed more strange than dangerous.

At our approach, all came to their feet, apparently startled at my mother's presence. The old man whisked off his cap, holding it over his heart as if he expected someone to sing "The Star-Spangled Banner." He teetered on a gimpy leg, and I wondered how he jumped moving trains. The red-haired man stared at both of us; I couldn't pinpoint the favored eye. And Minnesota grinned and said, "Here's a young man that knows fishing. I caught some swell trout."

Now their supper was rabbit sizzling in a long-handled skillet and baking powder biscuits in a makeshift Dutch oven. Two had been drinking 7-Up, the third held a can of Dad's root beer. So much for the colorful stories of Sterno and Vienna sausage Riley told.

Overall, the camp appeared fairly tidy, considering how dry and dusty the summer was. They had swept away the cheatgrass and pine needles to avoid starting a fire. Toiletry items were visible near the bedroll. The old man had been reading an adventure novel with a lurid cover.

Apparently Minnesota's remark didn't register on my mother or she chose to ignore it. Her accusing eyes shifted from man to man; none held her gaze more than a moment. "Well, you might as well tell me where Riley is."

No reply.

"I'm certain you boys know." She tapped her right foot a few times, waiting.

Out of hobo loyalty, all shook their heads, but it wasn't convincing. The redhead seemed to be looking all over the place at once. My mother's gaze had settled on a fourth bedroll apart from the others and a couple of Riley's shirts hanging from a juniper branch. One had been our birthday present to him three years back and featured small red locomotives on a blue background.

She shook the New Testament in their faces. "Put your hands on this and deny you know Riley. Take care now. Remember how ashamed Peter was when he denied Christ three times before the cock crowed."

They shrank away from the Bible as if its pebbled green cover belonged to a serpent. I admired the way she had them buffaloed. Triumph gleamed in her eyes.

I half wanted to confess about encountering Riley myself by the icehouse. That's how convincing she was.

"I'm certain you men haven't touched a Bible since the last time you appeared in court. You prefer to wallow in darkness and lust, I imagine." She glanced at the cover of the adventure novel.

The redhead's shoulders slumped, and the old man fidgeted as he tried blocking her view of his book. Minnesota cleared his throat and said, "Ma'am, Riley's off fishing right now. Usually he comes back way late."

"He probably lures them in with a lantern," she said. "I hope the game wardens nail him."

I was amazed she knew this trick of night fishing.

"You men tell him I demand a divorce," she continued. "Culver and I deserve a clean slate." Her eyes settled on Minnesota, who seemed the likeliest of the bunch to convey a message ungarbled. "*You* tell him."

"All right." He agreed, and the others nodded in unison like backup members of a singing group.

"And point out that should he ever beat up Franklin again, or anyone else in town, I shall be forced to engage the police. Understood?"

Again they nodded.

Turning her attention to the pan and its contents, she frowned. "Your poor supper's burning, I'm afraid." Her voice had softened. Taking the pot holder from the red-haired man, she seized the handle and shifted the skillet to the edge of the fire. "Rabbit's like chicken," she told them. "It requires a long time to cook. And you must do it slowly or it remains tough." She put a little pepper on the pieces, turning them over. "Delay adding salt until the last few minutes. That way the juices remain sealed."

"Would you and the boy care to stay for dinner, ma'am?" the red-haired man asked. "We don't get much gentle company." Until then, I had thought he might be mute.

"I don't believe so," she said. "Our own supper's at home waiting. But I can sit and visit a minute, supervise the rabbit. I trust it's not a jackrabbit. You might get tularemia. You must never eat a jackrabbit in a month that doesn't have an *r*."

She chose a place on a log and handed the pot holder back to the redhead. The old man offered 7-Ups and we both took one. Until then, I hadn't realized how dry my mouth felt.

After drinking, she sat on the ground, resting her back against a jack pine. A few stars were visible in the night sky, and Venus hung on the horizon. "I envy your lives in a way," she said to no one in particular. "So adventurous and free. Sometimes, I wonder — if I hadn't been born a woman needing to think about family responsibilities . . ."

They allowed that the traveling life had advantages. Most places they obtained day labor, lived off panhandling and church suppers. And as they watched out for their own, a kind of camaraderie grew. But it was no life for a woman, they agreed, at least not the kind of well-mannered woman my mother represented.

After the rabbit was properly cooked, if a little burned on one side, the men began to eat. Mom tried one of their biscuits, breaking off small pieces and chewing thoughtfully. Hungry, I gobbled two, and imagining the cold stove at home, longed for a rabbit thigh, but I was petrified of rabbit fever. Riley had told tales of men he'd encountered living along isolated sections of track whose diseased livers had turned them yellow as field corn. I settled for a third biscuit.

Over supper, each man catalogued his tribulations — divorce, bad business deals, crazy relatives, lousy breaks. Minnesota had served time for shoplifting in three states; the old man was wanted for armed robbery somewhere in the South. The red-haired man quietly confessed he hadn't paid child support in six years. "I'm a roofer by trade, but what's the point of sweating in the sun, freezing in the rain, when the government takes most of what I make?" He shook his head. "One day I'll fall off a slick roof and break my skull. For what?"

When my mother pressed him, he admitted he felt bad about the children. "They're in junior high by now. Lester had to repeat fifth grade. That's his mother's doing. She tried home schooling back in Kansas."

These were criminals all right, but not the hardened type I had imagined. Somehow they had lurched to the wrong siding and seemed unlikely to ever cross back to the main line. I realized they weren't much different from the back-room boys. A slow switch, a faulty coupling would land them here. Riley was proof.

Eventually the conversation lulled and my mother rose, brushing a few pine needles off her office clothes. The men rose, too. Once again, the old one removed his tan cap.

"We'd like to thank you for your hospitality," she said. "Please don't forget to deliver the message to Riley."

Before leaving, she handed the Bible to Minnesota. "I noticed one thing missing here. You men forgot to say grace."

12

THE LORD IS MY SHEPHERD, I was thinking when my uncle's voice cut in.

"You buy a boat and start running the rapids. After three years, if you've bought a lot of boats, look for another line of work." Jake grinned. "Now if you wreck Old Skookum, I've got to dock your wages."

I smiled, too nervous to laugh. He was teaching me to take the boat through Horse Head Rapids on our way to the memorial site, and I felt excited but scared, the way you might at a championship basketball game, when you want to make the big play but fear you'll goof.

"Tell me again, okay?" We stood on a railroad grade, studying the rocks and water below.

"Stay toward the right bank, not too close. Keep away from those overhanging trees." Jake drew an imaginary line through the rapids with his finger. "On the upper run, watch that bad rock this side of mid-stream. We call it the Can Opener. Real sharp edge will tear out a boat's side." He paused a moment.

"Slide past the Can Opener and you're in whitewater. See that groove of water below?"

"Right." I thought I saw the place. "It starts above those rock shelves."

"Teeth and Tongue, we call it. Hit that groove dead center and slide between those teeth on that long tongue of green water. That'll sweep you into the rooster tail. But hit it wrong, and I've bought a new boat."

"You don't pay me enough to dock my wages," I said.

"Listen. Once you're past the Can Opener and in the whitewater, take three good strokes with the left oar. That'll slide you right onto the Tongue."

Jake pushed the drift boat away from shore. His big rough hands on the gunnel made my own seem puny, but I gripped the oars, making certain they were secure in the locks.

He climbed in, water dripping from his hip boots. Making a show of tightening his life jacket and tugging his hat down, my uncle said, "I'm taking a deep seat, pardner." Picking up the spare oar, he brandished it over his head. "Might need to keep those teeth from biting the boat."

I rowed just short of midstream, then turned the boat to face the rapids. My hands were slick on the oars. As we approached the Can Opener, I kept stroking, giving us plenty of room.

"Not too much," he said. "We want to hit the green Tongue dead center."

As the Can Opener slid by, I could see the paint from other boats scraped along its jagged edge. We hit the whitewater, and I stroked three times with the left oar, then realized the current was sweeping us too far right.

"No!" Shifting his weight, Jake readied the spare oar to fend off the rocks.

I remembered to ship the right oar just as we began bumping along the rocky ledge. Jake grunted as he pushed us away, and I jammed my right palm against the mossy rocks. After bumping twice we cleared the shelf, sweeping through the rooster tail and slowing in the long calm pool beyond.

"Head for shore," Jake said, putting the spare oar back.

Mouth dry, I rowed the boat over to a sand point between two alders at the water's edge. At least I hadn't broken an oar or lost the boat.

Jake loosened his life vest.

"I'll do better next time," I said.

"That wasn't too shabby. It takes experience." He climbed out of the boat. "Come on. Let's pull Old Skookum out and take a look downstream."

According to Jake, "Skookum" was an Indian word that meant something like "powerful spirit." On this river, I was happy for any extra help I could get.

"Watch out for that goddamn poison oak," Jake said as we pulled the boat onto the lower end of Whiskey Dick Flat. "Sonofabitching stuff must've grown a foot in the last week. Maybe we can get the BLM to spray or something."

I was careful to follow Jake's footsteps around the patches as he led me to the memorial site. Whiskey Dick's was a long, low flat covered with ponderosa pine and junipers. Unlike the Barn Hole, this place had lots of shade and a beautiful view of the river. High redtop grass and a few cattails marked the flat's lower end, along with the poison oak. When I looked close, I realized a dozen saplings had been planted recently and would form a little arbor as they grew taller. "You did this?" I asked.

Jake took off his cap and rubbed his forehead. "Been planning awhile. When I'm not overloaded with dudes, I've brought down a few trees — black locust, red birch. With Juniper busy painting a few days, I thought we'd sneak down and take a look." He put on his cap. "This is one of the best spots on the river. Your dad loved camping here and I figured he'd like the trees. We'll bring some more down. The guides will make sure they get watered steady."

Three feet of chicken wire or cyclone fencing encircled each tree, protecting them.

"Beavers?" I asked.

Jake nodded. "They'll girdle a tree right quick. And cattle will rub against a trunk, knock it down. Can't do much about the deer, except pray for high grass."

"How do you plan to do the memorial? Put it right in those trees, I'll bet."

"Got a couple ideas," he said. "First, I want it *solid*. Make sure no flood or city dude can carry it out. We'll wrestle a big field rock down here, half bury it, fill up the hole with cement. We'll want a flat rock so we can drill one side, mount the plaque."

I didn't see any likely looking rocks nearby. Basalt rock was plentiful on the talus slopes, but I thought it would be too brittle to drill.

"I know some farmers with good field rocks," he said, as if reading my thoughts. "Granite should do the trick."

"You're going to need a pretty big boat to bring a rock in."

Jake pointed to a zigzag scar stitching the hillside. "This flat used to be a lambing site, and some bowed-neck old rancher punched a road out. Only took him eleven years. If we fill in a few slides, we can bring a tractor and trap wagon down. All we need's a key to the gate on top."

Following Jake's finger tracing the road, I realized what a rugged job it must have been. The hillside was so steep as to seem untrackable. "Tough country," I said.

"Tougher people."

After lunch, we took a nap, and when I awoke about three I noticed the blue sky smeared with dirty white smoke. "Think that's field burning?" I asked Jake.

He squinted. "Doesn't look too wild. But fire's always a threat in this country. Even in good years it's bad, and this year is terrible. Next trip down, we'll bring a propane stove. No open fires. Over the years we lost most of this country to fire. Half of Gateway burned once when a dude dropped his cigar in dry hay at the county fair. Hamilton burned up — that was a little mining town — Pine Crossing, Bright's Mill, and the Grand Hotel.

"When the old man got here he joined the fire department up on Juniper Flat, just a volunteer deal. The first time they got called to fight a grass fire, he saw the truck. Nothing but an old slick-tired flatbed with four fifty-five-gallon drums filled with water and burlap sacks."

"That was it? No pumpers or anything?"

Jake shook his head. "The old man couldn't believe it either. They expected him to beat out that fire with wet seed sacks. Problem was, the sacks kept falling apart. Most had been chewed up by mice. Otherwise the cheap farmers wouldn't have donated them to the fire brigade."

☆ ☆ ☆ ☆

That evening, when the wind kicked up a chill, Jake pulled an old Filson vest from beneath the seat of the boat. "Try this on for size. It's cotton duck, oiled to keep the wind from cutting."

"One of yours?" I asked. Big for me, the vest would be snug on Jake. Still, it felt comfortable.

"Your father's. It went down with the boat, but the scuba divers brought it up when they salvaged the gear. I dried everything out, put the gear back in the vest." He shrugged. "I figured someday it would hang on a good set of shoulders."

I was excited knowing the vest had belonged to my father. "Thanks, Uncle Jake." The pockets bulged, and I was curious to see the gear.

"Some guys are all tackle and no fish," Jake said. "Talk and act big shot but can't produce. Your dad was the genuine goods, like this Filson vest. He liked their company's motto: 'Might As Well Have the Best.'"

"Can't top that," I said.

"None better. When we first started the business and got in some of their equipment, I saw him eyeballing the vest. Awful pricey. Then we took some Denver dudes out and just slaughtered fish. Afterwards, one of them gave him a nice bonus. So he got the vest. It's a hunting vest, really, but he added a wool strip to dry his flies. Paid for it, too. That was your father. Some guys would just grab it off the rack, but he knew we were trying to build the business. He was always squared away."

I nodded, feeling good about wearing my father's vest, enjoying the gear's weight. This is what it's about, I thought, knowing I belonged right here on the river my father had loved so much, and his before him. Jake, too. Still, I felt a deep ache, because good as it was, something was missing.

"Check out the equipment," Jake said, jabbing his thumb at the vest. "Good reel there. Oiled it myself after he died, but most of the stuff, I just left alone."

I don't know if Jake had any idea what I was feeling, but he stood and walked down to the river, giving me a chance to explore the pockets and inventory the equipment.

The heaviest item was a Flueger Medalist reel. I loved the deep green metal casing with well-worn silver patches. The fly line was cracked, but I could buy a new one. And backing; that would be rotten. The reel's action was smooth though. Jake had oiled it well.

In other pockets I found pliers, Not-a-Knot leaders, a snakebite kit. Opening the kit, I discovered the Band-Aids and Merthiolate missing. In one pocket I found a fly box jammed with my father's favorites: Renegades, Spent-Wing Stones, Adams, a few Bucktail Caddis. The hooks were still sharp.

A plastic folder held his fishing license and steelhead tag from the year he drowned. Eleven punches in the tag showed he'd landed some big fish that spring. Underneath the steelhead tag was a small black and white photo of two men comparing catches of fish. One was my grandfather. The other I didn't recognize, but it seemed odd he was wearing a bow tie. I put the plastic folder on a flat rock so I could ask Jake when he came back.

Reading my father's signatures on the license and tag had sent a shiver down my back. And it made me curious about the vest and equipment. I wondered why my father wasn't wearing it when he drowned. Maybe it had been too awkward to get the life jacket over the vest, I decided.

My uncle was still bumping around in the boat and double-checking the tie-up, making certain the equipment was stored securely. He took pride in never losing a boat, except in the accident that killed my father, and he wasn't going to lose one at night, as dudes sometimes did when the river rose or a knot worked loose.

Old Skookum was heavy — some guides thought too heavy — because of all the extra equipment my uncle carried: spare hip boots, rods and reels, first-aid kits, flashlights and lanterns, fire extinguishers. His rule of thumb was to carry two of everything, just in case one failed.

"Anyone can have a bad day," he had explained once. "Lose a reel, break a rod, step in a hole and have to kick off your hip boots. What if it was the best day of the season and you ran short of flies or had a reel freeze-up? Once I had two reels give out the same trip. Might as well have plenty on hand. You can always put gear back when you're off the river."

Curiously, I had never seen him replace anything in the store except leftover sodas and a few bad fly patterns some dude might have insisted on trying after reading an article somewhere. Every time he went out, he threw in three or four rolls of toilet paper. "Film for the brownie," he called it; any given trip, the boat must have contained a dozen rolls.

After Jake came back from checking the boat, I held out the reel. "This must have been my father's spare, don't you think? His rod and reel probably went down with the boat."

Jake took the reel, turning it over in his hands before setting it on the flat rock. "That's his spare all right. Your dad never carried much equipment, but he always packed an extra reel." He shook his head. "Most likely he tucked that vest under the seat before we hit the rapids. When the scuba divers brought up the gear, the vest was with the rest of the stuff. Like I said, Dave traveled a little light. Me, I'm on the heavy side. Pliers and knives get dropped into the river; sunglasses fall off; tackle goes all over hell and gone. I remember one time when the fishing was red hot. A big caddis hatch was on and fish were boiling the water. I was hooking one every second cast, but when I went to check on Dave, he was sitting on a rock, watching the river. Turns out he'd dropped his fly box and it swept downstream before he could grab it.

"He kept a small plastic box in his shirt pocket — only held four big caddis flies. But the monsters had broken off three, and the last had a bum hook. So he just sat twiddling his thumbs, watching the fish rise. I gave him more flies and a heavier leader."

"Maybe he was counting on you," I said.

Jake mulled it over. "Think your dad was smart enough to make me mule-pack for him?"

I shrugged. "It's possible."

"Well, it worked out. He caught eight big redsides that afternoon, all over sixteen inches. And I only landed five. We cooked the two biggest for supper. 'You were fishing pretty puny this afternoon,' he said as he squeezed fresh lemon on his trout.

"'You wouldn't be eating at all, if I hadn't come prepared,' I told him. Your dad laughed. 'If it weren't for me,' he said, 'you'd have to munch on minnows.'

"Your great-uncle Harold and the old man," Jake said after studying the photograph I'd found along with my father's license. "Now that's a pair to draw to. Harold was the only man I ever saw actually fish while wearing his bow tie. Claimed the fish respected authority. But he still never caught as many lunkers as the old man. Pissed him off some, too, since he always bought tons of gear."

"Harold loved good equipment and he wasn't stingy. He'd lumber off the train from Minnesota, bristling with fishing rods and dragging two footlockers jammed with gear. A couple times he came out with nice Gokey outfits he bought in St. Paul. Whatever didn't catch fish, he gave to me and Dave. Said he'd probably borrow it next trip, but never did. Always came completely reequipped."

"Sounds like a character," I said.

"A gen-u-ine character," Jake said, emphasizing each syllable. "Big timber buyer for Weyerhaeuser. Self-made man. The old man and my uncle's father had been the coachman for Weyerhaeuser, so the boys grew up in 'coachman's alley,' just behind Summit Avenue in St. Paul, where all the muck-a-mucks lived.

"Harold always bragged that the top hands knew him from the time he started sucking lollipops. Frederick Weyerhaeuser, James J. Hill, the empire builder, A. B. Stickney, president of the Chicago Northern Railroad."

"Big shots," I said.

"The biggest," Jake agreed. "Big shots still call the plays. This whole country was built on timber and railroads. And a lot of them started back in Minnesota.

"Weyerhaeuser took a liking to the boys. They were full of vinegar and his kid was sickly. He paid them for shooting rats back in his horse stables. They killed those pests with twenty-two Hamiltons they got scrounging cigarette coupons off high rollers, and he thought they were go-getters. He appreciated that since he was a hustler himself — had to be.

"How he got his start, now there was a story. He had a contract to build a road through upper Minnesota, and the deal was he could keep all the timber they cleared building that road." Jake broke a stick and tossed it into the fire. "Nowhere in the contract did it specify how wide that roadway was to be." He squinted at me. "If you were building the road, how wide would you make it?"

"Pretty wide," I said.

"Pretty goddamn wide," he said. "Wide enough to jump into the timber business.

"Anyway, Harold saw everybody on Summit Avenue making big dollars and he vowed to grab a piece of the wealth himself. And I guess he did. Each time before he hopped that train back to Minnesota, he'd chide the old man about ever leaving, then put his arms around Dave and me. 'Boys, there's a wealth of opportunity in Minnesota. Your father's a brick head for ever leaving, but maybe you'll come back. I'll show you the ropes.'

"Harold had flair. When the snow got real deep at his winter cabin along the St. Croix River, he'd make a snowman. One Christmas he sent photos. His snowman had a creel slung over the shoulder and a fly rod tucked under the arm. His wife's snowwoman held a frying pan with some fish."

"Real fish?" I asked.

"Wooden. Otherwise the birds would get them. I'll say this about Harold. He came through with a loan when we needed it most. The old man was dead and the hospital bills staggering. Dave and I were foundering in the business. I thought maybe we'd have to give up and sell, but your dad wouldn't budge.

"'We got to nail our thumbs to the wall and try to hang on,' Dave said. And we did until Harold came through. Of course, eventually he wanted it back — with interest.

"Two kinds of people in the world," Jake said. "Those that wait for things to get handed to them. Others reach out and grab all they can." He closed both fists for emphasis. "That's why we got two."

"Whatever happened to Harold? If he liked you so much, maybe you'll inherit a bundle." I enjoyed the idea of cruising through the timber with another colorful uncle sizing up the trees for big commercial deals.

"Don't be a sucker," Jake said. "He got religion and gave almost everything away. Went on the road preaching. Once he came around here and we saw a poster describing Holy Harold. That night he drew a pretty good crowd to a little country Baptist church. Faith healing. A dozen people went up front. Whoever he touched jumped like he was a lightning bolt.

"Your dad and I stepped forward — just for a gag — but Harold spotted us right off. Drawing us close so his helpers couldn't hear, he said, 'Boys, I can't heal ugly.'

"We waited for him after the service, got him something to eat. He carried all his worldly goods in two small suitcases, one missing a handle. After dinner he said, 'Fishing for souls is all that counts. You should have seen me yesterday, boys. Put a brand new nose on a man and he dedicated himself to the good work.'"

"He really went a hundred percent, I guess."

"You're right." Jake stood and stretched. "There wasn't a half-assed bone in his body."

My uncle was working on his third drink. "Dave and I spent a lot of good times with Harold and the old man on this river just studying the sky, imagining things." Jake tapped his glass. "Dave always figured on having a kid, passing things on. Me, I wasn't so sure.

"The old man knew so much about the river, we expected him to know everything else, even the sky. Once we got past the Big Dipper, Little Dipper, and Orion, he was stuck. But he never let on." Jake craned back his neck and pointed. "'There's the Chinook Salmon,' the old man used to say. 'See the curved line of stars that make his back. That cluster is his tail. And those three that make a triangle — his fin.'

"He sounded pretty convincing. I kept believing that stuff long after I quit believing in Santa Claus. Of course, your dad played along with the old man, even after he had things figured.

"Whatever he knew about the river, that's what he saw in the sky. Watch." Jake pointed to a section of sky that contained clusters of stars, some stacked in columns, others forming graceful arcs. "There's the Sky Fisherman. Those stars closest to the mountain are the hip boots. Straight above is his vest, and the little curved line of stars is a pipe jutting out his mouth. That long row of curved stars makes up his fly rod. From the deep bend in that rod, I'd say he's hooked a dandy."

I stared at where Jake was pointing and thought I had the right stars. Sometimes the formations seemed to blur into one another and I couldn't quite tell. "And that fish will never get away," I said. "Maybe that's the best part."

"Sure," Jake said. "You can always imagine how big that lunker is going to be." Shaking his head, he added, "What always amazed your dad and me was how the Sky Fisherman dressed so much like the old man, right down to the crook-stem pipe. And when I got a little older and studied the stars at school, I couldn't figure why the teacher left out some of the most important ones. Even now, when I come out here on these clear nights and see all those stars, I'd rather think of them the way the old man had them, not the way some Greek or Roman said."

"That makes sense." Looking at the faraway stars made me think about heaven. Perhaps that was a place you could finally do what you wanted with those you loved — have a picnic with my father instead of Franklin. My mother and Jake would be there, too, of course. "Uncle Jake, point out all the constellations to me, would you? The way my grandfather had them?"

"Sure," he said. "Look over there to the east, right above the canyon rim. That's the Leaky Boat."

13

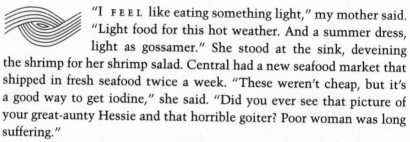

"I FEEL like eating something light," my mother said. "Light food for this hot weather. And a summer dress, light as gossamer." She stood at the sink, deveining the shrimp for her shrimp salad. Central had a new seafood market that shipped in fresh seafood twice a week. "These weren't cheap, but it's a good way to get iodine," she said. "Did you ever see that picture of your great-aunty Hessie and that horrible goiter? Poor woman was long suffering."

I had seen it and slipped it out of the family album a couple times to scare a fat kid at school. "Get one of these and you'll never wear a necktie, Delbert," I had told him. I squeezed a little lemon on one of the cleaned shrimp and popped it into my mouth. "They got iodine in salt now, Mom. You'd have to work pretty hard at getting a goiter."

"I'm sure you're right," she said. "But when I was growing up you couldn't get fresh seafood. Father used to put three iodine drops in a glass of water each Monday before he went to the office. When I saw the skull and crossbones on the dark blue bottle, I was positive he'd poisoned himself. I cried most of the day until he came home safely."

"Isn't Franklin going to be a little curious when he doesn't get to eat any of the shrimp he saw you buy?"

"I don't want to be predictable." She put the cleaned shrimp into the colander and ran cold water over them. "If a man knows everything you're going to do, it's no fun. You have to create a bit of flair, some mystery."

"And you get all that by not feeding Franklin these shrimp? Anyway, I'm glad he's not coming this time. It hurts to see him all beat up."

She flicked some cold water at me with her fingertips. "You were supposed to get out the good silver."

"Jake doesn't like stuff too fancy." I hoped the silver could pass inspection without being polished. I hated the smell of the polish.

"If I were thinking only of Jake, I'd fix steak and potatoes. This is for *us*." She softened. "And a little elegance now and then doesn't hurt."

I put the lace tablecloth, the sterling silverware, and the china on the kitchen table that we had moved into the front room for my mother's idea of "elegant" dining. Somehow most of the china had survived the moves, although only three teacups remained with handles. Two wine glasses survived, these being for my mother and Jake. Recently, I'd gotten used to putting out the good tableware for Franklin's visits.

My mother set the shrimp salad in the refrigerator and popped the cheese muffins into the preheated oven. Then she sat with me in the front room. "The table looks nice, Culver. But we're going to need the silver polished again soon."

"Thanks. I pretty much know the drill."

She frowned at the clock. "He's late."

"When the fishing's good, the dudes don't want to leave the river," I said. "This is the first trip he hasn't canceled in a couple weeks. Secretary of state or some hot shot."

"It's all right," she said. "Shrimp salad is delicious chilled. And this gives us a few moments to visit. It seems you're so busy I hardly see you. Is Jake paying you extra for overtime?"

"We've talked about it." He'd mentioned it once or twice but I wasn't counting my chickens.

"Well, he mustn't take advantage just because you're a relative."

"It's a good job, Mom. I'm learning all kinds of things about fishing and hunting."

"I'm sure you are, dear, but there are other things to consider, and school will be starting in about a month."

"Jake's said he wants me to work after school and weekends — at least through deer season."

"Well, we'll see how all that works out." She tipped her head slightly. "But let's talk about something else. I'm just curious. If you could go anywhere in the world, where would it be?"

"Is this some kind of trick question?"

She smiled. "Of course not. Don't tell me you're getting a suspicious mind. Just let your fancy take you. Pretend you have a magic carpet."

I tried, but as my mind ticked off the possibilities, I realized I wasn't interested in most of them. "I'd like to go to one of those big fishing resorts in Canada. Jake had some brochures and the guys caught salmon weighing over eighty pounds."

She sat a little straighter. "Yes, salmon. Okay, then, what would be your next choice?"

"Alaska," I said, but when I saw her mouth tighten, I added, "or probably England. My literature teacher talked a lot about the places there. A dead poet's buried under every tree."

She laughed. "Culver, you have an extravagant sense of humor, but yes, England would be ideal. Your father took me to Victoria on our honeymoon. That's very much like England."

"What about now, Mom?" I said. "Where would you like to go?"

"Anyplace I could be pampered," she said. "Waited on hand and foot."

Twenty minutes late, Jake smelled of Lava. His hands and forearms appeared well scrubbed. "Gateway's agreeing with you, Flora." He stepped in the door. "You're looking fit." Noticing the table, he added, "Nice spread. Haven't seen that china for a spell."

"Took dozens of newspapers to pack it," she said. "And those galoots Riley hired managed to drop a barrel or two. Please just take a seat. The cheese muffins are getting cool."

Mom brought in the shrimp salad and muffins as well as some white wine she bought in Central. I had to settle for apple juice in an everyday glass. As soon as I had filled my plate, I was ready to eat, but she stopped me with a look. "Jake, would you like to offer thanks?"

"Sure," he said without missing a beat. "Dear Lord, for this food and family and all thy blessings, we give thanks. Guide us, and especially watch over the young one, we pray. Amen."

After a moment's hesitation, she said, "That was very nice. Thank you." She lifted her fork and I knew we could begin eating.

"You know, these shrimp are terrific," he said after a couple bites. "Maybe just a bit more lemon."

I passed him the plate of lemon wedges and he continued. "Funny how fish smells like the water it comes from. A trout from the Lost tastes different than a trout from the Pine. And lake trout differ from stream. These shrimp smell like the ocean."

"I bought them fresh in Central," she said. "They fly fresh seafood in twice a week."

"Central would do that," he said, and I thought he might light into Central or the Water Pageant, but he didn't. "I ate crabs from the Chesapeake one time at a little place on the Eastern Shore of Maryland. Blue crabs, and they tasted just like the bay. That water's milder than here, more tropical. They boil crabs using a spicy seasoning called Old Bay."

"Jake, you're just full of surprises." Mom set down her fork. "I never knew you were in Maryland."

It was difficult to imagine my uncle anywhere but on the Lost. "When were you in the Chesapeake?" I asked.

Jake looked at me, not my mother. "After your father's death, I traveled around the country, tried to reckon with things."

"I remember you were out of touch a long time," Mom said after a moment.

He nodded. "Somehow, I always went to water. In Maryland, it was the Chesapeake and a place along the Choptank River. They study marine biology there."

"What was it like?" My mother broke one of her cheese muffins in half and slid a piece into her mouth.

"Nice country, but the water's pretty sluggish. Lots of mosquitoes. The official bird of Maryland." He winked.

"I'll bet you met a woman," my mother said, studying him. "Why else would you stay in Maryland?"

Jake nodded. "Later, she married a biologist. Now they've got three kids."

"So you were in Maryland and no one knew. I find that remarkable."

Jake poured wine for my mother, then filled his own glass. "Like I said, I always went to water. When I hit the Great Lakes, I was out of money, so I signed on as a deckhand for the Cleveland Cliffs boats. That's a steel company. When the captain learned I like to fish, once he anchored off Isle Royal in Lake Superior. We rowed the dinghy to shore, then hiked to an inland lake for walleyes. Caught a couple nice ones, but they don't fight anything like a Lost River steelhead. At night we heard wolves howling — spooky. Moose and wolves share that island. No people.

"We sailed all around the Great Lakes — Michigan and Superior. One time we anchored off a little town holding a memorial service to honor all the drowned sailors. Great Lake storms are wicked, especially on Superior. The big waves coming from all sides can rip a ship in half." He took a sip of his wine.

"Back in those days, fathers, sons, brothers, could work the same boats. But they changed the regulations since then, a couple years ago after the *Carl Bradley* sank." He shook his head. "I read about it in the paper. Twenty-two men were lost just from one city. Thirty-five altogether."

He tapped the side of his glass. "All that sadness. But I had realized a long time ago that my own grief was back here, so I'd come home."

My mother picked up her napkin, dabbing the corners of her mouth. Her eyes glistened and she blinked.

"Wolves and moose," I said, trying to keep the conversation going. "I'd like to see a wolf."

"They'll give you goose bumps." He laid his hand on my shoulder. "The only other time I heard wolves was in Alaska, when Dave and I tried longshoring to make money for the guide service."

My mother set down her napkin and stood. "Maybe that's enough stories for now. You're filling the boy's head with wild notions."

Jake tightened his grip. "She's afraid I'll tell you about the girl from Oberlin. In college she got knowledge, but in Alaska, she was *educated*." He let go of my shoulder and spread his hands. "What wild notions, Flora?"

She held the back of her chair. "School's coming up. He's got to study and get good grades. Right now he's got too many notions about fishing. Salmon in Canada, fish camp in Alaska. There's more to life than fishing. I plan for him to aim a little higher." She let go of her chair. "Now who wants coffee?"

Jake said he did, please, and she went into the kitchen. He scraped back his chair, intending to clear the table but she called, "Just sit still, I'm not ready for those yet. It's a small kitchen."

Jake leaned toward me and mouthed, "Canada?"

I shrugged, but for the first time since she'd invited Jake to dinner I realized her strategy. She wanted him to back off. She was laying out her territory. I didn't know how he would handle it, but I expected him to take her square on.

"How's Juniper?" she called from the kitchen, her tone lightened. We could hear her getting the coffee.

"Sold her painting of horses yesterday at the store. Guy wrote out a check for two hundred dollars like it was chicken feed." Jake paused. "I liked that painting and kinda hated to see it go."

"I'm certain the Central show will be a big success. Franklin and I are planning to attend the opening." Mom put two cups on the table and poured steaming hot coffee into each. When she offered cream and sugar, Jake shook his head. "Juniper must have a good head for business," she said.

He let Mom get the coffee to her mouth before he spoke. "Flora, I'm all for study. College, too, if necessary. We got no quarrel over that. But Culver needs to learn about business, and I can teach him."

"I'm not talking about fishing," she said, setting the cup down.

"Neither am I," he said and tapped his head. "It takes smarts to run a business these days, advertising, merchandising. All good skills. He learns a lot working in the store, and if it comes to college, I can help some."

I half expected my mother to say I could get a scholarship or we could swing it ourselves, but she didn't. She was already reading up on college expenses and knew we'd need help.

"Maybe the business at the store's okay, Jake," she said. "But I don't want him taking chances on the river. I don't." She put both hands on the table, leaning forward.

Glancing at Jake, I tried to catch his eye. I didn't want him thinking this confrontation was my idea.

Setting down his cup, he squared his shoulders and took her straight on. "Flora, don't try to tie him to your apron strings."

"Damn you, Jake, I'm not."

"Cut him some slack. Your own fears will hold him back."

"My fears?" She flared. "I've got reasons." Her wild eyes made Jake pause, and I realized how deep the hurt and anger were. I doubted she was ever going to change.

After taking a sip of his coffee, Jake said in a reassuring tone, "We never go on the dangerous parts, Flora. As for the rest, hell, college kids that don't know a paddle from a bailing bucket go through every weekend." He paused. "If you insist, I'll row Culver through the rapids. But we can't stay off the river. We're putting together a great project down there, aren't we, Culver?"

"That's right. We are." In some ways, I didn't want to be his accomplice against my mother, but I didn't want her preventing me from going on the river. "We're putting up a monument for my father, grandfather, and some of the other old guides. And we need your help to get the right words."

"Sure," Jake said. "I've been over to Silverdale to learn about metal plaques. They'll do a fine job. But saying the words, that's something else."

Her right hand went to the top button of her dress. She looked at me, Jake, then me again. "You're really involved in this, Culver?"

I nodded.

"It's something he'll always remember," Jake said. "We want to get it right."

She went into the kitchen to get some store-bought cookies for dessert, but she seemed to take a long time. After a while, Jake leaned toward me and said, "Coffee's cold. Tough getting a warm-up around here."

When I glanced into the kitchen, I could see my mother leaning heavily on the counter, totally still.

I don't remember much about conversation over the cookies and second cups of coffee. Jake helped clear the table and offered to wash or dry, but Mom said she'd get the dishes later. After he left, she put the leftover salad and muffins in the refrigerator, rinsed out the wine glasses and coffee cups. She filled each of the muffin tin containers with water, letting the crusty baked-on parts soften for the morning wash. "I can't face this right now," she said. When we moved the kitchen table back, she took out her manicure bag and started working on her cuticles, pushing them back with a little silver instrument until the moon slivers showed. "I've always had strong nails," she said. "They're one of my best features." She held up her left hand, inspecting the fingernails. "Even when I went to secretarial school and had to do all that typing, they never broke or chipped.

"A few of the other girls were jealous and when I found out, I told them Knox gelatin sometimes did the trick, even though I never used it myself. For a couple weeks they tried it but nothing changed. Then I discovered they had been *soaking* their nails instead of drinking it like they were supposed to." She shook her head and smiled at the memory. "Some of those girls didn't know sickem." She applied some clear lacquer to her nails and waited for them to dry, occasionally blowing gently. "Soaking them for two weeks. Can you imagine?"

Before going to bed, I took the garbage outside and placed a big rock on the dented can lid. According to my mother, cats were crazy about shrimp and she didn't want to find garbage strewn about the next morning.

Lying in bed that night, I felt a little sorry for her. Voices played over in my mind, especially the brief exchange she and my uncle had when she returned from the kitchen, composed, and set the cookies on the table.

"So you've gotten over it, I guess." Her words had been a challenge to Jake, rather than a question.

Reaching for a cookie, he stopped. "Not for a minute. I just quit hurting like hell."

14

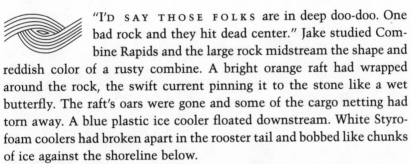"I'D SAY THOSE FOLKS are in deep doo-doo. One bad rock and they hit dead center." Jake studied Combine Rapids and the large rock midstream the shape and reddish color of a rusty combine. A bright orange raft had wrapped around the rock, the swift current pinning it to the stone like a wet butterfly. The raft's oars were gone and some of the cargo netting had torn away. A blue plastic ice cooler floated downstream. White Styrofoam coolers had broken apart in the rooster tail and bobbed like chunks of ice against the shoreline below.

Two rafters, a man and a woman, had scrambled up the rock and were stranded on a ledge three feet above the current. To my amazement, the man had no life vest. On the opposite shore, the third rafter waved feebly at his companions. Even at this distance, we could see the bloody scrapes on his legs from the sharp lava ledges of the sweeping rooster tail.

Jake had pulled our boat ashore to study the rapids, make certain a log hadn't jammed the chute he planned to run. "Sometimes a rock will roll, too," he said. "Always take time to look, even if you've run the thing a hundred times." When we had hiked around the corner on the railroad grade and seen the stricken raft, Jake had been almost as surprised as the rafters.

"They approached wrong," he said, pointing to the channel our side of midstream. "They stayed out there to avoid the overhanging trees along the bank, but the current swept them onto the rock. That's why it's also called Oh, fuck! rock. If you hit it, you scream, 'Oh, fuck.' Usually, a boat just bangs the side and hangs up for a moment. These dudes must have panicked and paddled the wrong way — something."

The man on the opposite shore finally saw us and started waving wildly, pointing. Then the two on the rock saw us and waved their arms, signaling distress.

"What are we going to do?" I asked.

"I'm wondering if we can get close enough to scrape them into the boat." Jake shook his head. "Look at that damn cargo net, floating on our side of the rock. Get tangled in that and you're dead."

Taking out his sheath knife, Jake made cutting motions at the couple on the ledge while pointing to their raft's floating cargo net, but they just kept waving.

"Maybe they don't have a knife," I said.

"There's a fool born a minute and only one dies a day." Jake sheathed the knife. "That's why this river's full of rafters. Guess we'll have to get them off."

The water churned and boiled around the rock. "Can we get close enough?" I wanted the pair to be rescued but hated the look of the water. "How about a helicopter or something?"

Jake reached into his pants pocket and held out a dime. "Go find us a phone booth."

I glanced at the steep timbered hillside, the stretches of rugged talus slopes, and felt dumb as a dude.

Jake started toward our boat. "I've heard other guides brag about pulling people from that rock. Always thought they were bullshitting."

Jake double-checked the buckles on his life vest and made sure I knew where the bailing bucket was. He had put an extra life vest on the seat beside me. When we got close, I was supposed to toss it to the man on the rock. That way, even if he missed the boat, he'd have a life vest for later.

"I'll pass by as close as I can," Jake said. "Throw him the vest as we approach. Let them try to jump in and *sit*. Knock them flat if you have to. Got it so far?"

I nodded, tightening the buckles on my own vest.

"If they hit the water, don't let them grab you or the boat. Might jerk you out or tangle us in that damn net. If they're too scared to jump, tough shit. Eventually, they'll get tired and fall off."

Pulling away from the shore, he continued giving instructions. "If we take on water, bail like hell. I'll yell 'right' or 'left' if I want you to shift weight.

"Now listen, if we get in *bad* trouble, I'll yell, 'The boat is lost!' Then get out. Go over the high side or off the end so she doesn't shift and pin you against some rock. Whatever you do, stay away from that fucking cargo net."

Even though I couldn't remember half of his instructions, I held two thumbs up.

"If you hit the water, clamp a hand over your mouth and nose so you don't suck in a lungful. A lot of drowned people float with their heads above water, cozy in their life vests. But they're dead as hell."

Maybe I looked scared because he grinned. "Now take a deep seat and enjoy the ride. I'm not figuring to lose this boat."

He rowed out to midstream, then let the boat slip down current.

We crossed the shallow rock shelf at the head of the rapids.

"Another damn can opener," Jake said as the boat scraped against barely submerged boulders. "It gets worse when the river lowers." He rowed toward the lapping green tongue between two submerged rocks. "This is the trick — Go right of the rocks and you hit the trees. Go left and you hit the Combine. You got to shoot straight through the middle. It's fast water — scares some people."

Sliding past the tongue and onto clear blue-green water, I glimpsed the rocky river bottom below us.

Approaching the Combine, I could see the gear still remaining in the raft's cargo net: soggy sleeping bags, a Coleman stove, folding aluminum chairs. Ten feet away, I waved the life vest at the man and pitched it sideways, a clean throw, but he didn't raise his arms to catch it, and the vest slid off the rock, falling into the water.

"Dumb shit," Jake muttered.

The woman leaned out toward us. She was wearing turquoise-colored shorts and a halter top but no shoes. Both knees and forearms were scraped from scrambling up the rock. The man had a wispy brown beard and stared straight ahead like an owl in sunlight. Maybe he lost his glasses, I thought.

Jake shipped the left oar so it wouldn't tangle in the cargo net. He ducked a little and braced for hitting the rock. "Jump," he shouted at the couple.

Bow first, we hit the Combine and the current swung the stern against the rock's side. The impact jolted me from the seat and I crouched on the boat bottom. For a moment we held steady, then started scraping along the rock.

"Jump," Jake yelled.

Holding her nose like a kid leaping into a summer lake, the woman jumped, crashing into my shoulder. Water sloshed over the side of the boat as momentum carried her past me, and she slammed against the gunnel.

"Shit, that stings," she said. The life jacket had prevented her from being hurt seriously.

Grabbing her arm, I pulled her down. Pain filled her eyes, but she was in the boat.

"Jump, goddamn you," Jake yelled, reaching toward the man with his left hand. The boat ground along the rock with a high screech.

"Look out below!" the man shouted. His arms came forward the way a large restless bird sometimes shifts its wings when it seems about to fly. But then he settled back on his perch.

"Chickenshit!" Jake pushed his fist against the slick red rock as if to shove the grinding boat free, and suddenly we were clear, hurling downstream in the foaming whitewater.

The man jumped, a full boat length too late, and disappeared into the churning water.

"Will," she cried out, half standing. "No, Will!"

His head appeared above water, dark as a seal's and he took several strong strokes toward the boat before going under again. Panic filled the woman's eyes.

"Bail, damn it! Wake up!" Jake strained at the oars.

I was surprised to see the ankle-deep water sloshing in the boat. Grabbing the bailer, I flung three bucketfuls of water over the side. Then I saw a hand and arm rise out of the water. Instinctively, I leaned over the side of the boat, reaching for the hand. Half standing, I reached further.

Jake was yelling, but I couldn't hear what as I grabbed the man's wrist and hung on. Then the other hand seized my arm, and I felt the terrible weight pulling me from the boat.

"Let go," I yelled as I slid over the gunnel. I felt the woman grab my right leg but she couldn't hold, and I knew I was going into the water.

After sucking a deep breath, I clamped my free hand over my mouth and gave in. The water was cold and so powerful it tumbled me and my captor over and over. We hit a smooth, deep underwater boulder, but he took most of the blow against his back. His grip relaxed a second and I wanted to go up for air, but had lost direction. Then he wrapped his arms around my neck and shoulders, dragging me down. I closed my eyes and went limp, hoping to lull him into letting go.

When we stopped tumbling, I opened my eyes and saw a sweep of clear blue-green water. Sunlight shone above, and below I saw a sunken boat, a broken oar still jammed in the oar lock, and I wondered how long it had been there, what fate its occupants met. I considered what an odd thing it might be to die here, drowned like my father, within sight of a sunken boat. Its bailing bucket, attached by a length of orange rope, pointed downstream five or six feet above the boat and turned slowly in the current.

Realizing I was low on breath, I struggled toward the light, but the man held me down the way a raccoon rides a dog's head underwater. I tried punching him, but my arms were tangled in his and the current spun us. I imagined how the searchers might find us in some quiet eddy, still entwined, the startling way one comes upon dead elk in a spring green meadow, their antlers locked in death's struggle. And I foresaw the uncomprehending look in my mother's eyes as Jake carried her the shocking news.

Coming out of the lull, I realized I couldn't allow myself to drown and resolved to do all I could to surface. I wanted to bite the man's nose or gouge his eyes, anything to make his grip loosen. With my right hand, I managed to grab his ear, pulling and twisting with all my might. A stream of bubbles escaped his mouth in a silent scream. One arm loosened.

Half free, I struggled to the surface and managed a quick clear breath before the current and the man's clinging weight dragged me under again.

Renewed by the oxygen, I managed to twist him downstream so his body would hit the rocks of the lower lava shelf, shielding mine. When we struck the first jagged ledge, the pain registered in his face and more bubbles slipped between his lips.

You'll drown first, you bastard, I thought, and if he did, maybe I could kick clear of him.

A bloodline rose from the torn ear. In the bright water, it seemed almost black.

Beyond anger, I was possessed by a kind of cold fury. Gripping the back of his neck with both my hands, I thrust my head forward, trying to break his nose with my skull.

My right leg scraped against sharp lava rocks and I gritted my teeth, trying to hold my breath and not cry out. Then he hit a rock. The shock of pain twisted his face and he writhed with renewed strength.

I braced for another blow against rock, but it never came. Instead, my left foot touched bottom and in a few more seconds the right touched as well. For a moment we struggled in the current, which swept us close to shore, until finally, I could stand and breathe.

Half carrying, half dragging him, I stumbled to waist-deep water. He was still draped all over me, but I managed to punch him in the stomach twice, and he slowly slid into the water.

Looking square into his owlish face, I hated his staring eyes and sparse wet beard. I understood that this was a complete stranger who had nearly drowned me, someone whose incompetence and cowardice proved he had no right to be on the same river my father had known, my uncle and I now treasured. I became furious with the man and punched him again, listening to the gurgle of water deep in his throat.

His eyes went from glassy to pain-filled as I started to rain blows on him. Finally, he lifted his arms to block my fists.

Shouts came from the bank. I heard splashing. The woman threw herself upon my back, and her weight, the unexpected thrust of it, knocked me to my knees. I tried elbowing her away, but only struck her life preserver.

"Stop it, you savage! Stop it!" Turning, I saw her face twisted in rage. Then her weight lifted off me. Jake dragged her by the life jacket toward the shallows.

Astonished, the man stood before me, breathing raggedly. Brushing his nose with the back of his hand, he stared at the smear of blood. Then he splashed past me toward shore, throwing himself across a grassy hummock. He vomited into the water.

My wrists hurt and my forearms bore angry red marks where he had stopped my blows. By evening they would darken to bruises. The woman waded out again and dragged the dazed man to land. "You're insane!" she screamed at me. As she touched his torn ear, he cried out. "You crazy bastard," she said. "He's hurt bad."

"I've seen worse," Jake said. "Just keep him warm. Get him off the river."

"We don't want any help from you," she said. Another party of rafters had pulled to shore downstream, and she started dragging the man in their direction.

She called back over her shoulder, "We're going to report this to the authorities. You don't belong on this river."

"Maybe you'd better figure out how to salvage your raft first." Jake watched them a moment and muttered, "Good riddance." Wading out to where I stood, he gripped my shoulder and steered me toward shore. "How you feeling, champ? Can you go another round?"

I nodded, but couldn't find the breath to speak. A yellow jacket landed on my bleeding leg and I waved it away.

We walked fifty yards upstream along a fisherman's path. I could see our boat, but my legs gave out. "Got to sit." Stumbling to a bleached log, I waited to catch my breath. I felt terribly cold. My knees shook.

"Be right back, champ."

Closing my eyes, I breathed deeply and waited for the shaking to stop. A slight breeze rustled the alder leaves. Opening my eyes, I saw pollen from the redtop dusting my thighs and legs. Sunlight bounced off the water like bright coins.

Jake returned with a handful of Fig Newtons and a Pepsi. "Sugar." He put a wool jacket across my shoulders. After a few minutes in the sun, I smelled the warming wool; it seemed to pull the chill from my body. After I had eaten the cookies and drunk half the Pepsi, Jake held up my arm the way a referee handles a winning prizefighter. "The winner and still cham-*peen!*"

I grinned and shook my head. "Maybe I shouldn't have hit him, but the bastard almost killed me."

"What the hell," Jake said. "I wanted to clobber him myself. She was okay, though. Feisty."

I lowered my head. The sunshine felt good across my shoulders, and I was just thankful to be above water, breathing.

Jake touched my leg. "We better take out early, get you a tetanus shot."

"Whatever." I was a little surprised I didn't mind leaving the river. We had planted some trees at the memorial site and planned an extra day's fishing to avoid the Water Pageant. But now, taking out early seemed best.

"Rafters." Jake pitched a stone toward the water. "One fool didn't die today. That means we owe two tomorrow."

"I LOVE THE EARTH TONES. So sensual yet rest-
ful." The red-haired woman wore a bright purple wrap-
around dress and matching cap. "Don't you remember,
Charles? We saw beautiful work like this in Santa Fe."

Her husband glanced up from his plateful of cheese wedges, crackers,
and dips. An enormous man with a full beard, he wore a Western-style
beige suit and alligator cowboy boots the same reptilian green as his
cowboy hat's band. "Those paintings were more vibrant." He selected
a cheese chunk impaled on a red-ruffled toothpick. "It's the light — the
slant of desert light."

"You're right." She tapped one painting's frame. "But these are more
unstructured. I *adore* the recklessness."

"With a little luck, I'll get these people on a river trip," Jake said, his
voice lowered. "A little more luck and they'll fall overboard. No, come
to think about it, that lard-o won't sink." He sipped a glass of wine, but
I could tell he wanted a beer or a hard drink. Still, he was being pleasant
enough, trying to put on a good face whenever Juniper introduced him
to the gallery owners or admirers who had come to the opening.

"See any blue-haired retired schoolteachers?" she had asked Jake
during a quiet moment.

"They're all at home taking a few shots of Geritol so they can stay
awake for the Festival of Floats."

Now she circulated with ease among the gallery crowd and other
artists while Jake worked his way into a section featuring Western art.
With his deep tan, military pressed pants, and light gray corduroy jacket,
one might have mistaken him for an artist. A roadrunner bolo tie crafted

from silver and turquoise was loosened at the collar of his denim shirt. The tie was a gift from Juniper, who had somehow talked him into attending the opening. Only when Jake had suggested heading for Central did I realize that this art show was his reason for taking out early, not his desire to make certain I had a tetanus shot.

Franklin and my mother attended the opening as well. Both wore Italian costumes. He talked on about the art in France and Italy, but they both seemed to be having a good time, even though Franklin appeared a little self-conscious about his wounds. "You could stand him in the corner like a statue," Jake said to my mother while Franklin was discussing Renaissance work with the gallery director. "Dangle a sign off him: BRUISED MAN."

"Don't get started, Jake," she warned.

Upon first learning that Jake planned to attend the opening, she had suggested we all ride up together. "I don't think so," he said. "Sounds too much like a bad double date. Anyway, I don't think I could resist Franklin's cologne round trip."

Juniper's paintings were titled in small capital letters with the prices alongside. WOMEN DIGGING CAMAS 300. HUCKLEBERRY FESTIVAL 350. Three paintings had a small red dot beside the price. "They've been sold," my mother explained. "That dot lets people know."

"Big deal, this art game," Jake said. "I sold two already and I'm not even a gallery. Besides, who knows how much commission these owners gouge?"

Jake deserved to be proud of the fact he had sold two of her works so quickly, both to dudes who claimed the paintings would keep their wives from protesting about the cost of Jake's fishing trips. Juniper suggested our adding the remaining three works to her show, but Jake insisted on leaving them in the store. I wished they had taken down the two of Kalim.

After she'd surveyed all the paintings, my mother cornered me about some clothes she'd seen in a men's store across the way. Franklin had been selecting a couple ties when my mother noticed a navy blue blazer she wanted me to try on. "Culver, I know you'd be even more dashing wearing that lovely blazer." With a lowered voice, she added, "They take layaway. Twenty percent down. The rest by Christmas. We can swing that."

"I don't need a blazer, Mom."

"Every young man needs one," she said. "It's part of the classic wardrobe. I remember your father's. He looked so handsome."

"Where would I wear it?"

"School pictures, the prom." She put her hands lightly on my shoulders and stood tiptoe to look square into my eyes. "You always act the way you dress. Not that I don't expect you to behave perfectly well no matter how you dress." She shook her head. "You're almost taller than your father. I swear, I'm going to put a brick on your head to slow your growth."

"Don't, Mom. Maybe I'll get a basketball scholarship." I paused. "Gateway's got a department store. I can look there later."

She stepped back. "Gateway's very nice, but as far as shopping goes, a little limited. Central has wonderful variety." Her eyes shifted to my pants. "Are those getting too tight? You're standing funny."

"I'm perfectly okay, Mom. Really. I just haven't worn these corduroy pants in a while."

"I think they're a little short. Right after Juniper talks, Franklin and I are taking you across the street. We've got to get you spruced up before school."

She didn't miss much. I was standing funny because the bandage the doctor had applied was stiffening my scraped leg. Before giving me a tetanus shot, he pronounced, "No sign of infection." Scraping off a little of the dressing Jake had applied, he asked, "What's this?"

"Bip," Jake said. "Bag balm and sheep dip. I mix it myself. Patent pending."

The doctor took a tube out of his white desk drawer. "If you run out of Bip, try this ointment."

When about forty people had gathered, the gallery owner tapped his wine glass with a small spoon and announced two upcoming shows, then introduced Juniper and the other artists.

Each offered a few comments. Juniper's talk was simple and clear. She pointed out that her works spoke for themselves, but she also explained they embodied a tradition of beliefs and ceremonies. In conclusion, she noted that her paintings were a way of returning thanks to her land and heritage.

After she finished, nearly everyone clapped politely, then returned to the wine and cheese. However, the red-haired woman pressed forward, taking Juniper's hand and announcing she was an artist herself. "Your words were a *gift*," the woman said. "A wonderful illumination at this very moment when I'm struggling to find my way through the dark night of the soul."

"Thank you," Juniper said. "It's always good to know people like your work."

"You're such a spiritual person. I was telling Charles earlier how enlightening your work is. Wasn't I, Charles?"

"Certainly." As he spoke, a few pieces of cheese leaked from his mouth into his beard and he tried combing them out with his fingers. I wondered where he was putting all the toothpicks.

Juniper kept smiling politely after the woman released her and then talked to several others who approached. When her admirers thinned, Jake handed her a glass of wine and touched her arm. "Now that you've sung for your supper, I'll buy. Let's head out, put on the feed bag."

She laughed. "Jake, I'd love to, but I've got to have dinner with some of these people. Why don't you come along. It's just a light dinner, nothing fancy."

Jake nodded at the man in the alligator boots. "That puny fella gonna turn up?"

She smiled. "How did you know?"

"I'm getting to know the art game. Hell, I'm already half your agent."

"That's Dr. Spears. Maybe I should introduce you. He loves fishing."

"Never mind," Jake said. "I'd have to buy a bigger boat. What kind of doc is he anyway?"

"You be quiet," she scolded. "He's a heart specialist."

"What does that tell you?" Jake answered his own question. "Never get your rig checked by a mechanic whose truck is headed for a breakdown."

"Go on," she said. "You're bad for business. Dr. Spears is thinking of commissioning some work for his office."

"I'll bet it's a painting of the First Foods Ceremony — huckleberries, salmon, caus caus, venison . . ."

She tried moving away from Jake, but he held her sleeve lightly. "I've got an idea for a series of paintings." He nodded toward Franklin. "The *Bruised Man* Collection."

My mother held Franklin's elbow. With his free hand he slipped something into his mouth.

"*Bruised Man and Breath Mint,*" Jake said.

Juniper laughed as she was trying to sip her wine and began coughing. He patted her on the back. "Excuse me," she said when she had regained control. "I've got to use the restroom."

Alarmed, I realized Mom was steering Franklin our way. "She plans to take me shopping, Jake," I whispered. "Get me out of it." I didn't want to go, especially with Franklin. And I suspected if I did, after the blazer she'd force me to try on slacks. I doubted I could keep the bandage a secret. No way did I want her to ask about the near escape at the Combine.

Jake was all smiles when they reached us. "Franklin, good to see you." He held out his hand and, after they shook, said, "Wasn't Juniper's talk splendid? Brief but spiritual, a real gift."

Franklin hesitated then answered. "Why yes, it was . . . spiritual." He smiled. "That's a good way to put it."

"I believe we've seen all the wonderful paintings," my mother said brightly. "Franklin and I were going to take Culver across the street to try on some clothes. We still have time before the Festival of Floats."

"That's a great idea," Jake said, and I wanted to kick him, until he added, "There's just a slight conflict." His eyes cut to the gallery owner who seemed about to close a sale on the huckleberry festival painting. "Flora, I don't want to put things in a quandary, but after the showing, the gallery owner and Juniper invited some people out to a light supper. She wanted me to sort of escort her and I thought maybe Culver should tag along. It's a nice opportunity."

"Really? Well, that's very nice."

I couldn't tell if she believed him entirely, but his next move was brilliant. "That distinguished-looking man in the alligator boots — Dr. Spears — is one of the West's top heart specialists. When the governor had that irregularity, they called in Spears for consultation." Jake tapped his chest. "And he loves to fish; that's my part in it. Don't you think Culver deserves a chance to associate with the best professionals Central has to offer?"

"Yes," she said, convinced. "I think so, too. It's a wonderful opportunity. Maybe we can shop later."

"No problem, Flora," Franklin said. "We'll bring Culver up another time."

She squeezed his upper arm. "Thank you. That would be lovely." Looking me over from top to bottom, she added, "I only wish you'd worn something other than those trousers. The wales appear a little worn." She brushed my cheek with a kiss. "Next time you'll be decked out in a brand-new blazer."

Her perfume, one I didn't recognize, suggested apple blossoms, and I knew this was a special occasion for her. "Love you, Mom," I said. "Have a good time." To tell the truth, I felt a little lousy for deceiving her, but I figured it would pass.

After my mother and Franklin left, Jake and I slipped out. "You owe me big time, Shotgun," he said.

. . .

The streets were festive, decorated for Venice West. Italian flags hung from the lampposts and the window boxes held colorful flowers. People wearing Italian costumes streamed toward the park beside the river. Many of them carried picnic baskets.

"All this excitement!" Jake stopped and thumped his heart with his fist. "Thank God it's not a heart attack. They'd have to call Spears away from the cheese plate."

I laughed. "Maybe you're hungry," I suggested, because I was. "We could try going to an Italian place."

Jake squinted at me. "Are you nuts? This is Central. They're only pretending to be Venice."

We stopped at the Branding Iron, which overlooked a stretch of river below the pond and park. The restaurant menu boasted they served only prime beef from registered Black Angus. "Say, do you know Dr. Spears by any chance?" Jake asked the waitress.

"You bet. He and his wife eat here all the time."

"This must be the place." Folding his menu, Jake winked at me. He ordered the Trail Boss and I had the Scout — both medium rare. They tasted terrific.

After dinner, Jake sipped his Seven and Seven. "Those gallery people put on a pretty good shindig. Wonder how they wound up in the art game, anyway."

"Maybe the way you got into sporting goods. Family business."

Jake nodded. "Could be."

After it grew dark, Central's symphony began playing in the park. I didn't recognize the music drifting across the water and through the open windows but thought my mother probably did. If not, Franklin would.

Fireworks flashed in the sky. Our waitress paused to view the display out the window. "Look there," she said. "The floats are just starting. Of all the lousy deals, I had to pull night shift. Still, you get a pretty good view from here."

After leaving her a big tip, Jake got another drink in a to-go cup, and we went outside to watch. The floats were at some distance, but we saw pretty well. Several resembled gondolas covered with fragrant blossoms. Men and women wearing bright traditional costumes waved as the floats glided on the mirror-smooth water. It was something to see all right.

When a siren went off, I thought it was part of the pageant, until I heard a fire engine race through town. More fireworks brightened the sky. Another siren sounded.

"Two alarms," Jake said. "Maybe their pyrotechnics got out of hand." Glimpsing the engine through the trees, he added, "That's their outlaw. Fire's outside of town someplace."

The tempo of the music quickened, and I suspected they were approaching the finale. A burst of fireworks outlined Italy's boundaries. The decorated boats faced the audience and we could hear ripples of applause.

"That was terrific," I said.

Jake nodded. "People like it. Of course, it's nothing like Gateway's fair and rodeo." He checked his watch. "I've got to hurry back and stick my face in a few bars. There'll be hell to pay if any of the back-room boys figure out I watched this damn pageant."

The magical boats shimmered like colorful leaves on the obsidian water. Deciding to add Italy to my vacation list of Canada and Alaska, I asked Jake, "You ever think of traveling to Italy?"

He pursed his lips. "I used to think about it. My worst fear is that it might turn out exactly like this."

16

THREE MILES OUTSIDE OF TOWN, we stopped on Rattlesnake Ridge to survey the fire. This spectacle illuminated the whole sky, and Jake guessed you could see the burning for fifty miles.

Most of the industrial buildings on the hill overlooking Gateway were blazing. The stud mill and plywood plant erupted with bright orange flames, and the fire threatened other nearby buildings — the Feed and Seed Co-op, the grain elevators, the historic railroad depot across from the plywood mill.

The cold deck, a log stack twenty feet high that stretched for two hundred yards, faced danger, too. Three sets of railroad tracks separated the cold deck from eight large fuel storage tanks that held gasoline, farm diesel, and home heating oil.

Jake seemed stunned by the fire's size. "They got two sprinkler systems at the mill," he said. "How'd they let that son of a bitch get started?"

Gateway's town siren shrieked steadily, calling all volunteers into action. In the distance, we heard the eerie wail of sirens and saw three red and white pumper fire engines racing toward the fire from the south.

"Central is in on this, too," Jake said. "We've got to hold that fire or the whole country burns up. Look at those goddamn fuel tanks."

We unhitched the boat and trailer at the store, leaving them in the main parking lot, because Jake didn't want to mess with the padlocked gate on the boat storage lot. "Drive across the street and fill up at the Union," he said, dashing into the store.

The kid pumping gas kept a wary eye on the hilltop fire. "My dad's up there fighting fire. He's a millwright at the plant." He pulled the nozzle out and returned it to the pump. "Told me to stay put. What if those tanks blow?" The kid looked at me for some kind of assurance, but I didn't have any.

Jake came running across the street carrying two big fire extinguishers. A short-handled shovel was tucked under one arm, and a pair of brand-new Wolverine boots hung from his neck by their laces. After tossing the gear into the back of the pickup, Jake handed me the boots. "Get those tennis shoes off and put these on. They're tough as hell and should keep your feet from getting scorched."

I saw they were just like Jake's but his were well broken in.

The siren continued blowing, but the town seemed empty except for the crummies and pickups filled with grim-faced men headed toward the fire.

Jake drove to the dry grass fields fringing the hill. A coach had his Little League baseball team fanned out checking for spot fires. Instead of bats, the players carried shovels. A few swung wildly at the burning cinders drifting on the wind.

My uncle stopped the truck and called to the coach. "What's the score, Pete?"

The man called back. "Where the hell you been? Off fishing?"

Jake pointed to the fuel tanks. "If the fire reaches those tanks, get these kids the hell out."

Pete gave him the thumbs-up sign.

"This is one the home team better win," Jake said.

The police had roadblocked the hill but allowed the firefighters through. "How long's this bastard been going?" Jake asked the cop at the block.

The cop checked his watch. "We got the first call two hours ago. Things were already bad. Fire really got a jump."

"Wonder why the sprinkler systems didn't slow it," Jake said.

The cop spit some tobacco on the ground. "Maybe my brother-in-law installed the fucking system."

The stud mill was completely enveloped in flames, and the fire had swept across the electrical plant that housed the generators, then burned on through to the lay up section where they actually made the plywood. Big enough to create its own wind, the fire roared like a train approaching a tunnel. The smell of burning plywood mixed with the rubbery stench from the belts and conduits, the singed hot metal scent of the burning saws. Thick black smoke poured out of the generator plant.

Men from six fire engines — tankers and pumpers — battled the blaze, but the mill was lost. The heat was so intense, half the water streaming from the fire hoses evaporated before it reached the fire. The hoses were manned by a mix of professional firefighters from Central and the volunteers from Gateway, Pinedale, Bridgeport. I recognized Sniffy hanging on to one two-and-a-half-inch hose.

Fiery embers carried by the wind rained on the roof of the Feed and Seed Co-op building. A few men had climbed on top of the building, dragging small hoses from the grass-fire trucks. More embers fell on the historic railroad depot, and a small pumper truck from Bridgeport had been deployed to soak the roof.

When Jake saw Sheriff Grady Simmons waving at us he stopped, and Grady thrust his head in the window. "Emergency vehicles only, Jake. Park that rig and help out on the hoses."

"You ramrodding this outfit?" Jake asked.

Grady touched his badge. "I'm in charge of emergency services."

"Then I hope there's no emergency," Jake said.

"Well, you're not the big shot," Grady said. "Some of us have been here two hours already."

"Then you should have enough sense to be soaking that cold deck," Jake said. "Pull those pumpers. The mill's a complete loss anyway."

Grady grinned, but it wasn't friendly. "Mule Mullins runs the fire crews. Speak to him."

"I haven't seen him," Jake said.

Grady swept his arm to indicate the burning buildings and fire. "You're the hotshot guide. Go find him."

Jake turned to me. "You know what I said — how a fool's born a minute and only one dies a day?"

I nodded.

He jerked his thumb at Grady. "When this sucker goes, that'll square things for a month."

Jake did find Mullins after a few minutes' search and told him about the cold deck. Mullins nodded. "The reservation's sending a couple trucks. I'll put them on it soon as they get here."

"I'd do it now if I were you," Jake said. "Pull that crew off the depot."

"Everybody's a chief," Mullins said. "Tangent keeps yelling to save his plant. The mayor says save the historic railroad depot at all costs. Thinks it'll bring in tourists after it's renovated."

"Bunch of jugheads," Jake said.

"Why don't you park it and help out for now," Mullins said. "We could use your know-how and some of these boys are pretty tired. Park over by the co-op."

Jake started driving toward the co-op, away from the fire, when he noticed a small fire starting in a wheat field beyond the building. No one was on it.

The orange flames burned close to the ground, but the wind was spreading the fire rapidly. Beyond the wheat field stood a line of small houses similar to the one Mom and I lived in. "Hang on," Jake said as he threw the pickup into four-wheel drive and headed into the field.

Ripening heads of wheat brushed the doors as we headed for the burning. Jake hunched over the steering wheel. "Two more weeks, this wheat would be so ripe you'd never get out the fire."

When we hit the burning section, Jake began driving back and forth, grinding the blazing wheat into the earth. The fire had spread and flames licked at the rocker panels and fenders. After making several swaths through the fire section, Jake started taking long turns in front of the fire, clearing a kind of fire line by turning the ripening wheat under the wheels.

On one turnaround in the soft dirt, the pickup slowed and the engine died. Jake tried starting it twice. A terrible look came over his face, not fear or anger, but disappointment, as if a good friend had let him down.

"Get one of the extinguishers out of the back," he said. "Leave the door half open and use it for a shield."

I scrambled for the extinguisher and did as he said. Crouched behind the door, I waited, measuring the distance as the fire closed. Two pheasants burst out of the flames and ran past us.

"It's getting hot," I said.

"Turn up the air conditioner if you want," Jake said. "I'm just waiting a minute. Don't want to flood it. Then she'd really blow."

When the flames were six feet away, I started spraying their base, making long sweeps back and forth, but I couldn't soak all the standing wheat, and tongues of fire licked at the door. The heat smacked against my forehead and I took shallow breaths.

"If she doesn't start, we'll bail out my side," Jake said. "Head straight for those houses. It's only fifty yards, but run like hell."

"We'll stop this son of a bitch," I said. My heart was thumping, and I kicked away some burning wheat around my legs.

Pressing the gas pedal to the floor, Jake held it a second to clear the carburetor. Then he tried the starter again. "Go, you sumbitch, go!" The engine roared. "Climb in, buddy!" He grinned at me as we were on the move again. "Remind me to kick the guy's ass that gave this rig the last tune-up."

Driving back and forth, back and forth, through the wheat ahead of the fire, Jake was relentless. After he'd ground a wide fire line, he took the pickup into the fire itself. The smell of scorched paint told me he'd need a new paint job, and I understood why he'd filled up with gas at the Union station — to avoid explosive fumes in a nearly empty tank. After twenty minutes, no flames were left, although the patches of blackened wheat smoldered and smoked. The field resembled a mangy dog's coat.

"Time to break in your new boots," he announced. Carrying fire extinguishers and shovels, we walked into the field, then sprayed and shoveled the hot spots. After they all seemed out, Jake stopped to piss on one of the smoldering places. "Make it count," he said.

He squinted at my new boots, now blackened with ash, dirt, and burned wheat. "Good thing you left your tennis shoes in the rig. When I was driving ambulance, I saw burn victims with their tennis shoes melted to the flesh. As the doctors cut away their shoes at the hospital, half the feet came, too."

We flung the shovels and fire extinguishers into the back and Jake dropped the tailgate. He fished a couple of Pepsis from the big Igloo cooler. "Let's take five."

As we drank, I watched the people across the field — the ones from the small row of houses. No men were visible and I figured they were fighting the mill fire. Several younger kids stood on ladders or the tops of cars, spraying their roofs with garden hoses. A woman in a housedress and apron kept banging out a back screen door and slopping pans of water onto her wooden porch. Her hair plastered to her forehead, and she stopped a moment, leaning in our direction and staring toward us or the fire behind. Backlit as we were, I didn't believe she could see anything but our silhouettes. After banging inside once again, she returned with a large pan, which she flung violently in our direction.

"She doesn't have to thank us or anything," I said.

"That's not it," Jake said, twisting around so he faced the burning plant. "Take a hard look. Dumb sonsabitches let that cold deck get started."

Fifty yards of the stacked-log cold deck burned furiously, sending orange and yellow flames leaping into the night sky. Sections of flaming bark broke away from the blazing logs, shooting baseball-size embers in all directions. As we drove closer, the heat intensified.

Jake kept clicking his tongue against the roof of his mouth. "Hope I remembered to pay my fire insurance. I know they piled those logs too close to the fuel tanks."

With the intense heat, the tanks expanded and sighed, groaning like goblins. "If one of those blows," Jake said, "you can wave bye-bye to Gateway."

The nearest tank, decorated with a big Shell scallop, shimmered and undulated. At first I thought it was an illusion, but Jake said the swelling was real.

Downhill from the storage tanks, emergency vehicles were evacuating the Rimrock Trailer Court. Occupants frantically threw their possessions into cars, pickups, makeshift wagons, while the voice from a loudspeaker urged them to move faster. I scanned the grassy fields for the baseball team, but they were gone.

Mullins had pulled back the pumpers from the mill fire. Now the firemen concentrated streams of water on the fuel tanks nearest the cold-deck inferno. Some firefighters held corrugated tin sheets as shields to reflect the heat while others manned the hoses, attempting to cool the fuel inside so it wouldn't explode. From time to time the men anxiously glanced over their shoulders, watching the advancing fire eat its way along the cold deck.

Billyum and half a dozen other Indians had shown up in reservation police cars. Red-faced, Mullins screamed at Billyum about the lack of reservation fire trucks, but the big man just turned away.

Spotting Jake, Mullins hurried over. "I need more fucking trucks. Can't talk to him." He waved both arms at the burning mill. "Son of a bitch is a complete loss. The idiots kept five hundred gallons of fucking gasoline in there to clean their tools. The explosion blew out the wall and torched the cold deck." He held his arms up like a man under arrest, then let them drop. "I don't know if we can save the town. We need more trucks." Taking off his helmet, he slapped it against his thigh.

"Go call Central again," Jake said. "Beg. And put your damn helmet on."

Mullins headed toward one of the fire trucks.

"You told him," I said after Mullins was out of earshot.

"He's doing the best he can," Jake said, calmer than I would have expected. "Mullins is in way too deep. As a volunteer you practice putting out garage fires, grass fires in vacant lots, or maybe some widow's tumbledown eyesore after she drops. Nobody's ready for something like this." Jake studied the disaster a moment. "The damn mill's sprinkler system should have controlled it."

"A lot of equipment and volunteers showed up," I said.

He nodded. "Beats whacking it out with feed sacks."

Billyum and the other Indians were staring at the fuel tanks. "Paint's blistering," Billyum said as we approached. "I'd say you city boys have a big problem."

"Did you forget where you parked the fire trucks?" Jake asked. "Drop the keys somewhere?"

Billyum shrugged. "Our boys are fighting fires way back in the woods. Got to protect our timber. Mullins must have got the message screwed up."

"He should have put the other trucks on it," Jake said. "Blood under the bridge now."

We all watched the fuel tanks for a few moments. Then Jake said, "I figure two things got to happen. Keep those tanks from blowing and put out that cold deck."

Billyum squinted at him. "Can't stop a cold deck, Jake. You better just clear the town."

Jake put his hand on Billyum's shoulder. "Don't go thinking negatory thoughts on me."

Billyum pointed downhill. "Trailer park's evacuated. Now they're evacuating this side of town. I'm taking my men down, see if we can help."

Mullins returned. "I've called Central and Pinedale. Begged for more trucks. We'll have real help in an hour." He glared at Billyum.

"You were smart to keep those tanks cool," Jake said. "But they're still heating and the cold deck's burning closer." He pointed to the blistering scallop on the Shell tank.

"I can pull the pumper off the depot," Mullins said. "What good's a depot if you got no town."

Jake shook his head. "Too much of the water is evaporating, and it's getting worse as that fire burns closer. We need hoses on top of the tanks. Open the nozzles wide and flood those suckers with cold water."

"I can't send anyone up on those tanks," Mullins said. "My guys are just volunteers. Most have families."

"Three of us can drag hoses up those ladders to the catwalk on top, then tie them off. Billyum said he'd help out."

"Bullshit," Billyum said. "I'm allergic to explosions."

"I'm going up," Jake said. "And Mullins here has got to look good so people don't blame him for letting this thing get so wild. You reservation guys forgot to bring any trucks." Jake paused. "Maybe you're chicken-shit."

Billyum seemed angry. "Goddamn right. You'd be too if your brain wasn't between your legs."

Jake jerked his thumb at me. "I'll take Culver if I need to, and you candy-asses can draw straws for third man."

I couldn't believe how Jake was goading them or that he'd volunteered me. I knew it was just a bluff, or hoped it was. The thought of going on those tanks made my stomach cramp.

Mullins had clenched his fists and took a step toward Jake. Billyum looked like he wanted to slug somebody, too. Jake stood his ground.

Punches might have been thrown, but a loud horrible belching stopped everybody, and we stared as a balloon of fire rose slowly from the tank top.

"She's blowing, Uncle Jake!"

The firefighters screamed and raced for cover. We all took shelter behind the pickup, but the tank didn't explode. As we stared from behind the shield, the fiery balloon rose in the air, burned with a loud hissing, then flamed out.

"It's venting," Jake said finally after he'd figured awhile. "Tank's got a pressure valve on top. The gases popped the valve and something sparked. Kind of like lighting a giant fart."

"I knew that," Billyum said, coming out from behind the pickup. "Still, I was scared."

Jake pointed at his crotch. "Your pants won't catch fire now, the way you pissed them up."

Billyum threw a slow roundhouse at Jake and grinned. "I didn't want to roast my weenie. Not without a nice warm bun."

"Jesus!" Mullins said. "What next?"

Half of the firefighters slowly returned to their hoses and corrugated tin shields. Some remained behind cover. A few straggled away. I saw Sniffy put on his helmet.

"Get those men back on the hoses," Jake said. "If the tank blows, the shrapnel will burst the other tanks. Gateway will be one big fireball. He turned to Mullins. "No choice. We got to climb those tanks."

"All right," Mullins said. "You son of a bitch."

"Get me some fire clothes, too," Billyum said. "I'm not letting this asshole get to be a hero all by himself."

Jake's grin was as wide as his face. "You don't want to miss the fun. This is a night you can tell your grandkids about."

Billyum glanced at the fuel tanks. "If that vents when we're on top, I won't have any grandkids."

"Don't worry," Jake said. "If it gets you, I'll tell them about it." He looked around. "I need to use a phone."

"They're still working inside the old depot," Mullins said. "Who the hell you gonna call?"

"What do you want on your pizza?" Jake yelled over his shoulder.

Ten minutes later, Jake, Billyum, and Mullins had on asbestos coats, thick rubber boots, gloves, and helmets. I knew they could use a fourth man to drag the hose up the ladder but no one was volunteering, including me. To tell the truth, seeing that huge fire balloon ignite and rise off the tank had taken a lot of starch out of people. Even if I had wanted to go, I knew Jake wouldn't let me, so that made me feel a little better. The tank vented again, a smaller fire balloon.

"We better move," Mullins said. "Lot of people below are praying these tanks hold."

Billyum chewed his lower lip and studied the tank. "Do you think it's best to rush over right after one of those fireballs or wait?"

"Ask Mullins. He's got the manual." Jake gazed into the smoky night sky like he was watching for a sign from God.

After a while I heard a faint humming, the way a mosquito sounds in a tent, barely audible but getting closer. At first I thought it was just another noise from the fire, the updraft whistling or damp logs singing as they burned.

"Is that damn tank making new noises?" Mullins couldn't take his eyes off it.

"Right there!" Jake pointed, and after a minute I could make out a little yellow biplane sliding past the tall grain elevators behind the co-op.

"It's a plane; it's a bird; it's superduster!" Jake waved at the plane. "My man Buzzy."

"What the shit?" Billyum seemed disgusted. "Is he sightseeing or what?"

At first I thought the little Stearman was just flying over to observe the disaster. But Buzzy flew dangerously close to the burning. The fierce updraft shot cinders toward the plane like tracer bullets. Some bounced off the fabric wings as the Stearman kept coming toward us, lined up with the railroad tracks and heading for the Shell tank. Buzzy flew so low I feared he'd hit the telephone wires, but he cleared them by inches, then aimed for the tank.

I remembered how Jake had bragged about Buzzy's crop dusting, claiming he flew so close to the ground he hiccuped to clear barbed-wire fences around fields of potatoes and peppermint.

Now he appeared to be landing the Stearman on the tank top, but as he skimmed past, Buzzy pulled the lever to the hopper, drenching the tank top and side with a reddish liquid.

"Bingo!" Jake turned to Billyum. "Extra tomato sauce for our pizza."

"Borate," Mullins said. "Where the hell did he get that?"

"Keeps it stocked now. He thinks these hardheaded Indians will hire him to fly fire patrol and put out lightning strikes on the rez."

Billyum put on his helmet. "Don't look at me. Take it up with tribal council."

"Okay," Jake said. "Let's act like we know what we're doing."

"How do you want to work it?" Mullins asked.

"We'll give Buzzy time for two more borate runs. Make sure the damn tank quits venting. I'm not keen about having my cookies toasted up there."

Buzzy made two more drops on the tank while Jake and the others checked their gear and dragged the fire hose into position. The Gateway airstrip was close by, and Buzzy had someone back there mixing borate, so a round trip took him only eight minutes. Since Buzzy had dropped the first load, the tank hadn't vented, but we were all holding our breaths. Reddish borate covered the tank top, oozing down the side in a thick red paste. With a little imagination, it did resemble pizza.

Jake gave instructions to the firefighters who had been hosing off the tanks. "Train your hoses on the ladders now. Cool off those rungs."

The firefighters crouched behind their tin shields, and I could only imagine how hot the ladders were.

"Watch it when we head up the side. Don't knock us off the goddamn ladders."

"Don't worry, Jake. They call me Deadeye Dick," one of the firefighters said.

"Your wife doesn't," Jake said. "And I've seen you piss all over your shoes down at the Elks."

The man laughed. "That was when I first got there. After a few drinks, I get steady."

"Let's hope you're blotto now," Jake said.

As the three started up the ladder dragging the hose, I crossed my fingers, prayed, cursed, made all sorts of bargains with God. They inched along — Jake packing the nozzle, Billyum lugging most of the weight, Mullins playing out hose and shouting directions to the firemen below. Each rung seemed a struggle.

As they crawled up the tank side, I considered the circumstances that brought them to that exact moment. How terrible, I thought, to have escaped drowning with my father only to be blown kingdom come by a fuel tank overlooking Gateway. If it happened, I didn't know how I could describe the scene to my mother. In high school, the gloomy shop teacher had lectured about various industrial accidents, embellishing his stories of reckless victims who ignored safety procedures only to wind up in Mason jars or other unlikely burial vessels. Out here in this emergency, I realized Jake had no rules to follow.

Finally, Jake and Billyum made it to the catwalk above the tank and began inching along. Mullins stayed on the ladder, keeping the hose unsnagged. I understood the plan. Tie the hose and open the nozzle to provide a steady flow of cooling water over the tank and down the sides. This, in combination with the streams from below, should prevent the tank from blowing until the cold deck was stopped or burned out. Thanks to the millpond and the farmers' irrigation ditches, water was available in spite of the general drought.

Behind me I heard someone remark, "That Jake would ride into hell with a bucket of water." I recognized Sniffy's voice, and at that moment I was terribly proud of my uncle. Billyum, too. And I prayed all the harder for their safekeeping. In spite of the water and borate, the tank could have exploded during the climb, but now that they were crawling along the catwalk, where the hot gases had vented, igniting into the fiery balloon, the danger seemed doubled.

I don't believe it took them over three or four minutes to secure the hose and nozzle, but during that time I don't remember breathing. Finally, they had it secured, and Jake waved for the men below to put water in the hose. A couple firemen started up the pumper and you could see the hose bulge and straighten all the way up the tank. Mullins had tied it to the ladder in a couple places, and it stiffened against those restraints.

As the water gushed from the nozzle, spreading across the tank top and washing the reddish borate down the sides, the men below cheered and whooped. A couple tossed their helmets into the air. Water and borate continued running freely down the sides of the tank now, giving the reflections of the cold deck flames eerie undulations. Jake and Billyum grabbed each other's shoulders and danced a funny little dance on the catwalk. With no room to move their feet and wearing the heavy boots, they bent and swayed like crazy men dancing on top of the reflected flames from the cold deck.

Everyone on the ground was watching the two act like firewalkers when I saw a flash of yellow. Turning away from the primitive spectacle of the dancers, I realized Buzzy and the Stearman were leveling off for another run. The plane had suddenly emerged from a dense cloud of smoke and now headed for the Shell tank.

"Christ, he's too close to see them," Sniffy said, and I knew it was true. The Stearman's front seat had been converted to the hopper that held the fluids, and the pilot sat in the rear seat, making it impossible to see the blind spot directly beyond the plane's nose.

"That prop will chop their heads off," Sniffy screamed.

Horrified, I watched the Stearman bear down on Billyum and Jake, imagining the fatal carnage of the 450-horsepower radial engine. In that instant while the fire roared, sirens screamed, and the men cried out, time hesitated and all sound ceased.

Jake's arms were still draped over Billyum's shoulders in the style of close dancing, and he forced the bigger man to his knees, pushing him out of harm's way.

Jake dropped a split second later, but not in time to avoid the plane except for the tiny hop that slipped it clear of both men and beyond the Shell tank. Jake and Billyum lay tangled on the catwalk, propwash fluttering their fire coats. Jake's helmet came loose, tumbling slowly toward the ground.

Fearful the helmet contained Jake's head, I followed its path to the cement skirt below the tank, listening for the high empty clang as it bounced high and away.

Jake and Billyum struggled to get untangled and regain their footing.

Buzzy dropped his borate on the Union 76 tank, then flew over them again, waggling his wings as he cleared the Shell tank by a good fifty feet. Billyum heaved his helmet at the plane underbelly and Jake flipped him both birds. Then the Stearman was out of sight, lost in the pall of smoke enveloping the co-op.

When Billyum and Jake made it to the ground, so many people lined up to thump their backs and pump their arms, I hung back. Someone gave each of them a beer, and they drank, heads thrown back, foam dribbling down their chins.

Sniffy pounded Jake on the shoulder. "Thought you'd fit in a short casket. Buzzy couldn't have missed you by a foot."

Jake rubbed his jaw. "Nothing shaves close as a blade. That sonofabitch Buzzy farted just in time or we'd be dead."

I DON'T BELIEVE I had ever been so proud of anyone as I was of my uncle Jake. A twinge of regret came over me, too, because I wanted to be a part of it, even though I realized I couldn't have climbed that tank for love or money. Dying was one thing, but being incinerated in a fiery explosion . . . that terrified me. Maybe it terrified Jake, too, but he wouldn't drop his brave disguise. I could tell Billyum and Mullins had been reluctant to drag the hose up the tank but had bent to Jake's goading.

Buzzy continued making runs with his Stearman, bombing the Union 76 and Chevron tanks. Mullins had managed to get several other volunteers to climb them and tie off nozzles. They hadn't vented fiery gases like the Shell tank, and because the first three climbers had lived, more of the young breaknecks stepped forward. Their eager faces flushed with the excitement of fighting fire, and they laughed and joked with one another as they buckled their equipment.

Older men and those with families stayed below to man the hoses and shields. Faces set, their eyes betrayed worry behind the dancing flames' reflections. Some had worked over twenty years at the plant and perhaps now suspected they were facing an uncertain future.

Mullins went from group to group patting backs and offering encouragement. "You boys will be getting medals for this," he said. "Damn right. We'll pass out boxes of medals. The price of silver's going up."

They grinned and shot smart remarks back, but no one was interested in medals. Somehow I realized that I was witnessing the best of Gateway, the best of small towns, where neighbors dropped their everyday grudges and risked their lives for the spirit of the community. Except for the professional firemen from Central, no one was getting paid for helping out. Years later, over drinks and memories, the volunteers would treasure the slaps on the backs above medals or money.

Jake and Billyum had been quietly drinking beers and studying the burning cold deck. Half the stacked logs were involved now, and the heat along the fire line was so intense that the railroad ties were twisting from the expansion.

"You want to have a go at that cold deck?" Jake asked Billyum.

"Forget it," Mullins said. "You can't stop a burning cold deck. Fire burns so hot it dries out the fuel ahead and just keeps eating away."

"I don't know that," Jake said. "Never saw one this close before." He tossed the beer can into the pickup bed. "What if we take some hoses, tie them up ahead where it's not burning yet. Soak the logs good. When you're camping, you can't get soaked wood to burn. It'll just char around the outside."

"Camping's for Boy Scouts," Mullins said. "She's burning too hot."

"Put a pumper on it, too," Jake said. "Worth a try."

"You should call the Forest Service," Billyum told Mullins. "Have them bring in those B-seventeens they use in forest fires and drop a few thousand pounds of borate on it. That should slow it."

Jake tapped his forehead. "Good thinking. Bomb the shit out of it."

Mullins said, "The farmers are going to raise hell for using their irrigation water and now I got to call the governor for an okay on the planes."

"Forget the farmers," Jake said. "They're always bitching and driving a hundred miles to save a dollar." He gripped Mullins's shoulder. "If you're scared, I'll call the governor. Took him fishing twice. Secretary of state last week. We're tight as ticks."

Mullins thought it over. "You trying to be head man around here, Jake?"

Jamming his thumb toward my uncle, Billyum grinned. "Your wife says he already is."

From the look on his face, Mullins didn't like that wisecrack coming from an Indian. But the way Jake and Billyum had volunteered for the tank, he couldn't say much.

"Just think," Jake said. "Everybody is going to want to interview you. Maybe this is your shot for Hollywood, the one in California, I mean. From the right camera angle, that mug isn't too unattractive."

"I'll give it a try," Mullins said.

"The dime you drop will save your ass," Jake said. "Maybe some hotshot reporter wonders why the cold deck wasn't protected better. Get it out and you'll be a hero, not a goat."

I was itching for action, but Jake wouldn't let me fight the cold-deck fire, so I joined dozens of volunteers swarming the co-op roof. With axes and crowbars, they pried up corrugated sheets of tin, then used one-inch hoses from their grass-fire pickups to douse spot fires flaring in the seed bins. They had ripped out the back of the co-op building, the side farthest from the blazing cold deck, and hauled away pallets loaded with ammonium nitrate fertilizer because it exploded if overheated.

Most of the volunteers were farmers trying to save their seed harvests. All had blackened faces from the cold-deck fire. None wore helmets or fire gear. A few scrambled across the rooftop in tennis shoes, and I thought of Jake's warning — rubber melting to flesh. Sparks and soot rained everywhere, driven by the fire's wind. The men soaked their clothing with water to prevent it from igniting. Those without caps soaked their hair.

In spite of their grimy faces, I recognized a few as avid fishermen who came by the store to stock up on equipment. Most used credit, waiting for harvest to pay Jake. They laughed at the dummy grenade hanging by the charge ledger. A huge "Number 1" tag hung from the grenade pin along with a sign that instructed IF YOU DON'T LIKE OUR CREDIT POLICY, TAKE A NUMBER.

When I scrambled up the ladder to the co-op roof, a man holding a fire hose waved me over. From his potbelly and tattoos I recognized Seaweed Swanson, the retired Navy man who raised sheep. "Come here, Little Jake. Help out."

Moving carefully to avoid the gaping holes in the ripped-up sections of roof, I scooted across.

"Take the hose, would you, kid? Getting parched up here without a beer. Hell of a note for an old swabby to be so dry. Some of these sick bastards" — he flicked the hose across the roof — "are so damn perverted they're drinking water."

After handing me the hose, Seaweed took a tallboy from his bib overalls front pocket and snapped the tab. Warm beer foamed across his hand, but he drank with gusto, then held the can to my lips. The wetness felt good in my mouth.

"This is a helluva fire, Little Jake. Saw your dad up on the tank. That took some balls." He belched and a little beer trickled out his nose.

"Well, *pardon* me. Saves wear and tear on the other end." He dropped the can into the gaping hole. "Man overboard!

"This here's a lulu all right, but nothing tops a fire at sea. Once I worked a grain ship that caught fire off the coast of Pakistan. Three days that fucking wheat smoldered, and we couldn't get it out. You lived with the smell — scorched Quaker Oats or something. Then the fire spread through the electrical system to the engine room. Lots of oil and grease, chance for an explosion." He shook his head. "No choice. We opened the sea valves and flooded the bastard. Put on our swimming trunks. Those pissant Pakistanis were supposed to send rescue helicopters but they took their own sweet time. We were swimming laps by the time they showed and lost three guys to sharks."

"No sharks here," I said, not knowing how much of the story to believe. According to Jake, Seaweed had more bullshit than the Pacific had salt.

He stretched, surveying the scene from the rooftop, while I concentrated the stream of water on the seed. I couldn't see flames, but there was plenty of smoke and sparks thick as raindrops. It smelled like someone was toasting birdseed.

The firemen at the fuel tanks and cold deck had taken off their heavy equipment and worked in boots, pants, and helmets. A few clustered at the millpond, dipping water with their helmets, then pouring it over their heads and shoulders.

"See how the track is buckling?" Seaweed pointed at the twisting rails. "Rails are swollen clear past the expansion joints. Now that's hot."

From this perspective, I could see the chaos of the fire, the jumble of hoses and equipment, tight knots of men trying to get some control. Jake, Billyum, and a couple of the other Indians had dragged hoses onto the log deck and were finishing tying them off. The hoses poured streams of water into the stacked logs. One of the Indians cocked his head and pointed toward the sky. The men on the co-op roof heard the deep droning too.

Not the high hum of the Stearman, this was an earthshaking rumbling similar to the ones depicted in old World War II movies as the big bombers throbbed over Germany's night skies. The entire co-op vibrated. Just knowing the converted B-17s had joined the fight gave me a thrill.

Below, firemen put on their helmets and took shelter in the trucks. Jake and the others scrambled off the cold deck, moving from log to log like frantic children at some kind of crazy jungle gym.

"Borate comes out in chunks!" Seaweed shouted, barely audible over the din. "Cover up, Little Jake." Dropping to his knees, he covered his head with both arms.

The first plane came in low, maybe three hundred yards off the ground, but it seemed the roar would shake the co-op apart. The corrugated roof rattled.

When I was younger, I assembled plastic models of World War II planes, including B-17s. These hung above my bed, twisting slowly on fishing line tacked into my bedroom ceiling. Now it seemed one of the big bombers had come to life.

Seaweed tugged my pants leg, urging me to kneel and cover, but I stood, waiting for the bomb doors to open.

And they did, dumping four thousand pounds of reddish borate mix, a huge red drench, most of it concentrated on the cold deck and vicinity. The updraft wind carried some of the mist in all directions and it fell around us like blood rain.

"You're bleeding like a stuck pig," Seaweed shouted, then grinned.

After the first bomber passed, I could hear better for a moment. The men on the co-op roof cheered, waving their hoses in the air.

As the second plane dumped its load, flames guttered and dimmed on top of the cold deck, even though the logs burned steadily below. But the top layer of logs between the fire and the drenching hoses was covered in a red paste, and for the first time I thought maybe they could stop the fire.

"Bomb the hell out of the son of a bitch," Seaweed yelled, waving his hose.

The B-17s droned into the distance, the noise of their big engines fading, but you could feel the surge of enthusiasm sweep the firefighters. On top of the co-op, men redoubled their efforts. Below, they dragged more hoses toward the deck, pouring on water.

Seaweed got so excited he dropped his beer. "Damn! Little Jake, go get me a couple more would you? How else can I endure fireman's fatigue?"

He pointed to a section of roof where smoke seeped between the corrugations and a makeshift crew was pulling up the tin. "Meet me in St. Louis, Louis," he called out, dragging his hose toward the new break. A man with a crowbar and ax hurried to join him.

I started toward the ladder, going cautiously around pried-up sections when I heard a cry. Looking back, I saw that Seaweed and the other man had disappeared. Seaweed's hose led to a broken section of roof.

When I reached the edge of the hole, I realized they had broken through a Plexiglas skylight. Careful to avoid a fall myself, I crouched and peered into the smoky interior. On the concrete floor thirty feet below, one man lay still. The second had landed on some empty pallets. Seaweed's hose had dropped halfway between the roof and floor. In the empty space, it waved and twisted like a frenzied snake, spraying the interior. Three stories below, the concrete floor rippled with water.

Scrambling across roof and down ladder, I raced through the torn-out back section of the co-op and into the smoky interior. After a couple moments, my eyes adjusted and I could recognize each man. Still clutching his crowbar, the younger man lay on the wet concrete. He wasn't moving and the odd twist in his back made me almost puke. Seaweed groaned on the pallets, perhaps three feet above the floor. Although his eyes were open, he wasn't alert. Nothing registered in them as I came closer. Blood seeped from the back of his head, soaking a T-shirt one of the volunteers pressed against the wound. "Where's the damn ambulance?" he said. Glancing at Seaweed, he shook his head. "Better goddamn hurry up and get here."

I touched Seaweed's shoulder. "Hey. It's Little Jake. Can you hear me? Just hang on tight. The ambulance is coming."

He didn't say anything until a few moments later, after the gushing hose swept by, whipping us with its hard stream.

"Captain. Captain. We're taking water."

I bent over Seaweed, shielding him the best I could from the wild hose.

"Pull the son of a bitch up, you idiots," the volunteer shouted to men on the roof. Heads appeared and disappeared at the broken skylight, but no one thought to lift the hose.

The ambulance arrived, backing through the hole they tore out to carry off the ammonium nitrate fertilizer. As soon as the attendants rushed out to help, the hose whipped by them and they cursed the men on the roof.

After a quick check of the young man on the floor, the ambulance crew lifted him on a stretcher and covered his face. They were more careful with Seaweed, trying to check his injuries. They asked the other volunteer firefighters and me a bunch of questions we couldn't answer before carefully lifting Seaweed, trying to prevent further injury. Even so he screamed twice, then lowered his voice to a whisper. "Getting dark, Captain. Should I put out the smoking lamp?"

Those were his last words. The ambulance door closed, and I knew I wouldn't hear him speak again.

No one cheered now, at least not around the co-op. The men seemed pretty glum, and the volunteer that had pressed Seaweed's wound picked up the crowbar lying on the floor and flung it straight up at the broken skylight. It sailed over and over, then thudded dully on concrete. Although his action was dumb, I understood, especially when he muttered, "Tyler had three damn kids, the little one barely walking."

Outside, I wandered around a little — in shock, I guess. The full reality of the fire's danger had hit, the sheer craziness of it. Here was this inferno at the mill and along the cold deck, but no one had been killed or blown sky-high on the fuel tanks. However, on the co-op roof, by all appearances a relatively safe place, two men had plunged to their deaths.

Stubborn firefighters still trained their streams on the cold deck and fuel tanks. Others climbed the ladders once again to the co-op roof. I gripped the rung of one ladder, then pushed away, scraping off a little mud with my palms. Everything was wet and slick now.

My hands shook, and I started walking again to keep my knees from buckling. Nothing could make me climb that ladder to the roof.

I wasn't too afraid to realize I was hungry and joined other firefighters straggling toward the makeshift food line Gateway's restaurants and bars had set up. The men looked like the wrath of God — covered with soot, mud, and reddish borate. In spite of their appearance, most seemed pleased to be there and shared a kind of jovial camaraderie. Nothing like this was likely to happen again in their lifetimes, so they bragged and joked like team members enjoying the locker room following a big game.

Finally one of them turned his attention to me. "You look like death warmed over, kid. Really you do. You're as ugly as my wife's first husband."

I grinned.

"You got more teeth though. I knocked two of his out myself."

They all laughed at that one. "She got two more with her high heel." The man kept the laughter going.

"Hey, this is Jake's nephew," another said. "No shit now, your uncle's a big hero. Saved the day as far as I'm concerned. Grow up with half his balls, you'll do all right."

I basked in my uncle's praise but tried to stick up for Billyum, too. "Jake had a little help."

"Sure, we seen that big Indian up there. He did all right."

✫ ✫ ✫ ✫

What I hadn't counted on was my mother. Along with other women from the community, she was serving sandwiches, hot coffee, apples, slices of pie. At the end of the portable tables were coolers filled with beer and soda. Grocery merchants had donated food and beverages. The bars had sent cases of ice-cold beer. Mullins was cautioning the firefighters about too much drinking. One or two beers was okay, but more could mean trouble. The way I'd seen Seaweed go down, I could have drunk half a case and never numbed the shock.

The women wore aprons that said, "Gateway Volunteer Firemen's Auxiliary." Where Mom had gotten hers, I didn't know, but she was the prettiest woman on the food line — and the only one wearing an Italian costume, so she must have come directly from the Festival of Floats.

Astonished to see me, she tried handing over an apple, but paused, unable to let it go. "Culver . . . What on earth? You and Jake were having supper with Juniper."

I gently removed the apple from her hand. "We left a little early."

I think she was going to comment on Jake, but then she saw my eyes. "You've been crying."

"Soot and ash, Mom." I took a beef sandwich from the next woman in line.

Mom left her place and followed. She seemed very flustered. "This fire's so dangerous, I want you home at once."

"Don't worry. I've just been helping hold hoses, watching for spot fires. Nothing too dangerous."

Reaching across the serving table, she gripped my wrist with surprising strength. "Go home, I say. You might get run over in all this confusion. I understand some unfortunate men fell through the co-op roof. The ambulance just raced by."

The man in line behind me cleared his throat and started to say something about the delay, but she glared at him. "First chance you get, Culver. I don't want any of you boys getting hurt."

"You should be proud, dear," the sandwich woman said. "My Jason's fighting fire and he's only fifteen."

My mother gave the woman one of her brightest smiles. "Of course I'm proud, fiercely proud of Culver. And as citizens of Gateway, we're very pleased to be helping out." She resumed her place in line and smoothed her apron. "I just don't want any of the young men getting hurt before their prime. I'm certain you'd have to agree that young men's judgment can be a little shaky." Not waiting for the woman to answer, she turned to the next man in line. "Here's a nice apple for you."

Scooting along, I grabbed a couple bags of potato chips. I craved salt. When Mom's head was turned, I snatched a beer from the ice chest.

I walked past rows of men sitting on tailgates and lounging on folding chairs someone had brought from the Lutheran church. Sweaty, muddy, they resembled war casualties, and the reddish borate stains seemed like blood. All were sooty; it was difficult to tell where their clothes stopped, wrists and necks began. I realized that I must have shocked my mother by looking as bad as they did — probably worse — because I had witnessed something they hadn't.

Choosing the tailgate of an empty pickup, I sat and began eating the sandwich. The roast beef tasted like smoke. Maybe it was my hands. The apple and chips tasted like smoke, too. At least the beer was cold.

After eating, I studied the area. Sections of the cold deck still burned, the stacked logs glowing like giant embers. But the top layers of logs, those smothered in borate, weren't burning, and where the hoses fired water into the deck, the logs charred and smoked. Taking a naked-eye measurement, I felt they could salvage half of it.

Equipment lay strewn about — helmets, fire coats, boots. Two men paraded around in their shorts; I believe they had spent more time drinking free beer than fighting fire. One stripped down to his briefs and tried diving into the millpond, using the tailgate of his pickup for a low board.

"Shit," Mullins said. "He's going to drown or break his neck. We don't need any more casualties." Disgusted, Mullins dragged the guy out of the water and tied his feet to the pickup spotlight. "By the time he sobers up enough to get free, he can drive again," Mullins said.

Axes, crowbars, shovels, seemed like toys left behind by careless kids. Waves and waves of heat coming from the glowing deck made the telephone poles seem eerily crooked.

A dozen men remained on the co-op roof, taking care to avoid the treacherous skylight. With the cold deck burning less furiously, the raining sparks slowed a little.

A man drinking a Mountain Dew sat next to me on the tailgate. Taking a wadded sandwich from his pants pocket, he started eating. "You look like dog shit, Bucko."

"Damn it, Riley! What are you doing here?" The *D* on his baseball cap had been entirely blackened by the soot.

He chuckled, but it sounded odd. One of his nostrils was packed with cotton, like he had a nosebleed. "Can't pass up a good fire."

I glanced around. "You better be careful. Someone will see you."

With the arm holding the can, he made a sweep of the cold deck and plant. "I been everywhere. Tied off a hose ten feet from Jake and he never knew me from Moses." He touched the can to his nose. "I held one of those tin shields awhile. Hot as a twenty-dollar pistol. Then my nose decided to get a period. But that's okay. The bosses want to see the workers' blood. Look at these dumb bastards risking life and limb to save the plant. What for? Tomorrow those same fucked-up heroes will be scratching for work. The owners will sell them downriver for an insurance check and a golf game." He paused. "We ought to torch the owners along with the cold deck."

Riley's anger made me realize that somewhere he had crossed the main line onto a dangerous spur and I doubted he'd ever get back. I voiced my thoughts without realizing. "You didn't start this fire, did you, Riley?"

He snorted, the blood bubbling up in the nostril. "What if I did. You turning me in?"

I shrugged. "Maybe." He knew I wouldn't, even though dozens of policemen were around. "Two guys fell through the co-op roof. Both are dead."

He removed his baseball cap, revealing a white line of high forehead that hadn't been smoked. Turning the cap in his hands, he seemed to be looking for some flaw. "The workers are getting screwed in this deal. Those two just checked out early, and I'm sorry as hell." He put the cap back on.

"I just want to know," I said when I realized he hadn't answered the question.

"Remember this, kid. When you're working in this society, you're a zero. Listen. Your mother and I were married for eight years, and I walked right past her. She gives me a sandwich, an apple, and a little dipsy smile. But she never had a clue. Working stiffs must look alike." He paused. "What's that stupid outfit she's wearing anyway?"

His remarks about my mother got me started. "She's exhausted, Riley. What do you expect? Anyway, you're not exactly working."

He drained his Mountain Dew. "Don't go getting snot-nosed on me."

But I was overheated. "If you didn't set this fire, why are you here? Not for the citizenship award."

"Let's just say it gives me a hard-on. Okay?" His voice softened after that. "Since when did you go drinking beer? You never did at my place."

"Since I felt like it."

"Well don't get too cheeky." He slapped my back. "Look at this damn soda." Riley held out the empty can for inspection. "How about you sneak back and grab us a couple beers. We'll have a drink — man to man, Bucko. If I go, your mom might get all excited and give me away."

I went. After dipping a couple beers out of the ice chest, I stood observing her, the cans cooling my hands. She greeted every weary firefighter, smiled at him, offered encouragement.

And it occurred to me then that if circumstances were different, if she had caught a decent break, my mother might have been the perfect hostess. The quick beauty of her smile, the slight forward tilt of her head — both suggested each word you had to say was important to her. I'd seen her act that way when she'd been a greeter in church, and I remembered how she always found something pleasant to say, even in the most difficult circumstance. I was tongue-tied as other church members poured out their woes: cancer, betrayal, accident. But in the most terrible circumstances, Mom found comforting words to make people feel better, to get them through the day — and perhaps the night.

Watching her greet the firemen, I realized how much she needed a divorce from Riley. She had to escape this two-bit box, even if a better opportunity only meant marrying someone like Franklin. He'd have screens on the doors, at least, and I guessed that would be okay, if she chose him. Not that I could ever call him Dad or anything. Still, even though I couldn't picture it, I'd be leaving soon — off to college or the service.

She glanced in my direction, although she didn't recognize me among the group of dirty firefighters, and I was struck again at how beautiful she appeared — a flower among all those exhausted workers, a bright crocus rising through dirty snow and winter ashes. At that moment I resolved to do whatever I could to help her.

Returning to the pickup, I handed Riley his beer.

He checked behind me to make certain no one had followed. "Thanks, Bucko. Took you long enough." As he drank, the beer foamed, running down his chin. "Shit. You shake this up?"

"Did you get our message, Riley? When we came to the camp?"

"I heard something." He studied me. "I've been your dad eight years now."

"I know, but things are different now. I can't see you coming to many ball games, Riley. When you torched Griggs, everything changed."

He wiped foam from his chin, leaving a black smear. "Everything changed before then. I finally had my say — loud and clear."

"You can see how things got pretty cramped for her."

He threw up his hands and some beer sloshed onto his wrist. "She can have a damn divorce. If that's what she wants. Sometimes people get back together."

I didn't say anything.

"If I went over there and talked to her, what do you think?"

"They might put you in jail."

He squinted at me. "Maybe she just wants to make it legal with pretty boy. Is he wearing the wallet these days?"

"We're carrying our own weight. Whatever she does, that's her business."

"Sure." Finished with the beer, he crushed the can against the side of the pickup but still gripped the metal tight. "Tell her to get the papers drawn. I'll let you know where to send them. Uncontested. I'll sign before a notary and ship them back. The declaration of her independence."

"Thanks, Riley." Reaching out, I tried to shake his hand, but he just brushed my palm.

"So long, Bucko." After tossing the empty can into the pickup bed, he started walking past all the firefighters and equipment, keeping to the raised track bed beside the twisted rails.

I wanted to laugh. Here he was, walking by dozens of firefighters and police officers, with no one, including me, making a move to stop him. To be truthful, I felt a great sense of relief, knowing he was walking out of our lives forever. And I thought with him gone we would be safe, because I didn't realize then that the seeds of meanness and betrayal lay buried in us all.

I wanted to believe that he didn't set this fire, but I thought he might commit an act equally reckless that could harm my mother and me or others, like Seaweed and Tyler, who never met Riley and just showed up by chance.

As he disappeared into the darkness beyond the fire's long glow, I felt unburdened of a terrible weight. In that buoyant moment, my thoughts returned to my mother and her chances. Free of Riley, she could do better than Franklin, I was convinced. She could marry a doctor or lawyer for another go-round. In one of my mother's magazines, I had read about a Supreme Court justice with several wives, the newest a beauty from the West. He appeared old and gray but they were hiking together over mountains, lovebirds basking in a spring start. Perhaps I would return from college to a justice's place.

While my imagination was running wild, I got an even crazier idea.

Maybe Mom and Jake would marry. They seemed an unlikely pair, but they shared me in common, and the way they quarreled made them seem almost married already.

Then my imagination dead-ended. Fear cut through my fantasies. Perhaps it was dehydration and fatigue or the shock of seeing two men dying. I took rapid gulps of air, fighting back the urge to puke.

Staring down the railroad tracks into the gloom beyond the glowing cold deck, my weary eyes conjured shadowy figures of Riley, Jake, and even my mother twisting in the eerie undulations from the fire's heat wave.

Tearing my gaze away from the haunting specters, I tried to find comfort in familiar objects. Fire hoses lay strewn along the railroad bed and fire equipment littered the blackened and muddy ground. The telephone poles and lines wavered in the heat. Even the railroad tracks had buckled into grotesque shapes. Try though I might, I couldn't follow a straight line anywhere.

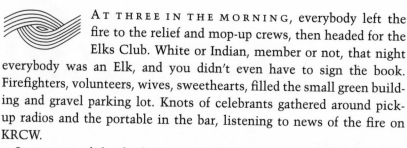

18

AT THREE IN THE MORNING, everybody left the fire to the relief and mop-up crews, then headed for the Elks Club. White or Indian, member or not, that night everybody was an Elk, and you didn't even have to sign the book. Firefighters, volunteers, wives, sweethearts, filled the small green building and gravel parking lot. Knots of celebrants gathered around pickup radios and the portable in the bar, listening to news of the fire on KRCW.

Soon some of the firefighters and the women got pretty happy and went around kissing everybody in sight. Jake, Buzzy, Mullins, and the other heroes collected lots of kisses. Billyum picked up a few, too, and seemed surprised. Usually the giddy women kissed him on the forehead or cheek, not the lips. A couple kissed me, and one tried to stick her tongue in my mouth.

The Cokes and 7-Ups I kept drinking didn't slake my thirst. Maybe it was dehydration or the beers I drank at the fire. Whichever. Jake put his arm around my shoulder, hugging me tight, and asked Gab, "Did you hear about the mother who knew her son didn't drink because he always woke up so thirsty in the morning?" They both laughed, and Jake told me to drink some plain ice water.

Inside the lodge, Ned Cabo, the combination cook-bouncer, dug into the walk-in refrigerator units and dragged out huge cans of crab they had planned on using for the annual crab feed. Doreen drove over from the Oasis with dozens and dozens of eggs. They asked me to hustle around and empty some candy jars, then make signs indicating donations would go to the dead firefighter's family. As the revelers came in for omelettes or beers, they put fistfuls of darkened bills and coins into the jars. "Don't matter if it's dirty," Ned said. "Spends the same."

The crab was shipped from a seafood place in Maryland, and the cans featured pictures of Chesapeake blue crabs. "Did you ever get steamed crabs like this and crack them up?" I asked Ned.

"No, but I got the other kind once," he replied, winking. "Jumped right off the toilet seat. They cracked *me* up."

He tried elbowing Doreen as she walked by with four big omelettes, but she sashayed past. "You never got 'em from me, honey. That must have been your wife."

Ned stuffed a handful of rich crabmeat into his mouth and tried talking. "Who wants to mess around with shells and a hammer? One of those funny bibs they wear back East? Here all you got to do is open the cans, set out crackers and ketchup."

We served breakfast until the light broke. By then we were out of crab and down to eggshells. Outside, red-faced men and women grew rowdier and started chanting the names of the fire's heroes. One by one they called them up, and the firefighters stood on the tailgates of pickups while the fans squirted them with beer, sort of like the players being interviewed after the World Series. Almost everybody got in on the act, including a bunch of fellas I never recognized from the fire at all. The biggest applause was saved for Buzzy, who wore his aviator helmet and pulled down the goggles to keep the beer out of his eyes.

He sprung from a pickup bed onto the cab roof and you could see it dent a little, but no one minded. While he flapped his wings and pretended to take off, the crowd made noises like buzzing bees.

They called for Jake and it became a chant. "Jake, Jake, Jake," but he and Billyum had slipped across the street and were nursing beers at the side of the Chinese restaurant.

I crossed the street, unnoticed by the crowd, and said, "They want you, Uncle Jake," as if he couldn't hear the noise.

He shook his head. "I've had about all of this fun I can take." He flexed his arms and shoulders. "Got to drink more beer. I feel like I've been beat up. More than once." Turning to Billyum, he asked, "Was it you?"

Billyum opened and closed his fists. His hands looked raw and sore. "Must be. I feel like I was in a hell of a fight." He cocked his head, listening to the continuing chant. "Better go take a bow, Jake. Kiss some more women."

"I'm going home," Jake said. "I'm not fixing to be around when sunlight smacks those poor bastards in the face and they figure out their jobs went up in smoke."

Jake dropped me off so I could get a little shut-eye, but he asked me to show up around ten. "I'm too pooped to pop. Going right to the store, try to catch some winks before the hotshots show up. At least two dozen guys will claim they put out that fire single-handed."

"Not me," I said. "I needed a little help."

"You didn't get any from him." Jake nodded his head in the direction of Franklin's Bel Air, which was parked directly in front of our house. "Say hi to your buddy," Jake said when I got out.

Franklin lay on the love seat, his legs covered with a beige terry-cloth robe that had been my father's. I had been quiet opening the door so he didn't waken. But it disturbed me to see him lying there just like he belonged, and I vowed to help my mother find someone a little better, if I could.

The early morning light filtered through the yellow curtains, defining Franklin's features. Parts of his face remained swollen and discolored, but where the skin was normal, it held a peculiar smoothness. Few pores were visible, even around the nose, and I wondered if he used Ivory soap the way my mother did.

The hands were smooth, too, unlike the working hands of the men who claimed the back-room territory. His left clutched the robe, and I could see the half-moons of his fingernails. They looked like they'd been manicured, and I realized why he held the fishing pole so awkwardly. These didn't look like hands to hold fishing gear at all. I checked the knuckles again in the clear light. If he'd swung on Riley, he hadn't landed much of a blow.

Franklin widened one eye. "You look terrible — like something the cat dragged in."

"Well, I've got lots of company," I said, not trying to hide my irritation. "Some of us stayed up all night fighting fire. Just about the whole town turned out." He seemed chickenshit for staying behind.

Franklin touched the back of his head with his hand, smoothing down some wild hair. "Doctor said I have a concussion, probably bruised a few organs. I'm supposed to take it easy a couple weeks."

"Seems like you've succeeded," I said.

He sat, swinging his legs to the floor. His ankles were thin and white. "Your mother was worried sick."

"Indeed I was," she said, opening the bedroom door. "Where on earth have you been?" Coming over, she gave me a long hug. "I prayed you weren't dead."

When she stepped back, I saw she had been crying. But her attention suddenly turned to the carpet. "Culver, you've tracked soot and mud all over. Please remove those awful boots at once."

"Sure, Mom. Sorry." So much for the hero's greeting, I thought. Backtracking to the front doormat, I sat and started unlacing the boots.

"After I saw you at the fire, I believed you'd come straight home. When you weren't here . . . Poor Franklin. He drove all over town looking for you."

"I was at the Elks, Mom. All the firefighters stopped there for a celebration."

Franklin shook his head. "Not much to celebrate. The mill's gone and the logs are burned up. The damage will total in the millions."

"At least the town's still here," I said. "That counts for something."

My mother turned to him. "If I were you, I wouldn't go poor-mouthing the hard work those men did last night. Remember, two lost their lives." She paused. "Didn't you go look for Culver at the Elks? I'm sure I said the Elks specifically."

"Yes I did." He spread his hands. "It was a mob. Lots of wild drunks. I asked everyone I knew."

I smiled a little. Probably he didn't hang around too long. Clean as he was, Franklin would have drawn ridicule, especially wearing his Italian costume. I believe my mother suspected the same but wouldn't admit it. Maybe she was starting to think he was a wuss, too.

"Well, the important thing is Culver's back safe and sound." She took my hand, giving it a squeeze. "You're getting too big to hold, but that doesn't mean I'm not your mother. And mothers worry. Now go take a shower and get some sleep." She examined some of the soot that had come off on her hands and nightgown. "Just throw those terrible clothes outside until I get a chance to soak them. I've never seen such a mess. Everything smells like smoke."

After placing my billfold and change on my dresser, I put the pants outside our back door. The billfold was damp from all the water and sweat, and I realized things still hadn't dried from my trip through the Combine, so I laid out the contents. The signatures on my fishing license and Social Security card were smeared. My Grass Valley student body card had turned to pulp, and a couple school photos of my teammates were ruined, too. I dumped them in the wastebasket.

I checked the kitchen clock. Almost eight. I was afraid I'd sleep through and miss helping Jake. "I've got to relieve Jake at ten, Mom. Can you call me? Wake me up?"

At the mention of my uncle, Mom's eyes flashed. "Taking a young boy to that fire. The man needs to be horsewhipped."

☆ ☆ ☆ ☆

We didn't sell much fishing tackle that day, but we sold out of emergency equipment — fire extinguishers, flashlights, thermos bottles, flares, Wolverine boots, all the short-handled shovels we stocked. People crowded the store all day long. So many crammed the back room, we made pot after pot of coffee, and Jake sent me to the store for more supplies. Homer carried over four trays of bakery goods; the fishing creel straps strained with the weight of all the coins.

Everyone was too excited to settle back into a routine. Rumors flew. A team of state fire investigators had arrived from the capital, and the insurance companies sent out their people, too. Lawyers from Central and the capital descended on the town.

"I haven't seen so many lawyers since that winter those California people hit the horses," Jake said. "God, it was freezing! We could have used some of the heat from the mill fire. Never saw it that damn cold."

"How cold was it?" I asked.

"So cold when the lawyers showed up, they kept their hands in their own pockets." Gab finished the punch line, so I knew I'd been set up. The back-room boys laughed, pointing at me. The hilarity covered their sadness about Seaweed.

My ears burned. "You guys can make your own damn coffee."

"See how you've got him swearing like a longshoreman," Jake said. "I want you damn bastards to clean up your language." At that point he added, "Fellas, I need for you to be quiet a minute."

After they quieted, he washed Seaweed's coffee cup and placed it upside down on the shelf above the sink. No one said anything for a minute, but Buzzy cleared his throat and Sniffy turned away. My eyes stung. "A good man," Jake said. "A *genuine* character."

Early reports said the fire had started in the stud mill. The whole operation had shut down two days for repairs and to allow the millworkers the opportunity to attend Central's Water Pageant. The theory was a spark from a welder's torch had smoldered in the sawdust, then ignited. Some claimed the automatic sprinkler system had come on until the fire swept through the electrical plant, disabling the generators. Others said the whole system had failed. All agreed the investigators would have a lot of questions.

Jake was dog tired. I had slept until ten, but I don't believe he managed even forty winks. He was running on nerves, coffee, and Homer's pastry.

Several times during the day, Jake took the donations jar from the front counter and passed it to the back-room boys and customers. "Give till it hurts," he said. "You'll feel better." If their wallets were thin, Jake kept the jar under their noses until they made out a check.

"I doubt if Tyler had much insurance." Gab nodded solemnly as he worked on another doughnut.

"Think about that," Jake said. "How much insurance did you have at twenty-two?"

We kept a pretty good crew until just before suppertime. Then those who had been up all night began to fade. I felt the fatigue too and wandered out by the pictures of Kalim and his grandparents. It was a weird summer, I thought. All my life, I'd never seen anyone dead except in a funeral home. Now I'd hauled a corpse out of the Lost and seen two men plunge to death. Crazy. And that didn't even bring Riley into it.

Just before noon, a reporter and photographer from the *Central Dispatch* had shown up, wanting to talk with Jake. "We're getting pictures of all the heroes," they had said.

"You need to get my nephew in the photo, then," he said. "How many sixteen-year-old heroes do you have in Central?"

We went outside so they could take the picture in front of the store. "Free advertising," Jake said with a wink.

The back-room boys lined up to watch. "It must be a slow news day," they teased. "They're getting a picture of next year's grand marshal, Jake."

"Got to hurry. I'm close to deadline." The reporter scribbled notes as he asked questions. "Were you on the fuel tank too?"

"No," I said. "I was on the co-op roof."

He wrote something. "Did you see those two men who died?"

"Yes. I was fighting alongside Seaweed. He was a regular customer here."

"One of a kind," Jake added.

"Too bad about that," the reporter said. "One more thing. How do you spell your name?"

Juniper stopped by in the early evening. When Jake saw her car, he ducked his head into the back room and said, "Fellas, there's a lady coming, and she doesn't think much of cussing. I'd appreciate it if you'd hold it down."

The boys had so much respect for Jake, they did stop swearing. It seemed quiet as a church meeting.

Juniper noticed right off. "You put a muzzle on them, Jake?"

"It's always quiet when they discuss religion and art," he said.

She rolled her eyes. "Give me a break." Touching his arm, she added, "Billyum was at the tribal center having coffee this morning. He looked terrible but claimed you were even worse, so I had to come see for myself."

Jake pulled down on both cheeks just under the eyes, so she could see the bloodshot whites. "What do you think? Death warmed over?"

"Stop it!" She laughed, turning away. "You look like one of those Halloween thingees with the eyeballs on springs."

"At least I didn't break any cameras. You missed the reporters. The *Central Dispatch* folks were here. I'll probably pull front page."

She shook her head. "Page eight. I bought some copies when I was in Central earlier. They sold two more of my paintings." She took several papers out of the bag and put them on the counter.

"Page eight," Jake said, opening the paper and winking. "We need a better agent."

Jake looked good and the store sign showed up well in the black and white photo. My eyes were half closed, a reaction to the flash. Underneath, the caption said, "Jake and Calvin Martin, Father and Son Fire Fighting Heroes."

The back-room boys teased us a lot about that.

"You're going to inherit this dump," Gab said. "Bad news. Poor Culver. Your lineage just got worse. You should never have posed with the old screwball. He just wanted to keep the camera from breaking."

Jake handed me one of the papers. "Show this to your mother. That should give her a conniption fit."

I grinned. It was kind of funny.

"Papers never get anything right," Juniper said. "They got the names of my paintings wrong at the gallery."

"I told you to let me keep them here," Jake said.

She pulled a wad of cash from her pocket. Noticing the donation jar, she slipped in a twenty.

"Page eight," Gab said. "That's where they put the lost dog notices.

Fall back one more page and you're in the obits along with poor Seaweed. I read them every day just to keep track of how I'm feeling."

After the back-room boys had settled down, Jake scanned the paper for more news of the fire. Gateway only had a weekly and it wasn't due out for two more days. "Blah, blah, blah," Jake said. "All about the heroic efforts and the damage assessments." His tone changed. "What they don't say is a lot of guys are going to lose their jobs. At first management will say they won't, but a year from now the millworkers won't need pants pockets."

"Maybe they can work on the rez," Juniper said. "There's talk of building a new mill out there."

Jake raised his eyebrows. "Who says?"

"A little bird. Ayyyy." She smiled. "I know some people on the tribal planning council. My uncle Sylvester. And Billyum mentioned it, too."

Jake seemed to think it over. "There's always talk of developing industry on the reservation. Still, you need a lot of start-up money."

"That's true." She took one of the beef jerky sticks from the jar on the counter and started to dig in her purse for change, but Jake shook his head. She nibbled the jerky. "But we've got the trees. You know those long-term timber leases are up next year. And if we make plywood from our own trees, we don't pay federal taxes."

"Lot more money for the tribe," Jake said. "Especially if the federal government gives you a start-up grant."

"Like I say, they've been talking about it. Around that little tribal sawmill, there's lots of room to build a modern plywood plant."

"Tribe's got to vote on it," Jake said. "Think they'll commit the long-term dollars?"

She nodded. "Things are changing. The mood is for more independence. It's different now than when I left for Albuquerque." She took another nibble of the jerky, then dropped it into the wastebacket. "Too salty. Some white guys must make this."

"If that plant gets built on the reservation under tribal supervision, a lot of boys lose their seniority."

"At least they'll be working," she said.

Jake nodded. "Who knows what's going to happen? We'll just have to wait for the guys in suits to open their briefcases."

"LET'S SHUT IT DOWN a little early tonight," Jake said around eight-thirty. "Could you make out the night deposit? I'm so tired I can't keep anything straight, but I don't want to leave all this money lying around, especially the donations."

We carried the three big jars into the office adjoining the back room, and I began counting the money while Jake started wheeling in the bikes. I finished the first deposit for Tyler's family — over six hundred dollars in checks and cash. Jake was singing one of his goofy songs as he rolled in the bikes, just trying to keep himself awake, I think. But he grew quiet and I heard a second voice.

"Everything out there's crooked as a corkscrew, Jake."

"Let's get the bikes in," Jake said. "Then I'll lock the door."

I quit working on the adding machine because I recognized the voice and wanted to listen. Sniffy sounded very upset.

For a few minutes I didn't hear anything but Jake wheeling in the bikes, then the door locking. Jake and Sniffy went into the back room.

"The fire couldn't have started the way they claimed . . ."

Sniffy was speaking and I moved across the office to hear better.

"If a spark from a welding torch hit that sawdust under the big saws, no way a fire'd take off like that. The water that cools those saw blades keeps that dust wet."

"The saws were shut down two days," Jake said. "It must have dried some."

"Not that fast." Sniffy paused. "I'm telling you things have gotten fishy. I've been walking clock, keeping notes."

"Don't go off the deep end," Jake said. "Maybe you're dreaming things up a little."

Sniffy became more agitated and his voice rose. "Did you know the big diesel generator was out of commission, missing a piston? That's no dream."

Jake grunted, seeming surprised. "So one of the sprinkler systems was completely shut down. How long?"

"Three weeks. The millwrights fussed around but couldn't fix it. Put that back in action, we might have saved the mill."

"Maybe you need to talk with someone else," Jake said.

"Like the insurance people?" Sniffy laughed, and it was bitter. "I'm not a rat. But I got my notes saved for a rainy day."

"All right then," Jake said. "The piston. You got anything else?"

"Glue," he said.

Jake didn't say anything.

"See, I know exactly how many batches I cook. But when I checked the records and saw what they were billing the tribe to make up their plywood, it was cockeyed. I'd cook up fifteen pots. They'd get billed for twenty. And they were billed for extra plywood, too. Somebody was skimming sweet."

"Glue and plywood must add up," Jake said.

"You better believe it. We're a big operation, and it takes a lot of plywood to rebuild the reservation. You could retire fat."

I heard the chair squeak as Sniffy moved. Opening the office door wide enough to squeeze through, I stepped into the shadows cast by the water skis.

"See, I been storing records at the glue house, but I couldn't leave them after the fire. That's about the only place left, and I was afraid one of the investigators might stumble across them." He paused. "I don't know what the hell to do."

Jake switched off the store lights, catching me unexpected. The office light shone through the open door. Hurrying back to my chair, I pretended to be mulling over the night deposit. When Jake stepped in to switch off the light, he seemed surprised, as if he'd forgotten I was back there at all. He studied the money, the empty jars, the checks on the desk. "How's it coming?"

"Slow." I rubbed my eyes. "These numbers just keep swimming."

"I didn't hear the adding machine." He looked around as if expecting someone else. "You're tired. Maybe I should finish. Go on home."

Just then Sniffy poked his head in, mouth open in surprise. "Jesus, Jake. The damn kid's back here working? What the hell!"

Jake rested his hand on Sniffy's shoulder, trying to calm him. "Mr. St. John is pretty upset, Culver. The fire and all. You understand?"

"Sure," I said, nodding.

Letting go of Sniffy's shoulder, he gripped mine. "Anything you heard tonight stays here. No matter what."

Sniffy was sweating more than anyone I'd seen who wasn't working outside. His mouth kept opening and closing like a fish's.

"That's a promise," I said.

Jake spread his hands. "The boy's my sidekick, Sniffy. My own flesh and blood. He's good as gospel."

"I got to take your word, don't I, Jake?"

My uncle perched on the edge of the desk, leaning forward. "Let's hear it all, Sniffy. What else you got?"

Sniffy seemed like he was going to collapse, and I scooted my chair under him. He sat and leaned back, closing his eyes. "Man oh man, what a pickle." His eyes opened. "Half the fire hoses were disconnected. Well, maybe not half, but a lot. I couldn't tell if it was plain sloppiness or someone doing it on purpose, but that first sprinkler system never had much chance either."

"Can't tell much now," Jake said. "That plant's all burned down. Machinery's blackened, walls collapsed."

Sniffy nodded. "This afternoon, soon as the ruin cooled some, one of the millwrights snuck out and put a truck piston in that diesel generator to make it look legit. Packed it solid with grease so the inspectors would miss it. I couldn't have told the difference myself if I didn't already know."

"You can't blame them for covering their ass," Jake said. "The insurance guys will try to welch every way possible. 'You were fully insured but not covered' is how they like to put it." He paused. "The question is how things got so broke down and why they weren't fixed sooner. Summer delays?"

Sniffy didn't say anything.

"What do you think. Italian lightning? Somebody torched it?"

"The plant was obsolete compared to the new places in the South and Canada. Way overinsured. And the Indians are going to control more of their timber, put the squeeze on."

"A match solves a lot of problems," Jake said so quiet I could hardly hear him. "But can you prove anything?"

Sniffy shook his head. "Slow down the payoff. That's about it."

Jake studied the cars dragging the gut outside the window. A Studebaker Starliner and a Corvette pulled into the parking lot, and kids started teasing each other through their open windows. A blond girl's face appeared blue in the blinking light of the neon fish. Sniffy shook his head. "I'm not going crazy, am I? Getting paranoid." He held out his hands. "See the shakes. Hell, I was in the war. Bombardier. After flying over Germany, we'd come back to England all shot up. Those Red Cross women would give us a shot of brandy. My hand was like a rock."

Jake took a bottle of Wild Turkey and a glass from out of the bottom desk drawer. I didn't know he kept one there and made a note. "You got big troubles," he said.

Sniffy took the glass in both hands and drank. "Thanks, Jake." He studied his hands. "Maybe another one would help."

Jake poured and Sniffy drank another. "Buy you one?" Sniffy asked.

"Why not? I feel like a priest." Jake poured himself a drink. "Might as well drink like one."

"You understand I can't prove anything."

Jake sipped his drink.

Sniffy's eyes darted around the room until they fixed on one of the donation jars for Tyler's family. He blinked. "If somebody torched that mill and those guys got killed falling through the skylight, is that murder?"

Jake rubbed his jaw. "It's something pretty damn bad, but not murder."

"That's how I figure." His eyes shifted to the floor. "You understand, I'm just trying out ideas."

"Two friends talking," Jake said. "Lots of guys tested out theories here today."

Sniffy's eyes settled on the painting of Kalim and the basketball team, then widened in recognition. "Man oh man. That Indian kid — he knew too much about the plant."

Jake had started to take another drink, but stopped. "What kid?"

Pointing at the picture, Sniffy said, "Him. You and the boy found him downriver."

"What did he know?"

"He and a couple rowdy white guys hung around. The white guys did hauling and cleaning. They were real wiseasses. Sometimes, when Kalim showed up, they went off and drank beer. Those three were always up to no good. Stealing loads of studs, stacks of plywood, anything they could get in their pickup. Hell, they even used my truck once when I was mixing glue. I'd been in there four hours and came out to find the engine warm, the gas tank down. Bastards had run to Central and sold a load of something. After that I kept the keys in my pocket.

"When I called them on it, the two white guys laughed and took off,

177

but not Kalim. He'd been looking at a notebook I'd left on the dash. His two buddies probably couldn't read, but he could. 'What's this?' he asked, waving the notebook in my face. 'All these figures about glue and plywood.'

"I tried calming him down, but he was half drunk and totally pissed. 'Somebody's always ripping us off,' he yelled. 'I'm going to see my old uncle Sylvester.'"

"I wonder if he did," Jake said, and I got to thinking about our meeting Sylvester on the river. Maybe he knew then something was going on.

"You could hear him yelling about Indians being cheated all over the plant," Sniffy said. "Other things, too. His two buddies had been painting up some old equipment, switching serial numbers. They planned on selling that junk to the tribe, even though it was obsolete." Sniffy tapped his forehead with the glass. "See, the way I figure, if the plywood mill got more timber leases, they'd keep ripping off the tribe one way. If the tribe built its own mill and got overcharged for obsolete equipment, they'd screw them another. Double payday."

"And you think Kalim figured all that out?"

Sniffy finished his drink and put the glass down. "Big braggers, those two white guys. Real loudmouths. And Kalim saw my notes. Hell, if I can figure things out, they've got to be crooked as a corkscrew." He looked at the glass, but Jake didn't fill it again. "The kid blows up and threatens to spill his guts. Two days later, he's staring at fishes."

"It's a hell of a story," Jake said. "Who were the white guys? Old ball players?"

"I'm no squealer. Don't get me wrong." Sniffy held his mouth tight.

"What do you plan to do?"

He wiped the back of his hand across his sweaty forehead. "Here's what I'd like to do — leave this town and go someplace warm. Maybe Arizona to help the wife's arthritis. It's pitiful how she hobbles in the winter." He leaned forward, almost whispering. "I get these wild ideas like selling the notes. Why not? Someone might be interested."

"Careful now," Jake said. "Don't catch your tit in the wringer."

Sniffy stood. "That's what I'd *like* to do. But I'm no fink. Maybe things will go all right with this investigation — smooth as a saw blade through white pine. But if it hits some big knots, I don't want to get cut up by flying metal." He paused. "Keep some papers for me, Jake. That way, if anything happens, you can clear my name."

Jake hesitated a minute, then stood and put his arm around Sniffy. "Whatever you say, buddy. But I think you're going off the deep end on this."

Sniffy pulled away. "Two men are dead. Three if I'm right about the Indian kid. Deep end, hell. I can't even see the shore."

After agreeing to bring the papers the next day, Sniffy drove away, the taillights of his pickup dimming. Jake relocked the door and leaned against the Pepsi machine. "You heard it here first."

"What are we going to do?" I asked.

Jake rapped the machine with his knuckles, then tapped the side of his head. "Too much glue. Too few brain cells."

I was astonished. "You think he's making it up? Sounded pretty convincing to me."

"Sure. He believes it himself. He sees something here, something different there, and tries to connect the dots. But maybe nobody else sees the pattern quite like he does."

"What if he's right? You said yourself the sprinkler systems should have stopped the fire. Sniffy explained why they didn't."

Jake seemed to be thinking it over. "If the fire investigators decide it's arson, then maybe his story will gain some credibility. Otherwise he's by himself in front of a grand jury, ticking away like a time bomb. Remember, this is the guy who sees flying saucers."

"What about Kalim?"

Jake spread his hands. "Maybe his buddies shot him. Or a jealous girlfriend. Once you start speculating about killing an Indian kid over glue and plywood, you'll split this town in half. It's damn hard enough already to keep the pieces together. Somebody's always squawking about getting ripped off."

"We can tell Billyum. Maybe he can get the FBI or something."

Jake pressed his hands against his eyes. "Haven't slept in two days. Can't think straight and neither can you."

"I caught a few hours," I said, but when my uncle looked at me and I saw the raccoon circles under his bloodshot eyes, I didn't say any more.

"No point running off half-cocked. Now grab that one night deposit and shove the rest of the stuff in the safe."

When I came back, Jake was watching the kids in the parking lot. The blond girl climbed out of the Starliner, slamming the car door. She started flirting with the guy in the Corvette. After a few moments, he opened the car door and she climbed in.

"When you're that young" — Jake nodded toward the car — "the only thing you worry about is getting her pants down and unrolling the rubber. Then you grow up and things get complicated."

20

"GATEWAY HAS A LOVELY LIBRARY. It's wonderful when a small town like this takes so much pride in education." My mother took a bite of her onion ring. "Hot!" She sipped her root beer. A thin line of foam clung to her upper lip, and after setting down the mug, she wiped her mouth with an orange and black napkin. "Remember that horrible library in Grass Valley? Those irregular hours? You could never tell when they were open or closed. I even kept a schedule in my purse, but they never stuck to it."

"Well, Gateway has some real advantages, Mom." She was always trying to point them out.

"Franklin's on the library committee," she said. "Their Northwest collection is even better than Central's."

"How about that." I took an onion ring.

"Don't burn your mouth." She had another, nibbling on the batter. "School will be starting soon, and I just wanted you to have a good place to study. Some of our country's best minds have been formed in small libraries — Lincoln, Carnegie, Edison. You don't remember, of course, but when I first took you for your aptitude tests in Waterville, the woman who administered the test kept asking me how old you were. 'Five and a half,' I said. She could hardly believe it. 'Well,' she said, 'he's sharp as a tack. Off the scale. However you do it, make certain you get this boy to college.'" Mom gripped her mug of root beer. "And we will do it. You can study at the library."

"The high school has a library," I pointed out. "Big one."

She wrinkled her nose. "Usually the problem students are sent to the library for detention. I remember how these things work. How can you study efficiently when they're giggling, writing silly notes, shooting paper clips and spitwads?"

"You must have been pretty familiar with detention to know so much about it. I never would have guessed."

She pretended to be annoyed. "For your information, I *worked* after school to restack the shelves. Anyway, the school library's not open weekends." She pushed the plastic basket toward me. "Have some more. You're not worried about calories."

Every Friday, Mom's payday, we walked the six blocks from our house to the A&W Root Beer Stand for root beer and a large basket of onion rings. She loved the frosted mugs that came right out of the deep freeze. As the frost melted, it slid into the root beer, almost the way melting ice slides down a window pane. "So good and so cold," she said. "I love the way my teeth ache."

What she didn't like were the kids squirreling in and out of the parking lot, gunning their engines and fishtailing in the loose gravel. I imagined these were the ones she thought would wind up in detention, but most likely they were offspring of school board members, prosperous merchants, or rich farmers who received cars for their sixteenth birthdays or high school graduations. As sons and daughters of the community's elite, they held special privileges and were unlikely to wind up in detention. Instead, they were elected Sadie Hawkins, prom king and queen, cheerleaders. I suspected my mother knew as much, but she didn't acknowledge it.

As for myself, I envied their advantages, but at the same time believed I was better than they were — smarter because I had to rely on my wits, tougher because I lacked their cushion. Even so, I was glad to have Jake now as a kind of safety net. Still, I longed for the ease of their lives. And more than anything, while I knew that a car was as out of reach for my mother as the moon, I admired the fancy ones like the Ford Thunderbirds and Chevrolet Corvettes. Not that I said much, but she saw me looking as they whizzed past.

"Cars are so terribly expensive," she was likely to say. "Upkeep and insurance. Even that old clunker Riley had cost a mint. Besides, walking keeps you in shape."

One time she stopped walking and studied her legs a moment. "Not bad. And my thighs haven't turned to waffles."

"It'd be nice to have a car," I said.

She put her arm around me. "You need to stay in shape for basketball.

After college, when you settle down, you'll have plenty of time for a car. Just promise you'll come take me for a ride — very first thing."

"Sure, Mom, but after college I'll be an old man."

Now she finished her root beer. "Wonderful. I feel so refreshed. But the onion rings tasted a little like smoke."

"Since that fire, everything tastes like smoke."

She smiled. "Except my cooking, I hope." She shook her head. "I feel sorry for those poor men. Some have applied to Sunrise Biscuits for elevator work, but we just don't have any openings. If they were in Minneapolis or Omaha . . ." She reached in her purse to pay the check. "Do you think they'll rebuild that plant?"

I shrugged. "Even if they do, things will never be the same. Jake says most likely they'll move it to the reservation. If the Indians build a plant and make plywood from their own timber, they'll get some big tax breaks."

"After what we've done to the poor Indians, I should certainly hope so. It's been one big disgrace." She shook her head. "Well, I don't understand all I know about it. The papers keep talking about this plan and that buyout, this deal and that offer. All big numbers and gobbledygook. The average person can't tell. However, Franklin does agree with Jake. The Indians will get some tax breaks. But we'll see. The older I get, the less I believe what I read and hear."

"It's pretty complicated, Mom." From time to time the back room crackled with talk of federal grants for the tribe, wheeling and dealing, political jostling. Speculation leaned to the Indians' controlling their own timber from the logging to finished product. This would require federal assistance, allowing them to build a plant on the reservation, managed by the tribe. Under these circumstances, a lot of townspeople stood to lose their jobs or seniority.

Still lurking behind the rebuilding of the plant was gossip about the fate of the old one. Rumors of arson persisted. The state police arson squad had listed the cause of the fire as "undetermined" but also cited the plant for negligence. The insurance company investigators hadn't reached a decision. No one was satisfied, and the bellyaching persisted.

My mother put enough money on the table to cover the check and tip. "Well, our society has certainly made a mess of things. That's perfectly clear." Reaching across the table, she patted my hand. "I'm very thankful the bright minds in your generation can unscramble the mess."

"I take it these are not the same hooligans staying after school in the library."

"Speaking of the library, they have lovely wildflowers from this area on display. Tables of them. Be sure to compliment the librarians when you're studying. People remember good manners and are likely to return the favor — order a book you need or something."

One of the farm kids pulled up in a white Ford convertible with a red interior and bucket seats. His muscular arms appeared even tanner because he wore a white sports shirt with little silver threads through it. When he removed his sunglasses, his blue eyes blazed. I regretted having to walk with my mother past his car and hoped he'd get an order to go.

Several of the waitresses gathered around the Ford, jostling one another to see who might take the order. Rising off the seat, he snatched away one's black and orange hat, holding it at arm's length when she reached for it, trying it on and mugging at her when she didn't.

"Don't I look just like a waitress?" he mocked. "Can I take your order, please, sir?"

"You better give that here, Price. Right this minute." The waitress had red hair and a lapel pin that said B E TS Y. Her face was becoming red. "I'm going to tell Shirley." Pointing to the empty passenger seat, she asked, "Where is she, anyhow?"

"Big deal, Lucille. That's for me to know and you to find out."

"She went to Central," another waitress said. "A sick aunt or something."

"Real sick." Grinning, he patted the empty seat. "Hurry and hop in before that old aunt recovers."

"That obnoxious show-off," my mother said, witnessing the scene outside.

The redhead started walking off but he called after her. "What about taking my order, Betsy? How do I get decent service around here? Where's the manager?"

The other waitresses offered to take his order, but he enjoyed tormenting the redhead. After stalling a minute, she went back, hatless. "All right, then." She flipped open her pad. "What can I get you?"

"Just a second, miss." He pretended to observe her. "You're out of uniform. Isn't that against A&W regulations? Can't take an order without your hat." He placed the hat on his lap. "Here it is, if you say 'Pretty please.'"

My mother took some coins out of her purse and tapped them on the counter, attracting the cook's attention. "I'd like another root beer, please. To go."

The redhead wouldn't reach for the hat. Her face was bright. She tried taking his order again, but he refused and threatened to call the manager.

"I don't need the lid," my mother told the cook.

"Listen, Mom," I started, but she was out the door, marching toward the car.

"Give her the hat right this minute, you silly hooligan." Her chin jutted straight ahead.

The sun was at her back, so he couldn't see clearly. Maybe he thought she was the manager. "I was just having a little fun."

My mother stood over him with the root beer, and I thought she was going to cool off his head or crotch. "Right this minute."

"All right, then." He had figured out she wasn't the manager but handed back the hat anyway. "You must be some kind of nutcase."

"Excuse me, please." Reaching across him before he could react, she poured root beer all over the passenger seat. The paper cup seemed bottomless as root beer ran everywhere. He watched, mouth agape, until she was finished and stepped back. "Now, what else can I get for you besides the root beer?"

He found his voice. "My car, God damn it! I just had it cleaned." The veins bulged in his neck when he stepped from the car. His white canvas shoes were spattered with brown root beer. He must have purchased the shoes in Central because no store in Gateway carried shoes like that.

My mother handed him a wad of napkins from one of the tin containers. "You'll want to clean that up before you get Shirley. I doubt she wants to sit in all that stickiness."

As we left, I could feel the looks of the waitresses and Price burning into our backs. "Who the hell is that woman?" he said. "Maybe I've seen that kid around."

"I don't know why you couldn't wait, Price," I heard one of the girls say. "We've got a restroom inside."

The others laughed.

Price had been in the store a couple of times, and he'd acted arrogantly there, too. He might try to settle up later, so I decided to start working out with the weights in the back room.

My mother remained casual. "Your father used to love going out for a root beer. When he got paid, we'd drive to a little place called the Hand Out for soft drinks and sandwiches. Way on the outskirts of town. They tore it down years ago to build tract homes. I believe the Hand Out had better root beer, but perhaps that's because I was so much younger then. Everything seemed so fresh."

"You're not exactly tottering on a cane, Mom. But it's sure too bad we can't still walk to the Hand Out. We could really get in shape. Maybe we should walk to Central. Thirty miles — we'd get in *top* shape."

"Stop it." She tapped my shoulder. "I'm glad you have a sense of humor. That was the single thing missing in your father. So serious."

"Maybe I got my sense of humor from Jake. The 'ho ho' gene."

"I certainly hope not. Humor is fine, but Jake carries things too far. All that horseplay."

I stopped walking. "How can you say that after your root beer stunt?"

"That boy made me a little crazy. I couldn't help it." She shook her head. "Most mothers would trade eyeteeth for a son like you. I consider myself very fortunate." We started walking again. "Do you think Price will come after you?" A worried line wrinkled her brow.

"Maybe," I said. "But Riley taught me a thing or two."

"Well, don't go breeding a scab on your nose. Always try to avoid violence." She paused. "But if that boy starts something, whip him good."

We had walked a little farther when she said, "Since you mentioned Central, I was thinking you and Franklin should go shopping for that blazer as soon as possible, before all the merchandise gets picked over. You might get a sweater, too. Brown to match your hair and eyes. Or burgundy."

"It's too hot to try on sweaters," I said.

"Once the school year starts, the holidays will be here before you know it."

"Maybe I should wait until then. They'll get in a bunch of new stuff."

Her brow furrowed. "By then the merchandise will be poor quality, very poor."

"For Christmas?"

She nodded. "They know people are anxious to buy. They get you coming and going."

She went on about the merchandising, but I quit listening because I had spotted Billyum's tribal rig outside the Alibi Tavern. The tavern was fringed by pickups and farm rigs, a few beaters that belonged to the field workers. Billyum's large arm hung out the window and he tapped his fingers against the side of the door, perhaps keeping time to the honky-tonk music. Neon glare kept me from seeing the other occupants clearly, but there were two. Billyum's head turned as he remarked to them.

Mom was still talking about the blazer, and I knew it had taken on a kind of exaggerated importance to her, suggesting the new improved life she planned for us. "Okay, Mom, stop twisting my arm. I'll go with Franklin to buy the blazer or something else. Whatever works. But there's one condition —"

"You absolutely must wear wool slacks," she said. "You're not getting by with jeans or cotton pants. You'd be so . . . mismatched."

I winced a little, remembering how my wool dress pants had itched back in the days she took me to church and I spent the minister's sermon time drawing airplanes in combat or studying the Zumwach boys, trying to determine which had the worst soup-bowl haircut. But that wasn't the condition. "I want to use some of my own money."

She stopped, and I first thought she was going to protest, but instead she put her arms around me and gave me a little hug. "What a lovely idea. Jake must be paying you pretty well, after all. I guess you can chip in just a little."

"Fifty-fifty, or else it's no deal." I knew my mother had been working hard. "Get something nice for yourself." I realized I could use Kalim's money and no one would be the wiser. I had half planned on using it to buy a new gun, but that didn't seem quite right, considering he'd been shot.

"I just hope Jake realizes how valuable you are."

"I'm the right-hand man," I said. "The glue. I hold everything together."

"You went awfully quiet back there for a minute," she said after we got home. "What were you thinking about? I hope it wasn't that obnoxious Price boy. You're not upset, are you, honey?"

"No, I'm not upset."

"Well then, a penny for your thoughts." She dug into her purse. "Here's a nickel. You were thinking something profound."

"Not really. I was thinking of the Zumwach boys and their crazy haircuts. Remember how they looked in church?"

Surprised, she laughed. "Whatever brought that up?"

"Your talking about wool pants got me to thinking about church and the gawky kids."

"Those poor boys. I know people do the best they can. And God knows we've been plenty strapped. But I've always managed to get you to the barber. Some people attempt those home haircuts, but I know my limitations. I imagine they put soup bowls on their heads." She clicked her tongue. "I wonder where those boys are now. I wouldn't be buried with haircuts like theirs."

☆ ☆ ☆
☆ ☆

But I had told a lie, because I wasn't thinking about the Zumwach boys all that time. As we passed the Alibi, the angle of light had changed and I could see inside the pickup. Jake and Sniffy were the other two occupants, a strange trio, especially the way they just seemed to be waiting outside the tavern, the truck sitting apart from the fringe of rigs driven by the patrons.

Maybe the third man wasn't Jake; his face was partially obscured. Sniffy I recognized for sure. He sat wedged between the other two and his look indicated he wasn't any too pleased. He seemed to have what Jake called a stiff iron supplement, a rod shoved up his ass. The three together struck me as odd because after Sniffy had spilled his guts that night in the store, he returned two days later to tell Jake he had been cockeyed about his suspicions at the mill. Fire and fatigue had worn him down, or so he claimed.

"I'm just sixteen months from retirement, Jake," he had said. "Who wants to see their old age go up in smoke?" He studied Jake, eager for sympathy.

"So I guess you're feeling better now?" Jake asked.

"One hundred percent. It's amazing what a couple nights' sleep can do."

"No bad dreams, huh? My sidekick's been having nightmares about Seaweed and Tyler."

Sniffy looked down at the floor. "Sorry to hear it."

After a minute Jake slapped his back. "Cheer up. I'm just sorry everyone else doesn't feel as good as you do. Lots of those mill fellas are looking at a pretty bleak future."

"They're young. Let's hope it's short term," Sniffy said. He tried to change the subject. "Say, I hope this unemployment doesn't hurt your business too much."

Jake smiled, a little too wide. "I'll do dandy. When times get tough, people buy guns. Fishing tackle drops off, but that's mostly tourist stuff anyway. Worried people buy guns. *Scared* people buy *lots* of guns."

Sniffy surveyed the rifles and pistols on display. "You're not kidding, are you?"

"I've seen it before," Jake said. "Out-of-work men start poaching deer and elk. Around here, they've got pride. No father's going to be standing in grocery lines paying with food stamps where some snot-nosed schoolmate can ask their sons and daughters about the funny money." Jake paused. "Takes a lot of meat to feed four or five growing kids. But you can do it poaching. Raise a few vegetables."

"So folks can get by," Sniffy said.

Jake rubbed his chin. "For a while. But you can't poach school clothes or shoes. Pretty soon the kids get kind of shabby. The wife starts looking haggard. She might get a job, wear a cute little outfit and serve the pushy tourists."

"They're still getting by, aren't they?" Sniffy had a worried look. "That's the main thing."

"Problem is, no one's happy with just getting by. Maybe the dad feels a little less manly, so he starts double-timing with some hard-eyed woman at the Alibi or Stardust. She's laughing at his jokes, not asking for too much money. One night when he staggers home, another woman's perfume clinging to him, the wife shoots him." Jake paused. "But that's not your worry, I guess."

"They might be planning to rebuild the plant, for Christ's sake. You got to look past these bad times," Sniffy said. "People can hang on."

Jake nodded at the paintings. "Kalim's not hanging on. Remember what you said about those fellas and Kalim? Think they came after him?"

Sniffy gripped the seat of his chair like he was about to be ejected from an airplane. "Jake, I'm telling you to back off, damn it. I was making mountains out of molehills. Now I've got things straight." Nodding at the painting, he added, "I was way off base about that Indian boy, too. Sorry."

"What about the notes you been keeping?" Jake asked.

"Just scribbles. They don't add up. For now, I'm holding on to them."

Sniffy seemed so confused and miserable that after a moment Jake stood behind him and rested his hands on Sniffy's shoulders. "I appreciate your coming by — clearing the air." His voice had softened.

Sniffy stood, holding out his right hand. "I've always considered you a friend, Jake." The hand trembled.

After a moment's hesitation, Jake took it. "Remember those Red Cross women and the brandy? You want some nerve juice?"

Sniffy shook his head. "The wife needs her medication. Got to get to the drugstore. If her arthritis gets worse we're moving to Arizona."

Jake walked Sniffy to the door. "Come by and talk, anytime. But listen, fella. Watch your back."

"I'm plenty jittery, Jake." His lip trembled and for a minute I thought Sniffy was going to cry.

We both watched him leave. "He sure changed his tune, didn't he?" I said. "He seems scared as hell."

Jake nodded. "Somebody gave him an attitude adjustment."

"I'll bet. They might have threatened his wife, too."

"Maybe he really was building mountains out of molehills," Jake said. "Who can tell?"

"Isn't there any way to check it out?"

"Not my job," Jake said. "I've got a hunch we're going to sell a lot of guns this fall. But first we've got to get through Labor Day, the last big fishing surge. I think you better get in the back room and start packaging up a mess of worms."

21

 I RECOGNIZED this guy's type by the way he slammed the pickup door and headed for the store. A high school athlete starting to fade, a wiseass in a baseball cap, a boozer and brawler — in short, a small-town troublemaker. He had a slight limp that could have been an old injury or too much summer celebration. I'd seen him before somewhere but couldn't name the place. Thrusting his head in the doorway, he ordered, "Get me fifty pounds of ice, buddy. No, better make it a hundred. And hustle it."

"Cube ice or block?" I asked, determined not to hustle for this guy. I pretended to be busy with some steelhead tags.

"In this heat? Block. Cube melts too fast. Any dumb shit knows that." His voice got louder. "Jake around? Lazy bum's off fishing again, I suppose. Some job." He flexed his bicep. "Six years at the plant. Just charge that ice would you, buddy?"

I began going methodically through the credit list. "What's your name?"

"F. T. Meeks," he said. "A steady customer. But right now I'm in a hurry. Say, what do you think I want that ice for anyway?" He raised an eyebrow.

"To keep something cool," I said. No point in being too nice to this guy. I had found his file in the credit ledger with Jake's scrawled "No Credit" across the top. Two checks returned for insufficient funds were stapled to the file.

"To . . . keep . . . something . . . cool." His mouth exaggerated each word. "Now I know why Jake hired you." He tapped his forehead. "Bright. Do you know how to make out a charge slip?"

"I do if you've got credit." Suddenly I realized where I had seen him. He was one of the half-naked drunk men at the fire. Mullins had tied Meeks's feet to his truck's spotlight. I tapped the file. "No credit, it says here."

He leaned over the counter, eyeing the checks. His hands were covered with what looked like dried blood. "That's my old man," he said after sucking in a breath. "Jake's got no credit beef with me."

"Jake's not around," I said. "He expects me to go by the book. If you still want that ice, you've got to pay cash." Jake always said be firm with wiseasses and bullies.

"What the hell?" He backed down sooner than I expected and pulled a five-dollar bill from his wallet. "How many rabbits do you think I've got in the back of my pickup?"

"Half a dozen," I said, "and they're all looking for ice."

"Come and see." He took a couple hitch steps toward the door, then beckoned.

Outside in the glaring heat, I peered into the bed. "Holy shit!" A jumble of dead rabbits were piled three or four deep, and they were beginning to ripen in the heat. Flies landed on their unblinking papery eyes and sucked at the blood clots in the bullet wounds.

I didn't want to get too close. "You're not planning to eat them, are you? Make you sick as hell."

He grinned — goofy and wicked at the same time. "This dumb bastard from the city — used to be a buddy of mine. We met at a North-South Shrine game. He called last week to see what was going on since the mill closed. I told him I shot forty-six rabbits. Son of a bitch called me a liar, so this weekend I shot eighty-two. Cruised those alfalfa fields all night with a spotlight and pow, pow, pow." He pretended to sight along his arm.

"The fun thing is he's gone all weekend. When he gets back late Sunday night, these rabbits will be partying on his lawn. That'll teach the rat fuck."

"He'll listen next time, all right," I said. "A hundred pounds, right?" My nose tingled and I moved toward the icehouse. "Why don't you help me load the blocks?" I didn't want to go near those rabbits. "You got a mess of them."

He held up a bloodstained thumb.

"Listen. I'll drag the blocks out. You load them." I planned to keep my distance.

"Teamwork," he said.

Inside, the icehouse was shocking cold compared with the withering heat. Using the ice tongs, I dragged two fifty-pound blocks of ice toward the door, then brushed away the flecks of sawdust insulation with a cotton glove. Grabbing the pick, I asked, "How do you want it? Ten-pound chunks?"

"Close enough."

Scooping up the first block I set out, he tucked it beneath his arm and zigzagged toward the truck, stiff-arming an imaginary opponent. At the goal, he spiked the ice into the truck with a sickening *whack* as it rebounded off rabbits. "Two-minute drill," he called, hurrying back to repeat the process.

"Better slow down in this heat," I said.

"You never saw me play, huh? Fred 'the Freight Train' Meeks. Scored eleven touchdowns my senior year." Beads of sweat popped out of his forehead, a combination of beer and heat. "Full-ride scholarship to Western. Really rolling until I got blindsided at Wyoming. That cowboy got a fifteen-yard penalty and I got a blown knee." He picked up another block and scooted toward the truck.

The last chunk was small, maybe five pounds, and he cocked it behind his ear like a passing quarterback, then threw, a wobbling missile that seemed about to crack the side window. "Shit," he cried as the ice hit the pickup spotlight, bounced off, then skittered across the asphalt, tiny pieces breaking from the main chunk. "Shit. Fuck. Never could pass. Look at that!"

I thought he meant the crooked spotlight in the pickup, but the sharp ice had cut his fingers. Drops of blood fell to the pavement.

"We've got some Band-Aids inside," I said. "Maybe you should come in and wash up."

He held up his hand. The blood was still coming. "Guess I better. No one's going to run off with those rabbits."

At the back-room sink, he pressed wet paper towels against the cut until it stopped bleeding.

"What a pisser." He gritted his teeth as I applied Merthiolate to the cut. "But Mercurochrome hurts worse."

"It might need a stitch," I said, applying a Band-Aid, "or one of those butterfly things. Pretty damn deep."

"I've had worse," he said. "But thanks." He stuffed some paper towels in his pocket and wiped his forehead with another. As he started to leave, he glanced up and saw Kalim's basketball painting. "Shit!" He stared at the painting.

"Did you know each other in school?" I asked.

He shook his head. "I'm older, but when that kid was hot, he could shoot the lights out. Fucking picture looks just like him."

"His aunt painted it," I said. "She's an old friend of Jake's."

"She caught him cold," he said. "I fucking can't believe it."

"Kind of gives me the spooks," I said. "My uncle and I found him. By then, you couldn't tell who he was."

He squinted at me, but didn't say anything for a moment. "You get around. Saw your picture in the paper a while back. Big hero at the fire. Hell, you've been all over this summer, haven't you?"

"I saw you at the fire, too."

He glanced toward the floor. "Not exactly my best night." He looked up. "So you found him? The way that river is, I'm surprised anyone did."

Outside again, he took a short-handled shovel from behind the pickup seat and stirred the rabbits and ice around. Some of the rabbits only had a foot or forequarter touching ice, so they'd continue to rot.

"Should have used some boxes, I guess. But what the hell. If I drive fast, I won't smell a thing."

"You got a helluva mess," I said. "If you get stopped, the cops won't believe it."

Melting ice was already leaking beneath the pickup's closed tailgate, dripping on the asphalt.

"Hollow points," he said, climbing into the truck. "Even with a lousy shot, rabbits slow down and crawl so you can club 'em. Ever hear rabbits scream?"

"Sure." Riley had gutshot a cottontail once. Remembering the horrible sound made me cringe.

"That's what I did when I lost that knee," he said. "Screamed just like a fucking rabbit."

After Meeks drove away, I couldn't help but feel a little sorry for him. When Riley had taught me boxing lessons, he had said I needed to toughen up, and he was probably right. Even so, I knew you had to be pretty good to play in a Shrine game, although I wasn't sure Meeks was telling the truth. Now he was just a small-town has-been playing cruel practical jokes and getting plastered.

What dark scrap of fate had cost Meeks the knee? I wondered. Or caused Riley to blow up and Kalim to lose his life? Looking up at Juniper's painting, I thought about Kalim. Juniper had said that in the All-Indian tournament he had been unstoppable, hitting from every spot on the court, bringing the crowd to its feet. I wanted to be that kind of player, too.

I studied my hands for traces of rabbit blood. One thing I knew, I didn't want my own future cut short by anything, including rabbit fever. At the back sink, I washed and washed with Lava until my hands ached.

When I came back out, I got a Pepsi and walked into the bright sunlight of the parking lot. After a few minutes my mind cleared and I took a deep breath, glad for the fresh start in Gateway. I studied the front wall of my uncle's store. Pumice block. Solid. Not even a tornado could take it apart, I decided, although one might tear off the roof. No, I said to myself, I wouldn't end up like Kalim or Meeks.

Inside, the phone rang but I didn't answer. Bathed by sunshine, I stood enjoying the cold drink. Vacationers drove by in a station wagon and some children waved. Smiling, I waved back.

☆ ☆ ☆ ☆

When I realized that school was about to start, I also knew I wasn't in top shape. I didn't want to wind up flabby like Meeks, so I started having Jake drop me off four miles from town, leaving me to run back and build endurance. I could have run out and back two miles myself, but I didn't like that approach because I might be tempted to cheat and dog back early. Jake measured exactly four miles on the truck odometer, increasing the distance a bit each time. Maybe he thought I was nuts, but he didn't disapprove the training. When Jake wasn't available, I'd ask Franklin. He didn't seem to mind, and I liked his car almost as much as Jake's truck. He had taken to sucking Sen-Sen and offered me some for the runs. "Keeps your mouth moist," he said.

I came to like the licorice, soapy taste, and it helped keep the saliva flowing. "Did you ever run, Franklin?" I asked him one night.

"Sure, but not like you're doing. Still, I know about training. Laps and laps and laps. I tried making the swim team at UCLA."

At first I had thought he meant track when he mentioned laps. Most of the towns we had lived in were too small to have swimming pools. Gateway was no exception, although people kept talking about building a pool, along with the hospital. However, with the mill destroyed and unemployment high, enthusiasm for those projects faded.

"Did you make the team?"

"Regrettably, no." His eyes saddened. "Not enough stamina. I had polio when I was young — not too bad — no iron lung, thank God. That

194

would have been worse than death, I think. But I ran a very high fever for a week and my left side was paralyzed ten days. Swimming was good therapy. I worked and worked at it, but that left side never quite got back the strength."

"How'd you get polio?" I asked.

"Who knows? My mother blamed the crowded Saturday matinees, and my dad blamed an irrigation ditch. People were scared to death. Now there's the vaccine." He pulled the car over onto the roadside. "Five miles. Give 'em hell."

I jogged in place a while, loosening muscles and getting my bearings. The constellations brightened the night sky, and I picked out the Sky Fisherman and the Leaky Boat, smiling at the recollection of Jake's story about the old man. Above Gateway, the sky glowed with the town lights, and I started off, taking a kind of joy in the tennis shoes' slap-slap on the pavement, the slight jar of contact in my knees, hips, and back. No weakness in my left side.

After running a couple miles toward town, I'd start to feel weary, then think of Grass Valley's track coach, "Doc" Lewis, who taught discipline and guts. Raw spring days when the baseball players stayed inside the warm gym practicing grounders on the hardwood floors, we ran muddy laps, towels wrapped around our necks to keep the rain from trickling down our backs. One day a freshman asked if we could practice inside. Rain dripped off Lewis's long nose and jutting chin as he gave the boy a withering look. "Track men don't melt."

The long-distance runners were Lewis's favorites. "Hard-asses," he called us. "You got to be a hard-ass on yourself, 'cause no one else gives a shit." If you ran a mile in four and a half minutes one day, he wanted four and a quarter the next. No excuses. We weren't smooth and we weren't pretty, but we won. Track, especially distance running, wasn't popular then as it became later. Sometimes at the end of the mile I was so exhausted I puked. "If you're not puking, you can run harder," he said. "It hurts too much," I complained once. He gave me a blistering look. "Pain is weakness leaving the body."

Long-distance running wasn't popular in Gateway either. On my night runs I owned the road's shoulders. Oncoming traffic would flick their headlights to see what the hell was coming. Big trucks honked as they passed. Polite drivers rode the white line, allowing me extra room.

Running hard, feeling strength in every sinew, I didn't even envy the people who sped by me in sleek cars, although the tinkling laughter of windswept girls tightened the emptiness of my belly.

Conditioning came now, I imagined. Given time, the cars and girls would come, too. From the the passing cars' radios I heard Hank Williams, Elvis, Brenda Lee.

The cars never stopped, although some slowed to pitch out beer bottles, cigarettes, religious tracts. Once a carload of boys slowed to my pace, and I expected trouble. But they were just curious. "What the hell you doing?" a moonfaced, blond boy asked. He had rolled up a pack of Winstons in his T-shirt sleeve.

"Training. Getting ready for basketball."

"Shit. You're starting early. Not even football season yet. You from Gateway?"

"That's right." I ran a little faster so they had to accelerate.

"We're from Pineville. Last year we whipped your ass."

"Not mine," I said. "I'm new."

"Well, shit. We better start running, too." They sped off.

Running toward the twinkling lights of Gateway, I believed they promised some important destination, a fulfillment one could accomplish by adhering to hard work, discipline, and smarts. If I ran hard enough and long enough, training for the right moment, I believed I could succeed. Other people might be born to privilege or money; hard work gained my advantage.

My mother believed this, too. After working all week at Sunrise Biscuits, she'd spend hours at the library studying to improve her knowledge of history, art, and music. She brought home every company publication and memo, improving her secretarial skills and studying up on the company's training and policies. On those rare occasions when a representative came out from Minneapolis or Omaha, she was ready — up to date and informed. Still, it took a toll. Much of the time she was dog tired.

If hard work was the main fiber of my training, resentment was the second motivator. Thinking of that farm boy at the A&W with his Ford convertible and others just like him, I ran harder, determined that when the moment came for a matchup, I'd beat him. I was getting ready, training to be tough, and he was still soft. Cocooned in his privilege, he didn't realize I was gaining on him, so that provided me the edge. It wasn't hate, the kind that settles when someone close betrays you. Instinctively, I resented this type, despised his arrogance and nonchalance. Make them pay, I thought, take their whipping — no apologies or excuses.

Doc Lewis taught me that, too. He was Grass Valley's basketball coach as well as the track coach, and our sophomore year we played Lakeshore in a state Christmas tournament. Three hundred miles from home, we were nervous in the big city and barely snuck by Crater, another podunk school, in the first round. Lewis didn't bother to have us scout Lakeshore's opening game. Instead, he loaded us on the varsity bus and had us tour the suburb. We saw Lakeshore's fancy houses, the foreign cars, the speedboats for water skiing. Most of the houses were decorated far more lavishly than anyplace in Grass Valley. A few had strung small white Christmas lights all around their possessions. Cars, boats, even a seaplane with pontoons, were outlined. "Isn't this pretty?" Lewis asked.

"I got to bring my dad back to see this," Jimmy Erickson said, and everybody laughed because his dad wasn't getting out of prison for three more years.

Before tip-off, Lewis stood pointing at the baskets. "They don't own those," he said. "If the bastards even try to get close, play smashmouth. I don't care if all of you foul out. When they start to drive the lane, make them pay."

And we did. Lakeshore was taller, more talented, but the way we played that night, basketball was a contact sport. Bump, hustle; slap, hustle; knee, hustle; elbow, hustle. Lakeshore whined and complained at the bruising style, but the referees let us play, except for the flagrant stuff. Pretty soon the crowd got behind our scruffy team from the boondocks. Jimmy and I broke Lakeshore's press like pretzels. Lewis pulled us when we got in foul trouble, but the subs did okay, too. Returning for the final quarter, hustling our guts out, we won by six. Lewis grinned a mile wide when the tournament organizers presented him with the trophy and game ball. In the locker room we laughed, too — and puked. Jimmy Erickson and I never played together again. After Christmas his mom took off with her boyfriend, dragging Jimmy to hell knows where, and I started at point guard the rest of the season.

On the homestretch, the road paralleled the railroad track. Some nights the silver streamliner swept by, its lights illuminating the road. Seeing me run, the engineer pulled the whistle as the train slid past. I wondered if the people in the coaches or dining cars noticed me, if someone in the club car laid down his cards and cigarette, then looked out the window, musing, "There's a young man on the move."

Hitting Gateway's outskirts, I sweated freely after five-plus miles. Passing the Tire Exchange, Krazy Karl's Gun World, the A&W, I kicked hard the last stretch, practically sprinting to the high school track. Now people could watch, and I imagined them admiring me and my training.

Through all this conditioning I felt a kind of inexplicable kinship to Kalim, and I thought if I could score enough points to gain some regional attention, I might dedicate the season to him. At the time, I fancied this was some type of altruism. Later, I recognized it as my own vanity.

22

 AT JAKE'S, Labor Day marked the division between fishing and hunting seasons, but it also marked a change in the customers' attitudes. Jake pointed out that Memorial Day was a happy occasion. In May, with the prospect of summer lying ahead — vacations and time off — people were enthusiastic and optimistic. But summer, like hope, fades. By Labor Day the customers had worked themselves into a frenzy, frustrated at all the activities they had planned but not accomplished, desperate for one last fling. A flabby guy from the city would come in and stare longingly at the fishing poles he had wanted to buy but wouldn't now because this season was almost finished. Even so, he'd try a couple, testing the limberness and weight. A frazzled wife, trailing a couple rumpled kids, would shuffle in on sunburned feet — all of them wore thongs — while they waited for their chicken order next door. "I hope you're not planning to buy that pole," she'd say. "You said that sundress I tried on in Central was too expensive and I passed it up. Anyway, we've got to hurry back and buy the kids some school clothes while they're on sale." Turning to me, she might ask, "Do you have sunburn ointment?"

I'd shake my head. "Sorry. We don't carry it. You've got to have a drugstore license."

She'd gather the kids, pulling them away from the baseball gloves and fishing lures, then go outside. "You coming, John? Now we've got to find a drugstore." He would acknowledge with a grunt but linger, trying a couple more flimsy casts, perhaps a pretense that he remained independent. Finally, he'd return the pole to the rack and drift out.

I never knew quite what to say to those guys, but Jake was masterful at hitting the right tone. "Come back and see us, fella" or "The fish will be bigger next year!" he'd say heartily. After they were gone, he'd add, "The poor bastard might get to retire before his heart attack."

Labor Day marked a change in fishing styles, too. Some of the great fishing would occur in the fall when salmon and steelhead left the Pacific, made their way up the big river past the fish ladders on the dams, and returned to the Lost, but the main recreational fishing enjoyed by the tourists and summer people was coming to an end. A hardier breed of fisherman tried the salmon and steelhead runs. It required more skill, especially when fly fishing for the lunkers.

Jake blacked out three days on his guide calendar, then wrote "architects" in the margin. "If anybody asks, you tell them I'm taking some muck-a-mucks from the city — the whole firm. The more important you make it sound, the more likely they'll believe you. Human nature."

"I can't believe you're going to leave me alone with the Labor Day rush." I didn't try to hide my annoyance. "It'll get frantic."

Jake tapped the calendar with a pencil. "I'm coming back Saturday. Anyway, you've got Jed to help out."

"Some help. He limps back to the toilet, contemplates existence for an hour."

I knew Jake didn't have a trip planned because I'd checked the guide calendar. "Where are you really going, just in case I have to send out the county Search and Rescue?"

His eyes widened as he pretended alarm. "Don't do that or I'll have to go rescue those lard buckets once they get themselves lost." After eyeing me for a minute, he said, "Scout's honor?"

"Why not?" I gave a mock salute.

Jake nodded. "Twice a year, old Billyum stretches tribal law a little and takes my white ass fishing — just to keep things in proportion. The reservation water looks so tempting . . . but it's not really much better than the water on the white side. Even so, Billyum shows me his second favorite spot — always keeps the best for himself. And I show him a few good holes along our side. That way, no one gets overcome with temptation." His eyes twinkled. "After all, the old man sent me to Sunday school and they taught me the lure of forbidden fruit."

Thinking of those sparsely fished stretches of Indian waters gave me shivers, but I tried to hide it. "So you're taking off for an unscheduled fishing trip?"

"It's scheduled, just not on the calendar. I got to go when Billyum beckons. Anyway, don't think of it as fishing. More like learning about the reservation culture. Promoting understanding. Last June, when the Salmon flies hatched, they covered the water like a blizzard. I caught eighteen big redsides in under two hours. My wrist got sore, no kidding, and I understood a hell of a lot more about their culture.

"Now the fall steelhead are starting to run. And a few salmon. Damn good fishing. Nothing like the old days before the dams on the big rivers. Back then, the farmers filled trap wagons with the fall salmon run. Anyway, you hold the fort until I get back."

I paused, deciding to try a bluff. "What if I quit?"

He shrugged, probably because he knew I wouldn't. "Suit yourself. But that might disappoint your mother."

"How about time and a half?"

He smiled. "Beats quitting. Try this. How about I take you goose hunting? Right before Thanksgiving, so you can plop a tasty grain-fed goose on your mom's table."

He had me. "You're not kidding." I pictured a bird on the table, glazed with orange sauce.

"I never kid about goose hunting." He winked. "Gab's got a great place that belonged to his father-in-law. Goose pits in a canyon below a wheat field — It's candy. I'm sure we can squeeze one more gun in the pits."

My elation dimmed. "I don't have a shotgun."

Jake waved at the racks of shotguns and rifles. "Put your name on one. You've been working hard. Your cost is store cost, plus ten percent. Consider it a bonus and quit bellyaching."

"You got a deal. Shake." He took my extended hand. "You just better be back Saturday."

"Cross my heart. But don't let on to the back-room boys."

"Not me," I said. "Architects. High rollers. I can see where you don't want anyone to know you're fishing illegal."

"Please." He put his finger to his lips. "An ill eagle is a sick bird. We got to protect our endangered species. What they'd really razz me about is the religious aspect."

"What religion?"

Jake glanced around but no one was coming. He lowered his voice. "After we fish, we go into a sweat lodge Billyum made down there. Get the impurities out."

"Nothing wrong with that."

Jake put up his hands. "I'm a tolerant guy — freedom of religion and all that. For Billyum, this sweat's a real serious thing, a regular ceremony. He gets going in different voices, talking to the river, the heated rocks, the pine and juniper he uses to purify the air."

"What's it like for you?"

"Damn hot." Jake paused. "And I guess a little spooky."

I didn't say anything.

"The Indians might be on to something," he continued. "Maybe it's a good thing to have spirits show up and tell you what to do. Point this way or that. If Billyum thinks it helps, great. Me, I got to bump along the current as best I can."

A car stopped outside the store and Jake's eyes focused on it a moment, then shifted to the stacked picnic tables. "While I'm gone, run a special on those damn things, would you? Make a sign: MANAGER'S LABOR DAY SPECIAL TWENTY BUCKS. If we don't move those pretty soon, we got to get dishonest or drastic."

When Jake returned from his outing with Billyum, he had two coolers filled with the big fish, which he kept on ice for a day. "Smart advertising," he called it, and we did a late spurt of fishing tackle sales that weekend to some fellas who imagined they might sneak back for a crack at the monsters. Half a dozen asked if their kids could pose with the fish and Jake obliged. The fathers chuckled with delight as they snapped photos of their kids holding lunkers that went over two feet and imagined the comments the photos would get at the office or plant. The mothers shuddered as slime rubbed off on their children's shirts and dresses, dripped onto their sandals and tennis shoes. The car ride home might be smelly, but the kids' giant grins showed they'd remember this moment. The smaller ones couldn't even hold the fish high enough to keep their tails from dragging on the cement floor. Photos finished, Jake would tousle the kids' hair, give them candy bars, and tell them to come back for a fishing expedition. They eagerly took the guide brochures Jake offered, but no one actually signed up for a trip. "We're building a future business," he said with a grin.

However, the current business was shifting to hunting. Archery season started for deer the second week of September, and men came into the store buying bows, arrows, scents, and calls. We sold camouflage outfits and face paint for stalking or waiting on the stand.

We also did good business with gag items Jake had picked up from one of the talkative salesmen — a camouflage bra and panty set. A placard above the display read, "Make Sure to Get Your 'Dear.' While You're in the Woods, She'll Be Waiting at Home."

In spite of this particular item's humor, most of the bow hunters were serious about their sport. A different breed from the casual fishermen, they came from the small towns and back country. Most drove pickups or four-wheel-drive rigs, chainsawed their wood. More than a few chewed tobacco.

As Jake had predicted, the unemployed millworkers bought rifles, planning to ensure meat on the table. He put some lever-action Winchester .30-.30s on sale, just a sliver above cost, and they were happy with the reduced price but balked at the ammunition prices. "Jake always used to give a free box of ammo with a new gun," they'd complain. "Can't do that at these prices, fellas," we'd say. A few threatened to run out to Krazy Karl's. Karl came on the radio each morning proclaiming, "I gotta be nuts to make these below-cost gun deals." But he was higher than Jake on most models. My uncle sent me out to check. Even though he wasn't supposed to, Jake started offering half boxes of cartridges for the guys who were really strapped, but few took him up on it. "You better hope you don't wound a deer with the tenth cartridge" was how he looked at it.

Nobody blamed the plant workers for worrying. Things were still unsettled, rumors flying. Whispers of arson persisted. Rebuilding the plant would take time, and unemployment benefits were going to run out long before Christmas. If the plant was rebuilt on the reservation, paychecks would be even slower.

Lean times lay ahead. Not that anybody had tightened his belt more than a couple notches, and they were a long way from putting popcorn and water in swollen stomachs. No one had sold the second car or camper yet. A few who could run field equipment managed to help out with harvest; others had taken jobs on the green chains in the area sawmills, settling for lower pay and no seniority. Still others put their wives to work as waitresses or motel maids, but with summer ending, those jobs would slow, too.

The farmers had money, although they spent little at our store and always complained about the prices, noting this item or that was cheaper at the discount places in Central. Because of the irrigation, their crops were doing fine in spite of the drought. They groused about the fire and all the water it had consumed, although the fact was the whole fire didn't use up any more water than a couple big alfalfa spreads or a few hundred acres of mint.

Of course, the farmers were already speculating about water shortages next year, if the rains didn't come and the mountains attain a decent snowpack.

The weather remained fiercely hot through most of September, but the slant of light shifted, and you got the sense that things would cool in spite of the long heat wave. The woods had become a worse tinderbox, and the Indians finally decided to hire Buzzy to drop fire retardant on lightning strikes, slowing the fires until their crews could get there. Adding fire patrol to crop dusting kept him busier than a rabbit with a credit card, Buzzy said. But he pointed out the rains wouldn't hold much longer.

"Deluge by Halloween," he predicted. "I got to talking with old Sylvester. Indians have ways of telling the weather. They study the woolly caterpillars, check how thick the hair grows on a coyote — stuff like that."

When Sylvester came in to buy ammunition for his .308, I asked him if he had special ways of predicting the weather.

"Sure." His eyes twinkled. "I check the *Farmer's Almanac.*"

23

THE DARK BLUE SHERIFF'S CAR pulled so close to the sidewalk that the wide chrome bumper was only inches from the line of bikes. The vibrations from the big Plymouth's engine made the front window of the store rattle. By the way Grady hitched his belt as he hurried in, I could tell he was on official business, and I braced myself for some bad news about Riley.

"Jake around?"

"Steelheading," I said. "Lots of fishing trips these last couple of weeks."

"I thought he might be off chasing that Indian skirt."

I measured each word. "No, he's on the river with some dudes."

Grady relaxed, letting his stomach sag. "Figured as much when I didn't see the pickup."

"That's why you're sheriff."

He sighed, releasing an exaggerated breath. "I got no beef with you, kid. It's a small town. Maybe we should try to get along."

"Fine with me, as long as you don't knock over my bike display." I nodded toward the big car's bumper.

"You got it." He took a manila envelope and set it on the counter. "I can show you these pictures. You're around more than Jake is anyway." He put two pictures on the counter. "A couple years older now, but they haven't changed all that much. Recognize this guy?"

"Sure." The first man sat on the tailgate of a pickup holding the head of a pronghorn antelope. He wore camouflage clothes, the kind appropriate for stalking game. "Freight Train Meeks. He was in here a couple of weeks ago. Bought a bunch of ice. The whole back of his pickup was loaded with dead rabbits. He planned on taking them to the city, dumping them on some poor dope's lawn."

Grady sucked in his cheeks. "I heard about that rabbit stunt. I didn't know if it was true or just Meeks blowing wind."

"It was true, all right. What a mess."

Grady handed me another photo. "Seen him?"

I studied the picture. At first it didn't ring a bell, but then I remembered the jittery, flat-faced man. "He was in here one night. Kept hanging around, acting strange. I thought maybe he was casing the joint and didn't come out from behind the counter. When he asked to see a pistol, I stalled him. Finally, someone outside in a car started honking. He left and they both drove away."

"Was the guy in the car Meeks?"

"Couldn't tell. He parked across the lot."

"This is a bad actor," Grady said, touching the man's face with his thumb. "He did three years in the Arizona pen for armed robbery. Once he came up here, they hired him at the plant. Odd jobs."

"Are they wanted for something now?" I asked. It wouldn't surprise me, but I had kind of liked Meeks.

"Just making some inquiries for now," Grady said. "Meeks's girlfriend filed a missing persons report on him two days ago. No one's seen either one for a couple weeks. Of course, that's not unusual during hunting season. A lot of guys go to deer camp for a week or two. Did Meeks say anything about going hunting, maybe traveling to a different state?"

I took a minute, trying to recall our entire conversation. "I don't think so. Mostly he talked about the rabbits. I guess he hurt his knee pretty bad playing football."

Grady pressed his palms on the counter and shifted forward. "You ever seen him play?"

I shook my head.

"All straight-ahead stuff. Nothing fancy. But he was tough. That's why they called him Freight Train."

"Good, huh?"

"Maybe not all that good. Gateway had a hell of an offensive line that year. But linemen never get any credit. You know how it works. I played guard myself. You could drive dump trucks through the holes we opened up, but the paper never said jack squat about us. I earned a scholarship to state — went to the police academy instead."

He slipped the photos back into the envelope. "I hate missing persons. A wild-goose chase, most of the time. Guys run away with another woman or take off hunting. Maybe they lose their shorts in Reno. Sometimes they show up married, other times divorced. Sometimes they claim amnesia." He grinned. "That's probably how this thing will turn out."

He tapped the envelope on the counter. "If it's not a wild-goose chase, then it's a mess. I don't even want to think about those messes. When Jake shows, ask him to give me a call. Maybe he remembers something."

"I'll tell him. But this time of year, he's a hard man to catch."

"Kind of like your father." Grady smiled. "Sorry. I couldn't let that one slide."

"Stepfather." I didn't mind. "Riley's my stepfather."

"Sure, kid. It's bad enough being related to Jake."

As he climbed into the car, I noticed he had left on the air conditioning. Coolant ran onto the ground, and I wondered how much of the taxpayers' money he had burned letting the car idle.

☆ ☆ ☆ ☆

Two days after Columbus Day, the back-room boys trickled in a little behind schedule, griping about the deluge. They wore water-repellent coats and boots; the water dripped from their hat brims even after the short dash from parking lot to store.

"Too wet to fly," Buzzy said, shaking off like a dog in the store entrance. "Better put some 'warm-up' medicine in that coffee. Winter's coming."

"I know," Sniffy said. "Been thinking about snow tires more than sex."

I'd noticed Sniffy's attitude had improved lately. He seemed more relaxed and talked less about moving to Arizona. Even the raw cold weather didn't seem to bother him.

Wheeling out the bikes had gone quickly for me. Only ten remained and the Christmas order hadn't arrived. After tucking the bikes far under the overhang, avoiding the rain, I studied the seven remaining picnic tables. The soaking rain made them seem even more forlorn.

"Fireplace fodder," Sniffy called them. "Pretty soon they'll be too soaked for kindling. Jake sure got beat on that deal."

The boys kept their jackets on and Buzzy poured a second shot of warm-up. It was colder than usual in the store, and I noticed Jake hadn't turned up the heat much, but business was slow and I figured he was just saving on overhead.

Even Homer complained, and that was unusual. "Going back to the bakery. I've been in morgues that are warmer than this."

Sniffy got one of the camping buckets and a small hatchet. "I'm heading out to the picnic table area to gather wood. We'll warm up in a minute."

"Stay put," Jake said. "Got something to show you fellas."

He was gone a few moments, then reappeared wearing an oversize hooded shaggy coat.

"For Christ sakes, get the gun! It's a Sasquatch!" Sniffy's eyes widened in mock terror.

"Looks just like your wife, Sniffy." Buzzy sipped his coffee. "Only she's hairier."

"Genuine, one hundred percent natural synthetic fiber," Jake said. "Guaranteed to keep you warm." He stroked the synthetic fur fibers. "The catalogue says they used the Alaskan brown bear for the model. Largest bear on the North American continent."

"Looks more like a mole's fur to me," Sniffy said. "Maybe a rat's."

Ignoring him, Jake continued. "I only ordered it in large and extra large. No puny people in Gateway. Get one of these and your wives will think you're a big cozy bear. It'll keep you warm until she can heat you up."

Buzzy shook his head. "Couldn't make it to the house. The dogs would attack me as soon as I hit the yard."

Jake took off the coat, handing it to me. "Put the coats on display," he told me. "This item will be the rage of Gateway this Christmas, but these yokels missed out." He nodded toward the boys, then followed me to the display section of the store.

I touched the fibers. They were over an inch long and had an unnatural sheen, the way gasoline looks in water. "Tough to sell these," I said.

Jake ran his hand over the fur. "I got to admit, they looked different in the catalogue," he said quietly. Patting me on the back, he added, "Everything's not as easy to sell as worms. Some merchandising takes a little imagination." He stroked his chin. "Tell you what. I'll give you a five-dollar bonus for each coat you sell. If they don't move by Christmas, you can take one as a present."

Later that morning, Billyum came in wearing a dark blue parka with an orange lining and fur-trimmed hood. He was soaked, his boots and pants smeared with mud and char. He smelled like a doused campfire and damp wool. Ordinarily Billyum didn't socialize much with the back-room boys, preferring to talk with Jake in private, but this time he took one of the spare cups and poured coffee, then helped himself to one of Homer's bear claws.

After Billyum was settled, Jake modeled the coat for him. "What do you think? You'd take an extra large."

Billyum took a hard look at the coat. "Every so often, someone on the reservation reports seeing something like that. I suggest they quit drinking."

Jake scowled. "That coffee and roll costs six bits. Put your money in the creel. You're not on the reservation now. No freebies."

Fishing in his pocket for three quarters and a nickel, Billyum smiled. He tossed the money into the creel. "Nice floor show, Jake," he said. "You need a younger model though."

When Gab came in, Jake didn't bother showing him the coat. "I'll talk to Priscilla when she comes looking for his Christmas present," he told me. "Those other fellas kind of spoiled today's selling atmosphere."

"I don't ever want another trip like that to Reno," Gab complained once he was settled. "Customer relations be damned. The hopper plugged up on the tour bus and we had to make potty stops every two hours."

"Maybe you should quit sweet-talking the old ladies," Sniffy said. "Start sugaring up to some of the younger customers. Better bladder control."

"Priscilla would just love that, wouldn't she?" Gab helped himself to one of Homer's jelly roll slices. "Old women weren't the worst of it." He lowered his voice. "Hate to bad-mouth a customer, but the real pain in the ass was Dunk Taylor. Something peculiar about that man."

Taylor owned two secondhand stores in town. Dunk's Junque featured pretty good collectibles. Mom and Franklin browsed there sometimes. Dunk's wife had managed Sheila's Swap Shoppe until she died and her sister Arletta took over. Tourists were always getting confused about the names.

"All right. I'll bite," Jake said. "What's so peculiar about the old coot? Sure, he mutters and makes strange noises, but that didn't start until after Sheila died."

"I can live with those noises," Gab said. "But every time we stopped the bus, he scooted off to some drugstore like he had to win the lottery. Then he'd disappear into a bathroom. Everybody would be back on the bus ten or fifteen minutes before he showed."

"Dunk would come out of the bathroom with his face glistening — that's the best word for it — and he smelled of medication. Others noticed it, too. Before long, he was sitting away by his lonesome."

"It can get hot down toward Reno," Sniffy said. "Maybe it was suntan oil."

Gab shook his head. "This trip wasn't hot. I make sure we have air conditioning. My advertisers travel in total comfort. Besides, suntan oil smells like coconuts." Gab got up and poured another cup of coffee. "Later on, when the bus overheated, Dunk took off his sport coat. His arms were entirely covered with the greasy stuff."

"Well, what was it anyway?" Buzzy asked.

"That's what I wondered, so I followed him while he searched along a drugstore aisle, muttering to himself and making those little grunts like 'pig, pig, pig, budda, budda, budda,' real quiet though. Then he goes 'Aha!' so loud everyone in the store looks. And he reaches for something on the shelf. *Unguentine*. That's it, I think. That's the exact smell, all right. But he doesn't buy just one tube. He takes all six or seven, whatever they got. He pays the pharmacist, who gives him kind of a fishy look, and then he goes down the street to the gas station and pops into the restroom.

"I followed him, not noisy, but not sneaky either, and he's sitting in the stall. He drops his pants, takes off his clothes and shoes, and rubs the stuff all over his body, even his feet. Then he reassembles himself and says just plain as a preacher, 'Now you can't burn me!' Practically shouts it, then adds, 'Hallelujah!'" Gab popped the last of the jelly roll into his mouth and took another.

"My wife had an aunt like that," Sniffy said. "Only with her it was Mentholatum. Sinuses flowed like the Jordan River. Don't think she put it on her feet though."

"Mentholatum's for coughs and colds," Buzzy said. "Plugged chests. Unguentine's for *serious* stuff. You guys don't know it, but up where I am, all kinds of activities go on, behind the clouds mostly." His eyes glimmered. "X-men from Mars. Whole squadrons with deadly heat rays. Only Dunk and I know."

"You should smell like Unguentine, too, then," Sniffy said.

"I'm on their side. At night, they land on my airfield. I'm surprised you haven't reported them, Sniffy." Buzzy sniffed his arms. "Anyway, I do smell a little like Unguentine. But you have to stand close. The way that glue's sabotaged your sniffer, you can't tell shit from Shinola."

Everybody laughed at that one. Even Sniffy cracked a smile.

"A-bomb tests," Jake said when things quieted. "Dunk protected himself from desert radiation. Too bad you didn't know, Gab. Now if you fire off a kid, radiation might give it two heads."

"Priscilla says we're too old for that anymore," Gab said. "All I know is I'm not paid to baby-sit nut cases. And that man is peculiar even if he is a preferred customer." He spread his hands. "I just don't know what to think."

"I think you better take Priscilla out a little more," Jake said. "Hanging around bathrooms watching men rub down with Unguentine sounds kind of sicko. Probably against the law, too."

Sniffy laughed so hard he blew coffee out his nose and had to retreat to the bathroom. Over the next few minutes we heard him chuckling, choking, and blowing.

"Gluehead," Gab said to no one in particular.

"Well," Jake said, "I sure regret missing that Reno trip. Sounds like a humdinger."

"You jokers can't carry on a decent, halfway intelligent conversation," Gab muttered, then turned to Billyum. "So what's new on the rez? I wish I could get some of the lodge people to go on my trips, improve our cultural relationships."

"Yeah, Reno should do that all right," Billyum said. "Especially the floor shows."

Gab didn't respond to the remark. "I want to go out there — drum up some advertising. What's new?"

Billyum stirred his coffee. "Found a burned-out vehicle — way back in the woods." He studied the boys one by one.

"That's hardly news," Gab said. He probably didn't want anyone trying to top his Unguentine story. "Lots of burned-out wrecks on the rez." Clearing his throat, he added. "Off the rez, too, of course. Somebody gets mad at his brother-in-law, stuffs a rag in the gas tank, and lights a match." He paused. "Whoosh! Instant pyrotechnics."

"This was a little different." Billyum finished the bear claw. "Two dead guys in it. Big elk in back. All of them black as charburgers."

Gab released a low whistle. "That is something. Any idea who they were?"

"Burned too bad to tell. But my guess is they'll wind up those guys from town Grady wanted to find."

"You think the dumb sons of bitches were poaching on the rez?" Jake asked.

Billyum nodded. "Indian meat cost them plenty this time. Damn sure."

"But they could be Indians," Jake pointed out. "Burned up, it's hard to tell."

"Maybe." Billyum stood and rinsed his cup. "But we're not missing anybody. You are."

"All burned up, huh?" Sniffy asked.

"You think that elk was smoking in the woods?" Jake glanced toward the place where the cigarette-smoking moosehead trophy had hung. Maybe he'd forgotten we took it down to hang Juniper's paintings.

Billyum shrugged. "They spotlighted that elk, most likely. Got drunk, fell asleep. Who knows? Dropped a cigarette in the pine needles. Maybe a spark from their exhaust pipe started it. They were right in the middle of a sixty-acre burn at the edge of Weyerhaeuser lease land."

Buzzy cocked an eyebrow. "Didn't I tell you about that vehicle almost a month ago? I saw a plume of smoke, and when I swooped down to drop retardant on the burn, thought I saw something funny under a canopy of pines. Couldn't get too good a look because of the smoke, but I went back after the rains started and things cooled. Sure looked like a car."

"Pickup," Billyum said. "But you were right. You win the diamond-studded stomach pump."

"How come you waited so long to send somebody out?" Buzzy asked.

"I was shorthanded. Everyone wants vacation time to go hunting. Anyway, like Gab says, lots of wrecked vehicles on the rez. When Squeaky got back after hunting, I sent him. He tried following an old logging road and got stuck up to the axles. Had to send another rig out with a winch and a hundred feet of half-inch steel cable. Used that outfit to winch around the mud holes, but some big trees had fallen across the road, so they had to walk the last few miles." Billyum shook his head. "They stumbled around in the mud and burn a few hours before they managed to find the pickup. Finally, Squeaky tripped on one dead guy lying about twenty feet from the wreck. Thought it was another chunk of charred wood, until his boot hit that soft flesh and everything started oozing."

Gab set down his jelly roll. "Jesus, Billyum. I'm trying to eat here."

Billyum studied everyone. Buzzy seemed somber and Sniffy had turned pale. Billyum cleared his throat. "I'm telling you fellas, it'll take a lot more than Unguentine to fix those two."

"I'm losing my appetite," Gab said.

"Some of us got weak stomachs," Billyum said. "Squeaky barfed all over himself. He could still barely talk by the time he got back. It'll be awhile before old Squeaky can eat a burned biscuit." He put down his coffee cup. "So that's the news on the rez."

"You tell Grady?" Buzzy asked.

"I'm fixing to do that soon," Billyum said. "After I talk with the coroner. They could be Indians, I guess. Either way, it's our jurisdiction."

"Bad rubbish." Sniffy spoke so suddenly everyone gave a little jump. "Good riddance, if it was them. Two troublemakers."

"No point in speaking ill of the dead," Jake said.

Sniffy made a face like his coffee needed sugar. "You didn't work around those wiseasses. I had to swallow a lot of shit."

"The hell you say." Gab put the last of his roll in his mouth. "I thought that glow was suntan."

Sniffy didn't reply, but his look stayed sour.

Billyum stood. "I better go check with the coroner. Then I'll let Grady know. Just as a courtesy. Don't worry. I'll keep you boys posted."

"Don't hurry back," Jake said. "You're lousy for business. Next time, try bringing a little cheerful news."

One by one, the boys drifted out into the rain; Gab stayed and tried another slice of jelly roll. "Appetite's coming back. I'm not paying for this slice, though."

Jake didn't say anything. He washed the boys' cups and replaced them on the rack. He took a couple of the other cups, including Seaweed's, and washed them, too. As he watched Gab lick jelly from his fingers, Jake paused. "How can you eat after a story like that?"

"I'm a radio man. A newshound. That's news."

"You don't even know who it is yet," Jake said. "Don't go stirring up rumors."

"Doesn't matter. It's still news, unless it was Indians on a toot. Then it's just news on the rez."

"Those fellas were hard cases," Jake said. "Maybe they finally hit a brick wall." He hung up the dish towel and replaced the liquid detergent. "Anyway, you're not the news director. You're head of advertising and promotions. That's why you're always hanging around dipping your hand in my pocket."

"I wear many hats. *Versatility* is the key to my success."

"You also married the station owner's daughter," Jake pointed out. "That didn't hurt."

Pretending to be stricken, Gab brought his hand to his heart. "It does hurt deeply, Jake, the way you belittle my talents. I'm a regular Renaissance man burdened by a small town's lack of sensitivity." He took a long breath. "As for Priscilla, she got a bargain."

Jake rinsed his own cup. "I wonder if Meeks and Chilcoat might have set that mill fire."

Gab stroked his chin, intrigued by the idea. "Now that would be something. Live by the sword . . ."

"Die by the sword," Jake finished.

Gab's mouth flew open in mock amazement. "Why, Jake. You're a Renaissance man, too."

"You, me, and Franklin," Jake said. "Tight as ticks."

ONE SMALL ADVANTAGE to moving from school to school was that none of my teachers realized what projects I had completed before, so at new schools I kept updating old projects, thereby minimizing homework. In Gateway this allowed more time for basketball practice and hanging around the sporting goods store. I had a pretty good report on Argentina that I'd updated twice for social science projects and one on the 1919 Centralia Massacre. In Washington State, Wobblies and veterans had clashed violently over labor rights during an Armistice Day parade, and several men were killed. Riley had put me onto that topic. According to him, the railroad needed more strong union sentiments. My mother never suspected I reused a lot of these projects until I mentioned I planned to enter a volcano in the Gateway science fair. Then she protested that I'd worked on a volcano two years before in Grass Valley.

The Gateway High School Science Fair was heralded with a lot of hoopla by the teacher and the local paper. Belief in American scientific know-how had suffered a setback with the early success of Russia's Sputnik program and other space launches. From the flyers the school sent out, one would think a successful fair at Gateway would enable our country to surpass the Russians. And when my science class had turned in ideas for the fair, the projects included a model satellite, Titan missile, torpedo, and similar hardware. I submitted a volcano.

I knew pretty much how these events worked because I'd seen smaller versions of the science fair at other schools. The best projects were made by the farm kids with access to their parents' machine shops and carpentry skills. Although adult hands-on help was taboo, it was pretty clear none of the sophisticated models were actually conceived and crafted by Junior. My little papier-mâché volcano with red food dye, baking soda, and vinegar lava seemed puny by comparison, but at least it met my mother's insistence that I enter the fair while keeping my time investment to a minimum. To her credit, I imagine she felt a blue-ribbon satellite or missile project would launch my career with the space program or at least open the doors at the Air Force Academy. But I was playing another angle, although I realized it was a long shot.

After the Science Fair, the next big project was the Future Farmers of America Livestock Show, where the ag boys demonstrated their cattle, sheep, and horses. Roughly a third of the Gateway boys belonged to FFA, and each Thursday they swaggered around in their blue whipcord jackets with gold lettering. While I had no use for a horse or cow, I wanted a dog and suggested to Mom that I could enter one in the small animal competition.

"A dog?" my mother said, glancing up from her ironing when I raised the idea. "Are you crazy? They live ten or fifteen years. In a couple years when you're off at college, I'll be stuck with a dog. Scratching up the drum table. Shedding hairs all over the love seat." She was working up a head of steam.

"I could take the dog with me to college," I offered.

"Culver, you know better. A dog would distract you from your studies. A dog is definitely out. Anyway, we can't afford a dog."

"Maybe I won't go to college. I might just stay around here and work at Jake's. Learn the business."

She put down the water bottle she used to squirt clothes. She had a steam iron, but the steaming holes had plugged up with minerals from the hard water in Grass Valley. "Don't even think about it. Do you want to wind up like Jed? Seventy years old. Perched on a stool selling worms and salmon eggs?"

"Not exactly." I had always imagined myself more like Jake — running the guide service. I'd get someone else to package worms.

"I should hope not. I should hope you'd have a little more ambition."

"That's why I need a dog," I said. "You told me to go a hundred percent at school. I can't even enter the FFA fair without an animal."

"When I said one hundred percent I was referring to your general studies and the Science Fair," she said. "You don't need to trot around the ring with some poor dumb animal." She paused. "Dogs. When we lived at that horrible siding in Black Diamond, the stationmaster kept two enormous dogs. I don't know what kind, but they were supposed to be a big deal. He was afraid those dogs would be run over by a train, so he kept them attached to the clothesline on long leads. I couldn't hang up clothes there because they pooped and peed under the clothesline all summer. Even after Riley went out and cleaned it up, that place still smelled so bad I wouldn't walk under the lines. We sure don't want any dogs." Red-faced, she returned to her ironing with a passion.

I knew I wouldn't win the dog round, but I'd scored a point about her not letting me enter school projects one hundred percent. In that peculiar manner of compromise each family has, what I'd gained was the option of making another volcano instead of committing to a more ambitious project.

Franklin had suggested a scale model of the Sunrise Biscuits plant and had been so helpful as to draw a model. With the railroad siding, tall grain storage elevators, flour mill, and business offices, I had to admit it could have made a terrific project, but I just didn't want to invest the time, even though both Mom and Franklin were a little disappointed.

Whatever I did was okay with Mr. Maxwell, the science instructor. To tell the truth, I think Maxwell had a thing for my mother. He had given her a pretty good lookover on parents' night and she had dressed up for the occasion. She had a bit of mystery about her. In those days single parents were not common, and I suppose Grady had spread the word about Riley. She was beautiful and might be dangerous.

Maxwell was an okay guy, too. He loved the desert and spent each summer there studying rocks and fossils. He wore flannel shirts and boots, so he looked like the guys who hung around Jake's. During summer, he had been in Jake's to buy gold pans and rock hammers and we had discussed his hunting plume agates and thunder eggs out in Oregon somewhere. I was pleasantly surprised to learn this fellow was going to be my science teacher.

On the night of the fair, half the town hurried to the high school gymnasium. During the afternoon, a committee of judges had awarded ribbons, but no one knew who had won until that evening when the doors opened. I didn't expect a ribbon, nor did I get one, although the volcano did receive an honorable mention certificate. I suspect Maxwell put it there himself, since he was sweet on my mother and I was a model student, paying attention most of the time, not goofing around with the chem lab, avoiding scraping mud on the chair rungs in front of me like the ag boys did.

Blue ribbons went to the Titan missile and satellite. A scale model of the Gateway Irrigation Project received a red ribbon, as did a study of pesticides and the insects they killed. I was a little embarrassed because these were costly, knockout projects that put mine to shame. However, for two hours I stood gamely behind my volcano and answered questions if anyone stopped to ask. Except for family, only a few did. The most memorable was a slightly tipsy ex-sailor who had seen volcanoes up close in Hawaii.

Across from me was a project entered by Alvina Toopah, sister of Thatcher Toopah, starting guard for the Gladiators. Her model was devoted to thermal energy and showed the reservation hot springs they used to heat the lodge and the swimming pool. She had won a red ribbon, too, and as far as I could tell, was the only Indian with an entry.

I was decked out in my blazer and felt a little uncomfortable because most of the other boys were wearing sports shirts and slacks. But my mother had insisted. "Parents and professional people will be there," she had said. "And you want to look your best. First impressions are always important." I think she even felt some Central people might come down, although I had no idea why they would. Their own high school was five times the size of ours.

That night my mother wore a green wool dress she had bought on sale. After the purchase, she had to lie down a little while, because strapped as we were, spending that much money on herself made her dizzy. But she looked terrific and several men's eyes cut her way when she and Franklin came through the door. "Pretty snertzy," she had said, trying on the dress again at home.

"Those your folks?" Alvina asked.

"My mom and her friend," I said. "Your folks coming?"

"I think so."

My mother and Franklin spent a long time looking at all the science projects, and my mother asked about each one, then listened politely to the explanations. When she saw my certificate, her face glowed, and I'm sure she saw Stanford or MIT just around the corner.

Jake and Juniper came, too, and seemed to spend almost as much time with each project as Franklin and my mother had. Juniper paused to study Alvina's model. "Mom used to grow the best vegetables out there at the hot springs. And the biggest. Everybody wanted some because they tasted so good. Maybe it was the minerals."

"I didn't know anyone lived down there," Alvina said.

"Before your time," Juniper said. "We had to move when those springs got sold off to a white doctor and he built the bathhouses. While I was growing up, Mom had a free pass, so we could use the bathhouse any-time we wanted. See, they saved one for Indians only, and I thought that was pretty great." She paused. "Until I realized that was to keep us out of the white bathhouses."

"I never could figure how he bought the land," Jake said. "It was on the reservation. The tribe should have kept it."

"Something was fishy," Juniper said. "Later, when the tribe wanted it back, that land cost us millions. And I imagine the doctor got pretty well situated."

"It's too bad you can't move back," Alvina said.

Juniper nodded. "They tore our family house down, those old bath-houses, too, when they built the lodge. But I have memories of sitting in there with my mother, feeling the good heat, the hard stones on my feet. And sometimes I hear those grandmothers, talking in the old lan-guage."

Juniper touched Alvina's model and fell silent, as if the heat from the stones warmed her hand and she could still hear the voices.

No one spoke for a moment. Trying to lighten the mood I asked, "Did you know what you wanted to do after high school?"

She laughed, shaking her head. "What I knew mostly was that I didn't want to be a teenage mother. They had us all take these aptitude tests. The counselors said I should try to be a checker in the grocery store or a typist. Right then, I knew something was wrong. I couldn't even type."

When she and Jake moved closer to my volcano, I asked if they wanted the complete spiel. Jake shook his head. "All this science is making me thirsty," he said.

One of the gymnasium tables was set up with sugar cookies and loganberry punch. Things were winding down, so I shucked my blazer and headed for the goodies. Maxwell was there, too, talking politely with all the parents and trying to figure out Franklin's exact relationship with my mother. His eyes seemed a little sad. But Franklin was asking him very intelligent questions without seeming like a weenie or anything and Maxwell was impressed by his knowledge of science.

Gab came in with a tape recorder and microphone. He planned to interview some of the exhibitors and play the show by delayed broad-cast.

"When will this be on the radio?" my mother asked. "We want to be sure to listen." She had hurried over when she saw Gab bringing in the gear.

"Six o'clock tomorrow morning. It's a little early, but we have to sneak it in before the regular network program. Specials are kind of hit and miss."

"We'll be up, listening." My mother motioned for me to return to my booth. "Put your coat back on, Culver. It's more professional."

Even though no one could see radio, I followed her instructions.

Gab spent a few minutes with the first-place winners and lingered over the Gateway Irrigation District project. I figured a lot of farmers would be listening at six in the morning. Then Gab approached me.

"Now here's a hot exhibit. This one will shake, rattle, and roll. Culver Martin has constructed a terrific model of a volcano. Culver, can you say a few words about it?"

"Certainly," I said. "Happy you asked." And I launched into the spiel I remembered from the science fair in Grass Valley, the same one I'd used for the text to accompany the project.

"Although many people fail to realize it, we live in close proximity to an active volcano range. Magma and hot lava exist just a few hundred yards beneath the earth's surface. While the mountains were being born, during a time of tremendous geological upheaval, all of this land was covered by lava flow." I took a breath.

"Well, you learn something new every day," Gab said. "And that's doubly true at the Gateway High School Science Fair. Anything else?"

When he put the mike close by, I steadied it with my hand. "Unlike the deep and fertile soil of the Midwest, here the topsoil is only a few inches deep, because it takes so long for the natural elements — wind, sun, and rain — to break down hard volcanic rock."

My mother was beaming and Franklin smiled too, although he was looking at her, not me. Jake and Juniper had been on their way out but paused by the doorway.

"Wow, you know this stuff cold," Gab said, signaling with his hand for me to continue. "But what we want to know is, Will one of these babies blow? Should we learn to duck and cover?"

"Scientists have recorded significant seismic activity throughout the western region. Many believe that these tremors are signals that a volcano could erupt and become active in the not-too-distant future."

Gab interrupted. "You mean one could blow at any time? I got to get a big helmet?"

"It's entirely possible that one of the mountains in the Lost River Range could experience volcanic activity within our lifetime."

Gab drew his finger across his throat and took back the mike. "I'm interrupting this program for an emergency announcement. Run home to check your insurance policies. Do you have volcano coverage? Do I? What about earthquake damage? Read the small print. You could be in for quite a shock." He chuckled at his little joke. Switching off the mike, he gave me a wink. "Some fun. That was pretty lively, Culver. You've inherited a bit of Jake's gift for gab. No kidding. You should consider a career in broadcast journalism."

"Gab's right," my mother said. "Or television. With your good looks, you'd be terrific on television."

"No doubt about it," Franklin said. "See how that blazer squared his shoulders. Good-looking kid."

Gab scowled. "TV is not as reliable as radio, Mrs. Walker. Culver has the charisma for radio. You know it from his voice. Those TV gadflies are all sizzle and no steak." He patted me on the back. "But you're a natural. Like Edward R. Murrow. And I discovered you."

"If he's so great, why can't he sell a picnic table or all-natural synthetic coat?" Jake asked. "Something must be haywire."

"Some crapola can't be pawned off on the public," Gab said. He slapped my back, then lowered his voice. "No kidding. You got the stuff, kid. When I tried to talk to that little egghead about his satellite, he was DOA. I heard people switching off their sets all over town."

☆ ☆ ☆ ☆ ☆

While Mom vaguely regarded science as a launch for my future, she was also making plans for her own. She'd been upset that Riley was at the fire, but any anxiety his closeness may have caused was relieved by learning that he agreed to sign the divorce papers. Still, as weeks went by without a word from my stepfather, her hopes began to fade.

Just when I'd about given up, too, he called the store late one night with his uncanny ability to catch me when Jake was out. Riley's voice was thick and I suspected he'd been drinking. "I'll tell you where I am, Bucko, but no one else can know. I want you to swear. Got a Bible around there?"

We had a couple spares at home but Jake didn't keep a Bible at the store. "Just the state fish and game regulations book," I said, half joking.

"That'll have to do. Swear and hope to die. Stick a needle in your eye." He paused. "You're the only one I trust, Bucko."

"All right then. I swear. My right hand's on the book." I hoped no customers walked in about then.

"The book doesn't matter. It's your word. I'm giving your mom a break here but taking a big chance."

"You got my promise, Riley."

He seemed to relax. "Traverse City, Michigan. It's the cherry capital of the world. Lots of tourists and farmworkers. People pass through, no questions asked. I'm not using my real name though." He cleared his throat. "Send the papers general delivery to Dwight Riggins." He paused, perhaps waiting for my reaction, then continued. "And don't use the Gateway post office. Drive up to Central."

"I hear you, Riley."

"Dwight." He chuckled. "You can't believe the money around this place. People from Chicago and Detroit have big summer homes on Lake Michigan. You could break into one and live like a king all winter. Who'd be the wiser?"

"You'd better take it easy," I said. "Don't go doing anything dangerous."

He chuckled. "I am dangerous. I'm one dangerous son of a bitch. The railroad people know that now. They've got a little respect since I smoked them out. But Dwight's been going to church. Met a rich old widow woman and even helped her with a little carpentry work. Maybe I'll wind up owning her cherry farm. Sit out on the porch swing in a straw hat eating fistfuls of cherries. No worries, except how to keep the juice from dripping on my white shirt."

"I hope things work out."

"She lives right on the peninsula." His voice became intense. "From her place, you can see those big old summer houses, the lights of town glimmer across the water. That's how the other half lives, kid."

When I closed my eyes, I could imagine him on the porch, but he wasn't watching lights. Near the dark water, a home blazed.

My eyes opened when the operator came on the line to tell him he'd have to deposit another sixty-five cents.

"This call is burning money. Listen, Bucko, don't smoke any trick cigars. Tell your mom I'm in clover and got a bead on this widow woman."

"I'll have her send the divorce papers, Dwight." The line went dead, so I didn't know if he'd heard me or not.

At dinner, when I told Mom he'd called, she started from her chair. "Where is he? Back in California?"

I knew she was excited but I kept my word. "I promised him I wouldn't tell."

"Okay, a promise is a promise," she said. "I don't really care where he is. I just wonder how many days the divorce papers will take to reach him. Well, things always drag out longer than you expect." She sat back down and shook her head. "Culver, I hope you don't regard me as being foolish for ever marrying that man."

"Of course not."

"I knew he lacked gumption, but he was always good to you. And I thought you needed a father."

"Well, now there's Jake," I said.

"Yes," she replied without a hint of enthusiasm. "Jake."

25

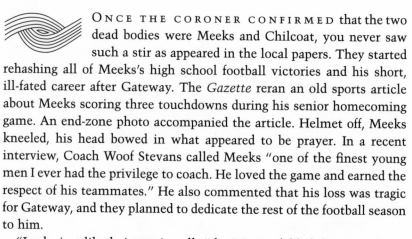

ONCE THE CORONER CONFIRMED that the two dead bodies were Meeks and Chilcoat, you never saw such a stir as appeared in the local papers. They started rehashing all of Meeks's high school football victories and his short, ill-fated career after Gateway. The *Gazette* reran an old sports article about Meeks scoring three touchdowns during his senior homecoming game. An end-zone photo accompanied the article. Helmet off, Meeks kneeled, his head bowed in what appeared to be prayer. In a recent interview, Coach Woof Stevans called Meeks "one of the finest young men I ever had the privilege to coach. He loved the game and earned the respect of his teammates." He also commented that his loss was tragic for Gateway, and they planned to dedicate the rest of the football season to him.

"Looks just like he's praying all right." Buzzy folded the paper, holding it close so he could study the picture. "Wonder how they ever got that photo."

"He's praying his buddies don't drink all the beer before he can shower and change," Jake said.

"Don't go speaking ill of the dead," Homer said. After making the pastry deliveries he had decided to stay. Identification of the bodies had made the back-room talk particularly intense that morning.

"We're putting together a radio show," Gab said, "interviewing some of his old teammates. It's a real human interest feature. Kind of whatever happened to the team. One got his leg cut off in a mint chopper; another got hurt in that water-skiing accident . . ."

"'Found dead under mysterious circumstances,'" Buzzy read from the article. "'Foul play not ruled out.'"

"Bullshit," Jake said. "The only foul play was those yahoos shooting that elk."

"The editor at the paper's always trying to stir up things," Homer said. "Remember when they had the noxious weed roundup last spring. 'Farmers Kill in Fields.' Earlier today the coroner stopped in to buy a cake for his grandson's birthday. His findings were 'accidental death.' No doubt about it."

"If you ask me, there's more to this than meets the eye," Buzzy said. "What were they doing so far back on the rez? When I first spotted that wreck, it was so remote, I thought it might be in the National Forest. You don't have to go that far from civilization to shoot an elk." He took a bite of his cinnamon roll. "You using margarine now?" he asked Homer.

"Never! God forgive you for even thinking it," Homer said.

"Probably the Indians aren't telling us everything," Buzzy said. He looked at the roll. "Maybe my taster's on the blink. Anyway, they took their own sweet time even checking out my report. Billyum always has been a little shifty, if you ask me. Sorry, Jake. I know he's your friend and all. But I wouldn't trust him as far as I could throw him — and he's a big man. All I'm saying is when you get on the reservation, there's not a thimbleful of real law."

"Or even a sense of fair play," Sniffy said. "For years the plywood mill kept the Indians' logging operations going. Then when the chance comes up, they plan to build their own damn mill without so much as a howdy or holler. Seems to me they're taking unfair advantage now because of government help. No regular outfit gets the same tax breaks and incentives the Indians do."

"What's that got to do with the guys in the woods?" Gab asked.

"I'm just putting in my opinion," Sniffy said. "Take it or leave it."

Jake raised an eyebrow, and I believe he was thinking of Sniffy's claim that the plywood mill had ripped off the Indians over the years. Now Sniffy was going along with the town.

"Grady thinks Billyum conducted a piss-poor investigation, too," Buzzy said. "By the time they got through mucking around, no one could even remember which body was in the pickup and which was on the ground. One's head was kind of bashed in. Maybe those two had a fight."

"Tree limb might have fallen," Homer said. "Of course, it wouldn't hit the guy in the cab."

"I still wonder why they were so far out," Buzzy said. "The longer they had to drive back, the greater the chance someone would spot them with that elk. Grady thinks it's peculiar, too." Buzzy finished the roll. "I don't care what you say, Homer. I know margarine. Can't trust anyone these days."

"Maybe they took a wrong turn." Homer was letting the margarine remark slide. "Reservation roads are confusing. If there's a sign at all, it usually points in the wrong direction."

"Could have been driven out there against their will." Gab raised an eyebrow. "A kidnapping?"

The back room was quiet for a few moments as they considered the idea. Then Jake began to speak with a lowered voice. "I know what happened. Billyum as much as said so, but it's all on the QT. If word gets back to him, I'm in dutch."

"You know us. Nothing leaves this room." Sniffy leaned forward.

"Put two and two together, you do come up with kidnapping," Jake said. "Someone pulled a pistol on them and headed out to the rez. Had a hell of a time driving the truck, holding the gun."

"I knew it," Buzzy said. "What did they want? Ransom?"

Jake waited for the hush. "Did I forget to say the kidnapper was the elk?" He grinned. "That elk knew it was going to be a lean winter and planned on feeding them to the little elks. But then it got to smoking, drinking, driving too fast. Big wreck."

"What a lousy story," Buzzy said. "I got a five-year-old niece lies better than that."

"Freak accident," Jake continued. "That's how one of those fellows wound up outside, the elk in the truck bed."

"You're full of shit as a Christmas goose," Gab said.

"Sometimes I don't know why I waste my time with you lowlifes." Buzzy put down the paper and left.

"When the truth comes out, you'll be laughing out the other side of your mouth," Jake called after him. "They'll vote me sheriff and I won't even have to run."

Juniper was steamed. I noticed the look the moment she stepped out of her van shortly after lunch. Inside the store, she nodded, then took coins out of her purse to buy a soda. "Got to cool off. I'm about to blow my top like some old Hawaiian volcano."

"I could say you're cute when you're mad," Jake said. "But I'm not even tempted. Just hoping you're not mad at me."

"Not so far, but there's plenty to go around. I stopped off at the *Gazette*, intending to give them a piece of my mind. These two poachers get page after page of news like they're some kind of saints. Kalim got murdered and only rated a tiny article on page six."

"So what did you do?" Jake asked.

"I parked in front of the *Gazette* office a long time, thinking about what I should say. But I couldn't go in. All those years, we stayed quiet whenever there was an insult. Say anything and you got tagged with being uppity or pushy." She shook her head.

"Most teachers treated us decent. Some didn't. But we kept our mouths shut or they made it worse. The other kids might jump on us, too. Find a weak point and they'd badger and badger until we broke down or headed back to the reservation." She frowned. "But the pressure was there, too. Always. 'You can make something of yourself,' teachers might say. What they really meant was 'Don't be like the rest of them.'"

"I still remember when you walked off the stage," Jake said.

She nodded. "That night I couldn't keep my temper. Later, when word got back to my mother and aunt, they scolded me and claimed I brought them shame." She sipped her drink. "Anyway, I'm getting sidetracked. Right now I've got another proposal to talk over."

Jake pretended to study his watch. "The consultant is in for the next hour and the back room is clear. Gonna cost you plenty though."

"Like what?"

"Lunch at the lodge. Fry bread and Indian chili."

Jake got a paper towel and wiped the pastry crumbs off a couple of the back-room chairs, but she sat at the high-backed work stool by the bench. Above her, Miss November on the Snap-On Tool calendar smiled at the wrench she was holding.

Jake tried handing Juniper a cup of coffee, but she shook her head. "I'll stick to my soda."

"So what's the deal?" he asked.

"It's pretty simple. They want me to manage a little gallery at the lodge. Sell Indian art to the tourists. I can set my own hours, leave time for my painting. Theoretically."

"Sounds perfect," Jake said.

She smiled. "It's not quite that easy. Living out there's pretty demanding. If you don't have family — an immediate family, I mean — they expect you to help out with all the ceremonies and dressings. You've got to cook, clean up, organize. I just don't think I could handle it all."

"Why not?" Jake teased. "You'd get first crack at all the food — eat the salmon cheeks and angel food cake. And you'd look good wearing a pom-pom cook's hat."

"Be serious. What do you really think?" she asked. "Running an art gallery at the lodge might not be so bad."

"Good opportunity," Jake said. "I wouldn't let it pass."

She shifted on the stool. "So many people never make it away from here. You know that relocation joke, about how they can shoot a man onto the moon but the scientists can't figure out how to get him back. 'Just send an Indian astronaut,' they say. 'He'll wander back all by himself.'"

Jake smiled. "You made it away. Now you're *choosing* to come back. Nothing wrong with that."

"I know." She sipped her soda. "But I just can't picture it permanently somehow. In Santa Fe or Albuquerque, I can concentrate on my work. No other demands."

Jake spread his hands. "Here you have a sense of community. And they love you in Central."

"That's good. But I have community there, too. I was planning a big art project in Arizona, down the Havasupai Canyon. It's magical. The water is absolutely blue-green, and rare moonflowers blossom in the shady spots. The Indians have found unusual petroglyphs and dinosaur tracks in the side canyons."

"Nothing's stopping you. You can still go —"

She shook her head. "A project like that could take over a year."

Jake seemed perplexed. "I can tell it's complicated."

"On the other hand, I love and respect the people here, and I've got so many good memories." She paused, smiling. "Yesterday I drove by that little Shaker church on the back side of the reservation. When I was a kid, my mother used to attend all the churches — Shaker, Catholic, Presbyterian — mostly to socialize. But she was shy and never talked much — just went to see what was going on, listen to gossip. Some mornings I'd be tired and try to sleep under the pew where no one could step on me. But once those Shakers got to ringing the bells and dancing, they kicked up so much dust I had to move or choke.

"The church was filled with crosses and candles. I remember smelling the burning candles, and Mom wearing an old shawl to keep the dripping wax from wrecking up her Sunday-best clothes.

"When people had troubles they moved to the center of the church while the Indian healers took the candles from the crosses. The bells kept ringing and they warmed their hands in the candles' flames, then touched the sick and troubled — patted them and stroked them, laid on the hands. You could feel the warmth from their hands just pass right through to you. After one of those healings, you'd feel so peaceful.

"After they were healed, the people circled the church like in the Washat — all four directions. They went under the big crosses on the east side and turned a circle, raising a hand to the Maker."

She smiled. "The healing was the best part, but I liked the cupcakes after the service, too. They were pretty heavy and had a sweet, sticky frosting. After a trip to the Shaker church, both my stomach and my mind felt good."

I stayed quiet, imagining the church, the candles, and the healing.

"Sounds to me like you should stick around here," Jake said.

"Like I said, I love the people here. Present company excluded." She winked at me. "I don't want your uncle getting a swelled head. This place is like a magnet. Keeps pulling at me. Still, you can get fooled. Right now, everyone is so nice, but I know if I moved back here they'd start taking me for granted. And I wouldn't have a moment's peace."

"It got to be like that for me, sort of," Jake said. "I was with the volunteer ambulance, the fire department, and the city council. When some people started drafting me for mayor, that was too much. I couldn't handle my own business."

"Fishing?" She kept a straight face.

He held out his arm, indicating the store. "This modest place that pays the rent."

She laughed. "You don't run it. Culver does. Everyone says he's twice as smart as you. They have trouble believing you're related."

I reddened a little.

"I hate to admit it," she said, "but in the old days I used to be pretty mean. Remember how Mavis Born-With-A-Tooth and I used to terrorize Bernadette, Billyum's cousin? She was a couple years younger, kept following us around like a lovesick puppy. Mavis and I were always cooking up trouble for her."

"Now she's a nurse," Jake said. "Works for Indian health."

Juniper nodded. "I pray nothing goes wrong with me. She'd love jabbing me with a dull needle after our stunts."

"Everybody horses around when they're younger," Jake said. "She's probably forgot."

Juniper shook her head. "We almost killed her one time. You know that steep section of the Kooskia Grade that has the one old crooked pine tree? When I was driving around the rez one day, I saw that tree and got to thinking about the time when Mavis and I found the old baby carriage at the dump. Two of the wheels were wobbly and it had something like tar spilled over it, but that sucker still rolled.

"We got to wondering how fast it would go down the grade — sort of like the soapbox derby. And we decided it would roll faster with more weight. We got Bernadette all gussied up after talking her into playing Baby for a Day, and we stopped at the store and bought her strawberry pop and Twinkies, whatever she wanted. Then we pushed that carriage out toward Kooskia. Took almost an hour.

"Bernadette was sucking on the bottle we filled with pop and making all kinds of goo-goo noises when we started pushing her up that grade. Man it was steep. Mavis and I both had to push. At the top, Bernadette got a little worried, but we told her everything was okay. Suddenly we turned that rickety thing around and let it roll downhill. Bernadette was riding backwards, facing us, and her eyes grew wild with terror. She started hollering and crying.

"Mavis looked at me and her eyes were wide. 'I think those soapbox thingees are supposed to have brakes,' she said, and we both started chasing downhill after Bernadette. She was flying by then, and when that carriage hit potholes her braids would fly up on her head. She was yelling 'Mama! Mama!' and she'd be rolling yet, if it wasn't for that tree.

"Smack!" Juniper slapped her open palms together. "The carriage hit that tree, skidded off to one side, then tipped over. Bernadette came rolling out in her fancy party dress. She thumped against a rock and just lay there, real quiet. We tiptoed up, thinking maybe she was too scared to cry out anymore, but she was knocked cold. Her eyeballs had rolled up so all you could see was white. 'I'll bet she's faking,' Mavis said. 'Check her ears for blood. That's a bad sign.'

"'I don't think she's even breathing,' I said. I looked in her ears. Dirt but no blood. Some ants were crawling on her face and she still wasn't moving. Both of us were afraid to actually touch her. The way we'd been so mean to her, a night ghost might grab us, carry us away with her spirit.

"'Let's call Cecil Funmaker,' Mavis said. He had that old rattletrap Dodge station wagon he called an ambulance. Sometimes when he wasn't too pie-eyed to drive, he'd run somebody with a broken arm or the DT's into Central.

"We both kept staring at Bernadette. 'She's dead for sure,' Mavis said. 'I wonder if I can have her bike.' Then she started crying around, and I was sniffling, too. Right after, we saw this big old snot bubble come out of Bernadette's nose. What a relief!

"'She's breathing,' Mavis shouted. 'All this time she's been faking, holding her breath to fool us!' She was about to give Bernadette a swift kick, but I stopped her. Good thing, too, because she had a broken arm. Just a hairline fracture. Both knees and one side of her face were skinned up good. A big lump rose right up on her forehead.

"We wanted to put her back in the carriage and wheel her home, but it was busted, so we had to walk and sort of support her. She kept holding that arm funny. We got her some more pop at the store and begged her to keep quiet, but as soon as her mother saw that purple egg on her forehead and the crooked way she carried that arm, she dragged her off to the hospital in Central. The moment she got back, Bernadette's mom called ours and we got spanked big time. I couldn't sit for a week and got grounded for a month. The only place I was allowed to go was over to Bernadette's, and I was forced to read to her every afternoon."

Jake laughed. "Maybe that incident caused her to become a nurse. A real life changer."

Juniper frowned. "That old baby carriage stayed right by the tree for ten years. Each year it got more faded and shabby. Mice ran off with parts of it to build nests. Everytime we drove by, my mother would fold her arms and scowl."

"I'll bet Bernadette is just waiting for her chance to get even," Jake said. "Go in with a splinter and she'll put you in a coma."

"Don't think I don't worry about it. On the rez, people got long memories."

When they had finished laughing, Juniper added, "I'll bet Billyum remembers that accident. He had to read to her all summer, too. *Little House on the Prairie*. I still hate those books."

She shifted the stool so she was facing Jake. "You know, when Billyum and I were talking earlier, he said something kind of odd."

"What about?" Jake asked.

"He said maybe Kalim knew those two guys that burned up. The way he said it was funny."

Jake didn't answer for a moment. I thought he might tell her what Sniffy had said, but he didn't.

"It's a small town," Jake said. "Everybody runs into everybody else. He might know them from the Alibi or the Phoenix. Or even the mill when Kalim brought in logs."

"I don't know." She paused. "Billyum had something more on his mind. I'm sure of it. He's so transparent, to me at least. I can read him like a book."

"Not the Bible," Jake said.

"No," she agreed. "That's not the book."

After Juniper was gone, I told Jake that it seemed funny how Sniffy had talked about those guys and now they were dead.

"Like Sniffy said, good riddance!"

"What if they had something to do with Kalim's death?" I said. "Do you think that's what Billyum had on his mind but couldn't tell her?"

"You know, I'll sure be glad when school starts and you can chase girls. That way you'll spend less energy on your goofy ideas." Jake took my arm. "Sniffy was firing blind that night. Even the old glue sniffer had enough sense to change the story."

"It's still a funny coincidence."

"What coincidence?" Jake cocked an eyebrow. "You don't believe the elk kidnapped them?"

I shrugged, knowing Jake was trying to change the subject.

"Maybe that elk wasn't smoking a cigar," Jake said. "Although smoking will spark the flames of hell quick enough to burn away salvation." Changing the cadence of his voice so he sounded like a revival preacher, he began pacing, stopping occasionally to throw his arms in the air. "Young sinner, you may call it a mere co-in-ci-dence." He raised his hands toward the sky. "I say di-vine Pro-vi-dence. Shout hallelujah. Holy Harold knows all, sees all. He sees how Providence struck down the wicked in their own iniquity — Sodom and Gomorrah, Ananias and Sapphira, Meeks and Chilcoat. Di-vine Providence."

He took a deep breath. "God saw the sinners poaching in His garden, and He was displeased, and struck them down." Jake slammed his fist into his open palm. "Sent them down to Big Smoky without passing Go or collecting two hundred dollars." He pointed his finger at me. "Struck them down with tongues of flame. And you, too, can be struck down if you don't obey the Commandments. Forget about adultery. That's kind of fun sometimes. But above all else, you must obey the Eleventh Commandment."

I held out my hands, pretending to ward off the evil. "I plan to. What is it?"

"Obeyeth your uncle." Jake continued, "When he saith, 'Sweep!' you sweepeth. When he saith 'Wheel the bikes,' you wheeleth. When he saith package the worms —'"

"But I always obey," I protested. "And for little reward."

"You're storing up treasures in heaven," he said. "And remember, you didn't sell all the picnic tables."

I laughed. "All right, you got me."

"Don't worry about taking up a collection at the end of this service. I'll deduct your donation straight from your wages."

I had enjoyed my uncle's antics, but they bothered me as well. It seemed as if I couldn't get him to be serious and answer my questions.

Later that night though, I laughed when telling Mom about Jake's imitation of Harold. She said it was sad but probably true he had acted just like that. "Your uncle's side of the family," she emphasized.

26

 AS WE WRESTLED with the stuffed deer on the icy roof, passing cars honked. A few people stopped to offer suggestions. The back-room boys had all kinds of wild ideas to improve the situation, but none worked too well in the sub-freezing temperature with a stiff wind driving sleet.

"Why couldn't you just do a window decoration like the other merchants?" I asked. "That window artist was around offering to do a holiday scene pretty cheap."

"It's not the same thing as a deer on the roof," Jake said. "This is a sporting goods store, not a wimpy dry cleaners or bank."

"No other merchant is dragging stuff onto the roof."

"Didn't you see the saddle shop? They rigged up a stuffed Shetland pony and outfitted it with red boots and a cowboy hat. Sneaky bastards are trying to steal my thunder."

"At least the pony doesn't have bullet holes," I said. Before it became a Christmas roof decoration, game wardens used Jake's stuffed deer as an open-field decoy to trap city dudes who stopped to spotlight and shoot it. Good for ten or twelve arrests each season, the deer took serious abuse. Some dudes even took time to reload when the deer didn't fall during the first volley.

Jake shook his head. "Don't go thinking negatory thoughts, nephew. This deer is a tradition. Kids love it. From a distance they can't see the bullet holes or raggedy rump. And I usually win a prize for merchant display."

I knew Jake was just blowing wind. Earlier he'd said that no one judged the merchant displays except a couple of tipsy old Realtors whose noses shone brighter than Rudolph's.

The roof was fairly flat, but it had taken me over an hour to shovel off the snow, given the accumulation, the wind, and the treacherous footing. I was wearing one of the Sasquatch coats. Before Thanksgiving, Jake had given me my Christmas present early because he thought some of my schoolmates might want one, and the fake fur had become so matted down with the sleet, I resembled an outlandish, oversize rodent.

Gab had done a practiced double take when he saw me working alone on the roof. "That's the ugliest goddamn elf I ever saw," he shouted up above the wind. "Santa's really scraping the bottom of the barrel."

I tried shoveling a load of snow on his head, but he ducked inside too fast.

While I cleared the roof, Jake had stayed inside keeping warm and patching a couple of the deer holes with catgut. My feet were freezing and my hands had turned numb.

Homer climbed the ladder to offer hot coffee and warm cake doughnuts. "Some job," he said, indicating the piles of snow I had pushed off the roof.

"Jake said this would take about an hour," I said. "After two, I'm leaving for sure."

"Good luck." Homer shook his head. "Last year when it was sunny and warm, it took three hours. Stringing the guy wires is no picnic. And I've never seen this much snow in mid-November."

"This is tough work," I said. "I can see why people in Minnesota have heart attacks." After I took off the parka hood, my head steamed more than Homer's coffee. Once the roof was clear, I went inside to get Jake. The coat was soaked and slick.

"Goddamn, I never saw a rat that big," Sniffy said. "Must've crawled out an open sewer somewhere."

"That's no rat. It's a nutria," Gab said.

"Same difference," Sniffy said. "They're cousins or something. People eat them in the Philippines."

"And they taste just like chicken," Gab said. "Everything tastes like chicken."

"Are you about ready to help?" I asked Jake. "You were supposed to come up sooner and clear the roof."

"Packaged up some worms," he said, "in case we get a rush." They all laughed, since fishing season had been over for a couple months.

"That's some coat, all right." Gab laughed. "I didn't think those coats could get uglier, but they look worse wet than dry."

"Your basketball team should wear them," Sniffy said. "Scare the opposition to death. Only way you're ever going to win."

"It might slow the players down," Gab said.

"They can't move any slower and still be breathing." Sniffy slapped his knee.

I didn't say anything because I'd shot only three for thirteen in the last game. Two of our starters had moved away with their parents, who had worked at the mill but were following job prospects to Arizona.

"Woof had to move guys up from the junior varsity," Jake said. "But I'll bet if he figured out a nutria play, we could go to state again."

I'd heard the story of Woof's trick play from the back-room boys early that season. Designed to create an easy bucket on an inbounds play under your own basket, he'd used it to win a regional championship. With two seconds to go and trailing by a point, Gateway had the ball out under its own basket. Talented Lewisburg usually guarded Gateway tightly on the inbounds and forced a long pass and a long shot. But this time Woof played his ace. As Woof's guard prepared to inbound, the Gateway center dropped to all fours and began barking wildly like a dog, shaking his head from side to side and snapping his teeth. Distracted, the Lewisburg players turned their attention to him, and the inbounds pass went to Gateway's forward for an easy layup.

The Lewisburg coach tried for a technical foul or unsportsmanlike conduct — anything to nullify the play — but the rulebook had no text on a barking-dog play, and Gateway advanced to state.

But now Sniffy was right. We had been playing poorly, and it would take more than a trick play to bring us up to speed.

Although no one could see the bullet holes from the highway, the deer was pretty shabby. The hair was worn off the left rump, perhaps from riding around in the game warden's rigs, but Jake had spray-painted a little tan marine paint on the ragged patch to make it seem more realistic. The rump appeared darker than the grayish brown color of mule deer, but at least he'd made the attempt.

The deer wasn't all that heavy, but awkward, especially in the wind. We hoisted it with a block and tackle and tried wrestling it to a high point on the roof. Clear of snow, the roof remained icy, and we nearly let the deer slide off before we caught it. Finally we managed to wire one of the hooves to a chimney.

Gab watched from below, keeping warm in a big parka and sipping coffee. "Hope your insurance is paid up, Jake. If that thing falls off the roof and injures a customer, you're looking at a big-time lawsuit."

"Like the carrier says, I'm fully insured but not covered. With a little luck, it might hit you," Jake said.

"I don't think most riders include dead deer falling off the roof and breaking people's necks. Acts of God but not acts of lunacy."

By the time we finally got the deer secure on the rooftop it was dusk. Jake rigged two spotlights on the roof corners to illuminate the deer. Then he attached the red light near its nose, securing the extension cord with baling wire. His teeth were chattering as we scrambled down.

"Light's too low," Gab said. "Looks like that deer is chomping a red lightbulb."

"How about you scramble up there and fix it," Jake said. "I'll give you directions for a change."

"Deer's gonna have a stomach full of glass. No wonder that critter's so full of holes. Next thing you'll have it swallowing a sword. I could work up a commercial spot for you. Come see Bambi the Magnificent. The Perforated Deer. I mean the *performing* deer."

After Gab was gone, Jake went out and admired the deer. "Maybe that light is hanging a little low. Up on the roof, it seemed okay."

"I'm not going back up there," I said.

He nodded. "It's close enough for Gateway. Tomorrow we've got to put up the sleigh."

"No way," I said and meant it. "Anyway, Mom says it's uncouth to put up Christmas decorations before Thanksgiving."

Grady stopped by two days later. "I like seeing that deer. Reminds me of when the state wardens caught those poachers at night. A stuffed deer makes a great tool for law enforcement."

"This one took some serious fire," Jake said.

"Seeing it up there got me to thinking about the two dead boys they found on the reservation," Grady said. "A strange business, so I used an old technique they taught us at the academy." He seemed pleased with himself. "I wrote down all the items that should be at the scene of a crime — what you'd expect to find. Then I listed all the things that were actually there. And I compared them."

"What crime scene?" Jake asked.

"On the reservation. You saw the *Gazette*. 'Foul play not ruled out.' Editor got that quote from me. Anonymous, of course. I suggested he run it like that."

"You're about to get everybody stirred up over nothing," Jake said.

"Tempers are already tight. If you go and say the Indians killed a couple guys on the reservation, it's going to be a lot worse."

"Didn't say the Indians did anything. I'm trying to be objective, Jake. Are you, the way you keep palling around with Indians day and night?"

"I choose my own company," Jake said.

"That's your business," Grady said. "Mine's the law. Anyway, I made that list and things didn't add up. I saw Billyum's report. Pretty sloppy police work." He handed Jake a sheet of paper with two columns. "Here, take a look."

Jake read it carefully. His brow furrowed.

"You see it, don't you?" Grady asked. "Remember why you stopped offering the Big Buck contest — quit giving away a new rifle every year for the biggest rack? Why was that?"

"The winners always went out at night and spotlighted," Jake said. He examined the list again. "Spotlight. Hell, they had a spotlight on that pickup. Didn't you see the photos?"

I nodded. "Sure. When Meeks was in here after slaughtering those rabbits, he bragged about freezing them with the spotlight. In fact, he hit it with a big chunk of ice. There was definitely a light."

Grady nodded and stroked his chin. "Well, howdy-do. Maybe that explains it. Meeks was down at the garage complaining the spot didn't work. Raised such a fuss they ordered him a new one."

"So what's the racket about a spotlight?" Jake asked.

"The new one's still sitting there. He never picked it up."

"Doesn't prove much," Jake said. "I get stuck with special orders all the time. Guys want something yesterday, place a special order, then buy it quicker someplace else. I'm stuck."

"I went out to the wrecking yard and checked," Grady said. "Original light is still on the truck. So what do you make of that?"

Jake shrugged. "I guess they used a portable light. I've got one Ray-O-Vac here that will throw a good beam over a hundred yards. You can pick up that kind of light about anywhere — Coast-to-Coast, Krazy Karl's."

"Those fellows ever buy one from you?"

"Not that I remember," Jake said. When he looked at me, I shook my head.

Grady squinted at Jake. "Now correct me if I'm wrong, but if I was poaching elk on the back corner of the reservation, I'd take along a pretty good light. In fact, I'd take a couple. Wouldn't you?"

"Yes, I would," Jake said. "But if those boys had been drinking a lot, Meeks might have forgotten his spotlight didn't work. Or they might have stopped to take a piss somewhere and dropped the portable."

Grady tapped the side of his head. "I like how you think. If you get tired of running this store, I'll put you to work. Anything's possible. Like you say, they can buy a portable just about anyplace. Billyum and Squeaky might have overlooked it. They didn't go over everything with a fine-tooth comb. All in all, it was a piss-poor investigation. Plus the burn and now the snow.

"Fire wipes out a lot of evidence. Hell, you couldn't tell shit after the plywood mill fire. The whole investigation was guesswork." He hitched his pants. "Anyway, the reservation's not my jurisdiction. Still, I don't want anything overlooked, so I'm sending off a letter stating my concerns to the regional office of the FBI. Let them have a crack."

"Fuckups, bullies, and idiots," Jake said. "The tribe isn't going to think much of the FBI futzing around. A missing spotlight seems pretty slim."

Grady smiled. "Sure it does. But I've seen cases turn on a lot less. A footprint, a button, broken shoelace. You start with a thread and see where it leads." He folded up the paper and put it in his jacket pocket. His eyes cut to the painting of Kalim. "You think those fellas knew that Kania boy?"

Jake seemed surprised. "Why would you think that?"

"I hear talk. Some of my boys moonlight a little at the mill. Used to moonlight, I mean. They think Meeks and Kania palled around."

"It's a small town," Jake said. "Everybody runs into everybody. What are you driving at?"

"Coincidences always make me wonder. Most of the time, people get killed by someone they know."

Jake laughed. "I can solve that one for you. Kalim didn't kill them, unless you believe that wandering Indian ghosts come looking for revenge."

Grady smiled. "You're smarter than most of my men, Jake. Like I say, you'd be great on the force. But you got this one ass backwards. I was thinking that if someone blamed them for killing Kalim, they might try to get some payback."

Jake didn't reply for a moment, and I stayed quiet, too. "Why would they kill Kalim?"

Grady's brow furrowed. "That's a puzzle, isn't it? But I didn't say they did. You never heard that from me. I'm just trying out a couple theories — shooting in the dark, seeing if I hit anything."

"It's your business," Jake said. "But I'd be careful and not get the town and reservation at each other's throats."

Grady shook his head. "Farthest thing from my mind. And I appreciate your concern." He fastened his coat. "I sure like that deer, Jake. Must be a powerful lot of work dragging it up there, using the pulley, attaching all the wires. Getting those lights on the roof."

"I got help," Jake said. "This nephew works like a mule."

"A good kid," Grady said, resting his hand on my shoulder. "He's not likely to wind up on the wrong side of the rule book, especially with his mother's influence. Can't say as much for the uncle."

For once he didn't mention my stepfather, and I was glad.

Grady shifted toward the door. "Hope nobody takes a potshot at that deer."

"I think it's safe from the dudes," Jake said.

"I don't worry much about dudes," Grady said. "What concerns me is the people close by." He stepped outside and looked up at the deer, then poked his head back in. "You ever think of outlining that critter in lights? They got lights on the horse down at the saddle shop. Looks sharp."

After Grady left, I studied my uncle. He was thinking hard but didn't speak until I asked, "Why do you think Grady is going after the Indians on this deal?"

"I'm not exactly sure," Jake said. He tapped the glass counter. "But he's not as dumb as he acts sometimes. And he's right about one thing. There should have been a spotlight."

"Maybe they used headlights. Caught a big elk crossing the road."

"Awful chancy," Jake said. "Most people heading toward a dark corner of the reservation would take along a damn good light."

☆ ☆ ☆ ☆ ☆

The deaths of Meeks and Chilcoat were having a bad effect on the school, too. Even before that mystery, tensions ran high between the children of unemployed millworkers and the Indians. On the basketball team, sons of plant workers wouldn't pass the ball to Indians and vice versa. I got caught in the middle. Needless to say, we lost. The opponents' defenses double-teamed white or Indian players, depending on who controlled the ball downcourt.

Probably Coach Stevans hadn't helped the situation any by dedicating the football season to Meeks. The *Gazette* kept the pot stirred and joined Grady in calling for an FBI investigation.

In the locker room after phys ed, clusters of Indians and white kids snapped one another with wet towels, raising angry welts. And after basketball practice no one kidded around much or played practical jokes like putting analgesic balm in jockstraps. Traveling to away games, the Indian players stuck to their side of the bus.

Woof Stevans was watching the season slip away but seemed unable to stop the hard feelings. When I walked the hallways between classes, I paused in front of the old trophies and banners, wondering if the season couldn't go better. Sometimes I browsed through old yearbooks. Jake and Billyum were in the championship team photo. Billyum posed like a downlineman, fist planted on the ground, leaning forward, his face twisted in a ferocious scowl.

Franklin and my mom came to every game. She looked terrific, but he always seemed a little overdressed in a blazer, ascot, and matching pocket handkerchief. During warm-ups, I'd give them a quick wave, then duck my head and concentrate on layups. Jake came, too, usually by himself. Seeing my uncle at the games gave me a boost. His confidence was apparent when he came through the door. He knew almost everyone in the place and stopped to talk with half a dozen people before he sat down to watch. Not growing up with a real father, I couldn't say for sure, but I think the love I felt for Jake was pretty close to how other guys felt about their dads.

The spectators divided into two groups. Most of the farmers, millworkers, and businesspeople sat on the bleachers behind the home team. The rally squad worked these bleachers.

People from Mission, Ace, and the RedWings sat on the bleachers opposite, not behind the visitors' bench but close to the gym entrance and the concessions. Everyone carried in tubs of buttered popcorn, garlicky hot dogs, soft drinks, and red licorice whips sold by the Girls Athletic Association.

The night we played Pinedale, Jake and Juniper arrived late, just as we were finishing warm-ups, so most of the crowd was already in. They hesitated in the doorway; she was leaning toward the Mission bleachers. Right then, Grady called out from the other side, "Hey, Jake. We got room here. Bring the little woman." Grady stood and pointed to a small section of bare bleacher. "Lots of room." He was grinning.

If Jake had a moment's pause, Grady settled it for him. My uncle and Juniper sat on the Mission side.

Pinedale was leading the league and figured we'd be a cinch. During warm-ups, I saw the moonfaced kid who had stopped and talked one night when I'd been running. He was beefier than I remembered, and I realized he'd be hard to outmuscle on the boards. "Hey," he said when he'd caught my eye. "I can't believe you pussies lost to Bridgeport. Our girls' team could beat them."

"In Pinedale, it's hard to tell the girls from the boys," I said.

Thatcher Toopah, our starting guard, grinned at that one.

"What's so funny, Calijah?" the Pinedale boy asked. "You look like a girl yourself with that braid. You know what they call an Indian with *two* bottles of whiskey on the reservation? They call him *mayor*." A couple of the other Pinedale players snickered.

I looked around to see if one of the refs heard, but they hadn't. Thatcher just kept smiling until someone tossed him the ball. Then he canned one from the top of the key.

"He won't make that when he's double-teamed," the blond boy said.

Before they announced the starting five, I sidled close to Thatcher. "You see any Indians on that Pinedale team?" I asked. "Come on. Let's get all five guys in the game and whip their butts."

Thatcher tapped my shoulder with his fist. "I don't want to see you casting off from the corner."

The first couple times Thatcher brought the ball downcourt, it looked like the same old shit. As soon as he crossed midcourt, Pinedale double-teamed both him and our forward Wilbur Tapish. First Thatcher tried forcing Wilbur a pass that got picked off and then he got called for a charging foul. Pinedale scored twice and led 4–0.

"I thought tonight was supposed to be different," Stork Whealey complained as he lumbered back to his high post.

"Pass the damn ball to the other guys!" Woof called from the bench.

"Don't worry," I told Stork. "Thatcher's just setting them up." I hoped it was true.

The next trip downcourt, Thatcher faked the drive, faked a pass to Wilbur, and slipped me a no-look pass as I cut for the basket. It was so slick, I almost dropped the ball but hung on for an uncontested layup.

"He must've gone color blind all of a sudden," the moonfaced kid said as I hustled back on defense. But Thatcher kept them off balance all night. He passed to the open man, drove the lane, and went on a red-hot shooting streak, casting off hip shots that had no business going in.

Pinedale was caught flat-footed, and all of us rallied behind Thatcher. Gateway fans stood and cheered, rocking both sets of bleachers. Every time Gab stood up from his broadcast mike to cheer, he dumped popcorn on the people in front, but they didn't mind. Everybody was too delighted watching Pinedale get drubbed.

After the game, Gab interviewed Thatcher and Stork for his radio show, and I stopped to talk with Franklin and my mother. "Great job, Culver," he said. "You got twelve points." He thumped my back, the most emotion I had ever seen him display. He had taken off his blazer and held it folded across his arm.

I looked around for Jake and Juniper, but they were gone.

"That your dad?" Thatcher asked as we showered after the game. "Guy with that funny thing around his neck?"

"No. But he goes with my mom sometimes."

"Could have fooled me." Thatcher grinned. "You look exactly like that weenie. Spitting image."

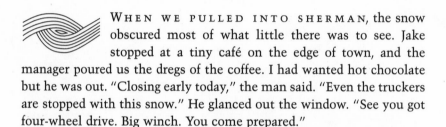

27

WHEN WE PULLED INTO SHERMAN, the snow obscured most of what little there was to see. Jake stopped at a tiny café on the edge of town, and the manager poured us the dregs of the coffee. I had wanted hot chocolate but he was out. "Closing early today," the man said. "Even the truckers are stopped with this snow." He glanced out the window. "See you got four-wheel drive. Big winch. You come prepared."

Jake nodded. "Triple A can't find this place," and the man grinned.

Across from the café were a couple acres littered with farm equipment, used appliances, flat-tired school buses. A weather-beaten old farmhouse rose from the middle of the junk. On the roof was a kind of widow's walk, and through the falling snow I could just make out what seemed to be a bundled-up person sitting in a lawn chair.

"That the mayor's place?" Jake asked.

"Old man Mossby and his two sisters. He tried to be mayor. Got four votes, but it wasn't enough." He poured Jake a little more coffee, thick and black, then rinsed out the pot. "With separate domiciles they collect three times as much support from the county. That's the law, believe it or not. Fact is, he can't stand the sisters, so he sits on the roof, watches the world go by."

"Not bad work," Jake said. "Where'd that fourth vote come from?"

"It's a mystery." The café owner placed the pot on a shelf. "Me, I don't care who wins, but they have to be Republicans."

Jake set a dollar on the counter and buttoned his coat.

"Honk as you drive by," the man said. "If the old fart waves, he hasn't frozen to death yet."

The cab was cold and we could see our breaths. "Heater's a little on the blink," Jake said.

As we drove by the junked-up yard, he honked and the bundled man waved. Jake honked again and the man gave a huge wave. "Likes his work," my uncle said.

A quarter mile from Sherman, we bumped across a double set of railroad tracks covered in snow and passed two tall grain elevators, larger than the ones at Sunrise Biscuits. Here the cement elevator remained in good condition, but the wooden one had partially burned. Smoke streaked the sides; part of the roof had caved in. "Some son of a bitch was torching these historic elevators last summer," Jake said. "Got five in this county alone."

"How much farther to Gab's place?" I couldn't see much but snow and an occasional farm light.

"Eight miles. This snow should keep the geese so low we can club them with our gun butts."

"You bet." I held my new Remington 870 pump to keep it from bouncing around in the cab as the snow-covered road turned to washboard. I had selected the deluxe model at Jake's suggestion because the checkered walnut stock seemed worth the extra price. I carried the shotgun in a padded case and could have left it behind the back seat with Jake's but wanted it closer. Under the heavy hunting coat, I was wearing my father's Filson vest. The pockets were filled with twenty shotgun shells and I felt the weight. I had intended to carry two boxes of shells, but Jake had insisted one was enough. After taking me out to the Gateway trap club and teaching me a little about wing shots, he had pronounced my shooting as "dude-gone good."

"Think geese," Jake said, grinning at the heavy snowfall. "Just like those skiers with their THINK SNOW bumper stickers. The geese will keep so low today they'll be big as bathtubs."

I felt exhilarated. Jake sped up and the pickup jarred over the snow-covered corrugations, almost rattling my teeth. Ahead, dark shadows blocked the road. "Hey, look out!" I jammed my foot into the floorboard.

When Jake saw them, he hit the brakes, sending the pickup into a long fishtail skid. "Shit fire!"

Turning the wheels into the skid, he straightened a little, and the pickup slid straight toward a herd of horses. The closest bolted as it saw the pickup loom out of the snow, but we grazed its rump with the spare tire Jake kept mounted high on the front. The others lunged toward the roadside, too, plumes of steam coming from their nostrils. Then they ran across the barrow pit and out into an open field. They stood, backs to the storm, their tails and manes shagged with ice.

"Fucking horses," Jake said. He leaned on the horn and they ran another fifty yards, then stopped, watching us closely. "Reminds me of an ambulance run."

"What about it?"

He shook his head. "Too long a story. Gab's place is dead ahead."

"Think that one's okay?" I asked. "We just grazed it."

"Sure. If not, we'll shoot the son of a bitch. Shoot the owner, too, for letting his horses run wild."

Billyum's tribal pickup sat in Gab's driveway. Jake hadn't mentioned his coming along, but I was pleased.

As soon as they saw our rig, the two rushed out the door carrying their shotguns and flasks of coffee. "Where the hell you been?" Gab asked. "Kept drinking coffee while we waited. Now I'm all jittery."

"Let's go," Billyum said, opening the door to his rig. "Feeding time for the geese."

"Just slow down a cotton-picking minute," Jake said. "Before we go any further, I want to see everybody's hunting license and waterfowl stamp."

I thought he was serious and started to take mine out.

"I'm not aiding and abetting any game-law violators in this great state." He looked at Billyum. "Got your federal waterfowl stamp, fella? The U.S. government says you got to have it."

"Gee, I think I left mine back on the rez," he said. "In my other pants."

"That's a piss-poor excuse," Jake said. "Limpy, gimpy, and lame. Sorry, but you can't hunt then. Like the sign says, 'The Game Law Violator Is a Thief.'"

"We own all this anyway," Billyum said, pointing to the land toward the river. "Geese belong to us, too."

"Don't give me that," Jake said. "I'm putting you on notice. Whose side is this anyway? White or Indian?"

"It's just a short-term loan," Billyum said.

"Let's get going, you loggerheads," Gab said, opening the passenger door on Billyum's rig. "We'll miss the geese."

"Just don't expect me to bail him out," Jake said.

From Gab's place, we drove six miles, then stopped at an old abandoned farmhouse crouched in a depression out of the wind. At the back of the farmhouse was a cistern filled with fifty or sixty empty farm chemical barrels and assorted junk.

246

Gab walked to the cistern and started peeing. "Damn coffee."

"It'll take you a while to fill that up," Jake said. "What the hell did they use that for? Swimming pool?"

"I don't know," Gab said. "It's always been dry long as I remember."

"What was in all these barrels?" I asked.

"Just farm stuff," Gab said. "People dump everything here. Look, there's an old sofa, a tricycle. I guess they think they're saving dumping fees, but it makes me mad."

In places the wind had scoured, wheat stubble poked through the snow. We walked a couple hundred yards across drifts and scours, then stood on the edge of the basalt rim overlooking the deep canyon. The bottom was swallowed by snowfall so you couldn't see the Lost.

"Over there." With a mittened hand, Gab pointed to a long saddle that ran about three hundred yards downslope, ending in a cliff face. "Those are the pits." Two dark circles stood at the far edge of the saddle.

"The geese come up both draws or fly low right over the point, depending on the weather. I love this kind of hunting," Gab said. "You don't have to drag out decoys or screw around with a boat. I even left the dog at the house. She's getting old. Loves to hunt but not when it's this cold."

We covered the distance to the pits in about ten minutes. The saddle was rugged and rocky, providing treacherous footing. The men were huffing and puffing by the time we arrived. I was a little tired, but felt in good shape because of basketball.

"You and Billyum take the left pit," Jake said. "Gab and I will shoot from the right."

"How come you always take that pit?" Billyum asked.

"I like shooting left-winged geese," Jake said. "They taste better. Anyway, our pit's more comfy."

Neither pit was luxurious. Each was a slight depression in the terrain circled with a pile of basalt rocks about five feet high. Some of the rocks had spilled off the wall with erosion and frost heaves, but the remaining walls seemed pretty solid, held by the frozen ice. The pits were about six feet in diameter, just big enough for two hunters. But the rocks were hard and cold. You had to sit, kneel, or squat so the geese couldn't see your head and shoulders above the pits. None of the positions were comfortable.

"These places get worse every year," Billyum said. "Let's take up a collection and buy some pillows or beanbag chairs."

"These pits are the *pits*," Jake said. "Next time we'll go to Billyum's place. Don't even need a federal waterfowl stamp to hunt there."

"Wind's getting worse." Billyum hunkered. "These rocks aren't much help. Cold wind just whistles through the gaps." He took out the thermos of coffee and poured a cup, then offered it to me. "Steady your nerves."

I took off my mittens to hold the cup, and the warmth felt good. Billyum had doctored the coffee with whiskey. "Makes the wait shorter," he said.

"Are you contributing to the delinquency of a minor?" Jake called. "I thought I smelled happy coffee on the faint summer breeze."

"No you didn't," Billyum said. "Wind's blowing wrong." He sneezed. "Damn it! I'm going to be pissed if I catch a cold for the holidays. Have to go take the old Indian cure."

"What's that?" I said. "A sweat?"

"Sort of. Vitamin C and lots of whiskey. That makes you sweat good."

"I'll bet you wish you were on the river instead of freezing to death in this goose pit. You and Jake sure caught some monsters."

Billyum shifted his position. "These are the coldest, hardest, most miserable rocks I've ever been around. I'm sure Jake and Gab went out of their way to make this the worst pit." He glanced at the sky. "I'll bet we catch double pneumonia for nothing. I've never seen snow like this before Thanksgiving. Even old Sylvester says it's deeper than he can remember."

"Jake thinks the snow will keep the geese low. He says not to shoot until I see their feet."

Billyum grinned. "Big advice. Jake can't shoot straight. He brings me out here every year just to try and beat me. So far eleven to nothing." He took off his right glove and put his hand inside his coat, next to his warm belly. "Thaw my trigger finger."

"You guys shut up!" Gab called from the next pit. "We're listening for geese here. Which way's the wind blowing? Upcanyon I think. We should hear them when they lift off the river."

"Have Jake stick his thumb up his butt," Billyum called. "Heck, that'll tell you what way the warm wind blows."

I smiled. "If they come, they'll look like bathtubs, Jake says. That's how low."

"Thinking of bathtubs, I'm going to get in a nice hot one tonight," Billyum said to me. "About two hundred degrees. Too cold this time of year to go to the sweat house — jump in the river." He shivered. "Thank God, I'm no Finn."

"Did you and Jake sweat and fish that whole time you were on the river?" I asked.

Billyum squinted at me, the snowflakes settling on his lashes. "We hit the great steelhead holes on both sides. Ate like kings. Went to the sweat house." He took his hand out and put his glove back on. "Why are you asking?"

"I could have used some help in the store. That's all."

Billyum chuckled. "Jake finds any excuse he can to get on the river. You got to admit it beats work."

"Did you ever take my dad to the sweat house?"

"No," Billyum said. "He and I weren't as close as Jake and me. Now I wish I had. Sort of missed the chance."

"Well, at least Jake's still here," I said. "Both of them could have drowned when the boat went down."

Billyum furrowed his brow, remembering. "Well, Jake could have drowned going in after your dad. But he wasn't in the boat."

"No, that's not right. They were both going through Bronco Rapids."

Billyum shook his head. "Jake wasn't in the boat. He worked hard at drowning himself, but he was diving in from the shore."

In spite of the cold, Billyum's words made heated blood flush my face. I was about to protest again, but Billyum put his finger to his lips. "Here they come," he whispered. "Don't talk."

I heard them, too, the honkers coming upcanyon from the river.

"Keep your head low," he whispered. "They might spook."

Kneeling, I kept my head down, and felt the shock of Billyum's words numbing my neck and back. The honking grew louder and louder until it sounded like the geese were flying straight into the pit. Billyum had pulled his parka hood forward but tipped his head to one side, so he could watch without showing his face. The cold basalt stones pressed against my knees.

Compelled to look, I turned to face skyward and saw the huge geese lumbering upcanyon, dark silhouettes against the snow-washed sky. The combined beating of their wings sounded like a train.

As soon as he heard firing from the other pit, Billyum leapt to his feet, but I was slower. He fired twice, flame leaping from the gun barrel into the darkening sky, and I stood confused, the gun silent at my shoulder.

A goose to my right dropped from the sky, hitting the snow and frozen ground with a sickening thud, then lying still as a sack of potatoes. Another goose glided on one wing, hit fifty yards uphill, and somersaulted, but after a minute began flapping and hopping one-footed toward the wheat field. The wounded goose made sharp warning honks.

"Shit. I wish we'd brought the dog," Gab said. "Jake can't shoot turds in a toilet."

"At least I hit something," Jake said. "Old Gab the veteran goose guide killed about three million snowflakes. Fellas, I can't do any more for him. He bought the biggest gun I sell."

"You jostled my elbow, you loggerhead," Gab said.

Billyum winked at me and called out, "Would you guys hurry up and chase that goose? Another raft of them might head up and he'll scare them off, honking like that."

"Let him stiffen up," Jake said. "He's bleeding. I heard those pellets thump."

The goose continued flailing toward the wheat fields. He would go a way, then stop, making an erratic trail through the snow.

"Time's wasting, men. And it's getting dark," Billyum said.

Grumbling, Gab and Jake climbed out of their pit.

"Would you fellows mind handing me my goose, as long as you're getting out?" Billyum asked.

"Maybe Culver got the goose," Jake said. "It'd be just like you to go claiming credit for someone else's kill."

"A little goose fever?" Gab asked me. "I never saw you shoot."

"He's waiting for the big ones," Billyum said. "Hurry up or they'll flare."

Jake dropped over to the right side of the saddle and Gab to the left. By staying below the crown, they figured they could get close enough to shoot the goose again. It had stopped moving but was still honking. The cries seemed to be answered by the geese that had landed in the wheat field above.

"If you guys hear another flock coming, drop down and pretend to be rocks," Billyum called. "Don't spoil this hunt for me and Culver, or I'm not paying." He climbed out of the blind to retrieve his goose. With lowered voice he told me, "I could get dozens of these on the reservation but I can't resist coming along and showing up Jake."

Billyum returned to the blind carrying the goose by the neck. A dark spot showed on the head and two red drops on the large gray breast. "I always aim for the head," Billyum said. "But two pellets hit the breast. Jake must have sold me some bum shells." When he held the fallen goose out for me to inspect, I brushed the snow away from its feathers with my mittened hand.

"Look at those snow clowns." Billyum pointed to Gab and Jake, stumbling and sliding on the basalt side slopes, trying to get close enough to finish the wounded goose.

"We'll be lucky if Gab doesn't trip and roll all the way to the river.

Go goose hunting in a wheat field and drown." Billyum paused, realizing what he had said. "Sorry, I didn't think . . ."

"It's all right," I said. "Anyway, I wanted you to finish telling about the river. You were saying Jake wasn't in the boat."

Billyum rubbed his thighs, trying to improve the circulation. "I figured you already knew the story by heart." He gave me a long look. "No harm in telling it again, I guess." Billyum seemed to be measuring each word, getting it right. "No one belonged on the river that spring, not until the water settled down some. But those two brothers were hell-bent to get some early fishing. Well, I was, too, but I drove down to Bronco. You can get fairly close on our side.

"I was fishing the big eddy about halfway through the rapids — damn nice spot when it's clear — but the high water made it too roily. I stuck with it all day, then toward night I looked up and here comes your dad bobbing and weaving through the rapids, the boat riding high as a cork. He was good with the oars. In fact, I thought it was Jake — they looked a lot alike.

"I waved and shouted, but if he saw me he didn't show it. How could he, the way he had to row like hell? Maybe he was a quarter mile below me when he hit a big submerged log that floated down in winter. Stopped the boat dead and he started taking water.

"The boat was sinking fast, I knew that, so I started running downstream like a wild man. I pushed through a stand of thick jack pines, and when I came out into the clearing, he was gone. Water swept him out, I guess. I ran downstream, seeing if the current carried him ashore. No luck. The bow of the boat stayed above water awhile. The boat could have pinned him against a rock.

"Then I saw Jake on the other side. For just a minute, I thought he got out, but when he started diving into the water, I realized he was after your father. Jake went in and got as close to those rocks as he could. I yelled, but he was concentrating on the river. He had an extra life jacket with him and he kept holding it out, like a parent holds out a child's coat while they look for him outside — you see that sometimes."

Billyum peered over the pit at the two men struggling toward the goose. The snow made it hard to see, but they were almost even with the bird, and both came stumbling up the side slope onto the saddle. Gab tried angling ahead of the goose, cutting it off, but he fell and didn't rise for a moment.

"I'll bet that hurt," Billyum said.

He returned to his story. "I never saw a man work so hard at drowning himself. Time after time, he went into that freezing water, until I knew he was going to stay under, too. 'Get out, you dumb bastard!' I shouted. Or something like that. But he wouldn't quit. Finally, I took my three fifty-seven Magnum out and fired a few rounds in his direction just to get his attention." Billyum chuckled. "When those bullets hit around him, he finally understood my drift. He crawled back to the bank and just sat there, holding the empty life preserver."

Billyum shook his head. "Those boys were too reckless that spring, I guess. But even if they had stopped to study the rapids, I don't think they'd have seen that submerged log. I went and flagged that bastard the next day, and when the water lowered, a diver went down and blasted it clear with dynamite. That's pretty much the story."

Jake started running helter-skelter over the snow-covered rocks until he was close enough to fire. Seeing him coming, the goose cut back toward us and Jake fired, a flame tongue leaping from the gun barrel in the dusk. Gab fired, too, and we saw snow fly around the goose, but it turned back toward the wheat field, flapping its good wing and honking.

Jake fell down, cursed, and was up again. Billyum slapped his knees. "This is better than a greased-pig chase at the county fair," he said. Jake stopped, planted himself, fired again. Finally, the goose lay still. Above us, we heard a raft of geese climbing high, away from the shooting.

"I'm not taking that goose," Billyum said. "More buckshot than bird." Taking out his pocketknife, he cut a notch in his own bird's wing. His cold hands fumbled with the blade. "Just so Jake doesn't try pulling an old switcheroo." He looked at me — eye level. "I thought you knew all about your dad's drowning."

"Pretty much," I said, trying to keep my voice steady. "I just always thought Jake was in the boat. That's all."

"Jake dresses up a story from time to time, but he gets the main parts right." Billyum chuckled. "By the time we hit town, he will have shot that goose seventy yards overhead, clean as a whistle. Like I say, he tells the main parts right. Probably he wishes he was in the boat. I know how bad he feels, even now. Sometimes I think maybe he'll talk about it during our sweats, but he never says a word. That's how I know."

Jake and Gab floundered back toward the blind. At this distance my uncle seemed small and clumsy as he picked his way across the saddle.

When they were about halfway back, Billyum yelled, "Get down! Geese!"

They both hunkered and I did, too, even though I hadn't heard the geese calling. After thirty seconds Billyum yelled, "Sorry, fellas, false alarm. I guess it was one of those Russian satellites. Looked kind of like a goose though."

"Smart-ass," Gab said when they were back. "Hit my knee on a rock. Scratched my gunstock falling down, too."

"The practice did you good. You seemed a little stiff getting up though."

"Twisted my ankle going after that damn goose."

"Let me see your goose," Jake said to Billyum. "I think this one's a little bigger."

"Bullshit," Billyum said. "Yours is *heavier* because you shot it six or eight times. Mine's practically a virgin. I notched the wing, too, so don't try to pull an old switcheroo."

Grumbling, Gab and Jake climbed back into their pit. It was almost too dark to shoot; we were past the legal hours.

"Getting late," Gab said. "Fifteen more minutes. My balls are blue."

"This is the time they come again," Billyum told me. "Don't go firing at the whole flock. Choose one target and keep shooting. Sometimes they're hard to bring down. Get one that's off a little ways. They fly so close, the shot pattern's too tight."

Another raft of geese lifted off the river, and we could hear them calling as they winged toward us.

"Last chance, ladies," Billyum said.

This time I stood and fired, selecting a big goose off to the left, giving it a solid lead. With my first shot it flinched midair, and with the second crumpled, falling to the ground with that terrible thud.

Billyum got another goose, too. Jake and Gab argued over which gun had knocked down the third. "You weren't even shooting out this side of the pit," Gab complained.

"I tried," Jake said, "but when I swung that direction, my gun jabbed your fat ass. That's the only goose you got all day."

"I thought that jab was your other thing," Gab said, "since I could barely feel it."

"I suppose I have to let you keep it," Jake said. "This being your place and all. It's not like you can't go hunting every damn day, if you want."

Snow continued falling as we headed back toward the rigs in the dark. Everyone carried a goose; Billyum packed two. I stayed quiet, unwilling to join their joshing about poor shooting and bloodshot geese. Jake claimed he was going to have to confiscate Billyum's birds because he didn't have a waterfowl stamp.

"Anyway, you shot those on the white side," Jake said.

"Hell, this is all Indian country," Billyum said. "Now we want it back."

Tripping on hidden rocks, I fell down twice. The second time I lay still a moment while the men walked ahead. Seeing I wasn't with them, Jake paused and called back, "Hurry up, nephew. What are you doing? Making snow angels?"

For a moment, I flapped my arms and legs in exaggerated fashion. They laughed and moved on. I lay still, snow falling onto my face from a dark sky.

By the time we reached the house, I was shivering with cold and anger at Jake. "You've taken a bad chill," Gab said. "Your teeth are chattering." He took me inside while Jake and Billyum headed for the garage to clean the geese.

"I'm sticking with Jake," Billyum said. "Can't trust him with my goose or Culver's. I've seen him notch every goose's wing. Try eating his goose, you'll be a victim of lead poisoning or die of the dentist bill."

On the back porch, I shucked my wet clothes and Gab offered me an oversized sweatshirt. "Put your wet pants on the heater to dry," he said. "It's okay to be around Priscilla in long johns. We raised a boy."

She had a big pot of chili on the stove and I could smell corn bread, too. On the way to the bathroom for a hot shower, I smelled something else, the fragrant scent of flowers. After showering and warming up, I found a good-size workroom filled with dried flowers, wreaths, and sachets.

Priscilla came into the room and I felt a little embarrassed in my long johns, even though she didn't appear to notice. "Feeling better? Gabby said you had a chill."

"Froze to death out there," I said. "Better now, thanks." Nodding toward the flowers, I added, "These smell terrific."

"I grow almost half an acre of flowers," she said, "then combine them with wildflowers. Domestics can be too sweet, even dried, and the wild are a little faint, so I like the mix." She paused. "I've got to do something way out here. Gabby's away so much. I go from one hobby to the next, what with the kids grown. Stewart was the last. Left three years ago."

She went down the hall a little farther. "Come here. I want to show you something. Opening a door, she revealed a young man's bedroom with pictures of sports figures, trucks, and cars. But what got my attention were all the trophies — elk, deer, antelope, even a moose.

"This is Stewart's room," she said. "He's away at the University of Montana. I wanted him to go to Minnesota, my alma mater, but he insisted the hunting was better in Montana." She laughed a little. "Just look at these. I swear, I don't know when he finds time to study."

"What's he studying?" I asked.

"Journalism," she said. "Gabby figures he can find him a spot. Maybe Boise or Denver. Of course, Stewart imagines he's going to do stories on big trophy hunts to Kenya, that sort of thing."

She had adorned the trophies' antlers with colorful flower wreaths. Some wreaths decorated their necks as well, and they reminded me of those surprised tourists arriving in Hawaii to have leis put around their necks by grass-skirted girls.

"I like hanging the wreaths in here and admiring them a little before selling them," Priscilla said. "The gift shops in Central and the flower shops seem to do pretty well with them."

"She's being too darned modest," Gab said. "She can't make them fast enough."

Gab had taken off his boots, so I hadn't heard him in the hallway. He was wearing his long johns, too, and that made me feel a little more comfortable. A bloodstain covered one of his knees, and I realized he had hurt himself falling.

"Gabby, you're hurt," she said. "We'll have to soak that knee with Epsom salts."

"Later. Right now, I'm hungry enough to eat a horse."

"Just a minute." She removed one of the dried wreaths from the elk's antlers and handed it to me. "Do you think your mother would like this?"

"Yes, thanks."

"I'll send along some sachets, too. They'll keep her house smelling fresh during winter. Gateway gets pretty bleak by February."

"Thanks." The smell of the room reminded me a little of my mother's room, with its perfumes and soaps. The trophies seemed odd among all the flowers. But it was good being in the house after freezing outside in the hard pits.

His parents were obviously proud of Stewart, and I wondered what it must be like to have a complete family. Until that afternoon, I felt that if anything happened to my mother, I at least had Jake. But Billyum's words had left me confused. I didn't understand why things couldn't be easier.

Gab and I sat at the table in the warm kitchen while Priscilla started ladling big bowls of chili. "Do you want to wait for Jake and Billyum?" she asked.

"We'll wait like pigs at a trough." Gab thumped the table. "Let's eat."

When my mother had time to cook, she made her potato soup, Riley's favorite. She fried bacon to put in the soup so the entire house took on that delicious aroma. Both Riley and I tried sneaking pieces of bacon when her back was turned, and she had to fry twice the amount she expected to put in the soup.

Now, sitting in Priscilla's warm kitchen, I enjoyed the chili, the sweet butter she spread on the corn bread. Temporarily, I forgot my anger and anxiety.

Cold air gripped my back and neck when Jake and Billyum burst through the door. I felt the harsh draft collapse my reverie and smelled the pungent odor of dead geese on their hands and clothes.

"For its size, you guys got the heaviest damn goose I ever saw," Billyum said to Gab. "Eat that thing and you'll sink like a stone if you try and go swimming." Turning to Priscilla, he added, "Things sure smell great."

"I'm starving," Jake said. "My stomach thinks my throat's been cut."

28

HALF AN HOUR AFTER LEAVING Gab's place, we were in the middle of a desolate flat and hadn't passed a farmhouse for miles. We rode along in silence, Jake's mouth tight as he concentrated on the road. I knew he was tired from the cold and hunt. Exhausted myself, I kept playing things over in my mind, the way you do when your body's fatigued but your mind refuses to shut down. One of the things I kept seeing was my father's clear signature on his license and the way my own had smeared after the near drowning in Combine Rapids. When I had placed the licenses side by side, the paper in mine had turned odd and brittle, the way it does after a soaking. More than anything else, I kept going over Billyum's account of the boat wreck.

Jake took one hand off the steering wheel and rubbed his eyes. "Damn near snowblind. I keep imagining horses."

"Nothing out there but snow," I said.

"I thought maybe you were asleep with your eyes stuck open. I've seen it happen."

"I keep thinking about things," I said.

"What kind of things? You got girl troubles? Your mom would have a shitfit."

"That's not it," I said.

He went on. "You know how to use a rubber, don't you? If you don't have any, we'll get some from the druggist. Can't have any accidents."

"I know how rubbers work," I said. "But I am thinking about an accident."

257

He caught my drift. He blinked the way people do when smoke shifts their way. "Having nightmares about Seaweed again? That's blood under the bridge."

I shook my head. "The accident I'm thinking about happened way back."

His eyes cut to me. "So."

I only knew what Billyum had said. "I know everything."

Jake laughed a little, trying to stay light. "That's an old joke. All the important men in town get an anonymous letter that says, 'They know everything. Flee at once.' And the scared sons of bitches bolt like rabbits trying to outrun crooked business deals, cheated wives, illegitimate kids —"

"I know everything about my father's accident." I watched Jake's face, but nothing registered at first.

"We've been over that." His tone seemed too normal.

"Sure, but Billyum was telling me about it, too. He said you weren't even in the boat."

Jake kept his eyes straight ahead and it took him a moment to answer. "Billyum was drinking like hell in those days. Hate to say it, but he was pie-eyed. I doubt he remembers much of anything."

Billyum's drinking was a possibility I hadn't considered. Even so, I didn't believe Jake. "Come on. Billyum's your friend. Don't go bad-mouthing him."

Jake swallowed. "What's the point of picking that old scab?"

"I don't want to be lied to," I said. "Especially about my father. For God's sake, can't you tell the truth about your own brother?"

His face went rigid in the glow of the dashlights. He concentrated on the road, the swipe, swipe, swipe of the wipers clearing the snow. Ice built up in the corners of the windshield.

"That vest you gave me never went down with the boat. My dad's signature on the license is as clear as the day he signed it. When I compared it to mine after I'd been in the Combine, I saw the difference plain as day. And that photo of him and Harold would be pulp, if it was on the river bottom like you said."

"I just wanted you to have the vest, that's all."

"Tell me, damn it. I've got to know the real story."

"All right, but it shouldn't go any further. Understand?" He took a long time before saying anything else. "Billyum wasn't drinking — let's get that clear first — and I wasn't in the boat. Your dad tackled Bronco alone."

"Why?"

"Don't rush me, damn it." Jake concentrated on the road, but his stare seemed to go beyond. "We argued, a bad one, and your dad clipped me good. He had taken off his vest and dropped it on the ground so he could hit harder. I glanced away, didn't expect it. But he was spitting mad.

"Worst punch I ever took. Made me groggy. I just lay there smelling weeds, and when my head cleared a little, the boat was in the river. 'Walk back, you son of a bitch!' Dave yelled.

"The high rapids took the boat, and it was a millrace. I stumbled along the bank, still groggy, but yelling for him to bring the boat to shore. He kept going, made it through the worst part of the rapids. That second stretch is bad, too, though. The boneyard.

"I kept running, scrambling up to the railroad tracks to make better time. He did everything right, kept to the best channel, approached the tongue right, but the boat hung on a submerged log. I was still a hundred yards away when it sank. He hung on as long as he could, but the current swept him out."

"You had his life preserver?" I remembered what Billyum had said about the extra preserver.

Jake nodded. "He'd dropped that, too, I guess, so he could really paste me. I picked it up by instinct. Anyway, there's that long, deep pool below the rapids. I kicked off my boots and kept diving in. I never stopped until Billyum shot toward me. I didn't even know he was watching. I was just concentrating on finding Dave in all that water." He paused. "Things might have been better if Billyum plugged me."

He didn't expect me to deny it and I wouldn't. "You lied to my mother?"

Jake nodded. "Flora didn't need to know everything. She already lost a husband and had a young boy. Things were going to be tough enough."

"What was the argument about?"

Jake shook his head. "That's just between your dad and me."

Neither of us spoke all the way back to town. Jake tried the radio and we got Patsy Cline and George Jones. The night announcer came on, warning everybody about the cold.

"It'll hit ten below," he said. "A November record. Cozy up to your sweetie and keep your dog curled by your feet."

Weary with fatigue, I closed my eyes and saw my father riding through the rapids. Standing high above him on a steep cutbank, I shouted a warning, but he kept rowing through the chute. When I tried running downstream, the earth gave way beneath me, and I plunged toward whitewater.

My eyes flew open, and I realized we were fishtailing on the ice. I was thrown hard against the passenger door.

As Jake straightened the rig, I slid toward him, but he elbowed me away. "That's always been a bad spot," Jake said.

My teeth began to chatter.

Jake fiddled with the heating control again, but it still seemed freezing in the cab. Glancing my way, he said, "You're shaking like a rat in a dog's mouth."

☆ ☆ ☆ ☆

I trudged through the snow carrying my shotgun, the goose, and the sack of flowers. All seemed incredibly heavy. I'd asked Jake to drop me off four blocks from home. I imagine neither of us wanted to face my mother that night, but I had no choice. Passing the illuminated windows of houses, I had the wild urge to load the shotgun and fire through the steamy panes at the curtains, shattering each family's outward tranquillity.

Reluctant to go inside once I reached our place, I remained on the doorstep. Then I brushed some snow from the goose and gun case and pushed inside.

"Goodness. You startled me." Putting down an issue of *Sunset*, Mom rose from the love seat and gave me a quick hug. "Did you have a good time, sweetheart? I was so worried you might get frostbite." She spotted the goose.

"Look at that! Did you shoot it yourself? I bought a turkey just in case you didn't have any luck, but we can freeze it for Christmas. A big holiday goose! I can't believe it. I selected a wonderful recipe out of a magazine."

She was genuinely excited, even though she didn't like game coming in the front door. "Where's Franklin?" I asked.

"Back at his place wrapping the pipes. He did that here already with some electrical tape. Wasn't that thoughtful of him? I'd hate to be without water for the holiday or have a big flood later on." Some snow was melting off the goose, and she stared at the water dripping from its feet. "Carry that right into the kitchen, please. And take off those wet clothes before you catch your death. Then sit down and tell me all about it."

I threw the goose and flowers on the table and went into the bedroom. Taking the shotgun out of the case, I worked the pump several times, making certain no shells remained.

She rapped on the door. "What's that racket? Have you taken off your boots yet, Culver? Honey, you've got to be more careful. You've dripped water all across the kitchen floor."

After pausing for breath, she continued. "Where did you get those beautiful flowers? I couldn't resist taking a peek. Hope I didn't spoil your surprise."

She moved away from the door and I heard her preparing tea. After a few minutes, I came out wearing dry long johns, wool socks, and my father's old robe. Keeping silent, I sat at the table. The flowers remained, but she had moved the goose to the sink.

As she stirred around, she kept talking. "I honestly believe you men are crazy, going out in this freezing weather. Culver, put your feet right over the heat vent. I turned up the thermostat. Getting chilled the way you have, I anticipate you'll experience chilblains. Now where exactly did you get those flowers?"

It was difficult to speak, but I managed to say "Priscilla."

"Oh, Gab's wife. Well, I'll have to write her a thank-you note." She glanced out the window. "Absolutely crazy to wander off in this weather. It froze your brain. I know you weren't born in a barn, but you never plop a dead goose on the kitchen table, until it's cooked, of course. Next time, please put it directly in the sink."

The teakettle began whistling and she poured two cups of hot water. Taking a pint bottle of Monarch rum out of the cupboard, she added some to each cup. "Just a splash. I don't think it'll stunt your growth, this one time. After all, a goose calls for a celebration. The girls at work are going to be so jealous when I tell them we had *wild* goose." She was beaming.

"It's some goose, all right," I said.

"It's a *marvelous* goose. And you brought it home. Culver, you could talk yourself up a little more. Sometimes you're as quiet as an oyster."

She set a teacup in front of me and sat. "Well, at least you spoke a whole sentence. I guess your tongue's defrosted." She sipped her tea, then touched the flowers. "These are pretty. I like the fragrance. So, how was the hunt? You better start talking."

I drank some of the tea, feeling the rum settle in my belly. I took another drink. "Mom, Jake wasn't in the boat when Dad drowned."

She brushed back her hair with her fingertips. "What's this about a boat? You were goose hunting." Her brow furrowed as her rush of enthusiasm faded.

"Mom, they argued. Jake wasn't in the boat."

Her mouth became a thin line. "Surely Jake had better sense than to take out a boat in this horrible weather. There's ice in the river. He told me you were going to Gab's place. Isn't that way above the river out in the wheat fields somewhere?"

"I'm not talking about today. Please listen. When Dad drowned, Jake wasn't in the boat."

"That accident was years ago." Her eyes clouded. "What are you talking about?"

I leaned forward. "They had a big fight. Dad knocked Jake down and took off through the rapids by himself."

She gripped the teacup, letting go when it became too hot. "Why are you bringing this up? Tomorrow's Thanksgiving and Franklin's coming over."

"I want to know what happened. That's all."

"*Your . . . father . . . drowned.*" She emphasized each word. "Those men had absolutely no business on the river that spring. I told them." She paused. "You were just a child."

"Mom, what was the argument about?"

She picked up the flowers and studied them. "I wonder how she dries them. The colors remain so vivid."

"Mom?"

She dropped the flowers. "Why don't you ask Jake? He's the one stirring up trouble."

I shook my head. "It wasn't Jake. Billyum told me."

"He's as bad as the rest of them," she said. "Just because he's Indian makes no difference."

"It was about you, wasn't it? They fought over you." I don't know how I knew, but I did.

Her eyes flashed. "I wasn't even there." Abruptly, she seized the flowers and stood. "Why would you even imagine such a thing? I knew Jake was a terrible influence, but who expected anything like this wild story? If you were younger, I'd wash out your mouth with soap."

Her eyes teared, but she didn't cry. I stood up, too, and we stared at each other across the table. I felt terrible but wouldn't lower my gaze.

"I'm not wallowing in the past," she said hoarsely. "What's done is done. I'm working for our future."

"If there's more to it, maybe we should get the truth out, Mom. Clear the air."

"I'm certainly not going to discuss this unpleasant matter any more tonight. I was upset all day long, worrying about you. Now, to tell you

262

the truth, I've had an even bigger shock." She moved toward her bedroom, gripping the flower wreath like a life preserver.

I remained sitting a few minutes, then threw open the back door and trudged out into the snow in my stockinged feet. Over and over again, I cursed as loud as I could, until the cold air stung my lungs and I couldn't regain my wind. Exhausted, I might have frozen to death, a numbed statue, if a police car hadn't stopped in front of our house.

A young cop came around back and shone his flashlight in my face. "You live here, kid?"

I nodded.

"One of the neighbors called in a complaint. You got anyone inside?" He shone the light on my robe and sock-clad feet.

"My mother," I said after a few moments. "She might be asleep." I could hear the police car engine running. A bulletin came over the radio.

"Well, you better pack it in and close the door. Pipes might freeze."

"We got 'em wrapped," I said.

He shone the light on my feet again. "All *your* plumbing might freeze. This cold weather's a bitch." He paused. "You going anyplace for Thanksgiving?"

I shook my head. "We're cooking a goose."

"Well, it's not New Year's, so try to hold it down."

I went inside, closing the door softly. As the cop drove away, I could hear the tick-tick-tick of his tire chains. Part of me wanted to climb into the warmth of that car and go someplace where I wouldn't have to think about anything for a while.

My teeth chattered a long time, even though I took a hot-water bottle to bed and wore wool socks and long underwear. When I awakened toward dawn, I wasn't cold because my mother had gotten in bed with me. Pressed against my back, she had flung one arm across my chest, holding tight. For a few pleasant moments, before recall struck, I thought I was a small child again. Turning to hold her, I smelled the cold in her hair and I awakened.

"I was freezing," she said. "The whole house was terribly cold."

I remembered leaving the door open and realized I had no idea how long I had remained outside. "The police came last night."

She shifted toward the edge of the bed. "Of course they did. I called them. You were making a horrible racket."

After getting up, she studied her reflection in the speckled mirror above my pine dresser. "I'm not stopping traffic this morning," she said. "Good thing it's hours before Franklin comes." She looked my way.

"You're not exactly Prince Charming either. Give me five minutes and then stir yourself." She hesitated. "I've decided to tell you what I remember, but you've got to get up. I'm preparing a big dinner and we'd better whip this house into shape."

The goose lay on the cutting board. My mother whacked off the head with a heavy butcher's knife, then chopped the wings just below the elbows. After dropping the pieces in the garbage can, she made a face. "Who wants to look at those eyes."

Shivering, I sat at the kitchen table, glad the oven was on preheat, the room warm. She rubbed the insides of the goose with lemon juice and salt. Taking a sharp paring knife, she pricked the skin on the breast and thighs in several places. "This allows the excess fat to run out," she explained. "Although maybe the shot holes already do that."

She rinsed her hands, then wiped them on the towel and sat opposite me. "Ready?" she asked. When I nodded, she said, "Here goes. It seems like a movie, not like anything that really happened."

I nodded. The past twenty-four hours felt like that.

"Your father was a wonderful man — considerate and sweet. There wasn't a mean bone in his body." She fussed with the shoulder straps on her apron. "But he worried so. Fretted and stewed. Blew things out of proportion." She paused. "I've never said an unkind thing about him. I've always held him up as a role model, but you wanted to know."

I nodded. "What kinds of things did he blow out of proportion?"

"The store, his father's illness, you — how to support the family." She counted each item on her fingers. "We were doing okay. Sometimes his worry ruined our good times. I remember the year after you were born, we went to the beach. It was a fabulous day. The sun was so warm, no wind, and we fed the seagulls stale bread. One took a piece from your tiny hand. Later you laughed and laughed as we held you in the waves." Her eyes shone, remembering. "But even then, as I watched your father in a quiet moment, he seemed troubled. When I asked, he only said, 'I wish the good times could last.'" She slapped both hands against her thighs. "Well, that's exactly how he could be."

She stood and returned to the goose, filling the cavity with chopped onions, apples, and celery. "Franklin doesn't like carrots in the stuffing." After placing the extra dressing into a bowl, she continued. "Your father's moods made things difficult at times. He gave me the sense things were so . . . transient. You see, it wasn't fair. I had you, I was young. It should have been the happiest time of my life."

I didn't know how to respond.

"Even when your grandfather died, although God knows it was a blessing, Dave mooned around for months. Jake just said, 'No clock keeps ticking forever. The old man had a pretty fair run.'"

She skewered the goose's legs and placed it on a roasting pan, breast side down. Measuring a cup of white wine, she took a couple sips, then poured half the rest on the goose. "Jake was always too confident. One time when your father was really blue, I went to see Jake." She refilled the measuring cup and had some more wine. "You know what I mean."

I didn't answer.

"Maybe it lasted three months. Of course it was a mistake, but I can't change it. We broke off right before that trip to the Barn Hole. God, but I felt wretched about everything. I never went fishing with them again." Turning to face me, she said, "I'm so terribly sorry it ever came up. The important thing as I see it is not to dwell on the past."

"But they fought about it, don't you see? Dad went into the rapids alone and drowned."

A veil seemed to hide her eyes. "I regret that. Don't think it hasn't been tough without him. But I'm not taking the responsibility. He and Jake had no business on the river that spring, especially your father. He had a child, a family . . ." She dropped her hands into her lap. "Well, I'm sure Jake goaded him into it." She drew a breath. "I just can't believe Jake lied about the accident all these years."

"He was keeping you out of it, trying to make you feel better."

Her laugh was harsh. "That sounds so noble. Don't forget, he was keeping *himself* out of it. When it comes to Jake, you're still wearing blinders. It was all self-interest."

I stood, moving to the back door and staring out its small window at the garbage can mounded with snow. Overwhelmed and confused, I had wanted to hear the truth, but believed I had made things worse now. The cruelest notion was that once I had dreamed Jake and my mother would get together. Learning they already had was a bitter pill.

29

 PIECES OF BURNED GOOSE lay scattered across Jake's backyard along with a blackened roasting pan and some burned carrots and onions. A cat had dragged part of the goose over by the woodpile and was chewing on a wing. Blackbirds picked at some fat scraps in the pan and scattered across the yard. Jake's rig was out front but he wasn't answering the door. I took the spare key off the tree limb and unlocked the back door.

Inside, the kitchen smelled like burned goose; dishes cluttered the table and sink. From beyond the kitchen came another smell — the rich odor of smoking tobacco.

Hunting and fishing gear were spread all across the front room. Jake had taken apart several reels and rifles for cleaning. But now he was sitting in the big armchair looking at photograph albums. A bottle of Seagram's Seven Crown whiskey and a tumbler filled with ice cubes were on a TV tray beside the couch. The tumbler featured a leaping deer.

"Did you help yourself to some goose, nephew?" His grin was a little crooked.

"What happened? It's a disaster out back. I thought you were taking that goose to Juniper's."

He shrugged. "The oven went kaput. Or maybe the recipe was lousy. Naw, I just fell asleep. Woke up to a houseful of smoke and pitched the whole mess out back."

"What about Juniper?"

"We ate at the lodge. Orange pheasant in a clay pot. Delicious but damn slow service. No one wants to work Thanksgiving. How about you? The holiday go okay?"

"We got through it," I said. "Franklin was all right. They're off shopping now. The day after Thanksgiving all the Christmas sales start." Jake hadn't opened the sporting goods store and I wanted to find out why. "You know, Franklin's real decent to Mom."

"Well, she deserves it." He lifted his tumbler. "Bully for him."

"If you want to know the truth, she and I talked about a lot of things before he came over."

Jake squinted. "What kind of things?"

"She told me what happened, you know, between you and her."

"Well, bully for her, too." Jake poured a little more of the Seagram's into the tumbler. "She's always had pluck. I'll give her that." He nodded toward the kitchen. "You want a drink?"

"Not exactly." But after a minute, I went into the kitchen and got a tumbler full of ice and a Pepsi, then returned to the front room. "I just want to know why," I said after sitting down. "How could you do such a thing to your own brother?"

Jake frowned at his glass. "That's the sixty-four-thousand-dollar question, isn't it? Answer it right and you come out of the isolation booth. Don't think I haven't asked myself that one a lot over the years. I think I've got it, more or less."

"Shoot. I'm listening."

He leaned forward. "I wanted Juniper in those days, but things couldn't work right between us. Times were different, between whites and Indians, I mean. She decided to head for Albuquerque, get involved in the art game down there. Maybe she wanted some distance, too." He set the glass on the table and clasped his hands. "Things went bust, like I say, and to tell the truth, I guess I got jealous. Dave had your mother. He had you. Still, he went around like a dark cloud spoiling a picnic."

Jake spread his hands. "So after Juniper left, I felt pretty lousy, mean-spirited, got to feeling sorry for myself. One day when Dave was being a real pissant, I saw this look in your mother's eyes. And I took advantage." He paused. "Maybe it went on a couple months. That's the whole sordid story, fella. The rest you know."

"No, I don't. How did he figure it out?"

Jake's voice seemed far away. "I always thought she told him."

I shook my head. "She didn't want to hurt him."

Jake shrugged. "Maybe he guessed."

Taking an ice cube into my mouth, I held it until the numbness spread. I felt as cold as my father lying on the river bottom. "Anyway, Juniper's back now. But my dad's not coming back."

"No, he isn't." Jake spoke quietly. "And she's heading south right after Christmas."

I was surprised but didn't say anything.

"Something about the Havasupais. People of the blue-green water. Petroglyphs, moonflowers. Waterfalls and deep pools. She plans to paint the whole shebang. But painting's not the only reason. There's a division between us again."

"What's that?"

"She's upset about this business with Kalim. Claims I'm holding something back. Billyum, too. She doesn't trust anybody." He laughed and it was bitter. "Hell, I'd do about anything for that woman. But you can't spill out everything that's in your guts. Nobody can take it."

"Do you blame her for not trusting you?" My words struck a blow and it felt good.

He took a drink and I heard his teeth break ice. "No."

"Meeks and Chilcoat aren't coming back either," I said.

He eyed me. "No," he said, "I don't believe they are."

"The way Grady keeps nosing around, I wonder if you know anything about that."

"Not really. I know one advantage of living in a small town is that wise guys have lots of opportunities to kill themselves. Driving drunk. Shooting each other over women. Hunting when they're liquored up. One thing I've got to admit, those boys chose unusual circumstances." He took a picture from the book in front of him. "Strange accidents happen. Come look at this."

I didn't move. I felt as cold as I had during summer in the icehouse, sitting on large blocks of ice until my spine numbed. "I don't feel sorry for you," I said. "All your life, you've done exactly what you wanted." I leaned forward.

"Maybe you're mad, got your dander up," he said. "Think you want to punch somebody?"

I straightened a little. "Last night I did. Today, I don't care. Maybe tomorrow I'll feel like slugging something."

"Hang a punching bag in the back of the store. Work out."

"I'm not going to be around the store much anymore." Flat gray ice was in my voice. "I thought with Christmas coming up, you better schedule Jed for more hours."

"I can do that," Jake said. "Suit yourself."

Leaning back, still holding the picture, he closed his eyes, and his deep breathing indicated he had dozed. I sat, drinking my Pepsi. I couldn't tell why I was hanging around. I knew things would never be the same between us, but I couldn't bring myself to leave yet. Riley was right, I decided. I was too soft.

"Stop!" Jake's body flinched and his eyes flew open. "Thought I smelled smoke!" After a minute he settled down. "Hell, I did smell smoke. Burned goose and Prince Albert."

"Did you start smoking the pipe?" I asked. It lay beside the chair in the ashtray.

"I'll have a pipe or two during the holidays," Jake said. "The old man always smoked Prince Albert. He'd sit in the chair, just like I'm doing, and read the *Gazette,* making sure all his work came out okay.

"After hunting season, Dave and I spread our gear across the living room for cleaning and inspection. The old man didn't inspect too carefully since he didn't want to leave the chair, but he was pretty good at giving orders. 'Clean this. Oil that. Keep your equipment in top shape boys. Take care of it and it'll take care of you.'

"Mom gave us two days to mess up the front room. After that we packed away our gear. Even though it was before Christmas, the old man usually had a present to add to our supplies. Oversized goose decoys one year since we could still hunt geese until late January. Hand warmers. Thermal socks. The front room smelled of banana oil, Huberd's shoe grease, silicone, Gun-Blu for the barrel knicks. And the old man's pipe tobacco. Whenever I smell that tobacco, I still think about those good times."

He flipped through one of the photo albums. "So I lit the pipe to get rid of that awful burned-goose smell. I tried opening the doors for an hour, but it was too damn cold."

I closed my eyes a moment and tried to think of my father, Jake, and the old man checking over the equipment. But all I could see was my uncle and father fighting on the shore, then my father going through the rapids by himself. "I think I better head out," I said.

"Hang on a minute." Jake held up the picture. "You got to see this first. It was taken right after your dad and I finished our volunteer ambulance training."

I moved closer. They were posed beside an ambulance. Both had their right foot on the running board and were grinning eagerly at the camera. They wore white coats with dark medical patches on the sleeves that read "G V F D."

"Didn't we look sharp?" Jake tapped the photo. "See the creases in those trousers?"

"You looked sharp all right." I tried studying my father's face for the gloom Jake and my mother had described, but I didn't see it in this photo.

"On the way to Gab's place you were asking about horses," he said, "why they make me spooky. Not long after we started driving ambulance, your dad and I answered a call about some California tourists who ran into a herd of reservation horses during a big snowstorm. That was a terrible winter."

"Like now?"

"Sure, but this one might get worse. Anyway, whoever called was frantic and garbled her speech. The lines were icing up, and that was the last call from the rez, until the telephone line crew got out there three days later.

"She said the old Mission cutoff road, about a forty-minute run, but it took us twice that long because road conditions were so bad. We chained up, but the roads were still treacherous. Half a foot of new snow on top of several inches of ice. Maybe thirty inches' total accumulation. Deep drifts and high banks where the snowplows had been. And still coming down.

"We got to speculating how tourists wound up on the old Mission road. The reservation signs were never too good, and the wind made wet snow stick to what markers they had, so probably they couldn't read where they were headed. When we saw lights pointed off the road at a cockeyed angle, we slowed way down. Here was their rig, off in the barrow pit, but not flipped or anything. Except for the dead horse in front of the car, things didn't look too bad. The other horses were milling around but none seemed injured. The car's taillights were still on, engine running. And we could hear the radio playing pretty loud. Classic stuff. Who knows where they pulled that station in from?"

"At night you can get some pretty far-off stations," I said. "Riley had one in Texas he listened to. The tower of power."

Jake continued. "When I heard that engine running, it seemed almost cozy. Figured these folks had filled up with gas before hitting the reservation. The sign says sixty-four miles with no services and most people are cautious. Afraid that if they run out of gas and go for help, they'll get scalped. As soon as I stepped out of the ambulance, I checked the tailpipe and was glad to see exhaust. Sometimes that will plug with snow, and people die from carbon monoxide. Just get sleepy and drift off. In fact, I thought they might be asleep, the way they kind of leaned into each other. 'Got tired of waiting, huh?' I called out."

Jake took a drink of the Seagram's and sloshed the liquid around in the tumbler. "The horse they hit was lying just in front of the car. Stone dead. One headlight was working and we saw the blood steaming in the snow, how the horse had torn the ground up, the sparkling glass fragments. At first we thought they were ice crystals.

"Then we got right up to the car. Both people were dead. The man and his wife were turned toward each other, like they were talking maybe. But the fronts of their heads were all bashed and their faces just pulp. Dave and I stood stock dazed. When that horse came through the windshield, they froze and it kicked them to death. They never ducked, not that they could have avoided those hooves. Horse goes into a frenzy . . ."

I nodded, realizing why Jake had been so upset at the horses on the way to Gab's.

"We tried calling the accident in, but the radio wasn't much good way out there. We only heard crackling. I don't think I was ever so glad to have Dave with me. This was far worse than when we tried scaring each other as kids. Telling ghost stories in our dark bedroom. Testing our courage in the old house where a guy committed suicide. The neighborhood kids believed ghosts hung around." He paused. "But this horse deal was flat-out eerie.

"Then we saw lights coming, and Dave struck a couple flares, because we didn't want another car coming along hitting the horses. But it was Billyum, driving slow. The same frantic gal had called the tribal police. We never found out who she was. Billyum took out his flashlight and looked at the dead people. We had left the doors open to check their pulses so he reached in and switched off the radio and the ignition. It seemed even worse then. No noise except for our car engines, and the occasional nicker of the horses.

"'Let's chase these damn horses off the road,' Billyum said.

"Right about then, they turned spooky. Those horses had just been standing around for an hour, but maybe the wind shifted or something and they smelled the dead people. Snorting and whinnying, they took off running. We all piled into Billyum's rig and went after them, hoping to chase them off the road.

"Loggers had been doing some clear cutting in that part of the reservation, and cat roads occasionally cut through the high snowbanks. We figured if we could get them headed up one of those cat roads into the logged-off areas, they'd be okay. Billyum honked his horn and fired his pistol. The damn horses wouldn't leave the road. We chased them three or four miles. Twice they wheeled and tried cutting back, but they spooked and reversed when they faced our headlights.

"Finally, a couple of lead horses left the road, and we felt good as the others followed. 'Oh shit!' Billyum said suddenly, and when we got closer to the cut I saw why. It wasn't the cat road but the train crossing. Billyum stopped the rig and cursed. We could hear the horses running down the cleared track. The sound carried a long way because it had stopped snowing by then and turned clear and cold.

"He set flares at the crossing, then stared down the track in the direction of the horses. 'If I walk up there and try to set more flares to warn the train, the ornery devils might kill me,' Billyum said.

"'You can't get ahead of them anyway,' Dave said. 'If they turn back, you're dead. Maybe this snow has stopped the trains.'

"'You can't tell,' Billyum said. 'They're running way off schedule.'

"After we returned to the wreck, Billyum helped us load the two dead people in body bags and put them in the ambulance. I don't care how cold it was, I was sweating like the Fourth of July. Billyum planned to spend the rest of the night at the crossing in case those horses came back to the road. No cars had come along, so it seemed like a quiet watch.

"I had just closed the back doors of the ambulance when we heard the train whistle. No one said a word as we stood there waiting, but when we heard it again, it was much closer.

"'Going pretty fast,' Billyum said.

"The whistle shrieked, staying on steady this time, and after a few moments we started hearing the deep crunches as the train hit horse after horse after horse. The whinnying and screaming went on. 'Stop that fucking train,' Billyum whispered. He started counting. 'One-two-three-four-five-six.' Finally, he covered his ears because he didn't want to hear any more, but there were eleven altogether.

"After they got the train stopped, you could hear the horses. 'I sure hope they got a rifle on that train,' Billyum said. He was wishing someone would be kind enough to walk the track and shoot the wounded horses. But we didn't hear any shots and then the train started up. We climbed into Billyum's rig again and went to the crossing. He tried to flag the train but it flew by. After it was gone, you could still hear the screaming.

"'Sonofabitching railroad,' Billyum said. 'I got to walk the track, shoot those mangled bastards.'

"'We better go with you,' Dave said. And he was right. Billyum might not see one of the horses in the darkness until he got too close. It could knock him down with its last kick, leaving him to freeze in the night.

"'I appreciate the offer,' Billyum said as he drove us back to the ambulance. 'You better get those bodies to Gateway, call some relatives. Maybe make some more ambulance runs.'

"I guess he was right. Things were a mess out there, but what was done was done. In town we might still help somebody." Jake sipped his drink. "Billyum was sure nervous about those horses. Who could blame him? He wanted to end their suffering quickly, but he wasn't anxious about walking the track.

"'A long night,' Dave said as Billyum dropped us off. 'Nobody's getting off early. Nobody's getting paid overtime.'"

Jake rested his elbows on the sides of the chair. "That's about it. We drove back and made the calls. Tough duty for us, too. We had a hard time getting somebody living in Southern California overlooking a golf course to understand the snow and horses. None of those dead horses could be used for anything but glue. The meat was all bloodshot."

I nodded. "That's some story."

"I don't know exactly why I'm telling you," he said, as if he'd lost the drift himself. "But I'll always remember how glad I was to have Dave along that night. Billyum, too. I thought you might want to know about it. Your dad and I had a lot of other ambulance runs. Women having babies, kids with broken arms falling off bikes, guys that didn't know how to handle a chainsaw. They were always bad. But that horse accident was the worst. Dave and I talked about it lots of times. We wanted things to work out better, but they didn't. The damage was already done; we just made things worse. Maybe that's the handle I'm trying to grab when I tell you."

"All right," I said. "Well, I got to get going."

"Put the key back on the tree," he said. "Don't go sticking it in your pocket."

When I stepped outside it was dark. I could still see the pan, outlined against the snow. Snow was falling and a fresh layer covered it. The goose was gone, but the smell of burned goose and Prince Albert clung to my coat. I returned the key to the tree branch and just stood a while in the dark.

I didn't know what to think. Things were falling away from me in ways I didn't understand. Although I had wanted events to be simple and clear, they weren't. Everything seemed muddled and confused. I didn't trust either Jake or my mother anymore, especially Jake. I even suspected he might know more about Meeks and Chilcoat, but whenever I thought of the possibilities, a cold hand seized my neck and my thoughts shivered to a stop. I decided I needed to distance myself from these events and people or they would stop me like submerged logs.

When I walked to the front of the house, I heard Jake inside talking. I peered through the window and could see past a gap in the drapes. He lit the pipe and took a couple of puffs. After the tobacco was burning good, he held the pipe in his hand, gesturing toward someone across the room. "Take care of your equipment, boys, and it'll take care of you."

He smiled, holding the pipe in front of him, close to his nose. After taking a few deep breaths, he set it in the ashtray and leaned back, closing his eyes. "I'm just relaxing a minute. I'll be coming to bed soon."

I watched the pipe smoke rise toward the ceiling and disappear as quietly as ghosts. I didn't want to see any more of my uncle then, so I moved away quietly, leaving a single line of footprints in the falling snow.

30

 A WARM CHINOOK WIND began blowing in mid-December and the snow melted at an alarming rate. After two days of wind, it started raining hard, but the ground was still frozen. Water ran everywhere. Each gulley, ditch, bottom, stream, and creek overflowed. In Gateway the parking lots became pools and people waded more than walked. "Hope this is enough water for the fucking farmers," Sniffy said when I ran into him at the post office. The rising water had taken out his wife's garden and flooded their basement.

Going to the post office had become my duty. I had mailed the papers as Riley instructed, but several weeks had passed with no reply. My mother grew so nervous waiting for the divorce papers to come, her hands shook when she tried to work the mailbox combination lock. "I'm sick of waiting for that man to act," she said.

I still felt a cold anger toward her and Jake and believed any anxiety she felt was well deserved. However, I became worried in early December when she actually caught a hard flu and stayed in bed over a week, alternating chills and fever, cramps and nausea. In lucid moments she fretted she was going to lose her job. "I don't understand it," she said between sips of strong tea, the only thing she could keep on her stomach. "I'm almost never sick. It's worry touches me off."

She grew better, but the doctor's bills and prescriptions had set us back. She insisted on paying as she went and managed to sign the checks with a wavering hand, but I filled in the names and amounts. The flu had to run its course the doctor decided; neither he nor the drugs did much more than the aspirin. However, the bills were almost as much as our rent.

I understood how disappointed she'd be when I returned empty-handed from the post office once again, so I tried to cheer her up by giving her sixty dollars of Kalim's money.

She seemed pleased but surprised when I handed her two twenties and two tens that I carefully removed from my billfold.

"Where'd you get this?" she asked.

"It was in the post office box." I shrugged. "Riley must've sent it."

She looked skeptical. "Why didn't he send the divorce papers?"

"Well, Mom, he's never been real predictable." Seeing how crestfallen she was, I added, "I'm sure they'll come soon."

A blanket over her lap and legs, she sat on the love seat, almost recovered. Even so, her arms and legs were terribly thin, and the dark circles beneath her eyes made her seem gaunt. I was relieved that she had been too preoccupied with the papers to examine closely my story about the money.

"Where's the envelope?" she asked. "I want to see the return address. The lawyer told me if I advertise at his last address for two months, I can get a divorce without his signature."

I paused, thinking over this new piece of information. It's true I had promised Riley not to tell his address. But why not let my mother get on with her life? Anyway, after all that had happened, I didn't feel as if I owed anybody.

"Traverse City," I said.

"What would he be doing there?" she said. "He doesn't have any relatives in Traverse City."

I hadn't told her about the widow woman, real or imagined. "Maybe he's working the Great Lakes. I think a lot of guys work the lakes if they're trying to hide out."

"He might be. If I remember my geography, that's on Lake Michigan." My mother examined one of the twenties. "And it does appear as if this was soaked at one time." She picked up a ten. "All of this money looks peculiar. You don't think he's involved in counterfeiting, something like that?"

"I think they'll spend, Mom. Anyway, we've been a little short this month."

Her eyes flashed. "This isn't your money, is it? You haven't been working for Jake?"

"It's not my money." I crossed my heart. "Do you want me to look around for the Bible or something?"

"I'm so tired." She leaned back, closing her eyes. "Well, we certainly need it. I just hope he didn't hold up a liquor store."

"Maybe he knocked over a bank," I said.

One eye opened. "He doesn't have the gumption for a bank."

Our house sat in a depression, so the water stood in pools all around. "They should have built this place on stilts." Mom was buckling her galoshes. She planned on going back to work, but I could tell she was still weak. "I've got to keep shagging along. They've already given me sick leave and let me use vacation time. That was very generous." She put on her coat and scarf. "I swear, it seems no matter how hard you try, you're just one disaster short of the poorhouse."

"Don't walk, Mom. Call Franklin."

"He had to go to Central on business. Won't be back until late this afternoon. Anyway, I've got a little business myself today."

"What's that?"

She put both hands on my shoulders so she was looking square into my face. "Riley sent the money from Traverse City? You could swear to that in a court of law?"

"Why would I need to?"

"I'm going to the lawyer. Pretty soon, I'll be a free woman."

"That's great, Mom. If I need to swear to it, I will." I was pleased to see her so happy. My reaction surprised me.

She took a bright umbrella out of the closet and opened the front door to a rising pool of water. "What a mess. By tonight this water will be over my galoshes. Call the city and make them do something about it. Bunch of loafers."

The high school had closed because so many roads were washed out the buses couldn't run. I felt guilty staying at home while Mom worked but felt pleased about giving her the sixty dollars. I decided to swing by at noon, maybe walk with her to the lawyer's office, just to keep her company.

At eight o'clock, someone honked outside and I thought maybe Franklin had come by after all, even though it didn't sound like his car horn.

When I opened the door, I was surprised to see Jake's rig towing his big aluminum guide boat with the twin Evinrudes. "The reservation's flooding," he said. "Lots of people are trapped in Hollywood."

I hesitated at the door.

"Hurry and get dressed. I need you to ride shotgun." He held up his hand. "Five minutes. These people need help."

In about three minutes, I had on my clothes and boots. At the last second, I grabbed my Sasquatch coat and headed out the door, splashing through the puddles.

When I climbed in, Jake looked at the coat, shaking his head. "That damn thing soaks water like a sponge. There's rain gear behind the seat." As he drove away, the tires threw up big sprays of water.

When we passed the burned-out plywood plant, Jake scowled at the hulk. "What an eyesore."

In spite of the cold, the char tingled my nostrils. For a moment it seemed to come from Jake's breath and clothes. I rolled down the window until the smell cleared.

"Don't play freeze-out," Jake said.

"Meeks and Chilcoat should have been deep-sixed." I rolled up the window. "Burning's a horrible way to go."

"You wouldn't want that," he said. "Think a minute. Your father's in the river."

That was as close as he ever came to saying he was mixed up in anything. "Well, those guys are dead," I said. "But the owner did all right for himself. Money in the bank. Lots of golf. The big fish got away, if you ask me."

Jake shook his head. "Just for the sake of argument, let's say some of the speculation is true. If that owner's guilty, he'll never bend over to putt without his ass puckering. And who knows? One hunting season, a stray bullet might wedge between his shoulder blades."

"I think Sniffy was pretty damn close to the truth," I said.

Jake's eyes narrowed. "Close only counts in horseshoes."

We remained silent for a few mintues. Then Jake said, "Plenty of times, your father and I didn't see eye to eye. That happens in families. After all, you can't choose your relations." He grinned. "But on ambulance calls, we dropped our quarrels and made a team. What say you and I bury the hatchet, at least for today?"

"All right." I swallowed. "How bad's the flood out there?"

"A damn big one. They're up shit creek without a bailing bucket."

☆ ☆ ☆ ☆

A flood will do strange things, just like a tornado that drives straws through a telephone pole. When we neared the main highway bridge that crossed the Lost going toward Mission, I was astonished to see that the floodwater had washed away both approaches. Only the center of the bridge, now an island, remained. A large egg truck had tried to make it across and remained stranded on the bridge, tilted against the railing by the water's force.

As evacuation headquarters, the Totem Pole Texaco and Snack Shop had become a hub of activity. This business was situated on high ground, perhaps a quarter mile toward Gateway from the bridge. In front were rigs from the Gateway Volunteer Fire Department, Sheriff's Department, Search and Rescue, Tribal Police, plus some sports fishermen. Behind the Totem Pole, a small bulldozer was scraping slush and ice from the landing strip dudes used for their planes. On the water, a dozen boats brought flood victims to high ground.

"Let's grab some coffee and a butter horn," Jake said. "No point in starting a rescue operation hungry."

"They got thirty thousand eggs on that truck," Gab said. "Driver says the way they're packed, he's convinced not a single one is broken. I figure that after we tame this flood, we'll whip up one hell of an omelette."

He was broadcasting a remote from the Totem Pole. Power had been out on the reservation for more than twenty-four hours and the phone lines were down, but he was giving people emergency instructions. "They can listen in their homes or in their cars, whatever's convenient. That's the beauty of radio."

"Nothing's convenient in a flood," Jake said.

Gab scowled at him. "Ask if television's done anything lately to help these flood victims."

"You're preaching to the converted," Jake said.

"Buy more advertising then. Put your money where your mouth is." Gab grinned. "We might even be able to sell the rest of those picnic tables. But right now, I've got to think of some ingredients for the Gateway omelette. What's in a Denver? Bacon, onions, cheese, green peppers. Green peppers? What the hell kind of an ingredient is that?"

"Maybe it's the Spanish influence or something," I said.

"This boy's a gold mine of ideas," Gab said. "You know how teenagers eat. What should we put in the omelette, Culver?"

"I don't know right off," I said. "Let me think about it. How'd that truck get out there, anyway?"

"The driver was heading to the tribal store," Gab said. "The water rose fast and got deeper than he thought on the bridge. Stalled the truck. Billyum went out and rescued him this morning while you were still snoozing."

"There's a fool born every minute and only one dies a day," Jake said.

Gab ignored him. "We're going to have a Gateway egg-stravaganza. I'm telling you it's a hundred thousand dollars' worth of publicity."

Jake rolled his eyes. "We got people to evacuate, Gab. You better perfect that recipe yourself."

"My very thought egg-zactly. Now listen, we're going live in thirty seconds, Jake. Put you on air. Tell these people what they can bring, what they can't."

"Tell them to travel light," Jake said. "No furniture."

"You tell them, Jake. You're on." Gab switched to broadcast and held the microphone in front of Jake. When my uncle didn't say anything for a moment, Gab announced, "Folks, we've got one of the heroic volunteer rescuers right here with us at the Totem Pole. I'm sure he'll tell you to sit tight and stay warm until help arrives. Jake Martin is just one of the good citizens offering his boat and energy to evacuate the people of Hollywood and bring them across to high ground. Now tell us, Jake, what should they do?"

"Dress warm," Jake said when Gab thrust the microphone under his chin. "Try to stay dry until we can pick you up. Be sure to bring any medicine your family needs. Lots of times people forget that. Try to cage your pets. No furniture. Just bring your prized possessions. Photos, scrapbooks, trophies —"

"No televisions," Gab said, taking back the mike. "Definitely no televisions. But be sure to bring along your radios. And remember to keep in touch with KRCW, twelve-sixty on your dial, for more emergency news and information."

☆ ☆ ☆ ☆

I had never seen a river high and out of its banks before. The angry brown water carried logs, debris, big chunks of ice. From time to time an unusual item floated by — sofa, pillow, rusted car body, the bloated carcass of a cow. Even one piano. Upstream, a lot of farmers and ranchers dumped their trash near the riverbank, and now the water had risen to claim it. Unlike the beautiful blue-green Lost of summer, this resembled a muddy, floating dump.

Sports fishermen, Jackson County Search and Rescue, the Sheriff's Department, all launched their boats from the Totem Pole side and were crossing to Hollywood, then bringing out the people. Kooskia Creek had flooded, too, taking out the bridge from the main road to Hollywood, so the residents were cut off and trapped against the high basalt bluffs behind the settlement. A few of the Indians who owned boats were evacuating people from the Mission side, but this was a limited operation compared with the efforts from the Totem Pole.

We used the highway itself for a boat launch, and it seemed odd how the pavement disappeared into the swift brown water.

"You're kind of late, Jake," a couple of the fishermen teased as they unloaded a Hollywood family and their dogs from their boats.

"Nephew needed his beauty sleep," Jake said. "But it didn't work." After waiting for their laugh, he added, "Actually, I was waiting until you fellas needed serious help. Kind of wondered when amateur hour was over."

"Glad you're here," one said after a moment. "My motor's been acting up."

"Where'd you get that lousy thing anyway?" Jake asked. It was a Mercury and we sold Evinrudes. "You fellas must have driven all the way to Central to get rooked. Next time, stop by my place. I'll treat you right. Meet or beat most deals."

They looked kind of sheepish. "Lots of debris, Jake. It really fouls the prop."

"You bet it does," he said. "I use two. If one goes kaput, I've got a spare."

Billyum and Squeaky were using the tribal boat to bring people from Hollywood to the Totem Pole side. "Not much point in heading for high ground on the rez," Billyum explained. "We got no uncontaminated water and the store's running out of milk and Coca-Cola. Some helicopters are supposed to bring in supplies, but so far they're busy with other rescues."

"That's a tragedy," Jake said. "When the helicopters come down, like gray doves from heaven, their cargo nets will be loaded with cases of Coke. Reservation manna."

Billyum agreed. "Miracles come in all shapes and flavors."

Several of the Hollywood houses closest to the riverbank had been swept away, and the row beyond that was flooded. People huddled back from the river, reluctant to abandon their homes. Some had dragged their prized possessions to higher ground, although Hollywood was dangerously situated on floodplain and high ground was scarce.

When we left the Totem Pole side, the first thing Jake did was hand me a pair of wire cutters. I didn't realize how much wire was around until we tried to get past the flooded houses and yards. Chicken wire, clothesline, barbed, phone, electric fence. Everyone had a couple cows or a horse, and I spent as much time cutting wire as I did loading people. Jake insisted I take the time to wrap the free wire around trees, stumps, or wherever, because trailing underwater it was bound to foul the props of the other rescuers.

Yazzie had dragged his guitar, rodeo trophies, and scrapbooks out of his robin's egg blue house and covered them with a gray tarp. As we loaded, I saw his possessions included posters from his music days. He also had a heavy suitcase and two garbage sacks filled with men's clothes.

"I hope you packed something for the wife," Jake said.

"To hell with it," Yazzie said. "She took off with my daughter, went to that big city mall with the ice rink. They always buy new outfits. Now I'm broke and got no home."

We tried to cover his loaded stuff with the tarp, but it was raining pretty hard and some posters were already soaked.

"How come you didn't hole up in one of the other houses? Keep this stuff dry?" Jake asked.

"The pink one, that's my daughter's." Yazzie pointed with his chin to a partially flooded house. The river had taken away one corner. "Guess my damn son-in-law switched the locks."

"You're getting soft," Jake said. "Used to be you'd bust out the windows."

"Yeah. Now I got religion."

As we were pulling away, one side of the pink house slid into the water so we could see right into the front room. A small table held a decorated Christmas tree and presents. As we watched, the water carried the table away. When the cord connected to the tree lights reached its limit, the tree was dragged into the water. Presents floated everywhere, and the current swept them toward open water.

"Damn, but my grandkids are going to be disappointed," Yazzie said. "I got a Daisy BB gun at your place, Jake."

"Then it's guaranteed one hundred percent not to rip, rot, rust, unravel, sag, drag, or bag at the knees." Jake turned the boat around. "Get the net, Culver. Let's save as much of this loot as we can, especially that gun. I don't want to deprive Yazzie's grandson the opportunity of shooting out the old fart's eye when he goes poking his nose somewhere it doesn't belong." He grinned at Yazzie. "I hope you didn't take advantage of my generosity by running up a big charge account."

"You know I'm good for it," Yazzie said. "Per capita payments come in January."

We spent five minutes dodging debris and ice chunks while we netted or grabbed presents before they became waterlogged and sank. As one bright red and green package was about to go under, I pulled it dripping into the boat. The package was about the size of a two-pound block of Tillamook cheese.

"Hope to hell that's not a fruitcake," Jake said. "You wouldn't have us out here risking our necks for a damn fruitcake, would you, Yazzie?" He picked up the package and held it over the side of the boat. "That stuff belongs on the bottom with the trash fish." He cocked his eyebrow. "Fruitcake?"

"Commodity butter," Yazzie said. "I just wrapped it up for fun."

Jake dropped the butter into the boat, then picked up Yazzie's guitar with his free hand, acting as if he was going to throw it into the water. "Sorry, but the boat's overloaded with these presents. By ditching this guitar, I'll be doing the world a favor."

Yazzie pulled open the coat he was wearing, flashing a Ruger .22 Blackhawk tucked into the waistband of his jeans. "If I put one between your eyes, I'd be doing the world a bigger favor. Save it from a flood of bullshit."

Jake grinned. "You know, I've always admired your singing. Come by the store more often and serenade the back-room boys. They can sing along with your tunes."

"Just like Mitch Miller. 'Yellow Rose of Texas.'"

"Oh, you're better than Mitch ever thought of being. Especially with that persuader tucked in your trousers."

Shortly after noon, Mule Mullins's Evinrude conked out on him, and Mule began drifting toward Deer Island. We were the closest boat to attempt a rescue, so we gave chase and threw him a tow line. I remembered that we had sold Mule his motor, and I wondered how Jake would handle him.

"Motor's not worth a damn, Jake," Mule teased. "You got to hang out on the river and rescue your customers. Hell of a deal."

"You must have bought some bad gas," Jake said.

Mule snorted. "Good thing I got your one hundred percent guarantee. Count on me bringing it in to be replaced. Unless you're going to say it's fully insured but not covered."

"Come on, Mule. Do I look like a slinking coyote to you? Fully insured means fully covered."

"That's good. I can relax." Mule leaned back in his boat, closing his eyes.

"Only problem could be the *exclusion* rule." Jake made certain Mule heard him over the roar of our Evinrudes.

Mule opened his eyes. "What the hell is that?"

"Acts of God are excluded."

"What act of God? The damn motor quit."

"I haven't checked lately," Jake said, "but the last time I looked, an act of God included floods. Wreck up a motor in a flood and you're standing outside the warranty. Way outside."

Mule leaned forward. "I don't believe it."

"You got no business out in a flood with a regular prop. Too damn much debris. Sooner or later the motor goes blooey. What did you expect?"

"Jake, you can't be serious."

"Talk to the Almighty. I didn't make the rules." Jake used his free hand to indicate the swollen river. "This is irregular, like hurricanes and lightning. I'm afraid you're out a motor, Mule. But don't feel too bad. Think of these poor Indian people. Lost about everything they have, then lose even more while I diddle around rescuing peckerheads like you."

Mule took a small crescent wrench out of his toolbox and banged on his motor a couple times, denting the casing. From the look on his face, I think Jake had him suckered.

"Now don't turn violent and start vandalizing that fine product. You've been a preferred customer over the years. We'll fill out the report just right. That's Jake's way. What Evinrude don't know can't hurt." He winked at me. "Old Mule was born without a funny bone."

After we had towed Mule and his boat safely to shore, we started back again. Billyum was crossing with another load of flood victims. "We're losing time rescuing the rescuers," he said.

"You're telling me," Jake said. "This whole operation would go a lot smoother if we didn't have so much help. These amateur Search and Rescue fellas are pimples on the head of progress." He grinned. "But that's just an opinion. I'm not thinking any negatory thoughts."

"Lettie Black-Eye is famous for her woven baskets," Jake said. "Juniper was going to display them at the lodge before she decided to head south."

I was helping Lettie carry sacks of baskets to the boat. They were plenty wet, but she said that wouldn't hurt them. The craftsmanship was superb; some were woven so tight they held water. Inside her house, Lettie had raised the furniture by placing large cans of commodity foods under the legs. The sturdy cans of lard and peaches had kept the furniture dry awhile, but now the water was as high as her sofa back and several pillows floated around the room.

After we had loaded her baskets, suitcases of clothes, and a couple bags of beadwork, she climbed into the boat, then whistled for her dogs, a black lab and a golden. "Get in Cola! Come on Bagel!" When the dogs got in, she gave each of them a small piece of venison jerky she carried in her apron pocket.

Jake shook his head when she offered one to him. "I'm already thirsty as hell. Seems funny with all the water rushing by."

The golden seemed nervous in the boat and she grabbed his neck, holding him down. "Take it easy, Bagel."

"There's a traditional Indian name," Jake said, grinning.

"Dr. Greenspan at Indian health put that name on him. I was planning to call him Biscuit. Dr. Greenspan's retired now. They gave us a real young man with a lot to learn."

I shoved the boat off. Lettie sat in the middle seat, a dog on either side. After taking a piece of jerky for herself, she folded her arms and stared straight at the Totem Pole shore. "I been in that house forty-five years," she said. Jake nodded. "I came out and got you a couple times in the ambulance. You were having that heart trouble."

"Your brother came, too," she said. "You were nice boys. I heard what happened to him and I'm sorry."

"His son helped you load," Jake said, nodding in my direction.

She turned back toward me just long enough to smile, then stared straight ahead again. She probably realized that by morning her house would be gone.

Loaded, the boat was sluggish, but at least this was a bigger one than the wooden drift boat we usually took on the Lost. That wouldn't have held much, especially with all Jake's gear. I sighed and leaned back, resting on the trip across.

"You got to eat more steak, nephew. I think you're getting a little puny."

"Worn out is what I'm getting." I was tired of being wet, tired of loading the boat, even tired of staying cheerful when I saw people losing almost everything they owned.

We ran steadily to midstream. I was thankful for Jake's skill and the twin Evinrudes. A lot of other boats had experienced difficulties and were out of the water. Only half a dozen still ran. Jake studied the water ahead for debris, ice. A small bloated doe drifted close by and Bagel growled deep in his throat.

We heard a rifle shot followed by two more in quick succession and my head snapped up. On the shore, Billyum was firing into the air and waving. Having gained our attention, he pointed the rifle upstream.

"Holy shit," Jake said. Two huge trees swept toward us, so large they seemed to cover the river from shore to shore. I expected them to wipe out the remaining section of bridge, but when they hit the concrete, the water swept one to either side, and they rushed toward us.

"You got to turn back," I said.

Jake's eyes cut from the trees to the far shore, measuring the distance. Against the current, our headway seemed pitifully slow and the trees were closing fast. No time to turn the boat.

Billyum fired three warnings again. A boat close to the Indian side turned back to Hollywood. The sheriff's boat surged toward the far shore. Only ours was caught midstream.

"These dogs are good swimmers," Lettie offered. "Lighten the load." She laid a hand on each one's neck, prepared to urge them into the water.

"Thanks," Jake said. "But we still couldn't make it. And they'd probably stick with us anyway." Turning the boat downstream, he opened the throttle.

As we raced toward Deer Island, I glanced backwards toward the trees. Terrified, but fascinated, I saw dirty clumps of ice and brown frozen ferns clinging to their roots. After separating at the bridge, the trees had locked root masses, forming an inverted V that threatened to swallow the boat.

I couldn't guess Jake's plan, but I didn't think we could outrun the trees too long. We bumped against chunks of debris, nearly knocking a box of baskets overboard. Gripping the sides of the boat with my hands, I tried to wrap my legs around the loose cargo.

When we hit the rapid channel around Deer Island, both dogs hunkered and whined. Lettie clung to the dogs rather than the boat. If she fell out, they would, too. We flew down the rapids with the boat chunk-chunking against the water with spine-jarring blows.

Over the roar of the motors, I heard a crash and limbs breaking with a noise like a giant falling tree snapping the trunks and branches of smaller trees as it crashes to the forest floor. I realized the two big trees were smashing through some of the flooded pines on Deer Island.

Reaching the foot of the island, Jake turned the boat upstream and we hovered in the current, using the island and its bigger trees as a shield. One of the floaters came by, seeming large as a ship when it passed. Jake pretended to wipe sweat from his forehead with the back of his hand. The other tree had hung at the top of the island, partially blocking the channel.

"I guess that bastard's stuck good," Jake said. "But I'm going to sit right here a couple minutes, make sure it doesn't bust loose. I'd take a piece of that jerky now, Lettie. My mouth is a little dry."

I asked for a piece, too.

She gave two to the dogs. "Cola knew we were going to make it," she said. "Bagel was kind of nervous though."

"Seeing those trees come straight at you makes you a little more sympathetic towards the loggers, doesn't it?" Jake said. "You know how some poor fella feels when a widow maker splits wrong and falls right toward him. For a minute there, I thought that sucker had our number."

Ten minutes later, Buzzy flew by us in the yellow Stearman. After circling the island's head, he came in treetop level and waved the all clear. Still, Jake waited, and I realized how scared he had been. We heard honking, faint across the water, and saw Billyum's rig bouncing along the bumpy abandoned railroad grade. Stopping across from us, he flashed his lights a few times, then got out of the car and waved that it was okay to head upstream.

"Guess that tree is hung good," Jake said. "But we'll take the opposite channel back up and hope nothing else sweeps down. If something catches us midchannel, we're deader than this venison."

As we made a late run, the sun's rays broke through the dark clouds. Jake blinked with the sudden brightness. His gaze swept the Hollywood shore and fixed on the chartreuse house now undercut by the floodwater. When I looked, I didn't see anything but orange light bouncing off the upstairs windows.

By the time we were almost finished loading Mrs. Sandoz, Juniper's aunt, and her menagerie of animals, it was growing dark. I could see the big red Texaco sign and the burn barrels illuminating the opposite shore.

"Last house," Billyum said. "Good thing, too." His boat and Jake's were the only ones left. Now they were filled with cages holding rabbits, raccoons, a couple descented skunks, and a fox. She had other animals, too, but we'd run out of room.

"I came out here on an ambulance run once," Jake said. "Damn skunk bit me. Waited a week to find out if it was rabid."

Now a couple of rabbits had gotten loose from their cages and Mrs. Sandoz refused to leave without them. They were a French breed with long floppy ears. "Paid top dollar for those rabbits," she said. "Maybe you can catch a rabbit. You stumblebums can't find Kalim's killer."

"Come on," Billyum said.

My uncle shook his head. "Your jurisdiction. I'm trying to stay on her sweet side."

Although we were clumsy in our hip boots, Squeaky, Billyum, and I came at them from three sides. Using the same net I'd used to snag Christmas presents, I got one before it could hop away. The second, frightened, bolted between Billyum and Squeaky. Lunging for it, Billyum missed, sprawling on the grass.

"Damn!" Crying out in pain, he stood, inspecting his bleeding hand. He'd hit some broken window pane and it was a wicked gash.

"How come you let my supper hop away?" Jake asked, and Billyum shot him a look. Jake tossed him a clean rag from the compartment under the seat. After wrapping his hand with the rag, Billyum stood by his boat and sulked. "Your turn."

With an exaggerated sigh, Jake left the boat. "Three men can't catch a baby bunny, for Christ's sake." He took the net and walked right up to the rabbit, which stood still for some reason. After scooping it into the net, Jake grinned at Billyum. "Technique. It's all in the wrist."

We caged both rabbits.

Mrs. Sandoz rode with us after deciding our boat had a better spirit. I think she meant to avoid Billyum's sulky mood rather than his boat. By then the river and sky seemed equally dark, and Jake kept his eyes peeled for obstacles. As we approached the far side, I saw Franklin's car parked up by the Texaco, and I could make out my mother's figure alongside one of the burn barrels. "The party's over," Jake began to sing off key. "The lights are dim." He had seen her, too.

"Better get ready for an injection of iron," he continued. "Your ass is grass and here comes the lawnmower. All the time she was warm and dry inside Sunrise Biscuits, you were busting your hump in this rescue operation, but she thought you were cozy at home."

"Stop riding me," I said. "I'll handle her."

"You might be able to handle her," Jake said. "She's been weakened a little by the flu."

When we nosed close to shore, I tossed the rope to one of the waiting men and they pulled us in. After we helped Mrs. Sandoz ashore, we started unloading her animals. Billyum arrived, too, but something was wrong with his motor. Coughing and sputtering, it barely made shore.

"You buy your gas on the rez?" Jake asked. "They must be using sludge again."

Billyum ignored the remark. As he unwrapped the bandage, we could see the wound was still oozing. "Shit. If I lose any more blood, I'll turn white."

288

"You go see the doc," Jake said. "We'll unload your boat. Later on we can check out the motor."

"Bad spark plug maybe," Billyum said. "We took it to the tribal shop a couple weeks ago. Squeaky's brother-in-law worked on it."

"You just located the trouble," Jake said, and they both laughed.

Mrs. Sandoz began talking rapidly and gesturing across the river. Billyum shook his head. "No, that was the last run," he said. "In the morning, we can look for your other animals."

Jake had climbed back into his boat and started the motors. "Shove me off, would you, nephew."

Billyum waded into the water, gripping the gunnel with his good hand. "Too damn dark. Don't go risking your life for a few animals." He lowered his voice. "Just because she's Juniper's aunt, I don't want you hotdogging and stealing the show."

Jake shook his head. "I don't care about those animals," he said. "Somebody's still over there. I saw his face in the window."

"Where?" Billyum asked, more of a challenge than a question.

At first I thought maybe Jake was showing off for Juniper, or even my mother, but that didn't seem quite right. Jake took big chances, but I doubted he'd take one with the flood in the dark.

"The chartreuse house sitting off by itself. I saw a face in the upstairs window. And that place won't last the night."

"Nobody's supposed to be there," Billyum said. "The whole family's back visiting people in South Dakota."

"Maybe somebody stayed behind," Jake said.

Billyum studied the opposite shore as if he expected to see what Jake had glimpsed. "You saw a reflection, trick of light. Squeaky checked that place earlier. Downstairs was already flooded."

"We'll see," Jake said. "But time's wasting and the water's rising."

Billyum started to climb into the boat. "I'll ride shotgun. The hand can wait."

"Bullshit!" Jake said. "You're not bleeding all over my boat."

The floodwaters had risen enough to free the boat, and Jake revved the motor a little, backing just enough to throw Billyum off balance, but he hung on. "Look," Jake said, "I don't want to be burdened with any one-handed, almost-turned-white peckerhead."

"I'm going." Billyum braced his legs and gripped the gunnel with his good hand.

Jake cut the motor. "What the hell. Get that sucker sewed up and then hurry back. Five minutes."

"You better wait." Billyum released the boat, pointing his good finger at me. "Hold him, Culver." He started double-timing in his hip boots toward the hospital tent.

"Runs like a duck with a ruptured asshole." Jake took a portable lantern from beneath the seat, securing it to the front of the boat with duct tape. Then he put on a battery-pack miner's helmet so he could use it as a minisearchlight by turning his head. "Shove me off, nephew!"

Billyum had reached the hospital tent. As he looked back, Jake waved, gesturing for him to hurry.

"It's awful dark," I said. "What if that guy's hurt or crazy? Why wouldn't he come out? You better wait for Billyum."

"Didn't say it was a guy. Might be a beautiful damsel. Rich, too."

"Let me go then."

He set his jaw. "Your mother would have a conniption fit. I'm already in deep dutch with her."

"I'll take care of it," I said.

"You do that, Shotgun. Just remind her you've done a good piece of work here today. When I come back, we'll go have a big steak. My treat."

"Sure." I was proud of what I'd accomplished that day, and the steak sounded good, if I didn't fall asleep at the plate.

"Be over and back before he gets out of that hospital tent. I heard about that young doctor. All thumbs. He couldn't hang on to his dick with glue."

Jake put the motors in reverse and I gave a half shove. The current took the boat until Jake opened the throttle. As he headed across, the motors sounded strong and even. Listening to the steady drone, I was glad Jake didn't trust anyone but himself to work on it. Buzzy felt the same way about the Stearman. Most of the back-room boys had that streak of self-reliance. Even Sniffy. "In the war, you learned to pack your own parachute," he was fond of saying.

After I had watched Jake's light reach midstream, I walked to the burn barrel where my mother and Franklin were keeping warm. Her face was as dark as a storm cloud, but Franklin tried to ease the tension. "You've been doing a man's work," he said, adding, "Of course, your mother was pretty worried. I'm afraid she might have a relapse out in this weather, but she insisted."

She gazed across the dark water. "Culver, you know how I feel about this river. And now it's more dangerous than ever."

"But we got everybody out, Mom. Almost everybody. Jake didn't talk me into it or anything. I volunteered."

Stepping away from the fire, she hugged me fiercely for a moment, then let go. "What's he trying to prove then?" She nodded toward the river.

"He thought he saw someone and went to check one of the houses. Place will be gone by morning."

"Well, thank God he had the human decency not to take you," she said. "Bumbling around on a flood in the dark like a blind man."

"At least you can find your way around over there," I said. "The houses are painted weird. The place he's headed for is chartreuse."

She touched the V of her throat with two fingers and a frightened look appeared in her eyes.

"What is it?" I asked.

She dropped her hand. "Nothing really. Just an odd memory."

"Like what?"

"It seems silly to even talk about such a thing."

"Tell us what it is, Flora." Franklin had come over and put his arm around her.

"All right then." She rubbed her arms briskly, as if she had goose bumps. "There was a yellow-green house a couple blocks from where the boys grew up. Who would want such a putrid color for a house?" She paused. "It seems a man hung himself in the upstairs bedroom. After that, no one would buy the place. Still, his relatives refused to lower the price."

"I remember that house," Franklin said. "All the kids thought it was spooky."

She nodded and continued. "Jake found a way in through the basement window, and the boys would test their courage by going upstairs. They had to stand directly at the bedroom window, where you could see their faces, and look out to prove they weren't lingering on the first floor but actually right in the room where the man had died. Anyway, one time your father went up to prove his courage to some neighbor boys, but he heard a sound or something and froze. Wouldn't move. The boys were too afraid to go in, so they sent one running to get Jake. He had to climb in and drag your father out."

She stopped to rub her arms again, and I felt goose bumps. "It's nothing really," she said. "That funny color made me think about it."

"Just a curious coincidence, Flora," Franklin said. "Happens all the time. Now we'd better get you home before you collapse."

"Whatever happened to that house?" I figured someone had repainted it since I hadn't seen a Gateway place that color.

"They never sold it," she said. "The place fell into disrepair and finally burned down. A tramp was trying to warm up inside, or so they said. Both your dad and Jake fought that blaze, but the house was a complete loss."

When I informed Billyum what had happened, he lost his patience with the young doctor sewing stitches in his hand. "Come on, can't you hurry it up?" he asked.

The doctor did seem clumsy, but he had been busy all day and was dog tired. "You're going to need a tetanus booster, and I'm out." He cut off the thread with long-nose scissors.

Billyum flexed his hand a few times, testing the stitches. "All right. I'll get one tomorrow." As he shrugged his coat on, he glanced around at the others waiting for treatment or just waiting.

Many flood victims had gathered in the hospital tent, trying to remain warm and dry before they were transported to Gateway's high school, where the gymnasium, showers, and cafeteria had been converted to emergency shelter. These people remained subdued and I was struck at the contrast between this atmosphere and the boisterous one at the fire. They seemed awed by the raw power of the river, their personal losses. Unlike the fire that destroyed a workplace, the flood took personal items and memories. Homes, cars, furniture, clothing, mementos. Everybody knew they would never rebuild Hollywood on that site.

Juniper had been busy calming some of the old people, holding their hands and assuring them everything would be okay. Mrs. Sandoz was crying about the animals she had left behind. Still, she held out hope Jake would bring them across on the return trip.

"I'm sure he'll do all he can," Juniper said. "But we wouldn't want him to risk his life —"

"He'll do it," Mrs. Sandoz said. "I know. When my Thompson had his heart attack, Jake drove the ambulance run with another nice young boy. They couldn't have been more considerate."

When Billyum was ready, we went down by the tribal boat. Squeaky had replaced the spark plug, but it still sputtered and died. "Carburetor," Squeaky said. "I'm pretty sure."

"That's the last time one of your relatives fixes our boat," Billyum said. "I ought to have my head examined."

"Hell, he's just shirttail on my wife's side," Squeaky said. "What's eating you?"

"Jake said he saw someone in that chartreuse house, but I went by it half a dozen times today. Never saw a thing. You were supposed to check it."

"I did," Squeaky said. "Waded right up on the front porch and yelled. No one answered. Jake couldn't have seen anyone."

All of us watched the faint ray of light work its way along the far shore. When it disappeared, we figured he was behind the first row of flooded houses where the structures blocked our view of the beam.

The light reappeared and everyone sighed. "That's close by the chartreuse house," Billyum said. "Check it and get the hell back," he muttered.

The boat seemed to linger there a long time, then the light disappeared again. We waited and waited. "What the hell's he doing?" Billyum scowled. "If he's stopping to get those animals, I'll fry that raccoon and make him eat it."

Then we saw the light, faint but steady.

All of us figured Jake had cleared the flooded houses and was heading for open water. "Here he comes," a couple people said quietly. No one cheered because he still had a long way to get across.

Three fellas drove their pickups to the water's edge and turned on spotlights, attempting to illuminate the water in front of the boat. But Jake was still too far across the river. "Keep those lights out of his eyes," Billyum warned. "He's got to keep them clear."

The light was coming toward us now, and you could see the smaller light from Jake's miner's helmet winking this way and that as he turned his head searching for obstacles.

"Wonder what he found over there," Squeaky said.

Jake was about a third of the way across when we could hear the motors laboring against the current. The fellas in the pickup adjusted their spotlights but the beams didn't reach far enough. They could only sweep the closest third of the river.

Suddenly, the boat light's direction changed, shining off at a cockeyed angle. It began pointing downstream, not following the natural arc a boat makes churning into a heavy current.

"What's this shit?" Billyum said.

The buzz of voices around the warming fires grew louder, and a couple people started up their pickups so we couldn't hear the boat motors clearly anymore, but I think they were still going.

Squeaky said something, Indian words that meant "Wet Shoes" and referred to the restless spirits of drowning victims, the same words Billyum had used a long time ago when we found Kalim.

Now Billyum swore, pushing Squeaky out of the way. He tried starting the motor with one hand, then both, pulling so hard he broke a stitch, but it wouldn't catch. "Come on, Jake. Shake clear." He rapped his knuckles against the front of the tribal boat.

The flickering light reached the head of Deer Island, gaining speed as it hit the swift current. The light went in a crazy half circle, first pointing to the shore, then sweeping the flooded trees of the island.

"Something spun him around," Billyum said. "Hit that damn tree, maybe."

Near the foot of the island, the light winked out.

Nobody spoke.

Buzzy took off in the Stearman, and the plane's roaring overhead offered comfort, even though we knew he couldn't help Jake directly. We traced the plane's dark silhouette against the night sky until it disappeared downriver. Buzzy didn't use running lights because he never dusted at night.

We waited, holding our breaths, half expecting the light of Jake's boat to reappear at the head of Deer Island. But there was only darkness and the deep churning of floodwaters.

When the faint sound of a motor droned from the distance, the outline of Buzzy's plane reappeared. Lining up on the burn barrels and the illuminated Texaco lights, he landed on the frozen air strip behind the Totem Pole. Billyum and I were waiting when he climbed out.

"What happened to Jake?" Billyum asked.

Buzzy took off his aviator glasses and shook his head. The glasses were wet and his jumpsuit was soaked. "Snag or a big stump maybe. I could see roots tangling the boat. Jake couldn't get free."

"Did he jump?" Billyum asked.

"I followed him as far as Picture Canyon. I think he was still in the boat. It was awful goddamn dark, and I had to watch those narrow walls."

"Was anybody else with him?"

Buzzy shrugged. "I kept making passes over the boat. A couple times I thought I saw someone, but it might have been a big root over the top. To tell the truth, my night vision is shot."

After Buzzy had been back awhile, old Sylvester went down to the water's edge and picked up some dirt and grass. Letting these sift through his hand into the water, he began chanting, bringing the empty hand to his heart. Continuing to chant, he reached into the medicine bundle he kept tied around his neck and tossed something into the water.

"What's he doing?" I asked Billyum.

"Sort of praying. Asking the river not to keep Jake."

"I hope it works," I said, remembering how things had turned out for Kalim.

"Don't worry about your uncle," Billyum said. "He's got more lives than a tomcat. Has more fun, too."

The longer Sylvester chanted, the more compelling his voice became. Billyum went down to join him, then Juniper, finally Squeaky and some of the other Indians. They didn't know all the words, but joined in the chant now and then.

I stood off a little way, saying my own prayers. It was best to go at it from all sides, I figured.

About fifteen minutes passed before Billyum left the group. "Let's drive down the railroad grade as far as we can. Maybe he jumped and Buzzy missed it."

"Sure," I said, glad to be doing something. Like Billyum, I wasn't certain if Buzzy had seen things clearly at all. He had to work pretty hard at not smashing his plane against the narrow canyon walls.

Others had started up their four-wheel-drive rigs and climbed the hillside to the old railroad grade. It went downriver almost a mile before dead-ending at a blasted tunnel. Now the drivers positioned themselves at spaced intervals, turning on their headlights and spotlights, forming a kind of beacon row along the flooded blackness. When I realized they were keeping watch, I wanted to cry.

"Look." Billyum pointed to the opposite hillside. Studying the high bluffs, I thought stars were coming out of the clouded night sky. Then I realized the lights were coming from Indian rigs high above the black basalt cliffs. They, too, were standing vigil.

For two hours we searched the flooded shoreline, poking among the piles of debris and calling out for Jake. Dozens of others joined us, but there was no sign.

When we found a waterlogged sofa that had floated down from Hollywood, Billyum said, "Let's take a break. I'm about asleep on my feet." He swept the flashlight beam across the sofa. "Wish old Jake was here taking a little snooze."

"Me too," I said.

Billyum shone the light in my face, just for a second. "Did your uncle have a fishing pole with him?"

"I didn't see one. Probably he had fishing gear stored up front."

Billyum put the light on his own face, so I wouldn't miss the grin. "If that sneaky bastard swam to the Indian side and is poaching our fish, I'll ticket his white ass, flood or no flood."

In spite of my weariness and worry, I grinned, too. "Hope he's catching some lunkers."

Billyum nodded. "More power to him . . . as long as they're on the white side." He focused the beam on his stitched hand. A crust of blood had formed across the broken stitch. "No kidding, Culver, we better get some rest. At first light, we'll take the boat down Picture Canyon."

"Sure thing," I said, then paused. "What boat?"

"If you got a spare set of store keys, we'll buy a new motor for the tribal boat. That'll be a hoot when old Jake has to pay you a big commission."

"I got keys." I could barely say the next part. "Think we'll find him okay?"

Billyum slapped some mud off his trousers with his good hand. "As Jake would say, 'Don't go thinking any negatory thoughts.' Remember, bullshit floats and he's full of it. Clear up to the gills."

"I hear you," I said. "Maybe old Sylvester's chanting will work, too."

Billyum lowered his voice. "If you promise not to tell, I'll level with you. The fact is, I put a lot more faith in Jake than I do in old Sylvester. But don't go spreading that information." He glanced around, but no one was near. "See, Sylvester misses more than he makes. Even his prophecies are all over the place. Take the World Series. I won bets off him five of the last seven years. My hunch is we'll find Jake tomorrow, if he isn't already walking out of the canyon tonight."

"That's good news," I said, but behind the hopefulness of Billyum's words I sensed his doubts. I didn't know exactly what to think, and remembering the way that boat light had spun around made me nauseous. I could feel slivers of doubt piercing my own heart.

"Listen, Billyum. There's one thing I need to ask, if you don't mind." He turned to face me. "Sure, kid."

"When you and Jake were fishing and taking sweats, did he stay on the river the whole time? I'm just wondering if he left at all."

His features turned somber in the lantern light. "How come you ask?"

"No real reason, exactly. I just keep thinking about that business with Meeks and Chilcoat. I know Grady and the newspaper editor keep trying to stir things up, but it is funny how those two drove so far out there and then burned up. Pretty weird." I wanted to tell him about the night Sniffy had come into the store telling the wild stories, and I wanted to ask about the time I saw the three of them in Billyum's rig outside the Alibi, but I didn't know how. Even so, I believe Billyum understood my drift.

"No need to go worrying about Jake," he said after a while. "He stayed with me all the time. Right there on the river."

"That's pretty much what I figured all along," I said.

Although I settled for Billyum's answer, I was too worried about Jake to sleep. Homer had shown up with fresh bakery goods, and throughout the night I helped him carry them to the men and women waiting in their rigs along the railroad grade. When they rolled down their windows to take the baked goods we offered, I smelled the coffee, cigarettes, air freshener, and damp wool. Now those scents mingled with the yeasty odor of doughnuts, butter horns, and bear claws. All these warm human smells offered comfort, a welcome contrast to the rising damp odors of the flood.

The people inside the vehicles kidded around about Jake, trying to make me feel better. "Don't worry about that crazy bastard," one said. "He'll ride that snag all the way to the ocean if he has to. He's a regular wild boat buckaroo." Another added, "Jake'll use that stump for a battering ram and knock out a couple dams along the way. Should help the steelhead and salmon return. And old Jake will be here waiting with his pole and a big fish-eating grin."

31

AFTER TAKING MY STORE KEYS, Billyum drove to town for a new motor. Attempting to get back on Billyum's good side, Squeaky and his relative installed it while Billyum caught a few winks. By first light we were on the river. Squeaky brought a chain saw to cut through brush and debris, if we needed. I didn't like the search dogs, two bloodhounds Billyum borrowed from a trainer. They smelled so bad I didn't understand how they could follow any scent other than their own. In the boat they seemed too anxious. On the riverbank, each time they nosed into a pile of debris, I caught my breath.

All that day we searched. Other boats tried, too, including one manned by Ace and a couple RedWings. Buzzy flew numerous passes over the river but failed to spot Jake or the boat. Once I found half a package of waterlogged Fig Newtons and showed them to Billyum. He shrugged and said lots of Hollywood people ate them, so they might have washed down from anywhere.

When we returned at dusk, the rigs had lined the old railroad bed again; some flew banners with Jake's name from their antennas. Gab had driven my uncle's pickup to the grade, so it sat there, keys in the ignition, waiting.

He reported that downriver, near South Junction, they had found two victims of the flood, both white, but neither was Jake.

"What do you think?" I asked Billyum that night when he dropped me off at our place.

Reaching across the pickup cab, he squeezed my shoulder. "Sylvester thinks he's dead and started the death chant. That gives me hope." He squeezed again. "I figure Jake and me should grow old together, cussing and spitting all the way to the grave."

After five days of fruitless search, I was convinced that Jake, like my father, had gone under to stay and that the boat had been ground to flotsam. But they found Jake a week later, after the water had receded. He and the boat lay smashed under a black stump, gripped by its tangle of roots. From the water the boat was scarcely visible, and only Billyum's persistence with the dogs led to the discovery. The temperature had dropped below freezing once again, so Jake's body was preserved. The broken boat and wiry roots sealed him away from the scavenger coyotes, and the sharp-beaked magpies couldn't reach his eyes.

For most of an afternoon, Billyum and Squeaky tried cutting him free with the chain saw but the effort failed, and Squeaky went upriver for help while Billyum built a warming fire and stayed with the body. He spread tobacco around to keep away the Wet Shoes.

The following morning they brought in a logging helicopter to lift the stump and then finished cutting free the boat and body. Billyum had the helicopter take out the smashed boat, but he brought Jake upriver himself. When he passed the vehicles standing watch along the riverbanks, they turned off their headlights one by one.

Billyum, Squeaky, and I carried Jake up from the river. The Gateway Fire Department ambulance crew wanted to put Jake in back, but we weren't ready to let him go. "I think he'd want to ride home in his truck, boys," Billyum said, and we loaded the body bag into the back of his rig. The keys were still in the ignition.

I expected Billyum to drive, but he climbed into the passenger seat, so I started her up and followed the ambulance's pulsing red light. We'd driven only a few miles when I started to sob. Billyum reached across the seat and squeezed my thigh. Then I settled down.

"I know how you feel," he said. "A fool's born every minute, but a good man died this time."

We arranged the service for the high school gymnasium, since no other facility in town could hold the crowd. The overflow sat in their pickups around the football field, and the janitor hooked up the outdoor loudspeakers so everyone could hear. Oars lashed into a cross, Jake's guide boat stood behind the makeshift pulpit. Flowers filled the boat and a couple dozen fishing creels. On the funeral program they used the Bible passage where Christ tells the disciples he will make them fishers of men. I figured old Harold would like that.

Everyone came — the guides and outfitters, the Elks, Indians from on and off the reservation, dudes with their wives and children, old high school chums, salesmen, Ace and the RedWings, game wardens, Fish and Game Commission officials. A few people thought they saw the governor, but it was actually the secretary of state. I recognized dozens of people with long-term outstanding bills at the store and realized this would probably be their excuse never to pay. Juniper was there, of course, Doreen, my mother. A few other decked-out women claimed to have been Jake's girl at one time or another.

I glimpsed Riley at the graveside service, but he slipped away before I could say anything. He wore a sports coat and tie, indicating better times, and I hoped his story about the rich widow was true. Franklin spotted him, too, but didn't let on. After the service we found divorce papers stuffed behind our screen door, so Riley had visited the house.

When they had finished the food and drinks at the hard-drinking wake, the back-room boys draped a big GONE FISHING banner across the front of the store. Sharing attention with the red-nosed deer and sleigh, the banner looked peculiar, but I liked the sentiment. Billyum turned Jake's coffee cup upside down next to Seaweed's.

Throughout that night and the next, Gab stayed on the air so listeners could call in and reminisce about Jake. I listened until three in the morning, enjoying the yarns even though I doubted half of them were true. Gab's voice coming out of the illuminated radio brought comfort to my darkened room. He played interviews with Jake from the year he started up the guide service and when he'd served as captain of the volunteer fire department. Hearing Jake's voice seemed magical, and I drifted off to sleep, nothing lost, since Gab was recording the entire program.

☆ ☆ ☆ ☆

The following spring we built the memorial for Jake, my father, and the other river guides on Whiskey Dick Flat. After Billyum brought down the smashed boat, my mother used it as a kind of giant flower planter. Balsam root, lupine, phlox, and Indian paintbrush bloomed until late summer.

Most of the trees Jake planted continue to grow. Fishing guides, their dudes, even the rafters, have all lent a hand watering them. People seemed compelled to leave mementos at the memorial or imbedded in the boat. Hand-tied flies, beat-up lures, feathers, river agates, adorn the gunnels. Juniper attached a bronze steelhead mask to the largest alder and no one has touched it, although it's a valuable work of art.

You probably know how her career took off after her paintings of the Havasupai were displayed all across the Southwest. And now her work is featured in major national museums. Still, she returns to Mission a couple times a year to offer workshops.

On the whole, things turned out well for my mother, so Gateway did offer a new start, although in a different way than either of us would have guessed. She and Franklin married — no children. She quit her job and does volunteer work at the library and Gateway's new hospital. Summers they travel. If anything, the excitement has made her more beautiful.

A couple of the mill boys moved away with their parents who were looking for jobs, and Thatcher was killed in a car wreck, so our basketball team barely scraped a winning season my last year of high school. I attended college in another state, where they had a good journalism program, and I suppose that was Billyum's doing, although he probably wouldn't take credit for giving me the nudge. Maybe I was tempted to hang around Gateway and follow Jake's footsteps, but Billyum laid a big hand on my shoulder once and said, "Cut your own trail. If you stay around Gateway, you'll always be Jake's nephew."

The store and the house both went to Mom, and she sold them after trying to ensure that the fellas who bought the store would try to run it pretty much the way Jake had. And they did for a while, but their style differed from his, so things changed as they always do. The new owners started carrying merchandise for new brands of dudes — water-skiers, rock climbers, cyclists. They even carry some golf equipment. Maybe Jake would have changed, too, but I doubt it. When I go to see Mom and Franklin at Christmas, a deer and sleigh still adorn the store roof. The deer came from a taxidermy shop in Central, and I know Jake's objection to that. I miss the mangy critter touched up with marine paint and held together by catgut. That was Jake's way.

32

W HAT I DON'T THINK MUCH ABOUT anymore
are those events that remain unclear but still cast long
shadows on my days and haunt my nights. My father's
drowning. My mother's infidelity. The mystery surrounding Meeks and
Chilcoat. After Jake's funeral, I kept thinking of the ambiguity of Billyum's words. While he was vouching for Jake, he also might have been
covering for himself. The two of them might have left the river to settle
the debt themselves.

And I don't think much more about the Wet Shoes, words I haven't
heard since the long night of the flood. I don't believe Jake saw my
father's face in the window or that my father's hand reached out of the
chill water to pull Jake in. My uncle was in the wrong place, and a snag
hit the boat. The face he saw in the window — that's anybody's guess.
The mind can play tricks. A reflection of light, as Billyum said.

I kept Juniper's painting of Kalim on the basketball court. She had
planned on taking it with her to Albuquerque, but I offered to buy it.
She seemed pleased but wouldn't take payment, just gave it to me with
that generous way Indians have when you admire their craft.

Over the years I marvel at the way Juniper got Kalim's expression
exactly right. The quick surprise you imagine at first is really in the
posture, the turn of the head. After studying the work longer, you see
the penetrating eyes that realize the calamities the rest of us fail to
notice in our day-to-day routines. Maybe that vision is truer for Indian
people because they've experienced so much loss, still experience it. But
after that time in Gateway, I understand loss, too, at least partway.

While the other players huddle heads down to concentrate on the coach's instructions, Kalim's staring at whatever's coming toward him. And now I realize what he sees — restless horses on a snowblind road, a slick black stump with tangled roots grasping like a claw, the snag of betrayal lying just beneath the smooth bright surface of a faithless lover's eyes.

Glimpsing my own reflection in motel mirrors, I sometimes recognize Kalim's expression, and I know that day I must remain especially vigilant. Now or soon, something rushes toward me. Keep alert, Kalim warns me. Stay on guard.

But when I dwell on those nightmare snags bumping along the dark current, I hear Jake say, "Don't go thinking negatory thoughts, nephew." And I realize I'm focusing only on the loss of that year. The time was magical, too.

When I'm on the road and chance into an old-fashioned sporting goods store, perhaps I smell coffee perking in the back room, catch the intoxicating ferrule cement as the owner rewraps a customer's favorite fly rod. While I ratchet the fly display case round and round, searching for some local, hand-tied special that's guaranteed to fool the lunkers, I listen to the customers bragging and telling improbable tales. None match the yarns of the back-room boys, but each storyteller has his own particular charm. If I feel especially comfortable, I'll reveal that Jake was my uncle, and they'll set aside their work long enough to swap a few stories. Everyone has a Jake tale and most remember him from the guide conventions.

At his funeral, the minister asked how do you say good-bye to a legend, and I suppose the answer is you don't. I can't, anyway, and I expect to be around to tell the story much later, when some of the wide-eyed youngsters from those Labor Day Polaroid shots grow up and ask about that grinning man who crowds the photo and shares his trophy fish.

After a little coaxing, I can usually get the locals to reveal a decent stretch of water off the beaten path where I can walk in and enjoy the quiet. I'll study the river a long time, imagining the people who fish it and realizing this river means as much to them as the Lost does to my family.

As I tie one of the local specials onto my leader, I can picture Jake standing at my shoulder, offering instructions. Downstream, my father and the old man fish the bright water.

I fish through the twilight. Venus appears on the horizon.

I locate the Sky Fisherman.

According to Billyum, old Indian legends claim the stars are campfires at the centers of villages. Around these campfires, the storytellers gather. Their words spark fires, warming the people until the sun rises. One by one, the fires dim and the storytellers slumber until the next night.

After Jake's death, I discovered a new light beside the Sky Fisherman, a blue-white star that shimmers like spring water. I expect he has built a campfire and is swapping yarns with my father and grandfather. Old feuds are forgotten. The smells of fish, biscuits, and whiskey mingle with the old man's pipe smoke. Harold approaches the campfire, toting a Bible in one hand, fly rod in the other. His bow tie remains impeccable and he has a string of glorious fish. Before he can shuck off his hip boots, the teasing begins.

I ache for their companionship. Still, despite the longing, I smile as I remember those friends, both white and Indian, who lined the riverbank and the high basalt cliffs, standing vigil for five days while waiting for Jake's gleaming light to reappear on the Lost.

From his campfire, Jake must have looked down each night, studying those sentries, smelling the good human scents of coffee, baked goods, and wet wool drift skyward. And when they spoke, he caught his name. Already, the storytellers were practicing.

Jake throws another log on the fire. He waits for the back-room boys, Billyum, Juniper, my mother. Even Franklin has a place. The last is mine.

Now I am finished casting. No twilight remains. Quick clouds of breath rise toward the night sky. I disturb the river with my hand. Reflected stars dance.

Thrusting my head back, I gaze at the countless stars. I stare and stare and stare until my balance falls away. Tasting water, I begin swimming toward the firelights.